3 5674 00646362 5

DETROIT PUBLIC LIBRARY

BROWSING LIBRARY
5201 Woodward
Detroit, MI 48202

DATE DUE

JUL 27 1991

A
FOR

PORTION

FOXES

JANE McILVAINE McCLARY

SIMON AND SCHUSTER · NEW YORK

RC. 3

COPYRIGHT © 1972 BY JANE MC ILVAINE MC CLARY
ALL RIGHTS RESERVED
INCLUDING THE RIGHT OF REPRODUCTION
IN WHOLE OR IN PART IN ANY FORM
PUBLISHED BY SIMON AND SCHUSTER
ROCKEFELLER CENTER, 630 FIFTH AVENUE
NEW YORK, NEW YORK 10020

FOURTH PRINTING

SBN 671-21151-X
LIBRARY OF CONGRESS CATALOG CARD NUMBER: 78-185626
DESIGNED BY EVE METZ
MANUFACTURED IN THE UNITED STATES OF AMERICA

SEP 27 '72

BL

2939-30-547

For
Nelson and Christopher

*Let them fall upon the edge of the sword,
that they may be a portion for foxes.*

PSALM 63
THE BOOK OF COMMON PRAYER

PART ONE
BALLYHOURA

PROLOGUE

I T WAS THE sharp, excited notes of the hunting horn, urging her on from across the valley, that drew Shelley back to Ballyhoura.

The vast turreted mansion had been empty, abandoned, its chimneys cold during her lifetime. As a child she had spent hours riding through the overgrown fields, exploring the ghostly ruins, sitting in the shingled rose-smothered gazebo dreaming of great hunts, heroic horses and heroic races run over the course her grandfather had built below the house. To Shelley, the estate was an extension of Shelburn Hall. Now that it had been sold and was being brought back to life, she felt as if something of hers had been taken from her.

It was the last day of the foxhunting season. After the usual morning chaos of breakfast to prepare, animals to feed and telephone calls to be answered—country correspondents calling in news for her husband Mike's weekly newspaper and invitations to hunt breakfasts and dinner parties—she had discovered that one of The Hunt's buttons was missing from her formal black hunting coat. By the time she found the needle, last used to dig splinters from her five-year-old son Cam's hand, and managed to resew the button on her coat, she was late starting for the meet.

At last she was mounted, had adjusted her stirrups and girth and was on her way. As she rode from the stable into the golden light of the early spring morning, the residue of tension remaining from confusion and hurry abated. The undefinable yearning and restlessness, which she could never be wholly free of, was temporarily stilled. On a hunting morning, with a fine horse beneath her, Shelley felt reborn.

Lookout Light tossed his head and took a quick dancing step. Joy seized her—joy in the green-turning land and in this horse she had worked on all season. The gray thoroughbred had been rehabilitated. Now he no longer refused the fences she put him at, fearing a heavy, hurting hand on the reins. His fear of pain had been replaced by a growing confidence in the light weight on his back, the featherlike touch against his mouth and the soft voice that sang to him.

Suddenly the horse shied. She glanced around, almost expecting to see a fox skulk from the honeysuckle bordering the road. There was nothing there. The March day was as bright and shining and empty of menace as a newly minted coin. The Valley, her valley, spread before her like a clean polished disc.

It was then that she heard the horn, laying its poignant heavy hold on her heart, calling to her to hurry. It would save time to ride through Ballyhoura.

It was a second or more before she realized the chimneys of Ballyhoura were no longer cold.

There were other changes. A new mailbox had been erected, with a blue stripe running diagonally across it. The iron-spiked gate opening onto the drive had been reset on its hinges. The entrance posts, with their carved inscriptions surmounted by stone foxes, and the gatehouse had been repaired. There was glass in the windows and geraniums in the window boxes. The potholes in the avenue had been filled in and rhododendrons and azaleas set out along the freshly graveled roadway. A new sign, Sean Shelburn's crest and emblem of The Hunt, the fox mask surmounted by the curving black brush, had been painted against a crimson background on which "Ballyhoura" had been lettered in blue. The sign was hung from a wrought-iron post. Beneath it a gardener was separating daffodil bulbs to plant around its base.

The iron gate was closed. A large "No Trespassing" sign warned that the police would be called to expel all unauthorized persons from the property. Obviously the new owners knew nothing of country living. In The Valley, nobody paid attention to such signs. Properties were posted against gunners and city people who drove out weekends, picnicked, and left a wake of litter. They were not off bounds to neighbors and foxhunters.

Shelley stopped singing. "Would you please open the gate?"

The man looked up. He had on khaki trousers and a matching shirt with "Ballyhoura" inscribed in crimson thread over the pocket.

"It's locked. Mr. Zagaran doesn't want any pony clubbers or people riding over his land."

His voice was low, with a rich, melodious quality. That, and a distinctness of enunciation utterly unlike the nasal drawl usually associated with the country people, gave it a foreign quality. She had heard that the Zagarans had imported artisans from Europe to restore the grounds and original gardens. Probably this man was one of them. The fact that he was foreign might also explain the amused light in his amber-colored eyes and the lack of deference which, as a Shelburn, the working people in The Valley accorded her.

Shelley lifted her hunting crop.

"Please unlock it at once. Surely you have a key."

The workman put his trowel down on the ground and straightened up. He was very tall, strongly built. His open-necked short-sleeved shirt displayed a chest and arms the rich golden brown color of the leaves on the ground. She saw his mouth, the planes of his narrow face. The nose, roughly cast and uneven, as though it had been broken, and the thin line of scar running through his left eyebrow added to the impression of strength and virility his features imparted. She felt the force of his eyes, strange and penetrating, dark brown shot through with yellow lights. She had the feeling she had seen them before, but where or when she could not say.

"Can't you read?" He nodded in the direction of the sign. Reaching into his shirt pocket, he drew out a package of cigarettes and a lighter. "You wouldn't want me to call the police?"

She stared at him, flabbergasted by his manner, the mockery in his eyes. Then, at the idea of Chester Glover, who was the "police" in The Valley and whom she had known since childhood, evicting her from what had always been considered Shelburn property, she began to laugh.

"I doubt that the police would evict *me*."

Lookout Light flung up his head. A quiver ran through his body. Then he became motionless, ears pricked, staring off toward the distant sound, the thin, striving cry of hounds, followed by the Old Huntsman's horn, blowing them away on the line of a fox.

Only the locked gate, as high and as unyielding as the iron from which it was made, stood between them and The Hunt.

Her laughter ceased.

"Nobody locks gates in The Valley. I suggest you tell Mr. Zagaran that in this country land is to be ridden over."

The man did not move. Instead he stood leaning against the iron post, smoking his cigarette.

"I suggest you tell him yourself!"

She was coldly furious.

"I intend to. I also plan to report your insolence."

"That's exactly what I'd do." He threw down his cigarette, ground it into the dirt, bent down and picked up his trowel. He was grinning as he started digging holes for the bulbs.

Shelley did not know what she would have said or done next if Freddy Fisher, the retired steeplechase jockey who had been hired as gatekeeper, had not emerged from the gatehouse. He, too, wore khakis with "Ballyhoura" inscribed in red over his shirt pocket. His face, eroded by years of wind and weather and alcohol, was clean-shaven and bore a glow of health that had not been there when she had last seen him in the liquor store.

"Hello, Miss Shelley." His eyes moved to the horse, seeing at a glance the beauty and substance, the quality and bravery in the soft wide-spaced eyes and patrician head. "Nice piece of work!" His voice was admiring. "Looks like a Pilot!"

"Freddy," Shelley cried relievedly. "Am I glad to see you! This man had the nerve to tell me I couldn't ride through Ballyhoura."

"Why, Mr. Zagaran—" The gatekeeper stopped abruptly, his face turning the color of his red "Ballyhoura" inscription. "I didn't see you there."

Shelley looked from one to the other aghast. Anger at having been mocked, made fun of by this rude raider, this impolite interloper, drove out all caution. With her whip hand she jammed her hunting cap down on her head, wearing it the way she met her fences, head-on. Beneath its velvet visor, her eyes flashed. "No locked gate ever kept a Shelburn from hounds!" she cried.

Lookout Light did not hesitate or falter. With the boldness of his breeding, he took off in his stride and arced into the air. Shelley felt his mane brush her face and was aware of the soaring exhilaration that jumping a big fence in complete rhythm and accord with one's horse always gave her.

She looked back and saw Freddy Fisher rooted to the ground, one arm raised as though in protest. She had a fleeting glimpse of Zagaran's dark face. The mockery was gone, replaced by grudging admiration. She heard herself laughing triumphantly as the horse sped along the avenue, spewing gravel onto the newly planted shrubbery.

The elegant society of the Virginia hunt country is threatened by the encroachment of 20th century ideals and conflicts.

ONE

BALLYHOURA blazed with light. Spotlights illuminated its towers and turrets and crenelated outlines. Colored lights played over the Ballyhoura Oak, the outbuildings, the terraced gardens, the swimming pool, the pavilion, and spilled from the windows of the great baronial house.

The furniture had been removed from the hall, from which one stepped down into a vast vaulted room so large that Andrea Zagaran's concert grand looked like a bedside table. Now it was being used by one of the men in Larry Lester's scarlet-coated orchestra, the number one band this year, who were playing dance music in the blue gazebo erected in front of the fireplace where the first Shelburns to inhabit Ballyhoura had roasted oxen. From the walls the dark oils in their old-fashioned gilt frames—paintings some of the guests maintained Zagaran had bought at auction to pass off as his ancestors—the seladang, rumored to have a wider horn span than the one displayed at the Museum of Natural History, the ferocious fanged tiger, the rhinos and elephant tusks, gazed down on the dancers.

Outside—Zagaran had bought an entire golf course in order to sod the expanse of terraced lawns—striped marquees had been built. Heated against the chill of the September evening, the tent city included bars and buffets serving everything from bourbon to banana splits, plus a pressing room, shoe shine parlor and a barber shop for the out-of-town collegians.

Around the floodlit Olympic-size swimming pool, tables with red-checked cloths had been set up in imitation of a Parisian sidewalk cafe. The marble pavilion, known locally as the Parthenon, was decorated in the Zagaran racing colors, sky blue and crimson, banked with blood-red roses from the famous Ballyhoura gardens and greenhouses, enormous blue and red lollipops and other intricate crepe paper decorations from Dickie Speer's interior-decorating firm in New York.

The ball, which was to be Tatine Zagaran's official debut, had been the talk of The Valley for months. In order that they might receive an invitation, a number of landowners had attempted to call on Andrea Zagaran, hoping that their names would be included in the guest list, along with the elite invited from Washington, New York, Boston and Philadelphia. None got past the padlocked gates.

During the time spent restoring the estate to its former grandeur—Hunter Jenney, the real estate broker who'd handled the sale, estimated that over a million dollars had already been put into the house and outbuildings, clearing the land and laying out an airstrip—the Zagarans had aided and abetted the air of mystery surrounding them by not appearing in public or accepting any invitations. Now, after all the rumor and conjecture, those who had received the formal invitations with the Shelburn crest pressed onto the thick expensive paper were having their first view of the extensive renovations made on house and grounds.

Until the man named Zagaran had bought the property the preceding spring, the great house, known locally as The Folly, had been empty and sinking slowly into ruin. The country people maintained it was haunted, that a sinister strain of black-brushed foxes lived in the wooded park. Whenever one of those foxes was viewed, it meant that death was imminent.

In the twenties it was bought by a man named Farrell who had made a fortune in oil and used the estate as a place to entertain members of the government. Some years later Farrell died of a heart attack. Mattie Moore, the Negro cook, insisted that the night before the fatal attack a black-brushed fox came out of the wood and was chased away from the house by one of the dogs. When the next owner went bankrupt—he owned a racing stable— the estate was taken over by the bank. The park became a jungle and the country people spoke of strange noises, the sound of a fox barking, of a ghost pack in pursuit, and of having seen a one-armed horseman galloping through the night.

Although strategically situated in the foxhunting country, an area rapidly becoming popular with Washington commuters, and the setting for the famous Shelburn Cup steeplechase run every spring over the high timber fences Sean Shelburn had built on the Valley floor, the crumbling crenelated ruins were classified as a white elephant. Hunter Jenney had given up all hope of selling the property and had even discontinued his expensive ads when he received the inquiry from the New York land broker. Not dreaming that the prospective buyer would accept the deal, sight unseen and at the price quoted, the local realtor did not bother to check with the Land Corporation.

Originally organized by Cameron Fitzgerald "to promote the best interests of The Valley" and "preserve it from undesirable people and commercial enterprises that would be damaging to the economic and aesthetic values of the countryside," the Corporation had no actual legal authority to bar anybody from buying property. Yet its power—due to the social and material means of Valley landowners—was such that no businessman dependent on local goodwill would deliberately defy what was in reality but a gentlemen's agreement. When it came to "letting in new people" the landowners forgot their individual feuds with one another and closed ranks.

Hunter's oversight caused several irate Hunt members to list their salable properties with other agents. However, as his commission on the Ballyhoura sale was enough to pay off the mortgage on his own farm and to put aside tuition for his three sons to go to the University of Virginia, Hunter wasn't, as Shelley Latimer put it, hurting.

Rumors, conjecture ran rife. Mrs. R. Rutherford Dinwiddie insisted Zagaran was a Russian Jew.

Her husband had it on good authority that he had been involved in shady transactions that had resulted in his expulsion from the Long Island community where he had lived prior to moving to Virginia. "On Wall Street they call him 'Under-the-Counter' Zagaran. When he goes back to Old Westbury he has to wear a bag over his head," Dudley Dudley-Smythe said meanly one night after a number of strong drinks.

"That's not true," Togo Baldwin, vice president of the bank, countered. "We ran a Dun and Bradstreet on him." Togo went on to say that by the time "Battle" Zagaran was thirty he had made his first million. At forty he had left the Buford Bond Corporation and become president of a unique company that financed the building of housing developments, bridges, turnpikes and municipal ventures on an international scale which, under his dynamic command, was continually expanding into new areas, absorbing less able competitors and spurring others into a desperate fight for survival. It was this love of challenge, of a good fight, which gave rise to the nickname "Battle." Nobody seemed to know what his real first name was—he signed all papers with just a B.

When renovations began, the stories spread and grew. Plans called for an Olympic-size swimming pool and a Grecian pavilion with a stainless steel kitchen for poolside buffets and dancing parties so that the Zagarans' daughter would have a place to entertain. A tennis court, skeet-shooting range, airstrip for Zagaran's plane, movie auditorium and a series of terraced lawns, each with a fountain operated by switches in the main house, were being constructed. John Taylor, the contractor, reported that even the old gazebo was being repaired and repainted.

"I'm told they're going to move the Ballyhoura Oak a half a foot left in order that the Terrible Tenth on the Cup course can be seen from the house," Misty Montague commented facetiously. Connie Jackson, who tried to infiltrate past the gate and garner a story for the *Capital Courier* on the changes taking place, was turned away by Freddy Fisher, who told her Mrs. Zagaran was not well and not receiving anyone. Connie asked Shelley Latimer in the supermarket if it was true that Andrea Zagaran was an alcoholic and Shelley replied that Simeon Tucker, who had been taken on as groom, told her groom, Virginia City, that Mrs. Zagaran spent all her time in her room with her Siamese cats, rearranging her shell collection.

"I don't know why people like that move into The Valley," Shelley said. "If they don't ride or hunt, what is there for them here?"

"I understand he's a developer," Connie replied. "There was a feature in the *Capital Courier* about a big modern housing project that he's backing near Washington."

"There are plenty of places where developments and factories would be welcome," Shelley said, "but not in the middle of the foxhunting country."

"Where are you going?" Connie called after her as she picked up the Army rucksack she used in place of a pocketbook and started for the door.

Shelley threw her a grin. "Home to hide the silver!"

She had not told Mike about meeting Zagaran. Nor had she seen the new master of Ballyhoura since.

Now Shelley saw the glow in the sky from the lights of Ballyhoura, heard the distant sensual throb of music, felt the enchantment of the soft September evening. Overhead the stars were beginning to emerge from behind milky wisps of cloud, as delicate as the scent of mimosa from the tree growing beside the ruined wing. Lance, the mastiff who followed her on her evening walk to check the horses, paused. Lifting his great head, he listened to the sound of the famous orchestra mingled with the nightly song of the tree frogs and the chuffing, rustling sounds from the pasture.

Returning to the house, she saw that the Jeep wasn't there. Mike still wasn't home. Although it was Saturday, he had spent all day at the plant working to get the press in running order for the first section of the paper on Monday.

She had a potato baking in the oven, the salad made and the steak ready to go under the broiler, and had read Cam a chapter of *The Wind in the Willows* when he returned. Mike stood in the doorway of the kitchen, his head almost touching the lintel. His blue shirt was torn at the top of the right sleeve and stained with grease. There was a smear of ink across his forehead and his gray eyes were shadowed with weariness.

"Why aren't you dressed?" he asked, observing Shelley's striped turtleneck, the blue jeans with the broken zipper—she had secured the fly with a sapphire pin inherited from her grandmother—and the high-laced men's shoes she wore to ride in.

She looked up, surprised. "I regretted the invitation."

"Daddy!" Cam jumped from Shelley's lap and ran to his father. Mike bent down and picked him up. "It's almost nine o'clock. Why aren't you in bed?"

"Mommy told me I could stay up until you got home," Cam replied, clinging to his father.

"All right." Mike smiled. "Up we go."

While Mike went to clean up, Shelley finished putting her son to bed. By the time Cam had brushed his teeth, said his prayers and snuggled down under the covers with Kitty-Kat, his frayed stuffed animal, it was long past his usual bedtime.

"I hear music," he said sleepily.

Shelley went to the window. The music was louder now, carried on the night breeze sweeping over the fields and woodlands.

Quickly she turned away, as though afraid to linger within the circle of the hypnotic spell that, like the crimson-painted plane which came and went over The Valley, bespoke the magic of money and power, and the glamour of far places.

"You're the one who's always accusing me of being a hermit." Mike emerged from the sunken tub, dripping water on the worn red Aubusson in their bedroom. "This is one time I want to go somewhere, and here you are, still in jeans."

"I told you. I don't want to be indebted to anyone named Zagaran."

"You might learn something!"

Shelley stood up. She was tall and slender, with long straight legs—"Excellent boot legs, madam!" said the man from Peal's when she ordered a new pair of hunting boots—and she carried herself with an air of pride and distinction that people who did not know her took to be arrogance.

As she turned toward him, he saw the set of her chin.

"In my father's day, a man with a name like that would never have been accepted here, no matter how rich and powerful."

"Shelley, ever since we've been in The Valley you've been forcing me to go to hunt breakfasts and cocktail parties and buffets with your buddies. Now, when I say that I want to go out, you dig in your heels. Look, Senator Bentley is supposed to be there. I have something to discuss with him. And I'm interested in Zagaran. He's just taken on an important government job," he continued, toweling himself vigorously. "He's apparently one of the *Sun*'s longtime subscribers, and he released the story of buying Ballyhoura to me before it was sent to the *Daily*. There've been articles about him in magazines."

Shelley sat down on Martha Washington's gilt bedroom chair and started to unlace her riding shoes. "I'm sick and tired of hearing Zagaran this and Zagaran that." She gave the leather laces a vicious jerk. "Imagine calling Mrs. Zagaran and angling for an invitation the way Connie Jackson did!"

"You should be glad your grandfather's place has been restored."

"By a man who locks gates. In a hunting country. He used my crest. The Shelburn crest on the invitations!"

Mike started to laugh. "Come now, Shelley, you really are being unreasonable. Virginia City said he'd sit with Cam. Let's go to the ball, dance and drink champagne and have fun."

"If you insist," she said finally, "but I haven't anything to wear."

She knew that she was being emotional and illogical, that there was no way to explain why she felt the way she did. It was all tied up with her heritage, her intense feeling for the land from which she had sprung, the feeling in her mind about people and places— how some people belonged to houses, were molded by them—and that somehow the Zagarans and the Schligmans, the "new" people pouring into The Valley, were outsiders who could never belong.

"I hate him," she said, standing up. Her sapphire eyes, the blue-violet Shelburn eyes framed by a thick fringe of curling black lashes, flashed, like her earrings, as she flung back her head. "I'm sick of the name Zagaran."

"Aren't you dressed yet?" Mike stuck his freshly shaven face around the doorway.

"I'll be with you in a minute."

She stared at her reflection in the antique gilt-framed mirror over her dressing table. When she'd been a child, Melusina, her nurse, had scraped her hair straight back off her high forehead with its widow's peak and small triangular scar where she had fallen off her pony onto a sharp rock, and tied it with a piece of twine or a ribbon. When she became older, Shelley had plaited her long, almost black hair into braids that fell below her waist or else went around her head two times. Grown up, she found it easier simply to do her hair up into a low loose knot at the nape of her neck. In the years she'd been married to Mike her hair style had not changed.

Now, suddenly, she was sick of it. Although the old pre-Cam dress with its utter simplicity and fine lines was a proper setting for the Shelburn Sapphires, the earrings and necklace that had belonged to her grandmother, it seemed to her dated. The people at the ball would wear the latest styles and hair sets, and she would feel as old-fashioned as her jewelry. This was another reason why she didn't want to go to the ball. To be shunted aside, patronized or, worse, ignored was something that, as more and more new people moved into The Valley, she was finding increasingly hard to bear.

"You look dazzling." Mike gazed over her shoulder at her reflection. "Come on." He pulled her to her feet. "Hmmm. You smell good. Darling, I've changed my mind. Let's stay home."

Shelley tensed. "As long as you insist on going, let's go."

"I can think of other things I'd prefer to do." His eyes traveled the length of her slim black sheath. "You have the best figure of any woman in The Valley." His gray eyes changed, softened. "Shelley, I love you."

"I know," she whispered. "No, don't. I've just finished doing my hair. Mike, no. We're so late now that if we don't go . . ."

He moved back. "There's never time any more."

Shelley had a sudden shattering sense of wrongdoing, coupled with a feeling of loss. Momentarily she yearned desperately for physical release, for a surging, blinding passion that would sweep away the debris of her thoughts—the fact that she had forgotten to buy butter for breakfast, new shoes for Cam, and that they were out of soap powder. Fighting to put down the queer sense of frozen inner tension that seemed lately to come over her, she sought to transfer her annoyance with herself, her housekeeping omissions and unresponsiveness to Mike.

As he drove the station wagon out of the driveway, Shelley sat tensely upright. Mike could not remember ever seeing her shoulders slump. Once she'd told him that her grandmother had made her stay for hours on that gilt-framed Martha Washington chair with a riding crop stuck inside her belt to teach her to sit properly.

Ahead, the road was a long, straight ribbon, cutting through the historic countryside. Originally it had been a footpath used by migrating Indians who camped along Buffalo Run. During the French and Indian Wars, Braddock's men had fought along it. Later, when King Shelburn began building Shelburn Hall, he hired a friend named George Washington to survey it. In order that his guests might not be discomforted by bumps and turns as they dozed in their coaches and carriages, the road was straightened and smoothed.

On either side the fields were all silver and shadow. Cattle and horses moved, shrouded in mist. A cool breeze, coming from the distant mountains, blew against them. Shelley felt it on her cheek. Gazing out of the car window, she could see the black lines of the hunting fences, the walls and rails and coops, all of which she knew the way she knew the bumps and undulations of the familiar road. And while one part of her mind wondered what the night held in store, the other played the old familiar game of picking her panel, the place she would choose to jump as soon as the hunting season began.

Mike slowed the car down. Ahead lay Ballyhoura, lighting the sky.

Since the day of the gate jump, Shelley had avoided Ballyhoura. Yet the comings and goings of the crimson-painted turbojet, circling over The Valley as it came in for a landing and then taking off again to ferry its owner to and from his appointments in the various places where new financial or building projects were under way, served as a disquieting reminder of the changes taking place in the countryside.

Now Freddy Fisher waved his flashlight, and his face, as leathery and cracked as his old racing boots, broke into a welcoming smile.

"Gate's open, Miss Shelley, ma'am," he said, weaving slightly. "Reckon there's no need to see *your* invitation. You'd be surprised, though, the people trying to crash. Kids mostly, but grown-ups, too. Seems like 'bout everybody wants to go to the ball. You all"—his words slurred—"just drive right on through."

"He's fallen off the wagon," Shelley said as they passed between the massive entrance posts. "A shame. He was doing so well."

As they drove between the freshly planted laurel and rhododendron lining the drive, the old spell of Ballyhoura was laid upon her. In spite of herself, Shelley was aware of the stirrings of anticipation.

In Shelley's grandfather's day the park had been a dark wood, sprawling and uncontrolled, alive with rabbits and squirrels and other creatures native to the countryside. Now trees had been cut down, the underbrush cleared. Grass was sown along the acres, with rhododendrons, azaleas, flowering fuchsias, and it was all surrounded by the high iron-spiked fence to ward off trespassers.

Suddenly a fox darted from the bushes lining the drive, directly across their path. Dazed by the headlights, he paused. In the darkness his eyes glittered, pinpoints of greenish-amber fire.

"Oh, he's beautiful," Shelley cried. "Don't hit him!" She clutched Mike's arm.

To avoid driving into the rhododendrons, Mike jammed on the brakes. "Damn it!" he exclaimed as the car behind them screeched to a halt. "You almost caused a wreck. All because of one of your straight-laced foxes. Country's too full of foxes anyway. One got our speckled hen last week."

"How can you say such things?" Shelley lashed out as he started up the car. "You know I hate seeing foxes killed. Anyway, they're straight-running, not straight-laced."

As the house came into view, Mike pointed out that she devoted a good many of her waking hours to the hunting field, chasing and killing foxes.

"You just don't want to understand," she answered helplessly. "It's the chase that counts, not the killing."

Without waiting for him, as Mike paused to speak to Zagaran's groom, Simeon Tucker, now in charge of the parking arrangements, Shelley hurried toward the house. The annoyance she felt toward her husband was replaced by a beginning excitement.

The cloakroom was at the end of the long, high-ceilinged hall. There Shelley handed the sable coat she had inherited from her grandmother to Community Brown. Ever since Shelley could remember, Community and her husband, Manassas, had served at local parties. Now that house servants were becoming almost as extinct as the bison that used to roam The Valley, people invariably checked with Community and Manassas to see if they were available before setting a date.

"Good evening, Community." Shelley smiled. "How is that knee of yours? Sound again, I hope."

"Evening, Miss Shelley. My knee's just fine, thank you, ma'am."

"And the boys?"

"All fine, Miss Shelley, ma'am." Community hesitated and then continued. "All but Mase."

Mase was the youngest of the Browns' five sons. For some time he had been working for a militant civil rights group in the Deep South. Recently Shelley had read in the *Capital Courier* that he had been jailed for leading a demonstration in Mississippi.

"Where is Mase now?" Shelley asked.

Community busied herself hanging up Shelley's coat.

"Manassas told Mase not to come home till he changed his attitude. Mase is full of hate. Manassas doesn't understand. It just isn't in Manassas to hate."

"I understand he was in town."

"I wouldn't know about that," Community replied. She turned away from the clothes rack to take a pile of wraps from a group of out-of-town guests and Shelley saw that her usually open and friendly face was set and closed in.

The dressing room had been done by Dickie Speer in crimson and blue. There were great crimson cabbage roses on hand-blocked wallpaper with matching curtains, gold fixtures shaped like mermaids on the old marble washstand. A silver vase of fresh roses was placed on the toilet tank.

A mass of pale backs and arms and vacant, beautifully made-up faces clustered around the two large mirrors. Tatine Zagaran's friends, no doubt, from Miss Shelburne's School, Farmington and Foxcroft, where they had been taught to move and speak and carry their heads with absolute confidence.

Maggie Bentley, the Senator's wife, whom Shelley had met pleasantly at the supermarket, came in followed by a woman in a sequined dress, whom Shelley recognized from her photographs as the Duchess of Glencoe. She was small and slender and contemptuously aloof, with smooth blond hair that, in spite of the elaborate upward trend in hair-dos, was worn in a simple page-boy. Transcendentally beautiful and famous—it was said that a member of European royalty had shot himself when she refused him permission to inspect the two bumblebees tattooed on her left thigh—she had begun her career as a stripper on Chicago's South Side. While starring in the international hit *Shady Lady*, she was the toast of New York and London. After divorcing her first husband, film star Victor Bolling, she had married Colin Campbell Bruce, the eleventh Duke of Glencoe, heir to a twelfth-century castle in the Scottish Highlands, and an inherited fortune.

Currently Bebe was involved in what the international press described as "the juiciest and most expensive divorce action in history." Accused by her titled husband of adultery involving the master of a famous hunt in Leicestershire, a British playwright, and a New York financier rumored to be Zagaran, she was quoted as saying tearfully that her relationships with the so-called other men had been above approach and that the Duke was barking up the wrong tree. "Barking up the wrong tree!" the Duke reportedly cried when he heard about it. "I'm barking up a whole bloody forest!"

Word in The Valley was that Bebe had returned to her homeland for "a little privacy"—she pronounced it "privvasee"—and had rented the Field House from Polo Pete Buford for the fox-hunting season.

"What a *de*vine party!" she cried now. Briefly her eyes traveled around the room, meeting Shelley's. Then with what Shelley took to be an air of dismissal and disinterest, she drew a lipstick from her purse and turned toward the mirror, where the young girls automatically moved aside to give her room.

"Our host seems charming," Maggie Bentley commented. "But where is Mrs. Zagaran? Nobody ever mentions her."

Bebe concentrated on painting her mouth with a pale pink lipstick. "Andrea's a frightful lush. Most of the time she's stoned. Poor Zagaran. Terribly hard on him."

"You knew him before?" Maggie Bentley asked.

"Yes, in London. I had just opened in *Shady Lady*. A friend brought him backstage. He was terribly young then, but he had been decorated for flying an incredible number of missions with the RAF. Maggie, whoever does your hair?"

"Why, Kenneth, of course. I fly to New York twice or three times a week."

Maggie Bentley suddenly noticed Shelley. "How nice to see you! Have you met our new neighbor, the Duchess of Glencoe?"

Shelley smiled and said she hoped the Duchess would like living in The Valley. The Duchess replied, "Charmed," and resumed her concentration on painting her mouth. Then Millicent Black and Cosy Rosy Dudley-Smythe converged upon her.

"Shelley," they cried in unison. "You said you weren't coming."

"I changed my mind. The music sounds wonderful."

"It is," Cosy Rosy cried enthusiastically. "Bones and I had the best dance."

"It was a very long one," Millicent said darkly and turned back to Shelley. "Sweetie pie, you look *marvelous*, you really do."

"I feel very Late Show." Shelley smiled at her friends. "I haven't had a new dress since I moved back to The Valley."

Millicent made a face. "I'm a basket case. Last Resort is full of fucking house guests." She rattled off a list of names familiar to newspaper readers, including a newly appointed Supreme Court justice, a famous ten-goal polo player from Texas and a blond divorcee who owned show horses and great chunks of Connecticut real estate.

As Shelley made sympathetic noises and offered to provide a casserole for the luncheon and keep the children, Millicent began hiking up the slipping shoulder straps of her orange dress.

"You know me, sport, not enough equipment to keep the damn dress up." She gave Cosy Rosy's full-breasted figure a sidelong glance. "Not like some people I know."

Shelley did not want to spend the rest of the evening in the dressing room listening to Millicent's complaints about her husband's interest in other women. She knew from experience that once she got started, Millicent would jump from Bones's misdemeanors to a denigration of Cosy Rosy, who seemed to be his current flame, and that this could run on all night.

"Let me know what I can do to help tomorrow," she said, starting to leave.

"Not a thing." Millicent's angular face broke into a grateful smile. "Sport, you're a sweetie pie and I kiss you on the nose. We'll manage. The farmer's wife can fry chicken, or somebody can go down to Delia's Kitchen. Just be sure that you and Mike turn up for lunch."

Alone in the shadowed hallway, Shelley wished for Mike, her security. He was probably still outside, discussing integration with the Negro car parkers. She lifted her head, gave her hair a final pat, straightened her shoulders and started toward the great brilliantly lit room filled with dancers. After all, she told herself, who had a better right to be here than Shelburn Fitzgerald Latimer, direct descendant of King Shelburn, who had owned the land on which Shelburn Hall and Ballyhoura were built, had founded The Hunt and been its first Master?

It was almost midnight. The receiving line had broken up and the ball was in full swing. Shelley wondered if she should try to find her hostess and decided she would wait for Mike.

Fax Templeton and Bones Black stood on the edge of the floor looking over the field, their friends' wives and ex-wives, old and half-known loves and anticipated loves, in the same manner in which they would have examined horses being paraded before potential buyers.

"Now that *you're* here, Miss Shelley, ma'am," Fax drawled, "the evening's off to a running start." Standing back, he eyed her appreciatively. "Ah declare, you look pretty enough to win the strip class at the spring show."

Bones elbowed him out of the way. "How about you and me doing a turn around the floor while Fax looks over the field?"

"No, you don't." Fax smiled and pushed his friend aside.

When Fax was in his element, in the ballroom or on a horse, his stutter was not noticeable. Now, despite numerous trips to the champagne fountain flowing in the adjoining room, he managed to say clearly, "As Master of The Hunt I have first choice."

Warmed by their admiration, secure in the friendship of long association, Shelley felt the old wild anticipatory eagerness beginning. As the music started up, she was aware of that sudden exultance that is like waiting for the signal to go away after hounds have opened. She wanted to undo the knot that held her hair in place at the nape of her neck, kick off her shoes, let herself be submerged in the music and the moment. Only the discipline drilled into her held her inherited wildness in abeyance, forcing it back beneath layers of reserve.

In his twenties, Fairfax Custis Templeton III, with his golden head and classic features, had been a celebrated and romantic figure. He had married twice. His first wife, Taffy Carlisle, of New York and Long Island, had paid off his gambling debts and completely done over Templeton, the historic house which had been in his family for five generations. Following a dinner at the Bufords', Taffy had retired to her hostess's bedroom to fix her face and had noticed Fax's distinctive needlepoint cummerbund hanging on the back of a chair.

"Recognize that?" Samantha Sue Buford inquired maliciously.

"Hell, yes," Taffy replied succinctly. "I spent months sewing that bloody fox for Fax!"

Thereafter Taffy pulled up the wall-to-wall carpeting at Templeton, stripped away the costly imported wallpaper, and moved out the period furniture.

Returning from two weeks at Hialeah with the wife of a Chicago meat packer for whom he had been training horses, Fax found his ancestral manse emptied of everything, including the tacks that had anchored down the rich carpets and the gold-plated fixtures Taffy had installed in the early nineteenth-century bathrooms.

Fax's next wife, Caddy McLean, had been a better housekeeper. (In Valley jargon, a good housekeeper was one who managed to keep the house following the divorce.) In return for paying off the mortgage, she acquired the deed to Templeton. Soon tiring of country life, she moved to Rome, where she married an Italian count.

Templeton had been on the open market for five years when the Schligmans bought it. Fax and his marital drop-outs who moved in with him had not improved its salability. Most of the land had been sold. Only the house and stable remained, and what had been picturesque and atmospheric in Judge Templeton's day degenerated into filth and decay. The stench of dogs and old clothing was overpowering. The wallpaper had peeled and lay in curling heaps on the rotting floorboards. The drawing-room walls were blackened with smoke from the fireplace where "My Boy Hambone" smoked the hams butchered from hogs raised in what had once been the rose garden. The ancestors, riddled with bullet holes from being used as targets during drinking bouts, hung drunkenly in their gilt frames. Empty bottles were everywhere. Windowpanes were cracked and stuffed with old newspapers.

There were boots in the bathtub and unpaid bills in the sink. The Nun, Fax's favorite broodmare, had foaled in the downstairs bedroom, which did not look as if it had been cleaned following the delivery.

"Such a lovely view," Katie Schligman said, averting her eyes and concentrating on the long green of pastures and woodlands.

"The best!" Fax agreed solemnly. "Ah can tell right away when it's breeding time!"

Because of the view—nobody could imagine why else the Schligmans would buy such a moldering ruin—the place was bought for the asking price, a third more, Hunter Jenney said, than house and grounds were worth, plus the condition that Fax be permitted to retain the stable and its upstairs apartment, dubbed the "Rakish Stud" because Fax brought his cronies to stay when batching between marriages. There, with the help of My Boy Hambone, paid spasmodically to do the stable work, exercise the horses, cook, wash, clean the apartment, and do valeting, Fax boarded and schooled young horses and controlled the Schligmans' waterworks. As the well that provided water for the house was on his property, Fax was able to do as he pleased. Whenever Augie Schligman objected to the cost of feed or the all-night poker parties, Fax simply turned off the water, leaving his employer with no alternative but to pay the stable bills and refrain from criticism of Fax's menage.

Although his hair was thinning and his waist thickening, Fax's charm, inherited from generations of cavalier ancestors, was unimpaired. His awareness of women and horses was instinctive and he could, on occasion, display true compassion. One night, not long after Dave, Misty Montague's husband, was killed in the Korean war, he arrived at Fairmont in George Blandford's cab, chauffeured by the local taxi driver, who, along with Raymond Hoe, the blind guitar player, had been hired for the evening. Persuading Misty that a change of scene would do her good, he ushered her into the rear seat. Then while George drove and Raymond serenaded them, Fax and Misty rode into Shelburn to the Inn, where Fax had ordered an elegant dinner.

"There should be an endowment fund for people like Fax," Mike Latimer once said. "They should be preserved and put under glass."

Fax was a beautiful dancer. And as Larry Lester began playing a nostalgic medley of songs that dated back to her youth, Shelley was transported back to the time when she had danced through the starlit nights with Fax, together with the closeness and understanding of a first love that had been nipped in the bud, cut off and ended the night Fax told her he was going to marry Taffy Carlisle.

"Honey, I'm not a stayer. Taffy now, she's like me, a stretch runner. Shelley, you need staying power, somebody with bottom for the long race."

The sense of rejection, of separation, had become blurred and finally dissipated by Mike's love, leaving memories and the loyalty of long association.

. . .

Mike looked around for Shelley. Now that he was here he felt out of place. In his black dinner jacket and with his slender, sensitive face he looked alien among the scarlet-coated, ruddy-faced foxhunters and collegians who all seemed cut from the same bolt of Ivy League cloth. The feeling was nothing new. He had felt uprooted ever since he had agreed to buy the weekly newspaper and live in The Valley where his wife had been born and brought up.

The way she had been sitting in the car, against the far door, was a reproach. A mental barrier seemed to have arisen between them. The things they now said to each other were symptomatic of a kind of sea change in their marriage, a growing difference of opinion, a gradual drawing apart.

The business of the fox had been typical. She had been furious with him, had jumped out of the car, vanished into the house when he stopped to speak to Simeon Tucker. Simeon, a member of the Human Relations Council, had held him a moment longer. He wanted to know the outcome of that morning's meeting with the owners of the local restaurants.

"We stressed the fact that a man of Senator Bentley's position couldn't live in a segregated community—not in the year of our Lord 1963," Mike told him. "We told them that outside Negroes from national organizations planned to picket the Senator on his way to church tomorrow, that if they did so there would be wide repercussions. They finally agreed to accept our recommendations."

"What about the drugstore?" Simeon asked.

"It took some doing"—Mike grinned—"but Doc Dickerson finally agreed to go along with the others." He looked at his watch. "I left word where I would be. The call from Mase should come any time." Feelingly, he added, "We'll be able to tell them not to demonstrate!"

"That's wonderful!" the big Negro said. "My people want to thank you. This was a bitter place before you came."

"Thanks." Mike's voice was husky. He clasped Simeon's callused hand as though they had made a pact.

Shelley was not in the hall. From the gallery he gazed down onto the great vaulted room ablaze with color. The music from

32

the famous band, the voices, the brilliance were almost blinding, like looking directly into the glittering prisms of light from the chandeliers. Slowly his eyes adjusted to the scene. Obviously, "everybody" was there. They were the rich and the powerful and the old school tie. Their names, on products ranging from cars and canned goods to airplanes and soap powders, were household words around the world. They were the people who should have been producing, promoting peace, "doing" for their country. Instead they sought to lose themselves in a violence of sport and of the senses. Even Major Southgate DeLong had emerged from the dank, musty, cobwebbed obscurity of DeLong Manor for this festive evening. One of The Valley's authentic characters—his father had ridden with Shelburn's Raiders—the Major had been in the cavalry in World War I. Because of his sideburns, pointed beard and proclivity for pinching the opposite sex, he was known as "Old Fur Face, the retired rapist." Now he was frolicking on the ballroom floor with Mrs. Talbot, wife of the State Senator.

With the exception of "Muddy" Watters, The Valley's general practitioner; Doc Black, the elderly veterinarian; Greg Atwell, lawyer and cattle farmer; Togo Baldwin, who was vice president of the bank; Telford Talbot, the State Senator; and a handful of other local citizens, the majority of Valleyites on the dance floor had inherited their money or married rich women.

With a sinking heart, Mike realized that Shelley hadn't waited for him. Instead, she was dancing with Fairfax Custis Templeton, that shining example of wiped-out Southern aristocracy who, with his courtly Old World manner, molasses-in-January drawl, and beautifully tailored, almost threadbare clothes, was Master of The Hunt and the most sought-after "extra" man in The Valley.

Now Mike saw that the Master was resplendent in scarlet full evening dress coat with the facings and collar of The Hunt, a white starched shirt, studded and cufflinked, a white waistcoat with The Hunt's bone buttons—these were so rare that nobody in The Valley other than R. Rutherford Dinwiddie and Shelley had a complete set—handkerchief folded exactly right and his grandfather's knee breeches and silver-buckled patent pumps. On anybody else the knee breeches and pumps would have looked ridiculous. On Fax, combined with the silver hunting horn tucked into his ruffled shirt and the therapeutic collar he had worn since a fall suffered schooling a young horse, they but served to give him additional glamour.

Perhaps Shelley had been right: wiser if they'd stayed home. It was doubtful if he would have a chance to warn Senator Bentley after all. Nor did it really matter. Perhaps it was better for him not to know of the proposed demonstration. Right now he was more concerned about Shelley.

The tension between them was probably his fault. He had been so busy at the paper lately, trying to repair antiquated machinery and get out of debt, that he'd had little time for his family. And perhaps, perversely, he'd refused to conform, accept the Valley mores and take them seriously. He knew it infuriated Shelley that he continually stood apart, judging, analyzing, mocking the beliefs and pretenses and traditions with which she had been brought up.

While the great ball was supposedly Tatine Zagaran's debut, the Valley people crowding the house were more interested in meeting their host and hostess for the first time than in being introduced to the Zagarans' only child.

For as Mrs. R. Rutherford Dinwiddie commented, lifting her thick unplucked eyebrows, Tatine hardly needed to be "introduced." Everyone who read the society columns knew of Tatine and her escapades. At fourteen she had been the best rider at Miss Shelburne's Finishing School for Young Ladies. Her chestnut horse, Warlock, garnered innumerable blue ribbons on the show circuit. In her junior year at the select institution, which had been founded and made famous by a member of one of The Valley's oldest and most respected families, she had been expelled for what people called "scandalous goings-on," and sent to a Swiss boarding school.

From Gstaad, word drifted back to The Valley that Tatine had climbed out of her dormitory window one night and eloped with a ski instructor. Another story was that she had run off to Paris with the drummer from the jazz band at the Palace Hotel. Whatever Tatine had done, and it seemed to include everything except studying, it had not in any way arrested her "development" or tempered her non-conformist tendencies.

Now, doing the Twist with one of the young men deemed eligible by Miss Marsh, the Washington social secretary from whose "exclusive" list the stag line had been culled, there was about Tatine a wildness as vivid and arresting as her undulating body and flaming red hair. Having revolted against traditional white, she was dressed in emerald green satin that looked, as Fax put it, as if it had been sprayed onto her figure.

With her flamboyant shoulder-length hair, amber eyes and arrogant aquiline features, she had an air of reckless daring bordering on insolence. From her disdainful expression, the mockery in her faintly slanting eyes, it was obvious to Mrs. Dinwiddie and her coterie that Tatine was well aware of the effect she made.

As the ball grew more raucous, Andrea Zagaran felt faint from exhaustion and the effort of remaining sober.

At one time Andrea had been a beauty. Now few traces remained. Her eyes, as they turned to focus on late-coming or departing guests, had the glazed, wounded look of a trapped animal. Her face was gray, drawn, and her body thin to the point of emaciation.

After murmuring, "I'm so glad you could come. Yes, the music is wonderful. Yes, the decorations are nice, aren't they? Have you had supper?" repeating the same phrases over and over again, her face felt frozen into a smile as meaningless as her marriage had become. A woman of gentleness and self-awareness, she moved in an alien country which, with its emphasis on the pursuit of the fox, was far removed from the pursuit of culture around which her life, before Zagaran, had been centered. Like one of her cultivated hothouse roses cut off from its natural habitat, she felt lifeless, uncared for. Pretending to ignore her husband's infidelities, her daughter's scorn, she moved trancelike through the days, blunting her loneliness with the contents of the bottles hidden in the hatboxes in her closet.

Now, after making sure that everything was running smoothly, the champagne fountains flowing freely, she sought to escape to her bedroom, where, after locking herself in, she could safely drink herself to oblivion.

"The ravages of drink," Mrs. R. Rutherford Dinwiddie commented darkly, apropos of the hostess's departure. "I knew her when she was married to Scampy Sage, of the Boston Sages, you know. So attractive . . ."

As The Valley's social leader and mentor of the Slap Leather Set (Mike Latimer dubbed them the "Four H's," hard, horsey, hell-for-leather heiresses) Terry Dinwiddie had missed little of the proceedings. Aged, aquiline and aristocratic—her father was a Talbot of the Tidewater Talbots and her mother a Telford from Charleston—her face, used as a windshield in all weather, was as worn and cracked as brown leather gloves left in the rain. Whereas her husband prided himself on his closets full of London suits and in always being immaculately turned out, his wife wore vintage tweeds, amber beads, battered felt riding hats and heavy English-made brogues, causing the couple to be known, in local society, as "Beauty and the Beast." Now a shapeless crepe covered her hunting underwear, worn as protection against the night air and protruding from beneath her sleeves and uneven hemline.

In World War I she had marched for women's suffrage and lobbied for Prohibition, she professed to hate children (those who were unkind said she refused to miss a season's hunting in order to have any of her own) and contributed largely to the Birth Control League, to which she had willed her ample fortune derived from the Talbot family's extensive orchards. She campaigned against pasteurizing milk (her own prize herd, which she had milked herself during World War II, had never been bested) and paving country roads. She got up petitions against pig farms and housing developments and sent her friends pamphlets on the evil of alcohol (once at a political rally when her brother Telford was running for public office she sampled some imported wine provided for the occasion, made a face and quickly added a tablespoon of sugar to her glass). Although she would never see seventy again, she still hunted three days a week during the season. Astride one of her aged, bony hunters, she rode as if driven by some deep inner need that compelled her to take desperate risks and jump fences even the most foolhardy pulled away from. She had broken so many bones and been concussed so many times that Fax Templeton said he could hear her brains rattle when he listened for hounds at covertside. The year before, she had almost drowned in Buffalo Run when her horse missed its foothold on the far bank and fell backward into the stream, crushing her hip against a rock.

Dr. Muddy Watters warned her that if she fell again she would be dead.

"That's how I want to go," she snapped. "In the hunting field. Dinny has promised to sprinkle my ashes by the high wall on Hunting Hill."

Since the fall she had been forced to walk with a cane and to be lifted onto her horse. At parties it was an unwritten rule that she should not be left sitting alone. Her neighbors and hunting companions took turns chatting with her on the sidelines.

Now Debby Darbyshire and Cosy Rosy Dudley-Smythe, her bridge partners on non-hunting days, had the duty.

"Probably her husband's to blame," Debby remarked bitterly.

Debby was big-boned and heavyset, built like a Percheron, Fax Templeton said. A divorcee, she lived alone on a farm near Priscelly Gate. A former alcoholic, she carried Coca-Cola in her hunting flask and rarely had a cigarette out of her mouth.

"What did you say, my dear?" asked the Beast, who was slightly deaf.

"I said it was probably Andrea Zagaran's husband's fault that she drank so much." Debby ground out her cigarette and reached into her evening bag for another. "I'm told he's a devil with the women. Look—that must be him now, dancing with Bebe Bruce."

Fax Templeton said that one of his biggest problems as Master of The Hunt was to keep the Four H's quiet while he was trying to listen to hounds. The sight of Ballyhoura's new owner accomplished what Fax was unable to do. As one, the women leaned forward in their chairs, mouths partially agape, yet speechless.

No question but that their host, whom most were seeing that evening for the first time, merited their fascinated stares. Zagaran's height was accentuated by his black evening clothes. As he whirled his partner around, he did not look ridiculous as the other florid-faced foxhunters did when they tried to compete with the collegians and dance gracefully around the floor. Instead, he moved with a feline grace, not unlike the tigers he was said to have hunted in India. His lean body and browned face suggested a man in prime condition, his age indeterminate between the thirties and the forties. There was about him a ruthless quality, a sense of power and vitality and maleness.

"I wouldn't mind it if he put his boots under my bed," breathed Cosy Rosy Dudley-Smythe.

Dark, with a heart-shaped face and melting brown eyes, she was distinguished by a bosom that Fax described as excessively mammiferous. She had met Dudley Dudley-Smythe, heir to the Dudley-Smythe Farm Implement fortune and known in The Valley as "Dash-Smythe," while riding at the Shelburn Horse Show. Dash-Smythe asked her to ride his show horses.

Surprisingly (for Dash-Smythe was a walking *Almanach de Gotha* and knew as much about the pedigrees of the First Families of Virginia as Fax knew about the bloodlines of his horses), he had left his last wife, a Lloyd of the Northern Neck Lloyds, to marry Rosy, who was far from being to the manor born and was twenty years younger. Now, while her husband raised Irish wolf-hounds, puffed on his bulldog pipe and cultivated his carefully waxed mustache (Cosy Rosy once confided to Debby Darbyshire that he put it up in Baggies at night), she struggled to learn to tie her hunting stock properly and achieve social acceptance. Toward this end she flirted with Fax Templeton, Bones Black and the other Valley husbands and had replaced Millicent Black (Mrs. Dinwiddie maintained that Millicent had hired Dixon, her long-time groom, away from her, and the former bridge partners were no longer speaking) at the Hunting Hill bridge table.

"What did you say, dear?" The Beast leaned toward her. "Rosy, I do wish you'd speak up so I can hear you."

"I said that our host is supposed to have collected more female scalps than you have brushes, Mrs. Dinwiddie."

"He does look attractive," the older woman conceded. "If it weren't for his clothes—they're really too well cut—and I doubt he knows beans about horses—you might almost call him a gentleman, despite his name."

"You haven't a chance." Debby looked across at Cosy Rosy. "Don't you read the gossip columns? He's supposed to be mad for Bebe." She raised her voice. "Terry, did you know that she wears a diamond in her navel and has two bees tattooed on her thigh? The bees are her trademark. No matter whom she marries, she never changes the monograms on her satin sheets."

"Well, I never!" The Beast lifted her eyebrows. The black ribbon circling her neck added to the impression she gave of gazing down her nose at the speaker. "Really, Debby—are you sure? Of course, I wouldn't put it past her. Not that I mind, mind you." She gazed pointedly at Cosy Rosy. "Look how utterly middle-class foxhunting's become, people like the Schligmans riding to hounds—oh, yes, I know, he just gave The Hunt a five-figure contribution."

"Bebe's problem is that she can't make up her mind whether she's Melton Mowbray or South Side Chicago," Debby said. "There's Samantha Sue Buford." Her leathered outdoor face took on an expression of distaste. "Polo Pete looks smashed and Samantha Sue angry."

"Now, Debby, you mustn't criticize our P. P.," Mrs. Dinwiddie admonished in a wrist-slapping tone. "We wouldn't have a hunt without him."

"Terry, you know as well as I do that he's positively revolting," Debby replied stubbornly. As the daughter of Bet-a-Million Brady, the steel tycoon, and the ex-wife of Clem Darbyshire of the Atlanta Darbyshires, she contributed almost as much toward the upkeep of The Hunt as Mrs. Dinwiddie or Polo Pete Buford. "Yuk," she concluded, refusing to be intimidated by the older woman. "Imagine going to bed with P. P. I don't blame Samantha Sue for looking around."

For a moment the women were silent, observing Samantha Sue Buford, small, slender and Southern, with a wide-eyed little-girl look of simulated innocence, gazing past her partner's head at Battle Zagaran.

"She looks as if she's out gunning for another affair," Cosy Rosy commented. "The thing with Story Jackson must be over."

"Story is the limit!" Debby volunteered. "Have you heard? He sold Black Magic to our host. That mare is a real widowmaker."

"You can't blame him for getting what he can out of Yankees," countered the Beast.

"Look!" Debby cried. "Do you see who I see?"

"Well, I never." Mrs. Dinwiddie leaned forward. "Shelley! I thought she swore on a stack of fixture cards she wouldn't be caught dead in her grandfather's house with that interloper."

"She called him a member of the Mafia," Debby added.

"A dear girl," Mrs. Dinwiddie went on, riding her own line. "Such a difficult life. Her mother abandoned her, you know. Did a bunk, as the British say, with my young brother. He was a Gentleman Rider, so handsome. The women were mad for him, but no bottom. Shelley's mother was a beauty, but"—the older woman shook her head—"there's bad blood there. The Shelburns are inbred."

"I wish I had a figure like Shelley's." Debby looked wistful.

"She does move well," Mrs. Dinwiddie admitted, "and, of course, there's nobody like her in the hunting field. I remember when she used to ride her pony, jumping fences higher than its head. I can't imagine why she married that penniless newspaperman. No family to speak of and he loathes horses. Shelley did get him on one once—and, my dears, he had the worst seat!"

In the Beast's Blue Book, nothing could be more unforgivable than a bad seat or bad hands. Only the year before she had refused to attend a showing of *National Velvet* put on for the benefit of the ASPCA because she maintained that Elizabeth Taylor had jerked her horse's mouth.

"Maybe she loves Mike," Cosy Rosy responded. "He's good-looking, in a bony kind of way."

Feeling as if he had been hired for the evening to keep track of the jewels, Mike plunged into the scarlet-coated melee on the dance floor, narrowly avoided R. Rutherford Dinwiddie, Esquire, gave the Blacks, obviously at odds, a wide berth and finally managed to run Fax and Shelley to ground in a corner.

"May I?" He tapped Fax's crimson-clad shoulder.

"Oh," Shelley said, "you!"

"Yes." Mike took her in his arms. "Whom did you expect to cut in on you? Senator Bentley? You might have waited."

The party smile left her face. "I thought you'd be out there for hours, with your Negro friends, holding a civil rights meeting."

"A wife generally waits for her husband. At least for the first dance."

"Please, Mike. Now that we're here let's try to enjoy ourselves. We used to have fun together."

"I know. I'm sorry." He felt ashamed, as if, deliberately, he had taken one of Cam's birthday balloons and popped it.

"Ouch!" Shelley cried as Major Southgate DeLong galloped past.

"Damn," Mike said. "Here comes Old Fur Face again, leading another cavalry charge." Desperately he sought to propel Shelley out of the way. As he did so, he collided with another couple.

He knew she was thinking that he moved as if he were shifting gears and wished she were back dancing with Fax, Story Jackson, or one of her other old beaux, and this made him feel even clumsier.

"Let's get a drink," he said resignedly.

Before Shelley could answer a voice cut in.

"Miss Shelburn, I presume. My name is Zagaran."

Mike stopped. "You presume wrong," he said, holding Shelley tight. "It's Mrs. Latimer. I'm Mike Latimer."

"Odd." Zagaran took her hand and lifted it almost to his lips, as he made a slight bow. "For some unaccountable reason I had the name Shelburn fixed in my mind."

Mike looked at Shelley. The indifference with which she sometimes gazed at people she didn't know had given way to a curious expression which he defined as something close to fear. Yet this, he thought, was ridiculous. As long as he had known her, he had never seen her afraid of man or beast. "It's time we left," he said.

Shelley's eyes widened. It wasn't like him to be abrupt, almost rude.

Zagaran's left eyebrow lifted. In the softened light the thin line of scar shone white.

"Then you'll have the last dance with me," he said, addressing Shelley.

She stood very straight, with her head up. Her lips were slightly parted and her eyes, fastened on Zagaran, wore a strange excited look—the same look, Mike realized, he had seen in them at the track when she had bet her last ten dollars on her horse's nose to win.

"A host's prerogative," Zagaran added.

Before she could reply, he made a slight bow of dismissal to Mike, took Shelley's arm and moved out onto the floor.

"Well, I never," Mrs. Dinwiddie cried excitedly.

"I wish a man would look at me like that," Debby said wistfully.

"Why, Debby," the Beast remonstrated, shocked, "I thought you had more sense."

"I'd rather have sex than sense," Debby replied bitterly. "I've been alone for ten years. I was told this was a wonderful place to find a husband." She paused. "What they didn't tell me was that you had to have a husband to start with."

It gave Shelley a perverse satisfaction to see the expressions, interest mingled with envy, on the faces of the Four H's sitting along the wall as Zagaran took her in his arms and danced off with her.

"I hear you're one for jumping gates," he said without preliminaries.

"I hear you're one for locking them."

"People can sightsee somewhere else." He whirled her out of the way of Sandy Montague and young Molly Atwell.

"I'm not people," she countered hotly.

"Yes, I know. You're Miss Shelburn. Tell me, what persuaded you to come to the ball?"

"My husband."

"That's not what I mean. I was told you said that wild horses couldn't drag you here."

She tried to look away but his eyes held her. "Mike wanted to meet you."

"And you didn't."

With an expertise that gave her a sensation of weightlessness, he twirled her past R. Rutherford Dinwiddie, dancing with Tatine. They danced to the end of the room. Larry Lester, bouncing up and down as he directed his orchestra, waved his baton and smiled at them.

"You've changed everything," Shelley said finally. "Even the old gazebo in the garden. I used to go there as a child. Sit and dream."

"I got rid of the wasps."

"And the roses. They smelled so good."

"My wife, Andrea, wanted wisteria. More Southern."

"And you lock your gates. I told you, nobody in a foxhunting country locks his gates."

"You can always jump them." There was an amused glint in his eyes.

"You're laughing at me."

"Laughing! I wouldn't laugh at you for anything. Imagine someone with the name of Zagaran making fun of a Shelburn."

"You'll change the countryside. Make The Valley different."

His arm around her tightened. "The aristocracy loves a raider."

He *was* a raider. He had taken her from Mike as though she were a rag doll, a chattel, without will or direction of her own.

And Mike had stood there blankly, doing and saying nothing.

It ended abruptly. Polo Pete Buford was cutting in. A strange look passed between the two men. Then, with a casual shrug, Zagaran released her, walking away without a word or a backward glance.

For a time the ball had been brilliant. At midnight Fax had blown a ringing "Gone Away" on the silver hunting horn that had belonged to his great-grandfather, who had hunted his own hounds in The Valley prior to the War Between the States, and which Fax always wore tucked between the second and third buttons of his ruffled evening shirt. Bebe Bruce, accompanied by David Rice, the composer, who was one of Millicent Black's house guests, had been persuaded to sing several of the songs from *Shady Lady*. The music, the decorations, the beauty of the women and the opulence of their clothes and jewels provided the glamour and gaiety that were to cause the newspapers to describe it as "fabulous, fantastic, the most sensational debut ever given in The Hunt Country."

Now, however, like one of Dickie Speer's balls of crimson satin ribbon hanging from the ceiling, it had started to unwind.

At the bar, where Manassas Brown was presiding, Mike asked for a stiff bourbon. A huge Negro with a scarred face and hands like skillets, Manassas had once been a professional boxer. Although a devout churchgoer and infinitely gentle in speech and action, his size and prowess made him invaluable when it came to coping with unruly guests.

It looked as though his services might soon be needed. In a darkened corner, Millicent and Bones Black were having an argument that was rapidly approaching a climax. Separated since the Horse Show Dance last June, they had come together again in order to start getting the horses fit for the upcoming foxhunting season. Now Millicent was accusing her husband of devoting too much time to Cosy Rosy. Bones, so named because almost every bone in his body had been broken steeplechasing, retorted that he was damned if he would be nagged at further and that he was moving back in with Fax Templeton.

Togo Baldwin, on the verge of passing out, sat morosely against the wall, nursing a drink. His wife, Betsy, was pleading with him to let her drive him home.

Fax was leaving the dance floor, heading toward the box maze with Tina Welford, whose husband, Donnie, had gone to sleep behind a potted hydrangea.

A growing slackness seemed to be taking over. Faces were flushed, ties askew. Plates, glasses and cigarette butts littered the terraces and lawns. A young girl, barefoot and with skirts held high, raced past, a man with tousled hair and lipstick on his shirt in hot pursuit. In the pool several guests, fully clothed, were playfully splashing one another.

Mike looked at his watch. Time to go home. Time to take Shelley away from Zagaran.

Setting down his glass, he noticed Andrea Zagaran hovering in the shadows of the terrace. The way she stood, hesitating on the perimeter of light, made him think of a small frightened rabbit. As he started toward the ballroom he saw Mrs. Dinwiddie confront her hostess.

"My dear Andrea, Dinny and I were just leaving. What a lovely party!"

"I'm glad you enjoyed it," Andrea Zagaran began, but the older woman overrode her.

"My dear, so many people. Why, I haven't seen Maggie Mallon —she married Senator Bentley—in years. Her parents used to bring her to Hunting Hill . . ." Mrs. Dinwiddie rattled on, giving a rundown on the assorted guests.

Mike had heard that Mrs. Dinwiddie's monogram, T. T. T. for Theresa Telford Talbot, stood for tall, tactless, temperance. Now Mike heard her saying, "But I mustn't keep you. Just one thing, my dear." As she towered over the younger woman, her untidy hair coming loose from its amber hairpins gave her an eerie witch-like appearance. "It's only fair to warn you—"

"My love, it's time to go," R. Rutherford Dinwiddie said, coming up with her wrap.

"Dinny always laughs at my psychic powers," Mrs. Dinwiddie said. "Nevertheless, my predictions do come true. Just the other day something told me that Fax was going to get a fall schooling that young horse."

"I must see if they need anything on the buffet," Andrea put in desperately.

"This concerns you, my dear." Mrs. Dinwiddie's voice rose. "You know, a curse is on Ballyhoura. Evil and violence—"

"The car is waiting," her husband announced firmly, taking her arm. "Good-by, Mrs. Zagaran. Wonderful party."

"Lovely," the Beast echoed. "Now, Andrea, do take care . . ."

Andrea Zagaran stared after them. Her face, splashed by light from the flares surrounding the terrace, looked pale and appalled.

Impulsively, Mike made his way to her side. "Mrs. Zagaran, I'm Mike Latimer. I haven't had a chance to speak to you before. My wife Shelley and I were late arriving. Mrs. Zagaran, may I get you something?"

Andrea started. For an instant she stared at him blankly. Then, as though the effort to remain upright was almost more than she was capable of, she began to sway.

"Mrs. Zagaran," Mike cried, reaching toward her, "don't you want to sit down?"

Her head swiveled slowly around. "Oh, no." She seemed to shrink back into the shadows.

"Then, may I get you a drink?"

"I'll take care of her," Zagaran said softly.

Neither of them had seen him coming. In the strange light, Andrea's eyes were two black holes in her white face.

"Darling," Zagaran said, "I thought you'd gone to bed. You came back for a nightcap? Is that it?" He beckoned to Manassas Brown, who had stepped away from the bar to clear a nearby table. "Manassas, fix Mrs. Zagaran a highball. Bourbon. You know the way she likes it. Have it taken to her room."

Manassas looked undecided. He started to speak and then, at the sight of his employer's face, thought better of it. Ducking his head in assent, he replied, "Right away, sir."

"She'll be all right now," Zagaran said curtly. Dismissing Mike, he put a proprietary arm around his wife's shoulders and started to lead her away. "I'll see you back to your room. Manassas will bring your drink—"

"Don't," Andrea cried desperately. Like a terrified animal, she sought to escape his grasp. "Zagaran, please."

"There, there, my dear." His voice was soothing. "Rest is what you need."

For a moment Mike stared after them. The glimpse of Andrea's colorless terror-stricken face filled him with foreboding. Should he have intervened? He did not know. Turning back into the light, he was sure of one thing. Andrea Zagaran lived in mortal fear of her husband.

"Mike," Misty Montague called, "come and join us."

Turning, he saw her sitting with the Reverend Chamberlain.

The sight of them was like a reprieve.

"Thanks," he said gratefully. "I should like to find Shelley and go home. Maybe just one drink."

When he was seated, Misty put her hand on his arm. "You look as if you'd seen a ghost. We'll get some more champagne. This bottle is almost empty."

In her long-sleeved blue dress, the bodice of which was held in place by an old-fashioned cameo, with her beaked aristocratic features and magnificent blue-black hair which she wore brushed up from her fine head like a crown, Misty was one of the most picturesque and arresting figures at the ball.

Mike's mood lightened. Of all the people in The Valley, Misty was one of the few he could talk to. There was about her a quality of sympathy, of understanding and maturity, that made her responsive in a way which was different from the rest of the Valley women. Lacking self-awareness, the others rode their own lines, making communication on any but their own equine or sexual levels exceedingly difficult. With Misty, one could communicate without words.

Now she seemed to sense his need for reassurance, for a renewal of strength.

"I read your editorial on civil rights. I thought it was wonderful. I told the Reverend so."

"You're in the minority. Curious that the foxhunters are so short-sighted. It's their hallowed country we're trying to preserve."

"It's always been that way. Nobody wants to rock the boat. This is a way of life that hinges on land and on The Hunt, and The Hunt is dependent on the availability of help. In this case and in this place, the help is predominantly Negro. Without a cheap supply of Negro labor, life wouldn't be nearly so pleasant. Remember, Mike, I warned you. The first time we met, I told you this community was a freak little vacuum, an intellectual desert. Yet somehow you've managed to put the paper on its feet."

In the candlelight, Misty's eyes, wide-set and flecked with

green lights, held a sudden warmth. "I thought the *Sun* was finished. I didn't see how anybody, not even Joseph Pulitzer himself, could rejuvenate it." She raised her champagne glass. "Mike, here's to you."

"I'll drink to that, also," said the Reverend Chamberlain.

And Mike, who moments before had felt adrift in an alien and hostile sea, felt suddenly heartened.

The Reverend Chamberlain was worn out. All night he had been keeping an apprehensive eye on his flock. Aside from comforting the tearful Millicent (on his way out the door, Bones had playfully tweaked the waxed ends of Dash-Smythe's mustache and his rival had retaliated by knocking him down), there was little he could do to deter his parishioners from overindulgence. The Valley's emotional laundry, soiled by broken commandments, was continually being laid at his door. The struggle to mend broken relationships and avoid the tragedies brought on by too much money, too much of everything, had taken its toll. Healthy, robust when he first came to Shelburn's Episcopal Church, he was now gaunt, wasted by a stomach ulcer.

Turning to Mike, he asked, "All set for tomorrow?"

"I think so. It worries me that Mase hasn't called. Too late now to phone him. I'll do it first thing in the morning."

"Have you told Bentley?"

Mike shook his head. "He's got enough to worry about."

"But you're sure Mase will call off the demonstration?" the Reverend persisted.

"No point in demonstrating if the town's desegregated," Mike pointed out.

"I hope you're right. A demonstration against the leading exponent of the civil rights bill could hurt the cause."

"How strange," Misty said suddenly. "Here we sit discussing something of vital import to all of us and yet practically nobody else here has the slightest inkling of it."

"They will tomorrow morning," the Reverend said, "when I announce from the pulpit that Shelburn has been desegregated."

At that moment, Polo Pete Buford lurched over. When he was sober, Polo Pete did not present an attractive personality. But Polo Pete drunk, combative, with a vicious gleam in his small eyes, was revolting.

Clapping the Reverend on the back, he demanded, "Want to

know your stand on this nigger thing. Understand you're in favor of desegregating The Valley." He waggled a white-gloved finger under the clergyman's nose. "Mustn't forget that building fund. New church still needs another coat of whitewash."

"Why, P. P.?" Misty interrupted mildly. "Why another coat of whitewash?"

"Not white enough," Polo Pete replied. "Not careful, Manassas Brown'll be sitting in my pew. Yankee editor"—he jerked his thumb at Mike—"has the nigras all stirred up. Between Wash Taylor and that preacher at Muster Corner, no telling what'll happen next. Somebody ought to burn that school down. They tell me he's teaching those nigra boys to chase after white women. Reminds me, have you heard the story about the nigger in the restaurant?"

Mike started toward him, but the Reverend restrained him.

"Mr. Buford," he said wearily, "if you'll please—"

"Relax, Reverend." Polo Pete pushed him back into his chair. Lurching off, he called back over his shoulder, "See you in church. That is, if your nigger friends haven't taken my pew."

Mike saw that Manassas Brown, his ebony face impassive, had been hovering deferentially in the background, waiting to replace the empty champagne bottle with a full one. He'd heard, of course. Mike sighed, sat down. No point in asking Manassas if he'd heard from Mase. Father and son were not speaking to each other.

After Manassas refilled their glasses, there was silence. The Reverend stared down at the wine in front of him. Mike felt compassion for the frail minister whose inner struggle was apparent in the deep lines of his face. In The Valley the Reverend walked a tightrope, seeking to reach a compromise between his conscience and his congregation.

Misty spoke finally. "You know, of course, why he's called Polo Pete?"

"Because of the Yale polo team?" Mike guessed.

Misty shook her head. "When we were teenagers, the boys used to play a game. They called it nigger polo. Pete thought it up. At first they rode horses and carried polo mallets. Later they did it from cars. They used to race through the colored communities—Muster Corner, Skunk Hollow and Screamertown. There were teams. One team in one car, the other team in another. The team that hooked the most Negroes won."

"Hooked?"

"They leaned out the car window with their polo mallets, and caught the person walking along the road by the neck. Then they dragged the Negro into the car, took him out into the woods and beat him up. They almost killed one of Manassas Brown's boys. It was hushed up."

Mase, Mike thought. So that explained his hatred. "What about the law?"

Misty gave an abrupt laugh. "Can you imagine Chester Glover picking up Freddy Fisher, whose father was District Attorney? Or Fax Templeton, whose father was a judge? Or the Talbot boys—or P. P.?" She shook her head. "Far as the law was concerned, it was just the gentry disporting themselves. Boyish pranks!"

"I have never understood why it is that a man like Buford is accepted—not only accepted, fawned over," Mike said.

"We all have our areas of hypocrisy, of compromise," the Reverend said resignedly. "I can lead my flock so far and no further. If I get too far ahead of them, I lose them altogether."

Slowly he gazed around at the floodlit pool, the glittering pavilion, the candle-lit tables. Speaking as if to himself, the Reverend continued. "It's taken me twenty-five years in the ministry to prepare for a place like this. A quarter of a century to learn how to write sermons that might possibly get a fraction of my message across." He shrugged helplessly. "What can you do with people like Mrs. R. Rutherford Dinwiddie, who stopped writing letters and, I might add, paying bills, when the new Lincoln stamp was issued?"

"The Northerners are worse," Misty said. "The types who move into The Valley and try to be more extreme than the Southerners in their attitudes."

"I doubt if there's another place in the world like this valley," the Reverend continued. "In Philadelphia, where I come from, we used to say that the Jews controlled business, the Quakers culture, the Catholics politics. Here you have no Jews or Quakers or Catholics, no industry, culture or politics. Subconsciously people, even Polo Pete, feel this lack. To give him credit, he did make a stab at running for the State Legislature."

"Might have made it, too," Misty said, "if he hadn't gotten drunk at the Cup Race Meet and fallen down in the paddock."

"Why should that stop him?" Mike asked seriously. "Senator 'States Rights' Talbot gets drunk every race day."

"But you don't understand." Misty's eyes gleamed with quiet humor. "It wasn't the getting drunk that ruined his political career. It was the fact that he frightened the horses."

Overcome by a need to escape from the noise and confusion and meaningless promiscuity, Shelley headed for the garden. Outside the perimeter of light she noticed a man standing behind one of the box bushes. Oblivious of her presence, he was gazing intently at the dancers in the pavilion. Shelley was about to continue on her way when something about the onlooker, the intensity of his watchfulness, like a deer poised for flight, caught her attention.

A couple, Tatine Zagaran and Sandy Montague, laughing and arms entwined, came across the grass. At the sound of their approach, the man turned.

As he did so, Shelley recognized the young, handsome face of Richard Doyle, The Hunt's new whipper-in, who had recently moved into the cottage by the stable. Wearing riding breeches and a tight-fitting turtleneck jersey that clung to his hard, muscular upper body, there was about him a reality, a rugged maleness lacking in the callow collegians dancing in the pavilion.

As Tatine approached, he stepped out from behind the box bush. Tatine's laughter died. Detaching herself from Sandy, she walked up to the Young Whip. Briefly their faces became silent, withdrawing into a sudden vast reserve which their eyes indicated was for themselves alone.

Abruptly the Young Whip nodded. Then he turned and was gone, vanishing into the shadows.

Shelley felt an emptiness she could not define, standing in similar shadow beyond the spectacle of the colored fountains. In the distance, the lights of Shelburn seemed part of the star-dusted horizon, as unreal and make-believe as the multicolored curtains of water.

Bending down, she slipped off her shoes. Beneath her feet the smooth turf felt rich, luxuriant. She took a deep breath. After the smoke and perfume and the smell of Polo Pete's stale breath, the crisp beginning fall richness of the air, the scent of earth and flowers began to restore her. The artificial conversations, the fumbled immature lovemaking seemed far away. Looking up at the stars, she was aware of the power of infinity, of something never ending. Ignoring bombs and the destructive forces of men, it would go on and on, long after the vines and underbrush grew back in the park, blanketing the ruins of Ballyhoura, choking the pampered, carefully cultivated countryside. Standing there alone, she had a sense of currents sweeping past her, stranding her in the backwaters of the present.

Carrying her slippers, she moved across the grass. From the house came the sound of music, barbaric, sensual. It filled her with a wildness, a recklessness, a need for some physical outlet. She wished she could run home, tack up her horse and gallop over the misted moonlit fields.

The outlines of the gazebo rose before her. The old latticed enclosure had a ghostly quality. It belonged to another, gentler age—that of crinolines and picture hats, poetry and tea served in delicate china cups. Amid the outcroppings of buildings jutting from the expanse of landscaped perfection, it was as incongruous as the recently completed bomb shelter rising hideously behind the stables.

Pushing through the vines obscuring the entrance, Shelley found herself inside the cool perfumed interior. Sinking down onto the circular bench, she dropped her shoes onto the floor.

The music stopped. Larry Lester was taking a break. In place of the primitive modern beat came the isolated bay of a hound and the sound of footsteps.

She looked up and saw him there. In the doorway, framed by the wisteria and the moonlight, as if he had materialized out of a dream.

"I thought I'd find you here."

"Hadn't you better go back to your party?" she asked coolly.

He brushed a cluster of wisteria out of his way. Bowing his head in order not to hit it against the latticework lintel, he entered the gazebo and lowered himself onto the bench beside her.

"Hmmmm." He sucked in his breath. "Nice perfume. Essence of vixen?"

She felt the color moving under her cheeks, like fire raked to life by his words. "Are bad manners part of the Zagaran charm?"

The sudden sound of hoofs beating against the walls of a stall interrupted her. "What is that?"

"Black Magic, the mare I bought to hunt."

"So you've given up gardening. Now it's horses and The Hunt! Somebody really should have warned you. Fax Templeton in his best days couldn't take Magic out with hounds. When she was at the track she almost killed three men."

"You're absolutely right. Somebody should have warned me."

She threw him a quick glance, but his face was expressionless. The mockery she sensed behind his words and manner drove her on.

"People who move into The Valley and buy horses without knowing what they're doing deserve to be done. I suppose the first thing you did was to buy a pink coat."

"Of course." He cocked an eyebrow. "Doesn't everyone? And black boots with brown tops and a high silk hat." He studied her. "What are you afraid of?"

"Afraid!" She really looked at him now, no longer dismissing him like a horse that had been led out for her inspection and then not measured up to requirements. "That's ridiculous. What would *I* be afraid of?"

"Then why do you cover your mouth with the back of your hand when you speak?"

The music started up again. The shadows and night scents and noises, the close intimacy in the gazebo struck her mind like the strains of the well-remembered tunes. The vitality, the aliveness, the power and passion that his presence transmitted to her gave rise to sudden hot excitement not unlike the elation she had felt when facing the gate. At the same time she, who knew no physical fear, was terrified of emotional involvement.

"I must find Mike and go home."

"Not before you answer my question."

She had been brought up to believe that showing one's innermost feelings was like wearing hair curlers in public, or going to church without white gloves.

"There is no reason why I should answer a personal question like that." She started to stand up. "I don't even know you!"

"No, but you will."

His eyes narrowed. In them something moved that, like the feather-light touch of his index finger on her wrist, had the power to force her backward, back down onto the bench. A strange trembling ran through her and all at once she felt shy and awkward, like a young girl at her first dance.

"Mike will wonder where I am."

"Let him wonder."

"What is it you want from me?"

"You," he said simply. "I want you."

Unconsciously, her hand went to her mouth. He reached up gently and drew it down.

"You have a beautiful mouth. Why hide it? Afraid of what you might say? That is, if you should ever permit yourself to speak the truth."

His face was close to hers. It was true, what he said. She was afraid, had always been afraid. She had been afraid of Fax when he'd tried to make love to her. She had begun then building a wall around herself that was as high and impenetrable as the wall that had once protected Shelburn land. Mike was the only man she had never been afraid of. Although she could not dominate him in matters of the mind, in matters of the flesh she held the upper hand. And somehow this had caused a growing dissatisfaction, an emptiness like the feeling that came after a young horse's schooling was completed, before the breaking in of a new one began. It was as if there was a phase of existence that still, despite the birth of her child, her return to The Valley, to the land that she loved, and the unceasing activity that revolved around horses and the newspaper, remained unfulfilled. Again she was conscious of his clean male smell, of the expensive shaving lotion, clothes and tobacco. Suddenly, like a breath of the night air turning cold, the feeling came over her that they were being watched. Turning, she saw pinpoints of greenish fire. A sense of the uncanny, of an intelligence more human than animal, made her cry out.

His hand holding hers tightened. "It's only a fox. One of the cubs I'm trying to tame."

She saw a tautness come into his face, a kind of excited wariness. A hunter's face, she thought, watching him, as if he were stalking a quarry.

As the fox, with a disdainful flick of its brush, continued on its way, moving without fear or hurry into the shadows, she felt burdened with the strange sense of guilt that had begun in the bedroom and which, all night, she had been unable to shake off.

The eyes had vanished. Yet the sense of the animal's presence remained. With all her strength, she twisted out of Zagaran's grasp.

There was a clinking sound as one of her sapphire earrings fell onto the stone floor.

"Wait!" she heard him call. "You forgot your earring!"

She was breathless when she reached the deserted terrace. She felt that she had been running for her life. Then she saw Mike coming toward her, carefully picking his way through the debris of abandoned furniture and empty glasses, and her sudden sense of deliverance was replaced with one of annoyance.

Why doesn't he get a haircut? she thought. And his evening clothes don't fit. He had not had time, he told her, to go to the barber, and in the months since he had last worn his dinner jacket he had, because of overwork and uncertain mealtimes, lost weight. These things had not bothered her before. But now, for some reason, she expected him to be different. The fact that he was the same made her annoyed with herself, with him, and with everything around her—the cigarette butts and plates and misplaced chairs, the disarray that was the aftermath of the ball.

"I was worried about you," Mike said as he came closer. "Shelley, you're missing an earring and where are your shoes?"

"I took them off," she said shortly. Aware that some further explanation seemed needed, she added, "They weren't any good for running."

"Running?" He looked past her, into the empty shadows. "Of course. Everyone runs, doesn't everyone?" As if to clear his head, he drew the back of his hand across his forehead. "Next time we go to a dance, I'll buy you a pair of track shoes. Well, Cinderella, it's long past midnight. Do you want to find your jewels and slippers, or shall we go home without them?"

"Let's go." She put her hand in his. "I'll come back and get them."

"You mustn't lose one of the Shelburn Sapphires."

"It's all right. He—" She broke off. "I mean, I'm sure someone will find it and return it."

He tucked her arm under his. "Come then. The ball is over."

TWO

WHEN Shelley awoke Sunday morning, it was with a sense of tension, of unease. As she lay still, listening to the sound of the wind in the century-old trees, she had the feeling of some imminent disaster, seeded long ago in a tangle of origins, influences and motives, and which now seemed on the verge of breaking forth with the accumulated force of years. The familiar sound of the wind, the banty roosters crowing, the cacophony of cicadas, brought back a sudden nostalgia for childhood, for peace and unhurry and that sense of wholeness taken for granted. As though seeking strength, reassurance, she reached for Mike. He stirred, mumbled something and turned over on his back. She studied his profile. Strong-featured, yet fine-grained. A good face. A face that was open and honest and sensitive to hurt.

Impulsively, she rested her cheek against his chest. In his sleep his arm closed around her, holding her against him. Slowly her tension eased. The hair on his chest tickled her nose. The sound of the wind died away. Overhead a mouse skittered across the attic floor. Miehle, the black Labrador, arose from his blanket and stretched.

"Good morning, Mummy. Good morning, Daddy."

Cam thrust his golden head around the corner of the doorway. Eyes wide and very blue. Cheeks flushed from sleep. Wisps of gossamer hair rose from the cowlick on the crown of his head. Fat rosy knees showed through the holes in his last year's sleepers.

As always, her son's beauty struck Shelley with renewed delight. In it lay a spiritual quality, a suggestion of gentleness and innocence not in any way feminine. At first Shelley had thought herself prejudiced. He could not be as beautiful to others as he seemed to her. But when strangers stopped to exclaim over his fairness and astonishing blue eyes, she realized that he really was a striking child. Looking from one to the other, people were puzzled. "No, he doesn't look like Mike or me," Shelley would reply.

"He must get his hair and coloring from his Grandfather Fitzgerald."

"I want to get in with you." Cam's expression was eager, expectant.

With one hand he clutched the sagging bottoms of his pajamas. The other rested lightly on Lance, the great fawn-colored mastiff that slept protectively beside his bed and never wandered far from his side.

A feeling of wonder, of love, engulfed Shelley. Sitting up in bed, she opened her arms. "O.K."

With an excited cry, her son ran to her. As she hugged him, he began to wiggle. "I want my daddy." Wriggling out of Shelley's grasp, Cam landed on his father's chest.

Mike groaned. "Ugh. Who's this?"

Lance put his forepaws on the bed. His black furrowed mastiff brow wore its usual expression of anxiety. As Mike tossed Cam into the air, the dog pushed his great head against him warningly.

"It's all right," Mike reassured him. "I won't hurt him."

The ritual of awakening was followed by coffee from the electric percolator plugged in beside the bed and the Sunday morning treat of "sticky buns," remnants of which Cam scattered in the bedclothes. During this close family interlude, the vast four-poster seemed an island of love and laughter and security.

Suddenly, unaccountably, it seemed to Shelley that a shadow, like that of Zagaran's plane rising from the airstrip at Ballyhoura and passing across the path of the sun, descended over them. Inadvertently, Cam jiggled her arm, spilling her coffee.

"Cam," she snapped irritably, "damn it, look what you've done."

When she spoke to Cam in what he called her "mad voice," his face crumpled. His blue eyes filled with tears.

"I'm sorry," Shelley apologized, gathering him to her. "Mummy's tired after the ball. Hurry. Get dressed. We'll have waffles for breakfast. This afternoon we'll take a walk."

"Is this Sunday School day?" Cam asked when they were at breakfast.

Shelley nodded. "Here's some melted butter."

She watched the butter spreading over the waffles. It was the color of his hair, of the sun pouring in through the opened windows, highlighting the black iron wood-burning stove that took up the length of one wall, glancing off the remains of King Shelburn's Lowestoft and Waterford glass, hidden away on the highest shelf of the glass-fronted cupboards, and the waxed sheen of the table at which they sat. When they had returned to Shelburn Hall the kitchen was a cavernous, echoing place, as gloomy and dark as the inside of a bourbon bottle. Now it was the family room. The great front ballroom-drawing room was closed off, left to the faded elegance of the maroon draperies and matching Aubusson; and the pine-paneled dining room, its alcoves filled with tarnished silver trophies and julep cups, and the refectory table large enough to seat all the members of The Hunt, was used only for the traditional Sunday lunches Shelley had started giving during the hunting season

The kitchen had been painted white. Melusina, Shelley's old nurse, sewed gay red curtains for the windows and replanted the geraniums in the green-painted pots. Shelley brought two rocking chairs down from the attic and placed them on either side of the Tiffany lamps set on the now defunct stove where newspapers, magazines and Mike's pipe rack had been laid out. It was a warm and cosy room which people never failed to exclaim over when they entered. Now fresh coffee simmered on the stove, the banties waiting for Cam to throw feed to them pecked at the window, the chameleon Mike had bought Cam at the Fireman's Carnival scurried about in his box, and the dogs lay on the floor. Shelley remembered the mornings in New York, smog and the sounds of traffic. She looked at Cam, his head bent over his plate, and found herself seized with delight in the golden day, her family, and all that was around her, wanting to hold everything to her and bask in the warmth and wonder of knowing it was hers.

"Mike, come to church with us," she said impulsively. "You haven't been in ages."

"You'll be in Sunday School."

"I just have the children during the sermon."

Mike glanced worriedly at his watch. "I'm expecting a call at the office." He put down his coffee cup. "I should be leaving now. I'll try to be finished up by eleven. Stop by the paper and pick me up."

"Do you have to go? This is Sunday. People aren't supposed to work on Sunday. We're asked to Last Resort for lunch. Mike, I wish you wouldn't get involved."

"Tomorrow's Labor Day." He went on talking to himself as if he hadn't heard her. "I have to get enough copy up for Josh to set if he comes in."

Shelley moved her plate aside. "Let's take a walk this afternoon. The three of us. We haven't taken a walk together in ages."

Mike stood up. "I'll try to be through in time for church. I'd like to hear the Reverend Chamberlain's sermon this morning." At the door he turned. "By the way," he said casually, "why don't you take Jimmy to Sunday School? I found him reading that book about Jesus we gave Cam last Christmas. He asked me a lot of questions."

Jimmy was the son of Jubal, the *Sun*'s drunken janitor. He had been living on a cot in the tack room and working at the paper through the summer. Afternoons, Shelley gave him riding lessons in order to have help exercising the horses.

"Mike, you're not serious! You remember what happened when Enid Jenney was teaching Sunday School and brought some of the Muster Corner children? Mrs. Dinwiddie, Polo Pete, the Jacksons, converged on Reverend Chamberlain and demanded that Enid be asked to resign. When the Reverend refused, P. P. yanked Buddha out of the class. The Blacks, Atwells, Baldwins —lots of others—took their kids out, too."

"What kind of Christianity are you teaching?" Mike asked. His voice was ominously mild.

"Mike, we've been through this before. This is the South."

"Simeon Tucker's children are a damn sight cleaner and better mannered than Buddha Buford."

"That's not the point," Shelley explained helplessly. "Some things are right and some things are wrong. After a certain age it's wrong for white children to associate with colored."

"And why in hell is that?"

"It just isn't done."

"Oh, for Christ's sake," Mike broke in. "Shelley, grow up. This is not 1863. Understand this. My son is not, I repeat *not*, going to be brought up in schizophrenic Southern style. He is *not* going to have his mind cluttered up with prejudicial claptrap. My God, Shelley, he's going to have to live and work in a world without a wall between black and white. Whether you like it or not, the clock can't be turned back." He strode out.

"Mike," she cried after him. "Mike, please—" She ran to the door, but he was already in the Jeep. "Mike, are you taking Miehle with you or shall I?"

"I'll take him. Obviously, *you* can't take him to Sunday School with you. He's black!"

Shelley clenched her fists. Her delight in the golden day was tarnishing, like the silver in the dining room. Last night, sitting alone in the summerhouse before Zagaran had shattered her composure, she had begun to understand some of the reasons that had drawn her back to The Valley. She wanted to show that she had made her life a success. Above all, she wanted to prove that she was invulnerable. In order to be safe, beyond anyone's power to injure her, it was necessary to accept the established order. Pony Club, Christmas Bazaar, the Women's Guild, the Hound Show and Sunday School, all the things she gave herself to, were part of the acceptable pattern. Now Mike was endangering her hard-won sense of security, the security she told herself was essential to Cam and his future. Mike had begun rocking the boat, had formed the Human Relations Council, blacks and whites working together to integrate the county.

Shelley stacked the breakfast dishes and fed the dogs. After putting on lipstick and foxhead earrings that matched her fox crystal watch and bracelet, she grabbed a pair of white gloves and the Shelburn prayer book. She was wearing her old blue tweed suit, her racing suit, which signaled the end of summer and the beginning of fall. Although it was ten years old, it was beautifully tailored—it had been made in London along with her last riding habit—and did not look out of style. Her felt riding and fishing hat, which was decorated with multicolored flies and resided on the hall table amid a welter of spurs, hunting crops, string gloves, toy trucks, unopened bills and her velvet hunting cap, completed her church costume.

She was fighting off the hound puppies that had come running from the stable and which threatened in their exuberant friendliness to tear her stockings and knock Cam down, when the crimson pickup truck came along the drive. Even before she saw the blue stripe painted across the door with "Ballyhoura" written above it, she felt the prickling excitement, the sudden anticipation.

"Morning, Miss Shelley." Sam Tucker, Simeon's brother, hired as chauffeur, doffed his black cap. "Mr. Zagaran sent me over with these." He indicated the back of the pickup. It was entirely filled with buckets of crimson roses.

"Surely they're not all for me?"

"Yes, they are, Miss Shelley. Mr. Zagaran told me, 'You be sure to get them over there this morning, as many as the truck will carry!' Dulany Douglas, he's gardener to Ballyhoura now, he's been cutting all morning long."

"Sam," Shelley gasped, "I can't accept them."

"Best take them, Miss Shelley," the Negro said, opening the back. "Mr. Zagaran will be angry if you don't." He began lifting the containers out of the truck. "Where should I put them?"

"Mummy," Cam cried delightedly, "we can put them in the bathtub, like the daffodils."

"I almost forgot." The chauffeur handed her a note. "Mr. Zagaran gave me this."

Shelley tore open the envelope. Inside was her sapphire earring wrapped in cotton, Scotch-taped to a piece of crested notepaper. In the center, a large Z had been scrawled.

Mike climbed into the secondhand Jeep he'd bought soon after acquiring the newspaper and drove slowly off. Miehle stood on the seat, his head out the window. The Labrador was a gift from Shelley's friend Millicent Black. A Black reject, Mike called him.

Millicent had wanted a retriever to train for the field. She had bought the dog as a puppy from a famous Eastern kennel, where she paid a big price for him. His breeder had warned that the Labrador was intelligent and high-strung and to start him slowly, with utmost patience. The day after the dog's arrival, Millicent tied his leash to her belt, took him out in the field and fired twenty-one shots over the pup's head. From then on, whenever the Labrador heard a sudden noise, he dissolved into panic. Millicent was disgusted. Bitterly she complained that the dog was a coward and that she had been robbed. Hearing that Mike was anxious for a Labrador as a house dog, she had been delighted to give the puppy away. Because it had come at the same time as the new press, Mike had christened him Miehle.

He had wanted a dog which would keep him company in the office on nights when he worked alone while Pete ran the big press in the back of the shop. But the noise of the old secondhand flatbed terrified the dog. The first time the Lab heard the rumbling of the press, he burrowed behind a pile of newsprint and lay in the dark corner shaking, until the noise subsided. Watching him, Mike wondered how it was that some of the hunting people who professed to care about their animals more than about their children could indulge in such unthinking cruelty.

Yet Shelley, he thought, was not like Millicent and the other Four-H girls, the Slap Leather Set, who rode to hounds with tense, anxious do-or-die expressions and cigarettes stuck in the corners of their mouths, animated splints with bashed-in heads and broken bones who considered it bad form to stop and inquire if one had a fall when hounds were running.

Shelley, in fact, was too much the other way. She was always rescuing stray animals, keeping other people's children and listening to other people's troubles.

A New Englander, descended from generations of abolitionists, Mike was astonished at the attitudes he encountered in The Valley. Lately, as he sat in the cluttered newspaper office wondering how to penetrate the ancient patterns of prejudice, the wall of material smugness against which he now seemed to be ineffectually butting his editorial head, and at the same time meet the bills mounting on his desk, he was aware of a sense of weariness and futility. Then some small thing would happen to counteract his mounting despair. In the eyes of men like Washington Taylor and Preacher Booker T. Young of the Muster Corner Baptist Church he would see the growing flame of hope which, with his pen, he had managed to kindle. Paradoxically, the very thing that kept him from selling the *Sun*, that gave meaning to the grinding work and compensated for his canceled advertising, was the same thing that now seemed to be threatening his marriage. He could almost understand how Shelley felt. She was a Southerner, a Shelburn. It was an attitude of mind, just as her sense of family and love of the land had been imbued in her bones. Although in some ways she felt closer to Virginia City, the stableman, and to Melusina than she did to her husband or her child, it was physically impossible for her to sit down at the same table in a restaurant with the old colored woman who had rocked her to sleep against her breast. Nor would Virginia City or Melusina have expected her to. It would not be fitting. Class lines were rigidly drawn and in some curious way their position, as family retainers, was stronger than his. It was all baffling and illogical and emotional.

Shelley's years in the North had in no way changed her viewpoint. If anything, the "uppity" Northern Negroes with their harsh voices and determined equality on buses and subways had only solidified her sense of difference, the feeling that "if God had meant the blacks to be equal, he would have made them white." Yet she could regale dinner guests with the story of her greatuncle, Carter Shelburn, who raised a son by his Muster Corner mistress. Known in the family as Carter's Ink—his actual name had been Thomas Shelburn—he had been raised on the island of Barbados, where he made a fortune in sugar and his descendants now owned one of the largest estates on the island.

Although Mike saw no difference whatever between white and black, and instinctively judged people as individuals regardless of the color of their skin or their religious beliefs, he respected his wife's feelings. Erroneous though he held them to be, her beliefs had been shaped by her heritage and environment.

Now, after living in the ghost-ridden house where on winter nights when the wind blew he listened to a thousand creaking sounds and it seemed he could hear the spirit of the infant born illegitimately to a Shelburn woman and bricked up in the wall struggling to be released, hear Shelley's grandmother's nocturnal steps and wild singing, he understood what she had not been able to tell him. Her grandmother, her mother, her father were all gone, yet in her, in the house, they lived on.

When he had first known her, when she was galloping the gray horse in the early morning light, she had been transfigured, free of the inarticulateness and self-doubt that came over her on the ground. He remembered how drab he had felt alongside Fax Templeton, Bones Black, and the others of her world. He wondered then why she had consented to marry him, a poor newsman without flair or fancy tweeds.

The first time he had seen her was at Belmont Park. He was having lunch with Tad Shapiro, the *Globe* columnist, at Bleeck's. Tad, a thin, wiry man with darting black eyes and a mind that many considered brilliant, had won a Pulitzer Prize for his combat stories on the Korean war. During one frozen, bloody march Mike had rescued the older man from a ditch where he lay

wounded and helped him to a medic who treated the bullet
wound in his shoulder. Although Mike did not consider that he
had done anything which anyone else wouldn't have done, Tad
boasted that Mike had saved his life. Through Tad he had been
promoted to doing features for the *Sunday Globe*.

"You need a break," Tad said, observing Mike. "Come to the
track with me this afternoon."

"You mean race track?" Mike concentrated on his club sandwich. "You know how I feel about horses. They're fine for some
people, like foreign cars or women. As for me, I can take them
if I have to but I'd rather leave them alone."

"Come on," Tad urged. "Marina says you look peaked, that you
need a girl—"

Mike held up his hand. "Now wait a minute, old buddy—"

"Seriously," Tad went on, "I ran across this girl. A horse trainer
and a painter. Make a good feature. Human interest stuff. She has
one horse, home-bred and homemade, and lives and paints in a
trailer with a dog the size of a pony."

"I know the type," Mike replied darkly. "Has two legs and
walks like a man—"

"This one's different. Old South and wisteria and all that."

"Oh, God," Mike groaned, "if there's anything I can do without it's Southern belles with a hollow ring."

Still, not because he wanted to but because he had nothing else
to do that afternoon and did need material for an article, he accepted.

Her horse was named The Gray Goose, and he was running,
at odds that were ten to one, in the brush race. The horse jumped
so big over the brush that he lost ground at each fence. At the
end, however, he came from fourth place to win by a nose.

Afterward they found her at one of the far barns, cooling him
out, doing the work entirely herself. Aside from the fawn-colored
mastiff lying protectively in front of the horse's stall and the horse
itself, she seemed totally alone.

She wore blue jeans, an old pair of moccasins which had come
unsewn, disclosing bare toes, and a man's blue shirt, ripped at the
shoulder. She had on no make-up and her hair was wild and
uncombed. Her eyes, blue-violet and fringed with thick black
lashes, were startling and she had an especially beautiful mouth,
short, with a full upper lip at the corner of which was an almost

imperceptible tuft of golden down. She had a look about her like that of the horse she was scraping the lather from—well-bred and high-strung.

He found himself watching her, the way she kept pushing the blue-black hair which came loose from the knot at the nape of her neck, obscuring the curving cheekline. The grace with which she moved was automatic rather than assumed. She was very thin, very hard—almost, but not quite, gaunt. There was nothing about her to indicate femininity, yet Mike had the feeling she was the most feminine girl he had ever met.

Tad explained that Mike had been in Korea, was now in the feature section of the *Globe* and was interested in doing a story about her.

"Not about me," she said quickly, "about The Goose." The way she put her hand on the horse's neck and looked at him indicated her feelings for him. "You saw him win today. Isn't he wonderful? He was schooled as a hunter, in a stone-wall country. So he refuses to go through the brush the way the others do. It tickles his stomach and he doesn't like it. If he didn't jump so big, over the top of it, he'd win every race by miles."

She picked up a bucket and went to a spigot where a line of grooms and hot walkers were queued up waiting to fill their pails. Mike offered to help, but the mastiff growled warningly.

"I'll do it," she said quickly, restraining the dog.

He watched her walk to the head of the line, where an old Negro in a battered straw hat quickly moved his bucket out of the way. "Here you are, Miss Shelley," the man said courteously. "You all go on ahead and get your water."

"Thank you, Stanley." She shoved her bucket under the spigot. While it filled up, she stood to one side discussing the afternoon's racing with the elderly Negro and the younger ones lined up behind him.

Mike was fascinated with the performance. Obviously, it had not occurred to her to wait in line behind the others. And although she seemed to be doing the same job that they were, there was unconscious acceptance of her as having privileges which they didn't, and this did not in any way seem to be resented. Instead, the word "affection" came to mind. Honest affection on her side for the old groom now telling her about his teenage son who

64

was breezing horses for a big-name stable and hoped to become a jockey.

As she walked the horse around, she told Mike his history. Her voice was beautiful, he thought. Low, musical, utterly unlike the nasal twang he associated with Southerners. The Goose, she said, had been bred on her parents' farm in Virginia. He was of the famous Galway Pilot strain founded by her grandfather. Rejected by his mother, he had been a frail, spindly-legged colt. In order to save him, she had sat up with him for three weeks, bottle-feeding him every four hours. As a two-year-old he had been so small that nobody wanted to bother with him. She had broken him and trained him as a hunter. Aware of his speed, she entered him in local point-to-points, all of which he won. He then started in Maryland, at Middleburg and in the Shelburn Cup, where he came in second. Thinking he might do well over brush, she had taken out a trainer's license. For the past year she had lived at the track.

"He's a real pet," she said as the horse lifted his right front leg and nuzzled her for sugar. "The first time he went to the post he tried to shake hands with the starter."

Then it was time to put the horse away and Mike realized he might not see her again.

"There are still some questions I'd like to ask you," he said quickly. "What it's like being a trainer—I gather it's a rather unusual profession for a girl—how you live and so forth."

"You don't want to hear about me." When other people said this he never believed them, but the way she spoke told him she was sincere. "But if you like you can come to the trailer. I'll give you a cup of coffee and show you some pictures of The Goose."

"I have to catch the five-twenty," Tad said, looking at his watch. "Marina is waiting for me. Mike, you can take a later train."

Mike turned, surprised. He had been so engrossed, he'd forgotten all about Tad.

The "trailer" was a pickup truck. The back had been boarded up and a roof added. The bunk bed, two-burner stove, small refrigerator and other basic utilities were routine. Books were piled under the bed and a pair of dusty field boots were thrust under the one chair. The table, converted from an orange crate, was covered with racing forms. On the tiny stand that served as a dressing table were no bottles of perfume or nail polish or any other cosmetics. Merely a hair brush and comb, a button hook and a shoe horn. There were no photographs, nothing that could be considered personal. What was astonishing was the oil painting hanging over her bed—a tall, thin pink-coated foxhunter on a beautiful gray horse. Two hounds stood at its feet and in the background was a turreted castlelike mansion.

"My grandfather," she explained. "His name was Sean Shelburn. He fought in the War Between the States."

"The Civil War?"

She shook her head. "It's never called that in the South. The War Between the States or the War of Northern Aggression."

He wanted to ask her more, but she was busy pulling an old suitcase out from under the cot. In order to do so, it was necessary to extricate first a drawing board and then a portfolio of sketches. One fell to the floor. He picked it up.

"Please," she said, reaching for it. "You don't want to look at those."

He stared at her drawings for a long time, ignoring her protest. He particularly liked the impressionist series, done in charcoal, of horses breezing on the track.

"It's very good," he said, studying the Dufy-type sketch.

She blushed. It had been a long time since he had seen a girl blush. It amazed him that one living alone in the back of a truck would be embarrassed about showing him work which he considered excellent. He was far more interested in seeing her drawings than he was in looking at photographs of the horse—pictures of the gray jumping, crossing the finish line, being presented with cups, parading in the paddock—all the usual horse pictures. He tried to make a show of interest, but all the time he was really observing her.

"Coffee?" she asked, after she put away the suitcase and the portfolio. "Do you mind if it's left over from breakfast?"

"No, not at all."

He tried to make her accept the one chair but she insisted on the floor, one hand on the mastiff's great head resting in her lap, her blue-jeaned legs doubled up underneath her like a schoolgirl.

Under the pretext of interviewing her, he worked to draw her out. But, as they drank the warmed-over coffee, he found himself doing most of the talking. He was not a talkative man, yet he heard himself deliberately dropping facts aimed at inspiring confidence, how he had left Dartmouth his senior year to go into the Navy, where he spent a year in the Pacific aboard a destroyer, how, afterward, he had gone back to college, graduated, spent a year working on the family-owned newspaper in New Hampshire and then gone to work for the *Globe*, first in the rewrite department, then on the city desk, where he had worked his way up to the Korean assignment. Irrelevantly, he added that his mother baked bread and knitted socks for himself and his three brothers, that his father had taught him how to handset type and that he, himself, could wiggle his ears.

"Let me see you," she said gravely.

He obliged and she burst out laughing.

"Brilliant." She sounded gay for the first time. "Positively brilliant."

It gave him the courage to ask if he could take her to dinner. "Or don't you eat anything but hot dogs, standing up?"

"Not tonight." She laughed. "I have some entry forms to fill out and I promised myself I'd go to bed early. I get up at five to work The Goose. But I do get tired of hot dogs, standing or sitting. Maybe some other time." Shyly, she added, "I mean if you need more information about The Goose for the article."

He had never enjoyed getting up in the morning. In college and in the Navy they'd had to drag him out of bed in time for class or to stand watch. Yet the next morning, as the sun was rising behind the jagged Long Island skyline, he stood on the rail with the trainers and timers and touts and watched the whip-thin girl on the gray horse gallop toward him out of the mist. Her hair glittered with diamonds of moisture and her cheeks were the color of the sunrise. As she reined in the race horse, she was laughing. He had an impression of complete confidence, competence, and a joyous freedom and exhilaration. Later, he was to remember how she had been then, that moment, when without really knowing anything about her, he had fallen in love with her.

He walked back to the barn with her.

"Do you usually interview people at this hour?" she asked.

"I wanted to make sure I hadn't dreamed you." He watched the color move into her cheeks.

"For the article?"

"No," he replied impatiently. "Not for the article. Forget the article."

Her color deepened. "I'm not sure I know what you mean." Not looking at him, she added irrelevantly, "I'm afraid— I mean, I'm not good with people. They consider me odd. Stand-offish."

He wanted to take her into his arms then. The impulse was not so much to make love to her as to comfort her.

But the horse stood between them.

In August she moved to Saratoga. He took his two weeks' vacation at the spa. Always before, his idea of a vacation had been to stay up nights and sleep during the day. Instead, he did just the opposite. Mornings he watched while she worked The Goose with other horses. Flattened against the gray's neck, her face buried in his mane, she came down the stretch, neck and neck with one of the exercise boys, the two of them shouting gaily at each other, or singing, then standing high in their stirrups and going half as far again before pulling up. Other mornings he observed her leading the gray from a piebald lead pony, saw how the thoroughbred arched his neck and strained against the shank that forced his long strides to match those of the fat, short-legged pony. Later, whenever he smelled wood smoke he would think of the fires the stableboys set under the trees to ward off the early morning chill and on which they warmed their coffee in tin mugs. In his imagination he would hear the soft crooning of the Negro grooms and swipes as, in the blue smoke-filled dawn light, they rubbed down the horses which had been worked. Although he never became wholly at ease with the high-mettled thoroughbreds that lunged and kicked and reared up en route to the post, he did come to understand the lure of the early morning stable, when the horses awoke to paw and nicker for the sleepy-eyed grooms who came whistling, caps back to front, rub rags sticking from their rear pockets.

On days when The Goose was running he stood outside the paddock watching her, trim in a linen dress, her hair held in place by an invisible hairnet, saddle her horse and issue last minute instructions to the series of pinch-faced jockeys who rode for her. With the jockeys and the other trainers, she exchanged greetings and stable talk and cheerful badinage. Yet when Alfred Gwynn Vanderbilt, Pete Bostwick, T. Patterson Gibson, and Polo Pete Buford paused to speak to her, she maintained a curious aloofness. The only thing that Mike could make of it all was that she felt more at ease with the working fraternity, whom she saw daily, than with the owners.

When the horses had been saddled and were on their way to the post, he walked with her to the stands to sit in the box of her friend, Millicent Black, or to the rail, where, with drawn, anxious face, she watched the race through binoculars, crying, "Come on, Goose, come on. There, he's over. Goose, come on."

He thought of what she had said about being stand-offish and wondered if the reason lay in the fact that she withheld so much about herself. Still, it was these things that drew him, her pride and her reticence. They gave her an elusive quality, an aura of mystery.

From the little that she did say, he acquired a strange, romantic image of an eccentric Southern family living in a crumbling mansion with turnips growing out of the tennis court and wisteria out of the west wing. Her mother had left her father for another man. Her father died shortly afterward and she was brought up by her grandmother, who paced the corridor at night, singing hymns. When her grandmother died, she closed the house and moved to the track. She did not seem to bear anyone any ill will. In fact, she told the story of her childhood as dispassionately as if it had been no different from anyone else's.

Her education consisted of a finishing school. "Like Versailles in its best days," she told him. "Miss Shelburne's was a school of superficialities. My father had a large library and taught me to love books, but on the whole I'm uneducated and uncultured. I spent most of my time drawing horses or playing field hockey in blue bloomers that itched."

When her grandmother died, she discovered that there was no money left, only the great house. Although the headmistress, in view of the fact that she was kin to the founder, offered a scholarship, she turned it down. After paying off her debts with money from the sale of the horses, she closed Shelburn Hall. Placing Virginia City, the old stableman, in charge of the property, she left the country.

He understood why she did not talk much. For most of her twenty-three years, aside from horses and dogs, there had been nobody to listen.

She was like the abstract paintings she kept under her bed. Just when he thought he'd grasped their meaning, it evaded him. The more he saw of her, the more he came to know her, the less he understood her. She was a creature of paradoxes. When he took her to a sentimental second-rate movie, she wept all the way through it. Yet when she saw a horse break its leg on the track she was coldly unemotional. He was never able to judge what her mood would be. Gay, hoydenish, girlish one moment. Serious and mature the next. Although she had read fewer books than he had and had not been to college, he sensed in her the ghost of a culture lacking in himself. She did not talk easily. But when she did, when she spoke of her family or the past, there was a mysterious intonation that hinted of things half said, of emotions charged with meanings of which she could not speak. It was as if within herself she harbored a secret passion and a potential that were, in themselves, an answer to all creation. But the promise of its disclosure, particularly when disclosure seemed the most possible, continually escaped him. This, her individuality and elusiveness, intrigued him, charging him with a desire to dominate, to force her to need him. He knew that they were mismatched, that she did not fit into the way of life he planned for himself. He knew, too, that whether he left her or whether he did not would not affect her. But try as he might—and he did try to let her go—he had the distinct feeling that if he lost her he would lose the most important thing in his life. Whatever it was that bound him to her had spoiled other women for him. When he saw her perched on the back of the gray horse, her hair loose and streaming in the wind, her face radiant, he knew that whatever the outcome, he had to have her.

At Saratoga she had a run of bad luck. In one race the gray got left at the post. In another he was squeezed out at the far turn. And she was worried about the filling in his right front tendon. On top of this, she was running short of money. She refused to borrow from her rich friends like Millicent Black. Instead, in an effort to recoup, she began betting. None of the horses she bet on came in. On a wild impulse, she put her last ten dollars on The Goose to win. Then the thing happened. Somebody had mistakenly left a sprinkler on the landing side of the liverpool. When the gray landed over it, he went in up to his knees. His jockey went over his head and when the horse staggered to his feet, it was obvious that both front legs had bowed.

The track vets advised shooting The Goose. Shelley refused, saying that when he recovered sufficiently she would send him home to Virginia. That night she stayed with her horse. The vets had given him a pain killer. With Lance lying in the straw by her feet, she sat in a corner of the stall. She had not changed from the blue linen dress she'd worn for the race. The skirt was stained. There were runs in both her stockings.

Mike unlatched the stall door. At sight of him The Goose raised his head and tried to take a step toward him. Lance awoke, saw who it was, and dropped his great head back down onto his paws. Without speaking, Mike sat down in the straw beside her, put his arm around her and drew her head down to his shoulder.

"Amazing," Shelley said.

"What's amazing?"

"Lance. He usually goes for anyone who comes near me. Once a drunk tried to break into the trailer. Lance would have killed him if I hadn't been able to calm him down. You'll get straw all over your suit."

"It doesn't matter. Shelley, will you marry me?"

He felt her stiffen.

With his free hand he reached for his pipe, then remembered he was in the stable and returned it to his pocket.

"There's a problem of money," he went on conversationally. "I'm not rich. I come from a long line of New Englanders. Farmers and Yankee editors. You come from quite a different sort of background." He paused. "I'm a fanatic on the subject of money. In college I was editor of the campus paper. There was a girl who laid out the ads. It never dawned on me that she was an heiress until one day when her father arrived in the office and accused me of being a fortune hunter. I picked up an inkwell. Luckily somebody came in just as I was about to throw it."

He looked at The Goose, standing dejectedly, his head bowed. The shots were wearing off and his silver coat was glazed with sweat. Shelley had told him that the horse would never race again.

"Surely you don't think that I have any money!"

"Well, then," he said quietly, "what are we waiting for?"

A week later they were married at the Shapiros' house in Westport.

"Well, old buddy," Tad said when the ceremony was over, "you've gone and done it." He gave Shelley a long, speculative look. "Take care of him." For her ears alone, he added, "Don't hurt him. He loves you very much."

She was indignant. "Why should I hurt him?"

He shook his head. "You're beautiful and talented, but you don't know the first thing about love."

They moved into his apartment in Greenwich Village. At first the newness of it all kept her occupied. She hung the painting of Sean Shelburn in the combined living room-dining room. She made curtains for the windows, cooked, took long walks, did some sketches of the people in Washington Square and began some abstract oils and collages. Occasionally Mike invited the Shapiros and some of his friends from the paper to dinner. In the tiny kitchen, Shelley turned out shrimp gumbo served in the pottery casserole he bought for her, and the hot breads she had watched Melusina make at Shelburn Hall.

The men and their wives were in their mid-thirties or early forties. They were all keen and alert and spoke animatedly on current affairs. Shelley, who knew nothing of politics, seemed left out. Mike would look at her and make a remark about "this must be boring to Shelley" or "you should hear Shelley talk about her days at the race track" or "Shelley, tell about the time Fax Templeton and Bones Black visited your friend Millicent at Saratoga and Fax hired the elephants from the circus and turned them loose in the garden so that when Bones woke up with a hangover he would look out the window and see them."

She would try, but then he would see that what she was saying was as foreign to them as some of their conversation was to her.

The bad time, though, came later when he tried to make love to her. She begged him to turn out the light and he did so, hoping that then, in the darkness, it would be less constrained.

When Cam was born, Mike's misgivings gave way to joyous wonder. Shelley softened. The nerved-up tautness, the flat, hipless hardness of her racing days were replaced by a kind of flowering. She laughed more and was more approachable. Drawn together by an overwhelming love for their child, they knew an enchanted period of communication. His own feelings were so profound that he felt his love spilling over to encompass all humanity.

Perhaps then the seed was planted, the desire to lead a more productive, useful life, to carry out his heritage by running his own newspaper and being his own boss. The idea of getting out of the city was nurtured by Cam's attacks of asthma and the yearning he began to see on Shelley's face, the wistfulness with which she gazed out the window at the sordid expanse of streets.

One day he suggested she job a horse to ride in Central Park and gave her the money to do so. That night he asked her how the ride had gone. She answered that the horse was so starved and seedy-looking that she had found a grassy plot, gotten off, removed the "Keep off the Grass" sign and allowed it to graze instead of riding the allotted hour.

"I'm sorry, Mike," she apologized. "I gave the man at the livery stable the rest of this week's grocery money to buy feed for the horse, but I'm afraid he'll pocket it instead."

She did not ride again. Like one of the land turtles Cam now picked up in the woods, she pulled the door shut against the city and its people.

It was at this stage that they received the letter from Misty Montague, Shelley's cousin, saying that she was being forced to sell the Shelburn *Sun*.

"Polo Pete Buford wants to buy the paper as a weapon to further his political career," Misty wrote Shelley. "He already owns the *County Daily*, which is now little more than a propaganda sheet for his own perverted ideas. I'd rather cease publication than sell it to him. But I'm afraid I can't swing it any longer."

For the first time in months Shelley's eyes lost their indifferent expression. "Mike," she asked urgently, "how much money is saved up?"

"That's an impertinent question."

"Mike, seriously, enough to buy the newspaper?"

"I think enough. I've got what I made free-lancing. We'd need a loan—"

"Oh, Mike." She clasped her hands together. "There's the income from father's trust. It's not much, but it's something to fall back on. We can live at Shelburn Hall."

"I didn't think you wanted to."

"It wasn't that," she answered slowly, "just that I couldn't bear to go home, knowing that I wouldn't be able to stay."

His innate New England caution kept him from throwing up his job with the *Globe*. He persuaded his editor to grant him a leave of absence while they drove to Virginia to see about buying the weekly newspaper. As they set about closing the apartment and packing, he told himself he could always return to New York.

Mike was so engrossed in his thoughts that he forgot to stop the Jeep at the end of the long avenue. At the last minute he saw the Bufords' Rolls, the chauffeur at the wheel, come over the brow of the hill. Automatically, he jammed on the brakes. The Jeep jerked to a stop. For an instant, after the car sped by, he sat shaken. His heart was pounding, his mouth dry. The entrance was dangerous. Although the rioting honeysuckle had been cut back, the hump in the road before the driveway obscured oncoming cars. Washington, the surveyor, should have eliminated the dangerous rise, Mike thought. He made a mental note to consult the highway department. Maybe they would put up a sign warning traffic to slow down.

The Valley was made up of a curious society, Mike thought. People who spent their lives on things that moved—horses, boats, skis. And they were always in a rush, always in a hurry.

Horses were an excellent antidote to thought. You could spend all the daylight hours with horses, knowing where the days belonged on the sporting calendar. People involved with horses were almost always late. Time, when you were in the hunting field, could disappear between the beats of your heart, and the seconds spent in the air over fences could appear to last for hours.

Others of what Mike called the "Go-Go Set" followed the same pattern. The frenetic horse activity in which they surrounded themselves was largely self-imposed. Millicent Black, for instance, always gave the impression of being rushed and overburdened.

"Sweetie pie, forgive me," she would apologize with a martyred air, "Betsy called. Her car was out of gas and I had to pick up her kids on the way. My itsy bitsy Jonesey had puppies all over my bed and I couldn't leave her."

It was as though the pace they maintained gave them a sense of importance, a feeling of "doing" that was bolstered by continuous self-induced crises. Horses bowed tendons and boats broke down. Servants departed and wells ran dry. Wives exchanged husbands and husbands exchanged wives.

The Valley prided itself on avoiding all elements of a resort area or suburbia. A country club, for instance. Time and again people had suggested turning one of the big places up for sale into a golf or tennis club and been voted down. The closest equivalent was the Halter Club, a shabby brick building at the north end of town where members had their own liquor lockers, subscriptions to the *Morning Telegraph, The Chronicle of the Horse*, the British *Horse and Hound* and other sporting publications, plus a direct line to their favorite bookmaker. Nothing else, other than the prestige of belonging, was forthcoming.

The community was characterized by an affluent dowdiness. Perhaps because many of the people were new, with new money, the old was the thing to aspire to. Old houses and furniture, clothes and cars. Fortunes were spent buying old farmhouses to tear down in order that new houses might be built from the old stone, wood and beams. At the Fox in the High Hat, the shop run by Tina Welford, secondhand Peal boots took precedence over new. It was the same with raincoats. They did not achieve character until the imported impossible-to-clean mackintoshes became stiff and streaked. It was agreed, however, that R. Rutherford Dinwiddie, Esquire, went to extremes. Whenever he acquired a new suit or coat from his British tailor, Winters, his valet, wore it for a month beforehand, in order to break it in for his master.

Hunting caps and pink coats became more cherished in proportion to their age. Blue jeans and khakis only became wearable after innumerable washings had shrunken and bleached them. Shelley's favorite pair was frayed and faded to a dusty blue. Having been brought up to dress either down or up but never in between, she wore them all year round. In winter, when she went to market in the open-topped Jeep, she threw on the sable coat. It did not occur to her that there was anything odd in her choice of clothing. She wore the fabulous floor-length sable inherited from her grandmother because it was the only warm coat that she owned, tossing it around, as Mike told her, like an old horse blanket.

In the supermarket, at the post office, the Covertside Inn or lunching at the Gone Away, where horse deals took place over hamburgers and coffee, it was difficult to tell the owners from their trainers or grooms. A stranger would have said that Donnie Welford was the owner of the Windsor Stud Farm, rather than T. Patterson Gibson, said to be one of the richest men in the world.

For whereas his trainer wore boots that shone like well-rubbed wood and well-tailored tweeds with patches of chamois at the elbows and drove a new Oldsmobile, his boss sported muddy rubber boots and a polo coat with burned places from his pipe ashes, and drove a disreputable pickup truck with crumpled fenders. Often Donnie and his blond wife, Tina, who ran the posh local shop, bejeweled and befurred, could be seen driving off to a cocktail party while T. Patterson Gibson, in coveralls and battered fedora, bounced over his extensive acres on a tractor, spreading manure.

Trucks, Jeeps, station wagons and foreign cars predominated, painted in their owners' racing colors—a colored stripe diagonal across the door and the name of the farm in small quietly inconspicuous letters. Nobody would have dreamed of attaching a fox brush to the radiator cap in the manner of teenagers. Most of the cars sported radiator caps of silver foxes or hand painted horses imported from England and sold at the Fox in the High Hat.

People like Millicent Black, internationally known for her vocabulary of four-letter words, her money and her menages, who either rode into town or drove her Rolls Royce, on the door of which was emblazoned a tiny replica of her orange and pink racing silks and cap.

At Last Resort, the beautiful old mansion purchased for her by her first husband, Randall Mason of the Mason Shoe Company, one could stumble on race track touts hobnobbing with foreign royalty. Through them all moved Millicent, in a cyclone of dogs or horses being brought into the living room to be shown off, wearing blue jeans—and the famed diamond necklace that had belonged to a Hapsburg around her neck. It was people like Millicent who gave the community its reputation for color and glamour.

Leaning forward, Mike saw that the road was clear and turned left toward the village.

It was a golden day, the colors so clear, fields and woodlands so sharply defined that the countryside had the clarity of a child's picture book. "*Je suis en paradis!*" Lafayette exclaimed when he first rode over the Gap in the blue mountains and looked down upon The Valley. Mike wondered what Lafayette would say now if he could see the beer cans and trash, thrown from passing cars, that littered the sides of the road, desecrating paradise. He thought of the editorials he had written, the litterbug campaign the *Sun* had promoted. Prizes for the best posters were given in county schools and local officials promised to provide signs and trash baskets at strategic spots alongside country roads. Yet passing motorists still threw paper bags and bottles, beer cans and lighted cigarettes which, because of the long drought, could cause fire. Somehow the litter symbolized the growing sense of irresponsibility, of dissolution, like the vandalism in The Valley School when, the preceding spring, windows had been broken and obscenities chalked on the walls, or like the growing rabies epidemic the foxhunters chose to ignore.

THREE

THE first time Mike had seen The Valley he had not noticed trash or beer cans. It was early April and, instead, he saw the daffodils, a green and gold host carpeting the entrances to the estates they passed and spilling over into the fields and pastures. The station wagon they had bought for the trip was crammed with suitcases, cooking utensils, his books and typewriter. Cam and Lance rode uneasily in the rear with the painting of Sean Shelburn.

After the great dual highway with its motels and shopping centers and hot dog stands that stretched from the heart of the nation's capital, the Valley road was like another world. Here was a different country, not country really, nor suburbia, but a unique area of manicured estates, protected by neat stone walls, white board fences and posts and rails behind which sleek thoroughbreds and registered cattle grazed in lush ankle-deep grass.

Long, graveled driveways, fronted by stone gateposts on which were chiseled the names of the farms and estates, led to mellow brick and fieldstone mansions.

Originally built by descendants of the early Tidewater families who had moved inland, Priscelly Gate, Fairmont, Misty Montague's house, Millicent Mason Whitman-Woolman Black's Last Resort, and Shelburn Hall were listed in *Great Houses of America* as some of the loveliest, most authentic examples of Colonial architecture in the United States. When the second Yankee invasion took place at the turn of the century, those that had fallen into ruin were carefully renovated in order to blend into the countryside in the same manner that the tweedlike woodlands mingled with manicured pastures the color and texture of polo fields.

There were stables and barns and dog runs—for in The Valley dogs were rated second only to horses—greenhouses, indoor squash courts, swimming pools and tennis courts, but all patinaed with an aura of age and deceptive simplicity, like the honeysuckle growing over the walls and rail fences. Overall lay a sense of peace, of stillness and serenity, almost a softness. It was as if two hundred years of what the Chamber of Commerce pamphlet termed "landed gentry and the ultimate in gracious living" had honed away the rough edges, leaving the fields without rocks or ruggedness, refining the vines and natural growth until, as Mike commented, the landscape was more English than England itself.

"Not a challenging country," he commented. "Doesn't make you feel like stopping the car and going exploring the way you would in New Hampshire or Vermont. I have the feeling of one long Sunday afternoon."

He glanced at Shelley and saw that she was sitting very straight on the edge of the seat.

"It's all so familiar," she said, "as though I hadn't been away. Look, Mike"—she clutched his arm—"see that line fence of the Baldwins? I used to jump that left panel. And that rotting coop set in the wire over there by the pond has a hole in front of it. A young horse I was riding once for Fax Templeton fell in it. See that wall?" She pointed to the dry stone wall that separated the road from a pasture in which brood mares and young foals were grazing. "It has a big drop on the other side and the day of the great Free Zone run The Goose overjumped and went down on his knees—"

"Look at the baby horses," Cam cried delightedly, pointing to the shy, thrusting faces of six foals peering at the passing car from over the wall.

"You'll see lots more," Shelley told him. "This is horse country. There's Priscelly Gate and around the bend we'll hit Four Corners, a famous meet in the Saturday country. Here's the road that leads to Muster Corner, the colored community. We're almost home now." She paused. Then, breathing deeply, she said with a kind of awe, "See those towers? That's Ballyhoura."

Mike slowed down. They were passing a woods surrounded by a high iron-spiked fence. Over the tops of the trees he saw a jumble of towers and turrets and crenellations. A gate between stone posts topped by stone foxes hung drunkenly on one hinge across the grass-grown drive that led through the wood. A lodge, obviously empty, stood by the gate. Some of the panes were broken in windows that gazed back at them with silent indifference.

"Ballyhoura," Shelley breathed. "Cam, that's where your great-grandfather lived, the one in the painting. The house is a ruin now."

"Can we go exploring?" Cam asked eagerly.

"Of course," Shelley replied. "But you've got to watch out for the ghost I told you about. And there's a pond to fish in."

"I expect Sean Shelburn to come cantering down the road," Mike said dryly.

"Oh, Mike." She put her hand on his arm. "Thank you. Thank you for bringing me home. Look, there's the creek that runs through our woods. The branch, they call it."

Shelburn Hall was the last place on the left before reaching the village. The road funneled through a wood, then up over a rise on the far side of which, abruptly, lay the driveway. Its only indication was a historical marker, now almost obscured by a tracery of vines.

"Built 1760 by King Shelburn. George Washington was often a guest. Lafayette visited here in 1824. Margaret Lee Shelburn, wife of Sean Shelburn, was born here. In 1928 it was restored by Cameron Fitzgerald, who married into the original family."

The entrance was barely distinguishable. The massive stone gateposts were choked in honeysuckle. The oak woods, originally cleared to resemble an English park, had become a jungle of vines and underbrush that, dark and uncontrolled, encroached onto the driveway. Overhead the branches of the great trees intermingled.

The road was green with grass and moss. Beneath the vaulted branches it wound upward, forcing its way between a sea of parasitic growth that, long neglected, had overrun the rhododendrons and azaleas and hydrangeas, choking out the careful planting that generations of Shelburns had cultivated. The way suddenly seemed endless. It was as if the distance, like the trees themselves, had multiplied and the road led not to civilization but deeper into labyrinthian wilderness, a wilderness shot through with rioting clumps of gold that seemed the final extension of the shafts of sunlight coming through the branches of the great oaks—daffodils that had spread and spread and finally gone wild.

"Aren't they beautiful!" Shelley clapped her hands in delight. "I'd forgotten how lovely they are in the spring. 'Fairy telephones,' Melusina called them. Then there are the ones with different blooms, more petals and more green. 'Spinach and eggs,' the country people call them. We'll have to pick lots and lots, put them all over the house."

Suddenly, it was there, the approach disguised by the growth spreading across the clearing that had once been acres of gardens, reaching to the walls, so that it seemed an outgrowth of the very land itself. A vast house of mellow rose-colored brick, fronted by five round white pillars reaching from the porch to the roof.

To the right lay the ruins of the burned wing. A small oak tree grew out of the center, its trunk furled with wisteria.

Mike stopped the station wagon and switched off the ignition. "My God," he said, awed. "Where are the ravens?" He looked at Shelley accusingly. "You never told me it was like this. So big." He reached for the starter. "We might as well turn around and go back where we came from. We can't possibly stay here. A pile of rubble would be more possible."

"Mike, please." She set her hand over his. Her eyes were pleading. "I didn't tell you what it was like, the number of rooms. I was afraid, well, that you'd refuse to live in it. That's why I never brought you to The Valley before."

With Cam running excitedly ahead, followed by Lance, Mike had no choice but to set out on a tour of the twenty-four musty rooms of Shelburn Hall that remained, following the fire which had leveled the west wing. The circular staircase rising from the center of the front hall was breathtaking.

"Nobody knows how it was constructed," Shelley explained. "In those days the great houses were built by slaves. Some were remarkable builders. Look." She showed him the ivory peg set in the newel post. "This is known as the amity button or 'Point of Satisfaction.' To have an amity button meant the mortgage had been paid off and you owned your property free and clear."

A suit of armor stood in one corner. Old gloves, stiffened and cracked by mud, lay with a welter of spurs and whips and a dented hunting horn. Lines of horseshoes engraved with the names of long-dead horses were nailed into the fine paneling along one wall. On the other side, fox masks grinned evilly from the gloom and dust. The hall opened onto a series of what Shelley called withdrawing rooms. Mike felt he should tiptoe. Their sheeted chairs and tables, settees, draped paintings and crystal chandeliers, peeling wallpaper and mildewed woodwork bespoke a past elegance, evoked a kind of awed reverence. Dust glazed the floors and tables and in the den the hunt fixture cards of seasons past remained tacked to the mantel. Shelley hurried from one room to another, showing him the bullets that had spattered the dining room mantel, bullets fired from Yankee guns in an attempt to capture Sean Shelburn, and the marks from the Union Cavalry officer's saber on the hall table.

In the ballroom she pointed out Lafayette's warming pan, hanging by the fireplace, and the windowpane on which the French general had inscribed his name with his diamond stickpin. The old square upright piano with its massive claw feet, the Aubusson faded to a pale rose, the dark, heavy furniture and crystal chandelier holding candles were as they had been in King Shelburn's day. From the walls the ancestors in their gilt frames and dark clothes gazed grimly down upon them.

"I know the title of that one," Mike commented facetiously. He pointed to a particularly severe-looking Shelburn wearing the wooden expression and depressing air peculiar to the eighteenth-century artists. " 'Our Horse Lost the Race!' "

"Mike," Shelley laughed, "you're silly. That's the Peale portrait of great-great-uncle Hugh, the scholar. He was a philosopher. Maybe that's why he looks so serious." She turned. "Cam," she called to the boy, who had paused to investigate the old crank gramophone on its stand, "when I was your age, my grandmother wouldn't let me eat dinner until I learned to identify the people in the portraits and was able to tell what relation they were to me."

As Shelley talked, pointing excitedly to one thing and then another, Mike wondered if she had the slightest awareness of all the cleaning that would have to be done, the repairs made, the money spent.

The bedrooms were enormous. The master one, with its massive four-poster, moldering curtains, fireplace in which lay the ashes of a long-dead fire, seemed to him to be large enough to encompass their entire New York apartment.

The bathroom, with its marble turn-of-the-century plumbing, was as big as their living room had been in Greenwich Village. The incredible sunken bathtub with steps leading down into it was filled to the brim with bundles of letters tied with faded ribbons, and the elegant gold-plated taps were webbed by spiders.

"It will be lovely." Shelley stood in the middle of the dusty floor. "I'd forgotten the size of the fireplaces and how high the ceilings are. Oh, Mike, don't you think yellow?"

"Yellow what?" he asked dismally.

"For the bathroom, of course. The color of the daffodils."

"There are leaks in the roof." He indicated the long stain on the wall. "And probably termites."

"Mike, it will be such fun to put it back the way it was. Much more sporting than if it had all been perfect, ready and waiting for us." She pointed to the window. "Look at the view. At the mountains and the woods and the flowers."

Mike looked down through the green-gold light at the daffodils beneath the tall oaks. Beyond lay the pond and in the distance, discernible through a vista cut long ago through the park, he saw again the deep blue secrecy of the mountains.

The old country kitchen was cold, damp, with peeling plaster. There was an ancient wood stove, black and rusted, with a pipe that vanished into the wall, a grimy porcelain sink and brown-painted cabinets. It was dark and dank and uninviting, about as friendly as a cave, Mike said.

"What's that noise?" Cam asked as Lance made a lunge for the corner by the stove. There was a sudden cackle, followed by barking as the mastiff reared back from the onslaught of the chicken sitting on eggs in the old woodbox half filled with dry leaves. A door banged and as the hen sat making angry throaty sounds and the dog stared, baffled and intimidated, slow steps approached.

"Miss Shelley?" a voice cried. "Thought it might be you."

And Mike saw a short stoop-shouldered Negro, his face eroded by years of work and living, his hair as white as the egg under the setting hen.

"Virginia City," Shelley matched his welcoming cry. "I'm home. I'm finally home!"

Shelley explained that the first thing she wanted to do when she got home was go riding. He told her to go ahead, that he and Cam would unload the car. She gave him a quick kiss, hauled an old pair of blue jeans from an upstairs closet and changed into them, adding moccasins that had come unstitched at the toes and a vivid orange turtleneck she'd bought on Fifth Avenue.

Mike watched her run out to the pasture, whistle for The Goose and vault onto the horse's back. She waved to him as she cantered past the house. Bareback, bridleless, guiding the old race horse by his halter. Her hair had come loose from its knot and blew wildly. Against the green of the budding trees and grass and daffodils, the orange sweater was as bright as her cheeks, filled now with color. Behind her, ears flopping, loped the mastiff, crashing delightedly through the underbrush. Then the only sound left was of her singing, the way she had those mornings at Saratoga.

He was standing on the veranda, leaning against one of the peeling white pillars, when she returned. He had finished unloading the car, explored the stable and outbuildings with Cam and Virginia City, who had already become fast friends, washed up with the cold tap water—Virginia City told him that the hot water system was "demised" and he didn't know how to fix it—and changed into khakis and a sweater. His pipe was in his mouth and he was staring at the rotting fence line and overgrown pasture when Shelley rode back up the woods path.

"Hi," she called. "Lord and master of all you survey."

He took the pipe from his mouth. "I was wondering if even a lifetime of footsteps would cultivate those fields. Incidentally, there isn't any food in the house."

"Oh, Lord. I forgot. What time is it? Stores should be open until six."

"We could eat out."

"No," Shelley said positively. "It's Saturday. The stores will still be open. There's time for a quick run to town. We'll have steak and champagne. I want you to see Shelburn. Cam can stay here with Virginia City. We won't be long. Oh, Mike, it's wonderful to be home."

Although Shelley was shocked to find that the shade trees which used to line the main street had been cut down and replaced by parking meters, Mike was pleasantly surprised to find the town as attractive as it was. The solidly built square houses, red brick, fieldstone and frame, were fronted by green lawns bordered with spring flowers and white or iron fences. Shelley pointed out Miss Letty Miller's house and yard, in which daffodils and tulips were in bloom, where Jeb Stuart, hiding from the Yankees, had stabled his horses in the cellar. The *Sun* building looked dingy and unpainted. He thought of stopping and then decided the morrow would be time enough for what he was beginning to feel would be a shattering disappointment.

There was the gray stone façade of the attractive Covertside Inn, then the post office and the new bank with the carved red-painted fox running over the doorway. They drove past Miss Kitty Luken's antique shop, actually her house, with a wide front porch on which resided three Hitchcock chairs and a corner cupboard waiting to be refinished, and the plate-glass windows of the ABC store. Centering the square, with its crowded complement of Jeeps, station wagons and pickup trucks, was the bronze monument of Sean Shelburn in Confederate uniform, astride his famous horse Shelburn Jack.

The town cop was directing the late afternoon traffic around the square. Holding up his right hand to stop traffic, he walked over to the station wagon.

"If it isn't Miss Shelley. Heard you was coming home." His face was hot and sweaty and his cap tipped on the back of his head.

"This is my husband." Shelley smiled. "Mike, meet Chester Glover. Chester is *the* law around here. When we were kids he made us toe the line, didn't you, Chester? Remember the time on Halloween when Fax Templeton, the Talbots and the rest of us dunked the Dinwiddies' horses' tails in whitewash? It was the night before opening meet and R. Rutherford was so furious he called you up and asked to have us arrested."

"Were you?" Mike asked.

The policeman grinned. "Miss Shelley, now, was just high-spirited. Mr. Dinwiddie knew I wouldn't put *her* in jail. Why, in our jail we just accommodate niggers. Ain't no place for a lady."

There was a line of cars behind them now.

"Well, I'd best get back to work. Nice to see you home, Miss Shelley. Nice to meet your husband."

The old chain store that Shelley remembered had been torn down. A new supermarket, air-conditioned and with automatic doors, had been built in its place. Mike found a space and parked. He dug into his pocket for change to put in the meter.

"Don't bother," Shelley said. "Chester wouldn't give me a ticket."

Mike glanced up and down the street. Almost all the meters showed violations.

"If I'm going to run the newspaper," he said, putting a nickel into the meter, "I better not get fined my first time in town."

The new supermarket, with its mosaic and elaborate crystal and gold chandeliers, was next door to the Fox in the High Hat, the show window of which disclosed neat round-collared shirtwaists, denim skirts, Tina Welford's tiles and Sion Atwell's distinctive sweaters with felt cutouts of horses and dogs appliquéd on them. A life-size wooden horse with a wreath of yellow daisies around its neck pranced gaily. On the opposite side of the street was the Gone Away drugstore, featuring old-fashioned bottles of colored water and posters advertising horse shows to be held in the area.

In the parking lot, battered pickup trucks and dusty, corroded coupes were democratically intermingled with shining sports cars and station wagons. Several sullen-faced unshaven men, accompanied by slat-thin women with protruding stomachs, carrying squalling infants and followed by grimy barefoot children, were loading groceries into a farm truck drawn up alongside a pink Cadillac.

"The Mellicks," Shelley commented. "They're Free Zoners. I see they still come into town on Saturday nights."

"Who are the Free Zoners?"

"They're the mountainy people," Shelley explained. "They live

85

on the edge of the hunting country, in the foothills. The Free Zone was founded during the Revolution. Deserters hid out there. They're a wild lawless bunch. Mean and inbred. They make moonshine and refuse to pay taxes and would as soon shoot you for trespassing in their territory as not."

Inside the door, in front of a large "No Loitering" sign, several Negroes stood against a pile of cardboard cartons gazing impassively at the people coming and going. As Shelley entered, the loungers shifted their feet.

They wore an air of uncertainty, as though not sure whether they would be acknowledged or not. Shelley stopped and smiled. An expression of genuine pleasure came over her face.

"Mike," she cried excitedly, "this is Nat. Nat's known me since childhood. Remember, Nat, how you used to pick flowers for me? Zinnias and petunias. I loved your petunias. And George Blandford—he's the local cab driver."

Mike extended his hand to each of the two elderly Negroes who, after a moment's hesitation, responded, beamed and bobbed their heads.

It was obvious that the supermarket was *the* meeting place in Shelburn. Shelley had no sooner acquired a chart and started along one of the aisles than she was converged upon by a number of women in tweeds and riding clothes who greeted her with hugs and excited exclamations. Mike saw a tall angular girl whom he recognized as Millicent Black, the heiress he'd met with Shelley at Saratoga. She had on scuffed brown boots, breeches with a rip at the knee and a man's orange button-down shirt. She was accompanied by two small terriers and seemed quite unconcerned that one was lifting its leg against the stand of canned goods on sale.

"Sweetie pie," she cried, "why, sport, I heard you were coming home."

"Millicent," Shelley responded. The two fell upon each other and embraced enthusiastically. "I'm so glad to see you." Shelley turned to a small trim woman, beautifully dressed by contrast, wearing wraparound sun glasses and an expensive-looking silk suit. "And Samantha Sue. I want you to meet my husband, Mike." She beckoned to him. "You remember Millicent, and this is Samantha Sue Buford. We grew up together."

"Ah'm so happy to meet you." The small girl put out her hand. "We've all been just dyin' to see Shelley's husband."

"Hi, sport." Millicent shook his hand with a hard, mannish grip. "I can't wait to get you and Shelley to Last Resort for a drink. Shelley, sport, I've got the most divine timber horse, a real sweetie pie. Wait till you see him." She tried to include Mike. "I've got a hunter for sale that would just suit you."

"Mike doesn't ride," Shelley said.

"Doesn't *ride?*" Millicent looked astounded. "But everyone rides!" She glanced up at the clock over the dairy section. "Shit, I've got to dash off. See a horse at Story Jackson's. Samantha Sue, you have paint on your skirt."

"Millicent, no!" Samantha Sue pulled her immaculate skirt up above her knees to examine the spot. "I was just on my way to the Beast's for tea." She made a face. "Now I'll have to go home and change."

At that moment a blond woman Mike had not noticed came along the aisle. She was large, with carefully dressed hair, a great deal of make-up, a large diamond ring, a flowered chiffon dress and high heels. Unlike the other blue-jeaned women aggressively pushing their bulging carts and calling out to one another, her manner was shy, hesitant.

"Oh, hello," Millicent said tartly. "I suppose you want to get by."

"There's no rush." The blond woman still retained her smile. Then, when no introductions were forthcoming, she said to Shelley, "I'm Katie Schligman. We've just moved to The Valley."

"I'm Shelley Latimer." Shelley smiled back. "This is my husband, Mike."

"How nice. Misty Montague told me you were moving back to Shelburn Hall. We bought Templeton."

"It's one of my favorite places."

"We'd love to have you come and see us. We've made a few changes."

"We'd like to. Wouldn't we, Mike?"

"Yes, indeed, Mrs. Schligman, we'd be happy to. Shelley," he added, "the ice cream will be melted before we get home."

Katie Schligman threw them a look of gratitude and went on past.

When she had rounded the corner of the cereal section, Samantha Sue turned to Shelley. "Honey, ah must warn you about The Valley. So many new people. Pushy. Nouveau."

"Real-ley," Millicent added, "all that blue eye shadow, like shrimp gone bad."

Samantha Sue leaned over her bulging cart. "He calls her Mama and she calls him Dad. He has six linear feet of custom-made shirts and she has a pink air-conditioned Cadillac."

"Shelley," Millicent said, "you'll flip, positively pee, when you see what they've done to Templeton. Barrels of draft beer in every room and a revolving bar in the living room."

"The Baldwins had a hunt breakfast and Katie came in sequins with a bare midriff and pink mink," Samantha Sue contributed. "P. P. tells me that they plan to hunt and have made a large contribution."

Her voice had a curious penetrating quality, like a rasp muffled in silk. Mike wondered if it carried to the blond woman, who had her back turned and was carefully selecting cheeses from a shelf in the dairy section.

"Once you get involved," Millicent announced flatly, "there's real-ley no end to it."

"Shelley," Mike pleaded, "the ice cream—"

Samantha Sue glanced at her watch. It was gold, with small fox crystals on either side of the face. "Ah've got to fly. Ah'll be late at Hunting Hill. Bye, Shelley, you must come to Silver Hill soon. Ah can't wait to have you see what Dickie Speer has done. You won't recognize the place." She started off, remembered Mike and turned back. "Ah'm so happy to meet Shelley's husband." She gave him a melting smile.

It was long past dark when they finished carrying suitcases upstairs, hanging Sean Shelburn in the blank space in the ballroom-drawing room and putting Cam, who had fallen asleep over a bowl of cereal, in the room next to theirs. It had once been Shelley's. From the walls old hunting prints and faded photographs looked down. Frayed horse-show ribbons hung on a string stretched over the sleigh bed and an entrancing carved wooden horse stood on the bookshelf over old copies of *Black Beauty* and *Somerville & Ross*.

Shelley assured Cam he'd be safe from the ghosts and went to change. She put on a long wool skirt and high-necked white blouse and, as an afterthought, the Shelburn Sapphires. She found candles and lit them in the hall and in the ballroom-drawing room, where in their soft flickering light the dust and disorder were eliminated, leaving the long, graceful room, golden with daffodils, to float in a kind of vapor of beauty and past elegance.

"We'll probably never eat here again," Shelley said, setting a round table in front of the fireplace, "but I feel that tonight we should."

Mike carried in wood from the pile outside the French doors and built a fire against the growing chill. A swallow's nest was dislodged and fell down with a swoosh. Then, while Shelley set the table with fine brown-stained linen from an upstairs closet, the heavy silverware carrying the Shelburn crest and the beautiful glass from the pantry shelves, the fire whistled and sang up the chimney.

They cooked the steak over the fire because Virginia City had forgotten to order bottled gas or hook up the "new" stove that had replaced the ancient iron wood-burning monster.

The fire blazed, a leaping frenzy of crimson shot through with blue like Shelley's eyes and the sapphires. The old house whispered with night sounds and the shadows lengthened over the crystal and portraits and fine furniture.

The champagne was warm because the refrigerator had not had time to grow cold. "In winter, we used to stick it outside in the drifts," Shelley told him. "When the snow melted we'd always find one or two bottles that had been forgotten."

Carefully Mike filled each of the fine glasses. Over the mound of daffodils that centered the table his eyes met Shelley's.

Afterward he lay in the monstrous bed. Shelley's head rested on his shoulder. Between the draping of the musty curtains he saw the stars, stretching like a sequined net. He heard the house noises, as alive and constant as the wind, and thought of how it had been that night, different from all the times before. For one vivid moment he felt that he, too, belonged.

The next morning Mike went to see Misty Montague.

A cousin of Shelley's, Misty belonged to the branch of the family known as the "Shelburnes with the E's but without the ease." Descended from King Shelburn's brother, Hugh, whose grandson Charles had founded the *Sun*, she was a woman of intellect and great charm. Her father, Scaisebrook Shelburne, had not only been editor and publisher of the family-owned newspaper, but had also written an extensive history of the Civil War that had made him celebrated as a historian. From early childhood, Misty was exposed to numerous writers, artists and musicians who came to visit at Fairmont, the rambling old fieldstone house overlooking Buffalo Run.

When her father died, Misty inherited Fairmont and the newspaper. Shortly afterward she married Dave Montague, then editor. When Dave was killed in Korea, leaving her with a son to bring up, Misty took over the paper. Although she maintained the quality of the *Sun*, her generosity and improvidence ran it into difficulties.

After the fall in the hunting field, when the specialists insisted she could never walk again, Misty set out to prove them wrong. Over her bed was a gymnast's iron bar rigged with pulleys which she still used for daily exercises that were exhausting and painful. Within a year she was able to walk with the aid of two canes. In two years, she was able to walk with only one and to drive a car.

During this period the paper was in the hands of a young journalism student who, with his youthful arrogance and brashness, managed to antagonize most of his advertisers and subscribers. When Misty was able to return to work—she insisted that running the addressograph was excellent therapy for her legs and that the long hours of writing copy, laying out ads and make-up kept her mind off her own problems—she fired the young editor and set out to build the weekly newspaper in her father's image.

Sitting at the long, battered table that served as the city desk, piled high with a conglomeration of advertising layouts, galley proofs, photographic cuts and copy, she demanded without preliminaries, "Why do you want the paper?"

Briefly he told her about the family-owned newspaper which his oldest brother had inherited. "I guess it's in my blood. I'm told I was almost born on an imposing stone and that when I was a baby, my mother kept me in a file drawer while she was at work. I learned my ABC's hand-setting type."

"It's only fair to warn you," she said, "that you'll break your back and your heart. The Valley is a freak little vacuum. Quite unlike any other place in the world. Not South. Not North. Not suburbia. Not real country. It's a withdrawal area where people don't want to be bothered. Most of them are retired from somewhere and something. Although many have made millions and are famous, they're more interested in idleness than ideas, in sex and scandal than anything spiritual. To be sure, in their fashion, they do a great deal for charity. The colored community center—built with Buford funds and segregated, of course—the new church, the health center and the horse museum which R. Rutherford Dinwiddie wants to get started. But there's no library, no bookstore, no art or music or even a movie theater. Nothing for the poor people to do but sit and watch the cars rust." In her intensity, she broke the pencil she had picked up from the desk. Rising from his nest of newspapers, her dog walked over to her and put his head in her lap.

When the dog had been comforted, she rose to her feet. Grasping her cane, she limped across the cement floor to a filing case that stood against the wall. She pulled out a drawer and extracted a thick folder. Returning, she handed it to him.

"Your first job will be to collect these. Maybe, because you're a stranger, you'll be better at it than I am. The richer people are, the less attention they pay to small bills. Look at this list. Millionaires with colossal farms and racing stables. Yet their two-fifty subscription to the *Sun* hasn't been paid in two years."

"Why do you keep on sending them the paper?"

Misty's grin was rueful. "They'd probably stop speaking if I cut them off. They wouldn't understand." She looked at him suddenly, her blue-gray eyes were speculative again. "You honestly think you can rebuild the *Sun*, make it a paper to be proud of, the way it was in Father's time?"

"I can try."

"Michael Latimer, you're out of your mind!" And then she smiled, with a sudden startling radiance that was like the afternoon sun streaming through the clouded windows, turning the dust in the office to a vague gold mist.

"You mean you'll sell?" Mike asked. "For the price I have to offer?"

"The money is meaningless. It's what *you* have to offer." She looked up at the bearded photograph he presumed to be her father on the wall over her typewriter.

"Michael Latimer," she said softly, "I have a feeling you're the answer to my prayers."

"That's wonderful, Mike," Shelley enthused when he told her what Misty had said. "You needn't have worried, though. I knew she'd agree to sell to you. Let's go see the bank."

The old bank, with its white pillars, wide oaken doors with gleaming foxhead knockers, and the red-painted running fox, the town insignia, carved over the entrance, had been remodeled and modernized. On the side street there was a drive-in window flanked with pots of geraniums. "A ride-in window," Shelley explained. "A lot of people like Fax Templeton still ride their horses into town."

Inside, the tile floor was freshly waxed. The old pens in wooden holders that would never write and the crusted dried-up inkwells had been replaced with ballpoints in order that people might sign counter checks decorated with the same running fox incorporated on local license tags, signs and on the flags that flew from lampposts on Shelburn Cup Day.

Hunting scenes looked down from the walls and a large silver bowl of spring flowers stood on the counter.

In the absence of Polo Pete Buford, who was at the track, Togo Baldwin ushered them into his office. The vice president was a man of middle age with thinning brown hair, a ruddy outdoor complexion and a body running to fat. He greeted them with a smile and a manner that seemed vaguely apologetic. Shelley had explained that he was a hometown boy, born and raised in Shelburn, the son of "Beanie" Baldwin, who owned the horse transportation service. After her divorce from Bones Black he married Betsy, Doc Watters's oldest daughter, who cheerfully bore him five children.

Unlike his slightly rumpled appearance, his office was almost austere. Papers were piled with ruled precision on the polished walnut desk. A large print of *The Foxhunter's Dream* graced one wall, while an early photograph of The Hunt hung facing his desk. The only other picture was a faded daguerreotype of Shelburn's Raiders at their reunion in 1895, some fifty or more bearded men staring into the camera from beneath peaked forage caps.

"My grandfather rode with Shelley's grandfather," Togo explained, noticing that Mike was staring at the photograph. He leaned his elbows on the desk. "It's good to have you back in The

Valley, Shelley. Your husband, too, of course." His voice turned vague. "So many new people. Not all are the Valley kind." He turned to Mike. His smile was as sudden and unexpected as the change in his manner, no longer apologetic now. "Mr. Latimer, what may I do for you?"

Mike was equally direct. "You can lend me some money." Quickly he explained about buying the *Sun*.

Togo looked past them, at the photograph of The Hunt on the wall. Then he asked, "What's your collateral?"

"Nothing," Mike said, "just me."

"Where will you be living?"

"Shelburn Hall. I need five thousand for a down payment."

Togo continued to study the photograph. "Better make it more," he said musingly. "At least twenty. To build up circulation and advertising, you'll need new machinery. Another linotype. A new press."

Mike's New England caution rose to the surface. "I don't want to get in too deep. What terms?"

"When it concerns a Shelburn," Togo said unctuously, "it's a matter of honor, not terms. In these parts, Mr. Latimer, Shelburn is a name that stands for something."

His eyes moved downward from the photograph of The Hunt. For a fraction of a second they met Shelley's. "The Valley needs the *Sun*," he said quickly. "Misty did a fine job, don't misunderstand. I didn't agree with a lot of what she said. It takes a man—" Pulling a memorandum pad toward him, he took the pen from its marble holder and scrawled some figures on it.

"It's our policy to make loans on character rather than collateral." He leaned back in his chair. "As long as people don't do anything to destroy the image of The Valley—we want to make sure, for instance, that a developer doesn't get in and start putting up a lot of tacky houses—I tell them the same thing. Black, blue or white, it's all the same to me, long as their money's green."

He made a tent of his fingers. "Of course, all loans of the size of what you have in mind must be taken up at the directors' meeting. However, the next one won't be for a month and I assume you'd like the money without delay. In this case"—once again he looked at Shelley—"I think we can make an exception. I'm sure our president would agree. As long as it's for Miss Shelley here, I'll be glad to assume the responsibility."

His blue eyes swung around, aiming at Mike. "The name of Shelburn is all the collateral that's needed."

Shelburn!

Because of the name he was now, on this beautiful Sunday morning, editor and publisher of the weekly paper. The name spelled collateral, made it possible to purchase a paper founded in 1863 and published weekly ever since in the same brick building that had originally been a livery stable. One of Mike's first improvements was to eliminate the sliding doors and replace them with a plate-glass window, so the townspeople could look in and see the paper being printed. Then he had one of Washington Taylor's men inscribe the name, date it was founded and its slogan, "Veritas vincit" (Truth Conquers), in gilt letters on the glass.

This September day as he parked the Jeep in front of it he saw that the window was badly in need of washing and that some of the paint had rubbed off the word "Truth."

The old rolltop desk which Misty Montague's great-grandfather, Charles Shelburne, had used when he founded the weekly was piled high with papers, mail and unread galleys. Instinctively Mike glanced around the office, as if in tabulating each hard-won gain he would find the renewal of strength that suddenly seemed vitally necessary.

The beaverboard walls that separated the office from the back shop were covered with carelessly tacked unframed citations and photographs. The certificates were very old, presented to Misty's father and to Misty by state and national press associations for features, news stories and editorials.

There were snapshots of Shelley astride The Gray Goose, and an autographed portrait from the Governor, grateful to the *Sun* for its aid in the "Keep Virginia Beautiful" campaign. Directly over his desk, where he could see it when he looked up from his typewriter, was the daffodil-colored abstract Shelley had painted for him soon after the move to The Valley, bringing light and color to the dark, cluttered surroundings. Books were stacked along the wall and cuts were piled haphazardly on the shelves by the entrance. They had not been filed away since press day and the floor had not been swept.

Jubal Jones hadn't been in all week. The last time Mike had

bailed him out of jail he warned him that he would have to fire him if he got drunk once more.

Jubal had been janitor at the *Sun* when Mike bought it. "He's a real loser," Misty warned him. "He'll set civil rights back a hundred years. I don't know why I keep him on."

Mike knew why. There was no place else for Jubal to go. He was a prime example of what generations of substandard living, lack of education—plus several centuries of what Washington Taylor called brainwashing—could do.

The most incredible things happened to Jubal. When a slug flew out of the linotype it struck his right eye, almost blinding him, blackening it for days. Jubal had curious nosebleeds that came without apparent reason, causing him to shuffle around as he swept, a blood-soaked rag held to his nose.

When they were transferring a roller from the Miehle press, the iron bar fell on his foot, breaking several small bones. Each week when he was paid on Friday, the money was gone by Monday. Jubal never knew where. And hardly a day passed that Jubal's creditors didn't come to see Mike, demanding payment for such things as a transistor radio, padded ski jacket, or the milk that was delivered to the crumbling shack where his two sons, Jimmy and Bardy, abandoned by their mother, lived.

Now Bardy had gone to live with a relative near Bellevue and Jimmy was at Shelburn Hall, learning stable work from Virginia City, and receiving riding and drawing lessons from Shelley.

The jangling of the telephone broke into his thoughts. Mase! Mike thought, grabbing it. But it was not the Washington call. It was Jubal.

"Mr. Editor, I'm in jail!" Jubal spoke as if he had accomplished a remarkable feat. When Mike only sighed, refusing to sound surprised, a note of chagrin crept into his voice.

"I'm incarcerated for fuckin' her ass off!"

Chester Glover broke into the conversation. He was laughing. "He means felonious assault. He and one of the Bellevue niggers had a bust-up at Delia's Kitchen. When he sobers up, I'll let him out."

The problem of the janitor was minor compared to the problems that faced Mike now. It was obvious that when the role he had played in the desegregation of the county was made clear, he

95

would lose the support of the political and moneyed powers. The loss of legals and county job work would be a bitter blow.

There had been a time, during the period of rebuilding, when each new day had meant a promise, a new advertiser, more subscribers. Shelley worked with him, coming in afternoons to provide tea and cookies for himself and the staff, to read proof and muck out the office—sweep up the cigarette butts and empty the wastebaskets—and help fold the paper on press nights. The brutal work, the coping with temperamental printers and machinery, going to meetings, then staying in the office until the early morning hours in order to find an uninterrupted period in which to catch up on the paper's editorial content had been rewarding. In one year, circulation had tripled. Local and national advertising had increased.

Because he had been told so many times that the North did not understand the South, that only the Southerner knew how to manage the Negroes and it was only when there was Northern interference that any problem evolved, he had gone along with the prevailing opinion. He joined the local civic clubs and glad-handed the supervisors and politicians, and refrained from all controversy. He had managed to please everyone except himself.

By the end of the year he was able to pay back part of the money owed to the bank and buy the Miehle press. There was plenty of advertising and goodwill. Shelley boasted of the success of the paper to her friends.

Money and his wife's acclaim, plus the warming, heady sense of his own personal popularity, battled against his sense of decency and fair play. Could he run a newspaper and at the same time remain invulnerable, untroubled, withdrawn? Neighboring papers did. The Buford-owned *Daily* was as bland, as uncontroversial as country butter. And they made money.

The *Sun*'s folding parties provided the atmosphere for the change.

Once Ambrose Webster stopped in on press night. "Ay," commented the farmer, "so you bend 'em by hand."

When Mike, fresh from a big city daily, learned just how primitive the *Sun*'s back shop actually was, he was horrified. That "bending 'em by hand" could be part of producing the paper had not occurred to him. Newspapers, he had been led to believe, went in one end of the press and came out the other, neatly folded and ready to be whisked away by trucks and distributed.

At the *Sun*, however, the process of getting the paper out was little different than it had been when Benjamin Franklin invented the stove that, in winter, served to warm the office. The shop consisted of the bare mechanical necessities installed at the turn of the century when Misty's grandfather had bought what appeared to be one of the first linotypes ever built. Every week the paper ran to five thousand copies, twenty-four pages each. This meant that 120,000 sheets were folded over, the inside sheets inserted and the final fold of the assembled paper made, all by hand.

Folding the *Sun* took anywhere from three to eight hours, depending on the number of workers and the topics under discussion. Egged on by whoever happened to be writing the Teen-Talk column for the moment and lured by Pete the printer's wisecracks, local high school students joined in as folders, happy to have something to do aside from baby-sitting that would provide spending money.

At five o'clock on press day evening, the door would crash open and what Misty described as "the goon squad" would roar in.

In the beginning of Mike's tenure the folders, left over from Misty's era, ranged in age from fourteen-year-old Janie Gilbert, whose father ran the service station, to seventy-year-old Miss Letty Miller. After working all day at the post office, Miss Letty said she didn't have enough to do and liked to help out whenever possible. Invariably she breezed into the shop with her hat slanted over one alert brown eye and a pocket full of second-class mail culled from the post office wastebasket where the material had been dropped by the boxholders to whom it was addressed. After scanning it and surreptitiously reading all the post cards mailed and received by local residents, Miss Letty was a fund of miscellany and up-to-the-minute information as to who was in Palm Beach, at Saratoga for the racing, or skiing at Aspen.

Had it not been for Jimmy Jones, the janitor's oldest son, the folding parties might never have become integrated or the Human Relations Council formed.

That first summer the folding parties came to represent a sort of private youth movement. Parents asked Mike to take on their children, explaining that working at the *Sun* kept them off the street. Jimmy was one of the leading troublemakers. On the nights that the paper went to press, Mike became accustomed to seeing Jimmy, holding his smaller brother Bardy by the hand and standing in the door of the supermarket, wistfully watching the arrival of the folders. One night, when they were short-handed, Mike impulsively asked Jimmy if he would like a job.

For an instant the boy's thin black face came alive. Then, almost immediately, it subsided into lines of hopelessness. "I've got to tend Bardy," he said.

Aware that he was breaking the child labor laws, Mike offered recklessly, "Bring him."

"You better be careful," Chester Glover warned darkly when he heard about it. "Them niggers is light-fingered. First thing you know you'll see your typewriter goin' out the door."

Chester, known locally as "Chester the Arrester," had been proven wrong. Jimmy worked silently and well, and when the folding was finished he lingered behind to sweep up.

One press night Mike learned at the last minute that, because of a baseball game at the county seat, the regular folders would not be able to come. After he had exhausted all possibilities for help, Jimmy timidly suggested that he call Preacher Young at Muster Corner. Only a few days before, Mike had noticed the Negro minister shopping in the chain store and asked one of the checkers who he was.

"That's the old codger who runs the colored school at Muster Corner. He takes on problem kids from the city."

Without asking any questions, the preacher replied that he would be delighted to cooperate. Shortly afterward his ancient pickup, laden with husky teenagers, drove up.

Thus, the Muster Corner boys became regulars. Standing between Misty, sitting on her high stool, and Miss Letty, in her denim apron and exotic hat, the colored preacher in his dark ministerial clothes also joined in the folding.

As the weeks passed, Mike's admiration for Preacher Young and the work he was doing grew. Frail, light-boned, with white hair and an ascetic face, the preacher was raised, as he put it, "at my best knowledge with schoolin' through the fourth grade." By reading everything he could get his hands on, he learned to discourse and preach on a variety of subjects. His voice was soft and mellifluous and his skill as a preacher and educator was famed among his people. Melusina said the test of a good minister was whether or not she tapped her foot during the service, adding that whenever she went to Preacher Young's church she stayed so still that she didn't even fan herself in summer.

With his abilities he could have had almost any Negro church he wished. Instead, he chose to remain at Muster Corner, where, several years previously, he had started a unique summer school.

His pupils were Negro delinquents from slum areas. At first, without dormitories or other facilities, the students were housed with local Negro families. The surrounding countryside rose up in arms. Polo Pete Buford posted his property and Major DeLong peppered trespassing students with buckshot. On Saturday afternoons, when the students were permitted to come to Shelburn in the battered pickup driven by the black-garbed preacher, Chester the Arrester invariably found some excuse—loitering in the streets or disturbing the peace—to send them scurrying back to the farm truck with orders to leave town.

Following several arrests for petty theft—the policeman insisted they had been shoplifting, while the boys argued they were just looking—Preacher Young forbade his students to leave Muster Corner. Although it was later discovered that Buddha Buford had taken the missing bags of candy from the Gone Away drugstore, there were no further trips to town.

When Washington Taylor, the local leader in the struggle for civil rights, urged sit-in demonstrations and more concentrated action, the minister preached patience, moderation.

"We've got to meet and learn the people," he said, "not just sing and preach, but teach."

To prepare his people for the day when they would be free to go to the Covertside Inn and order dinner, instructions included the proper use of knives and forks, the correct procedure for ordering a meal. Speech, manners, dress and general decorum were gone into, and speakers from Howard and Hampton discoursed on subjects ranging from modern art to anthropology.

Mike's story on the Muster Corner School was picked up by a wire service and written up in a national news magazine. Civic-minded teachers volunteered to join in the combined effort. Contributions poured in.

When the combination school and dormitory building, built by students and faculty in conjunction with Washington Taylor and his crew, rose out of the honeysuckled ruins of Charles Shelburne's original academy, the Muster Corner Summer School became an all-year-round institution where Negro teenagers could acquire a high school education away from crime-breeding environments and where all ages were welcome to join in the "integration classes."

During this period Mike came to know Washington Taylor.

It was Preacher Young who suggested that he hire Washington's contracting firm to replace the old livery stable sliding doors with a plate-glass window. Washington stood six feet three inches, and his grandfather had been a white man. Those whose memories were long said that if you looked closely, you could see the Shelburn look in the high cheekbones, the hawklike features, the smoldering eyes. And although his manners were impeccable, there was something about him that people found disturbing. It was as though he saw behind them and around them and through them and was inwardly mocking them.

A superb stonemason and carpenter, well versed in all the facets of the building trade, he was the only Negro in The Valley to own his own business.

When Washington Taylor bought the land next to The Valley School and set about building a stone house for his family, Polo Pete tried to run him off the property by setting up a pig farm on the adjoining land, which he owned. But as the pig farm also involved the school attended by his only son, Peter Junior (known as Buddha), Polo Pete was forced to abandon the project and try other measures. This took the form of calling in outside contractors to do the work on his numerous farms and trying to persuade his neighbors to do the same. This also failed.

After the war, when more and more new people began buying up and renovating the old houses, Washington Taylor and his men were the only craftsmen capable of beveling century-old cornices and replacing hand-hewn beams and fine old woodwork in such a way that the new was indistinguishable from the old. When Zagaran began rebuilding Ballyhoura he contracted Washington Taylor's firm. Now Washington's oldest son, John, was expanding the business and becoming rich.

Of his many children and grandchildren, Washington cared most for his ten-year-old granddaughter Lucy Mae. The little girl's legs were paralyzed as a result of polio. Her grandfather devoted long hours to reading to her and instructing her in history and mathematics. One night, at a folding session, he showed Shelley a pencil sketch that Lucy Mae had done of him. Shelley was so impressed by the child's talent that she volunteered to come twice a week and give Lucy Mae instruction. From then on, when her schoolwork was complete, Lucy Mae spent her time drawing.

Afternoons, Washington could be seen wheeling the little girl to the Gone Away for an ice cream cone. Because Negroes were not permitted to sit down at the marble-topped counter, Lucy Mae remained outside in the wheelchair while her grandfather made the purchase.

Over a period of time, Mike found that the guarded fencing that generally passes for conversation between whites and Negroes broke down. He began to see Negroes as individuals rather than as part of an amorphous mass. To his shame, he realized that like most whites he had fallen into the trap of speaking of them as "they" rather than as separate entities, with names and habits and independent characteristics. Slowly his education evolved. He began to question, to listen and to notice the subtle distinction between the way the Negroes he knew spoke when they were with him, as opposed to the way they were with one another and with other whites. With each other they spoke a language as far removed from the shuffling head-bobbing subservience accorded white people as Swahili. With him it was somewhere in between. Although they were never familiar—they always called him Mr. Editor or Mr. Latimer—they began to accept him into their confidence. Sensing his concern, they spoke of their employment difficulties, of their yearnings for better housing and educational opportunities. As he became more perceptive, the deep-seated anguish, the despair buried under centuries of oppression, transmitted itself to him. He talked to the Reverend Chamberlain, to Misty, Hunter Jenney and others who would listen. One night he invited them to the *Sun* office to meet Preacher Young and Washington Taylor.

That night the Human Relations Council was born. And that week the first of Mike's series on integration began.

Nobody took him seriously. "He'll get over it," Polo Pete Buford said, "when he's been here awhile." Major DeLong, the former mayor, agreed. The *Sun* had lauded the Major in an editorial when he retired, and he owed the new editor a debt of gratitude. "What you'd expect," he said. "He's a Yankee. And Yankees think they can come in and change something that's gone on for hundreds of years."

Shelley's friends began according him the same condescending, slightly ironic indulgence they reserved for those who were outside their inner circle and yet in some way connected. At Rotary, the VFW and the PTA and the other civic clubs and committees to which he belonged he was now granted a kind of humorous tolerance. "You don't really believe the things you're writing in that paper of yours?" When he said that he did, they nodded wisely and commented that after he'd been in the South awhile he would change his tune.

It was only lately that the temper of the community had altered. It was an atmospheric thing, something sensed in the averted eyes, the guarded way people now spoke to him. During the recent drive, some subscriptions had not been renewed and a few of the standing ads had been canceled. There had been one or two anonymous letters and telephone calls saying that he was a "nigger-loving Communist son of a bitch."

Right now, on this golden Sunday morning, the Valley people were sitting on a powder keg and didn't know it. The problem of desegregating the local eating establishments had been brought to a head the preceding Sunday. A militant civil rights worker, on his way to organize a demonstration in a neighboring county, had been refused service at the Gone Away drugstore. His name was Mase, and it turned out that he was a local boy, the son of Community and Manassas Brown. A tall, lanky student in his twenties, he had been beaten in Birmingham, jailed in Florida and stoned in Mississippi. A long, livid scar ran down his cheek and one eye had been permanently damaged.

As he was leaving the drugstore, Senator Bentley, accompanied by a visiting chief of state and followed by a carload of reporters, drove past on his way to church.

A meeting had been called at Washington Taylor's house. Mase had argued that now was the time to demonstrate. With representatives of the wire services on hand to cover the activities of the Senator, famed for his liberal legislation and sponsorship of the civil rights bill, a demonstration would receive worldwide publicity.

"A hundred years is too long," he cried violently. "Now is the time to achieve our rights, to overcome—"

"Listen," Mike said urgently. "We'll desegregate, but let's do it ourselves."

"Amen," Preacher Young put in. "Mr. Editor is right. We don't want outsiders telling us what to do."

"Bunch of Uncle Toms," Mase cried bitterly. "Whitey won't change. Nothing is going to change unless you force it."

"We don't want any name-calling here," Washington Taylor said. "We'll do what we think is right."

After a lengthy discussion, a compromise was reached. It was agreed that the Human Relations Council would be granted a week in which to desegregate the community. If the job was not done by the following Sunday, buses and possibly heads would roll!

The following morning Mike, Reverend Chamberlain and Dr. Watters went to see the owners of the various eating establishments. Hunter Jenney, who owned the Covertside Inn, was the first to go along. Hunter was a local citizen who had left the Marines to return to his home place, farm and sell real estate on the side.

"No sweat," he told his surprised supplicants. "We've been desegregated all along. It just so happens no colored people have ever come in. If they had, I'd have treated 'em just like white folks." Leaning across the counter, he said to Mike, "Hell, there's no segregation in a foxhole!" He rested his tattooed forearms on the clean-wiped formica. "Seems to me the sooner folks around here forget Appomattox and start thinking about 1963, the better off we'll be."

By Friday, all but Doc Dickerson at the Gone Away drugstore had agreed to desegregate.

Past seventy, with thinning gray hair and an ingratiating manner, Doc Dickerson was the third generation to operate the family-owned pharmacy.

"My help will leave," he groaned. "Mrs. Winecoop and Ethel won't serve niggers. I'll be ruined." Behind his spectacles his faded eyes filled with tears. "Maybe it's wrong, but I'm too old to change."

When Mike reported this conversation to Preacher Young, the Negro said softly, "This is new to white people. My people must realize this and be patient. Doc Dickerson was one of the contributors to my school. Last year he gave a hundred dollars to the church. Nobody in The Valley has done more for my people. He's provided medicine for the sick and given credit to the poor. I'll tell my people to leave him alone."

Before returning home the night of Zagaran's ball, Mike received the final telephone call from the Washington headquarters of the demonstrators.

"The buses are ready to roll. We'll picket the churches and have a sit-in at the drugstore."

"The town's desegregated," Mike replied. "The job is done."

"I don't believe it," Mase said flatly.

"I tell you, it's true," Mike insisted desperately. "Come and see for yourself."

"I'll call back," said the organizer, and hung up.

Mike went to see Doc Dickerson. He told him what Preacher Young's attitude was, and about the telephone call from Washington.

"For the sake of Shelburn," Mike begged, "please serve them if they come in." Hating himself, but convinced of the necessity of it, he added, "You told me the Bentleys were your biggest customers."

"Not as big as the Bufords."

The two men stared at each other. Then, aware that he had done all he could, Mike started for the door.

"Wait," Doc Dickerson called after him. "I'll serve them. By God, I'll serve them myself. God forgive me, I never thought I'd live to see the day." His voice rose. Shaking a finger at Mike, he cried, "But I'm warning you. If there's any trouble, no nigger will sit at my counter again!"

Mike looked at his watch. Almost time for church. Within the next hour the desegregation announcements would be "shouted" from local pulpits. Since the preceding afternoon he had not talked to Washington Taylor. All morning he'd tried to reach the number Mase had given him and been told that it did not answer. Was it possible that the demonstration was still planned to come off? Mike shuddered at the thought. Without police protection, it could degenerate into violence. If it did, the efforts of the committee would be negated. The moderate element in the business community, softened by the arguments of the Human Relations Council and at the point of accepting the new order, would revert back to their original thinking.

Again he dialed Washington.

Still no answer. Slowly, Mike returned the receiver to its cradle.

"Michael," Misty Montague said, "may I sit down?"

He had been so lost in thought he hadn't heard her come in. Leaping to his feet, he drew up one of the straight-backed chairs borrowed from Shelburn Hall and not yet returned. "Good heavens, Misty, of course you can sit down. Forgive me. I was cogitating."

Leaning her cane alongside the desk, Misty carefully lowered herself onto the chair. Obviously she was on her way to church. She had on a blue and white silk dress and a hat, the wide brim of which had been strengthened by a steel knitting needle woven through it. She looked cool and fresh and very clean. Over and beyond the familiar scent of dust and ink and molten lead came the faint, elusive odor of mimosa.

"I know what you were thinking," she said softly. "I used to sit there, where you're sitting now, and wonder how I would get the paper out. Now it's you who has to worry. But I'm taking up your time."

"No, Misty, you're not." Suddenly he knew he meant it. He did not want Misty to go. Whenever he was with her, sitting as they were now, either surrounded by people or alone, that special quality of hers, a kind of inner tranquillity, transmitted itself to him. That, and a certain inborn courage that could not be put down.

"Michael," she said now, "I thought it would be fun to retire, to have time to play the piano and take care of the animals, bake bread and make preserves and read all the books I never had time for before. But with Sandy away, I'm lonely. Do you think I could help out here? My spelling doesn't speak well for Miss Shelburne's School for Young Ladies, but if you can correct my copy, salary isn't important. You could pay me what you thought I was worth—"

"Misty, I could never pay you what you're worth." Mike

picked up his pipe. As he did so, he realized his hand was shaking. Irrelevantly he heard himself saying, "Nobody but my mother ever called me Michael before."

"Well, Michael"—Misty smiled—"may I come to work?"

He rubbed the back of his hand across his forehead, leaving a smear of ink. "Frankly, I don't know what to do. After today's announcement you know darn well there'll be cancellations, and I'll bet Buford will see to it that the county legals and printing we've been getting stop. The new press and restoring Shelburn Hall—" He puffed hard on his pipe and then continued, "I've got a payment due at the bank—"

"Polo Pete still wants to get his hands on this paper," Misty said. "Mike, I couldn't bear that."

He handed her an anonymous card congratulating him on becoming an "Honorary Nigger." "After this morning's announcement, will you still want to be associated with the *Sun?*"

Misty dropped the card onto the desk. "Of course."

"It will get worse before it gets better."

"I know that. That's why I want to be here."

He was aware of a slant of sunlight from the window crossing her, giving her a smooth, golden look. Instinct told him, from the way she was looking at him, that she was lonely. Some people, he thought, were like Virginia City's hens at Shelburn Hall. They could make a snug, safe nest in which they could live. But he sensed that Misty's wall, like his wall, was a thin thing, like the beaverboard he'd put up to separate his office cubicle from the bustle of the back shop. The pulse and rhythm of life came through, sometimes with such a cutting edge, such hurting force that one needed a person to lean on, and when you found somebody who felt the same way, then it was a fine thing not to have to explain.

Impulsively, his wide-palmed ink-stained hand covered hers. He did not know how long he'd been sitting there, holding her hand, gaining strength and decision from her touch when he realized the golden shaft was cut off. He looked past Misty and saw Shelley standing outside the plate-glass window, blocking off the sunlight.

"Shelley." He jumped up and ran to the door. "Shelley," he called again, but she was already in the station wagon driving away.

I might have known, Shelley thought, turning away from the *Sun*'s windows. Feeling angry and defiant, she slid behind the wheel of the station wagon and without looking back drove quickly down the main street. My cousin, Misty. The "brain" of the family. The one who was always right.

When they'd been children, Misty was the one with her head in a book while the others went riding. The Shelburnes with the E's had always considered themselves superior to the Shelburns without the E's. Probably Misty had been feeding Mike full of what Melusina used to call "reconstruction ideas," about equality and such. Hell, Shelley thought. She slammed on the brakes to avoid hitting a news photographer crossing the street. Why can't things stay the same? Why must everything change?

FOUR

ON THIS Sunday morning Shelburn, with its shop-bordered Main Street, its air of leisure and unhurry, resembled any other small community. Along with the monument in the square, the town's most prominent feature was the church.

Shelley could never pass it without a certain nostalgia for the old ivy-covered stone church with its modest white interior, the stained-glass window over the entrance donated by the Ku Klux Klan, the slave balcony, the spacious yard where three hundred wounded had been cared for following the battle of Bull Run. Here, beneath the oaks on Christmas morning, hounds met following the early service. Then, after the blessing of hounds by the Reverend Whitcomb, The Hunt moved off along Main Street, horses plaited with red rosettes, their riders sporting sprigs of holly in their buttonholes. The old church, with its high box pews, dated back to Revolutionary times and had possessed the charm of simplicity. The new church, designed by a New York architect and built with Buford funds, was ornate, elaborate, featuring wall panels of the chase (one depicted a cassocked priest blessing hounds) painted at great cost by a leading modern artist. Gone, too, was the Reverend Whitcomb. The red-visaged pastor had been a famous local character. People liked to reminisce about the time he ran out of communion wine following a Hunt Ball on Saturday night. "Sorry, boys," he apologized from the rail. "I underestimated."

The pastor, who boasted that he "suffered sinners, sweat and hangovers," had hunted three days a week until the Roman-nosed widow-maker which he had bought from a dealer in Bellevue ran him into a tree and killed him.

"It was the way he would have chosen to go," Mrs. Dinwiddie observed at the funeral. "Still, it's a great loss. Just last Sunday he preached the most marvelous sermon. All about the race—"

Mike had not been able to resist asking, "Horse or human, Mrs. Dinwiddie?"

Shelley recalled that the Reverend Whitcomb once commented that the same people who suffered through pages of hound pedigrees snored through Genesis. Yet had you accused the sporting element of hypocrisy, of coming to church to cleanse themselves of Saturday night's dissipation, or to exchange information about what horses were for sale, they would have been indignant. The Sunday morning service was part of their way of life, the one time during the week when the men appeared in white shirts and dark suits and the women were transformed from ruddy-faced wind-blown creatures of the hunting field to fashion plates in tailored tweeds, cashmere sweaters, pearls and hats.

The crowd of photographers and non-Episcopalians on the sidewalk and clustered on the lawn indicated that the Bentleys were attending. Reverend Chamberlain observed dryly that it was astonishing how many residents had taken suddenly to coming to church. But although there were many new members of the congregation who were obviously thrilled to be worshiping under the same roof with the noted Senator and his style-setting wife, The Valley Church had always contained its hard core of the old guard, to whom the morning service was as much of a social event and chance to visit on the lawn, before and after, as it was a time of worship.

The Bentleys' gleaming limousine was in glaring contrast to Major Southgate DeLong's dilapidated buggy. Artaxerxes, the Major's old black horse, named for Mr. Jorrocks's favorite hunter, was tied to one of the parking meters that lined the main street. Joe, his flea-bitten yellow hound, lay curled on the buggy's seat, which was torn and stained with an accumulation of chicken droppings. Although Joe, with his graying muzzle and mournful yellow eyes, looked as harmless as one of the fleas that spasmodically roused him to frenzied scratching, the usual cluster of colored people who loitered on the bank corner and all the local passers-by were aware of the old hound's prowess as a guard dog. For had any one of them attempted to untie Artaxerxes and make off with the rickety conveyance that was the Major's sole means of transportation, Joe would have gone for his throat.

As Shelley parked she saw Buddha Buford "shooting" at the churchgoers as they came up the walk. Buddha was one of those children who are always shooting at somebody or something. His father encouraged him by giving him expensive military toys, tanks, guns and rockets that were the envy of the other boys. At Christmas, Buddha had received an elaborate cosmic ray gun created by a comic book character currently popular with the children. Buddha called it a zap gun. Since then he'd gone around "zapping" people at every opportunity.

"Zap, zap," he cried, aiming at Mrs. Dinwiddie. "You're dead!"

"What a repulsive child!" the Beast exclaimed, holding a torn lavender chiffon handkerchief to her nose. Guiltily she darted her head around to see if Samantha Sue, descending from her new blue Mercedes, had heard her.

"Check your firearms at the door," Shelley commanded firmly.

"Zap, zap, you're dead," responded Buddha.

She could not help feeling sorry for the Bufords' only son. Times when she had taken him fishing with Cam he had relaxed and become more amenable. It was not his fault that, as everyone knew, he was ignored by his mother and spoiled rotten by his father.

"I'll zap you," she said jokingly, "if you're not inside the parish house in one minute, with your prayer book open to the lesson. It's about the prophet—"

"Ha, ha," Buddha interrupted. He was a pudgy little boy with coarse black hair that would not stay slicked down and braces on his teeth. "No Sunday School. Reverend Chamberlain wants everybody in church. Anyway," he concluded, "I know all about profits. My father keeps them in his bank."

"The Reverend Chamberlain told us he had something to say," Bitsy Baldwin put in. "Something important to children."

"I wannasitwithyou, Shelley," Buddha cried.

"All right, if your mother doesn't mind." Impulsively she added, "Buddha, how would you like to come home with us after church? We might have a picnic."

"Can we go fishing?"

"Maybe."

"Goody." With uncharacteristic generosity, Buddha added, "Cam, you can play with the gun while I go ask my mother."

"Cam," Shelley said, "you can play with the gun this afternoon. Now go with Buddha while he leaves it in the car. Here"—she dug into her shoulder bag—"here's a lollipop, one for each of you to eat after church. Remember, I said after—"

"Do I get one, too?"

Shelley jumped, as if she'd been shot by Buddha's gun. She turned to find Zagaran gazing down at her. He wore a dark suit, a white shirt, a red rose in his buttonhole and matching maroon tie. He was bareheaded, and his amber eyes were amused.

"Red, like the roses. Speaking of roses—" Shelley stopped in confusion. Misty Montague was coming up the walk, her cane tap-tapping on the flagstones. She looked cool and aristocratic and summery. Shelley thought of the tweed suit she had taken from the moth closet this morning in honor of the changing season and wished she hadn't worn it.

With a quick glance from one to the other, Misty nodded and said good morning. Zagaran held the door open for her. She thanked him smilingly.

"The ball last night was wonderful. A beautiful party. I'm afraid I didn't get a chance to make my manners. I hoped to see your wife."

"I'll tell her," Zagaran said quickly. "She thought she'd better stay in bed this morning and rest, particularly as we're going to the Bufords' dinner tonight."

"Oh, I see." Misty gave Shelley a quick questioning look and went down the aisle.

Shelley turned to find Zagaran watching her and for an instant she had the same sense of menace she'd known the night before in the gazebo when she saw the fox's eyes fixed on her.

At that moment the church bells, denoting the beginning of the eleven o'clock service, chimed with a loudness, a clashing dissonance that indicated Freddy Fisher was off the wagon. In hopes of rehabilitating Freddy, one of the community's most hopeless alcoholics, Wiley Matthews, owner of the Dependable Store and president of the Shelburn chapter of Alcoholics Anonymous and also choir director, had persuaded the Reverend Chamberlain to give him a job. Sober, Freddy caused the bells to peal forth with perfection, but on Sundays, following the dissipations of Saturday night, the dissonance was almost unbearable.

As the sound of bells died away, the churchgoers in the yard ended their conversations and started toward the entrance. Shelley was only vaguely aware of nodding and smiling in response to their called greetings as they went past. Zagaran's eyes held her pinned to the spot on the grass by the rose of Sharon which the Guild ladies had planted after the spring plant sale.

"Last night must have been too much for Freddy," she said sadly. "And he seemed to be doing so well with the job you gave him."

The little lights that came and went in his eyes, making them seem mocking and amused, went out. Now they were no longer the color of bourbon in sunlight. Instead they were as dark and cold as polished marble. "I was a fool to listen to Wiley Matthews. Last night your friend Freddy got drunk and abandoned the gate. He's off the payroll."

"No!" Impulsively, Shelley put her hand on his arm. It was like the muscles in a horse's quarters that's racing fit. Quickly she drew her hand back. "If you do, it will be the end of him."

"My mother says I can come," Buddha interrupted.

"Mommy," Cam put in, "do I have to go to church? Can't Buddha and I stay out here?"

She had forgotten the time and the children. All but Buddha, eating his lollipop when she had told him not to, were inside with their parents.

"No, Cam, I want you to sit with me." She grabbed his hand, grateful for a reprieve from Zagaran's presence. Their conversations seemed to take an unpredictable turn. They left her confused and shaken, irritated and unsure of herself.

"Come along, Buddha." She started toward the door. "You'll want to sit with your parents."

Buddha clutched her skirt. "I want to sit with you. Daddy's in bed with a hangover, Mommy doesn't like me beside her. She says I get her clothes sticky."

The congregation was standing, singing the opening hymn, when Shelley, head high and pretending to be unaware of Zagaran behind her, started down the aisle, accompanied by Cam and Buddha. The Schligmans were sitting in the Shelburn pew. Augie Schligman, heir to the great Schligman beer fortune, was a huge expansive man with a loud voice and loud vests—violent checks in the daytime, orange and crimson brocade at night. His wife Katie, considerably younger than her husband, leaned toward flowered chiffon, diamonds and furs. Because they entertained lavishly and spent money freely, they had been accepted by all but a handful of the old guard, who considered "those beer people" common.

Shelley resented their calm assumption that simply because the church was crowded it was permissible for them to make themselves at home in her pew. Coolly she acknowledged their nodded greeting, and knelt down on her grandmother's needlepoint cushion to pray. Cheek pressed against her knuckles, she tried to concentrate. Instead, she was aware of the musty church scent of wood and leather, wax and smoking candles, and that Zagaran, sitting with Samantha Sue Buford two pews behind, was staring at the nape of her neck. Closing her eyes, she struggled to thrust back the images and fragments of unrelated thoughts battering against her mind like insects against a screen. The roses, for instance. She had forgotten to thank him. She would write a note with the Shelburn crest on it. Dear God, she prayed, help me. But how and to do what? She did not know. That moment she was aware only that the future had acquired a further dimension, veiled and dangerous, from which prayer rebounded.

Sitting back in her pew, she wondered why it was she could never keep her white gloves white, like Misty's, and then remembered she had fended off the hound puppies with them. She straightened her shoulders. The suit felt heavy, and there was an itch in the small of her back. As though seeking reassurance, her eyes traveled to the plaque on the wall beside the pew.

To the Glory of God and in memory of Lt. Col. King Shelburn and Nuala, his wife, of Shelburn. Born in 1730, King Shelburn settled in Bellevue County where he built Shelburn Hall.

In 1784 the General Assembly granted him 6000 acres and in 1787 he dedicated 50 acres of this land for a town site to which was given the name of Shelburn.

Justice of the peace 1769, co-author of the Resolution of 1774, Major of Minute Men. Member of the County Committee of Safety and Correspondence 1775. Lt. Col. of the 16th Va. Regiment Continental Army with which he served at Whitemarsh and Valley Forge 1777–78. Fiscal Agent of the Federal Government 1778–81, Member of the Virginia Convention of 1778 for ratification of the U.S. Constitution. Presidential Elector 1796. Member of Congress 1799–1801.

He served his country well as

PATRIOT   SOLDIER   STATESMAN   CITIZEN

Patriot, soldier, statesman, citizen. What of King Shelburn's descendants? Had they measured up to this heritage of duty? Or had the family, like Shelburn Hall, slowly over the generations, run down? Now she was the last remaining direct descendant, and the burden of her heritage hung like a pall across her shoulders.

The choir rose to sing. Under the direction of Wiley Matthews, it was made up exclusively of AA members. There was Donnie Welford, manager of Windsor Stud Farm, who had once, following a Hunt Ball, kidnaped Millicent Black's tame bear, led it into the lobby of the Mayflower Hotel at five o'clock in the morning and insisted that the bear and himself be given a room. Dudley Dudley-Smythe, who hadn't had a drink in two years. Greg Atwell, who had abandoned his wife and children, been rehabilitated by Wiley, and had recently been reunited with his family. Along with Greg there were several other graduates of "Drop Kick Kelly's Drying Out Center," the name by which the famous New England sanatorium was known locally. There were also several women like Debby Darbyshire, who had been a public problem until Wiley persuaded her to accept the AA philosophy. The fact that these people were members of the choir had nothing whatsoever to do with their vocal ability. But as Wiley explained, "Surely the congregation would rather have them off the tune than off the wagon."

The front pews were reserved for the members of the old families, such as Misty, whose small proud head was on a level with the bottom of the marble plaque hung on the wall at the end of the family pew in memory of her father, Scaisebrook Shelburne.

In another pew sat Miss Letty Miller, her flowered hat cocked over one alert eye. Major Southgate DeLong, eyes straight ahead, back ramrod straight, sat behind her. There was a limp daisy in the buttonhole of his old-fashioned linen frock coat, and his high starched collar was rusted with age.

In a middle pew sat the Bentleys. The Senator's arms were crossed, his head slightly bent. His wife, Maggie, was chic as always in a blue suit with a matching pillbox hat atop her teased hairdo.

Wearing a dejected air and a discolored eye, Bones Black sat in the Templeton pew, chin resting in the palm of his hand. Obviously, after last night's row, the Blacks had separated again, for whenever Bones appeared in church alone it meant he had "turfed out," moved back to the Rakish Stud with his friend Fax.

By contrast, the Baldwins and their five tow-headed children, including the baby on Betsy's lap, presented a picture of family solidarity.

Shelley's eye caught Fax's bloodshot gaze as she reached for her prayer book. He gave her a brief smile and then, as though any move or change of expression was painful to him, directed his eyes back to the Reverend Chamberlain, who was reading the lesson.

His profile, Shelley mused, was that of the eternal patrician. His hair, graying now, was brushed back from a high forehead. His skin, nicked where he had cut himself shaving that morning, was pulled taut over the too-perfect features. In his beautifully tailored tweed, the elbows reinforced with chamois, he looked overbred, undernourished. As if it required too great an effort, Fax seldom stood or sat straight. He lounged. Yet no matter what clothes he wore, faded khakis and scuffed cowboy boots or a London-tailored suit, there was about him an air of consummate elegance.

Shelley thought of the effort it must have cost him to get out of bed, shave, dress and come to worship. Mike could have made the effort, she thought resentfully, if he'd wanted to, rather than sitting in the office holding Misty's hand. Last Sunday he had also refused to accompany her. Instead, he had gone to a mass meeting at Muster Corner Church, Misty with him.

"We will read Psalm 63, page 414 in the Book of Common Prayer."

"O God, thou art my God; early will I seek thee."

The voices rose and fell, like the leaves whirling past the tall windows.

"Let them fall upon the edge of the sword, that they may be a portion for foxes."

Some compulsion made Shelley turn.

Her eyes met Zagaran's. They held their half-smiling hooded look and seemed to see through her outward defenses, penetrating deep inside to the indecision, the trembling uncertainty. Quickly she looked away.

The congregation was seated again. The latecomers, who had been waiting at the door, entered. Millicent Black, in the harsh morning light slanting across the aisle, looked tired and drawn. Her two children, by Bones, were with her.

With a joyful cry, six-year-old Merry broke away from her mother and ran up the aisle. "Daddy, Daddy," the little girl cried. "I want to sit with you."

Ineffectually Bones tried to shush her. Undeterred, Merry clambered over Fax and snuggled up against Bones. "You weren't in Mommy's bed this morning. I looked and look—"

"Shh," Bones admonished. "I spent the night with your Uncle Fax."

Shelley dared not look at Cosy Rosy Dash-Smythe sitting tensely across the way, or back at Millicent, who unwittingly had slipped into the Dinwiddie pew with Archie, her eight-year-old son.

Millicent knelt down to pray, not realizing until she straightened up that the Dinwiddies occupied the other end of the pew. When Millicent moved into The Valley with her first husband, Randall Mason of the Mason Shoe Company, Shelley had taken her foxhunting as her guest and introduced her to the old guard. Millicent and Mrs. Dinwiddie became inseparable, in the hunting field and at the bridge table. Although they still saw each other almost every day, they hadn't spoken since last spring, when Dixon, the Dinwiddies' groom, went to work for Millicent.

"Other people's husbands are fair game," snorted the older woman, "but hiring away somebody's groom is unforgivable."

Millicent retaliated by telling everyone that "the old biddy refused to give Dixon a raise. Everyone knows what a skinflint she is," Millicent said. "She even rewrites the addresses on the free return envelopes that come in the mail—and reuses them!"

"Mommy," Archie whispered, "if Merry can sit with Dad, why can't I?"

"No, God damn it!" Millicent cried out. Aware that her exclamation had been clearly heard by the congregation, she added hastily, "Scuse me, God."

The hymn ended. The Reverend Chamberlain moved to the lectern.

"And the men said unto Lot . . . we will destroy this place, because the cry of them is waxen great before the face of the Lord: and the Lord hath sent us to destroy it." In his rich, vibrant voice, the minister was quoting Genesis.

The Reverend's eyes focused on the rose window over the entranceway. Speaking softly, as if to himself, he continued.

"A hundred years ago the armies of Abraham Lincoln, of the Federal Government, swept through Northern Virginia. They fought to make all men free, to give the Negro citizens of this great nation their constitutional rights. A hundred years ago the soldiers of the Confederacy who opposed them, the wounded from Manassas and Bull Run, were laid in this churchyard. The men who died were buried in the graveyard behind the church. I am saddened and ashamed that after almost a century the bitterness remains. Here, amongst us now, are those whom we cannot ignore, cannot forget . . ."

Deliberately, Samantha Sue Buford yawned and stared pointedly at the stained-glass window over the minister's head. Major Southgate DeLong adjusted his glasses, opened his prayer book and started to study it. Millicent Black reached into her shoulder bag, brought out her needlepoint and began to sew.

The minister's voice sank almost to a whisper. Yet his final words were clearly audible. "It is time to set our own houses in order. Time to end the evil of segregation, in public and in our hearts." He paused. Then he raised his head. His voice gathered strength. "There is but one God. The only supremacy exists in Him. In His eyes we are all equal."

Suddenly his voice underwent a change. His eyes swept the congregation seated below him. Leaning forward and gripping the edge of the rostrum, he seemed to be speaking personally to each individual.

"Last Sunday, outside this church, there appeared a civil rights worker from the nation's capital. Discovering that the community was segregated, a demonstration was planned to take place this morning."

Those who had been nodding and stifling yawns sat bolt upright. As if stopped by a camera in mid-scene, Miss Letty Miller's fan ceased to move back and forth. Senator Bentley's shoulders stiffened. Mrs. Matthews, who played the organ, sat forward on her bench. The only sound came from Merry Black saying, "Daddy, I want to wee."

Now the Reverend looked directly at Shelley.

"Our town is fortunate in having a fearless and dynamic newspaper editor. A man unafraid of what the neighbors think. Due to Mike Latimer, possible violence has been averted. It was Mike who organized the Human Relations Council, Mike who visited the owners and proprietors of the local eating places and persuaded them to open their doors to our Negro citizens. This took tact and persuasion and considerable courage." The minister's smile was rueful. "Thanks to Mike and the Human Relations Council and the high type of Negro leadership in our community, the outside organizers were put off, the village has desegregated and the demonstration planned for today, which would have embarrassed our good neighbor and friend, Senator Bentley, has been avoided. Shelburn has been integrated not by the sword, but by the pen. Let us pray."

Usually Shelley lingered to greet her friends, catch up on the news and make plans for the coming week. As she walked out of church, nodding and smiling like an automaton, she felt a subtle difference, a strangeness in the air, that was like the echo after the bells had rung.

Samantha Sue Buford grasped her arm, pinching the flesh.

Shelley whirled around. Samantha Sue's eyes in her heart-shaped face were a clear, cold powder blue, the color of the French import that she wore, and her smile resembled the rigid expression people wear when trying to even out their bite in the dentist's chair.

Whenever Samantha Sue was under duress her moonlight and magnolia accent ripened.

"That nawthern boyee," she said distinctly, "that yawl married, Shelley, should know bettah." The smile became even more pronounced and Shelley noticed that Samantha Sue had a mole on her right cheek with a black hair growing out of it. "Couse ah knows it isn't yawl's fault, Shelley." Her voice assumed a caressing quality. It made Shelley think of a caterpillar crawling on her skin. "Ah thought yawl had moh control. Anyway, honey"—her clasp on Shelley's arm tightened—"long's we all know where we stands. Ah'm sure yawl will straighten out that Yankee husband of yours, show him that the Southern way is the right way, just as surely as Robert E. Lee's birthday falls on January tenth."

The Dinwiddies were approaching. Although Samantha Sue's smile and voice softened, the pressure on Shelley's arm did not. "Bye, now, Shelley honey. See you this evening. Seven-thirty sharp. Just a simple little get-together. A few fun people. Come along, Buddha."

"But Buddha was going on a picnic with us," Shelley called after her. "Cam will be disappointed."

"Sorry about that," Samantha Sue said crisply, with hardly a trace of accent. "I just now remembered that his daddy wants him home this afternoon."

Church services had begun when, in the burning sunlight of the September morning, the cars drew up beside the highway. From their opened windows bristled crudely lettered placards. "Desegregate Shelburn." "Senator Bentley speaks for integration but lives in a segregated town." "Who are you kidding, Senator?" "No freedom in Bentley's town." In the quiet fields on either side, unconcerned by snatches of songs and handclapping, horses and cattle grazed.

Chester Glover was routing Sunday traffic around the parked vehicles. From beneath his new shining crash helmet, his heavy florid face streamed with perspiration.

"Why wasn't I told about this?" he demanded angrily of Mike. "These people ain't got no permit. They ain't got no right to demonstrate."

"We didn't know they were coming." Mike stared at the crowd of curious onlookers gathering in the field and alongside the highway. Colored families from Muster Corner and a handful of white teenagers. Town boys in T-shirts and dungarees, with slicked-down hair and a swaggering air. Should there be trouble, they would provide the source.

"How we gonna get rid of 'em?" the policeman asked worriedly. "What I hear, these people ain't afraid of jail. Anyway, we ain't got the space."

"Let Washington handle it," Mike replied. "He's the only one who can make them listen."

A historical marker indicated the beginning of the town limits. "Near this place on June 8, 1863, Shelburn's Raiders held off Federal Forces, and kept the town of Shelburn from falling into enemy hands."

Standing in front of it, the local civil rights leader and the "outside organizer" faced one another.

"There's nothing for you to do." In his dark Sunday suit with his white shirt and black tie, Washington Taylor stood very tall, very erect. "The town's desegregated. Even the drugstore. The job's been done. Thanks to Mr. Latimer and our white friends."

"Don't kid yourself!" Mase interrupted violently. "You sound like my pa. You haven't got any white friends!"

Washington Taylor was indignant. "Your pa didn't bring you up to talk that way. He brought you up to be mannerly. Now get back into your car and turn around and head back to where you came from. We don't want or need your help."

Mike felt a glow of accomplishment. He had not expected to hear the contractor on the side of moderation. But during the past week doors had been opened—doors closed for centuries. Washington Taylor had seen it happen. But that any black could trust the white man's word was evidently beyond the understanding of the younger man. In Mase's taut, angry face, in his muttered blasphemy, Mike saw the bitterness, the hate. Had he been beaten and bombed, clubbed and condemned, might not he, too, be as bitter, as militant? Yet Mike knew that Mase's way was not the answer. The only answer which Mike could accept lay in non-violence, in the line taken by the Reverend Martin Luther King, of whom Preacher Young was a disciple. Now, in the face of the growing restlessness of the crowd, Washington Taylor sought to hold off the demonstrators with arguments of reason and logic.

As though in a dream, Mike heard his own words: "If you

demonstrate, you'll undo the progress that's been made. You'll antagonize those who are for us as well as those against us. Our next step is to desegregate the schools. The board is receptive. We don't want to jeopardize our chances."

Mase could not comprehend such an approach.

"Man, you've been brainwashed," he interrupted furiously. Glaring at Mike, he continued. "You think Mister Charley here is on your side. Man, you're crazy with the heat!"

"Now you listen to me," Washington said coldly. "I don't care what you think. The fact remains that Senator Bentley is a famous man. He is majority leader of the United States Senate. It's up to him to put through civil rights legislation. You want to march against him? Make him angry?"

The demonstrators were becoming restive. From the crowded cars the singing and handclapping were accelerated. At that moment one of the Free Zoners who had stopped along the highway threw a rock. It glanced off the windshield of the lead car and rolled to the ground beside the highway. Mike recognized the man Shelley had pointed out at the supermarket as a Mellick.

"Go!" Washington Taylor said, pointing to the car. "Now, before there's trouble."

A murmur ran through the crowd. Then silence. Bareheaded, standing very tall, with his arm raised and his hooded eyes flashing fire, Washington Taylor could have been the reincarnation of his kingly ancestors repelling invaders from their African village.

Involuntarily, Mase took a step backward. He saw the impassive, staring faces, felt the sudden hostility, not only from the whites but from his own people. He was too well trained not to know when he had been impulsive. Carried away with visions of the worldwide publicity, he had misled his superiors into believing that the demonstration was wanted by the local Negroes. He had not believed that the community could be desegregated in a week and had been sure that when the deadline came, the demonstration would be acceptable. This was not the case.

Without local sanction and a police permit, he would have to call off the demonstration. Without losing face, he must explain to the students he had routed from their beds that morning to letter signs and placards that the march was not to take place.

He looked around. From experience he sensed the mood of the moment. Any sudden movement, another stone or a cry, and the quiet people watching could turn mob. There was a time when it was worth it to fight, but this wasn't it. No point in having his head bashed in and languishing in jail when he was desperately needed elsewhere. No point risking censure from his higher-ups for a bunch of Uncle Toms who didn't have the sense to appreciate outside help when it was offered.

"All right. You win," he said gracelessly. "But when your white friends cut out, don't call on us."

Finally the last car vanished over the rise, heading homeward. The local onlookers sighed, turned back into individuals and began to disperse. Although it was not yet noon, Mike wished there were someplace he and Washington Taylor could go together and have a drink. Yet even if there were, he knew it would not be fitting. Despite all that they had been through together, the apartness, the formality which characterized white-Negro relationships was still present.

"Thank you, Mr. Latimer," the tall Negro said with dignity.

"Thank *you*, Mr. Taylor," Mike replied feelingly, clasping the outstretched hand.

"I guess we told 'em off," Chester Glover commented smugly. "Reckon they know better than to come back."

Mike drove slowly to the office. He wondered what the local reaction would be to the announcements that had been "shouted" from the local pulpits. Doubtless he would find out soon enough.

Shelley drove out of town. The Sunday traffic was heavier than usual. A lot of colored people seemed to be on the sidewalks. She saw Fax Templeton's My Boy Hambone and Simeon Tucker, both in their dark Sunday-best suits, and John Taylor's wife, Linda, pushing Lucy Mae in her wheelchair past Miss Letty Miller's yard.

"Why didn't Buddha come?" Cam asked. "He was going to bring his gun. He said I could play with it."

"Mrs. Buford forgot that his father had plans for him." She reached over and patted Cam's hand. "Maybe tomorrow . . ."

Her voice trailed off. She felt as if a tightly balled fist had hit her in the center of her stomach. Samantha Sue's words left her experiencing feelings she had not known before—anger, fear, and finally burning shame.

Samantha Sue would never have dared to talk to her in such a manner unless she knew about the loan.

Shelley realized that by keeping the knowledge from Mike she had walked right into the trap which Polo Pete could spring at any time he wished, playing her like one of the bass with which he stocked his farm pond, until the time when it would seem propitious to net her and squeeze her pride, her life's blood, from her.

Once she had actually started living at Shelburn Hall, anticipation dwindled to reality, a reality of mice and musty discomfort and repairs which, if taken as a whole, seemed impossible. For instance, the old wooden reservoir leaked badly. Before winter a new furnace was required. There were broken windowpanes, and the electrical system had to be carefully gone over. In the library, a leak had rotted away the fine paneling, and six generations of valuable books were mildewed and mouse-eaten. The grounds were so overgrown that it had taken Mike days of hacking at the honeysuckle to uncover the former terraced garden, fallen-in swimming pool and tennis court.

The income from her trust fund and the amount delegated to her for household repairs from the initial loan that Togo Baldwin had put through went for the basics—patching the roof, plumbing and a new stove. Such refinements as repairing the paneling in the den and the antiques that had been taken from the downstairs rooms as they disintegrated, and stored in the attic, painting, sanding the floors, re-covering the chairs and sofas, had yet to be accomplished. When Shelley mentioned such items, Mike told her that if she was determined to live in The Valley, the newspaper would have to come first. Until it became solvent and their debts could be paid back, they would have to forgo the luxuries.

Shelley could not have borne it if she'd not been able to foxhunt. The Goose had died soon after her return and been buried in the horse graveyard in the woods. Since then she had not had a horse of her own. Luckily, she'd been able to open and maintain the stable by taking in boarders, mounts for the foxhunters who commuted from Washington and New York on weekends, and young horses which people wanted broken and schooled. Although these horses, along with ones that her friends asked her to hunt for them, kept her in the field almost every time that hounds went out, she yearned for a horse of her own, one that she could school herself and that might someday realize her dream of winning the Shelburn Cup.

Shelley would not have permitted herself to become financially involved with Polo Pete Buford if she hadn't seen him riding Lookout Light that day in the hunting field and fallen in love with the gray Pilot colt. Lookout Light was of the great Shelburn strain, descended from the stallion Galway Pilot that Sean Shelburn had imported to The Valley. He was a beautiful blood horse, gray flecked with black, with strong, clean legs and a short, compact body which made him look smaller than he actually was. In every inch of him, the long, gently arched neck, the graceful doe-soft muzzle, the liquid wide-apart eyes, there was the Pilot breeding—that special thoroughbred quality that captures the imagination and sets up a singing in the heart.

Shelley's immediate thought was that here, finally, was a Shelburn Cup horse and if the glory of winning the coveted race was ever to be hers, this was the horse that could do it. Her next thought was that Polo Pete, with his impossible seat and hands like bags of cement, had no business riding a thoroughbred, let alone one with the temperament of a Pilot.

She had ridden up and asked him where he had gotten the colt.

"I bought Lookout Lady at your dispersal sale." He leaned over and pinched her knee. "I bred her to Fax's stallion Moonlighter. This was the mare's last foal. Fax broke him and schooled him for me." His eyes, a very light blue, seemed to look at and through her. "You like him?"

Shelley fought to control her revulsion as his fingers pressed against her flesh. "Yes, P. P., I do."

The gray started out jumping well, but as the hunt progressed and his rider continued to snatch him, to jerk his mouth at each obstacle, the horse began rushing his fences and hitting them. Finally he lunged into a fair-sized coop. At the last minute, instead of jumping, he wheeled with such speed and agility that Polo Pete was sent flying over his head. Shelley caught the colt and returned him to his owner. Grim-lipped, furious at being thrown in full view of the field, Polo Pete waited until he thought Shelley and The Hunt were out of sight. Then taking a chain that had been wrapped around the gate beside the fence, he began beating the terrified horse.

Some instinct caused Shelley to look back. The sight filled her with fury. Returning at a gallop, she jumped off the young horse she had been schooling, ran up to Polo Pete and grabbed the chain away from him. The gray, eyes rolling with fear and nostrils dilated, reared up, breaking away. Reins dangling, he galloped off in the direction The Hunt had gone.

"How could you?" Shelley demanded scathingly. "How could you abuse a horse like that?"

The force of her contempt was such that for an instant the fat man had the grace to look abashed. "I lost my temper." He gave her an ingratiating smile. "Stupid of me. Unsporting. He's not really my type. He should be yours, Shelley, considering his breeding and all." He paused, and then his eyes slid away to where Roy, his English groom, was leading the colt back to him. "How would you like to have him?"

It was as if she had put all her money on a long shot and it had won. Then hope died. "If I bought a horse Mike would never forgive me. We can barely keep our heads above water now."

Roy led the gray up. She saw the beauty, the breeding, and as Polo Pete advanced toward him, the fear. She knew suddenly that she had never in her life wanted anything so much as she wanted this horse.

Polo Pete was watching her closely. "Tell you what, Shelley," he said, taking the reins, "come to my office in the bank tomorrow and we'll make a deal."

She had her first real argument with Mike that night. The initial dissension began at dinner, which was late and not very good. She had stopped off at the Dinwiddies' hunt breakfast and it was after six when she reached home to find Suellen, their sometimes helper, was already departed, leaving Virginia City to watch Cam until her return.

Mike announced he had had a terrible day at the paper. At home, a raccoon had killed two setting hens. The pump was broken and there was no hot water to take a bath. The electrician still had not come to fix the hall lights, and a section of the paddock fence had collapsed, allowing the young horses to get out onto the road, where the filly that Shelley was boarding for Millicent Black had fallen and been cut.

Cam upset his milk and when she chided him he burst into tears and ran out of the kitchen.

"Damn it, all I do is maintenance," she cried, starting after Cam.

"Shelley," Mike said wearily, "you were the one—"

"Who wanted to come back to The Valley. I know, I know. Just don't say it."

She went to bed finally with her world spinning on an axis of household disasters, of trivia and tension, accented by her physical weariness. She was tired of not having enough money, of making do with everything old—house, furniture, clothes.

For a long time she lay awake, resenting Mike's even breathing beside her, the fact that he could sleep when she could not. She thought about the gray colt, and in her mind's eye she saw the horse's fear, sensed the abuse he would be subjected to if he remained at Silver Hill. Lying tensely on her back, she stared at the shadowed ceiling and told herself that it was her duty to rescue Lookout Light from Buford hands.

The next morning she went to see Polo Pete.

He was beaming and affable and oddly humble. He complimented her on how well she looked, how good it was to have her living in The Valley again, how well Mike was doing with the paper. "It's a banker's job to do more than just loan money," he said sanctimoniously. "In a small town like this it's our responsibility to help one another and to get things started. Now the *Sun* is giving my paper a run for its money." His pale blue eyes seemed suddenly as cold and analytical as the tax table on his desk. But when he continued, his manner was warm, almost too friendly. "Naturally, I wouldn't have it otherwise. Competition is the heart, the very foundation of the capitalistic system. Without it we'd have Communism instead of Christian brotherly love."

Then he got onto the subject of the horse, how it was only right and proper that a Shelburn should have Lookout Light, that she was really the only person who could ride and understand the Pilot strain and that all along he'd really just been keeping the colt for her, hoping she'd return to The Valley and take him back to Shelburn Hall where he belonged.

He explained that if she needed money for the additional repairs to the Hall, he would be glad to lend it to her. "It's one of our great houses," he said. "Part of the Valley image." He told her he would be glad to let her have the horse and to lend her five thousand in a private transaction. This, he explained, would make it unnecessary to bring up the matter at the directors' meeting. "In that way," he added, "you don't need to tell your husband." Leaning back in his chair, he gazed benignly at the silver-framed photograph of Samantha Sue holding Buddha in her lap, which sat at an angle on his desk. "Your husband has enough to worry about right now without assuming further financial burdens."

Shelley mentioned collateral and he gave her an ingratiating smile and answered that all he really required was her word, but that for the sake of doing everything nice and legal like, all she had to do was give him a temporary assignment on her personal and her land holdings, plus 7½ per cent interest payments on the loan, which was the same amount of interest that the bank would demand. "Take those paintings," he remarked thoughtfully. "The Gilbert Stuarts and Peales must be very valuable."

He showed her to the door and repeated in a cautionary tone that it might be best to keep the matter from Mike. "It would just worry him, and right now he needs all his energies to get the paper on its feet."

Now, fresh from her encounter with Samantha Sue and on her way home from church, she realized what basically she had always known but refused to face. Polo Pete Buford was small-minded and vengeful. Historically the Bufords had always resented and been jealous of the Shelburns. When Misty refused to sell him the *Sun* and sold it to Mike instead, Polo Pete improved the *County Daily*, which he could now use as a weapon against Mike. Polo Pete had ridden Lookout Light deliberately that day as bait, and she had swallowed it. Horses and Shelburn Hall were irresistible lures.

So far, she had been able to meet the interest payments with the income from the boarding horses in the stable, and the secret had been kept from Mike. It was only that whenever she saw Polo Pete and remembered her indebtedness to him, she was aware of a vague apprehension, part shame, part guilt, as if she had been a partner in some dishonesty. It was the way she had felt the only time she went gigging, when at sight of the frogs impaled on the pointed stick, she had felt as though she'd run full face through a cobweb, bits and pieces of which she could not brush away.

The sky was cloudless, the country on either side of the road tranquil. Nothing in sight but trees and green fields, farm ponds shimmering in the sun like round silver dollars, and fat cattle. A scene of enchantment and profound peace. Yet Shelley had a deep sense of foreboding.

FIVE

WHEN Shelley was "in pieces," as Melusina used to say, she turned to that which was known and understood. Green fields and blue mountains, their colors constantly changing, their shades of blue as varied as there were paints with which to capture their particular essence. She would have liked to go to the upstairs bedroom with the skylight which she had fixed up as a studio and work, experimenting with the abstract shapes and vivid colors she had discovered in New York, or painting the landscapes she loved. But lately there seemed to be less and less time.

She glanced at the bulletin board Mike had put in the hallway and on which were tacked invitations, a listing of fall race meetings and horse shows, and "things to be done." The invitations were tacked one atop the other, three to luncheons that very Sunday. She had accepted Millicent Black's invitation, knowing as she did so that Mike would probably object, saying that they were never home any more and that he had too much to do around the place or at the office to go gallivanting off to Sunday lunch where he would have Bloody Marys and wine and be rendered ineffectual for afternoon work. Briefly she noted three or four invitations to cocktails that afternoon. Well, she'd explain to the people when she saw them that night at the Bufords'. Mike would think it odd if, after having pleaded with him to go to the party, she suddenly said she didn't want to go. She did not admit to herself that in spite of Samantha Sue's insulting remarks she still wanted to go to Silver Hill for dinner—or why.

She telephoned Last Resort and left a message that she would not be able to come to luncheon. After changing into her blue jeans, she made sandwiches for Cam and herself.

The Sunday afternoon walks that Shelley took with Cam and the dogs followed a pattern. The mellow holes in the old wall that had once separated the rose garden from the park were a good place to begin. Shelley had shown Cam the small hollowed-out place where as a child she had kept her special treasures, a peach or an apple to ripen, and sometimes an especially beautiful marble. Now they each had a secret place, off bounds to others.

The week before, they had gone to see Melusina. The old woman had given Cam apples from the tree in her front yard. Cam pinched one and decided it was still not ripe.

"Give it another day," Shelley advised.

"O.K.," Cam agreed, and while she set out toward the stable, he went to search out eggs that Virginia City's banty hens laid in strange and unexpected places, like the seat of the breaking cart in the wagon shed, or in a flowerpot in the old greenhouse.

Inside the archway Shelley paused, standing for an instant on the hard-packed red clay that Virginia City kept swept and wetted down. The cheerful sound of horses moving in their stalls, the heady odor of hay and clean straw were reassuring. Her mind stopped, changed into a different gear, acquiring new strength, a new set of values, the way it always did when she entered there.

The barn at Shelburn Hall had originally been built for many more horses than were stabled there now. At least a dozen stalls were fastened up, the names of their long-ago occupants fading away on the painted plaques nailed to the doors.

At the sight of the dogs, Virginia City's big striped tomcat rose from where it had been curled, arched its back and hissed at what it considered interlopers. A banty hen that had been setting in the abandoned wheelbarrow outside the tack room door flew off to join the flock pecking about in the manure pile.

Lookout Light had been brought in from the field in preparation for the cubbing season. He stopped stall-walking and came to her. The hound puppies rubbed up against her as she spoke to her horse, whispering of the joys they would experience the following morning, when hounds met at Ballyhoura.

. . .

The wood surrounding Shelburn Hall was a mile or more of tall overly ripe oaks that swung their century-old heads over the rides which long ago had been cut through the undergrowth. The path that Shelley and Cam now traveled wound alongside a clear bubbling stream, a tributary of Buffalo Run, which ran through the old orchard by the graveyard.

Ringing the gray-green fields were the inevitable mountains, blue, hazy, ever-changing but always blue, easily maintaining their steadfast, lingering enchantment. From the pasture came the raw caw of a crow, and in the swampy area around the distant pond sounded the hypnotic rise and fall of the frogs' song. There was the dry aromatic fragrance of grass in the sun, and she knew then that no other part of the world would ever mean what this land and its associations did, and that beyond reason, beyond time, she would always love this place where her roots were sunk.

Leaving the woods, Cam and Shelley moved across the meadow, brilliant with goldenrod and crimson sumac and clouded with yellow butterflies rising at the dogs' approach. Maples mottled with golden leaves rippled in the breeze. The square, stocky beef cattle raised their heads. After a desultory glance, they returned to their grazing.

The stillness, the beauty of the golden afternoon had a healing quality. Here, for an hour or more, she could piece together the parts of herself that daily, because of the process of living, became unraveled.

They reached a clearing by the stream, a kind of fairy circle where in the spring violets made a lavender carpet.

Cam sneezed. Guilt returned. She had forgotten to take him to Dr. Watters for his hay fever shot. Tomorrow she would do it. "Allergies," the doctor explained. "We can test and test and not find what causes asthma. Goldenrod and house dust. Strawberries and detergents."

Lately Cam had been very well. Still Dr. Watters advised against letting him be around the horses. All summer Cam had been unable to ride the old pony which Hunter Jenney had given Shelley when his son Sam outgrew it. The fact that Cam could not ride or participate in the Pony Club was a disappointment to Shelley.

In the overgrown apple orchard they sampled the small round

apples clustering the gnarled, broken lichen-covered boughs bending beneath their weight. Abandoned, uncared for since Mr. Hatch, the old farmer, had died, the trees continued to bear fruit. Despite wind and weather that had severed branches, leaving them like amputated limbs lying on the ground, productivity had not ceased. Biting into the cold, hard, tart fruit, Shelley thought how much more flavor they had than the big rosy polished apples from the supermarket.

"Don't eat too many," she cautioned as Cam reached for a second.

"Please, Mommy, just one more."

"You'll get a tummy ache."

Cam gazed longingly at the apple in his hand. His skin, like his hair, was very fair. In the sun it gleamed like the golden fruit.

"Then can I take it home with me?"

"May, not can," Shelley replied automatically. "Yes, you may take one home with you."

"And one for my daddy?"

Shelley nodded.

Tossing away the core of her apple, she shivered. Instinctively, as though expecting to see a fox bolt from the honeysuckle, she looked around. There was nothing there. In the golden light of the Indian summer afternoon the countryside was as before, carefully cultivated meadows beaded with brown walls and white fences, serene, beautiful. A plane droned overhead, a crow flew lazily toward the mountains. From the Ballyhoura pasture came the lowing of cattle. In that present-day setting of pastoral peace, the past seemed distant, unreal.

They sat on the bank beside the stream to eat their sandwiches. Afterward Shelley watched Cam absorbed in tossing sticks into the water. As Lance plunged after them, snapping and snarling with pretended ferocity, her son's delighted laughter bubbled up like the clear water rippling over the rocks.

Next to the orchard between Ballyhoura and Shelburn Hall was the family burial ground. The stone wall that had once surrounded it had fallen down and been obscured by weeds. Above the encroaching greenery rose the ancient gray headstones. Here, ashes to ashes, dust to dust, was her heritage. Dark, murky, as tangled as the vines embracing the untended graves.

I must get it cleaned up, she thought. Mend the wall, get rid of the weeds, straighten up the lurching headstones.

Every time she rode or walked past the graveyard she made this resolve. Then something else took precedence. Like the roof at Shelburn Hall, the paddock fence and the new furnace. With Mike so busy at the paper and only Virginia City left on the place, there was not enough help to take care of necessities, let alone the incidentals like cutting back the overgrown entrance to the drive, trimming the box, or clearing the famous rose garden.

Slowly Shelley picked her way through the maze of graves. Prickers tore at her blue jeans. Burrs attached themselves to her sweater. Bending down, she read the inscription on the grave of Nellie Shelburn, who had died bearing an illegitimate child in 1790.

> She is gone, O she is gone
> to Everlasting Rest
> To Christ, our Saviour who
> Loved Sinners best.

Stopping beside the largest headstone, she tore away the honey-suckle obscuring the chiseled epitaph.

    King Shelburn
    Died Shelburn Hall

The rest of the epitaph had been worn away by time and weather. Here and there Shelley was able to pick out the words "Reputable Character," "Consummate Frugality," "Prudence," "Indefatigable," "Inseparable Friend," "Useful Man." At the bottom of the gravestone, beneath which foxes had tunneled to make a den, the words "Disconsolate Relations" were barely legible.

Cam stood staring at the grave. His face wore a puzzled expression. "What do those words mean?"

"They're good words," Shelley answered. "When you go to The Valley Day School you'll learn how to say them and what they mean. They were written about your great-great-great-grandfather, King Shelburn. Cam, those words are your heritage. It's up to you to give them meaning once again."

"Is he the man in the painting?"

Shelley shook her head. "No, that's your great-grandfather, Sean Shelburn. He was the leader of Shelburn's Raiders."

"Tell me about him."

"All right. Sit down." She put her arm around him and drew him down onto the sun-warmed ivy. "But I have to go back to the beginning. Now . . ."

Their backs rested against King Shelburn's headstone. The leaves of the dogwoods, shriveled and inverted like aging hands holding their clusters of red berries, made brittle sounds as the breeze blew from the mountains. A chipmunk skittered gaily along the wall and disappeared into a hole.

"Once upon a time," Shelley began, "in a country across the sea . . ."

The origins of the name dated back to antiquity. The first known English Shelburne was a Sir Hugh Shelburne, an officer in Thomas Cromwell's army. As a reward for his services, he was granted the lands and buildings of a convent, Ballyhoura, in County Cork. According to correspondence in the state papers at the time of Cromwell, he was the first of the English Shelburnes to live in Ireland. It was said that when he appeared at the convent to dispossess the nuns, the abbess and the community went on their knees and cursed the family, praying that "the new owner should never see the smoke of its chimneys."

Undaunted, Sir Hugh proceeded to ignite all the peat fires laid in the convent fireplaces, so that the smoke of its chimneys could be seen all the way to the sea. He then set out to win himself the daughter of a fashionable lord who had fought long and hard against the Cromwellian infidels.

After the elopement, Sir Hugh brought his bride back to Ballyhoura. He was forty-five, she but twenty. He was a warrior, she a gentlewoman who knew nothing of life in a bleak country house far removed from the gaiety of Dublin. Also her father, enraged at the elopement, began a blood feud with her husband that culminated in battle. Aware that his enemy was about to make a furious charge against him, Sir Hugh mistakenly turned to face his opponent and fell dead, a musket ball in his brain.

When the grandsons of Sir Hugh and his lady, who inherited the property, were in their twenties, the nuns' prophecy came to pass. Ballyhoura was burned to the ground, leaving only its chimneys to rise gray and cold against the mountains. Fleeing from lawsuits and the violence resulting from Parliament's bill "to prevent the further growth of Popery" that had incited Catholic to rise against Protestant, Hugh and Richard emigrated to the New World.

Hugh, the scholar, settled in Boston, where he became renowned as a philosopher and essayist. His descendants became professors at Harvard, book publishers and playwrights, ranking in prestige with the Cabots and the Lowells and other famed New England families.

"That is your cousin Misty's branch of the family," Shelley told Cam. "The Shelburnes with the E's because they were supposed to be smarter and could spell better than our side of the family. But it was our side who made the money that built Shelburn Hall."

"Do we have money now?" Cam asked, looking around at the overgrown cemetery.

Shelley looked at the towers of Ballyhoura in the distance. "Once we owned the land from here to Bellevue, all you could ride over in a day. Now it's all gone but Shelburn Hall. In those days gentlemen didn't work. They were farmers and went foxhunting. If they had to earn a living they went into real estate. Richard Shelburn, our direct ancestor, settled on Buffalo Run and became a successful tobacco planter. He built Ballyhoura as a replica of the Irish Ballyhoura."

From the outset, Ballyhoura seemed cursed. A workman was killed when one of the great boulders used for the foundations rolled on him. Another lost a leg falling from the tower. Richard Shelburn's young wife died giving birth to a son who was named King Shelburn because, as the oldest son, he was to be king of Ballyhoura and all the land he surveyed.

Richard Shelburn married again, a country woman by the name of Carter, who bore him a half-brother to King. Carter Shelburn was a rake and a rascal who wenched and gambled and was, in Valley jargon, "just plain no good." King Shelburn inherited Ballyhoura. A deeply religious man, he believed that a curse of God had been put on the house, and that those who lived there would be doomed to disaster and distress of the heart. Thus he deeded it to Carter, who let the once great plantation go downhill into debt and dissolution. When there was no longer money to meet his expenses, Carter decamped and went to Barbados, where his son, Thomas, born to him by his Muster Corner mistress, became a highly successful sugar planter.

At Ballyhoura, the smoke from the chimneys ceased and the hearths grew cold. The windows were boarded over and the great gloomy fortresslike house became a ghostly ruin. The park grew into a jungle where foxes prospered, poachers walked, tramps hid out and young girls and boys came in pretended fear and trembling to find solace and safety in each other's arms.

King Shelburn was the opposite of his half-brother Carter. A good man, respected by his friends and neighbors, deserving of the accolades carved into his headstone. Inherent in his blood was a love of buildings and fine horses. Like his friend George Washington, he was a "real" foxhunter, "one whose greatest interest was in hounds and the results of the chase as a game." In return for his services during the Revolution, he was granted six thousand additional acres, becoming the largest landowner in The Valley of Northern Virginia. There he proceeded to devote the remainder of his life to building a gracious country house and to the breeding of superlative horses and hounds.

After years devoted to planning, assembling materials and actual construction, Shelburn Hall was completed. The gleaming white-pillared brick structure, fronted by a wide door over which was carved the Shelburn crest—the white horse tied to the tree with "Keep Tryst" written beneath it—had a storybook quality.

Silhouetted against the hyacinth rise of the blue mountains, it faced out over the historic Valley. At the foot of the great park flowed a sparkling stream along which, a century before, migrating Indians camped and buffalo grazed in the lush grass. Beyond the river lay a patchwork of luxuriant meadows, crisscrossed with split-rail fences and dry stone walls which slaves had built with rocks cleared from the fields.

Outside the high walls that surrounded the estate, King Shelburn dedicated fifty acres of land, on which were built a tavern, a blacksmith shop, the first flour mill in that section and stone cottages for his slaves. This center was given the name of Shelburn.

Next to the graves of King Shelburn and his wife, who had been kin to the Lees and borne a number of daughters but no sons, lay the remains of Shelley's grandmother, Margaret Lee, King's granddaughter, known as Miss Marlee. Miss Marlee married her cousin, Sean Shelburn, son of Carter of Ballyhoura. Described as "wild as a hawk, handsome as Lucifer," he had been born in Barbados, the result of his father's late marriage to a titled Englishwoman with a considerable fortune.

"Tell me about the man in the grave that isn't marked." Cam pointed beyond the crumbled wall. "The man you said lived at Ballyhoura and was bad."

"He was my grandfather. Your great-grandfather . . ."

As though not to contaminate the graves of his respectable relatives, Sean Shelburn had been buried outside the compound. His grave was overgrown. His only marker had been a crude wooden board, long since rotted away, on which were written the words of the poet Shelley: "It is a man of violent passions, bloodshot eyes and swollen veins that alone can grasp the knife of murder."

Nobody knew who had written it. It could have been one of the Mellick clan, his wife Margaret Lee, or any one of the numerous local girls and matrons he had taken to bed following the all-night revels at Ballyhoura.

There was about his memory a legendary aura, a glamour envied by the conventional, the earthbound. Fearless in battle and in the hunting field, he had taken what he wanted.

The painting of him which now hung at Shelburn Hall showed a dark high-boned face dominated by piercing black eyes. Something about it caught the onlooker, so that one was drawn to study it again and again.

When Sean was eighteen, he left Barbados to attend the University of Virginia and make the acquaintance of his Virginia cousins. Ballyhoura was his inheritance, and at sight of the house he determined to restore it and live there. With money left him by his mother, the great gloomy mansion was rebuilt and furnished. The grounds were cleared and the fences repaired. Sean never returned to his island birthplace.

During the latter half of the Civil War he was leader of the guerrilla group known as Shelburn's Raiders that captured two Union generals and was instrumental in prolonging the war.

At Ballyhoura the Hanging Tree, the great oak where it was said he had hanged deserters and Yankee prisoners, and where he had once hidden when the house was surrounded by Union cavalry, was pictured in many Virginia histories, as were the marks made by his charger's hoofs when he galloped the horse through the house and leapt the stone steps descending to the drive. When he returned from the war, his left arm had been amputated and his left leg shattered by fragments of shrapnel.

These physical ailments did not deter him from entering wholeheartedly into a life of foxhunting and carousing. For years the woods adjoining the great fortresslike house had proved the best cover in the hunting country, rarely failing to yield a straight-running fox. In this cover the country people spoke of having seen a black-brushed fox so tame that he failed to run at the approach of humans. In defiance of this, Sean designed a set of raised bone buttons, which he had made up in England, bearing what was to become the emblem of The Hunt—a fox's mask over which curved a painted black brush. This same emblem was chiseled out of stone and set over the iron-studded front door.

From the moment that Sean Shelburn returned to Ballyhoura, the doings at the great gray house on the hill became the main topic of conversation. His entertainments were lavish. People came from miles around to stand on the hillside overlooking the race ground, later to become the Cup course, where the famed match races between his great stallion Galway Pilot and other famous horses of the day took place.

Three days a week a liveried servant rode around to the houses of the landowners in order to leave word as to the time and place of the meet. The Thanksgiving Day Lawn Meet became a tradition. From miles around, the gentry came to partake of the port and brandy, smoked turkeys and other delicacies set out on tables on the lawn. When the foxhunters rode away on their gleaming thoroughbreds, the country people followed on foot, exclaiming over the sight of the Master, resplendent in scarlet, astride his gray hunter, Shelburn Jack, as he led off over the five-foot wall that separated Ballyhoura from Shelburn. When the field returned from hunting, there was feasting and dancing far into the night.

In order to entertain guests, and the refugee remnants of his Confederate raiders, a wing known as the bachelor quarters adjoined the main house. Here a valet pulled off the hunters' boots after a day in the field. The boots were then taken to be cleaned, before they could damage the Aubusson carpets and polished floors. Following this, each guest was handed a toddy, a tall silver tumbler of bourbon, and ushered into a steaming tub set into a huge walnut coffinlike receptacle. Then they were helped into the clothes that had been laid out for them. Scarlet full-dress evening coat, with the facings and collar of their respective hunts, braided trousers and patent leather shoes. On the bed would be a white starched shirt, studded and cufflinked, a white waistcoat with the hunt's buttons, collar, white tie and carefully folded white handkerchief.

Nightly, the gleaming mahogany banquet table, with the elaborate carved border which could be removed in order to extend the table the length of the room, was set for a minimum of thirty guests. At these long dinners, clear soups, roast game and fine wines were featured. When the finger bowls had been removed, the Master raised his hunting horn and blew "Gone Away," signaling the coffee and cigars in the drawing room. After dinner Sir Hugh's Cromwellian goblet was set out. Traditionally it was filled with a bottle of claret. Silver dollars were placed in the bottom. Whoever could empty the glass without pausing got the money.

While these parties were in process it was said that one servant saw to it that the guests' collars were loosened so that when the gentry fell onto the floor they would not choke to death.

Following these stag affairs, it was customary for the men to ask Gabriel to provide Negro women. The well-trained butler watched and listened and measured. He knew just how Marse Shelburn liked his dark meat—young and vigorous and black as midnight—and that if satisfied he would pay well. He knew that Colonel DeLong required older women and ones versed in certain types of perversion and that it was necessary to collect the money beforehand or he would conveniently forget what was owed. He knew that Squire Bolling preferred young virgins and that Armistead Talbot could not make love to his young wife, but that when he was with Clemmie Taylor he could do it two, sometimes three times a night. It never occurred to "Old Gabe" to tell of the things that he knew, any more than he would have registered amazement at the happenings at Ballyhoura.

Yet, however badly he was regarded by his neighbors for his temper and his excesses (it was said that whereas it had required a Confederate garrison to populate nearby Bellevue, the county seat, Sean Shelburn alone was responsible for doubling the population of the Negro community at Muster Corner), the Squire of Ballyhoura was a power in horse-racing and breeding circles. By importing the great stallion Galway Pilot from Ireland, he founded the famous Ballyhoura strain including Pilot Light, winner of the Derby, and Shelburn Jack, in whose memory the Shelburn Cup was presented each spring to the winner of the steeplechase later run over the course laid in The Valley below Ballyhoura House.

Sean Shelburn was past fifty when he married his cousin, beautiful Margaret Lee of Shelburn Hall. Despite his profligate life and excessive drinking, he was still a dashing and romantic figure. Long days of hard riding in the open air had kept his piercng black eyes clear, his body lean and hard. Marlee, not quite twenty, fell madly in love with him. The marriage was ill-fated from the start. Sean Shelburn was too old to mend his wild ways; and once the challenge had been met, his in-laws thwarted and the shotgun relatives defeated, boredom set in.

When Marlee became pregnant and was unable to follow him in the hunting field, marital fidelity began to pall. He started to indulge himself with Marnie Mellick, the predatory young wife of Tom Mellick, the Covertside innkeeper. When Marlee was delivered of a daughter, Sean was at the Covertside Inn drinking with his foxhunting cronies. On hearing the news of his daughter's birth, he failed to return home. Instead, bitterly disappointed that Marlee had not borne him a son and heir, he suggested to his drinking companions that they race by moonlight from the Shelburn church steeple to that of the neighboring town of Bellevue. In time-honored fashion, as depicted in the hunting prints, it was decided that the competitors would wear nightshirts and that the winner would receive a replica of the Cromwellian goblet.

That night's race, the forerunner of the current-day steeplechase run each spring for the Shelburn Cup, was to become part of Valley legend. Old-timers, sitting around the fire in the pine-paneled barroom at the Inn, still regale newcomers with tales of the wild race across country in which two horses fell and had to be destroyed and Squire Bolling broke his neck jumping a gate. They tell how Sean Shelburn came riding victoriously down the Valley road at dawn, his nightshirt ripped to ribbons from leaping through hedges, his horse dripping and exhausted from the five-mile gallop; how he delegated Tom Mellick to care for his horse and then, still attired in his nightshirt, stood at the bar providing drinks for all comers and giving an account of the race.

When Sean Shelburn finally returned to Ballyhoura, he found

that his wife and baby had been moved home to Shelburn Hall.

Shortly afterward, Tom Mellick mysteriously disappeared. A week later, Marnie, with her passion for blue bonnets tied with pink streamers, moved into Ballyhoura as housekeeper.

At this time there lived in a hollow behind Ballyhoura an old colored woman who, along with an assortment of cats, chickens, skunks and a pet raccoon, kept a tame fox with a black brush believed to be from a Ballyhoura litter. Her name was Carrie Charity and she was said to have second sight and be versed in voodoo. Believing her to have healing powers, the colored people went to her for herbs to cure their illnesses. The gentry discounted her as "that crazy old woman with the pet fox."

One chill gray November afternoon, hounds got on the line of this fox. After a long, cold, blank day both hounds and their followers were frantic for sport. Although John Pope, the young whipper-in, shouted to him that said fox was the one belonging to the old woman in the hollow, Sean Shelburn did not order hounds whipped off.

Coming upon the scene of the kill, the old woman stood silent, staring at the mangled remains. Then she looked up at the Master, mounted on his tall hunter. Sean Shelburn was not one to be kept from his post-hunting pleasures, a warm fire and a hot toddy after a long day in the saddle, yet the expression on the old woman's ancient lined face gave him pause.

Speaking clearly in her singsong voice, she said to the Squire of Ballyhoura: "I see disaster in what you did today. Because of this the Shelburns will wear woe on their heads like a crown of thorns." Slowly she glanced around at the members of the field. "From this day on, whosoever first views a black-brushed fox will meet his or her death!"

Sean Shelburn did not believe in curses and dark doings. Laughing off the old woman's words as superstitious nonsense, he called his hounds to him and galloped home to Ballyhoura. After filling the Cromwellian goblet to the brim, he embarked on a night of drinking and carousing that lasted all through the following day.

From then on he seemed intent on dissipating his fortune and himself. The years passed. The beautiful furniture, originally built by master carpenters who had come to the New World as indentured servants and been employed on the great plantations throughout the South, was removed to the attic or broken up into kindling to feed the vast fireplaces. As the kennels and stables fell into disrepair the house became a shambles of burr-matted hounds, saddles, crops and clothing. Rooms were never dusted and the Aubusson carpets were stained with spilled food and liquor.

Decent servants refused to remain in the employ of a woman of Marnie's reputation or to put up with the Master's drunken rages. Shocked at the goings-on, the conservative element in The Valley dubbed Ballyhoura "Babylon-on-Buffalo Run."

When there was nobody to build the wood fires and the chimneys became cold, Sean Shelburn spent his time drinking at the bar in the Covertside Inn.

The following season rabies destroyed many of the foxes in The Valley. Sport was bad. Day after day hounds went out, only to draw the neighboring covers blank.

Yet, despite the epidemic and the avid hounds now permitted to roam the premises, the untended park and grounds continued to be alive with prey. Then, as now, it was every landowner's ambition to make a good show of foxes. Ballyhoura, known as the most famous cover in the country, lived up to its reputation. When all others failed, the dark wood was sure to yield a straight-running fox.

The traditional Thanksgiving Day Meet brought out a large and optimistic crowd. The day was chill, with a hint of snow in the air. House and grounds wore a dark, brooding air. As they waited for the hunt to begin, people sat shivering in their saddles, almost as much from dread of the gaunt ivy-covered house jutting from the top of the hill as from the frigid air.

Old Squire Bolling, riding a big rangy bay, banged his gloved palms together to restore circulation. Turning to Colonel De-Long, he remarked, "How Sean can live in this mausoleum beats me." He shook his head. "A shame to see a family wear out, go downhill the way the Shelburns have. Too much inbreeding, like his hounds. For a hundred years everything in this valley has been Shelburn. Then the family took to marrying cousins. Now they're cousined out."

As he spoke, the Master emerged from the house. Without glancing right or left, he mounted his Shelburn Jack. Calling to the lean, frantic hounds rioting over the overgrown lawns, he moved off.

"We'll draw the wood," he said to Squire Bolling as he rode past. "I viewed a fox there last evening."

His face was pale and drawn, his lips jerked nervously and one eye was almost closed.

"My God, he looks like death!" exclaimed Colonel DeLong. "Must have had another fight with that woman. Did you notice his eye?"

At Ballyhoura the slatternly maid whom Marnie had hired from the Free Zone waited to serve Thanksgiving dinner.

Four o'clock came. Then five. Then six o'clock. Still the Master did not return. Everyone knew that a fox had been gotten up in the first cover, Ballyhoura Park, and gone away across The Valley toward the blue mountains. Gazing out the door, the maid saw it was starting to snow. Slamming it shut on the frigid night, she wished the hunters would return. The house, she thought, was spooky enough in the daylight. Now, with the Missus gone, lock, stock and bonnets, following the awful row the night before, the wind howling and nobody but herself in that great barn of a place, she was frankly terrified.

Suddenly, over and above the sound of the wind, she heard the distant chiming cry of hounds. As she listened, it seemed to come closer. Running to the front entrance, she saw what appeared to be hounds racing through the snow driving across the park. Then came the neigh of a horse, a sobbing kind of whimpering noise, as though from an animal far spent.

The ghostly pack and the weird sounds filled her with terror. At that moment Shelburn Jack stumbled into the courtyard. His white coat was streaked with mud and lather and blood. Astride his back was the body of his master, tied to the saddle with his own hound couplings. His scarlet coat was streaked with black rivulets of blood, and two of the famous foxhead buttons were missing. When Sean Shelburn was cut down off the dying horse, a small hole hardly bigger than the head of a match was found in his forehead. Around his neck was his hunting horn. In his pocket was a matted blood-soaked black brush.

The murderer was never discovered. By late afternoon the people who had hunted that day had pulled out. When the huntsman had started to blow hounds off, the Master had taken the horn from him and continued alone. After that nobody could say for sure what had happened.

The Valley assumed the murder was an act of revenge. Marnie Mellick's husband was judged to be the murderer. However, the Shelburn relatives, wanting only to forget the whole unsavory mess, did not press prosecution. Until R. Rutherford Dinwiddie, Esquire, published the story in his book about The Hunt, the scandal had been largely forgotten.

Cam's eyes were big as he listened to the whitewashed, summarized version tailored to his years by Shelley. "Tell me about my other grandfather," he urged when she had finished.

"He started The Hunt," Shelley said. "Before he came, there were outlaw packs, but no organized foxhunts in The Valley."

In the annals of contemporary sport, Shelley's father, Cameron Fitzgerald, was a legendary figure. A descendant of John Fortune Fitzgerald, who had amassed great riches from coal, steel, railroads and a series of daring stock manipulations, he was one of the country's wealthiest and most eligible bachelors. A lover of hounds and of fine horses, he had organized a foxhunt in a New Jersey area that was rapidly becoming a suburb of New York. He thus decided to move his hunt and staff to new country.

Traveling the length and breadth of the South in his private railroad car with its grand piano and gold bathroom fixtures, he had seen nothing comparable to this Virginia valley, bounded on the east and west by pale blue hills.

Under the mastership of Sean Shelburn, the kennels had fallen into disrepair. The hounds had been permitted to run wild, ravaging the countryside for food. This, Sean Shelburn maintained, made them keener. Ravenous, savage, they took to killing sheep and livestock, causing the country people to rebel against his hunt and its followers.

At that time a large number of farmers who were avid and individualistic foxhunters still lived in The Valley. Almost all kept a couple or more "dawgs," which were permitted to run freely, foraging for their food under the pretext that it kept them keen and made them better hunters. These outlaw packs were hunted without pomp or protocol, in the old-fashioned manner. While their owners sat around a bonfire on a fall night on a high hill, passing an earthenware jug of corn likker from one to the other, they made bets as to which hound would speak first and which would "win the hunt" by killing or driving the fox to earth.

These men, some of whom remembered hiding out from Union soldiers who had sacked and burned their property, were united in their hatred of Yankee interlopers. Determined to destroy the Yankees' sport, they studied the fixture cards issued by The Hunt, then systematically looted the covers planned for hounds on the morrow. In this way they managed to make sure that the recognized Hunt did not find a fox or have sport.

Cameron Fitzgerald called on these men. He bought horses from them and helped them to become prosperous. Gradually they stopped hunting their own hounds and began hunting with The Hunt.

One of the last hold-outs had been Colonel Southgate DeLong, a chicken farmer who continued to hunt an outlaw pack and to do all he could willfully to destroy The Hunt's sport.

One day, when The Hunt's hounds ran over DeLong acres, "Young South," the Colonel's son, then in his teens, rode boldly up to Cameron Fitzgerald and ordered them off his property, promising that so long as he was alive "no damn Yankee would ride over DeLong land."

The following day, when Young South came to deliver eggs, the Fitzgerald butler ordered him to the back entrance of the private railroad car drawn up on a siding at Shelburn. Overhearing Young South's outraged refusal, Cameron Fitzgerald rushed to the doorway. Sensing that the DeLong's fierce family pride had been offended, he urged the boy to enter, saying, "Mr. DeLong, sir. Glad to see you, sir. Come in. Put the damned eggs on the piano and have a spot of bourbon."

When young DeLong returned home that night, it was with the understanding that he would no longer hunt his hounds in The Hunt's country.

Shelley's father had been tall, with the slender build of an athlete, and had warm brown eyes. Innumerable local belles set their hunting caps for him. He, however, cared for but one.

A week after their first meeting on the hunting field, he proposed to Sean Shelburn's daughter, Nuala.

"I'll marry you if you win the Shelburn Cup" was her reply.

Cameron Fitzgerald did not win the Shelburn Cup. Instead Tommy Talbot, the leading Gentleman Rider of that time, had won the race and Cameron Fitzgerald had fallen at the first fence.

In The Valley it was believed that Tommy Talbot and Nuala

would eventually be married. Nuala's mother, however, was bitterly opposed to the match. Hating the genteel poverty which forbade repairs on the leaking roof of Shelburn Hall, Miss Marlee determined that her daughter would marry money, even if it meant breaking with tradition and giving herself to a Yankee. When Nuala threatened to elope with the handsome race rider, she was locked in her bedroom. At the end of three days, Nuala bowed to her mother's will and agreed to marry Cameron Fitzgerald.

Valley memories are long, and some are still alive who recall the deal Shelley's grandmother made with "Yankee" Fitzgerald. Although many of the fine heirlooms dating back to Revolutionary times had been sold in order to keep Shelburn Hall from falling into the hands of Northerners moving into The Valley, the famous Gilbert Stuart of King Shelburn in his Revolutionary uniform still remained over the drawing-room mantel. The story told was that Cameron Fitzgerald bought it for a hundred thousand dollars, paid to his future mother-in-law. The painting was then presented to his bride as a wedding present and returned to its original position in the drawing room.

The portrait of Nuala, done by Augustus John during her honeymoon in England and still hanging in the dining room, showed a tall, slim girl walking in a park. Behind her spread an arch of tall oaks, whose massive trunks accentuated her willowy delicacy. It was only when you looked closely that you saw the look of not-too-well-controlled wildness about the eyes and mouth of this remarkable face. The furious racing blood of her forebears may have accounted for her restlessness, her inability to accept the routine of normal living from which she was eventually to escape.

Yet Cameron Fitzgerald was destined to be forever in awe of the prize originally won.

Shelley did not learn until years afterward that there are some men to whom pain is a stimulant, that in being hurt they love the more. Her father loved her mother, but was afraid of her. Using pity as a shield, he refused to face his wife's fury, defending himself against her paranoiac tantrums and accusations by walking away, going foxhunting or closeting himself in his den.

Shelley's memories of her mother were vague and fantastic. She remembered a vain woman, fond of flattery, with sea blue eyes that seemed to change color with her mercurial moods, paling to glittering turquoise when angry. Somehow she managed to live her life without resilience or awareness. Everything was always done "the right way," the Shelburn way.

Shelley's parents spent their days in the hunting field and dined out or entertained almost every night. The long, leisurely Sunday luncheons at Shelburn Hall began with buckets of imported caviar surrounded by cracked ice and served with the best champagne. The guests then sat down to five courses, rounded out with finger bowls, followed by coffee poured into cups that once belonged to Dolly Madison. Afterward, people went to polo, beagled or shot skeet. It was as though Nuala cared only for the superficial in love and living, ignoring all that lay beneath the surface of mind and body. Her contempt for her husband was obvious. She considered the Fitzgeralds upstarts, nouveau riche and in no way to the manor born. Yet such was her concern for the noble house built by King Shelburn that she went to the extent of forgoing a hunting season in order to provide an heir. That she had borne a daughter rather than a son seemed to her to be a conspiracy on the part of the fates, and it wasn't until years later that Shelley came to understand the reasons behind her mother's abandonment.

Shelley's upbringing fell to Melusina, and to her grandmother, Miss Marlee, who lived in an apartment set aside for her in the west wing. She was free to spend the timeless sunlit days of summer riding beside cool streams, along honeysuckle-choked lanes, or at picnics beneath the willows by the old quarry pool where the local children, Hunter Jenney, Telly Talbot, Fax Templeton, Story Jackson, Freddy Fisher, Dave Montague, her cousin Misty, the Baldwin girls and the others who lived along the Valley road went swimming. They played "Shelburn's Raiders" or hide and seek amid the ruins of Ballyhoura, where the park was a magical place for foxes and rabbits and an occasional deer, the pond full of fish and the rotting rose-covered gazebo a wonderful spot to sit and dream.

Her life revolved around the stable. This was Virginia City's domain. His job was to see that the stalls were mucked out properly and banked with clean, sweet-smelling straw, that the long ranks of bridles hung like a frieze on the dark-paneled tack-room walls and the saddles on their stands, towering one above the other, glistened with long rubbing with saddle soap, and that the bits and stirrup irons shone like the dining-room silver.

Shelley's father had discovered Virginia City when he was a child hanging around the barn where the Fitzgerald horses had been stabled at Saratoga. Something about the boy, his thinness disguised by ragged too-big clothes, or his intensity, caught his eye. "Hey, boy," he called, "what's your name?" "Roanoke, Mr. Fitzgerald, sir." "Roanoke!" Cameron Fitzgerald snorted. "That's a city, not a name." "Yessir," the boy agreed, "a Virginia city."

Cameron Fitzgerald always said that because he could never remember to call the boy Roanoke (and kept calling him Norfolk or Newport News or Winchester instead) it was easier just to sing out "Virginia City" when he wanted him. The name stuck. Virginia City had been orphaned and abandoned on a Roanoke stoop. At the age of twelve he ran away from the overburdened family that had raised him—itinerant farm laborers with seven other children to care for. He'd lived from hand to mouth walking hots and as a swipe at various tracks. Aware that the boy's build—his growth had been stunted by years of near starvation—and native intelligence would make him a good exercise boy, Cameron Fitzgerald hired him.

When the race horses were sold, Virginia City was assigned to the hunter barn at Shelburn Hall, where he spent long hours directing Shelley in the pony ring, comforting her when she fell off Jack Spratt, the stubborn, willful Shetland on which she learned to ride.

In the fall, when the sounds of hounds and horn echoed throughout the red-gold countryside, the groom took her foxhunting. By the light of the orange October moon, the hunter's moon, Virginia City introduced her to coon hunting with his "dawgs." Laughing, they scrambled up and down hillsides, over rocks and through "branches," muddying their shoes, scratching their faces and hands and knees. The stumbling, breathless physical exhilaration of the chase was the exciting part. When hounds treed the coon and Fax or one of the other boys climbed the tree and shook it down into the midst of the snarling pack, Shelley turned her face away.

On special occasions she was allowed to stay up and go night foxhunting with the DeLongs and some of the old-time farmer foxhunters. Feeling grown up and important, she sat silently, out of range of the light from the great roaring fire on the hilltop around which the men sat drinking home-brewed corn likker from the jug and listening to the music of their hounds. Coming to know the hound voices until she, too, could lay bets as to which would take the lead, feeling an infinite wholesomeness, a closeness to nature, and knowing that never-to-be-found-again sense of peace and timelessness that is rarely understood or appreciated except in retrospect.

This acceptance—the sense of wholeness, of entity—for which she strove was later to be found only in the hunting field. When she went foxhunting, she thought of nothing else. If she could not stay out until hounds came home, she did not want to go foxhunting at all.

For Shelley it had been an inward life evolved around the changing seasons, the animals in the barn. Outwardly she had grown straight and clean-limbed, like the thoroughbred foals in the pasture, clumsy in the growing but at the same time with that natural grace which is the essence of beauty.

Templeton was the meeting place for the neighborhood children. As the court at Shelburn Hall was almost always being used by her parents' friends, Shelley learned to play tennis on the old clay court at Templeton, where the tennis net was pinned together with the big horse-blanket safety pins. Before they played it was necessary to fill in the holes left by the horses who pushed down the rotting rails separating them from the tennis court. The tennis balls that were lost in the roses which climbed over the fence and were never cut back would have filled several bushel baskets.

It was at Templeton that Shelburn's Raiders had been organized. The rallying cry was "Ride, Red, ride!" With Fax at the head of the troop, they had "terrorized" the countryside, galloping madly over walls and rails and across seeded lawns, giving the high, shrill Rebel yell—and when pursued by imaginary foes had gone full tilt over whatever stood between them and the sanctuary of Templeton's stone barn. The Templetons never minded how many children cantered over the flower beds, playing hide and seek on their ponies amid the priceless English box bushes, or had tournaments in the field. Judge Templeton had been a tall, distinguished-looking white-haired man who wore a long frock coat and a pointed beard. He had resembled the bourbon ads of Kentucky colonels drinking juleps and gazing out across emerald pastures. When his inability to see eye to eye with the Talbot machine forced his retirement from the bench, he had ensconced himself happily in a small dark-paneled den, surrounded by bulging file cabinets, great dark-bound leather tomes, faded photographs of dock-tailed horses leaping high fences, and of long-dead relatives, a few mothy brushes, fishing rods, tarnished horse-show trophies, old caps, broken hunting crops, newly born puppies, bottles of Absorbine, liniments and whiskey. Mrs. Templeton had been fat and jolly and cheerful. Occasionally she would have a go at clearing out *the* room. Then the Judge's bellows of indignation could be heard all the way to the stable.

When the Raiders took up nigger polo, Fax warned them that the Judge would skin them alive if he heard about it. This was the most dangerous and exciting game of all. Pete Buford thought it up, and girls were not permitted to play.

One night, just after dark, Pete, Telly Talbot and Fax, and one of the Mellicks from the Free Zone, where they'd gone to get corn liquor, set out for Muster Corner. Bible classes were in session and they waited in the weeds until the children came out of church. Pete had provided monogrammed sheets from Silver Hill, and when the colored children saw the sheeted horsemen galloping at them and brandishing polo mallets, all but Mase Brown fled down the road in terror. It fell to Pete to make the first goal by throwing Mase into the ditch with a blow on the side of the head.

Telly's father, serving his first term as Senator, heard about it from Washington Taylor. A delegation from Muster Corner called on Judge Templeton, who forbade Fax the privilege of riding his new young horse for a month and gave the Raiders a talking-to which Shelley never forgot.

"You are gentry," he said, his blue eyes flashing. "As such you have a responsibility to your inferiors. Noblesse oblige. If you don't know what that means, I'll explain. It means courtesy at all times and thinking of others."

"But they were just niggers," Pete argued. "You can't hurt niggers."

The Judge turned on him, his voice shaking. "It's not my busi-

148

ness to teach you morals." Judge Templeton raised his hand. "The mark of a gentleman, a Southern gentleman, lies in how he treats his nigras. He should accord them the same treatment he accords his animals. You wouldn't harm a good horse?" He looked around at the circle of faces. "Would you now?"

Up until the time that she was twelve, Shelley considered herself one of the fortunate, accepting without thought the fact that she was a Shelburn, and thus removed from the Bufords, who had bought Silver Hill and rebuilt the old stone walls, only to disguise their new look with plantings of the destructive honeysuckle the rest of the population strove to do away with. Then the foundations on which her world had been built crumbled, never again to be the same.

During the Depression years her father lost a large part of his inheritance. In an attempt to rebuild his fortune, he made a series of desperate speculations, all of which proved unwise and which, augmented by years of extravagant living, dissipated what remained of his capital. By 1945, when Shelley was twelve, he was bankrupt.

Shelley's grandmother told her that her mother had gone away for a rest cure. One afternoon in the Gone Away drugstore Shelley learned the truth. Pete Buford, Fax Templeton, Samantha Sue Hulburd and Betsy Watters were drinking Cokes and gossiping.

Betsy Watters, face flushed and still perspiring from having made the winning goal that afternoon on the hockey field, was animatedly discussing Shelburn's latest scandal.

Chester the Arrester had been locked into the town cemetery by Nat, the caretaker, when he made his midnight round. It had been necessary for the policeman to leave Daisy, the checker at the grocery store, in the car while he chased after Nat to unlock the gate and let them out.

Shelley spoke up indignantly. "How revolting. Chester's a married man."

"Revolting," echoed Betsy. "Now come on, Shelley. What would you do if you were married to that stone-faced wife of his? Daisy is cute."

"A policeman is supposed to set an example," Shelley said hotly.

Pete Buford broke his silence. "People who live in glass houses—"

"You have a lower lip as long as a blacksmith's apron," her grandmother once told her. From that time on, in moments of stress, Shelley instinctively covered her mouth with her hand.

At sight of Pete Buford's face on that long-ago day in the drugstore Shelley's hand went to her mouth.

"Why shouldn't she know the facts? Just because she's a Shelburn, she thinks she's better than anyone else."

"Pete—" Betsy interrupted.

"Well, she does," Pete insisted. "Anyway, she must know about it. Everybody else does."

"Know what?" Shelley's hand was clasped tight over her mouth, making her voice barely audible.

"About your mother and Tommy Talbot. They've run away together."

The fact that it was Polo Pete who had given her the news made it even more of a blow. She could tell from the expression on his face that he relished being the one to tell her. His delight came from the age-old feelings of bitterness and inferiority stemming from the uneasy relationship between the two families.

Polo Pete Buford bore one of the most prominent names in the history of American finance. His grandfather, P. G. Buford—the initials stood for Peter Galtee—had left the Irish village in which he was born, shirttails protruding from the holes in his homespuns. After emigrating to the United States he worked his way west to Virginia City, Nevada. There, not long after his twenty-fifth birthday, he discovered one of the richest deposits in the surrounding hills. By the time he was forty he was internationally known as a financial genius comparable to Ralston and Mills in the West, Carnegie and Harriman in the East.

His native love of horses and a superstitious belief that the name Virginia spelled luck drew him to The Valley, where, in the early 1900s, with money derived from banking and shipping concerns, railroads and munitions, the second Yankee invasion was in process.

Aware that its verdant beauty and proximity to the nation's capital would continue to increase land values, P. G., in the manner of one of the pirates who selected the Caribbean as a base of operations, began buying land and building the vast Victorian house at Muster Corner which, with its landscaped gardens and

Italian statuary, its greenhouses, dog runs, stables and private railroad siding, was named Silver Hill.

P. G. married twice. His first wife, Belle Fleurey, was the daughter of a Virginia City saloonkeeper. She was big and buxom and cherished illusions of social grandeur. When Silver Hill was finished, the organ installed in the domed "music room" and the tropical plants in the conservatory, Valley society was invited to a soiree.

The most exotic foods and wines, catered from Delmonico's in New York, were shipped via P. G.'s private train, and a famous quartet was imported for the evening to provide chamber music among the potted palms. Negro footmen, dressed in scarlet livery, were hired to stand behind each chair in the banquet hall and Belle's pink gown and long white kid gloves had been imported from Paris. No expense was spared. Nothing left to chance.

Belle never understood why it was that no return invitations from the Shelburns, the Talbots, the Dinwiddies, the DeLongs, the Templetons or any other Valley family were forthcoming. Purposely she had refrained from drinking too much champagne and had told only faintly risqué stories, none of the bawdy ones that had sent the miners into paroxysms of laughter. Even when one of the waiters had dropped an elaborately decorated platter of pheasant, she had not used bad language. And the gloves had been the greatest concession of all. Although they were too tight and hampered her when it came to smoking her favorite cigars, she had deliberately kept them on, all through the interminable dinner, noting with satisfaction that none of the other women, even that young Mrs. Shelburn from Ballyhoura, had the good manners to follow suit.

This was the first and last party Belle ever gave at Silver Hill. Shortly afterward the Bufords left for Europe, where they traveled to all the fashionable spas on the Continent and bought a house in London. There Belle, with her gloves and cigars and stories of the Old West, became a favorite of Edward VII and achieved the celebrity she had always craved.

Belle bore four sons, of whom the eldest was named Peter Galtee II. Galtee Buford was said to have inherited all of his father's vices and none of his virtues. Of his generation he was the only one to refuse to work for the Buford Foundation or any of the multitudinous Buford enterprises. Instead he left Harvard in his junior year to join the Lafayette Escadrille. After surviving the war, in which he became a famous ace with twelve German planes to his credit, he proceeded to start around the world on a motorcycle. After nearly dying of thirst in the Sahara desert, he abandoned the machine and the rest of his journey to live in Paris, where he became a favorite of Gertrude Stein and a drinking companion of Scott Fitzgerald. During his Paris period he had an affair with a black-haired bohemian from Iowa who was studying modern dance.

This was Polo Pete's mother, and Galtee had married her for form's sake. When she left Galtee for a young painter of the impressionist school, she left behind her infant son. Galtee, in turn, abandoned the baby to the scandalized care of his grandparents.

When the baby was two, his grandmother, Belle, died, and his grandfather promptly married a young Italian marchesa, a widow with several young children of her own. When not traveling or foxhunting in Ireland (with his first million P. G. had bought the castle in which his mother had worked as a chambermaid and had made his mark by introducing modern plumbing to that part of the country), the Bufords lived in a villa on the Italian Riviera. Not wanting to burden his new bride with Galtee's son, an ugly, unattractive child with heavy features and a habit of sucking his thumb, he put the boy in the charge of an austere British nanny named Miss Dill and sent him home to Silver Hill.

When P. G. died (he was seventy-eight and passed away during the night following a long day in the Irish hunting field), Galtee inherited Silver Hill and the surrounding farms.

Unlike his father, Galtee had no interest in furthering the family fortune which, luckily, had been left in trust. But although he had not inherited his father's business acumen or his mother's warmth and sharp intelligence, he had charm and a lust for life which, along with his money, endeared him to women. His next wife was a British actress, whom he divorced in order to marry an Austrian countess he met skiing in the Arlberg. When this marriage ended, Galtee decided to return to Silver Hill.

P. G. III was six when his father came home. Behind his back the servants and the Valley children called him Piggy, a name suited to his fat figure, thick neck and overly large head. He was a compulsive eater and could not stop sucking his thumb. In order to break him of this habit, Miss Dill bound it in a bandage saturated with red pepper. This caused him to sneeze until his eyes ran and to compensate by biting his nails and picking his cuticles. With his overly long hair worn British style and his too-short gray flannels, he was rejected and made fun of. Patrick, the stud groom, and Miss Dill found him unlovable and backward. When forced to ride—the ponies Patrick supplied were overbred and too much for him—Piggy was more often on the ground, weeping with terror, than in the saddle. When he heard that his father was coming home, the lonely little boy looked to him for salvation.

"When my father comes home," he told the governess defiantly, "you won't be able to tie up my thumbs or hit me any more."

Daily he waited, hope building to a climax. Other children, he knew, had fathers and mothers and this had nothing to do with being rich. Even the poor, the colored, the pigtailed girls and ragged boys of Muster Corner all had families. In the soft summer dusk he could hear the laughter and music coming from the cabins at the Corner. He did not know what it was that reached out to him, drew him to the wall that separated Silver Hill from the Negro community. The Negroes, Miss Dill insisted, were dirty and bad. When Washington Taylor's son, John, showed him how his father made and baited the box traps in which he caught the rabbits that went into his mother's savory stews, Pete longed to invite him up to his room and show him the model plane his father had sent for Christmas. He knew, though, that he could not. Like his spaniel that was relegated to the kennel, dogs and colored children were not permitted in the house.

The Negroes showed him the only kindness he knew. The wall that separated Silver Hill from Muster Corner was the dividing line and he longed to cross over it, move into this different world that seemed filled with love and warmth and rich laughter. And because of this, the division, and not understanding, mingled feelings of guilt and envy and longing gripped him, choking him like the strands of honeysuckle. The aching emptiness that, like his physical hunger for cake and candy, was never satisfied became a black, violent feeling that made him want to strike out with his fists, stamp out the light and laughter.

Hiding behind the honeysuckled wall beyond which he was forbidden to go, he gnawed and tore at his cuticles until his hands bled.

The day of Galtee's homecoming finally arrived. Since early morning delectable odors wafted from the kitchen, where a magnificent dinner was being prepared. When nobody was looking, Piggy managed to sample the cakes and grab a handful of chocolate bonbons from the silver dish on the sideboard. After he was dressed in his white sailor suit, he slipped a few into his pocket.

The private train and siding had been abandoned. With the advent of the automobile age, people drove to and from the city. Washington Taylor, who was then combination butler and chauffeur, had gone to Washington to meet Galtee.

For a long time Piggy stood on the veranda with Miss Dill and the lined-up servants. It was hot and the governess kept plucking at him, straightening his collar and ordering him to pull up his socks. When her head was turned he managed to stuff a melted chocolate into his mouth. At that moment the car whirled up the drive and stopped in front of the box-bordered walk. Washington got out and opened the rear door. A tall man in a gleaming white linen suit and a straw boater emerged and came swinging up the walk.

Before Miss Dill could restrain him, he ran down the steps. Sobbing, he flung himself at his father.

Galtee was embarrassed. He knew nothing about children and overt emotion. Even when expressed by a child of six who was his only son, it made him uncomfortable. He did not mean to be cruel. He was merely anxious to remove himself from this snuffling creature with the chocolate-smeared mouth who was clinging to his leg, get the greetings from the staff over with, and have a drink.

With a motion more instinctive than deliberate, he reached down, loosened his son's hands, which were locked around his leg, and gave him a slight push.

Miss Dill, who had run up behind, caught Piggy.

Aghast, the governess saw the brown streaks from the boy's hand on his father's immaculate white suit.

"Oh, sir," she gasped. "Mr. Buford, sir, I'm so sorry." Her long fingers were digging into Piggy's back like pincers. "The child has dirtied your suit." Putting on her martyred air, she continued,

"I do the best I can. But it's difficult. I'm afraid, sir, you'll find the boy deceitful, disobedient—"

"It's quite all right," Galtee interrupted impatiently. "Now if you don't mind, I'd like to see my room."

He did not look again at his son.

Piggy was nine when his father took as his mistress an exotic dancer, Maria Christian, then starring in a hit musical.

Maria was the rage of New York. The result of an illicit liaison between a mulatto mother and a white planter on the island of Martinique, she had been brought up in Paris, where, when she went on the stage, she became an immediate hit. Aside from her beauty she had something more. A quality of compassion, a sense of the spiritual, a certain *gentillesse*. The fashionable artists of the day, who painted her in innumerable poses, never wearied of her constantly changing expressions or the vibrancy of her beauty. For the first time in his life, Galtee fell madly in love. Nothing, neither the outrage of the local citizenry nor the Virginia law that forbade miscegenation, was to deter him.

Despite the Bufords' vast land holdings, this was too much for The Hunt. At his mother-in-law's insistence, Cameron Fitzgerald went to Galtee and told him he would no longer be accepted in the hunting field or at the Halter Club. Thus began one of the classic Valley feuds. When Galtee retaliated by surrounding Silver Hill and his other farms with unjumpable five-foot fences topped with wire, The Hunt warned local businessmen that, if they accepted the Buford account, they would no longer receive The Hunt's business. As it was a question of economic survival, all but Henry Jenney complied. When Henry continued selling feed and grain to the Bufords, his store was fired and burned to the ground and despite appeals to Richmond and to Colonel DeLong, then a State Senator, the arsonist was never found to be brought to trial.

Galtee delighted in the fight. Flaunting his defiance, he galloped up and down the Valley road in his lemon yellow Tallyho, Maria, swathed in mink, beside him. At that speed only the coach, drawn by four spanking bays, was spectacular. But when it came to a standstill at the races or in the village, Valley residents could not help taking a second look at That Woman.

To Galtee's son, Maria gave the only affection he had ever

known. When she caught Miss Dill rapping his knuckles, she saw to it that the governess was fired. For a time Pete Buford came as close as he would ever be to happiness.

Then tragedy struck. It was Shelburn Cup Day. Maria stayed at home. But Galtee, in pearl gray topper and spats, his coach equipped with thermoses of iced juleps and filled with weekend revelers, including a famous Russian choreographer with an unpronounceable name, drove his matched team of bays home from the race at a full gallop.

It had not rained for some weeks and the then-unpaved road, clogged with race traffic, was thick with dust. Consequently, Galtee did not see Judge Templeton in his new Duesenberg when, without slowing down, he recklessly attempted to make the turn onto the Muster Corner lane that led to Silver Hill.

The coach overturned and although no one else was seriously injured, Galtee was flung onto a pile of rocks left beside the road when the highway department had filled the potholes. His skull was fractured, and by the time Dr. Muddy Watters arrived he was dead.

Immediately following the funeral Maria hired Washington Taylor's Aunt Ruth to stay in the house and take care of Pete. Ruth agreed under condition that she could bring her children with her, and Maria prepared to depart. The next morning, with a sinking heart and a sense of inescapable loss, Pete watched her go.

He was never to see her again.

At twenty-one Pete Buford inherited the money his grandfather had left in trust. He had never done a day's work in his life. After college, where he took up boxing and polo, he lived on Long Island, where his Buford cousins had big houses, and played polo at Westbury.

While Galtee Buford had been lecherous and pleasure-loving, he had lived his life fully. His son was lecherous and pleasure-loving without his father's individuality or boldness. As a child he had been made aware of his father's contempt. As an adult he determined to gain the one thing his father had never achieved. Social acceptance.

His first step toward this end was to marry Samantha Sue Hulburd and return to Silver Hill. Of an old impoverished Valley family—the Hulburds had been kin to the DeLongs, and Samantha Sue's mother had been a Talbot—Samantha Sue was small and calculating. With that pretended helplessness and coquetry characteristic of the old-fashioned Southern belle, she was as deadly as the pearl-handled derringer which, she boasted, her pappy had made her promise always to carry "as protection against the nigras." With her sweet talk, silky brown curls, magnolia-white skin and long-lashed blue eyes, and by presenting him with a son whom he adored, she coiled herself around Polo Pete, throttling his interest in poetry by giving away all his old dog-eared books to the Salvation Army when she redid Silver Hill, smothering him in simulated adoration, manipulating him to her will and whims until, like some poisonous vine, she managed to arrest whatever growth he might possibly have been capable of. The result was that Polo Pete had become an alcoholic nonentity, almost pathetic in his desire for acceptance on some level not connected with his money.

In order to achieve this he seemed forced to disguise the banal surface of his own personality with a compulsive desire to gain attention. Just as his automobiles were plated with chrome, his mind, slowed and coarsened by years of constant drinking, was plated with vulgarity.

His jokes, like his clothes, were loud and in bad taste. His body, like his torn fingers hidden by the cotton gloves which Samantha Sue urged him to wear, was bloated by his excesses. Yet because of his money and power—he owned the most valuable land in The Valley as well as the county newspaper—he carried weight with the politicians in Richmond. As the older generation died off, people forgot that his grandmother had been the daughter of a saloonkeeper and spoke of her as the fabulous Belle Buford who had been the consort of kings—and the scandal of Maria was buried in the mists of time. When he was named President of The Hunt, the Land Company and the bank, it could be said that Pete had achieved his ambition.

After hearing of her mother's elopement from Polo Pete, Shelley became unreachable and fiercely competitive. On The Gray Goose, the hunter she had schooled herself, she won local point-to-points and blue ribbons at the shows. She no longer drank Cokes at the drugstore or went to parties. Instead, she devoted herself to schooling horses, building fences, carpentering and working like a field hand. It was as though she was determined to show The Valley that the Shelburn name still stood for something, although what that intangible something was nobody, including Shelley, seemed quite to know. Whereas adults caused her to draw into her shell, she was completely natural when playing with children or animals. Sensing this, they responded accordingly. When she started her riding classes at Shelburn she was overwhelmed with applicants. Children adored her and she could do anything with them she wished.

With a horse, it was the same. As Connor, the Dash-Smythes' Irish groom, expressed it, "Her hands on a horse's mouth were that soft she could braid a cobweb and not disturb the dew."

There was a wildness about her that found its release in riding fast horses over the highest fences. For the most part this wildness was kept in check. "Under wraps" was the term used at the track when horses were restrained from showing their best speed. At home or with other people, Shelley was behind the bit. It was only when she was riding alone or hunting, on a fast horse with the wind in her face, singing, that she was able to forget self, forget the torment of ambivalence, of rebellion against her grandmother's worn-out world coupled with an instinctive resentment against the new.

The truth of her father's facetious remark that the family was like the famous circular staircase that rose from the ground floor to the attic without visible means of support was borne out. Shelley and her father, in a desperate effort to keep up Shelburn Hall and maintain The Hunt, decided to take in paying guests.

This period lasted two hunting seasons, a chaotic time of coping with unsound horses and temperamental cooks who objected to serving round-the-clock meals, and cleaning boots—there was nobody else whose job it was—until early morning hours.

At times the memory of this queer interim period seemed to sharpen, sweep in upon her. Curiously, she wanted to step back into that past which, by the time of her grandmother's death, had become an unhappy thing.

The rose garden went to hay, turnips were planted in the tennis court, the water in the swimming pool was muddy and there were snapping turtles in it. When her father missed the meet or turned up too drunk to ride, Shelley acted as Field Master.

As time passed, Shelley's father began to spend most of his waking hours in his den. Once, when Shelley asked him what he did during those hours locked away in the pine-paneled book-lined room, he replied, "I struggle with my conscience. Shelley, remember this. You can never evade it."

Aware that she was staring at a bottle half hidden by the unpaid bills in his desk drawer, his expression changed to one of resignation.

"I'm sorry," he said, raising his head. He looked directly at her and she saw tears in his eyes. "Shelley, it's up to you to find the future and reshape your heritage."

Shelley had come home from school and was waiting dinner for him when, wearing his scarlet coat stained with mud, he was carried into the great front room of Shelburn Hall. Virginia City told her that he had been drinking, and that he had done his best to persuade him not to go hunting. Her father had refused to listen. He had jumped the high wall that separated the property from Ballyhoura. A low-hanging branch had fractured his skull.

Shelley would always remember that his white stock had been loosened and sagged in crumpled folds around his neck, and that one of his boot garters had broken. Her father had been a stickler for appointments. Long before Shelley knew how to tie her high brown shoes, she had known how to tie a stock. Patiently her father had instructed her on such small details as boot garters and straight gold stock pins as opposed to ornate diamond or silver pins. Curiously, these details were so imbued in her mind that she did not think of any of the big things—death, the fact that her father would never ride with her again. Instead, she wanted to retie his stock and adjust his boot garter.

Cameron Fitzgerald had been a weak man. Yet he had been well liked. The fact that he had been wronged, abandoned by his wife, had made him an object of sympathy and, before he began drinking too much, he had been sought after by local widows and divorcees. Too, he had been generous, considerate of others, and possessed of the ability to communicate with people of all walks of life without affectation or condescension.

As Judge Templeton commented, the funeral drew a good gate. The street in front of the old stone church was lined with cars and buggies, and the Dinwiddies' coach, drawn by four shining hackneys and with two men on the box, was pulled up behind the hearse. The sidewalk was jammed with local Negroes and townspeople.

The old stone church was packed. Farmers and tradesmen, grooms and gardeners, ambassadors and the Undersecretary of State. Those too late to find seats stood along the wall or in the churchyard, the snow falling silently onto their bowed heads.

Her father, Shelley thought, would have hated the fuss and the flowers. Particularly the bunches of violets arranged around the casket. "Look at those stinking violets," he snorted every spring. "Means the end of another foxhunting season."

The Reverend Whitcomb's words and the service meant little to her. But the sight of the acolyte carefully snuffing out the altar candles was vividly imprinted on her mind. Nor would she forget the sudden jarring sound of the carillon tolling the strains of "John Peel."

As the casket, covered in green and gold chrysanthemums—the Fitzgerald racing colors—was slowly trundled down the aisle, the sound of the bells seemed louder and the ache in her throat became almost unendurable.

Behind the casket walked the pallbearers: R. Rutherford Dinwiddie, Esquire; Judge Templeton and the Old Huntsman, Timmy Glasscock, who had whipped-in for twenty years; Ikie Smith, the butler; Freddy Fisher and Fax Templeton, who had ridden the race horses; Sidney Merrywood, his trainer; the farmers Fletcher and Fuller and Webster, over whose land The Hunt had ridden for decades; Young South, who had once put his eggs on the grand piano; Lord Desmond, the British Ambassador; and Virginia City, his combination stableman and valet, who brought up the rear.

During the service the white pallbearers sat in the front two pews reserved for them. The Negroes walked to the rear, where they stood with their heads bowed.

Cameron Fitzgerald was the only Yankee buried in the family graveyard behind Shelburn Hall. He had been laid to rest wearing his pink coat, his famous racing silks draped over his arm. Virginia City had seen to it that his boots were boned, his white kid breeches immaculate, his stock tied perfectly, his hunting crop at his side—that for this, the long ride into the unknown, the Master of The Hunt was properly turned out.

The snow fell on the bared heads of the Negroes who stood

deferentially to one side. It clung to Mrs. Dinwiddie's veil, to Lord Desmond's mustache. From across the hills came the faint, distant sound of the carillon. "D'ye ken John Peel, at the break of day. D'ye ken John Peel with his hounds far away . . ." The refrain went around and around in Shelley's head, muffling the minister's final words like the distant melancholy cry of hounds coming from the kennels.

The casket was lowered, a handful of snow tossed onto it. The Old Huntsman raised his curving cow's horn to his lips. Putting his head back, he blew "Gone Away." As the last echoing spine-tingling note was carried away by the wind, those at the graveside knew that the death of Cameron Fitzgerald marked the end of a sporting era—an era which those who had not known it would never understand, and that those who had would not find its like again.

A month later word came from England that Shelley's mother and her lover had been killed in a car crash while going to Newmarket to look at a horse.

The deaths of her parents flung a shadow across Shelley's adolescence which life at Shelburn Hall but deepened. Like its owner, the Hall was reaching the last stages of decay. Miss Marlee would not spend any money on it. There were no more Shelburns, she said, to carry it on. Therefore, she intended that the house would die with herself.

Sinking into a twilight zone of senility, she relinquished all responsibility. The house took on an air of impenetrable gloom. Eyebrows of wisteria twined around the pillars and formed a tangle over the windows, cutting off the light. The woodwork, long unpainted, and the pillars began to rot. In the great front room paintings cracked, tapestries unraveled, and the beautiful French wallpaper peeled away like layers of skin. The maroon curtains which had never been cleaned in Shelley's lifetime were limp with grime, and the dogs, Shelley's mastiff and the hound puppies, had stained the fine old furniture and the floors.

People rarely came to the house now. The few who did were dried-up dowagers, the Misses Talbot and old Mrs. Hulburd, contemporaries of Miss Marlee who came to complain about the new people, gossip and fill the salon with ancient scandals. They gazed at Shelley with faded, suggestive eyes, gloating on her innocence.

She wondered what their glances meant, why they nudged each other and cackled with laughter. The musty odor of decay that surrounded them, their withered cheeks and shriveled fingers, made her skin crawl.

After her mother's death, her grandmother's madness deepened. In Shelley she saw the daughter who had betrayed her and the husband who had abandoned her. Instead of the awful caresses, Shelley became the object of screaming fits of passion.

At night the sound of her grandmother's cane could be heard tapping along the ghostly cobwebbed hallway. This was accompanied by the sound of her high cracked voice singing hymns. When Shelley sought to lead her back to her room, the old woman raised her walking stick. Pointing it at her granddaughter, she screamed, "You're the way she was. Like her. Sinful. Sinful!"

Her grandmother's accusations seeded a growing guilt. It was as though life's secrets, held in her body, were things to be ignored or, if they could not be ignored, defiled. Instead of pride, Shelley felt shame at being born female.

Whatever love and human warmth she was to know as a child came from the servants' quarters, out of the darkness and mysteries that flowered below stairs. Here she smoked her first cigarette and drank the champagne left over in the glasses from the Sunday luncheons. She came to associate pleasure with that which is forbidden, with remorse as the natural aftermath.

When she was twelve, Shelley felt the growth within her of a kind of mystical awareness. Lying in bed at night, she could feel her breasts starting to expand and flower. When she touched her nipples she felt a tingling, excited sensation. She was deeply conscious of the fact that now, when she rode, her breasts bobbed beneath her polo shirt. She was certain that the convicts who worked on the road, who raised their heads and stared, their faces impassive, expressionless as she passed them, saw through her shirt to the pointed mounds of flesh. This gave her a burning sense of shame and to avoid displaying her breasts, she bound them as tight and flat as she could with a horse bandage.

One day she was riding The Goose bareback along the stream behind Muster Corner when she saw two figures lying beneath a tree in the clearing by the quarry. The girl lay on her back, long, black hair fanned out on the grass behind her. The man lay on top of her. His body, naked from the waist, was dappled with sunlight. As he moved his head to one side, Shelley saw the girl's face. Her eyes were closed. As the man's hands and lips moved over her body, her lips parted and her face twisted as though in pain. As Shelley watched, mesmerized, the motions of the lovers became increasingly violent. Oblivious now to all that was around them, the golden-winged butterfly circling the girl's hair, the noisy squirrel in the tree overhead, the man extended the girl's arms from her sides and covered them with his own. As she lay helpless, as though on a cross, Shelley saw the muscles swell on the man's glistening ebony back and the dark hairs of the girl's long legs as she wrapped them around his buttocks. Then the silence was rent with a final convolution and the girl's ecstatic cry.

Shelley's body was soaked with perspiration. As she forced herself to ride on, the motion of the horse increased the sensation of melting, of detachment and curious serenity. Unconsciously she found herself pressing down against the horse's withers. The resulting sensation, an agonizing, blissful, cutting feeling, as though a knife was being drawn between her legs, was unlike anything she had ever experienced.

The world around her was a golden glaze. Her body seemed totally separate from her conscious mind. Frantic for relief, it made motions entirely on its own. The Goose, unconcerned by the strange movements on his back, continued slowly along the path. Bending low, Shelley rubbed her aching breasts against his coarse mane. As she strained against the horse, the melting sensation became almost unbearable. As though to wrest away the throbbing, pulsating feeling, part pain, part bliss, she put her hand between the horse's body and her own. There was a second of increased excitement and this was climaxed by a sensation so all-consuming and exquisite that when it was over she was limp. Had the horse shied or increased his speed she would have fallen.

Shelley was appalled at what she had done. When she rode into the stableyard she was sure that her sin must be obvious, in her burning eyes, her sweat-soaked shirt. She also felt tired and, for the first time in months, at peace.

For days afterward she fought off temptation. It came to her at the oddest times. Listening to Melusina, or watching Virginia City work, the muscles moving like water beneath his shirt. Or on a horse, after jumping a big fence, or when in some scene of nature, the golden light of late afternoon, sunset, with the sight of hounds in full cry across a green meadow. The ecstasy she had experienced was associated with horses. At the same time horses, the unending activity surrounding them, stilled the shameful need.

The madness and decay would not have been bearable without Melusina. Although she had married John Taylor, Washington Taylor's father, and had borne him eleven children, her life had been devoted to the Shelburns. For over half a century she had traveled from the "home place" at Muster Corner to cook and clean and care for Miss Marlee.

Miss Marlee believed that she was born with money the way one is born with a need to defecate and that therefore it was a topic that was simply not discussed. When some of the tradespeople who were not native to the area wrote rude letters and refused credit, she blamed their attitude on the spread of Communism in the world. When the manager of the old chain store, whose mother had been a Mellick from the Free Zone, refused to cash a worthless check, Miss Marlee shrugged and commented that his disrespect was to be expected from poor white trash.

Melusina was the only one who would put up with the lack of pay, accusations and insults. During the last months of Miss Marlee's life, Shelley and her grandmother subsisted on the chickens and an occasional hog killed at the home place, and the turnips, cabbages, lettuces and tomatoes that Melusina grew in the old clay tennis court which one of her sons had resodded, planted and fertilized.

Shelley's grandmother lay helpless and insane in her huge canopied bed. Melusina fed her by hand and emptied her bedpan. Miss Marlee's periods of lucidity grew rarer. Mostly she lived in the past. She remembered her mother's key basket, the tattered bag containing the heavy iron keys to the front door, the closets, the meat house and outbuildings. She told of the time her mother had crowned the Yankee officer on the head with the big iron front-door key when he tried to break into the smokehouse and the Yankee's reply, "Any woman with that much courage deserves to keep her damn ham," how the officer then ordered his soldiers to leave Shelburn and the "brave ladies" in peace. She demanded that Melusina lock all the doors at night and then bring her the ancient tattered carryall filled with rusted keys. This she kept hidden beneath her mattress along with a box of Confederate bills which, long ago, had been buried with the silver in the hole dug beneath the oak, down by the old well. She spoke endlessly of Sean Shelburn, and how when she was a little girl he had galloped up to Shelburn Hall at the head of his Raiders. She described his dark strange beauty, the sleeve of his ash-gray uniform pinned to his side, his worn boots shining like the mahogany dining-room table, how he flung the reins of his horse to old Solomon, swung his right leg over the horse's withers and jumped down. She had been wearing her white muslin with its pink sash and belled-out skirt. He had seen her standing by the doorway, picked her up with his one good arm, swung her high into the air, kissed her roundly on the cheek and cried out, "Men, this is my cousin Marlee, the prettiest lil ole girl in Bellevue County." The long feather from his hat had swept her face as he set her down. Then everyone laughed and cheered and clumped into the house, where the servants were hurriedly bringing out musty bottles of wine that had been locked away from the Yankee looters in the cellar.

After telling this story, Shelley's grandmother would begin to weep. Melusina would then rub her mistress's back with cologne and after a while Miss Marlee would become quiet.

" 'Sina," she would say sleepily, clutching the colored woman's hand, "won't be long before we meet in heaven."

"Yessum."

"I'll be sitting in the parlor with my needlepoint and you'll be in the kitchen."

By the time the fire was discovered, the west wing was an inferno. Although the firemen were able to save the rest of the Hall, there was nothing they could do to save Shelley's grandmother, whose charred remains were found in the ruins.

All the rest of her life Shelley was to remember the look of horror on the faces of the people who came to make the funeral arrangements, and along with this memory lay guilt. For she had not felt sorrow or even surprise.

She knew then that the tragedy lay not in death itself, but in what death did to the living. The awful thing was that she had not felt grief. That in itself was worse than any grief she could have experienced. For it made of her grandmother's life a waste. She had wanted to cry and not been able to. For she had known then that she was no more alone, in reality, than she had always been.

The horses were sold at a dispersal sale, the proceeds of which went to pay off the most pressing debts. The income from the small trust fund her father had set aside for her enabled her to buy and fix up the truck-trailer. Leaving Virginia City in charge of the place, she led The Goose into the trailer and drove north.

The sun was lowering now, sinking to meet the ridge of blue-gray mountains rimming The Valley, painting the fields and woodlands and waving broom sedge with rust pink afternoon light. Aside from the rustle of the wind in the ancient trees and the snuffling of the hound puppies investigating a groundhog hole, there was nothing to destroy the atmosphere of pastoral peace.

Cam, tired of sitting, had gone to see what the puppies had found.

Shelley sat motionless, feeling the healing warmth of the sun on her face, the soft scented air.

The sound of hoofs followed by an explosion of laughter caused her to look up. A girl on a chestnut horse was cantering over the field toward her, followed by a man. The girl's hair was blowing wildly behind her, and Shelley saw that it was the orange-pink color of the broom sedge.

"Oh, hi," the girl called out, coming to a stop on the other side of the cemetery wall. "I'm Tatine Zagaran. You must be Mrs. Latimer."

"Hello," Shelley said and smiled. "I didn't get a chance last night to thank you for a wonderful party."

"At least it's over." Tatine wrinkled her nose. Her unbelievable eyes, green with yellow flecks like the changing fall foliage, were set far apart. Close up, her hair was the exact color of the brandy that Mike liked to sip after dinner. "It would have been cheaper and simpler to paint the front gate blue and hang up a sign on the door saying, 'Marriageable daughter. Step up, gentlemen.' Hi, young man. Who are you? Hey, whatcha got there?"

"I'm Cam," Cam said. He extended a fat green caterpillar. The tiny feelers growing from its head resembled horns. It looked like a miniature dragon.

"Gee!" Tatine exclaimed, leaning down to observe Cam's prize. "What a ferocious-looking creature."

Shelley noticed that the young man, whom she recognized as the Young Whip, had reined in his horse and was waiting deferentially in the background. While Tatine and Cam continued to discuss the caterpillar, Shelley asked the Young Whip how the hounds were getting along.

"We'll see tomorrow," he replied. "Mr. Templeton says hounds are to go out at seven o'clock at Ballyhoura." He glanced at the sky. "If you ask me, it's mighty hot and dry, but Mr. Templeton says it's because of the party, guests and all."

The image of the Young Whip's face as he had stood outside the ballroom talking to Tatine last night flashed across Shelley's mind. Now she noticed that he was looking at Tatine in much the same way. Shelley could not blame him. As the girl listened intently to Cam explaining about his mellow hole, she was no longer the cynical, worldly-wise debutante of the night before. Instead, wearing frontier pants and a polo shirt, and without a trace of make-up, a yellow leaf caught in her tangled hair, she looked fresh and beautiful and about fifteen years old. She started to speak further and then did not. The Young Whip had forgotten Shelley, had forgotten to disguise the contents of his heart, all of which shone in his countryman's vivid blue eyes, focused on the slender girl astride the graceful chestnut thoroughbred.

The horse shook its head, chewing on its bit. "Hush, Warlock," Tatine admonished. "Settle down, love."

"He's beautiful," Shelley said sincerely. "I remember reading about him in *The Chronicle*. Didn't you win a lot, that year you went on the show circuit?"

Tatine nodded. "We were lucky." She leaned down and hugged the horse. "Warlock, I love you. He's pretty old now," she told Shelley, "but he's got another season or more left. After he bowed I couldn't show him any more. But he hunts like a dream."

"You'll be hunting?"

Tatine nodded. "I adore The Valley. I never want to leave."

"Will your parents be hunting?"

"Dad will," Tatine said. "Mother, no. My mother isn't well. I'm afraid the party did her in." She glanced at the lowering sun. "Hey, gotta go. Left my house guests spread out by the pool. See you, Mrs. Latimer. Tonight at the Bufords' bash, I hope. And you, sport"—she gave Cam a melting smile—"we have a date to go fishing."

Shelley watched Tatine and the Young Whip ride off. The way the girl had looked and the way she spoke to Cam were as unexpected as her sudden appearance. After the stories she'd heard, Shelley had expected her to be hard, coarse. Instead she was struck by her beauty. She turned to Cam. From his bemused expression as he stared after the riders, still holding the caterpillar on his flattened palm, it was obvious that Tatine's power over the male sex transcended age.

As the riders vanished over the hill, Shelley saw the sun hovering over the tower at Ballyhoura, the shadows lengthening on the blue mountains. The world of her afternoon crashed. She would have to go home, face Mike, remind him that they were expected at the Bufords' for dinner. She could not tell him what Samantha Sue had said after church. If she related the conversation, he would be so angry he would refuse to go. Just as she could not tell him about the loan. If she did, he might never forgive her or trust her again. The only answer lay in making it appear that nothing had happened to change the relationship between the Bufords and herself.

As she turned to walk back to the house, the fears she had been fighting off all day came flooding back. Past and present seemed intermingled, the face of Sean Shelburn, who had been so much in her thoughts as she told part of his story to Cam, alternating with that of Zagaran in her mind.

If she went to the Bufords' she would see him. It would give her a chance to thank him for returning her earring and for the roses she suddenly remembered were still in the bathtub. When she finally admitted to herself why she really wanted to go to the Bufords' dinner, she felt as if her soul was slowly being stained, and from somewhere deep inside herself came the knowledge that if the staining process, the deception she had begun by borrowing money from Polo Pete, was allowed to continue, the time would come when not even the stiff brush she had bought at the Saddle Shop to knock the summer dirt from the horses' coats would be able to scrub away the guilt of deceiving Mike.

The sun was a scarlet globe now. It seemed to be hanging directly over the distant mountain where the Free Zoners lived. On the hill, dark, majestic, medieval, brooded Ballyhoura. A plane droned overhead. Crimson and gold against the sky. Beyond the Shelburn Cup Course it dropped down onto the private airstrip, taxied along the concrete runway and came to a stop. When the sound of its engines ceased, she heard the cry of the hound puppies chasing a rabbit through her overgrown pasture. It was past time to return to the house, give Cam and Virginia City, who would stay with him, supper, and dress for the Bufords' dinner.

"Cam," she called, "time to go. Come, Lance. Here, hounds."

The mastiff came at once, lumbering after Cam. The puppies, loath to leave the chase, ignored them. "I guess they'll come eventually," Shelley said. "Still, I worry about them going out on the road."

In the brilliant light of late afternoon, sifting through the branches of the great oaks, the park was the color of polished brass. It was the light she remembered best. It held a green-gold quality which seemed characteristic of her Valley and which she had never seen elsewhere. Pale yellow-green filtered through the great trees. Vivid. Acidy. She had painted it from memory in New York. She must get back to painting, she thought. Maybe she could make Christmas cards. Or get some orders for horse portraits from the hunting people. The money could go toward paying off some of their debts—that secret loan.

Cam ran ahead to put the apples from the orchard in his mellow hole. The dogs raced at his side. Shelley felt a rush of love and pride in his now sturdy, healthy boy's body, his glowing cheeks and golden hair. He's our collateral, she thought, he will inherit Shelburn Hall, keep it from going out of the family.

Cam stopped. There were two box turtles beside the path. One had yellow markings, the other orange. The first turtle sought fruitlessly to escape, its head and legs flailing wildly. The second turtle curled up in fright, its shell closed tight.

"Let them stay in the sunlight," Shelley said.

"I want to take them home and show them to my daddy."

"All right. We'll put them in a box."

The hound puppies came bounding up the path. Lookout Light extended his fine-veined head over his stall door and whinnied. The horses in the field raised their heads and cocked their ears. Wheeling suddenly, they galloped toward the gate, manes and tails flying like dark ribbons against the dying light.

Holding Cam with one hand, carrying a turtle in the other, and warding off the eager snuffling hounds threatening to trip her, Shelley was caught up in the habitual conditions of her life, her child, her horses and her dogs.

SIX

FOR the second night in succession, the Latimers drove along the Valley road. The dryness of the countryside was almost audible, like the sudden crack of a stick, and when the animals moved in the fields, puffs of dust rose behind them. They were half an hour late for what Samantha Sue had described as "just a simple Sunday night supper for Tatine Zagaran and a few of her friends, a fun party."

They turned onto the dusty washboard road that led through the village of Muster Corner to Silver Hill.

Although the Shelburn property and other extensive plantations in The Valley had been broken up, sold and resold, Muster Corner remained as it had always been, a handful of moldering cabins populated by Negro families crushed to subservience by hopelessness and an inadequate diet. At the turn of the century, when it was bought by P. G. Buford, who proceeded to build the vast Victorian house, with its conservatory and cupola, curlicued woodwork and impressive garden, with money he had mined in Nevada, the Muster Corner Negroes again found full employment in the house and stables and on the farm, where fine horses, cows and beef cattle were raised.

Now the Negro residents sat in the twilight in front of the cluster of unpainted shacks. Some of the children played around the tireless derelict cars abandoned in dusty yards. Others thronged the sides of the road, staring impassively at the cars turning into Silver Hill. Anywhere else it would be considered a slum, Mike thought, recalling the rats he'd seen running through Jubal Jones's shanty when he had gone to pick up the janitor following one of his periodic binges. Here it was considered picturesque.

Muster Corner had always been there, he thought. It would be there long after he was gone. There would always be Muster Corner because the people who lived in the great houses drove by daily without seeing. To them Muster Corner was faceless, its inhabitants as lacking in identity as the Bufords' cattle grazing in the fields. For years Polo Pete had run his vast farming enterprise with convict labor, parolees who lived in the crumbling shacks with outside privies and one well to supply water for thirty-two families. Any complaints, any hint of rebellion or slacking off were answered by a phone call to the parole officer, and those involved would be returned to the penitentiary. For Polo Pete the arrangement was eminently satisfactory. Of all the landowners in The Valley, he was one of the few who did not have a help problem.

Ahead lay the entrance to Silver Hill and its complex of farm buildings. On either side of the cattle guard stood imposing stone posts topped with swooping granite eagles with spread wings and open beaks. A mailbox built in the shape of a small house and painted with windows and window boxes by Tina Welford stood by the entrance. The words "Silver Hill Farms" were lettered on its side.

The long avenue wound past a farm pond, over an arching stone bridge and through a series of fields separated by cattle guards. Mike slowed down for the bumps, placed at intervals in order that the Bufords' only son, Peter Galtee IV, known as Buddha, and the house dogs would be safe from speeders.

"You've known Pete a long time, haven't you?" Mike asked as they rattled over the last cattle guard.

Shelley turned to look at him, wondering why he should ask this now. Irrelevantly she noticed that his hair was too long, a few tendrils curling down over the collar of his white shirt.

"You know I have. P. P. and I grew up together."

"You must know the kind of man he is."

"I've always taken him for granted," Shelley answered defensively. "You do, you know, about a person or place which you've always known."

The incongruous house with its peaked roof, ornate woodwork and stained-glass windows stood on a knoll surrounded by pristine pastures. Miles of board fences encased the fields and trees, carefully planted to provide shade for the beef cattle, horses and prize dairy herd.

It was almost dusk now. Julep time, Mike thought. Fun time in old Virginia. Behind the ornate façade of Silver Hill the sky was pink-purple. On either side of the walk stood the tall magnolia trees that Samantha Sue, at great cost, had moved from the back garden when she redid the house and landscaped the grounds. Their flat smooth leaves had a sleek oily look and the white waxen blossoms held an artificiality, like the flares that outlined the turning circle and the lanterns hung in the trees around the swimming pool. In the flickering light Mike saw the preoccupied anticipatory look on Shelley's face, as though already, at the sound of music and laughter coming from the gaily lit terrace, she had forgotten him and was thinking of the people she would see at the party.

He was not a man to display emotion, particularly in public. Yet as they reached the foot of the divided stone stairway with the symbolic cut glass pineapples balanced atop the iron balustrade, he felt a sudden weakness, a loss of direction, as though he did not know which steps to take, the ones to the left or the ones to the right. Reaching out, he clutched Shelley's arm. The gesture was instinctive, like that of a man who, fighting a heavy sea to reach the safety of shore, gropes for a tangible object to cling to.

She stopped, surprised. He felt her stiffen, and anger, as sudden as it was uncharacteristic, swept over him. It was because of her that he was here, in an alien country, among people with whom he had no rapport. He wanted to fight her, batter down her resistance. His hand tightened on her arm. At the same time he wanted to hold her against him, force her to want him.

"Hey!" It was Fax Templeton.

His therapeutic collar was gone. In place of the high white ruff was a maroon silk foulard cravat, and there was a yellow rosebud in the buttonhole of his slightly frayed but beautifully cut gabardine jacket.

"Why, Fax," Shelley said, "your collar is gone."

"Yep." Fax nodded. "I got so hot under it terpsichoring last night I called Muddy Watters. He told me to come in after church and he'd take it off. Said all it amounted to anyway was a bog spavin of the neck. He said I could go hunting in the morning, ride shotgun on the Duchess here, long as I don't buy any more ground for a while. Hey, what were you two doing? Necking?"

He turned to Bebe Bruce. "Fancy a married couple who talk to one another. Bebe, meet the Latimers. Mike and Shelley. The Valley's most devoted couple."

"But I have met them," the Duchess answered in her Melton-Mowbray voice. Her eyes slid to Mike. Her mouth curved into a smile. "You're *the* Michael Latimer. *The* editor."

The way she said it, in her softest, furriest, carefully accented voice with its emphasis on the "the," as if he were the editor of the *Capital Courier*, had the effect of Buddha's zap gun, if real and directed at a human being. Instead of collapsing, Mike smiled. With courtesy he mentioned that he had met her at the ball and hoped she would like living in The Valley.

"You must put me down for a subscription to your paper," Bebe said, going ahead up the steps. Trailing her hand along the balustrade, she gazed back at him. "I'm told it's terribly amusing."

At the look in Bebe's blue eyes, Shelley's own turned quickly to her husband. He was forty-two now, but he looked older. His fine-boned sensitive good looks had not altered, but the looseness of his jacket around his waist indicated the loss of weight. His face, too, was thinner and about his eyes there was a look of strain. And yet it struck her, looking at him purely objectively in the same manner Bebe was doing, that he was a very attractive man. Why, then, she wondered obliquely, did she feel this ennui, a kind of weariness of the senses, when she was with him and was forced to accept his touch?

Then they were in the hall. David, the Bufords' very proper butler (paroled years previously for good behavior following the axe murder of his wife's lover), greeted them warmly.

While the Duchess went to the ladies' room to perfect her already perfect make-up, Shelley gave herself a desultory glance in the ornate gilt-framed mirror that had come from a Virginia City saloon and that Samantha Sue kept as a conversation piece.

Now, after three generations, Belle Fleurey had been accepted into the family. The Bufords boasted of her colorful past and her connections with European royalty. When Samantha Sue had Dickie Speer do over the house, the famous decorator had been entranced by the massive furniture, stained glass, dried flower arrangements under domes and extravagantly framed oils, some of which had been painted by Nevada miners as barroom decorations in exchange for liquor, and the other bric-a-brac stored in the attic. Amazingly, he managed to blend the relics of that gaudy, gilded era, which, with its utter disdain for pastels or graceful outlines, made a striking contrast to the Swedish modern decor that was his specialty. The result was fascinating and ingenious and although the house was not what Shelley would call livable, it was unforgettable.

As Shelley turned away from the mirror, Fax eyed her appreciatively. Turning to Mike, he said, "I wonder if you have any idea how many men hate your guts for snatching the most charming girl in The Valley out from under our cotton-picking noses."

Mike smiled. "I have a good idea."

"Right now he's ready to auction me off to the highest bidder," Shelley answered, grateful to Fax for always providing the light touch. "To be honest, Fax, there are times when I hardly blame him."

Something in her voice caused Fax, who steered away from discord in the manner of a rabbit twisting and turning away from a pack of beagles, to direct his attention to Bebe coming from the ladies' room.

Wearing black velvet pants, a white silk blouse and demure black bows in her smooth blond hair, the slim Duchess looked deceptively girlish and unsophisticated. Until you saw her undulating walk and the way she looked at men, it was hard to believe that her affairs were legion and that the number of lovers whose names were inscribed on her platinum cigarette case and who had been privileged to see her famous trademark, the bees tattooed on her left thigh, could, if laid end to end, stretch the length of the Valley road.

Fax gave her his teasing little-boy grin—slightly rueful, with a touch of wistfulness, an expression that never failed to make each woman he met think that she, above all others, had been destined to mother him, reform him, shape him into something of her own creation. Simultaneously he whipped his hunting horn from the place where, like Napoleon's hand, it was carried between the buttons of his evening shirt. Putting it between his lips he announced their arrival by blowing a series of rousing toots.

At the sound of Fax's horn their host detached himself from Kevin Martin, the TV commentator who had recently bought the Jenneys' house, Meadowview. Polo Pete was wearing his at-home uniform—bottle green smoking jacket, soft shirt, black bow tie and needlepoint slippers emblazoned with his monogram. On

174

his torn fingers were the habitual white cotton gloves. As he focused his attention on the Duchess, his voice boomed forth like one of the green-glass-domed lamps, seeking out the corners of the crowded room.

"S-pleasure. A real pleasure. Drink. Boy." He snapped his gloved fingers. Manassas Brown, his face impassive, came forward with a tray of drinks.

"Want champagne?" Polo Pete asked Bebe. "Got lots. Always have it on hand for an occasion. Forn-i-cation, got it?"

The Duchess gazed at him coldly.

"One of your juleps will do nicely." She accepted a frosted silver cup with a sprig of mint in it. Gazing past her host as if he were one of the wooden white-painted Ionic pillars holding up the doorway, she said to Fax, "Dahling, who *are* all these people? For instance, who is that old biddy wrapped in burlap and held together with diamond brooches? She must be a hundred and ten."

Fax laughed. "That's Mrs. R. Rutherford Dinwiddie. She still hunts and goes like a bomb. I wouldn't know her age. I've never looked at her teeth."

Aware that the Duchess had slipped from his immediate grasp, Polo Pete put his gloved hand on Shelley's forearm. Forcing herself not to shrink away, she stood patiently while her host said, "Got a new one for you." Acknowledging Mike's presence for the first time, he continued, "Editor here won't appreciate it, but you will. Know what N. J. stands for?"

Shelley shook her head, dreading what was coming next.

"Niggers and Jews." He gave a loud guffaw. "You thought it stood for New Jersey, didn't you? Didn't you?" he repeated insistently, pinching her arm. "I wouldn't expect *him* to understand, but you, Shelley—you're one of us!"

"I'm sorry, Pete," Shelley said, jerking out of his grasp, "I don't think it's funny."

For an instant the fat man looked abashed. In his eyes was an expression like Miehle's when the dog heard the press at the *Sun* start to roll, a cowering, fearful look as though waiting to be struck. Then he took a long swallow of his drink and that look was replaced by one that was crafty and calculating.

"Shelley, I'd like to have Lookout Light back. Naturally, I'll pay you a price. After all you've done for him. But come, right now you need a drink. Later we'll talk business." As he tucked his white-gloved hand under Shelley's elbow it was all she could do to repress a shudder. She had not been honest with Mike. Had she been, she would have told him that from earliest childhood she had always detested Pete Buford.

"Mr. Latimer, would you like a drink?" Manassas Brown, his face looking as though carved from one of the massive mahogany tables, stood holding a silver tray.

At sight of the bartender, embarrassment mingled with revulsion flooded through Mike. If I had any guts, he thought, I would grab Shelley by the hair and yank her out of here. Then he told himself that until she recognized Polo Pete for what he was, saw the bigotry and the button-down mind, nothing would change.

"I need a miracle drug to get me through this evening," he murmured under his breath.

Mike's eyes met those of the colored man. Briefly Mike saw a flash of understanding. Then once again they became hooded, inscrutable.

"Thank you," Mike said. "Bourbon and water will be fine."

In order to enter the living room, it was necessary to circumvent the Jones terriers and a crescent-shaped hunt board. Originally it had been designed to stand in front of the fireplace, where in olden times it had been laden with cheeses and port wine to be devoured by the foxhunters when they returned from the chase. Now it was used to support half a dozen thick scrapbooks, placed at carefully measured intervals and expensively bound in green morocco. Each album bore a separate title written in gold block letters: HORSES, DOGS, SHOOTING, RACING, FOX-HUNTING and, finally, FUN.

Bones Black and Cosy Rosy were on the sofa. Bones looked thin, drawn. Years of dieting and of running along the Valley road in a rubber suit had given him a hollow look. Race riders, Mike thought, all tended to look as if horses had fallen on them when they were children, arresting their growth, leaving them flattened, concave. Cosy Rosy, small and pretty with a short upturned nose, was gazing up at him with wide, admiring brown eyes while Bones filled her in on how he had won the Maryland Hunt Cup on a horse that nobody had thought could go a yard.

R. Rutherford Dinwiddie, Esquire, and Dudley Dudley-Smythe were at the bar. It would be hard to say which of the two was the worst snob. Dash-Smythe was an intense Anglophile who generally managed to work into the conversation that his direct ancestor had traveled to the New World aboard the *Mayflower*. He was proud of his resemblance to the Duke of Windsor and emphasized it by the knot in his tie, his British-made suits and shoes from Lobb in London. He was discussing his oldest daughter, Diana, out of his first wife, Sion, who had become fed up with his ancestor worship and divorced him to marry Greg Atwell, the lawyer. Now Mike overheard him tell R. Rutherford that Diana, who had defied him and gone north to Radcliffe, planned to add insult to injury by marrying a Harvard man.

"Oh, I say," R. Rutherford exclaimed, shocked, "spoil the bloodlines, what?"

Polo Pete leaned over the top of the bar and snapped his fingers. "Boy, where's my bourbon?"

He turned to the men. "Take my dairy herd. Most people care about how much milk their cows give. *I* care about purebred cows—and people." His eyes met Mike's. "Breeding and Christian brotherly love is what counts."

Mike looked around, hoping to escape, but he was pinned to the bar by the crowd.

"I tell you, hee-ar, the reason why America is the greatest country is because she is Christian, and her early Christians had an ideal." Jabbing Mike's chest with his index finger, Polo Pete continued, quoting Senator Telly Talbot's latest speech almost word for word. "We can only combat Communism by spreading Christianity throughout the entire world. France, England, all corrupted by paganism. But we know the living God. He is right hee-ar in this room!"

Mike saw Bones Black and Cosy Rosy vanishing into the shadows behind Samantha Sue's magnolias. Returning to the conversation, he felt compelled to point out that during the past few decades Christians had killed some fifty million of each other. "Is this brotherly love?" he asked.

"Look how the underdeveloped nations are sunk in poverty," Polo Pete replied, ignoring Mike's question. "If they are starving, it's their own fault. They have not shown Christian brotherly love. And I would rather they be shot than not show brotherly love by allowing each other to starve."

Mike thought of the Smith family at Muster Corner. The father was employed by Buford as a farm laborer. There were nine children in a three-room shanty, all with the bloated, rounded bellies that indicated malnutrition.

"Luckily there's county welfare—" He got no further.

"Nobody wants to work. And they all have television sets." R. Rutherford bristled.

"Why should they, when the government pays them not to?" Dash-Smythe said flatly.

"I tell you"—Polo Pete waggled his finger under Mike's nose— "those people in Washington, those Communist agitators, will destroy us. Instead of Christian brotherly love we have creeping socialism."

Mike saw an opening in the crowd around the bar and made for it. Polo Pete put out his hand to restrain him. "I wouldn't have let the bank loan you that money," he said soberly and distinctly, "if I'd known you were a damn nigger lover."

Mike rallied to make a retort, but Polo Pete had vanished and again Mike was left on his own. Standing on the darkened terrace, his eyes swept the crowded room like a broom, seeking out people he could talk to, or rather who would talk to him.

He had never had trouble finding people to talk to before. Wherever he had gone, there were always people to talk to about his work, people who were interested in what he was doing. But here they spoke to him about the newspaper as though it were a hobby, something like Tina Welford's tiles or Millicent Black's needlepoint.

When one had a Valley party, even a "simple Sunday night supper," it was almost impossible to limit it to a handful. Mike saw that Samantha Sue had invited almost everybody. Even the Dinwiddies were here, providing the hostess with a real coup. For the elderly couple had more or less retired from the social fray, preferring to save their energy for the hunting field. Yet they were always invited. As authentic members of the old guard, Beauty and the Beast gave a certain intangible style to the functions they attended. Millicent Black, wearing a long pink and orange wraparound evening skirt that resembled a horse blanket, was ensconced on a sofa. With a wave of her needlepoint, she flagged him down.

"You really must stop writing those fucking editorials," she said without preliminaries. "It's too hard on Shelley."

Before Mike could reply, she was diverted by her bête noire, Mrs. Dinwiddie, en route to the terrace. Millicent's lips pursed. Taking in the Beast's unfashionable flowered chiffon and amber beads, she turned to Debby Darbyshire sitting beside her. "My dear, she looks just like one of Samantha Sue's dried flower arrangements."

Mike made his way past into what Samantha Sue called the card room, where the young marrieds had gathered. After seeing them in the post office or the supermarket or at PTA meetings in riding clothes, often with a crop or a racing bat which they rolled in their hands or slapped against booted legs for emphasis, he had dubbed them the Slap Leather Set. In spite of their evening clothes, it seemed to Mike that the faint acrid odor of horse still clung to them.

Millicent Black was their leader. Mike had never understood why Shelley was so fond of her. He supposed it was due to their long association, having known each other first at Miss Shelburne's, and later when Shelley rode Millicent's horse show string for her. Shelley had told him about helping Millicent through her last divorce, sitting up nights listening to her complain about her current husband and profess her love for Bones.

Mike wondered, too, what it was that gave her an international reputation. It was not her intelligence. She boasted that the only book she had ever read was *Black Beauty* and that she had been one of the very few to earn the distinction of flunking out of Miss Shelburne's. Yet Terence Glyndon's latest travel book had been dedicated to her and almost every prominent figure in the contemporary worlds of art, literature, sports and politics eventually turned up at Last Resort.

Nor was it her beauty. Millicent was squarely built, flat-chested and big-boned (Mike could never see her without thinking of Dylan Thomas's remark about hard-faced horsey women wearing heavy stockings full of hockey muscles). Her face had a brown dried-out look. Her hair, wiry and cropped short, was prematurely gray, growing from her head like steel wool. With her square hips and matching jaw she reminded Mike of one of her great-grandfather's clipper ships, sailing through life, pulling people, horses, dogs and her children in her wake.

Mike suspected that Millicent's prestige stemmed from four generations of Back Bay Bostonians from which was derived her impeccable social position, coupled with an enormous income from the family-owned import-export business. Both facets had been augmented by her marriage to Randall Mason, of the Long Island Masons, who had bought and restored Last Resort, the historic plantation where Jeb Stuart had defeated a Yankee cavalry unit. The marriage had been short-lived. When Millicent refused to have children, saying that they would interfere with her fox-hunting, he had given up the ghost, in this case the ghost of the original builder, who had bled to death on the drawing-room floor following a duel. Mason had named the terriers as corespondents in the divorce action, testifying that the bed was so damned full of dogs there wasn't room for him. His remarks had been quoted in the press under the headline "Heir to Mason Shoe Fortune Gives Wife the Boot—says she prefers canines to connubial bliss."

Millicent, who was as tenacious as her clipper ship ancestors, held out for Last Resort and a million-dollar settlement. Following the divorce, she began building up one of the largest stables in the country. Nobody knew, least of all Millicent, how many horses were turned out on the mountain behind the house or resided in the numerous barns. House and gardens were overrun with animals, dogs of every description, a parrot who knew almost as many four-letter words as his mistress, two monkeys, a tame raccoon and, for a while, a bear who served to sober drunken visitors by licking their faces until they regained consciousness.

Millicent's second husband had been a jazz pianist, culled from among the celebrities who flocked to Last Resort. This marriage had been of even shorter duration. Millicent paid him off with a grand piano, after finding him one night in her circular larger-than-king-sized bed with Tina Welford, who, until that time, had been her closest friend.

Her third husband was a big-game hunter and a drunk. After he winged her on the shoulder one night with his elephant gun, she set him up on a farm in Kenya with the provision that he remain an ocean away from Virginia.

Then she fell in love with Bones Black. A son of Doc Black, the local veterinarian, he was younger than she and did not move in the same milieu. After graduating from the local public school he had been drafted and sent to Korea. He returned to find that his marriage to Betsy Watters, the doctor's daughter, had come unstuck. After the divorce he moved in with Fax and started riding races. Fax brought him to Millicent's annual prerace luncheon on Shelburn Cup Day. Bones had broken his collarbone the week before and was not able to ride. Millicent found him tall, dark and impossibly handsome with his empty coat sleeve and bright-colored silk sling. She took him with her to the race atop her miniature orange-painted coach, drawn by the four white ponies, which was a fixture at the Shelburn Cup Meet. Afterward she lured him back to Last Resort, plied him with the imported champagne with which Randall Mason had originally stocked the cellar and lured him upstairs to bed.

Bones made love in such a way that she found herself reaching her climax almost immediately. He was the first man ever to satisfy her. She even agreed to have his children if he would marry her.

After she promised to buy him a Jaguar and put him in charge of her racing stable, he decided that marriage was the line of least resistance. Millicent and Bones were married at Last Resort with all the dogs in attendance and Nautilus, her Shelburn Cup horse, standing in the doorway, his halter decorated with orange poppies.

A short time afterward Fax married Caddy McLean, whose father had parlayed a certain oil filter for automobiles into a billion-dollar business.

"If those boys don't beat all," commented Charlie Woodruff, the news dealer. "Darned if they didn't fall into a tub of butter."

But old habits do not die easily, and when Millicent's organizing became unbearable, Bones "turfed out," gladly exchanging the butter in the tub for today's margarine diet at Fax's Rakish Stud.

In the end Millicent inevitably had the last word. Now Mike heard her saying, "I warned the sport after church that if he didn't come home I'd stop payment on the new XKE and send the horses to Maryland to be trained."

"What did he say?" Debby asked eagerly.

Millicent glanced up from the tapestry of a fox and hounds that she was doing for prayer cushions for the church and nodded triumphantly. "He came home, dragging his ass behind him. He knew that this time I meant what I said, that I'd take Nautilus away from him, and Bones wants to win the Shelburn Cup more than anything."

Listening to her, Mike felt a deep sympathy for Bones. He recalled the story of Miehle and thought of how Millicent forced her six-year-old daughter, Merry, to ride by threatening her with her hunting crop. And he thought back to the previous year when, every morning for three months prior to the Shelburn Cup, Millicent "trained" Bones by "leading" him from the Jeep, clocking him as he ran three miles along the Valley road in a rubber reducing suit.

Even when wearing a long evening skirt and high heels, she walked as if she had on her hunting boots. With her long, mannish stride she sailed through life presenting an air of such positiveness and decision that those around her, prone to self-doubt, found themselves envying the very quality that annoyed and intimidated them.

Now she sailed into Mike. Deliberately setting her needlepoint to the side and reaching for a cigarette, she said, "I say, sport, what are you trying to do? Give the country over to the blacks and the Communists?"

Somehow Millicent always put him on the defensive.

"Millicent, you amaze me." He fumbled for the comfort of his pipe. "With your background and education I would have thought that you belonged to the more enlightened element of The Valley. It stands to reason, in the light of what's happening in other parts of the country, that unless the moderate whites get behind the moderate Negroes and give them support, there will indeed be trouble.

"It's a matter of freedom," he continued, knowing he sounded stuffy and dogmatic. "Freedom to eat in restaurants, go to decent schools—"

"Real-ley, Mike!" Millicent interrupted, sitting up straight. The heavy gold bangle she wore on her bracelet for her puppies to teeth on gave an emphatic clank. "I say, sport, you can't real-ley mean you want them to go to The Valley School? Mike, do you real-ley want Cam to marry one?"

He bit down on his pipestem, wishing he could find a match. "No," he admitted finally, feeling tired and defeated. At the sight of Polo Pete's flushed face as he stared over in their direction, he felt called upon to add, "nor would I want him to marry Polo Pete's daughter if he had one."

"Sport," Millicent said archly, "you're a riot."

Thinking that she had backed him into a corner and could thus afford to be magnanimous, she picked up her needlepoint and began working at it once again.

"The *Sun* gave the School Pony Show such mar-r-velous publicity last year. I know, Mike, that you'll help us again this fall."

"You've almost finished that bench cover," Debby said admiringly. "Millicent, whenever do you find time to do it?"

"In the back of the van, going to race meets," she explained.

"What do you do on the way home?" Mike asked innocently.

"The horses and I drink beer," replied Millicent.

Ever since she could remember, Shelley had anticipated going to parties only to find that once she got there everything was the same. The same people. The same conversations. And inevitably, the old shy sense of inadequacy came over her at being unable to sparkle the way Samantha Sue and Cosy Rosy did, with gestures and a dropping of the eyes.

Moving on, she heard the Four-H girls talking about Zagaran.

"Honestly," Debby said admiringly, "he *is* attractive with that battered face and that curious elegance."

Millicent shrugged. "He may be a financial genius, but he cahn't know a fucking things about horses. Imagine buying that bitch of a mare."

Shelley drifted away. The buzzing voices around her held a monotony, like the droning of frogs from the fields and ponds. Down through the black silhouettes of the transplanted magnolias and spreading crab apple trees drifted the silver light of a beginning moon. When she turned, the silver blobs and patches were swept away by the floodlights that illuminated Tatine Zagaran and her friends around the pool. The Zagarans had just arrived— Tatine in a very short striped dress and very long earrings and convoyed by her entourage of long-haired young men, followed by Zagaran and Andrea. Because they were so late, dinner had been held up and the cocktail period had extended over a far longer time than Samantha Sue, whose household was run with scheduled precision, liked.

"Ah declare, people today have no manners," she complained to Mrs. Dinwiddie. "Me-mah brought me up always to be on time."

Yet when Andrea and Zagaran stepped out onto the terrace, she was all smiles and graciousness. "Andrea, B." She extended both hands. "How good of you to come. After last night you must all be in a decline."

Andrea Zagaran looked ghastly. Her make-up failed to hide the tone of her skin, which, in the glow from the candles and lamps, was the color of the nicotine stains on her fingers. Her eyes held a haunted look and as she walked out onto the terrace, she staggered. Without her husband's supporting arm she would have fallen. Still the traces of beauty could not be totally obscured, the good bones, the generous mouth. And in those sad, frightened eyes there was also an intelligent awareness.

After the second or third round of drinks the animation that came from seeing people and having the first cocktail receded, like waves from a beach, leaving conversations stranded and people languishing. Now with the arrival of the Zagarans a change came over the party. It was as if Zagaran generated a sudden new electricity. His entrance was like a gust of wind, causing the conversation, like the candles in the hurricane lamps, to flicker and then to flame up once again.

Shelley watched him move across the room, seeing the beautifully tailored gabardine jacket, gray flannels, foulard tie and patent leather evening slippers. His white shirt was immaculate and on the breast pocket was a crimson Z, slanting, bold, imperious, like the Z she had received on the note with the roses. In his buttonhole was a matching rosebud.

Her blurred sense of futility vanished. She found herself sitting rigidly, fighting the impulse to rush to meet him. And when his eyes went past her to focus on Bebe Bruce, her heart gave a lurch of disappointment.

Taking another glass of champagne from Manassas Brown's tray, she realized that she had expected him to come immediately to her, that subconsciously she had been waiting for the moment when he would cross the room, lift her hand and make that abrupt, faintly foreign bow that from anyone else would seem affected. Quickly she sipped her wine. Her mouth felt dry, and she had a breathless sensation which, when he continued to ignore her, began to change to annoyance. She watched him turning his charm first toward the Duchess, then Samantha Sue, mouth curving into her predatory smile as she met his dark gaze, to Debby Darbyshire and even to Mrs. Dinwiddie, sitting down beside her and appearing to give her his full attention as she told him about Millicent's betrayal and listed the number of championships her horses had won on the show circuit that summer. Furious at herself for wanting him, Shelley deliberately sought sanctuary on the darkened terrace.

Tatine Zagaran was regaling the Martins and the Atwells with a description of the after-party. "I got Warlock and rode him into the pond," she announced.

"In your dress?" Sion Atwell exclaimed.

Tatine looked askance. "Of course not. I took it off."

"You mean you were naked?"

Tatine shrugged. "So was Lady Godiva. Honestly"—she grinned—"don't look so horrified. I had on a bikini. Otherwise I would have been rubbed raw."

"Did Warlock enjoy it?" Shelley asked.

"He loved the champagne. Afterward I poured half a bottle down his throat to warm him up. He took off across the lawn, cleared the garden wall, and I didn't get him stopped until we got to the stable. The after-party was a real gas," Tatine continued. "Nobody felt like going to bed so we moved the orchestra into the wing where the boys were staying. Hilaire Huntingdon picked a fight with Borgie, you know, the Italian count with the mustache. Bitsy Baldwin poured champagne on them to make them stop, but it didn't work. Pretty soon everybody was in on the act. Sandy Montague and Timmy Talbot began tossing pillows and blankets out the windows. Tommy Atwell went to the clinic with some teeth knocked out and Marty de la Tour got a cut on her arm when she put it through a pane of glass."

Shelley gazed at her in horror. "Why did you do it?"

Tatine stiffened. Her long eyes narrowed. "For kicks, what else?"

Shelley suddenly wanted Mike. She turned and saw him leave the table where he had been sitting with Debby Darbyshire and go to the bar.

"How about getting me a drink?" she asked, coming alongside him.

"You, who you? This one's for Debby. Shelley, *meine Frau*, you don't drink!"

"I do tonight." She sounded a little desperate. "I'd like some of that lovely bubbly, as the Duchess would say."

"All right," Mike said to David behind the bar, "champagne for Mrs. Latimer."

"Scotch and soda for me."

Shelley spun around. His expression was the one she had carried with her all day—wry, wary, amused.

"I thought you Southerners liked your liquor neat," he said as Mike poured additional water from the pitcher on the bar into his bourbon.

Mike turned slowly. "There are some things we like diluted."

"I see," Zagaran said, looking at Shelley. "Bloodlines, for instance."

"Now just a minute," Mike said. "In the first place, I'm from New Hampshire."

Zagaran gazed at him blandly. "How could I forget? It's your wife who's an FFV."

"Michael, where's my drinkie-winkie?" Debby Darbyshire called imperiously from the table where he had left her. She had gone off the wagon the night before and was obviously feeling no pain. Mike ignored the summons.

"Mr. Zagaran, I don't like your tone of voice."

Zagaran looked at the glass in Mike's hand. "Sometimes it's a mistake to combine alcohol with the wrong kind of altruism."

"Michael, sweetie," Debby called louder, "I'm tired of waiting for my drinkie-winkie."

Mike picked up the glasses. With deliberate politeness he said, "Mr. Zagaran, let's talk about it sometime. Perhaps you'd be interested in knowing what's going on."

"Michael," Debby called.

"This isn't the time," Mike concluded quickly.

The change in Zagaran's manner was as sudden as his smile. "Please don't misunderstand. I'm in favor of what you're doing and I'd like to know more about the county in which I live."

"You can always reach me at the *Sun*," Mike said, turning away.

When he had left, Zagaran asked, "The earrings? You're not wearing them."

"Not for a simple Sunday night supper."

With an abrupt gesture he reached up and touched the round white collar of her linen dress. "*Mädchen in Uniform*. Nobody can be that demure. And that hair. Tell me, do you ever let it down?"

Her head came up. She stared at him coldly. "What business is it of yours what I wear or how I feel?"

"Dinner is ready," Samantha Sue said, materializing beside him. She put her arm through Zagaran's. "Have you noticed the sunset? It's quite spectacular."

"Excuse me," Shelley said. "I seem to be blocking the view."

"It's a marvelous view." Lowering his voice, Zagaran said, "I see through you, Shelley."

"Come along, B.," Samantha Sue purred. "You're next to me."

Who in hell was *Mädchen in Uniform*? Shelley thought angrily. Amid the custom-made evening pants and vivid Puccis her white linen with its tailored lines and round collar seemed suddenly overly plain, drab. "Damn him," she whispered under her breath. "Damn him to hell!"

She found herself sitting next to Bones Black. The effects of the wine had been quelled by Zagaran's mocking words. She looked over at him, head bent to listen to what Samantha Sue was saying, giving her the benefit of that total concentration women seemed to find irresistible. Then abruptly he lifted his head and his eyes met hers. Shelley turned quickly to Bones and began talking. With diabolical intent, Samantha Sue had placed Cosy Rosy next to Bones. Fax Templeton and Debby Darbyshire, Millicent Black and Dash-Smythe sitting opposite, made up the remainder of the table. Mike, Shelley noticed, had been corralled to sit next to Mrs. Dinwiddie, and Polo Pete had placed Kevin Martin's wife, Marjorie, on his left. Andrea Zagaran, looking dazed and lifeless, was on his right. Samantha Sue could not have thought up a more incompatible seating arrangement. It was as if she had put all the names in a hat, then drawn them out without thought as to who was speaking or sleeping with whom.

Many of the people had been drinking all day. Starting with Bloody Marys at the Atwells', they had gone on to a long liquid lunch at Last Resort. Now, following the extended cocktail hour, the effects of the long holiday weekend were beginning to be obvious.

The iced vichyssoise had just been served when Andrea, looking as white as the soup, asked to be excused. After a whispered conversation with his hostess, Zagaran rose and followed her.

Shelley heard the front door slam shut. She felt as if her chair had just been pulled out from under her. So that was to be that, for tonight. She stared at her soup and wished she could vanish from the table like the puffs of smoke from the cigarettes. A splash startled her. Heads swiveled around.

Someone—it turned out to be Buddha's newly hired nursemaid, who was helping to serve—had tripped with a tray of dishes and fallen into the pool. Just as she was going down for the second time, one of Tatine's long-haired escorts dove into the debris of plates and silverware and retrieved the spluttering, terrified girl.

Mike was enjoying the rich chocolate dessert when Mrs. Dinwiddie spoke to him for the first time that evening.

"Mr. Latimer, I hope you're doing something about the Indians in that newspaper of yours." The Beast's tone was conversational but her eyes, intent on her husband, who was absorbed in talk with Bebe, were cold and watchful. She pushed back her chair. "If we're going to hunt tomorrow, we'd best be off. Good night, Mr. Latimer." Although Mike had met her numerous times, she still called him Mr. Latimer.

Quickly he got to his feet. "Let me," he said, helping her out of her chair.

The Duchess of Glencoe, a long ivory cigarette holder in one hand, a glass of champagne in the other, was saying to Mr. Dinwiddie, "Do tell me more about those darling hounds and their pedigrees."

"Dinny," the Beast said firmly, "time to go."

"Oh, no." Bebe made a gesture of dismay. "You cahn't take him away now. I've been so enthralled hearing about his books I quite forgot to swing with the cutlets." She gave Crocker Stephens, the headmaster of The Valley Day School, on her other side, a melting smile of apology. "Do forgive me."

"Come, Dinny," his wife repeated. "Shelley's husband has offered to see about the car."

Millicent Black, eyes narrowed, lips pursed, sat brutalizing the elegant petit fours and glaring at her husband, deep in conversation with Cosy Rosy, who, until Zagaran's ball, had been a close friend. Suddenly Millicent vanished beneath the pink damask tablecloth. Cosy Rosy, sitting opposite her, let out a shriek.

"She bit me!"

Millicent surfaced, calmly picked up her spoon and began methodically to eat her dessert.

"Bitch!" she observed to the table at large. "Imagine holding hands with my very own husband before my very own eyes!"

Cosy Rosy sat nursing a perfect set of toothmarks on the back of her thumb. "Dudley," she cried imploringly, "do something!"

"What would you like me to do?" her husband replied. "Cut off her head and send it to the Board of Health?"

Cosy Rosy gazed wildly around the table. Then abruptly she pushed back her chair and fled, tears coursing down her cheeks.

Millicent's extraordinary action was the turning point. As Mike said later, it was then that the bloodletting began. By the time dinner, with its assortment of wines, was over, Polo Pete had reached the stage of drunkenness that usually resulted in the terrier chase. Fortunately, Mrs. Dinwiddie had persuaded her husband to go home, for the masks and brushes hanging on the walls of the den were named after members of The Hunt. One, newly mounted, was called Beauty. The other, old and bedraggled, the Beast. Taking it down from the wall, Polo Pete dangled it under the terriers' noses. Then with whoops and yells he took off on a chase that led out onto the terrace and back, on and off sofas and chairs, knocking over Samantha Sue's priceless artifacts, glass-domed flowers and ashtrays. When Polo Pete could run no farther, the dogs were permitted to tear at the Beast's mask and further denude it of fur.

Subsiding into a chair, Polo Pete mopped his brow. "Boy," he shouted to Manassas Brown, "bring me a drink."

In the drawing room the rugs had been rolled back. Raymond Hoe, who had serenaded them at dinner with his guitar, was replaced by records on the hi-fi. Tatine and her friends were dancing. Millicent Black squared her chin. With her do-or-die, I'll-get-over-that-fence-if-it-kills-me-to-win-the-hunt expression, she grabbed two gourds from one of Samantha Sue's carefully arranged table decorations, kicked off her high-heeled shoes, unbuttoned her silk blouse and stuffed the gourds into the front of her Pucci.

Moving to the center of the floor, she began doing a wildly abandoned version of the Twist. What made the performance embarrassing was not the incongruity of the gourds, but that her gestures had the awkward self-consciousness of the amateur attempting to copy the professional. There was nothing of Tatine's graceful eroticism. Instead, Millicent's movements and undulations were curiously pathetic.

Mike had never before seen Millicent let down her arrogant guard. But now as he saw the deep uncertainty, the awareness of her lack of physical charm and the fear of losing her husband that lay behind her desperate bid for attention, he felt a sudden burst of pity.

One by one the younger people stopped dancing. Millicent was left alone on the floor. Roused from the stupor into which he had fallen after the terrier chase, Polo Pete grabbed an empty champagne bottle, thrust it between his legs and proceeded to become Millicent's partner. While Millicent gyrated with unrhythmic and self-conscious stiffness, Polo Pete made obscene gestures with his white-gloved hands.

Had he been asked beforehand, Mike would have guessed that if anyone misbehaved it would have been Tatine or Bebe Bruce. But when he saw the expression of disgust on Tatine's face as she gathered up her group and went to say good-by to Samantha Sue on the terrace, and the manner in which Bebe was fending off Fax Templeton's advances on the sofa pushed up against the wall, it was brought home to him that background, breeding and bitchery had nothing to do with a certain basic honesty, taste and innate decency that were either born in one or not. Mike admired Bebe's adroitness.

"Dahling"—carefully she removed Fax's hand from the front of her blouse—"have a cigarette? What? You don't smoke? Only cigars? Dear boy, you really should. It would give you something to do with your hands. What? Bad for the wind? Dear boy, surely you have enough to spare."

"Speaking of air"—Mike sat down beside them—"Fax, why don't you go out and get some?"

"Yes, dear boy, why don't you?" Patiently Bebe removed Fax's arm, which was stealing around the back of her neck. Then she opened her purse and extracted a platinum case. Two bees were engraved in the corner. The rest was covered with signatures. It was the famous cigarette case that Mike had heard about, the one on which Bebe had inscribed the names of her lovers.

"Damn"—she flipped it open—"I'm out."

"Honey," Fax said thickly, "you'll get c-c-c-cancer."

"Dear boy, I too read the Surgeon General's report." She snapped the case shut. "I also read the Kinsey report. From the evidence presented here tonight, it would appear that neither report has been taken to heart."

As she stopped speaking, the bottle that Polo Pete had been holding crashed to the floor. Pulling Millicent to him, he began chewing on the gourds. Millicent pushed him away. Reaching into the unbuttoned front of her long-sleeved shirtwaist, she removed the gourds. Polo Pete's flushed face went slack. Avidly he stared at the shriveled purpled nipples while Millicent, with the awful gesture of one unaccustomed to sensuality but in whom all shame and modesty had been dispelled, dangled her breasts lewdly before him. Suddenly Millicent staggered. Polo Pete clung to her. For an instant it appeared that they both might topple down onto the sofa.

Bebe stiffened. Mayfair and Melton-Mowbray went by the boards. "I'm getting angry, sweetie." Her eyes narrowed dangerously. "For Chrissake, get off my feet. If you two want to fuck," she cried in clarion tones, "why in the bloody hell don't you get it over with?"

Samantha Sue came from the terrace and took in the scene at a glance. Totally ignoring Millicent, the hostess marched up to her husband and hurled the contents of her champagne glass into his face. Then she reached onto a tray where Manassas Brown had placed the soiled glasses he'd collected and methodically began throwing them, one by one, at her husband's head.

Manassas and the other servants found sanctuary behind the bar. Arms crossed over their chests, they stood motionless, staring impassively into space. Mike was reminded of the three monkeys —see no evil, hear no evil, speak no evil.

"How could you"—Samantha Sue hurled the last glass—"in front of the servants!"

"S-s-s-starting to r-r-r-riot," Fax said, coming from the men's room. "T-t-t-time to h-h-h-horn 'em in."

Somewhat unsteadily he extracted his silver horn. Puffing out his cheeks, he managed a few muffled toots.

"Fax Templeton, you just shut up. Oooooo." Samantha Sue put her hands to her face. "My party is ruined."

The moon was almost full, bathing the fields in milk-white light. Ahead the long drive stretched like a silver ribbon.

"My God!" Shelley exclaimed. "What's that?"

A long-skirted figure, wearing high heels, was walking unsteadily down the center of the avenue.

"Millicent," Shelley breathed. "Millicent, walking home."

"Home? But it's eight miles."

"You know Millicent, once she makes up her mind."

After the incident at dinner—Mike later referred to it as Millicent's biting sarcasm—and Cosy Rosy's tearful departure, Bones had cornered Shelley by the pool.

"What will I do? She takes the dogs to bed with her and doesn't leave room for me. The other night when I got home late from the track one of those damned terriers bit me."

Shelley could hear the sounds of revelry coming from the living room. She longed to break away and find out what was going on.

"I'd leave her for good," Bones said plaintively, "I'd turf out tomorrow if it weren't for the kids."

Fax's horn put an end to Bones's self-pity. Together they appeared on the scene in time to hear Samantha Sue's final outcry.

Then Millicent finished buttoning her blouse, retrieved her shoes from under the sofa, picked up her sweater and skirt and ran from the house. Now she was marching down the center of the drive, ignoring Bones, who, his head thrust out the window of the new XKE, was pleading with her to be reasonable and get into the car.

"Fuck you," Millicent responded violently. "Fuck everybody. I'll walk down the middle of the Valley road and get myself killed. Then you'll be sorry."

"Sweetie," Bones called plaintively, "you're not shod for a couple of miles on the flat."

Stopping in the middle of the avenue, Millicent turned and faced her husband. In the glow from the headlights, her steel wool hair stood out wildly, her blouse was ripped and her skirt torn. "I'd rather die than ride with you," she cried dramatically.

"Sweetie"—Bones was abject—"I *had* to sit with her. Samantha Sue put us there."

"I'll bet you switched place cards." Millicent about-faced and began marching again. "Sport, this is the last straw," she shouted back over her shoulder. "You can have that bloody car, but I'll keep the horses and the dogs and the children."

"I'll bet she means it," Mike said. "In that order, too." Looking back, he saw a line of cars queued up behind them. "Want to let us past?" he called to Bones. "Maybe she'll go with us."

Bones obligingly pulled over to one side.

Mike drove up behind Millicent. "She's your friend," he said to Shelley. "See what you can do."

Shelley leaned out the window. "Millicent, please let us drive you home."

"No, thanks," Millicent choked. Her heel caught in a rut and she almost fell. "Damn it to hell, I've broken a heel."

"Sweetie," Bones's plaintive voice called from behind, "you'll never make the cattle guard."

Millicent paid no attention. Squaring her shoulders and setting her jaw as though about to pilot one of her grandfather's clipper ships around the Horn, she continued determinedly along the center of the driveway.

"Might as well stop," Mike said resignedly, switching off the engine.

"Will she or won't she?" Bones asked obliquely, standing by the door of the Jag.

"Will she or won't she leave you? Probably." Millicent's march was becoming unfunny. Mike wanted to go home and go to bed.

"I meant will she or won't she make the cattle guard," Bones answered.

"What g-g-g-goes on?" Fax Templeton called. He was in his pickup truck behind Bones's car. The night air had sobered him up. "The Duchess here wants to go h-h-h-home. I've got h-h-h-horses to get to a seven o'clock m-m-m-meet."

"You're bloody well right I want to get home," Bebe said. She was sitting very straight on the high front seat of the dusty pickup with "Rakish Stud" lettered on the door. "Besides, I'm out of cigarettes."

"I've got one." Bones handed his pack to Bebe. "Keep them.

We may have to wait awhile. Want to make book on whether she makes the cattle guard?"

"Who?" Bebe asked.

"My wife." Bones lit her cigarette. "For some reason she refuses to ride home with me."

"You don't mean it," Bebe answered brightly. "I cahn't imagine why. Can you, Fax?" Leaning back against the seat, she took a deep drag on her cigarette.

"What odds are you g-g-g-giving?" Fax asked, suddenly interested. Reaching into his pocket, he pulled out a crumpled bill.

"Even money," Bones answered. "Knowing mah wife, ah reckon she'll make it. She'll hike around for a piece, steam coming out of her nostrils, but then she'll be back."

"We can't sit here all night," Crocker Stephens called from behind them.

"What's going on up there?" asked another voice.

"For Chrissake, somebody's blocking the driveway."

A chorus of cries came from the cars lined up behind them.

"We're making book," Bones called back brightly, "on whether or not Millicent makes the cattle guard."

"T-t-t-tallyho!" Fax cried, tooting his hunting horn. "She's almost there."

"Is it safe to fasten my seat belt?" Bebe asked wearily.

"Now, D-d-d-duchess." Fax sounded rueful. "That's not f-f-f-fair. All this t-t-t-time I've kept my hands in my p-p-p-pockets."

"Hmmm," said Bebe.

Bones made a final try. "Sweetie, won't you please be sensible and get into the car?"

This decided Millicent. Tentatively she put her foot on the first round pipe. For an instant she stood, teetering. Then with the assured air of one used to negotiating all manner of obstacles in the wake of a pack of beagles, she sprang across the remaining pipes. Unfortunately, she'd forgotten her restraining skirt and remaining high heel. She landed on the last pipe off balance. Her foot twisted under her and with a cry of pain she went down.

Bones was at her side in a flash. Lifting her up, he carried her to the side of the road.

"Anything we can do?" Shelley asked as they drove alongside.

"I've sprained my ankle," Millicent moaned. "That new exercise boy from the track didn't show up this morning. I've got all those damned horses to exercise."

"I'll do the horses," Bones reassured her. "Let me carry you to the Jag and drive you home."

"J-j-j-just my l-l-l-luck," Fax said, returning to his pickup. "I should have t-t-t-taken that b-b-b-bet."

Mike shifted gears, and the station wagon picked up speed. Suddenly he started to laugh. "A quiet Sunday supper in the country!"

Shelley looked at him. At the memory of Millicent marching down the drive in the moonlight, she began to giggle. Then she was doubled over, laughing with him. Putting his arm around his wife, Mike drew her to him and drove home.

PART TWO
THE HUNT

PART TWO

THE LIGHT

SEVEN

SEPTEMBER was that time of imperceptible quickening, of golden mornings and wood smoke, of coolness and change that Shelley had always loved. Already the green of the gums, the oaks and maples had begun to turn, deepening to yellow. And here and there swatches of scarlet, dogwood and plumy sumac threaded the tweedlike tapestry of fields and woodlands, reaching to the hazy pastel-colored mountains that rimmed The Valley.

The hunters had been taken up out of the pastures. After their long, indolent summer spent under the willows bordering Buffalo Run, stamping lazily and switching their tails at the flies, they had been brought to the stable, groomed and shod prior to the fox-hunting season.

Cubbing began that Monday morning. Three mornings a week The Hunt would meet at daybreak. As the sun rose, burning away the glitter of cobwebs, clotting the luxuriant grass and spilling through the trees onto the woodland "rides," the young entry, the hound puppies, would be trained in the age-old sport of seeking out and running foxes. Of all times during the five-month season that opened officially in November, Shelley preferred this informal period when only the hardy regulars, the integral core of The Hunt, turned out.

The alarm jolted her to consciousness. Quickly, she rolled over and snapped it off. For a moment she lay rigid, her body long and flat beneath the bedclothes, hands tightly clenched at her sides, as if to beat off the fragments of fears, the tatters of anxieties already starting to fill her mind the way her grandmother's grab bag had been filled with bits and pieces of colored cloth, pointless and lacking in design. Memory of the Bufords' dinner the night before moved from the edge of her mind inward, like a snake lifting its head to strike. Deliberately she drove it back and yet despite her conscious effort Zagaran forced himself upon her, the dark eyes filled with that maddening insolence and mockery, the lifted eyebrow with its narrow scar.

It would be Zagaran's first time out with hounds. That killer mare, Black Magic, would accomplish what she had been unable to do, would shame and humble him. A rooster crowed. One of the hound puppies barked. Behind the black outline of trees the beginning light touched the horizon, filling Shelley with a sense of urgency. In one long sliding motion she got out of bed. Her bare feet against the board floor tingled with cold. Hastily she grabbed the underwear, jodhpurs and red turtleneck that she had laid out on Martha Washington's gilt chair before she went to bed. The night air was shiveringly cold. She debated whether or not to wear a sweater under her tweed coat and decided against it. When the sun rose up, the day would turn dry and hot.

In the light from the retreating moon that filtered through the tall windows, she bent over and laced up her high men's shoes. Furtively, she tiptoed into Cam's room. Lance, lying on the rug beside the bed, lifted his head. Shelley gave the mastiff a reassuring pat. Assured that Cam was safe, the dog lowered his great head to the floor and went back to sleep.

Illuminated by the dim glow of the night light, Cam lay on his side, his fists curled like rose petals. His enchanting profile clutched at her heart. She kissed him on the forehead and pulled the covers up around him. The child stirred, clasped the frayed Kitty-Kat closer, sighed and lapsed back into deep slumber.

In the vast subterranean kitchen, damp and chill now that the nights were turning cool, she plugged in the electric coffeemaker and set about preparing the oatmeal that Mike and Cam would eat when they arose. Waiting for the coffeepot's cheerful hiccuping to conclude along with the thickening of the cereal, she read the note Mike had left propped against the sugarbowl.

"Happy Hunting!! I'll stay with Cam until you get home. Shelley, I love you."

She stood stock still, holding the note. A twinge of guilt told her that in the absence of Suellen, she had no business leaving

Mike to tend Cam and the household while she pleasured herself in the hunting field. But *this* morning . . . The wind and pre-dawn darkness seemed to carry a message, telling her to hurry.

The grandfather clock chimed the hour of six. Its final notes echoed through the silent house. She imagined the fields and woodlands emerging into the pink dawn light, saw the eager members of the field gathered at the meet, sensed Lookout Light's excitement and felt a shivering anticipation.

Sudden energy filled her. Quickly she ate a bowlful of dry cereal and gulped the hot coffee. After scraping the remaining cereal into the dog's dish, she rinsed out the bowl and cup. Cam's turtles were in their box by the stove. The adventurous turtle made scraping sounds against the cardboard as he continued to struggle to escape. The other turtle, when she looked down at it, receded into its tightly closed shell. In the box filled with old newspaper and scraps of kindling for the wood stove, the speckled banty hen had laid an egg. Shelley picked it up. It was still warm. Cam or Mike could eat it for breakfast. She carried it to the stove.

Anxious to be away, she set the egg down carelessly, causing its fragile shell to crack and its contents to slither out onto a burner. Exasperated, she wiped it up and threw the shell fragments into the garbage pail. It took her a minute or two to extract her ragged tweed coat from the welter of raincoats and jackets in the hall closet and find her hunting cap and whip buried on the table be-neath the summer's accumulation of newspapers, hats, magazines and unpaid bills. Quickly, almost furtively, as though if she lin-gered any longer invisible hands would reach out and reel her back to the reality of breakfast, dishes and domesticity, she went out the door and closed it quietly behind her.

At the stable the sharp, clean, pungent smell, the sound of the horses' welcoming whinnies, the twitter of sparrows nesting in the beams overhead greeted Shelley. Bathed in orange light, the old dark varnished wood, the brass fittings on the doors, and the horses' coats gleamed.

Virginia City stood waiting, holding Lookout Light.

The short bandy-legged Negro with his soft voice and inordi-nate patience was a symbol of solace, something solid and un-changing and predictable, in the sense that the dogs and the horses and the woods creatures were predictable. That, and a strangely impersonal quality that was comforting, predictable like the bricks of Shelburn Hall, the great oaks and the mountains that by their very inanimateness were positive and undemanding. In the dim light his eyes and his face were the color and texture of the old and yet still supple and gleaming leather, the lines of bridles and saddles in the tack room that were his pride. Although Shelley knew him to be past seventy, he looked fifty. In face and bearing he was ageless, composed, intractable, unchanging—as much a part of her life as the misted blue mountains.

"Good morning, Miss Shelley," he said now, inclining his head. "Going to be a nice morning."

"Good morning, Virginia City." A wave of affection for him ran through her. Arthritic, tortured by what he termed his "misery" in damp weather, the old Negro's lifework was maintained with dignity and composure. Doing the work of three men, he kept the stable with a pride and diligence that made it the envy of The Valley.

"Virginia City," Shelley said, "you shouldn't have gotten up. I told you I'd tack up the colt. How is your misery?"

"Tolerable, Miss Shelley, tolerable." There was a note of apology in his voice. "I don't rightly know how much longer I can keep going. But long as I can hold together, Miss Shelley, I'm not gonna let you go out hunting on a horse that isn't clean." He ran his hand along the colt's glossy shoulder. "Took me 'bout an hour to knock out that summer dirt."

"If we can just get through this coming season . . ." Shelley's voice faded out. Every morning they had the same conversation. Grooms had come to help with the boarders and gone. None had been trustworthy. Virginia City went on coping alone.

"I wouldn't know how to manage without you," Shelley said sincerely.

"Long as I don't cord up I can do my work." A note of pride strengthened his voice. "Tell the truth, Miss Shelley, I prefer doing it myself to putting up with the kind of stable help that's around these days. Horses, they're different. They's all kinds and colors. This here Lookout Light, now . . ." As he led the colt out of the stall he continued talking to him, a soft, crooning flow of loverlike words to which the horse responded by grabbing the material of his old frayed riding coat at the shoulder and playfully tugging at it.

Lookout Light came quietly, confidently, a beautiful blood horse, his youthful gray coat still flecked with black. As the groom halted him at the mounting block, he raised his lovely head. For an instant he stood motionless, curved ears pricked, staring off into the predawn darkness, gazing at some imaginary object of the mind.

"He's feeling might good," Virginia City warned, as the colt pranced away from the mounting block. "Mind you sit chilly, Miss Shelley. Best horse we ever had on the place," he mused, as if to himself. "Better than The Goose. He could have won the old Shelburn Cup." He gave her shoes a final dusting with the rub rag he carried in his jacket pocket.

During the hours she had spent sitting in a corner of the colt's stall, talking softly, offering carrots and stroking his head and ears in order to win his confidence, regain his trust in humans that had been destroyed by the abuse he had suffered, she had come to love Lookout Light in a way she had never before loved another horse. When she began his schooling, starting from scratch, lunging him riderless over the cavalletti in the field to vanquish his fear of being hurt, she had been thrilled by his ability, the grace and elegance with which he moved and jumped.

Leaning forward, Shelley reassured him with her voice. The dark wood closed around her like a cloak. Stable and house vanished into the shadows. Inside Shelley, something gave. Tensions unknotted. Her anticipation rose like the colt's ears, rigid, alert to every rustle in the underbrush. With the scuffling of hoofs against dry leaves, the wind against her face, the sense of freedom and escape and aloneness built like the approaching sunrise, to an intensity of awareness that was almost tangible.

She nudged Lookout Light into a trot. Ears pricked, shying at the shadows, he moved with a lightness, a buoyancy that matched the rising of her heart, rising to meet the morning.

In The Valley, The Hunt was as integral a part of life as the food that came from the supermarket. It was, in fact, the reason for The Valley's way of life, a way of life that had, since plantation days, been made easy and effortless by abundant land and cheap labor.

The Hunt was as exclusive as the Halter Club. Only a handful were permitted to wear the green collar and raised buttons. Shelley was one of the few whose buttons dated back to the original days of whalebone. The current buttons that had been presented to Debby Darbyshire, Millicent Black and the other large contributors and landowners were brass. Fax was fond of saying that although he was the sixth generation of Templetons to live on the home place, he had not received his buttons officially until he had been made Field Master.

In those pre-World War II days, The Hunt reached its peak. Most of the men wore scarlet and the women rode sidesaddle. There were second horses, which grooms produced when The Hunt paused for lunch, eaten from the old boxlike wooden station wagon that carried each family's assortment of food and drink. Then, while the staff kept hounds packed in and to one side, the men and women relieved themselves in the woods (the women taking much longer due to the voluminous complications of their sidesaddle skirts and imported woolen underwear).

In Shelley's childhood, the foxhunting people had truly loved and understood the sport. They gave it flair, dignity, purpose and pageantry. They believed sport necessary to keep the proper balance between man and machine. They believed the same qualities that made a first-class horse and hound were essential in a first-class man—honesty, determination, courage, drive. How often her father had intoned, pounding the dining-room table for emphasis, "Foxhunting demands courage and a proper understanding of nature and animals, and it's the only sport in the world that cannot be commercialized."

A true autocrat of the hunt breakfast table, Cameron Fitzgerald maintained that you could tell what a man was by the way he rode across country, and that this was more important than his money. Thus, he permitted only true lovers of the sport to hunt, and then by invitation only. In some instances, those who had hunted a season and been found wanting were not on the mailing list for fixture cards the following year. In other cases, hardworking farmers and local residents unable to contribute toward the paneling fund were invited because of their principles and love of sport. Honor, a certain code, manners, were of great concern to Cameron Fitzgerald.

"One of the troubles with the world," he once told Shelley, "is that everybody is trying to push the other fellow out of the way, get ahead of him. There's a right way and a wrong way to do this. You can wait your turn and get there just as quickly, or you can run overtop of the other fellows. Anybody who overruns my hounds or deliberately cuts another off at a fence, hasn't a right to be in the hunting field. It's the same in everything you do. In order to earn respect, you must first respect others as individuals. Big or little. The fellow with five acres is just as important to The Hunt as the landowner with five hundred. Those without respect for the fox or the hounds or their horses or The Hunt's landowners will find that pretty soon the landowners will close their land and there won't be any for The Hunt to ride over."

Like all great masters of foxhounds, Cameron Fitzgerald was a diplomat. Hardly a day passed that he did not visit the farmers and country people, saying a word here, a word there.

In this way there grew a bond between the country people and the foxhunters, a bond strengthened by the customary Christmas visits to each homestead, where the Master sat at the kitchen table partaking of holiday cheer and chatting with the farmer and his family about country topics. As a child, Shelley had loved traveling the back roads and byways to the cheerful farm kitchens redolent with the smells of holiday baking, followed by the cold drives home behind one of the old hunters pulling the pony cart in the frosty starlit night, her father's great bear rug pulled up under her chin.

After Cameron Fitzgerald's death, The Hunt had gone downhill. Shelley had taken over as Field Master. When she left Shelburn to go to the track, the Dinwiddies had become joint masters, running it arbitrarily as they pleased. Panels had fallen down and been replaced by wire, and no money had been raised to rebuild the fences. Finally they retired, turning over the mastership to Fax Templeton.

Fax made a colorful and hard-riding MFH, but he was not reliable. Often when he went out of town for a racing weekend or to a party given on Long Island by one of his old girls, Shelley would receive a long distance call on Monday morning, saying he had missed his ride home or the plane he had intended to take, and would she cover for him as Field Master. There were times when this was very inconvenient and meant a frantic series of telephone calls and changes in plans. Yet because of The Hunt, her heritage and feeling for it, she had never yet failed to appear, dressed and on time, to take over the field.

There was another difficulty with Fax. He paid no attention to management problems. Hunt stables and kennels had fallen into disrepair and no new blood had been introduced to the famous pack.

Now The Hunt was very different from what it had been in Cameron Fitzgerald's day. Many of the members were new people from Geneseo and Lake Forest, Connecticut and California. Gone were most of the farmers who had owned the land traversed by The Hunt. In their place had come an artificiality, a caring more for appearances and the social aspects than the sport itself. And somehow the atmosphere in the field had changed. Shelley could not explain what it was that she felt. She knew only that some element, some intangible, had been introduced that had done away with the old joyous attitude of sport for sport's sake.

Ahead rose the chimneys of Ballyhoura. As she turned onto the drive, the gathering light of dawn filled the wood with wraithing mist. She could feel the hairs prickle along her forearms. At moments such as this, she could well understand why the colored people said that Ballyhoura was haunted. It was as though any moment now Sean Shelburn, his hunting horn around his neck, his face streaked with blood, would come riding out of the mist.

As though he, too, sensed a supernatural being, the colt pranced nervously, casting his head from side to side, snorting at the shadows.

Suddenly the silence was shattered by a high, shrill neigh. As she moved from the dark wood into the growing morning light, Shelley saw Simeon Tucker standing in the stableyard holding Black Magic. The mare was alternately pawing the ground and trying to pull away from the groom.

"Whoa there, mare," Simeon was saying. "Whoa there."

So he really is going to try and hunt her, Shelley thought, and suddenly, for some unaccountable reason she could not define, she no longer wanted to see Zagaran made a fool of by the horse.

Nobody, so far as she knew, had ever hunted Black Magic. Bred by T. Patterson Gibson, she was one of the erratic Witchcraft strain that had produced Gypsy King, winner of the triple crown, as well as Voodoo, currently a leading contender for the Kentucky Derby. Magic, however, was a notorious rogue. Ruled off the race track as a two-year-old—she had deliberately savaged and seriously injured an assistant starter—she had been sold to a succession of owners, all of whom had given up trying to subdue her deliberate viciousness. Polo Pete had been unaware of her reputation when he had bought her. Because of her beauty and breeding, he considered that he had made a fine bargain. When she went over backwards with him and crushed his leg, laying him up for six months, Polo Pete ordered her shot and sent to the hounds. Story Jackson heard about the mare and, hoping to be able to sell her, had gone and taken her back to his barn. The fact that Zagaran had bought her seemed an indication of how little he knew about horses.

Dooley Wright, the blacksmith, had told Shelley that Magic had savaged Tom Mellick, the groom Zagaran had first hired off the mountain. The man retaliated by sticking a pitchfork into the mare's chest. Luckily he'd managed to get out of the stall before she killed him. There had been several grooms after that, none of whom would handle Black Magic. Finally Simeon, who loved and understood horses, agreed to the job.

"Simeon has all them children," Virginia City told Shelley. "Reckon he needs the money Mr. Zagaran's willing to pay." He rolled his eyes. "Not easy to get help at Ballyhoura, not with all them hants roamin' the woods. Simeon says the only reason they have *any* help is because Mr. Zagaran is willing to pay a heap of money."

Shelley rode past the stable into the open space before the great house, where cars and trailers were already pulling up.

In that gentle countryside the jumble of towers, turrets and crenellations was as famous as The Hunt. Early General Grant Gothic, somebody once called it. But although lacking in architectural symmetry, age, history, legend and its own heavy incongruity had instilled it with glamour. In The Valley it was a place that was always pointed out to strangers.

Now it was like a grande dame who has had her face lifted, her eyebrows plucked, and presents a new façade to the world. The grounds had been landscaped, the Ballyhoura Oak patched with tar and cement, and the rail fence that separated the lawns from the Cup course rebuilt. Somehow its shaggy charm, its fascination had, like the ivy that clung to its gray walls, been eliminated, leaving only a gaunt, somber edifice that seemed strangely lifeless, like a child's cardboard castle.

Shelley glanced around. In spite of the late night before, the regulars would not miss hunting. Many had already arrived. On Opening Day and during the rest of the season they would be immaculate in black or scarlet coats, clean light-colored breeches and polished black boots. But this early in the season nobody wore formal attire. The young housewives with children and ponies to get ready wore blue jeans or frontier pants and cowboy boots, turtlenecks or open-necked shirts.

There was Debby Darbyshire with her hard leathered look and her graying hair crammed carelessly under her hunting cap. Wearing corduroy pants tucked into cowboy boots and a quilted jacket, she was on her old hunter just out of the field.

"Filthy!" She slapped the horse's flank and a cloud of dust arose. "Those damn niggers. That no good Harper hasn't turned up since last Tuesday. And Roosevelt left me with forty-eight head of Angus to feed and went to work for the Schligmans. They've gone in for beef cattle and are hiring everybody's help away from them. Roosevelt said he couldn't turn down such a good-paying job with a wife and eight kids to feed. I told him it served him right for having so many kids." She paused to light a cigarette.

Sion Atwell, astride one of her husband's quarter horses, rode up. She had on blue jeans and a cowboy hat. "I'm supposed to be moving cattle, but I couldn't bear to miss the first day of cubbing."

"I was just telling Shelley the Schligmans are ruining the labor market," Debby said, blowing smoke. "I forgot, Shelley, that they're friends of yours. They were sitting in your pew yesterday. Still, I think it's a crime when people like that move in and start changing the status quo."

Shelley had never before felt the need to defend the Schligmans, but the bitterness in Debby's voice, a bitterness she felt was somehow directed at her, compelled her to do so. "I think Katie and Augie are good people. Katie volunteered to run the Red Cross Blood Bank—you know what a thankless job that is—and is doing the church rummage sale."

"They don't know a thing about foxhunting," Sion said. "They've been riding in Story Jackson's show ring all summer, 'learning to hunt' is the way Katie puts it."

Debby exhaled smoke. "Hell, they can't even spell horse, let alone ride one."

Shelley felt a sudden distaste. She had never bothered to analyze the hunting people or dig beneath the surface. It was as though instinct warned her that if she did so her entire world might crack, shatter like the banty egg she had broken that morning.

Determined not to let her joy in the morning be spoiled, she rode over to Betsy Baldwin. Betsy was on an old polo pony and accompanied by three of her children, including five-year-old Spunky on a leadline.

"Morning, Shelley," she called out. "Spunky, try not to let the pony get under my feet. Lovely morning, isn't it? Buttons, watch out for hounds. The pony might kick."

Cosy Rosy and Millicent Black, trailers hitched behind their cars, arrived simultaneously. Cosy Rosy, who was ahead, tried to turn in the space in front of the stable and head out again. Unable to make the turn, she was forced to stop in the middle of the circle. Behind her, Millicent sat stonily at the wheel of her Rolls, ignoring her once best friend.

"Oh, dear," Cosy Rosy cried helplessly, lifting her bandaged hand from the wheel, "I don't know how to back the damn thing."

Shelley dismounted. She turned to Buttons Baldwin. "Hold him a minute, will you please?"

She walked past Millicent.

"Hi—I thought you sprained your ankle."

"I promised Merry I'd take her hunting." Millicent's face, wreathed in smoke from her cigarette, looked drawn. "I taped my ankle with an Ace bandage. I can ride the old lead pony sidesaddle. If that idiot would get out of the way, we could unload."

Shelley glanced at six-year-old Merry, sitting tensely by her mother. "Hello, Merry," she called. "Got your new pony out this morning?" The little girl's face puckered. Her fist clenched around her whip. Unable to speak, she nodded to Shelley in reply.

Shelley thought of the day Merry had fallen off the show pony Millicent had bought at Devon and broken her wrist. "Serves her jolly well right," Millicent had said. "Now, maybe she'll learn."

But the little girl hadn't learned. Obviously she was still terrified. Why couldn't Millicent be honest, Shelley thought suddenly, and admit Merry wasn't the reason she had come hunting. The reason, Shelley realized with new insight, lay in something deeper, as though paradoxically by being her most masculine she could in some curious way compete and prove herself as a woman.

Shelley slid behind the wheel of Cosy Rosy's Scout. The sound of kicking came from the trailer. "Dudley's new horse." Cosy Rosy looked pale and strained. "He's just off the track. What a morning." She adjusted her hunting cap on her honey-colored hair. "It's Jennifer's last chance to hunt before school. Shelley, can you back the bloody thing so I can get him out before he shakes the trailer to pieces?" She glanced at the bandage around her hand. "I feel so awkward."

Shelley skillfully managed to straighten out the trailer and park on one side of the drive.

"About time," Millicent said loudly, driving past to turn her trailer around. "I never knew a more helpless female."

"Never mind." Shelley grinned at Cosy Rosy. "Her bite is worse than her bark!"

Millicent was directing Dixon, her groom, and Merry in unloading the horses. Accompanied by a constant flow of advice— "Now, Merry, don't let your pony run up on other horses. Merry, for God's sake, don't let him eat. Merry, fix your girth."— the tearful child was finally mounted on the striking-looking bay show pony. "For God's sake, get out of the way of that horse!" Millicent cried, limping over to a stump in order to mount Bones's lead pony. "Some people haven't any sense," she muttered darkly, glaring at Cosy Rosy. "Taking a horse like that out hunting with kids." Throwing away her cigarette, she ground it out with her good leg, encased in blue jeans and a cowboy boot. Still muttering to herself, she managed to mount and put her injured leg, in its horse bandage and sneaker, over the sidesaddle pommel.

Meanwhile, Cosy Rosy was trying to mount. "Shelley," she cried frantically as her horse continued to circle and lash out at the ponies, "please hold him so I can get up. He's never seen hounds before."

"Calm down, old fellow, nobody's going to hurt you." Shelley spoke soothingly to the horse. At last Cosy Rosy was in the saddle, adjusting her girth. Letting the saddle flap fall back, she took her racing bat out of her mouth. "This maniac will probably kill me." She finished buttoning the crash helmet Dudley had bought her after her last concussion and picked up the reins. Grimly she added, "Millicent would be delighted."

Shelley continued patting the race horse. "Relax, why don't you?" She was not sure whether she meant the horse or Cosy Rosy.

"I haven't had any sleep." Her small Valentine-shaped face, with its candybox features, tiny tip-tilted nose and mouth that parted to show small white teeth set apart, crumpled, like Merry Black's. "Dudley's furious at me. He refused to come hunting. I don't care about Bones. Honestly, Shelley, I don't. But he keeps following me around, telling me those things . . ."

"My father maintained that the outside of a horse was good for the inside of a man, but there are times when tennis or swimming or some other sport that doesn't require so much money and preparation would be more sensible." She gave the nervous horse a final pat. "Rosy, you shouldn't keep riding rank horses and breaking yearlings and getting those falls."

The girl smiled at her gratefully. "He'll be all right once he settles. You're a dear, Shelley. Thank you."

"Well, what do you know," Debby said. "There's Polo Pete. I could have sworn he'd never make it."

Since the fall when he had broken his leg, Polo Pete had carried a shooting stick instead of a cane. Taking it from Malakai, his chauffeur, he started toward the mounting block where Roy, his groom, stood holding his big brown hunter. After the hectic activity of the night before, his limp seemed more pronounced than ever. He wore dark glasses and two Band-Aids. His green stock looked as if he had had a wrestling match with it and the stock had won.

"He looks gimpy," Debby commented. "Probably timber shins from leaping the furniture."

"I'll bet his head hurts worse than his shins," Sion Atwell commented as she rode up on her chestnut.

The sky was filled with pink-gray dawn light. Mist hung over the valleys, a silver sea above which the higher land and trees rose like islands.

The silence and strangeness of the nighttime woods were displaced by the noise and commotion of the field's arrival, in cars and horse trailers and astride their hunters, hacking along the drive in gaily chattering groups.

"Where is our host?" Cosy Rosy asked as she passed Mrs. Dinwiddie. She lifted her bandaged hand to brush away a fly. As she did so, it was obvious that she wore nothing underneath her V-necked polo shirt. The year before, her horse had stepped in a groundhog hole and given her a hard fall, knocking her out. The men in the field, who normally refused to stop for anybody, had pulled up and rallied round. Bones Black had unwound her stock to give her air and discovered, to the fascination of the field, that she did not wear a shirt or underwear under her heavy black hunting coat.

"Damned if I know how she does it," Debby Darbyshire commented. "Did you ever try to ride a horse without a bra?"

"I understand Mr. Zagaran will be hunting with us today," the Beast said, changing the subject as William, her new groom, carefully put her up on her aged bay hunter and began adjusting the sidesaddle skirt of her blue habit which Busvine had made for her some forty years before. Although faded now, and shabby, it retained its original elegance. Throwing her husband a resigned look as he stood in his beautiful tweeds, leaning on a cane and talking to Bebe Bruce, the Beast picked up her reins and rode off with Debby.

Bebe seemed oblivious of the looks the women gave her. Wearing jodhpurs, close-fitting tweed jacket and hunting cap, false eyelashes and the tiny gold bees that were her trademark fastened in her pierced ears, the Duchess was the radiant point of the men circled around her.

As Shelley walked back to collect her horse, she noticed Staunton, the Schligmans' groom, riding up the drive. Staunton was a Valley fixture. Years before he had been brought from England by Sidney Merrywood, who had been trainer for the Shelburn Stables. When Sidney retired to his cottage at Priscelly Gate, Staunton had been employed by T. Patterson Gibson. Unable to resist the lure of higher wages, he went to work for the Schligmans. Staunton, always correct in black coat and bowler, considered himself a distinct cut above the other grooms, Negroes and young white boys from the Free Zone. Now Shelley saw that he was leading Augie Schligman's roan and Katie's mare, recently bought from Story Jackson's show stable for a fancy price. Both horses' manes and tails were braided with green rosettes. As Staunton reined them in to speak to Roy, the Bufords' man, his face was rigid with disapproval. "I told Mr. Schligman it wasn't proper to braid during the cubbing season. But he said the Madam wanted her mare's hair done." Staunton rolled his eyes skyward. "Did you ever? Next you know I'll be running a bloody hair shop instead of a stable."

The groom's indignation, sparking the snobbery that cracked his veneer as a well-trained servant, implied the Schligmans were not the Valley type. Augie was self-made and made no bones about it. He was as round and heavyset as one of the barrels in his Milwaukee brewery. Katie, or Mama as her husband called her, had starred in *Peg o' My Heart* on the road and been in light opera. She was big-breasted, with bleached blond hair, too much make-up and no eyebrows. Community Brown, who had helped out until the Schligmans acquired their own staff, reported that it took Mrs. Schligman a good forty-five minutes every morning to put on her eyebrows, and if her hand trembled it took longer.

At first she made timid overtures to Mrs. Dinwiddie and the other Valley matrons she met at the supermarket. "She invited me to tea," the Beast commented. "Did you ever? I never heard of the Schligmans except on television when they keep interrupting my news program with that awful jingle about beer, beer, beautiful beer, beer of the evening, beer of good cheer."

After the Schligmans bought several horses and put Fax in charge of their stable, the Master had been duty bound to put them up for membership in The Hunt. A recent meeting of the board had been devoted to the pros and cons. The pros had been financial. Augie, who, as Fax put it, looked as if he'd learned to ride on one of his cart horses in the brewery, was willing to pay the stipulated thousand-dollar membership and give a five-figure contribution to the paneling fund. This meant that the Schligmans would have to be included in Hunt activities.

"It's not that they're Jewish," Mrs. Dinwiddie insisted. "It's just that they've put up that awful scrolled sign saying 'The Schligmans' and have painted everything pink."

The discussion went on until Togo Baldwin brought out the past year's financial statement and pointed out that The Hunt was a good five thousand dollars in arrears and that if the Schligmans were not accepted, each steward would have to dig down into his or her pocket and make up the difference.

The following week the Schligmans and their daughter Judy received an invitation to become members of The Hunt.

Now, at sight of Augie Schligman emerging from his pink Cadillac, those assembled along the drive looked stunned. Although the morning was already becoming hot and airless, Augie Schligman wore black boots, heavy hunting breeches and a scarlet coat. His white stock was correctly tied and aside from his high silk hat, which he had on backwards with the ring for the hat guard hanging down over his forehead, he was turned out in full fox-hunting kit, as though for the formal opening meet in November, rather than for the first day of casual cubbing.

Katie also wore formal hunting clothes, black coat, white stock, canary-colored breeches and gleaming black boots. Her face was elaborately made up, penciled brows, blue eye shadow and carefully applied rouge which made two round pink spots high on her cheeks, which fear, combined with the early hour, had turned ashen. Her blond hair was coiled into an elaborate platinum bun that tipped her derby forward over her nose. But the thing that stopped all conversation and brought gasps from the Hunt members was that her new black hunting coat was decorated with The Hunt's buttons and green collar.

"Well, I never," the Beast managed finally.

"All that make-up!" Debby Darbyshire exclaimed. "She must have to chip it off with a chisel."

Shelley saw the smile leave Katie Schligman's face as one by one the women turned away from her.

"Buttons!" Mrs. Dinwiddie exclaimed, looking down from the top of her tall bay. "My dear, you must know that only people who have hunted with The Hunt for years and years have a right to wear them!"

"We didn't know." Katie's blue eyes filled with tears. "Nobody told us."

Augie put a protective arm around his wife's shoulders. "The man from England who came to the Fox in the High Hat asked Mama what hunt she hunted with when he took the measurements for her coat. She told him *The* Hunt, and he went ahead and put on the buttons and the collar."

"I assumed he knew what he was doing," Katie added sadly.

"Mrs. Schligman, I think you look marvelous," Shelley said quickly. "Mrs. Dinwiddie, doesn't she look well? The coat is beautifully cut."

The glance the Beast threw Shelley was as hard and cold as the diamond that flashed on Katie's finger when she took off her string gloves to grope for her handkerchief.

"My dear Shelley, you of all people should know what appointments are correct."

Katie tried to smile. "Maybe it would be better if we didn't go hunting."

"We can't give up now," Augie whispered as the Beast rode off. "Come on, Mama, don't let them get you down. Up dog and at 'em!"

Shelley, smarting from the Beast's reprimand, looked at her watch. "Five after. Fax is late as usual. There's the hound truck coming now."

Not since Sean Shelburn's time had the hounds been kenneled at Ballyhoura. Cameron Fitzgerald had bought a farm beyond Shelburn where the Hunt horses and the hounds were kept, to be roaded or trucked to meets. Now the hounds tumbled out of the green-painted hound truck, with its cagelike wire sides, like spaghetti spilling from a strainer. A black and white sea of waving sterns was presided over by Tom Pope, the Old Huntsman.

"I see they're taking out the bitch pack," Millicent said.

"All those dear little hounds," said Cosy Rosy.

"Yeah," Millicent replied dryly, "with their tits dragging along the ground."

In the great days of The Hunt, three dozen horses were kept up during the season for the staff and guests. The majority were perfectly matched and turned-out grays. Every effort had been expended to hire the best staff available. Cameron Fitzgerald's huntsman had been John Pope, who had come from the Free Zone, to whip-in for Sean Shelburn. When he died, as the result of a fall one day when his horse stepped in a hole, his oldest son, Tom, carried the horn. Then but a boy in his teens, he had gone on to the realms of hunting greatness, reaching his peak in the thirties, when his hounds defeated some of the best packs in America at the National Foxhound trials.

The previous spring, following the fall that had broken his shoulder, some of the stewards had argued that Tom should be replaced by the Young Whip. Shelley, recalling the great runs of her youth behind the Old Huntsman, had argued that it would break his heart to be pensioned off and that he should be permitted to hunt hounds for another season.

"I know he's slowed down," she argued. "Who wouldn't after forty years? Still, there's nobody who can hunt hounds the way he can. Let him continue for another season and train the Young Whip."

Backed up by Fax, R. Rutherford Dinwiddie and some of the other old-timers, her arguments had won out. Thus the Old Huntsman remained, a little heavier, less supple, wearing his worn velvet cap, patinaed with age, carrying his cherished cow's horn supported by a leather thong tied around his neck.

Anticipating his commands, Richard Doyle, the Young Whip, stood to one side flicking straying puppies with the thong of his hunting whip, calling out, "Pack in there, Bomber. Get along, Bouncer."

The Young Whip, Shelley observed, was tall and well built, with the lean, hard-muscled look that came from a life spent in the open. She was thinking how well he looked on a horse when she glanced around and saw the Master.

Fax was riding The Saint. The horse had won most of the major steeplechases on the timber circuit. Fax had retired him and kept him now as a hunter. Tall and leggy, with a long back, narrow, veined head and long flowing tail that My Boy Hambone kept well brushed and full, he resembled a Herring painting.

On a horse Fax was as dashing and picturesque as he was in a ballroom. Although his drawl was slower and his compliments more flowery, indicating that he had already had a nip or two from his silver flask, My Boy Hambone had seen to it that his tie was carefully knotted, his breeches and field boots clean, and he wore a yellow rosebud in his lapel. After telling Shelley how well she looked, how well Lookout Light looked, how well they both looked together, he whipped out a liquor-soaked cigar.

"Ride all day and drink all night," he announced jubilantly, sticking the cigar in the corner of his mouth. "Shelley, honey, that's living. I keep my boots alongside my bed, where I can jump up and pull them on. All I ask of the good Lord above is to be allowed to die with my boots on." He broke off, staring. "Unless my eyes deceive me, that's Millicent. Ah declare, that lil ole gal is made of iron, like one of those pipes she fell over."

As though he hadn't seen any members of the field for months instead of but a few hours beforehand, he told Mrs. Dinwiddie that he hoped she had summered well, asked her husband if he had seen any foxes in his woods, and nodded and spoke to all the children. After helping Bebe Bruce onto the young thoroughbred which My Boy Hambone had been schooling during the past months, adjusting her stirrup leathers and tightening her girth, he remounted and faced the assembled field.

As Shelley had often remarked, when Fax was on a horse he never stuttered. As he himself explained it, "Out there in front, aboard The Saint, I feel like a king."

Now, in spite of the nips he had already taken from his flask, he addressed the people gathered before him, speaking clearly and distinctly.

"Countryside's so dry, I'd appreciate it if you'd not smoke." With an elaborate gesture he tossed his cigar onto the drive. "We'll try to be as careful as we can and meet as early as possible until the first killing frost. Rosy"—he swung The Saint out of the way of the race horse—"can't you keep your horse from trampling the rhododendrons? As I was saying, the countryside's mighty dry. We don't want any fires blamed on The Hunt."

He signaled to the Old Huntsman, who started along the drive. The riders fell into line behind the Master, and The Hunt moved off, past the stone entrance posts fronting the stableyard surmounted by the carved stone foxes with François Villon's definition of the chase that Sean Shelburn had inscribed beneath them: "Image of war without its guilt."

He's not coming, Shelley thought relievedly. She realized that she had been deliberately submerging the hope that she would see him. This was combined with the growing fear that he would appear wrongly turned out and be made an object of ridicule, like Augie Schligman. Pity, hers or anyone else's, was something she could not associate with Zagaran.

Then she heard the sound of hoofs striking the cobbles in the stableyard, and in the growing morning light she saw the man and the black mare.

Zagaran, she noticed at once, was a dazzling contradiction of her preconceived idea. His ratcatcher was immaculate. He wore a bowler hat, a well-cut coat of reddish-brown tweed, tan breeches and superbly fitted and polished brown boots. While Simeon made motions with his rub rag and kept up his chant, the mare permitted Zagaran to approach. Suddenly, with a quick, decisive motion, Zagaran placed his hands on the saddle and before the groom could give him a leg up, vaulted onto the mare's back.

"Whoa there, hawse," Simeon cautioned. "Whoa there."

"She'll be all right," Zagaran commanded. "Let her loose."

The groom dropped the mare's reins and jumped aside.

"I thought he was joking when he said he was going to hunt Black Magic," Debby Darbyshire said.

As she spoke, the mare burst into an explosion of striking legs and gleaming hoofs. Within seconds, she was a whirling black savage, a killer. The stableboys clustered in the entrance hurled themselves out of the way as the horse came at them, swerving at the last minute, almost striking the wall that surrounded the cobbled yard.

Zagaran rode her like a rodeo cowboy or a Cossack. The more furiously she bucked and twisted and sought to dislodge him by running him up against the wall, the better he seemed to enjoy it. The smile, the triumphant glitter in his eyes, never left his face.

Then as suddenly as it had begun, it was all over. Black Magic stood motionless, head down, sides heaving. Zagaran threw his right leg over the pommel and dismounted.

"Take her," he said to Simeon.

"I thought you were going to hunt her," the groom replied, looking confused.

"I was, but some business has come up. I'm flying to New York."

He gazed at Black Magic standing quietly, passively. Then without looking back or at the riders on the driveway, he walked quickly toward the house.

"Whoa there, mare, whoa . . ." Simeon continued his monotonous singsong as he led the mare back to her stall.

"Well, I never!" commented Mrs. Dinwiddie.

"Now that little performance is over," Fax said dryly, "let's go foxchasing." Shelley let out her breath in a long sigh. She had not realized she'd been holding it.

Shaking their heads wonderingly, the field moved on along the drive. Shelley and the Schligmans brought up the rear. Staunton followed, his mouth pursed in a thin, disapproving line.

"I don't want to go hunting," Katie cried, taking a stranglehold on the reins. The nervous mare began to throw her head.

"Don't take such a tight hold," Shelley cautioned, wishing Story had sold the beginning rider a quieter, more suitable mount, but the dealer liked nothing better than taking on newcomers, especially Yankees, and sticking them for high-priced horseflesh. "Let your reins go."

"I can't," Katie wailed. "If I do I'll never find them again."

"Be a sport, Mama," Augie said. He was on the big roan heavyweight that Story had imported from Ireland. "It'll be okay once we get started."

"I took two tranquilizers this morning," Katie said, "and some orange juice. Then I threw up."

The horses were herdbound. As Augie rode off, Katie's mare whirled to follow her stablemate. Katie's face was ashen, her derby was askew and a wisp of blond hair had come loose from its restraining net. "Dad, wait," she cried tearfully. "Wait for me!"

Simeon and the mare had gone back to the stable when Tatine Zagaran rode out on Warlock. Dressed in her faded Levi's and turtleneck, her flaming hair hanging in a ponytail from beneath her velvet cap, she was as thin, as graceful, as lovely as the morning light. She stopped her horse to let Shelley and the Schligmans ride by.

"Hi, Mrs. Latimer," she called gaily. "Mr. and Mrs. Schligman. Glad to see you made it."

"They say my clothes are all wrong . . ." Katie could not go on.

"Mama's upset," Augie said quickly. "We looked at pictures of The Hunt. We thought we had the right gear."

"I think you both look great," Tatine consoled. "Don't let the bitch pack get you down." She glanced at Shelley. "Sorry, Mrs. Latimer. I guess you think I shouldn't have said that."

"No," Shelley said. "Well, yes—" She felt torn in all directions, the peace and mindlessness of the morning, of riding her horse had gone, along with Zagaran's extraordinary performance and departure. "I hear your mother's sick."

Tatine shrugged. "No more than usual."

"Your father put on quite a show."

Tatine's worldly-wise green eyes gazed into hers. Then looking away, she said bitterly, "He should have been an actor. He digs drama." She put up her hand. "Listen! I hear hounds!"

Aware that the horses ahead were getting away from him, Augie's roan began to plunge. The big man was very unsteady in the saddle. At each lunging motion he became more out of position. Katie's horse, determined not to be separated, followed suit. "Dad," she called desperately. "Don't leave me, Dad."

At that moment hounds burst out of the wood. In full cry they raced across the jeweled meadow, past the great house and the Ballyhoura Oak and down the long sweep of hill. The fences of the Shelburn Cup course rose from the green valley floor beyond which gleamed Zagaran's plane, parked on the newly constructed runway.

"Please go ahead," Katie urged between clenched teeth.

"Yes, Miss Shelley," Staunton agreed, his face impassive. "I'll take care of the Madam."

"You do that," Shelley ordered. "Come on, Tatine, looks as if we might have some fun."

When they were out of earshot, Shelley said, "That was kind of you."

"That old biddy Dinwiddie thinks she controls creation," Tatine answered. "I'm surprised she doesn't have everyone who comes into The Valley vetted beforehand."

As hounds swept on toward the deepening golden light of the dawn-filled morning, Lookout Light shied at the skeet-shooting range, at the rabbit that streaked out of a clump of goldenrod, at the hound puppy that darted across his path. Going down the hill, he let out an enormous jolting buck that would have unseated a lesser rider. Snatching his head up, Shelley heard herself laughing, reveling in the challenge of quieting the high-mettled thoroughbred.

Beyond the concrete airstrip that bounded the far side of the Cup course, hounds overran the line. As the Old Huntsman carefully cast them in the high cobwebbed grass, Shelley waited, patting the colt, calming him, teaching him to wait patiently despite the intoxicating activity around him.

"Sure 'n' there ought to be plenty of foxes this year," Shelley overheard Connor, the Dash-Smythes' Irish groom, comment to the Bufords' man, Roy. "They put out a plenty last spring."

"We've got a bunch, too," Roy replied. He was board-thin and rode with the shortened stirrups and shoulder-slumping nonchalance peculiar to professional horsemen. "Had to shoot one the other day. A gray. Right in the broodmare pasture. Acted like he had rabies."

"Grays don't count," Connor said relievedly. "A red, now, that's different."

Just then a cub broke from behind a pile of rocks. Bathed in sunlight, he stood for an instant, dazedly observing his pursuers. His coat, rich russet brown, was shot through with shimmering light. Then his brush, its white tip gleaming, flicked upward as, in a leisurely lope, he set off across the Valley floor.

Lifting his cap, the Young Whip waved and shouted, "Tallyho!"

Simultaneously the Old Huntsman's high-pitched Rebel yell echoed from the hillside. "Oyee," he screamed. "Hark to 'im, my beauties. Hark to 'im!"

Hounds came together as one, the music of their voices swelling, bursting into an eager, screaming chorus as their noses picked up the fox's scent.

"Gone away!" the Master shouted exultantly, waving his arm for the field to follow.

The sun was up now, absorbing the dew, drying away the delicate handkerchief-size cobwebs. Ahead lay a sweep of open country patterned with gray walls.

Between the colt's sensitive curved ears, black-rimmed and sharp-pointed, stretched the panorama of The Hunt. Black and white hounds plunging through the grass, the Old Huntsman on his gray horse cheering them on, then Fax on The Saint.

Thought receded. Time stood still. It was the moment that Shelley had waited for, when all the pieces in the kaleidoscope came together and there was no past or future, only the now. That and a piercing sense of beauty, a feeling of closeness to all that was around her and of which she was a part.

The thrusters surged down the hill. Tatine on her long-striding chestnut, hard on the Master's heels. Mrs. Dinwiddie on her big-striding bay. Polo Pete, legs well ahead of his saddle flaps, bouncing unmercifully on his horse's kidneys. Off to one side, riding with long-legged, relaxed grace, galloped Richard Doyle, cheering the lagging puppies onto the line.

The cub, hearing the clamor behind him, gave a quick look, then increased his speed. Jumping up onto a wall, he paused briefly as though debating which way to go. Then he leapt down again, becoming lost from sight as his own rich color blended with that of the broom sedge in the overgrown meadow.

As the older horses went away from them, Lookout Light's trembling increased. His heart beat a tattoo against her knee. His excitement, his urgency, transmitted itself to Shelley.

"All right," she cried, releasing him. "Let's go."

The colt leapt into a gallop, seeming to catch up with the horses ahead in one long bound. With effort, Shelley steadied him for the wall. Taking off in his stride, he cleared it with a foot to spare. "What a leaper you are," Shelley whispered, elated. Forgetting her original intention to hilltop, to bring the colt along slowly and not let him take part in the run, she let him gallop across the meadow.

In the distance she could see the pack, running as one, the young hounds true to their instinct, giving tongue with their elders. As the colt's lovely long strides lengthened and he continued taking the fences that rose before him, Shelley felt transported by a wave of pure joy. Throwing her heart a fence or two ahead and riding effortlessly, it was as though the sun, the wind and the beat of a universal rhythm became one, fusing her senses until the problem of self, a separate being, was gone.

"They go strong together. Like a picture," observed Connor. "The heart of her and the heart of him are one."

On they went, skimming through the whispering grass decorated with clumps of blue flowers and the high white blooms of Queen Anne's lace, splashing through streams, pushing up banks, the muscles in Lookout Light's strong quarters moving like pistons.

In the Websters' woods the dogwoods were a deep red, their crimson berries shining against the leaves curving in protection against the cold weather to come.

Beyond the Webster land, the fox circled and headed toward Muster Corner. While innumerable relatives and grandchildren stood out by the peach tree, they jumped the old snake fence encircling Melusina's "home place" and swept over the grass and through the stream to the lane that led past the pool in the clearing where the local children swam in the summertime.

"There goes Miss Shelley," cried the children as she galloped past. "Hi, Miss Shelley."

She called out to them, raising one arm from the reins to wave, as they stood delightedly watching The Hunt stream by.

The Hunt tore along the dusty washboard road between Muster Corner's ramshackle houses, scattering children, dogs and chickens. A three-legged dog hopped onto the Smith family's rotting, broken porch, where it stood barking defiantly at the elegantly clad people who galloped past without looking to the right or left, leaving little puffs of dust that rose from their horses' uncaring hoofs.

Beyond Preacher Young's school, hounds converged on the Muster Corner junkyard, a surrealistic mound of rusted, broken cars, tin cans, glass and other kitchen midden, where they made a loss.

The Old Huntsman blew hounds to him and crossed the road into Silver Hill. Roy held the gate beside the cattle guard to let the riders through. In the pasture next to the road the members of the field circled their horses.

Cosy Rosy took her lathered race horse to one side, out of harm's way. Merry Black's pony tried to eat grass.

"For God's sake, Merry, pull his head up," Millicent commanded. Unaccustomed to riding sidesaddle, she looked tense and uncomfortable. Nevertheless she had managed to get across the countryside and keep up with The Hunt.

"I can't," Merry answered desperately as the pony thrust its head down, jerking her forward onto its neck.

"Of course you can. Just pull."

Merry tugged helplessly at the reins. "I can't," she said. Suddenly racked with sobs, she fell forward on the pony's neck, burying her face in its mane.

Millicent turned to Debby Darbyshire. "Real-ley, sometimes I wonder if it's worth it, trying to teach her to ride." Digging into the pocket of her pants, she brought out a cigarette and her lighter. "Damn it, I'm out of fluid."

"Fax asked us not to smoke," Debby reminded.

"For Chrissake," Millicent answered defiantly. "My ankle hurts like hell. You don't think I'm going through an entire morning without a cigarette, do you?"

Shelley rode up to the sobbing child. "Don't cry, Merry. Tomorrow's the Pony Club. We'll have some fun."

Millicent had her cigarette lit now, and her anger was spent. "Shelley, she'll be all right. She's got to learn control."

"Some of us never do," Shelley answered pointedly. "There's no reason to scare her to death."

Millicent's eyes narrowed dangerously. Slowly she took the cigarette out of her mouth. "It's about time you started minding your own business. And that goes for your husband, too."

"If her ankle hurts, why doesn't she go home and go to bed?" Bebe Bruce asked Fax.

"Old Ironpants?" The Master threw a glance in Millicent's direction. "Now if you ask me, what Millicent needs—"

"I didn't ask you," Bebe said.

The morning was not to be, as the sporting books said, without further incident. While hounds busied themselves in the grass, seeking to recover the scent, the Schligmans caught up. Because of Staunton's knowledge of the country and where the gates were located, they had managed to stay with The Hunt.

Suddenly hounds refound the line and started toward Silver Hill. Augie Schligman's roan leapt into a gallop, unseating its rider. Katie's mare, determined to remain with her stablemate, raced behind him.

"Hold hard," Fax yelled. "You'll override hounds."

Augie, caught off balance, was helpless to respond. The heavy-headed roan had no intention of stopping until it had passed all the horses. Augie, his face the color of his scarlet coat, caromed past, heading for the center of the pack.

Katie's mare followed. Katie's derby had fallen off and her blond hair had come loose. Screaming with terror, she clung to the neck of the runaway horse.

"Stop that damned purple cow," Fax shouted to the Old Huntsman.

The Old Huntsman, who refused to admit to the deafness that had been coming on for the past year or so, did not hear the Master. But the Young Whip did. Turning his horse around, he galloped back from the edge of the field where a puppy, out for the first time, was in full cry after a rabbit it had surprised in a clump of goldenrod.

Unable to head off Augie's horse, he reached out to grab Katie's reins. The mare saw him and swerved, throwing Katie to the ground. The Young Whip pulled up and jumped off.

With a great clamor, hounds clambered over the rail fence and raced across the Bufords' pasture.

"Get back up and whip that puppy onto the line," Fax commanded. The Young Whip hesitated. Then at the sight of Staunton riding to the rescue, he remounted and rode off to do the Master's bidding.

Confronted by the rail fence, Augie's roan stopped. The run had gone out of him now. He did not object when Augie turned him around and headed back to where Katie lay on the ground.

"Mama," Augie cried, dismounting. He turned his horse loose and ran to his wife's side.

" 'Ware loose horse," Debby Darbyshire cried. "Catch him, somebody."

Shelley started to pull up. Cosy Rosy almost ran her down. Wildly excited by the cry of hounds and the horses galloping ahead, the race horse was completely out of control. Shelley had a glimpse of Rosy's frightened face and then she was gone, racing toward the high rails. The rest of the field followed suit. The fact that the groom had arrived on the scene absolved them of having to stop. With hardly a glance at the fallen rider, they concentrated on getting into position for the fence ahead.

Foxhunting was not for the fainthearted. Falls were to be expected as part of the game. During the cubbing season, when people rode green, untrained horses and the older hunters had yet to settle down, accidents were numerous.

Nevertheless, Shelley was struck by the field's lack of concern. On this strange morning it was as though the sun that had burned away the cobwebs and now shone down on the countryside with harsh intensity had also burned away the mist before her eyes. She had always taken the hunting people for granted, excusing them to Mike and, she realized now, to herself. Millicent had shaken her. That, and the sudden change of attitude from friendly admiration to hostility.

Lookout Light, frustrated at not being permitted to go with the horses vanishing from sight over the rise by Silver Hill, chewed on his bit and pawed the ground.

Shelley got off and led him over to Staunton and Roy, who had stopped to assist his friend. Both grooms stood looking longingly in the direction hounds had gone. "People like the Madam have no business in the hunting field," Staunton muttered darkly. He won't be with the Schligmans much longer, Shelley thought, handing him Lookout Light's reins.

Katie was sitting up now. Her husband had loosened her stock. Yet she was still blown. Mascara smudged her cheeks and there was a scratch on her forehead.

Augie was making crooning noises of sympathy. "Mama, baby, it wasn't your fault."

"I feel such a fool," Katie choked.

"It happens to all of us," Shelley said sympathetically. "Are you hurt?"

"I think my collarbone is broken." Katie tried to turn her head and winced. "I'm so ashamed." Her tears fell free now. "I was so scared. Practicing in that ring all summer with Story Jackson yelling at me. But I wanted to make Dad proud."

The roar of an airplane was loud. Looking up, Shelley saw Zagaran's plane, a streak of crimson climbing to the blue sky.

"I'll ride back to the road and find Roosevelt and the car."

"You'll miss the hunt," Augie said.

"It doesn't matter." Shelley was surprised to find that she meant it. "Lookout Light's had enough."

The big man threw her a look of gratitude. He picked up his silk hat and began to put it on.

"Mr. Schligman," Shelley began, "mind if I tell you something?"

"Little lady, you can tell me anything you want," the big man said, "long as you call me Augie."

"Well then, Augie." Shelley took a deep breath. "You're wearing your hat backwards. The ring goes in back. You ought to get a hat guard, one of those stringlike things. You attach it to the little ring and the loop in the back of your hunting coat. Then if your hat falls off you won't lose it."

"I'll be damned," Augie said wonderingly. "I wondered what that little ring was for."

Shelley eventually found Roosevelt proudly displaying the pink

Cadillac to his friends at Muster Corner. After dispatching him to pick up the Schligmans, Shelley started to ride home. She could hear hounds in the distance, running toward Priscelly Gate, and once or twice she saw riders outlined against the horizon.

The sun was high now, the blurred golden softness of early morning dissolved by its white hot glare. The joy she had known earlier was gone, too. She did not want to believe that Millicent and Debby and the others were the way they seemed. If she did so, the golden quality that lived in her mind and diffused The Valley, her valley, with its light, would vanish like the fresh dew of dawn.

Fax Templeton and Bebe Bruce were opening a farm gate onto the lane.

"Hi," he called out. "Where have you been? You missed a right decent hunt for this time of year. Hounds denned back of Silver Hill."

"I'm absolutely cooked," Bebe said, looking as cool and flawless as she had at the meet.

"I stopped to help Katie Schligman," Shelley explained. "Nobody else bothered."

"They wouldn't dare," Bebe said with mock horror. "Their horses would never stand still long enough to allow them to get back on. Poor Katie," Bebe added. "Dinwiddie gave her such a rocket. Somewhere in that old woman's pedigree a bitch got over the wall and coupled with a mongrel."

Shelley threw her a quick glance. It was hard to remember that she had only known Bebe since Saturday night, when they met at Zagaran's ball. Now she had the strange feeling that she knew Bebe better than she did Samantha Sue, Millicent and the others. She's like Tatine, Shelley thought suddenly, the same spit-in-their-eye attitude and basic honesty.

Fax, who had long ago learned that the only way to survive in The Hunt was never to take sides or become involved in prevailing feuds, moved onto safer grounds. "Lunch!" Drawing a banana from his pocket, he began to peel it. "Shelley, Duchess, how about lunch?"

"Dear boy," Bebe replied, "you must be joking. I told you this morning I'm due in Washington at one. I'm going to be frightfully late. We really should jog on."

"I was just offering you a bite of my banana."

"Dear boy." Bebe broke into her raucous laugh. "Why didn't you say so? Darling," she continued between peals of laughter, "by all means give me a bite of that lovely banana."

They all laughed then, and for a short interval, before Fax and Bebe turned off the lane in order to reach Templeton, they talked about the night before, about their horses, The Hunt and the need for rain. They were three people riding home from hunting and it would have been hard to imagine that any one of them had a care in the world.

"Good-by," they called to Shelley. "See you."

Shelley waved and rode on alone.

When she reached the stable it was almost noon. Leaving instructions to rub the colt down and lunge the other horses that needed to be exercised, she turned Lookout Light over to Virginia City.

As she reached the turning circle, the front door flew open. Lance and the Labrador, full of love, hurled themselves at her. Behind them came Cam and Mike.

"I've been helping Daddy," Cam announced proudly. His face was grimy, his blue jeans covered with mud and his sneakers untied. "Daddy and me have been carrying logs in for the fireplace."

"Daddy and *I* have been working," Shelley corrected automatically. Picking him up, she gave him a hug. "Did you eat your breakfast?"

Cam nodded. "Did you see a big red fox?"

Shelley hesitated, remembering. "I saw a little red fox. A cub."

"Oh." Cam nodded knowingly. "A little bitty fox. Was he running and running?"

"Yes," Shelley acknowledged sadly. "He was running and running."

"I'm going to turn you in on a new model," Mike said, shaking his head in pretended despair. "Do you know what time it is?"

"I'm sorry." Shelley's sense of pressure began building. "I couldn't get back any sooner."

"Couldn't? What do you mean, couldn't?" Mike took a deep breath. "I go to considerable lengths to see that you enjoy yourself, go to fun parties, like last night—" He broke off. "There aren't any shirts in my drawer."

Shelley felt the bright mirror of the morning splintering further. "I meant to put in a load first thing—before going hunting."

"I found one in the dryer."

"Daddy ironed it himself," Cam put in.

"Did you really?" Shelley was impressed. "Mike, you never cease to amaze me."

"You'd be surprised at the things I know." He grinned at her and she felt an immense sense of relief.

"You're the world's worst laundress, but I love you anyway." Shelley smiled at him. "I'll make a casserole for dinner. Please try to get home on time."

Cam stood looking at them both. Assured that his world was intact once again, he grabbed his mother's hand. "Come on, Mommy, you said you'd take me to Rob-Rob's."

"I forgot." As her son's eager face clouded with disappointment, she said, "Okay, as soon as I get straightened up here."

EIGHT

SHELLEY fed the dogs, the goldfish and the turtles. Cam checked on the little speckled hen and her chicks, and scattered feed for the other chickens. He was distressed that foxes, or the raccoon that overturned the garbage at night, had gotten two sitting hens. Then, while he zoomed back and forth from the kitchen to the laundry on his tricycle, she made a casserole of leftover chicken, mushrooms, and artichoke hearts for dinner, put clothes into the washing machine and made a mental list of what she needed at the supermarket. Coffee, flour, cookies and soft drinks for the Pony Club meeting the following afternoon. Meat, vegetables . . .

The station wagon started reluctantly. Dating back to their New York days, it was long past its prime. Now it was too late to get anything on a trade-in. The Jeep was essential to Mike for his newspaper rounds. She must be content with the old car.

At the entrance she came to a complete stop. We really must

cut away the underbrush, she thought, craning her neck to see if any cars were approaching. Since the road had been paved, cars whizzed over the hill at reckless speeds. Leaning forward, she saw that the road was clear and turned onto it.

Now in his fifties, Dr. Watters, gruff and outspoken, was the traditional country doctor. Once, following a midnight delivery in a farmhouse, his car had been swept away while fording Buffalo Run during a springtime flood. The doctor, his bowler floating beside him, had emerged well downstream, covered with mud. Since then he'd been known as Muddy Watters.

He was a foxhunter and a polo player. Some of his patients accused him of being more concerned with polo and hunting than sniffles and sarcomas. One story concerned R. Rutherford Dinwiddie, Esquire, who went to see Dr. Watters about a lump in his chest. The doctor insisted that the elderly foxhunter go to the hospital at once.

"But I can't today," R. Rutherford gasped. "I must make certain arrangements. Perhaps I could tomorrow."

"Can't tomorrow," Muddy Watters replied definitely. "It's Opening Meet."

Dr. Watters's house and office, known as Pill Hill, was on a side street. It was an old stone house with a wide front porch hung with wisteria and furnished with a rickety swing. The pillars were dingy from lack of fresh paint, and Carlene, the doctor's housekeeper, had failed to sweep the fallen leaves from the walk and porch. After ringing and entering, Shelley and Cam went into the waiting room, crowded with an assortment of country women with babies and farm laborers. That was the trouble, Shelley thought. There was always such a long wait that by the time you did get into the inner sanctum you had almost forgotten what it was you had come to see the doctor about. Once Virginia City had spent an entire day in the waiting room. Just as his turn was about to come up, the doctor rushed out of the office on an emergency call. Returning home, Virginia City told Shelley he had waited so long to see the doctor that "his misery cured itself."

"Did you have a good hunt?" Dr. Watters asked without preliminaries when, an hour later, Shelley and Cam finally found themselves in his office. Sitting down in his swivel chair in front of his littered roll-top desk, he observed them through his thick bifocals held together with Band-Aids. "Lovely morning. Wish I could have gone out with you. Sorry Katie Schligman broke her collarbone. I just finished taping it up. Cosy Rosy Dash-Smythe came in wanting a tetanus shot for a bite on her hand. I asked what bit her and she said Millicent Black." He shook his head. "Honest to God, Shelley, I sometimes wonder what kind of brew the Valley people drink that makes 'em do the things they do." He ran his hands through his thick iron gray hair. "Well, young man, ready for another shot?"

Manfully Cam bared his arm. "May I have a lollipop?" He eyed the jar on the doctor's desk. "If I'm a good boy?"

The doctor smiled. "You're a very good boy. Certainly you may have a lollipop." He turned to Shelley. "How is his asthma?"

"It comes and goes. Lately he's been very well."

"I wish I could give you an easy answer," the doctor said. "We can keep on making tests, trying to find out what causes his allergies. But as far as I'm concerned, it's a waste of time and money." He shrugged. "Could be anything from house dust to horses. Let's just keep on with the shots and hope he outgrows it."

"Can he ride yet?" Shelley asked, thinking of the Pony Club meeting.

"Wait until it rains. Less dust and pollen." Digging into the jar, the doctor extracted a green lollipop. "There you are, young fellow." He handed it to Cam. "Come back and see me soon."

"By the way, Shelley," he said, holding the door open for them, "all this rabies business. Keep an eye on Cam in the woods. Might go hard with him if he should be required to take the Pasteur treatment."

"I'm told it's those damn gray foxes that are spreading it." Shelley paused. "You don't seriously believe all that business about the foxhunters refusing to allow the epidemic to be stamped out?"

"My dear girl, reds, grays, dogs, cats, raccoons—all the same when it comes to rabies. If the dens are contaminated, they should be blown up. I had three cases here in my office last week. Cam could easily be allergic to the vaccine. So just don't take any chances."

Shelley swallowed. "All right, but . . ." Her voice dwindled off. Already the doctor's mind was on his next patient.

"Now can we go to Rob-Rob's?" Cam took her hand.

"Okay. But not for long. I have to go home and fix dinner and iron clothes for school. It starts Wednesday."

"Buddha's birthday will be soon," Cam said hopefully. "Last year they had puppets."

As they turned onto the Valley road, Cam talked about the party. Buddha's birthday came soon after the opening of nursery school. It was always a major event. Shelley had overheard Samantha Sue mention that this year she hoped to hire the clown she had seen on television. "We'll have pony rides and do the whole thing with a circus motif," Samantha Sue had said.

"Maybe there's an invitation in the mail now." Shelley glanced at her son's excited, anticipatory face and suddenly felt chilled.

She took a deep breath. The fields on either side of the road were thatched with a second cutting of hay that lay where it had fallen, filling the air of early fall with its grassy odor. A sense of well-being stole over her. She reached up with one hand to pat Cam. "We'll be at the Jenneys' soon," she said, "and you can play with Rob-Rob."

Mike maintained that Enid and Hunter Jenney were the only people in The Valley with whom he felt completely at home. Self-supporting and hard-working, Hunt farmed his one hundred acres that adjoined Silver Hill, raised chickens and Welsh ponies, which his sons Sam and Billy exhibited in the local horse shows, sold real estate and owned the Covertside Inn. Too poor to fox-hunt and too proud to be patronized, the Jenneys kept to themselves, caring for their children ("home-from-school parents," Shelley called them) and livestock, living in a house of warmth and love in a kind of happy chaos, amid the material plenty and moral turbulence surrounding them.

Whereas Hunt was large and slow-speaking, with a craggy, weatherbeaten face and kindly gray eyes, Enid was small and dark and talented—her prize-winning short stories had been reprinted in several anthologies—with a flashing wit and strong moral sense.

The Jenneys were hated by the rich and powerful in The Valley. For one thing, Hunt was Southern, a fragment of the past that had not yet been obliterated. It was his land, his Valley, and paradoxically those who came later, the outsiders, resented the fact that he had managed to retain his independence.

232

The first schism had come with the paving of the Valley road. Winter and early spring it became a rutted, impassable morass of mud. Hunt petitioned the state to hard-surface it. His neighbors argued against it. They used it to exercise their horses, and the worse the road became the better it was for keeping out tourists and traffic. By going against his neighbors and persuading Richmond to convert the clay to macadam, Hunt antagonized the fox-hunters.

The Jenneys provided other irons in the fire of public vilification, all of which left them completely indifferent. It was not true, for instance, that Hunt closed his land when someone left open a pasture gate and Sam's pony filly got out onto the road, was hit by a truck and had to be destroyed. All Hunter ever said was that The Hunt shouldn't be so careless of other people's property and that from then on, when any livestock was out in the field, he intended to wire up his fences and lock his gates. Nor was it true that Enid was a nudist. The story had gone the rounds one day after Millicent Black had stopped by to pick up Merry, who had spent the day with Rob-Rob. Millicent saw Enid walking unconcernedly down the driveway wearing a hat, white gloves, high heels and nothing else.

It turned out that Enid had been to Washington to see a magazine editor. She returned hot and tired and decided to go for a swim in the pond. While she was swimming, Hunt, who had been mowing, scooped up her clothes, leaving only hat, gloves, and shoes. Enid pretended not to notice the clothes were missing and proceeded nonchalantly home along the driveway.

"Really!" Millicent had exclaimed, regaling members of the hunting field with the tale, "there she was marching along the middle of the road without a fucking stitch on. Anybody could have come along."

During the time that Shelley had known Enid, her admiration had grown. Although Shelley's compulsive outdoor life left little time to read or paint, she respected Enid's artistic talent and her courage to live her life as she saw fit. Along with bringing up her four children, she ran her household with relaxed efficiency, gardened, put up pickles and read every book and periodical she could get her hands on. Somehow she also found time to write. Her predominant characteristic was one of inner quiet and tranquillity. Once Shelley offered to keep the children so Enid and Hunt could go away for a weekend together.

Enid looked at her in amazement. "Why would we want to get away? We have everything we want. Right here."

Although the Jenneys were always busy, they gave the impression of having all the time in the world to spare for their friends. While Cam and Rob-Rob played in the yard, Enid would be mending a piece of furniture, knitting, cooking or pounding her ancient typewriter. Hunt, when he was at home from work, could be found cleaning the chicken house, supervising the boys as they schooled the ponies, or spreading fertilizer on the fields.

Occasionally Shelley and Mike joined the Jenneys in a simple supper. While the children ran about with joyous abandon and the soft Virginia night closed about them, Shelley would feel a renewal of faith in The Valley. For the Jenneys exuded a kind of glory, a vitality and love for life and each other that rubbed off and restored those around them.

The farm lane that served as their driveway followed a winding stream. Trees arched overhead, and in the sunlight that spilled through their branches the hard-packed clay lane shone pink.

After fording the creek that crossed over the road, the trees gave way to green meadows where the ponies grazed and the family was busy completing the last of the year's haying.

Pulling over to one side, Shelley parked the station wagon. As the engine died, Hunt's shouted commands and the sounds of happy laughter drifted across the meadow. Primroses climbed on the old brown stones of the wall that bordered the hayfield, and the distant tinkling of bells from adjoining meadows where the Bufords' cows grazed filled the air.

Cam scrambled over the wall and began running toward the workers. Shelley followed. They were lucky to have any hay at all, she thought, noticing how the crackling dryness detracted from the sweet sun-filled smell of orchard and grass and clover. She looked up at the sky. Not a cloud. If it didn't rain soon the entire countryside would burn up.

Enid was driving the tractor. She wore a wide-brimmed straw hat, a checked shirt and blue jeans. With the help of the older boys, Hunt lifted the bales as they came from the baler onto the wagon. The younger children, riding on a pyramid of packed hay, helped Cam to scramble topside.

"Now sit still," Hunt cautioned. "There. Next to Rob-Rob. Okay." He nodded to Enid. "Start her up."

"Let me help," Shelley said.

"No need." Hunt grinned. He took off his raveled straw hat, wiped his face with a colored handkerchief and then set it back on his head. "I've got a first-class crew."

"Go on down to the house," Enid called. "This is the last field. We wanted to wind it up while the boys had a holiday."

Shelley started toward the house and then thought better of it. Along with the noise of the machinery, the rumble of the tractor, the whirring of the baler as it scooped the loose hay and transformed it into string-tied bales, came the cry of crows chattering in the apple trees in the orchard. That and the light, gay voices of the children. The remembered sensations, the tired ache and sense of accomplishment and peace of haying she had known in former times, before the farm and surrounding fields had been sold off, and when they had made their own hay at the Hall, came back to her. Turning, she began walking alongside the slow-moving wagon. Hunt and Billy kept moving, swinging the bales up onto the wagon, where Sam stacked them. They did not show any signs of weariness, but Shelley, after lifting five bales, felt at the end of her strength. Hunt glanced around.

"For God's sake!" he exclaimed. "Don't lift those. They're too heavy for you."

She had considered stopping. She was out of practice and already her arms and back ached. But when Hunt looked at her in such a way, as though to say, "You're a girl; you can't do a man's work," the compulsion to show him, to prove herself, asserted itself.

"Go on," she said. "Don't worry about me."

Hunt shrugged helplessly and went ahead. Shelley followed. Lifting the bales became harder and harder.

Hunt stopped, wiped his face, started to say something to her and then did not. After a momentary pause while Enid turned to drive back along the second row, he went on his way. This long row was slightly uphill and very hard work. Sweat poured down Shelley's face and drenched her shirt.

The work went on, up the length of the long, slightly sloping field, then back again. Another row and yet another, while the bales that fell from the mouth of the baler like pale tan dominoes on the stiff dried short-cut grass were heaved back up off the field and onto the wagon.

Shelley no longer knew if it was late or early. Now she worked without consciousness, without thought of what she was doing. Drenched in perspiration, she lent a dogged energy to her labor, a vigor that increased with her growing, expanding sense of happiness.

It was only when she had to break off the motion and think that her hot, moist shoulders felt suddenly chilled and when, after detouring a boulder, breaking her rhythm to wait for the baler, the work again became an effort.

They came to the end of the final row. Shelley glanced around dazedly. The sun was sinking behind the trees. The afternoon was spent. Her hair was wisped with bits of dried grass, her clothes were plastered to her skin. Her ankles were raw and scratched. As she straightened up, the pain between her shoulders was like a knife. And yet, she thought suddenly, I'm happy now, the way I was this morning before The Hunt began, riding to the meet in the dark.

"Who wants to swim?" Hunt shouted.

Within seconds the boys had stripped off their shirts. Rob-Rob and Cam, wearing shorts and T-shirts, went in as they were. Without taking off anything but her shoes, Shelley plunged in after them.

When Mrs. Jenney died, Hunt sold the big house, Meadowview, to Kevin Martin. Retaining one hundred acres, he converted a wing of the stable into living quarters.

In the midst of the vast estates patterning the countryside, the simple abode, abounding in children and animals and decorated with hand-painted Tyrolean figures, was charmingly incongruous. Beside the wicket gate there was a blue-painted merry-go-round horse with one hind leg missing.

"Whew!" Enid wiped her sunburned face with a red bandanna from the pocket of her sawed-off blue jeans. "Let's get a cold drink."

Shelley looked down at her sopping pants and bare feet. "I can't come in like this. Besides, it's late. Almost time for dinner."

"Stay," Enid urged. "I'll lend you some dry clothes. Call Mike and tell him to come on over. I have some home-cured ham and fresh bread. Salad from the garden—"

"I wish we could, but we can't." Shelley thought of all she had to do at home. Iron clean clothes for Cam to wear to nursery school. Call Samantha Sue about the car pool. Samantha Sue had said she would do it alternate weeks. There were the horses to check on. Supper. Prepare for the Pony Club meeting the following afternoon.

"Come and sit for a while anyway," Enid said.

Shelley followed her inside. The kitchen and dining-living room had been converted from stalls, the partitions knocked out to form one big room. From the old oak beams and the walls hung an extraordinary assortment of dried herbs, copper pans, crockery, raincoats and rag dolls. At either end was a stone fireplace. Beyond the kitchen were the bedrooms, reconverted stalls facing onto the hallway.

The atmosphere was one of cluttered intimacy, emanating not only from the wood fires but from the inmates themselves.

"An elephant could lose its young in this place," Enid commented. She shooed the cat off a rocker. "Hunt says this room is like the disturbed nest of a dormouse."

Striking a match, she put it to the wood fire laid in the fireplace. "Fall's almost here. As soon as the sun goes down it gets chilly."

Shelley sat in the rocker and watched Enid slide crusty brown loaves of home-baked bread out of the oven. Cam, wearing Rob-Rob's clothes, was helping Hunt and the boys with the evening chores. Shelley did not want to move. She would have liked to sit there forever, smelling the heart-holding odor of the bread. Here, where the sense of reality was as overpowering as the scent of the bread, it seemed incredible that she had ever been at the Bufords'. Now the ball, the dinner, The Hunt, even Zagaran seemed like a dream, a dream tinged with overtones of nightmare.

Suddenly she remembered the Schligmans. She must call and find out how Katie was.

While Enid sat knitting a sock, she told her about the morning.

"You don't mean it!" Enid exclaimed indignantly when she was finished. "Katie's one of the nicest women I know. This summer when Sam was in the hospital with his tonsils and I had nobody to look after the baby, she took Rob-Rob for a whole week."

"I offered to—"

"I know you did. But you had your hands full. Katie really wanted Rob-Rob. She said little Augie is so lonely."

"Why do people like the Schligmans come here?" Shelley wondered. "They don't fit in."

Enid was gazing at her strangely. "Neither do I," she said slowly. "But then I have Hunt and all this. The only way to survive in The Valley is to detach yourself, make your own life apart. That is if you want a life of your own." She paused to pick up her knitting and then continued. "Funny thing about you, Shelley. I don't really know you. You're establishment. Mike isn't, and this is pulling you apart. Why, for instance, do you come here?"

"Maybe it's because you and Hunt are people people. Human. What Mike calls 'not bread alone' people. I can't explain—"

"Afraid to lose the old," Enid murmured as if to herself. "Afraid you won't be able to find the new.

"It's like writing," Enid continued. "At first it all seems simple. You begin with a nice clean piece of paper. The longer you work, the more difficult it becomes. You're in despair. When you most want to forget it and give it up, you can't. Like love. Because it's only then that you start to get a glimmer of what it's about. Most people are afraid to do this. It's safer on the surface. But instinctively they know they're missing something. This makes them suspicious. They're afraid of people who see something else, something beyond—" She broke off, staring at the sock she was knitting. Deftly she turned it.

"I dropped a stitch. Look." She turned the sock inside out. "Rough, uneven. If you go beneath the surface, Shelley, you'll come up with a lot of dropped stitches. You'll find this Valley is a seething petri dish. Culture gone haywire. What everyone seems to have lost is moral indignation. The light's been blown out. People burning in Birmingham—does anyone mention it? No, that wouldn't be good taste. Oh, I know you don't feel the way I do, but for once you should listen to what your husband is trying to tell you. He's a good man. He really believes there is a right and a wrong. He believes that if the Constitution doesn't speak for some, in some parts of the country, then it doesn't speak for anyone. That's why The Valley is against him. Here, people believe there's only one sin, to lose The Hunt or to lose status.

One and the same. Play musical beds. Take someone else's husband. Good fun. Par for the course. But get involved. Try and give another human a fair shake and, baby, you're in for trouble. That's going *too* far!"

Shelley had never seen Enid so wound up. She was like the yarn in her lap, coiled into a tight ball.

"Know what they used to call Virginia?" she went on. "Mother of slaves. It should have been father. Right here in this Valley there were stud farms. Slave studs. Plantation owners brought men like Washington Taylor's ancestors from Africa to breed to their slave women. Today they make life unbearable for self-respecting Negroes. Oh, I know—we don't have a Klan or lynchings. That wouldn't be aristocratic, well-bred. Here it's much more subtle. We don't even bother to close the schools the way they did in Prince William and the other counties. We just tell them when they apply that their marks aren't up to scratch, or that they live too far off the bus route for transportation and that they'd be better off in the colored school. What happens to any card-carrying member of the Human Relations Council? The deep-freeze treatment. Do you think anyone asks *us* out any more? They pretend it's because of the fence that The Hunt got so angry about. Nobody would dream of being so crude as to say it's because we believe Negroes should have equal rights, sit in restaurants, go to school, and vote!" Enid stopped knitting. "They just ignore you," she said intensely. "They just don't see you any more. Sorry, Shelley. I didn't mean to get carried away. But I'm warning you, if you start peeling away those protective layers. By the way, why don't you paint any more?"

"I haven't time."

"All that time you spend on Pony Club! Surely you don't want to make Pony Club your life? You've outgrown it. You can find time to do anything if you really want to. You're escaping. You don't want to see what's happening around you. You don't want to recognize that money and status have replaced justice and human dignity and compassion." Enid shook her head. "No, Shelley, maybe you're better off—not seeing."

Shelley was suddenly indignant. "Why better off?"

"Because The Valley will zap you."

Shelley's eyes flashed. "They wouldn't dare. I grew up here. This is my Valley, my country."

"Don't kid yourself." Enid picked up her knitting. "You've got skeet feet like everyone else."

"Skeet feet?"

"Feet of clay," Enid said.

Shelley drove slowly homeward. Shadows moved on the fields, and the face of her country was suffused with the brassy brilliance of the dying light. If she thought only of the immediacy of everyday things like getting Cam to bed, checking the colt to see that he was sound after his hunt, and outlining her schedule for the coming week, she could keep her thoughts from turning first one way and then another, like the leaves on the trees, shimmering and pewter gray as they twisted in the wind.

"Mommy"—Cam clutched her arm excitedly—"here comes Tatine."

With a roar, the sports car shot past.

"She didn't wave to me," Cam said dispiritedly.

"She was going too fast. Someday she'll kill herself, driving that way."

NINE

AT THE sight of the oncoming station wagon, Richard Doyle hunched down lower in the bucket seat of Tatine's new sports car. By now he knew that discretion was futile, that even if Mrs. Latimer had not seen him speeding past with Tatine, it was but a matter of time before The Valley found them out. Still, his strong countryman's sense of class distinctions cried out for secrecy. At the same time he was aware of dazed wonder and disbelief. Somehow it did not seem possible that he, but a whip for The Hunt and the son of a Free Zoner who still made moonshine on the mountain, could be riding in this expensive car with a girl whom society columnists described as the nation's number one debutante.

The first time he'd seen her was the day after she'd returned from Europe, not long after he and his wife, Darlene May, had moved into the cottage that The Hunt had rented for him at Ballyhoura. It was mid-August and very hot. He'd been roading hounds in the lane back of Ballyhoura, exercising the puppies that were to be shown at the hound show, when he heard the sound of hoofs. Looking around, he saw her jump her horse over the rails in the field.

As she galloped toward him, her slenderness moved in rhythm with the gelding's long, raking stride. Her hair, the color of an Irish setter, streamed out behind her like a banner. She looked like a goddess, he thought, one of those he'd read about in high school.

"Hi." She yanked the old chaser to a stop. "I'm Tatine Zagaran. Who are you?"

He mumbled that he was the new whipper-in.

She had on blue jeans and a white polo shirt that seemed molded to the contours of her pointed, upthrusting breasts. He could see their nipples straining against the fabric. There was a thickness in his throat and he felt the color spreading over his cheeks.

"Good morning, miss," he managed finally. "It's nice to see you home."

"Home!" She gave a hard, abrupt laugh. Throwing a glance at the great house on the hill, she said scornfully, "You call that home?" She shrugged. "Oh, well, I guess it does keep the rain out."

Boldly, lingeringly, her eyes traveled over him. Her mouth, with its full, sensual upper lip, parted slightly. For an instant he saw her tongue, its tip caught between even white teeth. Suddenly, as though reaching a decision, she said, "Let's go across country. I hate to jump alone."

Without waiting for a reply, she spurred the chestnut into a gallop.

Briefly he debated. His horse was just out of the field. The Old Huntsman had told him just to road hounds. On the other hand, if she had a fall out there larking alone, he would be held responsible.

In the third field, hounds went away on the line of a fox.

"Gone away!" she cried jubilantly. "Now we'll have some fun. Just us, without a lot of people fouling things up."

His grass-soft horse had trouble keeping up with her. Galloping over the fields, taking the overgrown walls and line fences that stood in the way, she rode with a reckless exuberance, a wildness that he found firing his own blood with the desire to match her, beat her at the game she had devised.

Riding up alongside her, hearing her triumphant laughter, he forgot he was the Young Whip, a servant in The Hunt's employ. Pulling ahead, he chose a high panel in the snake fence rising before them. As his horse landed safely, he looked back, elated. She followed, her body bent low on the chestnut's neck, her legs urging him to a lovely fluid, surging leap.

Hounds lost in Webster's woods. They pulled their blown horses up in a grassy, sun-speckled glen. Dropping her reins, without bothering to run up her stirrup irons, Tatine threw her right leg over the pommel and slid to the ground. Leaning against her horse's shoulder, the puppies surging about her feet, she looked up at him.

"Let's rest a minute."

"We ought to keep the horses moving," he said, aware of the steam rising from their lathered sides.

She kept observing him, a strange speculative look in her green eyes. When she spoke it was with uncharacteristic meekness. "Okay. Let's walk them around until they cool out."

He glanced at his watch. It was going on toward noon. The Old Huntsman would wonder where hounds were. Then he looked back at her. She had not moved. Yet, subtly, her expression had altered. Her eyes were half shut, her lips parted. Dropping the chestnut's reins, she slowly, languorously, in the manner of a cat stretching, arched her back. As though lifting an imaginary object, she raised her outspread hands. Resting her palms flat against the sides of her breasts, she slowly ran them over her upper body, letting the rigid spread fingers relax only when they closed around her slender waist.

Richard felt the roaring in his blood. A melting sensation dissolved the words he'd been about to speak. Through the haze in his mind he heard himself say huskily, "All right, but it's getting pretty late."

Dismounting, he ran up his irons and loosened his horse's girth.

As his fingers fumbled with the billets he became aware of her behind him. Rubbing up against his back. The tips of her breasts seemed to be burning through the fabric of his shirt, singeing his skin like coals. Laughing, she reached around in front of him.

"You're very good-looking."

"The horses—"

"Oh, the horses! Fuck the horses."

He felt the color flooding his face. Desperately he tried again. "The hounds! My God, where are the hounds?"

Then she was touching him in such a way that he could no longer speak. "Darling," she said huskily. Quickly she slid down her jeans.

It was she who called the signals, begging him to fondle her stiffened nipples, crying out to him to bear down harder, all the while making moaning animal-like sounds, caressing him until he was afraid of losing all control.

When he thought he could stand the feel of her hands no longer, she cried out to him to hurry. Had he not been so aroused, he would have been overcome with shame at the sound of the words she whispered in his ear, words he had never heard before, spoken breathlessly in some foreign language and yet the meaning of which was as obvious, as blatant, as her frantic seeking fingers closing around him, forcing him into her.

Afterward, lying on the bed of crumpled green, he was appalled. Hounds and horses had vanished. My God, he thought. They've gone home. The Old Huntsman will be coming to look for us. In his hurry to pull up his khakis, the zipper stuck. She started to laugh. Arching her back in that catlike manner of hers, she cupped her naked breasts with her hands.

"Forget your goddamned pants, let's do it again."

"No, ma'am." He didn't dare look at her. "I've got to find those hounds. The Old Huntsman will skin me alive."

"I hope not." Her voice was mocking. "That would be a dreadful waste."

My God, he thought frantically, stumbling along the overgrown woods path that led to the abandoned quarry, where can the horses and the hounds be?

Then from the direction of the Webster farm he heard sounds that sent a chill through his stomach.

Ambrose Webster was a crusty ancient with whom The Hunt

was always having trouble. Only last year the field had left its copyright in the form of a downed fence and somebody had ridden over a seeded field. It had taken funds for a new fence and all of the Master's diplomacy to persuade the farmer not to close his land. Just his luck, Richard thought, to have hounds escape to the Websters' and inflict further damage.

The scene that greeted him filled him with horror. From the pigpen came lurid sounds of snarling, cursing and the panic-stricken squeals of young shoats. In the middle of the oozing mud stood the farmer, shouting and beating off the puppies with a stick.

Frantically wielding his hunting crop, Richard waded into their midst. When the pigpen was finally cleared and the rioting hounds under control, he looked up and saw Bouncer trotting proudly around the corner of the barn. In his mouth was a large and very dead turkey. After persuading the reluctant hound to unclamp his jaws and drop his prize, the Young Whip turned to face the raging farmer.

"Done kilt my Thanksgiving turkey. Tore up my garden and scairt my pigs to death." Shaking his fist in Richard's face, he concluded ominously, "I'll see that The Hunt pays for this. It'll be a cold day in hell before anybody hunts across my land."

Richard opened his mouth to speak, but no words came out.

"Mr. Webster, please." Tatine, fully clothed, stood smiling at the infuriated farmer. Miraculously she was holding both horses. "I promise to make it right for you."

Richard was reminded of a slim English prince, like the one he had seen pictured in one of the school library books, addressing his subjects.

"Please don't be angry with us. The puppies rioted and ran off. We've been looking everywhere for them." She dug the toe of her jodhpur shoe into the mud. Looking up again, she gave the farmer the full benefit of her wonderful eyes, filled now with a look of entreaty. "If you tell anybody, Richard might lose his job." Her voice broke. Then, taking a deep breath, she continued tremulously, "I do so love to ride out mornings, help Richard with the young hounds."

The farmer's stern faced softened. "Well, miss," he replied finally, "I used to follow the dogs myself. Back in Cameron Fitzgerald's day. The Old Huntsman's a friend of mine." He looked at the Young Whip. "Reckon I knew your dad. Wasn't he a Doyle from the Free Zone? Married one of the Walker girls. The Walkers are kin to my wife." He looked down at the dead bird. "Reckon we'll have our Thanksgiving tonight."

Tatine's smile was brilliant. "Oh, Mr. Webster. How can we ever thank you? You'll have the biggest and best turkey in The Valley for your *real* Thanksgiving. Richard and I will deliver it in person, won't we, Richard?"

"Wow!" Tatine exclaimed when they were out of range, the subdued hounds trotting obediently alongside. "I thought our goose, I mean our turkey, was cooked."

Richard's mouth was less dry. His heart began beating almost normally. "Lucky you talked him out of telephoning the kennels. If he had I might as well have begun packing soon as I got home." He gave her a quick glance. She looked cool and composed. Had it not been for a green leaf caught in her hair, what had happened in the woods might have been a dream. "Where did you find the horses?" he asked wonderingly.

"Grazing beside the lane." She patted her horse's neck. "Warlock broke a rein, but I tied it together."

She looked at him demurely and smiled. Her eyes were shining, and without make-up she looked about fourteen. Again he felt that sudden melting warmth. At the same time he had an illogical desire to reach over and remove the leaf from her wind-blown hair.

An anguished yelp distracted them. One of the puppies had strayed into the field. In an effort to rejoin the pack, he had gotten himself caught in Mr. Webster's barbed wire fence.

"He's hurt," Tatine cried. In a flash she was on the ground, running to the aid of the hound. Scrambling up the bank, the horse's reins still in her hand, she started to extricate the struggling puppy.

"It's Bellboy," Richard said. "Watch out. He'll bite."

"He's bleeding."

"You hold the horses," Richard commanded. "I'll get him out." Using his wire cutters, he quickly freed the frantic hound. Bellboy bounded down the bank, leaving a trail of blood from a cut pad.

"He's hurt. Oh, Bellboy," crooned Tatine. Disregarding the

mud in the lane, she sank down onto her knees and took the wounded dog in her arms.

Richard stared in amazement. "It's just a scratch."

She lifted her head. The puppy began licking her face and there was blood on her white shirt. "He is too hurt. Look at the blood."

"It's just a nick." Richard leaned down and gently took hold of the hound's paw. "I'll put some disinfectant on it when we get home and he'll be as good as new."

"Are you sure?" She sounded relieved.

"Yes," he answered, baffled. How could she be so concerned over a simple scratch on a dog's foot? How could she take such a small thing to heart when with something big, like back there in the woods . . . ? He was at a loss to understand.

The narrow dirt lane descended to a clear rippling stream, then wound upward once again, through trees. Pools of sunlight dappled their path. It must be long past noon now. Darlene May would have fixed their midday meal and would be waiting. It was the first time he had thought of his wife.

"What a smashing morning," Tatine said suddenly, joyously. "Let's do it soon again."

Since that morning, the ecstatic abandonment, the savagery and soaring flights of passion that he had come to know through Tatine seemed an incredible dream, the reality of which reached him only when the sudden shattering fear of discovery swept over him.

Fortunately, due to her pregnancy, his wife made few demands on him. As time passed she spent more and more time in front of the television, wearing her shapeless pink wrapper, her hair up in pink rollers. Had she asked why he no longer thrust himself upon her to make quick, furtive love in the closed darkness of their cottage bedroom, he would not have known how to reply.

Following the first morning, he had noticed Tatine coming and going, whirling along the drive past the cottage in the new red car which her father had presented to her as a coming-out present. Generally she was with Sandy Montague or the others in her crowd, lanky collegians and long-legged, long-haired girls, with that self-assured air that came from money and privilege.

Then one evening he was walking home when she passed him on the drive. She jammed on the brakes and stopped.

"Know what?" Her voice was gay. "I've got the Websters' primitive plumbing on my behind."

"Pardon?" He hadn't a clue what she was talking about.

"Must you say 'pardon'? It's terribly bourgeois. Poison ivy, silly. My bottom is covered with it. That's why I haven't been riding."

Now he understood. Color flooded his face.

"What do you suppose Farmer Webster would say if he knew?"

The idea was so appalling, so ludicrous, that he found himself starting to laugh.

"So long," she said huskily. "See you." With a casual wave she was gone.

The afternoon before the ball she was waiting outside the kennels when he finished feeding.

"Come on," she said urgently. "Come with me now."

He looked at her smooth, beautiful face with its tilted nose and pointed nostrils and saw a look in her eye, a look not unlike that of the young mare he'd been given to ride when she was in heat. "My wife's expecting me for supper."

"At five-thirty?" She stared, wide-eyed. "My God, how country can you be?"

Suddenly he was angry. A bitch, he thought. A spoiled rich bitch with all the demanding ferocity but without the gentleness of the bitches he tended in the kennel. Then the image of her bending over Bellboy's pad came to mind. At the same time he saw his wife, her hair bristling with the omnipresent pink rollers, eyes glazed from television, moving about the kitchen in the soiled, shapeless pink wrapper. He was filled with distaste and with it a reluctance to return to the cramped cottage permeated with the smell of cabbage and pork grease.

"Come on," Tatine repeated huskily. "Hurry."

He jerked his head in the direction of the great house. "Won't they miss you?"

"Miss me?" Her laughter was hoarse, bitter. "Are you kidding? Mom's locked in her room with a bottle and Zagaran's off to dinner with one of his harem."

She shouldn't talk about her parents that way, he thought. Calling her father Zagaran made him uncomfortable, like her use of four-letter words.

As though reading his mind, she said defiantly, "I know you think I'm sinful. Well, I've news for you. Nobody's going to change *me*."

"It's not for me to change you," he said helplessly. "But this isn't right. What if your father finds out?"

"Well, now, wouldn't that be something?" Her eyes narrowed dangerously. "The pot calling the kettle black."

"What about that boy, Mrs. Montague's son?"

"Sandy?" She hooted. "He's an infant." She took a step toward him. "Now you—"

"Not here," he said quickly. "Somebody might see."

"I parked behind the rhododendron bush," she said breathlessly. "Up the drive. I'll meet you there."

For a second he stood motionless, looking after her, observing the swinging motion of her flat boy's hips beneath her short white skirt. She's so clean, he thought suddenly. She smells of soap and water and drying grass.

He telephoned his wife from the stable. "I've got to go into town and get some disinfectant. One of the hounds cut himself. Don't wait supper. I'll get something later."

"Not again!" Darlene May's voice was petulant. "I've just finished fixing the food. Pork chops—and you know how cooking affects me. It makes me sick to my stomach. Dr. Watters says—"

"You told me what Dr. Watters says. My ride's waiting."

The sports car was long and low and powerful with four speeds and a speedometer that went up to a hundred and fifty miles an hour. Soft music came from the radio turned down low. She shoved a battered stuffed rabbit and a large bulging shoulder bag under the seat.

"I just parked here for your sake," she said pointedly as the car shot away up the drive. "I don't give a damn who sees us."

The rush of wind in his face eliminated the need to reply. In order not to look at the speedometer, he busied himself adjusting his seat belt. Hers, he noticed, was unbuckled.

"Shouldn't you fasten yours?"

Taking one hand off the wheel, she made a disparaging gesture. "I can't be bothered. It's like those things men wear. It spoils the sensation."

How many men had she known, he wondered. She couldn't be more than eighteen, nineteen at the most, the same age Darlene

May was when they married. Darlene May, from a hard-core Baptist family, had been a virgin. Once before they were married he had almost made her. Carried away by her softness, the big breasts and rounded stomach, he found himself losing control. Just at the crucial moment she had screamed and pushed him aside. Her new organdy, bought for the church social, had been stained and crumpled. She had been terrified that her mother would find out. He was mighty careful after that. He didn't want that brother of hers coming after him with a shotgun. Now that he was head of the family, following her father's death, Tom Mellick took his job too seriously for Richard's comfort. It was also true that he wouldn't have married her if she hadn't been a good girl, if she had been passed around like one of the covered dishes at the church suppers, going from hand to hand, running off into the bushes with every one of the grooms and farmhands who asked her, the way some of the other girls did. He hadn't let himself go until their wedding night, shut away from her Bible-quoting mother and the violence of her brother Tom and the other Mellicks who had come from their cabins hidden away in the fastnesses of the Free Zone for the wedding. He had put his arms around her as soon as the door was closed behind them. "Not now," she said, pushing him away. "Let me put my hair up first. Tomorrow we're going to Grandma's for dinner."

He had said urgently, "I want you now."

She hadn't put her hair up. But he had been forced to wait a long time while she did things in the bathroom. By the time she did come to bed, his desire had lessened. The corn likker provided for the festivities had worn off and he was sleepy. He tried to do his best but she was very coy, moving away from him just when the urge came upon him. He had done it finally and she had cried out and said he was hurting her. Later, he had taken her roughly and she'd told him he would make her pregnant and she didn't want to be pregnant right away.

Pregnant. A stab of terror shot through him. Tatine couldn't mean—but obviously she did. What if she became pregnant? What if, back in the woods amid the poison ivy, it had already happened? At the same time he thought about how much he liked his job. Despite his cantankerousness, the Old Huntsman had taught him a lot. Once or twice he had intimated that it might not be much longer before he retired. All his life the Young Whip had wanted to be Huntsman for The Hunt. Although he had served his apprenticeship with a neighboring pack, it was The Hunt that belonged to legend and story which drew him. When the countrymen gathered around the fires and spoke of foxes and hounds and great runs, it was always The Hunt they talked about. Now he had an opportunity to achieve his ambition. He did not want to jeopardize his chance of becoming Huntsman for The Hunt by fooling around with a rich man's daughter.

Suddenly she slowed down and turned off the Valley road.

"Where are we going?" he asked.

"Wait and see."

After several jolting miles, Tatine turned left onto a private driveway.

He knew where he was now. A month before he'd come here with Simeon and some of the foxes that The Hunt had brought in from the West to set out in various parts of the hunting country. Simeon pointed out the old stone house and barn that had once belonged to the Mellicks. It had come up at auction and Zagaran bought it. It was far removed from the heart of the hunting country and stood on a lonely, uninhabited area of the Free Zone. Simeon explained that the boss had fixed it up as a guest house and place to entertain business acquaintances during the bird season.

"Ever find yourself this way after a long hunt," the colored man said, "you can put your horse up for the night. Stalls are bedded down and there's feed in the bins. House is kept stocked, too. Wouldn't know why, would you?"

Richard had glanced at him quickly. However, the groom's face was inscrutable. Despite the talk about Zagaran and his carryings-on with women, it wouldn't have been fitting to discuss his boss's business.

At thought of her father, sudden panic overrode his desire. Bad enough to have his wife wondering where he was, but to have Zagaran come and find them! He'd be out of his job before he could holler, "Gone away." And just when he was finally learning how to blow a hunting horn properly.

In front of the stone farmhouse Tatine jammed on the brakes and switched off the ignition. Once again she seemed to guess his thoughts. "Don't worry about Dad popping in on us." Her eyes mocked him. "He's tied up with Samantha Sue Buford."

Suddenly she caught her breath. Her lips parted. Her body

tensed. Then, in one long sliding motion, she threw herself against him. Avidly she sought his mouth. "God," she whispered. "It's been so long." Sliding away from him again, she opened the door of the car. "Well, aren't you coming?"

The night of the ball he found himself unable to stay in the cottage with Darlene May and the television. He had been drawn to the great house, where the lights from the windows and pavilions and the sounds of music and revelry spread across The Valley. He stood watching from the shadows. He had seen her dancing in her long green dress. He had thought of her firm breasts, her wonderful body, and the way she cried out and clutched him, raking his back with her long polished nails. Standing there in the shadows he had known such a paroxysm of desire that walking back to the cottage afterward he felt weak and spent.

Sunday afternoon she had telephoned, saying breathlessly that she had to get away for a while and to hurry and tack up the horses.

He had promised Darlene May to take her home to see her folks. "I'm sorry," he said to his wife, "but some of the out-of-town people are coming to the kennels to look at the hounds. The Old Huntsman wants me there to help show them off."

Darlene May had given him a strange look but had not said anything. He had left her, hair still in rollers in preparation for her visit, looking at the Sunday movie on the TV set.

They had ridden hard for an hour. On the way home they'd encountered Mrs. Latimer and her little boy.

"What will she think?" he asked as they rode back to the stable.

"I couldn't care less." Tossing back her long red mane, she added defiantly, "Nobody's going to tell me what to do or think."

At the meet that morning, in the early dawn, she had ridden up and spoken to him in plain view of everyone. She had told him to meet her that afternoon behind the big rhododendron bush just off the drive.

He had been afraid to look at her, afraid that his desire would be written on his face for all to see.

Now, finally, they were together. Soon she would be in his arms. As though she, too, was aware of the same urgency, Tatine put her foot down hard on the accelerator. As always, she drove very fast but with dexterity, a skill and concentration that reminded him of the way she rode and made love, seemingly reckless but with a knowledge of what she was doing.

Now they were doing eighty. A car was approaching. He recognized Mrs. Latimer's old station wagon. Tatine appeared not to notice. Holding the left wheels to the center line, she stared straight ahead.

"That was Mrs. Latimer," he said, just for something to say. "Her and her little boy."

"Cam? I didn't notice. Oh, dear, he'll be hurt that I didn't wave." Suddenly she sounded angry. "Can't you learn to speak correctly? It's not 'her and her little boy.' Just say 'her little boy was with her.' "

He stared, incredulous. She did not mind hurting him, reducing him to a quivering mass of uncertainty. On the other hand, she couldn't bear to hurt an animal or a child.

As though sensing his sudden recoil, she said apologetically, "Richard, I'm sorry. Darling, forgive me. I *am* a bitch. But don't you see, I would have liked to be a nice normal housewife with a nice normal husband and a nice normal little boy, like Shelley Latimer. Now I never can be. Do you know," she went on conversationally, her words coming to him like the wind thrusting him further down in the bucket seat, "I had a room full of stuffed animals. There must have been a thousand. When I was a child they were my only friends."

The road leveled out, flat and straight but for deceptive rises from beyond which, in the deepening dusk, came the occasional faint glow from an approaching pair of headlights. Aside from a fiery crimson line separating the purpling hills from the matching sky, it was almost dark.

On the horizon hanging above the blue hills was a single bright star.

They turned onto the now familiar rutted lane. Ahead loomed the farmhouse. Tatine stopped the car and switched off the ignition. The seat belt hampered him. Somehow he could not unfasten it fast enough. Then he was fumbling with the handle of the door, pushing it the wrong way.

"Up!" She was laughing. "Everything else is up. Why not the door handle?"

Then, her skirt whirling around her legs and her hair flying, she was running up the walk.

The faint elusive scent of her was on his shirt, in his heart and all around him. Suspended there in the doorway of the farmhouse, beckoning to him, she was like the star overhead.

TEN

WEEK nights Mike and Shelley generally ate an early supper with Cam. This Monday night, Labor Day, they'd been asked to several parties, which Shelley had turned down. Suddenly she realized that she had been up since before dawn and was very tired. Since Suellen had been sick— she'd announced several days before that she had "dire-rear" and did not know when she'd be back—the house seemed to be in a perpetual state of chaos. Laundry was piled sky-high. She would have to iron some clean clothes for Cam to wear to nursery school. Mike was right. The horses took up far too much time. Then there was Cam's birthday, the Pony Club, collecting for the Red Cross. The annual church bazaar was in the offing also. And just when she thought she was caught up and might find time to paint again, something came up, like taking Melusina to the clinic for a check-up.

She was relieved that Mike wasn't home yet. It gave her time to put the casserole in the oven, bathe Cam, take a shower and change into green pants and a green and white overblouse.

At seven Mike still hadn't come home. She wondered if he might have stopped off on the way to see Misty. Several times lately, when she had asked him why he was late, he'd mentioned going to Fairmont to ask some question about the paper.

She opened the oven door and looked at the casserole. The bread crumbs on the top were burning. Bending down, she reached in to remove it. As she lifted it up, the handle broke off. Instinctively she grabbed the dish to keep it from sliding off the rack. The casserole crashed to the floor. For an instant she stood transfixed, feeling the throbbing pain in her burned hand, starring at the chicken mixture and pieces of broken crockery at her feet. With sudden fury, she slammed the oven door shut, so hard that the old rusted hinges gave way and it, too, fell to the floor with a crash.

Aroused by the noise, Miehle began to moan and quiver. Trembling, he came to her. Sitting down on the floor, the ruins of the meal around her, Shelley took the Labrador in her arms. As she rocked back and forth, tears of anger and pain and frustration ran down her cheeks.

"Mommy, Mommy," Cam cried, alarmed. "Why are you crying?" He looked at the debris on the floor and then back at her. "You broke the dinner," he accused.

"I know." She shoved Miehle out of her lap and stood up. "I'll scramble some eggs and we'll go ahead and eat."

Cam looked as if he, too, were about to cry. "I want to eat with my daddy. Mommy," he asked plaintively, "where is my daddy?"

"Damned if I know," Shelley answered violently. "He said he was on his way home."

The clock over the door into the print shop chimed six. Mike stopped typing his editorial. Because of constant interruptions during the day, it still wasn't finished. He knew from having grown up in his father's newspaper shop that these interruptions were a part of the price of success as a local editor. And yet they exacted a toll in the form of unfinished work and late nights. Now in order to have copy ready for Josh when he came in to set type the following morning, he would have to return after dinner. But then there was the Human Relations Council meeting to attend at Muster Corner.

Labor Day, he thought ruefully. Everything else in town had been closed. But people seeing his Jeep out front had stopped by to place classifieds, give him social notes, harangue him about typographical errors in last week's ads, and simply to converse.

Surprisingly little notice seemed to have been taken of the desegregation effort. Mike had expected a further rocket from Millicent when, with her ankle taped up by Dr. Watters, she hobbled in with the aid of a shooting stick. Instead, she had poured out her shame at her behavior the preceding night.

"You won't mention it in the paper, Mike?"

"Of course not. What do you think we are, *Playboy?*"

Then she began on her marital problems. Finally he got rid of her by advising her to see the Reverend Chamberlain. She departed reluctantly, only to be replaced by Mrs. Dinwiddie, still wearing her habit from hunting and on her way to a meeting at the parish house. Her laundress had left and she wanted to know if he knew where she could hire one.

"It's getting to the point where it would be cheaper to send it out," she said indignantly. "The servant situation is unbelievable. Yet all those people in Muster Corner are on relief. I've offered them jobs over and over and they still won't work."

"Perhaps if they had a chance to go to decent schools, have job training—" Mike began.

"Governor Berkeley—he was kin on my mother's side of the family—said that mass education would lead to rebellion and heresy in the world. Anyway, nobody wants to work. All they want is to sit and look at television."

Mike ran through the classifieds piled on his desk. "I'll let you know if I hear of anybody."

"If I could get a decent colored laundress, or anyone for that matter, I'd pay them almost as much as I pay my white cook."

Mike's patience ran out. Without thinking, he heard himself say, "You might consider doing the laundry yourself. I do."

The Beast stiffened. She gazed around at the cluttered office with distaste. "Young man, it's time you were taught not to override the line." She started to say more, then apparently thought better of it. Picking up her cane and her string gloves, she departed.

Mike sat looking after her. He knew he had made an enemy.

Shelley would be home by now, preparing dinner. He knocked out his pipe and started out the door.

"Just stopped to find out how things were going," the Reverend Chamberlain said apologetically. His face was deeply lined and he stood with a slight stoop as though now at the end of the day the effort to remain erect could be relaxed. Although it was obvious that Mike was on his way home, he made no effort to leave.

Once the Reverend began, he would go on talking for at least an hour. In Shelburn, few shared his views. Mike was one with whom he could, as he put it, discuss. Therefore, once he got going on one of his favorite subjects, integration or predestination, he was like a rusted faucet—hard to turn on, but once started, a gathering force which becomes a steady outpouring.

"I'm late now," Mike said resignedly. He reached for his pipe. "I don't suppose it matters if I'm later." He moved aside to let the minister by. "Come in and sit down."

The Reverend crossed his long, thin black-clothed legs and stared over Mike's head at the framed citations on the wall. "I'm told the locals held the line against the outsiders, repelled the invaders at the city gates."

"The situation could have been explosive," Mike agreed. "Washington Taylor handled it with reason and rationality. Thanks to him the demonstration was called off."

"Yet because he's a member of the NAACP he's considered a Communist and an agitator," the minister said thoughtfully. "None of it makes any sense. What I really came by for was to tell you that I may not be in Shelburn much longer."

"What!" Mike swiveled around and stared at him.

"Buford," the Reverend said. "Directly after church he called the vestry together. Togo Baldwin came to see me. He was very sheepish about it. Just said that the vestry had met and come to the conclusion that I'd be better suited to some other parish. Preferably in the North. It would be better for my health, was the way Togo put it."

"What are you going to do?"

There was a new light in the Reverend's eyes and when he spoke again it was with determination and purpose. "At first I was inclined to agree. My ulcer has been misbehaving. I haven't felt well. Then I began to think. I recalled that when I first came to Shelburn I felt a sense of guilt. I wasn't serving the Lord's or my purpose. After nine years under fire in Norfolk, where I started an interracial committee and was forced out of the parish, the bishop sent me here because he thought there wouldn't be problems. In The Valley, in a retirement community made up largely of Northerners, I could relax and be non-controversial." Uncrossing his legs, he sat erect. "Now that the battle has begun, it seems wrong to pull out." He looked at Mike. "Particularly when there are so few on our team."

"Then you'll stay?"

The minister nodded. "They may force me to leave by cutting my salary, but I won't resign of my own accord." He gazed at the quote from Edmund Burke which Mike had taped to the wall over his desk: "I know no better way for evil to triumph than for good men to remain silent."

As he drove home, Mike felt a sense of accomplishment that somehow made the dying light of the early fall day brighter, his heart lighter. If only, he thought, Shelley could come to see it the way he did.

After parking the Jeep in the drive, he walked toward the house. The evening breeze swept at him through the oaks. A fallen branch lay disconsolately across the walk and the geraniums in their pots banking the steps leading up to the wide front door were wilting. I must move them inside, Mike thought. Before the frost.

Shelley stood at the sink filling an ice tray. She lifted the tray and turned, facing him. As always he was struck by the curious, impersonal quality of her beauty, a beauty of bone structure and breeding, doubly effective because she was so totally unaware of it.

He had a sudden unaccountable desire to run to her, as Cam would, and pour out the day's happenings, dump them into her lap like an offering of precious stones.

He started toward her.

Just as he reached her, she held up the ice tray, as if to fend him off. He stopped, and for an instant they gazed at each other silently. Then she walked past him and began stirring something in a pot on the stove.

"You're late. The casserole is burned. I put Cam to bed. He's waiting for you to say good night."

He stood without moving.

"You'd better go, or he'll never go to sleep."

"Why did you put him to bed? It's only seven-thirty and we always have supper together."

She put her hand to her mouth. It was a gesture that always irritated him, even when he loved her the most.

"Damn it," he exploded, "I asked you a question."

"As a newspaperman, you should be more accurate. You mean we *used* to have supper together." She stopped stirring and flipped off the burner. "How was I to know when you'd be home? For months now you've been going to those Muster Corner meetings with your colored friends, not getting home before midnight—"

"It's time we had a talk." He fumbled for his pipe and realized he'd left it in the Jeep.

"Oh, Mike, we've been over it all so often."

"Not about that. About us."

"Daddy," they heard Cam calling. "I want my daddy."

"I'll go see him. I know I'm late. I'm sorry. But I'm tired. I'd like a drink before dinner. Would you mind pouring me one?" He left the kitchen without looking at her.

"Daddy, where were you? I've been waiting and waiting." Cam looked warm and clean, all pink and gold and blue, blue eyes and blue pajamas, the worn Kitty-Kat minus an ear and a leg clutched against one rosy cheek. As always, he tried to prolong the moment when sleep and aloneness became unavoidable. Now he pleaded for a story.

Mike sat down on the bed and, for the duration of a Mr. Bear tale, the rest of the world was well lost. During that brief interim thought and tension, worry and anxiety faded into shadow, leaving only father and son and the current of love and understanding flowing between them. Finally, after a final drink of water, a last hug, the moment of parting could no longer be prolonged.

"Make me all snuggly, Daddy," Cam said resignedly.

As Mike drew the blanket up over his firm, sturdy body, he was aware of a deep thankfulness that his son was no longer thin, frail, prone to the colds and croup and respiratory difficulties that had plagued his infancy.

Mike switched off the lights. For an instant he lingered. In the warm September darkness that sheltered them, he stood gazing down. He did not want to move, to think beyond Cam, to end the security of the moment.

Returning to the kitchen, he saw the single glass sitting beside the single place set at the table.

Shelley was drying the dishes in the rack.

"Won't you join me?" he asked.

"I had one before dinner." Carefully she rubbed Cam's silver mug.

"You've already eaten? You didn't wait?"

"No," she replied. "Mike, I'm tired. I got up at four-thirty this morning. Tomorrow I have four horses to get out by afternoon when the Pony Club comes."

"And the horses are more important than your husband."

"If you say so. At least I have the horses as company. God knows I haven't seen much of *you* lately."

"You always did prefer horses to humans." He drained the glass and picked up his pipe. "Shelley, this is your house. Your Valley. I bought the paper because you wanted to come back here. I'm trying to make a go of it." He indicated the bills piled on the iron stove. When they had moved into Shelburn Hall and the first bills for repairs had begun coming in, she had made a joke of them, saying she would put them all in a hat, like a pool. She had dumped them into her hunting cap and asked him to pull one out, promising to pay it promptly.

At first he had found her unorthodox bookkeeping endearing. But when her listing of stable costs, which ran to hundreds of dollars each month as etceteras, had caused the Internal Revenue people to investigate them the previous year, he no longer found it amusing.

Now he asked her when she planned to attend to the bills.

"They've been sitting there for weeks. Some haven't even been opened."

She slammed down the dish towel. "Those people have been nasty. I see no reason to even put their bills in the hat!"

"Nasty or not, the bills aren't going to stop coming. The fact that we owe everybody in town doesn't help my job as editor and publisher of the paper."

"Making us a laughing stock doesn't help either! Do you want people like Suellen and Jubal running the country?"

Mike shook his head. "No. Nor do I want Polo Pete Buford or Major Southgate DeLong or Mrs. Dinwiddie running the country. However, I wouldn't mind Preacher Young or Washington Taylor. They are superior in anybody's league. The Sherpas are less suited to running the Shelburn bank than Togo Baldwin. That doesn't mean Sherpas can't be trained as bankers. Nobody wants to leave government in the hands of an untrained quantity. But they must be permitted an opportunity for education. You can't close the schools and then say that the Negro isn't capable of equality because he isn't educated to it. You were born into a society as people are born into the Catholic Church. The Negro isn't."

Shelley's eyes were blazing. "You want us all to be one big mud-colored race?"

"I might as well eat." Mike sighed. "That is, if there's anything to eat. Or would you rather I went to the Gone Away and had a hamburger?"

"Now that the town's integrated, you can meet your friends there!"

Putting down his drink, he tried to eat the food she placed silently before him. "Eggs?" he asked between mouthfuls. "What happened to the casserole?"

"I broke it. It was in the oven too long. It started to burn. When I took it out, the handle came off. It fell on the floor." She looked at the blisters on her palm. "I burned my hand."

"I'm sorry." He shoved his plate away. "If you can find the pieces, I'll glue them together. It was a nice casserole. Do you remember? We bought it in the Village, just before we moved into the apartment."

"I put them in the trash can." Sweeping his half-empty plate out from before him, she scraped it, ran it under the tap and put it in the rack to dry.

He started to remind her that lately, because of washing the dishes without soap, either he or the succession of cleaning women who had been coming in since Suellen's illness had to rewash them in the morning. But something about the rigidity of her back and the way she jammed the dish into the rack caused him to refrain.

Instead he said quietly, "Shelley, you must be tired. Neither of us got much sleep last night." He did not dare tell her that he had to go to a Human Relations Council meeting. "You go on up. I still have some work to do. I'll put the dogs out and lock up."

When she didn't turn or reply, he could no longer hold back the things he wanted to say.

"I appreciate your help and understanding." He laughed a short, harsh laugh. "Do you *know* what I've been doing? Working like hell to save this beautiful, benign, corrupt Valley, this hallowed ground of your ancestors. Slaving to stave off violence, bloodshed." He knew he was being foolishly dramatic and couldn't help himself. "So that people like you and Polo Pete, your dear Fax and now that Heathcliff, Zagaran, can fornicate and foxhunt."

"Mike—" She sounded shocked.

"Oh, I know you haven't been unfaithful. You don't like to be touched. My God, I almost wish you would be. It would make you more human, more approachable." As soon as he had spoken, he knew that he had gone too far. When she brushed past him he realized that she was crying and suddenly it no longer seemed to concern him. Locked as he was in his own anxieties, she seemed a stranger to him.

Mike felt duty-bound to attend the meeting of the Human Relations Council at Muster Corner Baptist Church. Innumerable times it had been brought home to him that his presence, a white presence, gave Preacher Young and the pacifically minded non-violent Negroes a feeling that they were not entirely alone in their determination to keep the peace.

So far as Mike knew there had been no trouble. Washington Taylor and his family had eaten Sunday dinner at the Covertside Inn. Dr. Watters, Misty Montague, the Jenneys and the Chamberlains, who had been asked to serve as "sit-withs," had dined at adjoining tables.

When Mike asked Linda Taylor, Washington's daughter-in-law, how she had enjoyed her Sunday dinner, her only comment was that the meal was terribly expensive and the fried chicken not half as good as that which came out of her own kitchen.

"Think you'll go back?" Mike asked.

"No, sir." Linda was positive. "John makes good money, but we can't afford that place. Mr. Editor, all we want to know is that a person can go into places like that if a person wants to."

Turning off the Valley road, one struck the rutted washboard lane that became a lake of dust during the dry season, almost impassable during the snow months. A historical marker gave the only warning of a turnoff.

> MUSTER CORNER
> Near here, on July 8, 1863, Company B, 44th Battalion of Partisan Raiders, known as Shelburn's Raiders, was formally mustered. Sean Shelburn was elected captain. Fairfax Templeton, lieutenant. Members were . . .

The list duplicated the names in family burial plots throughout The Valley.

At the time when Sean Shelburn "mustered" the Raiders, who,

because of their daredevil feats, were to be romanticized in song and story and become part of the legend and lore of the Civil War, the Corner had been part of the original tract granted King Shelburn. The little stone church and whitewashed cabins had been slave quarters for Shelburne Academy, the young ladies' finishing school founded by Patrick Shelburne, who, bearing a crate of books, had come riding out of the North to visit the Southern branch of the family and been persuaded to stay on and found the Academy. When Patrick Shelburne died, his oldest son, Charles, who had inherited his father's intellectual bent, took over the running of the Academy. Because his sympathies were with the Union and he refused to join his Shelburn cousins in secession, he was branded a traitor to his kind and cause.

Charles Shelburne was a Quaker and a pacifist. The Academy had long been a stop on the Underground Railroad and when there were no more young ladies to attend his classes, he opened them to Negroes and became the first white man to educate Negroes openly in the South. To the colored people he was known as "Yankee" Shelburne and looked upon with reverence and awe.

In the fall of 1863, the Academy was burned. It was believed that the fire was set at the instigation of Sean Shelburn, and although this was never proven it was known that the dashing Raider came almost nightly to the Corner, where he bedded down with fifteen-year-old Marcy Stuart. Later, when she was delivered of the light-skinned child with the Shelburn nose and eyes, Marcy confessed that the night of the fire she had told her lover that she was learning to read and write at Yankee Shelburne's school. It was a mistake. Sean had been drinking, and he retaliated by giving her a furious beating with his hunting crop. Then, after violent lovemaking, he rose from the grassy place by the stream where they had been meeting for months, and went forth in the righteous wrath of God's chosen to "put a stop to Charles's damned nonsense."

After the fire, Yankee Shelburne moved to Fairmont. In order to carry on his crusade for peace, he started a weekly newspaper, the first to be published in The Valley. Named the *Shelburne Sun*, it was pledged "to let the light of truth shine on the facts and print them in the public interest."

As his car rattled over the rocks and potholes, Mike could visualize Shelburn's Raiders mustering at the crossroad. In his imagination he could smell the horses, hear the softly flowing curses and the creak of saddle leather, feel the crammed tension and excitement. "Come on, boys, tonight we'll give the Yanks a run." Above the sound of the car's motor came the imagined drumming of galloping hoofs as the ghostly cavalry swept by, to be followed by eyes, filled with awe and wonder, watching from the cracks in the cabin doors.

The people in the chinked cabins had not understood, Mike thought. Any more than Sean Shelburn had understood. Nothing clean-cut like slavery or states' rights or Northern oppression had fired the gray hordes with their plumed hats and colored sashes to ride out into the night, but something so shrouded, so dim and yet so keenly felt as to be a religion itself. A clay road and dust in the sun. White pillars and candles in crystal chandeliers. Skirts as wide as the second-floor gallery whirling to the scrape of fiddles. The cry of hounds on a November afternoon and a certain fragrance. A wide, slow river and a Negro fishing. Wild pink blossoms in the spring and the savagery of black flesh. A timelessness, a way of life, a clinging until the third and fourth generations that was as strong, as binding as the wisteria that had wrapped itself around the pillars of Shelburn Hall. A guilt-filled dream as elusive as the mist that lay on the fields at dawn.

A hundred years ago. Yet what had changed? Tired of being hungry and homeless in the postwar chaos, many of the freed Negroes had found their way back to their original cabins, some of which were now occupied by their descendants.

In the latter part of the nineteenth century, Muster Corner had been a contract convict labor camp. Members of the chain gang built Silver Hill and some of the other great houses in the area. Although the camp had been disbanded long before World War I, some of the convicts who escaped or had served their time returned to Muster Corner to live, to die, and to contribute to the heritage of the local Negroes. A few of the original shacks remained, rotting and rat-infested, inhabited by slatternly women, carping matriarchs and innumerable children wearing runny noses and open sores like badges of degradation. Polo Pete Buford was now their landlord.

When Mike had once suggested that the shacks be leveled and rebuilt, Polo Pete pointed out that the present housing was more than adequate. "They could clean the place up if they wanted to,"

Buford retorted. "But they won't. Give them a decent house and it would be a pigsty in a week. Why waste the money?"

To be sure there were decent houses. Manassas Brown, the Tuckers and members of the Taylor family had built bungalows on the outskirts of the community. They had acquired television aerials and automobiles. One or two had telephones, and the year before Washington Taylor put down a well and installed a bathroom at the home place where Melusina, his mother, lived. But the fine words, like flags unfurling, that had been spoken at Gettysburg had yet to be resolved.

The little church was very old. It had a scrubbed, threadbare quality, a simplicity that was pleasing. The walls were white-painted. The pulpit was of brown-stained wood. On either side of the altar was a can wrapped in silver tinfoil and filled with artificial roses. Beside the battered upright piano stood a solitary green rubber plant.

The meeting was already under way when Mike arrived. Though the evening was not cold, women with infants cradled in their arms and the children huddled around the pot-bellied stove that was crammed with slow-burning pine knots.

The Muster Corner congregation was distinguished by the Taylor family. Of all the Negro families in the country, the Taylors stood the highest. They were the oldest and most aristocratic and most prosperous. Melusina was undisputed matriarch. As she sat in her side pew, her back ramrod straight, her face beneath her flowered hat was the face of an African carving.

On this Monday evening Mike was wrong if he hoped to escape unnoticed. Preacher Young finished reading from Chapter Four, St. Mark: "And have no root in themselves, and so endure but for a time: afterward, when affliction or persecution ariseth for the word's sake, immediately they are offended—that seeing they may see and not perceive, and hearing they may hear and not understand . . ." He gazed down from the podium. "I see our good friend Mr. Editor Latimer has arrived. I think we should give him a big hand. If it hadn't been for Mr. Editor, Brother Taylor would have been home on Sunday, tending to business, instead of socializing." He paused to let the laughter die down. "Sister Taylor"—he nodded in the direction of Linda—"tells me that the Covertside Inn needs some advice on how to fry chicken." Again he waited for the laughter. Then he continued.

"Seriously, Brother Smith here asked me tonight if Mr. Buford had died. I said I hadn't heard any such news. Brother Smith replied that he'd heard Mr. Buford say that if a colored person entered a local restaurant it would be over his dead body. Therefore, he presumed that Mr. Buford had passed."

Mrs. Cindy Smith and Mrs. Leona Stuart, sitting in front of Mike, shook with laughter. "Hear, hear," cried the congregation.

When the Reverend could again be heard it was to say, "And so, my friends, let's give Mr. Latimer our thanks."

"Amen, amen," echoed the congregation. Nodding their heads in accord, they clapped strenuously.

When the clapping subsided, the minister wound up the routine business of the evening. As he thanked various committees for the bake sales, the clothes collected for his students, the books received for his library, and congratulated the Ladies' Auxiliary for money raised through chicken dinners and socials, Mike was struck by the instinctive courtesy that these Negroes extended to one another.

Now Preacher Young turned the meeting over to the contractor to report on "D-Day in Shelburn." Mike found himself studying the tall blue-eyed Negro. No matter how distilled, no matter how vast the accretions of corruption that slavery and segregation had silted upon the original stock, certain nobilities remained. Washington Taylor was descended from kings and, it was universally believed, from the last of the Shelburn men. In the fine shape of his head, his high-bridged nose with its flaring nostrils, and remarkable hooded eyes lay the proofs of his heritage. That such a man could have spent his entire life in a town the size of Shelburn without ever before being permitted to eat in a local restaurant seemed incredible.

Although he was largely self-taught and held no degrees, Washington Taylor's speech was more precise, more eloquent than that of Preacher Young. In Washington's talk there were none of the usual Negro homilies or euphemisms. He did not call members of the audience brother or sister. And just as it would never have occurred to Mike to presume upon their friendship by calling him anything more familiar than Mr. Taylor, it would not have been natural for the contractor to call Mike anything other than Mr. Latimer.

Now Mike heard him say, "Today, thanks to Mr. Latimer, the

Reverend Chamberlain and our other white friends, local restaurants were desegregated. But"—and his voice jerked the audience to attention—"our fight is just now beginning. After two hundred years of segregation, of separate schools and unequal opportunities, we've taken just one small step. We have many more to take. A long way to travel before we sleep. The price of civil rights, of gaining our legal and moral rights, is eternal struggle." His eyes swept the congregation. "Our cause is just and right. There is no longer room for the fearful, the weak-kneed, the Uncle Toms, afraid to register and vote for fear of annoying a handful of bigoted white people. We cannot. We must not let down now. Our next step is to register in order that you and you and you may vote. Until enough of us do this, we cannot hope to have proper leadership. Another and longer step is school integration. We all know what separate but equal facilities means." His fist came down on the rostrum. "Cast-off desks from the white schools. Desks so scarred and broken they cannot be written upon. Damaged, inadequate primers. Not enough paper or pencils or playground facilities. Toilets that don't flush." Pausing, he glanced at his watch. "It's late. We've talked enough. God doesn't want our words. He wants our works. Now is the time for action. Actions that speak louder than words. Actions that tell the white people we mean what we say."

He glanced at his wife, sitting in a side pew with Lucy Mae, whose wheelchair had been left at the door. His voice softened. "A few years before I was born, Virginia went Jim Crow. Before God calls me home I want to see my people free. Now at last the day has come when Lucy Mae and I may sit at a drugstore counter and eat the food that we order in the company of white people. If those of us here tonight have done nothing else in our lifetime of struggle, we have at least accomplished this." Again he paused. "Tomorrow Lucy Mae and I will sit in the Gone Away drugstore. We will sit at the counter. We will sit there, if we choose to, until our ice cream melts."

"Where are my eggs?" Mike asked the next morning.

"Aren't any," Shelley answered. "Yesterday was a holiday. Labor Day, remember? I'm going to town this morning."

Mike looked out at the magnolia outside the kitchen window

where the banties roosted. "My God, with all these chickens. Don't they lay eggs?"

"I haven't had time to collect them. Cam, eat your breakfast."

"I don't like cornflakes," Cam said.

"You've got to learn to eat what's put in front of you. Think of the poor children like Jimmy and Bardy who don't have anything to eat."

"I hate green beans," Cam said irrelevantly. "Girls and green beans are my worst enemies. Daddy, did you like beans when you were little?"

"No," Mike said. "I can't say that I did. Shelley, please sit down. You make me nervous."

"I'm waiting for the toast to pop up."

She wished she could sit down. But she couldn't. Like Cam, she could not stay still. Anxieties, omissions, guilts beat against her mind like the speckled hen tapping at the windowpane. Chicken feed. They were out of chicken feed. Out of almost everything. Breakfast had been the remaining can of frozen orange juice and the last of the cold cereal. All that remained of the bread were the two crusted ends now in the toaster.

"Please eat something," Mike said.

"I'm not hungry. Honestly."

The toast popped up and she carried it to the table. She put one piece on his plate, one on Cam's.

"Is there any jam?" Cam asked.

"No," Shelley answered. "I'll get some this morning."

"I have to pick up copy from the country correspondents," Mike said. "Shelley, come with me."

All that she had to do came crowding in on her. "I can't. The horses, marketing. The Pony Club's coming this afternoon for a practice session."

"You told me you were going to get out of the Pony Club."

"I know, but there's nobody else. I promised to work with the younger kids. I was hoping Cam could ride in the School Show."

"He doesn't want to. Why force him?"

"You do so, don't you, Cam?" Shelley asked.

"I'd rather play baseball with Jimmy." Cam looked at his slightly burnt curled-up crust and began crumbling it on his plate.

"I wish you'd come with me," Mike repeated. "Shelley, you

used to like to come with me. Miss Abby Cooke at Cooke's Store said she hasn't seen you in months."

"I wish I could," Shelley said. She thought of the first weeks with the paper, when once a week they piled into the station wagon or the Jeep and drove to the far ends of the county to collect the weekly columns from the country correspondents. Miss Abby always made them pause for a chat, gave them coffee or a Coke, talked about the Shelburns and the old days and sent them off with vegetables from her garden or homemade relish or preserves from her store. There had been time then. Why, now, was there no longer time?

"I want a zap gun like Buddha's," Cam said.

"Cam," Shelley said, "if you've finished you can start feeding the dogs."

"There isn't any dog food."

"Oh, Lord, well, we'll have to wait until after I've been to town."

"I wish you'd come with me," Mike persisted when he was leaving.

"I'd like to," she repeated, "but the Pony Club—"

"Damn the Pony Club," Mike said and went out the door.

Following the June rally, Shelley had agreed to give up what Mike called the Four-Footed Little League. Then Millicent and the others persuaded her to continue. "You're so good at it," the mothers argued. "The children are so fond of you."

She told Mike it was because of the children that she stayed on. Still, when it came actually to relinquishing her authority, Shelley procrastinated. It was as if the frenetic activity of working with children and horses fulfilled a basic need, that of absolving her from more demanding pursuits, painting or helping Mike with the paper.

Because nobody was home and somebody had to do it, she had made up the fixture card of Pony Club events for the fall season and mailed it out to the members. The first meeting, a schooling session in preparation for the School Show to be held in October, was to be that afternoon.

She'd tell Millicent that afternoon, she decided, starting for the stable to see Virginia City about tacking up Millicent's young horse that needed to be exercised.

The telephone stopped her. It was Washington calling, the *Cap-*

ital Courier, for Mike. "He's just left," she told the operator. "I'll give him the message to call you."

It was another golden day. For over a month there had not been rain. The corn in the fields was shriveled and the late hay had gone to seed. In order to fill their lofts, the owners of the big stables were being forced to buy it off trucks from the West. Now the town well was in danger of going dry and Mike had been asked to warn his readers to conserve water. The preceding spring, when a water main burst, Mike had learned that the system was dangerously antiquated. Laid out at the turn of the century, when the population had been half the size it was now, it consisted of a well from which the community's water supply was pumped into a rotting wooden tank at the north end of town. Mike warned editorially that such a system was primitive and inadequate and that funds should be appropriated for a new and modernized system.

Nothing had been done. There was no local industry and but a handful of business concerns. Consequently, taxes provided little income and the town treasury held no funds for improvements.

It was like everything else, Mike thought, frustrated. Sewage disposal, street lights, parking meters and the water supply. Until the stench became overpowering, somebody was killed at the corner and the well ran dry, no changes, no improvements, would be made.

The more Mike thought about it, the more his New England conscience rebelled. How was it possible, he wondered, to instill in this strange community, characterized by the *Gone with the Wind* "I'll think about it tomorrow" concept of the Old South, compounded with Northern disinterest, the basic lesson learned at his father's knee and from New England town meetings, that there was a price to be paid for everything.

Mike had collected the copy from the country correspondents, Miss Emily at Mooreville, Mrs. Loganberry at Mount Sinai and Miss Abby Cooke at Cooke's Store. He had listened to their comments on the drought, rabid foxes, and the failure of the corn crop. It was after noon. If he went to the office now, he would be inundated with the usual weekly problems of making up the first run of the paper. Might as well stop by the Gone Away and have lunch first.

He left the car at Gilbert's gas station to be inspected and set off down the wide, sunlit main street. As he approached the *Sun* building, he saw how dingy the plate-glass window had become. It reminded him that before he could have it washed he would have to bail Jubal out of the old brick jail that had rusted iron bars, moss in the cracks and clay-packed floors, smelling of urine, and where in warm weather you could see the heavyset policeman tilted against the wall in a straight chair, spitting reflectively in the red dust of the back street.

Passing the *Sun* building, Mike continued by the bank and the newsstand, where Charlie Woodruff sat behind the counter hunched over the *Morning Telegraph*. As he came to the post office, he noticed Major DeLong's dilapidated unpainted buggy parked behind Millicent's Rolls. The bony horse, his reins wrapped around a parking meter, stood with his head down. His ears were at half mast and he appeared the soul of dejection. On the driver's seat lay Joe, the Major's yellow hound, grown so old now that he no longer knew friend from foe, his legs hanging down in front of him, one baleful eye cocked at the passersby.

"Hi, Joe," Mike called out.

At the sound of his name the old dog lifted his head, stared malevolently at Mike and emitted a low warning growl. Simultaneously, Major Southgate DeLong came out of the post office.

The Major, a widower, was the last of the DeLongs. (Charlie Woodruff had once had the temerity to suggest to Miss Letty, the community's leading old maid, that instead of the *Saturday Evening Post* what she really needed was a *Country Gentleman* like Major DeLong.) A man of stiff heel-clicking courtesy, of antebellum manners and ante-bellum airs, the Major evoked a melancholy sense of anachronism, like that evoked by DeLong Manor, the big crumbling white-pillared ghost of a place where he lived with his dogs, pistol collections and memories of past grandeur.

The Major's attitude toward money was also ante-bellum. After the Civil War, many of the best families had been left penniless. Those with money were suspect, as if they had come by it through ill-gotten gains, gun-running for the North or selling ill-fitting shoes that fell apart to the Confederate armies. It would not have occurred to him to replace DeLong Manor's broken windows with anything other than cardboard, or to remove the icebox rusting in the weeds smothering the backyard. He was a

Southern gentleman, one of the last of a dying breed who kept fighting cocks in the basement, hounds on the second-floor gallery, and made their own corn liquor. To the Major's mind, any kind of a moneymaking job was unthinkable. Poverty, like his pointed beard and the pearl-handled pistol Sean Shelburn had presented to his father, was a prideful thing.

In The Valley there was an old saying to the effect that as long as you had a roof overhead and a horse below, you weren't really poor.

There was no question but that the Major in his faded scarlet, high silk hat, held over a steaming kettle of boiling water to make it smooth and shiny, and the tall bony horse lent tone to the hunting field. When arthritis forced him to give up foxhunting, the sight of him standing up in his stirrups and halloaing away a fox was sorely missed.

Elected mayor (nobody else wanted the job and it was thought that his presence would add a certain distinction to the community), he soon became a public menace. Daily he stood on the bank corner, clad in well-fitted jodhpurs, ancient English tweeds, string tie and cloth cap, passing the time of day with Miss Letty's yardman, Raymond Hoe, who played the guitar for local parties, Jubal Jones, Mattie Moore and other local Negroes who, congregating there, observed the comings and goings of the community.

Typically, neither the Major nor the Negroes saw anything contradictory in the fact that while inquiring about Raymond Hoe's rheumatism or Lucy Mae Taylor's progress with her painting, the dignified white-haired old gentleman passed out inflammatory hate pamphlets supplied by segregation groups.

To Mike, one of the most puzzling aspects of the civil rights issue lay in the Major's relationship with Negroes. Although a violent racist, he seemed to be loved and looked up to by the local colored people. Naomi Brown, Manassas Brown's older sister, had worked for the DeLongs since childhood. She cooked for the Major, put up with his drunken rages and verbal abuse, and had not received any wages since Young South's death. Yet she accorded the old man the same deference and devotion that Joe, his hound dog, kicked and beaten and half-starved, gave him. Whereas the Northern residents, who paid high wages and gave their employees countless days off, complained of continual servant troubles, Naomi, who rarely left the crumbling home place and collected mustard greens from the fields for food when the larder was empty, would have given her life for the last of the DeLongs.

At first Mike attempted to reason with the Major. Quickly he realized that reason, when it came to the question of race, Republicans or damn Yankees, was nonexistent. Dowdey's *Life of Lee* was the Major's bible. Once he told Mike that every time he read about Gettysburg, he became so excited that he cried out, "This time, by gum, we'll lick those Yankees!"

When Mike compared the North to the Roundheads, calling them "right but repulsive," and the Southern cause to that espoused by the Cavaliers as "wrong but romantic," the Major replied stiffly, "Sir, I don't consider that we were wrong!"

Eventually, unable to work because of the mayor's constant interruptions and tirades, Mike was forced to bar him from the *Sun* office. The mayor retaliated by having "No Parking" signs put up in front of the office and ordering Chester Glover to fine any vehicles parked between the signs.

Because the price to be paid for his picturesqueness was being harangued to death, Major DeLong was not re-elected mayor. This removed him from the street corner and forced his return to the crumbling manor house and the solitary drinking bouts, punctuated by wild interims of target practice that succeeded in peppering the family portraits with bullet holes.

Now he rarely appeared in town except to attend church or gather up a pitiful supply of groceries, consisting largely of dog food for Joe.

If the old man cared for any living thing, it was Joe. Joe was the last remaining descendant of the Colonel's outlaw pack. According to his owner the hound, as thin and ugly a specimen of canine as one could hope to encounter, was the most accomplished dog in dogdom.

When South, Jr., died in the Korean war, there was nobody left at the home place but the Major and Joe and Naomi. With his son gone, it was as if the Major gave up, worn out like his land and his family. Bit by bit the land was sold off. Finally only the great house and surrounding yard remained. Sitting in his den, a dark, gloomy room filled with moth-eaten fox brushes, his father's Civil

War saber, mildewing tomes and guns in glass cases racked along the wall, the Major sipped the toddies that Naomi brewed in the tarnished silver cups won long ago by DeLong horses and brooded over the rising black tide. This he saw as part of the Yankee plot that had overthrown the old order, causing the war with those yellow Korean bastards who had killed his only son.

When Jonathan Bentley moved into the house on Wildcat Hill, Major DeLong focused his hatreds and his old brass Civil War cannon on the rise that lay across The Valley from his front door. Every evening at sundown he played what The Valley called "Boom the Bentleys." This consisted of loading the cannon with gunpowder and firing it at the house belonging to the leading senatorial exponent of civil rights.

When the farm truck disintegrated, the Major took Artaxerxes from the field and hitched the aged hunter, now almost twenty years old, to the once-elegant phaeton that had stood in the shed since his father's day and which the fighting cocks used as a roost. While the abandoned truck went to ruin in the yard, the Major drove to town with Joe, now almost blind, curled on the seat beside him.

Now as he came out of the post office, the Major looked seedy and unkempt. His beard needed trimming. The buttons were missing from his frayed tweed jacket (on the lapel of which Naomi had pinned her market list with a clothspin) and his shoes were filthy. Gone, Mike thought sympathetically, all of it gone. The wife and son, the horses and the land. All but the name and the pride and the prejudice.

Mike spoke politely. "Good morning, sir. Nice day, isn't it?"

The Major stiffened. His body straightened. For an instant his eyes turned on Mike. Then, as though in response to some inwardly spoken command, the Major's head snapped forward. Tight-lipped, wordless, he marched past.

Mike felt a kind of sickness in his stomach as he turned into the Gone Away drugstore. He thought of what Washington Taylor had once said. "If you are spoken to by the white people, you nod and say good morning. If not, you get out of the way."

ELEVEN

SHELLEY noticed that the oaks were turning a golden yellow and the maple at the entrance to the drive had a sprinkling of crimson leaves. She called to Lance and Miehle and the hound puppies to "Stay!" Reluctantly they backed off from the station wagon.

"I wish we could take them," Cam said. "Everyone else does."

"I know," Shelley agreed. "But your father is right. They could be run over, and they're not allowed in the supermarket."

She looked right and left and then, seeing that the Valley road was clear, turned onto it.

"Can we go to the Gone Away and have ice cream?"

"We'll see."

She waved to Bones Black, running along the side of the road in his rubber reducing suit. Shelley wondered why he bothered to lose weight in order to ride at the fall Hunt meets. After the night at the Bufords', Millicent would probably take the horses away, send them to Maryland to be trained.

Shelburn was crowded. The people who went to the Cape, to Maine, to Newport, out West or to Europe for the summer were home now. After the long holiday weekend, everyone seemed to be in town, at the post office, the liquor store, or replenishing their larders at the supermarket. Chauffeurs and colored boys trundled laden pushcarts along the sidewalk to waiting station wagons, farm trucks and Jeeps, while mothers clung to their children and dogs to keep them from running out in front of the out-of-state cars attempting to make their way through the local traffic blocking the street.

Eventually a car pulled out from the space behind Millicent Black's trailer. Two of the children's ponies were in the trailer munching hay. Millicent's tan terriers perched on the rear seat of the Rolls, behind the rolled-up glass that separated the front from the back and which Millicent maintained kept children and dogs seen but not heard.

Shelley backed the station wagon into the space behind the trailer. As usual, she didn't have any change. When she had asked Larry Gillespie, now one of the bank tellers, to find out the balance in her checking account, he'd returned with the amount written on a slip of paper. One dollar and seventy-nine cents. This was to last her until the middle of the month, when the small income check from the trust left by her father was due. Fortunately, there was food stored in the freezer and although the supermarket had a rule against charge accounts, she had persuaded Mr. Johnson, the new manager, to let her have credit until her income check came.

"You didn't put any money in the meter," Cam stated accusingly.

"Damn it, I haven't any change." She took his hand. "Come on, we won't be long."

Cam hung back. "Daddy says it's dishonest not to put money in the meter."

Artaxerxes stood tied to the meter in front of the market. The red marker was up. Almost all the meters lining the street showed violations. It still annoyed Shelley to have to find the proper change to feed into their metal maws. Almost everybody else felt the same way. The result was that the meters had yet to yield more than a pittance to the town treasury. Because of Chester Glover's reticence about handing out tickets to people like the Bufords, the Dinwiddies, the Dash-Smythes and T. Patterson Gibson, the amount that would have compensated in fines was not forthcoming. When the actual placing of tickets on the windshields of cars long overparked became unavoidable, the policeman did it with a furtive air of apology, as if hoping that nobody would notice. Generally the tickets were torn up and the dollar fine disregarded.

Mike considered this part of the pattern of irresponsibility, like building farm ponds with government money when you weren't a farmer, and cheating on the income tax.

"Mommy," Cam persisted, "Daddy says—"

"I know what Daddy says, God damn it!" Shelley was hot and in a hurry to get home and set up schooling fences for the Pony Club. "Oh, all right. I'll borrow a dime and come back."

The supermarket was the women's meeting place. Divorces were discussed by the diet section. Dinner parties were planned over Produce. Horse deals were made, servants hired and fired, and the latest gossip exchanged over the pushcarts.

On the morning after Labor Day it was a madhouse, as crowded as Friday night, when the farmers and Free Zoners and the Negroes from Muster Corner did their weekly shopping. Aisles teemed with bulging pushcarts, children and dogs. After several rousing dog fights resulting in broken glass and damaged property, the manager had tried to keep dogs off the premises. Finding his signs and his pleas disregarded, he had given up. Now when Millicent came in with her Jones terriers or Debby Darbyshire with Butch, her German shepherd, he merely shrugged and glanced the other way. It hadn't taken him long to realize that these people were laws unto themselves and that if he wanted to remain as manager of the market he would have to accept the occasional checks that bounced, the complaints from people like old Mrs. Dinwiddie, who intimated it was his fault that food prices were so high, and Major Southgate DeLong's paranoid anger at the checkers he insisted were trying to cheat him. From his glass cage by the entrance the young manager had seen the mask of refined living slip away, as when Mrs. Dinwiddie accused Mrs. Black of stealing her groom and the two women had almost come to blows in the dairy section—or when Mrs. Darbyshire cornered Mrs. Atwell by the canned goods and blamed her for cutting her off at a fence in the hunting field.

Now as he observed the crowded aisles and the long lines at the checkout counters, he sensed a kind of electricity in the air, a tension that seemed to penetrate through the glass into his cubicle. From the remarks he overheard, he realized it had something to do with the business of desegregation that had taken place on Sunday. The name Latimer was mentioned. The blame and the animosity, triggered by the announcement made in church, seemed now to have crystallized and be focused on the editor.

"I went along on the campaign for a new sewer and water for Muster Corner and his other crusades," he heard Mrs. Black say to Mrs. Darbyshire when they paused by his cubicle to buy cigarettes. "But this is real-ley going too far!"

As the automatic doors swung open, he saw Mrs. Latimer and her little boy come in.

Normally Shelley enjoyed her trips to the supermarket. She thought of it as a warm and friendly place where she saw friends, exchanged news about the weather, the Pony Club, the hunting and other local activities. Generally she picked up news items for the paper and saved the time spent telephoning by accepting or turning down invitations and making arrangements concerning Cam's activities.

At the nearest counter Tina Welford and Sion Atwell waited to be checked out. They leaned across their bulging wire baskets talking animatedly to each other. As Shelley started toward them they glanced up. For an instant their faces became blank, closed, like the automatic doors swinging shut behind her. Then their odd, faintly guilty expressions were replaced by smiles that suddenly struck Shelley as vague and meaningless. It was the same smile they reserved for the colored people lounging in front of the "No Loitering" sign by the doorway, for people like Katie Schligman and Connie Jackson, people who were not quite, quite—

A chill ran through her, like that of coming from the heat of noonday into an air-conditioned building. As though seeking escape, she glanced around. The eyes of the Negroes dropped. She felt a sudden compulsion to speak to them, make them look at her, recognize her as Miss Shelley of Shelburn Hall. Taking Cam by the hand, she moved as though in a receiving line, calling each Negro by name, shaking hands and making appropriate remarks.

"Mommy." Cam tugged at her hand. "The meter."

"I forgot."

"Miss Shelley, I'll put some money in the meter," Russell Grimes volunteered, taking a nickel from his pocket. The young Negro had grown up at Last Resort, where he worked in the stable. Shelley thanked him warmly and started toward the produce section. "I'll pay you back later."

"Hold hard," Betsy Baldwin cried as Cam, piloting Shelley's cart, rammed into hers. This was followed by the sound of cereal boxes crashing down as her Spunky climbed onto a lower shelf in order to reach one of the brands that boasted a prize inside. "Pick them up," Betsy directed, grabbing her six-month-old baby, who was about to topple out of the cart.

"Spunky, here's a penny and one for Cam. Go and get some bubble gum. Whew"—she smiled at Shelley—"it'll be a relief when school starts tomorrow."

What is happening to me? Shelley thought. For an instant she had expected Betsy to be different, distant, Betsy, whom she had always known. But Betsy looked and acted the same, her too-tight blue jeans enlarging rather than compressing her growing middle-aged spread, hair unpermanented and unfashionably cut, and the faintly anxious, harassed expression that a big house and numerous children to take care of, without enough money or adequate help, had caused to become habitual. Following her divorce from Bones and her marriage to Togo she had given up trying to keep up with the group, the cocktail set made up of the Blacks and the Bufords and the young marrieds, resigning herself to what Debby Darbyshire termed narrowing the mind and broadening the hips.

"Hmmm," she said now, studying the long list in her hand. "I need some more jars. We're still putting up tomatoes and pickles."

Turning the corner into Paper Products, Detergents and Household Supplies, they came upon Millicent and Merry. Millicent was inspecting an assortment of paper napkins. Her ankle was still taped. She had on pants, a red-striped silk turtleneck, and dark wraparound glasses shaped like a brassiere. She was lighting a cigarette.

"Got to have one to think," she said, blowing out the match and dropping it onto the floor. "Oh, hi, Betsy. Hi—" Her eyes slid away from Shelley and she began busily pulling out packages of napkins.

"Hello, Merry," Shelley said. The little girl gave her a shy, delighted smile. Merry was dressed for Pony Club in clean blue jeans and a checked shirt. Her dark hair was neatly braided into two pigtails and tied with red ribbons. She was holding one of Millicent's puppies on a leash.

"Mrs. Latimer, will you take us for a ride this afternoon and let us go swimming in the Ballyhoura pond?"

"I don't know if we'll have time. We're supposed to practice for the School Show. I love your puppy." She bent down to pat the Jones. The tiny puppy rolled on its back, its entire body wiggling with pleasure.

"Yes, he's sweet," Betsy said.

"He's Mother's precious-darling-love," Millicent enthused. "His father was Best of Opposite Sex at Westminster. Merry"— her voice sharpened—"for God's sake, don't let him piddle."

But Merry, distracted by Cam offering her some bubble gum,

was too late to keep the puppy from squatting beside a large box of laundry detergent.

With a resigned expression, Millicent reached into her enormous handbag. Lifting the flap with the brass horseshoe on it, she extracted a piece of absorbent tissue. "Mother's precious-darling-love doesn't know any better, does 'um?" she crooned, dropping the tissue onto the puddle beside the soap box.

"What on earth?" Betsy stared at the tissue.

"Oh, want to see?" Millicent beamed at her husband's first wife. The dog's "teething bracelet" with the bangles that she always wore tinkled as, digging into her shoulder bag once more, she brought out a handful of tissues. "I had Bergdorf's make me up a carload. See, it has 'Mother's Precious-Darling-Love' printed in the corner, in our racing colors. Perfect for mopping up after the dogs. And you know how Bones hates dog do."

"Yes," Betsy said dryly, "come to think of it, Bones is quite fastidious."

Millicent nodded. "Never lifts a finger and wants everything just so." She turned back to the paper napkins. "I'm going in for paper napkins and plates. Clara hasn't turned up since Friday and I'm sick of doing dishes." She rolled her eyes in the direction of Shelley. "Real-ley, the servant problem is getting unbelievable. Anyway, Bones has moved back to the Rakish Stud. So who cares whether we eat off the Worcester or off paper? Sometimes I think you were right to divorce him."

Shelley was so intrigued listening to this conversation she forgot that Millicent seemed to be deliberately ignoring her presence. Now she wondered what Betsy was going to say.

Betsy, however, was saved from having to reply.

"God, I wish somebody would clock me." Debby Darbyshire strode up. Butch, her German shepherd, was tied to her overflowing cart. "This is the third time around looking for Alpo. Butch, no!"

"Take him away," Millicent screamed. "Merry, you idiot, keep Mother's precious-darling-love away from that monster."

But Merry was too late. Butch lunged toward the puppy, towing the cart behind him and spewing an assortment of groceries onto the aisle.

Shelley pushed Merry out of the way and scooped up the puppy.

"Christ, the caviar!" cried Debby, lunging for the falling jars.

"Fuck the caviar and curb your dog!" Millicent screamed at Debby. "That undisciplined beast could have killed my little love."

"Ladies. Ladies." It was the manager. At the sound of the fracas, he had come running from his cubicle. "Ladies, please!"

Laboriously he began picking up the boxes of dog biscuit, jars of caviar and cans of tomatoes and other items that had fallen out of Debby's cart.

Shelley waited for Millicent to thank her for rescuing the puppy. Instead, Millicent grabbed the trembling animal and began stalking toward the checkout counter. With a shy, apologetic smile, Merry followed, pushing the cart.

Shelley stood looking after them. Was it her imagination or had they deliberately excluded her? Although she rarely had time or the inclination to join them for lunch, they had never before failed to ask her. "Come along, Shelley. Do you good. You're too thin. Have some coffee. Have a milkshake."

At sight of the Beast at the meat counter sudden shyness came over Shelley. Would the old lady turn on her also?

Mrs. Dinwiddie resembled one of the scarecrows her farmer put up in her garden to ward off scavenging birds. Yet in spite of the long burlap skirt she wore both summer and winter, the man's felt hat with the moth holes in the brim, and the cracked high shoes with their leather laces, her spare build and imperious manner gave her a distinction that set her apart from Tessie, Samantha Sue's maid, who, wearing one of her mistress's cast-off Chanel suits, waited for Mr. Compton, the butcher, to finish discussing the rising cost of meat with Mrs. Dinwiddie and take her order.

"Mr. Compton, be sure to trim off the fat. Oh, Shelley. Good morning. I didn't see you standing there. The only beef we buy now is for the dogs." Mrs. Dinwiddie lowered her voice. "Shelley, I meant to speak to you this morning. Yes, Mr. Compton, top round! Dinny and I will eat frankfurters." She directed her attention back to Shelley. "My dear, I've known you since you were a child. Your mother and my youngest brother—well, never mind. What I want to say is this. People are saying—"

Shelley was aware of the heavy chilled feeling that had come over her in the hunting field. "Just what *are* people saying?"

Mrs. Dinwiddie's eyes dropped. "You know. About your activities! My dear, why doesn't the *Sun* do something about the Indians? Think of what those poor people have had to put up with all these years. Why, thank you, Mr. Compton." She graciously accepted the bundles of meat that had been wrapped for her. "Shelley, do speak to your husband about the Indians. Dinny is waiting. I must fly."

"Wait," Shelley called after her. "You haven't told me which tribe!"

Shelley doubled back by Produce. Although only half her list was completed, she determined to leave the market as soon as possible.

She waited for Leslie, Wiley Matthews's daughter, newly employed as a checker, to ring up her order. She wished the new girl wasn't so slow. She wanted to be away, back home with the horses and dogs. At that moment, even the turtles seemed preferable to humans.

Leslie was having trouble. Frowning, she studied the prices marked on each item. When it came to the dozen cans of dog food she rang each one up separately.

"Mommy," Cam said plaintively, "I'm hungry."

"Please, Cam, be patient. I have to write a check."

"Mommy, I saw Mr. Buford go into the Gone Away. You can ask *him* about Buddha."

After what seemed an interminable time, Leslie finished ringing up the order. Forgetting the state of her bank account, Shelley wrote a check to cover the amount listed on the register and to pay Virginia City the money owed him for chicken feed. Without waiting to count the change Leslie laid on the counter in front of her, she picked up the bills and stuffed them into her wallet.

The groceries were loaded into the station wagon. Russell had been tipped and repaid the nickel he had put into the meter.

"Please, Mommy, aren't we going to the Gone Away for lunch? Mommy, you promised," Cam pleaded.

"Oh, Cam, we're so late. I've got to get the food put away. The Pony Club's coming at two." She switched on the ignition.

"But, Mommy, you promised."

Shelley turned it off again. "Cam, I know, but would you mind?"

"Maybe Daddy's at the Gone Away."

Shelley remembered that she had forgotten to call Mike and give him the message about the *Capital Courier*. "All right," she agreed resignedly, "but it will have to be quick."

"The meter," Cam said. "There's Mr. Glover now. He looks cross."

Shelley opened her change purse and handed Cam a nickel. Before he could put it in the meter, the policeman had gone by. His face was grim as, without looking to the right or the left, he shoved Lucy Mae's wheelchair out of his way, flung open the door of the drugstore and marched in.

Lucy Mae's empty wheelchair stood in front of the Gone Away. Washington Taylor's triumphant words rang in Mike's ears. "I'm going to carry her into the drugstore, set her down on a stool, and then we're going to sit at that counter and eat our ice cream cones."

The drugstore was crowded with local businessmen having an early lunch, jockeys from the track with emaciated bodies and pinched old-young faces eating Spartan midday meals of grapefruit and diet bread, owners and trainers, the mink and manure set drinking coffee. Usually horses were the main topic of conversation. Mike had once set a fifty-cent piece in front of him. When Doc Dickerson was plainly insulted by what he thought was a tip, Mike hastily explained that the money was not there for that reason. "I have a bet with myself. If the day ever comes when I hear talk about some topic other than sex and horses, I'll treat you to a drink."

Generally when Mike entered, Doc hailed him from behind the prescription counter. "Hiya, Editor, what's new?" After he exchanged greetings with the customers at the tables and counter, accepted change for classified ads, subscription money or advertising copy, Mrs. Winecoop or Ethel took his order.

Today there was a marked difference. Instead of the usual hubbub, voices were muted; and the atmosphere of good-natured camaraderie, friendliness and courtesy, fostered by the old-fashioned furnishings, the wire-backed chairs and glass containers filled with colored water, had been replaced by a sense of tension.

At the counter, sitting on the center stools, were Washington

Taylor and Lucy Mae. Although several people lingered by the tobacco counter, obviously waiting for a seat, the remaining stools were unoccupied.

Mike walked slowly toward them. As he threaded his way between the tables, the solid disapproval displayed on the faces of his subscribers seemed to squeeze the blood from his heart. He wished that, like Cam, he could go to Dr. Watters and be given some sort of shot that would immunize him against this draining emotional hurt. He knew, however, that to let his feelings show, by word or action, would be an admission of defeat.

Millicent Black and Debby Darbyshire and Sion Atwell were at the table by the lotions counter. They sat with their elbows on the table and their legs apart. It was the way they sat on their horses. With a kind of implacability, Mike thought, as though nothing could or would throw them.

He paused. "Good morning." Turning to Millicent, he asked, "How is your ankle?"

He saw her lips tighten and realized that by reminding her of her midnight march, he had been tactless.

"Muddy Watters taped it up." She did not look at him or take the cigarette out of her mouth. "I can still ride, sidesaddle."

Mike was aware of a sudden convulsion of dislike, part of which was aimed at himself. He was more of a hypocrite than they were. He had forced himself to stop and speak because he needed them, as subscribers and opinion makers. They belonged to the power structure. If he could get them to support his paper and its policies, the rest of the community would fall in line.

"I received the publicity about the School Show," he said deliberately. "I'll try and get it in this week." He'd gone so far, he might as well continue. "You wouldn't consider running an ad as well?"

"You know the Show is for the benefit of the building fund," Millicent drawled. "Surely you can afford to give us that much space."

Mike felt trapped. Millicent knew the contributor list for the new gym. His name was not on it. Next year Cam was due to enter first grade. It was within Millicent's power, as chairman of the Valley Day School Board, to see that Cam was refused admission. "All right, Millicent," he answered pleasantly, "we'll give you the space."

Apparently Mrs. Winecoop and Ethel had made good their threat to "resign rather than serve niggers." For Doc, a white apron wrapped around his waist and a worried expression on his face, was behind the counter. As he slapped hamburger patties onto the grill, his every motion registered disapproval.

Mike sat down on the stool next to Lucy Mae. "Good afternoon, Mr. Taylor. Good afternoon, Lucy Mae. My, you certainly do look pretty in that dress."

The little girl resembled a fairy, a café-au-lait fairy in a beautiful blue dress. Its skirt was full and starched and blossomed from the wide sash at her waist like the petals of an inverted flower. It had been hand-made by her great-grandmother Melusina, and all of Millicent's millions could not have duplicated the loving attention to detail and the delicate embroidery.

From the skirt, belled out over the stool, Lucy Mae's wasted legs and feet, encased in white socks and shiny new patent leather slippers, dangled helplessly.

In reply to Mike's greeting, she turned her head, bristling with neatly braided pigtails, and gave him a shy, delighted smile.

Mike felt a sudden renewal of strength. The image of the little colored girl, dressed in her Sunday best and sitting at the white marble-topped counter, compensated for the hate letters, the averted faces and canceled subscriptions.

In place of his workday khakis Washington Taylor wore his shiny black Sunday suit, white shirt and stiff starched collar and black tie. The suit was carefully pressed, the shirt meticulously clean, and the black shoes held a gloss rarely duplicated by the shoes of his white contemporaries.

"We could use some rain," Mike said conversationally. "Countryside's burnt to a crisp."

"I understand the town water supply is low," the Negro said.

Mike nodded. "Council asked me to put a notice in the paper about conserving water."

Doc turned around. He put two hamburgers, placed on napkins, down on the counter, one in front of each of the Taylors. Going to the coffee urn, he began drawing coffee.

"Excuse me," Washington Taylor said politely, "but we'd like plates for our hamburgers."

For a moment the proprietor stood rigid, his hand holding the coffee cup poised in mid-air. Then with the resigned expression of a man ordered into battle against his will, he reached to the shelf. Slowly his hands moved along past the heavy china plates served to the customers, until they fell on the pile of paper plates used for take-out orders. Methodically he unwrapped the outer covering and lifted two from the top of the pile. After what seemed an interminable time he turned, walked back to the counter, and grudgingly slid the paper plates across to the Negroes.

"Anything else you think you oughta get?"

"Yes," Washington Taylor said, "we'd like glasses of water."

Doc's face reddened. Controlling himself with a mighty effort, he walked back to the container on the wall, extracted two paper cups, ran them under the faucet and returned with them to the counter.

Dixie cups, Mike thought. Had it not been for the proprietor's face he would have laughed.

"What's *your* order?" Doc didn't look at Mike. "Ham, cheese on rye, tuna salad?"

During the years in which Mike had been running the paper he'd eaten at least once, sometimes twice a day at the Gone Away. Often Doc joined him as he ate "the usual." Mike's "usual"— cheeseburger and coffee—had come to be a standing joke. Once Doc ordered Ethel to serve Mike a cheese sandwich instead. He'd laughed uproariously when Mike absent-mindedly ate half of it before realizing it wasn't "the usual."

In the early days of the paper Mike often went to Doc for advice on how to handle local issues. The druggist had been a loyal supporter, persuading his customers to subscribe to the new *Sun* and advertise in it rather than the *County Daily*.

Now Mike realized that the past had been wiped away as cleanly, as deliberately as the drops of water that had sloshed over the edges of the paper cups when the proprietor set them down. As Doc continued to polish the counter, as if determined to eliminate some invisible spot, Mike looked at him steadily. "I'll have the usual, please."

Doc did not acknowledge the order or return his gaze. He gave the counter a few more swipes with his cloth, turned, and picked up a patty of raw beef. With a hand which trembled slightly, he dropped it onto the grill.

Mike realized he had been holding his breath.

Sensing the need to break the tension, Washington Taylor began talking about repairs at the *Sun* office. "We could be starting pretty soon," he said.

Mike shook his head. "I can't afford it now, Mr. Taylor. Some things have come up."

"Makes no difference, Mr. Latimer. You got to have the roof fixed. Not safe the way it is. It don't—" Quickly he corrected himself. "It doesn't matter when you get around to paying." His eyes, as blue as the liquid in one of the glass containers in the window, met Mike's.

Lucy Mae had been eating with quick, almost furtive gestures, as if fearful that her plate would be snatched away before the last crumb of bread and piece of meat had been consumed. Now, with a sigh of contentment, she turned expectantly to her grandfather.

"Ready, child?"

Slowly, solemnly, Lucy nodded.

"Two vanilla cones, please," Washington Taylor said.

Doc scooped the ice cream into a cone. Without tamping it down or bothering to wrap the cone in a paper napkin, he extended it across the counter to Lucy Mae. Lucy Mae's hand reached out. Then quickly she restrained herself.

"Is it all right, Granddad? Is it all right to take it?"

Washington Taylor's eyes softened. To his own family he had, with furious industry and his own native ability, given the economic independence that served as a measure of safety, a bulwark against bigotry. But this child, with paralyzed legs and heightened perception, the pale skin and the blue eyes so like his own, was utterly dependent, vulnerable. "Go ahead, child," he answered gently. "Eat it. It's your right."

"Thank you." Lucy Mae smiled at Doc. For an instant after taking the cone from him, she held it in her hand, wonder and disbelief flooding her face. Then, slowly, she brought the ice cream cone to her mouth. Her hand trembled, her eyes widened. Then her tongue darted out to meet it and on her face came a radiance that seemed to burn from some deep inward place, long dormant and just now ignited.

"Two hamburgers. Two cones. That's eighty cents," Doc said, not bothering to write out a check.

Washington Taylor brought out his wallet. Taking a dollar bill, he placed it on the counter.

Doc picked up the paper plates with one hand, the dollar with the other. Walking over to the trash basket, he dropped the plates into it. Then he went to the cash register and rang up eighty cents. Returning to the counter he placed two dimes in front of Washington Taylor. The colored man made no move to pick up the change. Staring into the mirror behind Doc, he continued to eat his ice cream.

Doc's generally colorless face was apoplectic. For an instant he stood motionless, his hands at his sides, clenching and unclenching. Then his eyes fell on the two paper cups left on the counter. Grabbing one in each hand he crumpled them up with a furious gesture and hurled them into the trash.

At that moment the door was flung open. Polo Pete Buford entered the drugstore. He wore his "racing suit," coat, trousers, "tatty" vest of the same livid black and puce checks as his racing colors, and his "lucky" hat, a green Tyrolean felt decorated with pins and badges, the gold United Hunt's horseshoe, the miniature halter with its tiny gold chain that was the emblem of the Halter Club, the buttons that gave him entry to the clubhouses at Aqueduct and Saratoga and status in the horse world.

In his right hand he carried his shooting stick.

Halfway to the tobacco counter Polo Pete stopped dead. At sight of Lucy Mae and Washington a look of stunned incomprehension came over his face. The color rose in his already ruddy cheeks and his eyes began to blink rapidly. Mike was reminded of Lance when a rabbit leaped up in front of him and it took a second or more for the mastiff's slow brain to react.

Ignoring the people at the tables, Polo Pete reached the counter. In a voice shaking with rage he addressed Doc. "So, it's true!"

"Mr. Buford, Mr. Buford, sir. This ain't my choice."

Mike felt the eyes on his back as he sat stiffly, aligned now with Washington Taylor and Lucy Mae.

"Get up!" The words boomed out like Major DeLong's cannon.

Washington Taylor turned slowly. Something about the unhurried quietness of the movement, the lack of subservience in his manner, was further salt in the raw wound of Polo Pete's fury, spreading now throughout the room. Grabbing the lapels of Washington's black suit, the fat man jerked him upright. There was a ripping sound as the buttons came loose. Then Polo Pete sent his fist crashing into Washington Taylor's face.

Polo Pete had not forgotten his college boxing lessons. For years his prowess with his fists had stood him in good stead at the race track, where he once got into a famous hassle with a bookie, and at Hunt Balls when the gentry got into free-for-alls. He hit the Negro with a deft right to the jaw. Washington Taylor went down like a giant tree, banging the side of his head on the stool. Like a furious child, all control gone, Buford grabbed his shooting stick. Prodding the fallen man in the ribs, he pushed him back down against the base of the counter.

For one awful moment nobody moved. Doc stood behind the counter, his face ashen. Lucy Mae sat like a graven image, the ice cream from her cone dripping onto her immaculate starched skirt. Her very stillness and the ice cream melting slowly down over her clenched fist seemed to Mike more terrible than any outward sign of fear or anger.

It was as though Mike had an ulcer that had been festering for months, growing daily under the pressures of restraint. Now, provoked by Buford's unwarranted attack, it burst suddenly into action.

Without thought of the consequences, he rose and grabbed the shooting stick from Buford's hand. Caught off balance, the fat man staggered. Falling sideways against the tobacco counter, he sent the pyramid of cans rolling across the floor.

"My God!" Millicent cried, taking the cigarette out of her mouth. The little jockeys giggled nervously. Herm Gillespie, owner of the General Store, a large part of whose income came from Silver Hill Farms, arose and went to assist Polo Pete.

Simultaneously the street door was flung wide and Chester Glover crashed in. Behind him Mike saw Shelley, one hand at her mouth, the other holding Cam's.

Taking in the scene at a glance, the policeman purposefully marched toward Washington Taylor, who, with Mike's assistance, was up off the floor and leaning dazedly against the counter. Grabbing the Negro roughly by the shoulder he started propelling him toward the entrance.

"Take your hands off him!" Mike cried involuntarily. "Mr. Taylor didn't do anything."

This was too much for the policeman. "Mr. Taylor," he exploded. "So it's *Mister* Taylor now, is it? Reckon when I book Mattie Moore on Saturday night for being drunk and cutting up the folks in niggertown, I'll be calling her Missus Moore!" Aware that he had the full attention of his audience, including Mrs. Black, who gave the biggest contribution to the VFW banquet which he chairmanned annually for the benefit of the local organization, Chester put one hand on his hip. Holding Washington Taylor with the other, he assumed a falsetto voice. "Missus Moore, please, ma'am, will you kindly follow me? At your convenience, that is."

One of the jockeys laughed openly and the policeman threw him a look of appreciation. Then he returned to the business at hand. "Come on. I've had enough of you and your friends, *Mister* Taylor. 'Bout time you learned your place in this here town. We'll see what the Judge says about disturbing the peace."

Mike stepped around in front of the policeman. "Chester, for God's sake. You were there on Sunday. You saw Washington Taylor hold off that mob. Then you really might have had a disturbance. I tell you he hasn't done a thing. He was sitting at the counter, minding his own business." Out of the corner of his eye he saw Cam trying to come to him and Shelley holding him back.

"Mr. Buford hit my granddaddy," Lucy Mae said distinctly. "He knocked him down. My granddaddy hurt hisself."

They had forgotten her, sitting helplessly on her stool. As one, all eyes in the store turned to focus on the little girl clutching her soggy ice cream cone.

Chester Glover sighed. "You say that gentleman there—" He pointed to Polo Pete, sitting at a table now, rubbing his arm where he'd fallen against the tobacco counter. "Do I understand you to say that gentleman knocked your grandfather down?"

Lucy Mae's eyes were like blue marbles dropped in clean white. "Yes, sir."

The policeman assumed a martyred air. "What in hell am I supposed to do?" With an expression of pained resignation he glanced around, hoping somebody would get him off the hook.

"The less said and done the better," Mike offered. Walking over to Polo Pete he extended his hand. Fighting off his revulsion, he said evenly, "I'm willing to forget if you are."

Buford looked down at Mike's palm and then up into his face. His eyes narrowed, and in their bloodshot depths Mike saw the hatred that had previously been directed at the Negro focused now on him.

With a sudden violent gesture Polo Pete sent his chair crashing over backward. "Nigger lover! I don't shake hands with nigger lovers!" Grabbing the shooting stick that Mike had leaned against the table, he strode to the door.

Cam stood in his path. "Hi, Mr. Buford." Shelley, a look of horror on her face, snatched him out of the way. Then she was pulling her son toward the car.

"But you promised I could have a cone," Cam cried, looking back over his shoulder.

As the door banged shut behind Buford, the policeman, absolved of the responsibility of making an arrest, let go of Washington Taylor's arm. The Negro straightened. His clothes were ripped and there was a rising bump on his forehead where it had struck the stool. His lip was cut. There was blood on his white shirt and in his eyes, which, as he stared after Polo Pete, were savage.

Turning, he walked back to the counter. He did not look at Doc Dickerson, still cowering behind it, or at the two dimes lying on the white surface. With infinite gentleness he lifted his granddaughter up into his arms. Without looking to the right or the left, he strode between the tables to the door.

TWELVE

THE *Sun* office was strangely silent. In the back shop the usual banter that went on between Pete, the printer, and Josh, the linotype operator, was nonexistent. Instead the men went about their business with almost funereal quiet. Even the cheerful tinkling of the linotype, the grating noise of the saw, the hillbilly music coming from the portable radio and the ga-boom of the flatbed running off the first section seemed muted.

After he finished the editorial and before starting to lay out the handful of ads he had gotten for that week's paper, Mike decided to go to Charlie Woodruff's for tobacco and a chocolate bar. The cheeseburger he'd eaten at the Gone Away that noon seemed a long time ago.

As he passed the drugstore he felt that if he looked down he would see his shirt going up and down from the beating of his heart. How clichéd can you be? he thought wryly. Here was the stock situation in so many movies. The fearless crusading editor walking down the main street of "his" town after the bads have been sent packing and the community made safe for democracy.

In the newsstand, crowded with members of the business community who had stopped to pick up their afternoon papers, Mike had the brief satisfaction of causing at least three conversations to come to an abrupt end. He asked the news dealer for his usual brand of tobacco and nodded and spoke to the businessmen, who suddenly seemed vitally interested in their papers.

Charlie Woodruff's response was guarded. After providing Mike with change from the bill he'd given him, he said mildly in a low voice, "Got a lot of rejects this week. Won't be needing so many papers Thursday. Not unless folks want to use it to wrap up the garbage."

Mike looked at the stack of *Shelburne Suns* on the floor. "They all rejects?"

"Some picks up their papers at night."

Mike leaned his elbows on the counter. "Charlie, I've known you since I came to Shelburn. You've given me good advice."

The news dealer looked away. Putting the cigar he'd been smoking in an ashtray, he said, "It's the wheel squeaks the loudest gets the grease. Mr. Buford owns the bank and most of the real estate in town. He owns this here building I'm in. He stopped by this afternoon to pick up his papers. Usually he has David do it, but today he come in by hisself. We had a little talk. For some reason he didn't explain, he just don't want to see the *Sun* get ahead."

"Maybe Mr. Buford doesn't like competition."

Charlie picked up his cigar and began puffing leisurely.

"They'se a lot of things he don't like." He gazed soberly at Mike. "You're kind of controversial, Editor. Tain't the best way to win friends."

At two o'clock the trailers and Betsy Baldwin in her farm truck, with three ponies crammed in behind the high removable partitions, began arriving. By two-thirty the stable area was a chaos of children and ponies, shouting parents and barking dogs. "Why do people bring dogs to houses where they know there are other dogs?" Mike had demanded one day after he'd restrained Lance, who was hurling himself at the rolled-up windows of Millicent's Rolls. Shelley warned Millicent but Millicent paid no attention. Whether it was to the Cape for the summer or Shelburn to go shopping, Millicent moved in a confusion of children, dogs, tack to be mended, groceries, and generally the trailer, loaded with ponies or race horses going to the training track, hitched behind. "The Terror of the Valley Road," Debby Darbyshire called her. "When you see that Rolls coming, duck!"

In spite of always traveling at top speed, Millicent was never on time. Now she was half an hour late. Just as Shelley had decided she wasn't coming, the big car and the trailer came hurtling up the drive. With a suddenness that threw the ponies against the padded partitions and caused the terriers to fly against the glass partition, Millicent narrowly missed a tree and the Baldwins' truck, pulled in front of Katie Schligman's pink Cadillac and jammed on the brakes.

"Archie, Merry," she commanded. "Unload the ponies."

Children and terriers spilled out of the car. At that moment Lance, Miehle and the hound puppies came bounding from the stable, where Shelley had secured them in a box stall. Buttons Baldwin stood by the open door. "Oh, dear," she apologized, "I thought it was empty. I just wanted to put my pony in so I could go to the bathroom."

"Lance! Miehle!" Shelley cried desperately. She knew it was hopeless. Their territory was being invaded. The dogs would not stop until they had routed the trespassers.

Millicent forgot Mother's precious-darling-love on her lap. As she jumped out of the car to call back the loosened terriers, the puppy fell to the ground. Lance was upon it in a flash. Millicent's scream rose above the sounds of the other dogs crashing after the terriers in the woods.

The next few seconds were ghastly. Millicent, shouting epithets, was beating the mastiff with her shoulder bag. Merry was sobbing. Archie stood by the car, his face ashen. Mothers and children, holding their ponies, ringed in a horrified circle. Staunton, who had brought little Augie Schligman's pony, and the other grooms tried to help Shelley pull Lance away. Buttons Baldwin, who had been the cause of it all, forgot to hold onto her pony. It wandered off to eat grass, stepped on a rein and broke it. While Betsy tried to help Shelley, Virginia City stood holding two of the Baldwins' ponies. As Cam, Jimmy, Bardy and little Augie returned with the other terriers they'd rescued in the woods, the third Baldwin pony, frantic at being left behind in the truck, pulled the partition he was tied to down on top of himself. While Betsy and the grooms tried to untangle the pony, the awful struggle continued.

Satisfied finally that the ratlike object in his mouth was still, Lance dropped the puppy. At sight of its mangled remains, Shelley turned her head away, ran behind the oak and was ill.

Grabbing the puppy's broken carcass, Millicent clasped it to her, alternately weeping and cursing as the front of her turtleneck turned red.

"My poor, poor baby. Mother's precious-darling-love. His father was a champion—Archie. Merry. Get the other dogs. We're going home." Tears running down her cheeks and the puppy's remains still in her lap, she started up the Rolls and backed the trailer into Katie's pink Cadillac.

"Oh, dear," Katie gasped. "First my flamingo flew away and now this." She gazed at the smear of pink that had been transplanted from the fender of her new car to the ramp of Millicent's trailer. "Whatever will Dad say?"

"Shit!" Millicent retorted. "Send me the bill for your fender." She glared at Shelley. "That dog should be put down."

"I know how you feel, Millicent," Shelley said miserably. "I'd give anything if it hadn't happened."

Millicent jerked ahead. The trailer scraped past the tree. She put her foot down on the accelerator and headed down the drive, children, dogs and ponies sliding and bumping against the partition behind her.

Shelley did her best to salvage what was left of the afternoon. After she had dragged the reluctant mastiff into the house and locked him in the den, and Jimmy had put Miehle and the hound puppies back in the stall, she directed the subdued Pony Clubbers into the field.

She forced herself to keep on as though nothing had happened. She let the children take turns jumping the fences in the ring and play Simon Says. Generally they enjoyed putting their hands on their heads, lying down on their ponies' backs, touching their toes and going through the other motions that Simon demanded. Now they played silently, mechanically, without enthusiasm. Shelley found herself missing Millicent, the loud, abrasive quality the children had come to accept as part of the program, her bossy, blasphemous commands: "Buttons, you idiot, don't let your pony get so close to Archie. You know Chrysanthemum kicks like a bloody steer." "Shut up, Merry. Pay attention." "Augie, tighten your girth. Haven't you the sense God gave you?"

Millicent could get more out of the children than she could, possibly because they were afraid of her. They had seen her whip Merry with her hunting crop and yell at Archie until the little boy turned away grim-faced, controlling himself until out of sight, where he gave way to his anger and frustration by beating his long-suffering Welsh pony.

After an hour in the hot sun, Shelley let the children untack their ponies and have lemonade and cookies in the tack room. She invited the mothers to the house. Instead of the usual quick acceptance—Connie Jackson's surreptitious inspection of the bulletin board where invitations and "things to be done" were tacked, and the eagerness of new people, like Marjorie Martin and Mary McFarland, to inspect the portraits and the antiques—there was a rash of apologies.

Now she stood in the courtyard gazing after the last departing car. Cam and Jimmy were helping Virginia City feed and finish up his chores. She turned back toward the house. Silence and the oncoming darkness pressed down upon her. In the half light the ruins of the west wing, the rubble smothered in vines, held a menacing quality. It was as if mingled with the whisper of the evening breeze and the cry of the tree frogs she could hear her grandmother's halting steps, her voice calling from the top of the stairs. As the ghostly outlines of the great house rose before her, the silence, the darkness and the solitude were suddenly terrifying. She had a chilling sense of déjà vu, as if she had lived through the scene before. She felt herself to be old, her steps halting, her body feeble, deserted and left alone with the house.

Panic seized her. She longed for Mike, for shelter, comfort and safety, the way Cam wanted a light at night.

She went into the house, turned on the lamps and called the *Sun* office. The telephone rang for a long time. Slowly she replaced the receiver. Fear rushed at her, like the approaching darkness.

Shelley gave Cam supper. She heated up a bowl of soup for herself, sat down and tried to eat it. Lance rested his great head against her knee. When she rose to clear away the dishes the mastiff followed her. He seemed to know that he was in disgrace. As she washed the dishes he rubbed his head against her knees.

As though sensing her thoughts, Cam looked up from his Jello and asked, "Mommy, you won't take Lance away? Please, Mommy, no matter what Mrs. Black says."

"I have to talk to your father. We can't have him killing other people's dogs."

Cam's eyes filled with tears. "But, Mommy—"

"Darling." Shelley put down the dish towel and walked over to him. She put her arms around him and held him against her.

Lance butted his head against Cam and began to whine.

"It will be all right," Shelley said, "I promise."

She cleaned up the kitchen and set the table for breakfast. Twice the telephone rang. She ran to it, hoping it was Mike, or Millicent having a change of heart. The first time there was a click after she said hello. She put the receiver down and picked it up again, but there was no one on the line. She had no sooner returned to the kitchen when it rang again. An unknown voice asked to speak to Mrs. Latimer.

"This is Mrs. Latimer," Shelley replied.

"This is to let you know that you are now an official member of the white niggers' affiliate of the NAACP." This information was followed by a series of obscenities and a click as the person hung up.

Shelley stood stunned, holding the receiver. She was shaking, as though a cold wind was blowing through the house. Slowly she replaced the receiver and returned to the kitchen.

Desperately she wanted Mike. Several times she thought she heard his car and went to the window. But there was no one there. She sat down to wait for him. The afternoon's horror returned. Lance came to her and rested his head on her lap. He gazed up at her pleadingly, sorrowfully. She ran her hand along his head and neck, feeling the fawn-colored pelt. Slowly she stroked him, thinking of loneliness shared. Days at the track when The Goose had failed to win and her funds ran low, nights in the horse's stall when he was hurt, the long, lonely period in New York when the mastiff had been her sole link to The Valley and the past, moments during this year when they had been alone together, waiting for Mike to come home, when the dog's devotion and undemanding companionship provided comfort, solace. Bending over, she rested her cheek against the mastiff's wide brow.

Tomorrow, she thought, she would see Millicent and make her understand.

When Cam finished his supper Shelley sat in the old leather chair beside the wood stove. He climbed into her lap. Lance lay down at her feet. From the stable, where the hound puppies were shut in a stall, came a long, doleful howl. The mastiff lifted his head and let it fall back down onto his paws. There was a scratching from the cardboard box as Cam's turtles moved. Outside the wind rose, bending back the tops of the trees, setting up its cacaphony as it blew against the eaves of the old house. Shelley read a chapter from *The Wind in the Willows*. It was a long chapter, but when she had finished she could not remember a word of what she had read.

It was eight-thirty by the time Cam finished his bath, brushed his teeth, said his prayers and finally crawled into bed. Shelley finished laying out his school clothes, bent over to kiss him good night. Rotary should be over by now, she thought. Maybe Mike would be back in time to say good night to his son.

When Mike looked at the clock he realized that it was too late to attend the Rotary meeting. Just as well, he thought. After what had happened that day his presence would have embarrassed the others.

He was not conscious of driving past the entrance to Shelburn Hall. It wasn't until he was beyond Priscelly Gate that he realized he was almost at the road to Fairmont. As though the car had a will of its own, it turned left into the narrow rutted lane that served as the drive to Misty's house. On either side of the lane ran an old rail fence draped with honeysuckle.

As the car jangled and bumped over 'the rough road, dark shapes snorted and raised their heads. Misty's horses, horses that had been starved and beaten, broken and bowed. Misty was a kind of one-woman ASPCA. Although she could no longer ride them, or afford in reality to feed them, she collected horses from barn-yards where the lame or the halt or the blind had been abandoned, from friends who wanted to give their retired hunters a good home and from trainers at the race track.

Misty had Shelley's Shelburn outlook on money. Long ago she had gone through the sum received from the paper. Now she lived literally from hand to mouth, depending largely on the daily double. When she won she blew her winnings on a huge meal which she cooked for her friends—jockeys and trainers down on their luck and whoever happened to drop in at the time.

When she lost at the races, Misty starved herself in order to provide for the horses, the nine dogs that came in all sizes and shapes, and the geese that wandered the premises, honking and flap-ping their wings at all comers. Through it all she was gay and gallant.

"As Fax Templeton says, I haven't two n-n-n-nipples to rub together," she told Mike one day when he came upon her collect-ing mustard greens for dinner. Imitating Fax's stutter, she added, "Who n-n-n-needs it? I've got the sky overhead and the greens in the fields."

The Valley, Mike knew, was strewn with male hearts which had been bent and bowed by Misty, salvaged and put together by other loves, but never completely whole. For what man, Mike thought, could ever be entirely the same after being dis-carded in favor of a newborn foal or a young one that might make a Shelburn Cup horse?

The lane had not been graded in years. Grass grew in its crown and there was a spring-breaking bump in the hollow by the weep-ing willow that guarded the springhouse. Then the lane wound upward and around a turning place, girdled with untrimmed Eng-lish box higher than a man's head. Horses grazed on what had once been a well-kept lawn and a fat goose waddled across the drive in front of him. Mike parked, got out, shooed the banty chickens out of his way and walked up the uneven walk to the round millstone that served as a stoop. He pulled the cord attached to the brass cowbell. As the ringing died away he heard the dogs barking. Then Misty's voice shushing them and the sound of her footsteps.

Funny, he thought, one never noticed the sound of a person's footsteps until there was a dissonance, an off beat. Because of Misty's limp he could tell her approach in the dark, without seeing her. Then she was tugging at the heavy oak door that always stuck. Mike pushed against it. It gave suddenly and the moonlight flickered in with him.

"Mike!" Misty sounded faintly breathless. Her hair was loosely pinned in a pompadour. He fought back the sudden impulse to reach out and bring it tumbling down. She wore a red felt wrapper like a monk's robe, tied at the waist with a cord, and a pair of sheepskin slippers, flat and built up on the sides like the ones that Cam wore. In the moonlight filling the hall, her face looked white and cool and smooth, like marble. At the same time there was something soft and warm . . .

Her hand went to her hair. "I wasn't expecting company. I was working on the column."

Saber, the black shepherd, sniffed at his trouser leg. Some passing motorist had dropped him out onto the side of the highway in a bag. Misty had come along shortly after and released him. He had been vicious and half starved and at first refused to let her touch him. Now he followed her like a shadow. Mike reached down to pat him and the dog, satisfied that he meant no harm, turned back into the hall.

The clock struck ten. Misty must wonder why, at this hour, he was calling.

"Funny," he said. "Now I'm here I don't know why. I just started driving—"

"I'm glad you are," Misty replied simply. Her voice was low and musical without the underlying whining quality he associated with Samantha Sue. A proper Southern voice like Shelley's, vibrant with a singing sound that seemed to linger in the air after she had spoken. "But come in. You look as if you could stand a drink. I'll get you one."

It seemed perfectly natural to follow her down the worn uneven steps to the old basement kitchen with its wide wood-planked floor and low beamed ceiling.

"Watch out for your head," she warned as he stooped to enter the room. "When Tom Wolfe visited my father he always banged his head. He was well over six feet . . ."

As she moved about, talking of Thomas Wolfe, Hemingway and the others who had come to Fairmont when her father was alive, he was aware of that special quality of hers, that inner peace and tranquillity, which was like coming in from the cold. Sinking into the rocking chair in front of the great stone hearth, he watched her make him a drink.

Holding the silver mug in her hand, she turned toward him. At sight of the expression on his face her smile faded and then suddenly was reborn.

"You were looking at me," she cried delightedly. "You never really looked at me before."

"You're wrong. I always look at you and each time I see something I haven't seen before."

Briskly she brought up the column she wanted to do for the paper. " 'Something for the Girls,' " she said. "How about that for a title? It can be a little of everything, from how to tie a stock to how to make mulligatawny stew."

When she had finished telling him about her ideas, he told her what had happened in the drugstore.

When he stopped speaking she sat very still. Her eyes were wide and candid. "Does Shelley know?"

"She was there." Mike took quick puffs on his pipe. Despite his efforts, the glow in the bowl burned out. He took it out of his mouth. "I haven't been home tonight. She doesn't— I mean. Hell, I don't mean to sound like a misunderstood husband. I love Shelley. It's just—" He did not know how to go on.

As though drawing strength from his surroundings, he glanced around the room. At the Dutch cupboard containing Misty's collection of blue Canton china, at the rack by the door that held the hats, an ancient derby with a dent in it, Misty's hunting cap, green with age, the brown felt riding hat from Nardi that she wore to church and to funerals, and the World War I shell that held a collection of shooting sticks and umbrellas. The far side of the room was taken up by the ancient iron stove, no longer in use other than as a catch-all for an assortment of books, magazines, newspapers.

Leaning against the back of the stove was a dart board. A picture of Senator Joseph McCarthy, torn from a newspaper, had been pasted on it. Misty had told Mike that during the McCarthy hearings she had been so angry that she had let off steam by throwing darts at the Senator.

"I put a hex on him," she said seriously. "It's an ancient Irish curse I found in a book of Father's. The book warns you to be careful, to use it only when absolutely necessary. I became so incensed over what McCarthy was doing to the country that I invoked the curse. The darts all struck at his throat. Next thing I knew he had laryngitis and couldn't speak. A short time after that he was dead. I've never dared invoke the curse since."

The paper face was now so pierced and torn it was almost unrecognizable.

Following his gaze, Misty said, "I'm going to change it to Governor Wallace. But you were talking about Shelley."

"You're so different in outlook," Mike said. "I sometimes wonder how you can be cousins."

Misty turned her face away. Instinctively she reached for the black dog lying by her side. Her hand stroked his sleek head. "We were brought up differently. My father's people, the Shelburnes with the E's, were 'feet on the fender' people. Father was a direct descendant of Hugh, the philosopher. He read Latin and Greek in the original without having to get up from the hearthside in order to look up a word in Dr. Johnson's Dictionary. Heaslip Hunt, the Negro writer, was one of Father's best friends. I remember how shocked The Valley was when he came and visited us. Nobody called. Nobody asked us to dinner. Yet Heaslip was brilliant. When you were with him you had no thought of color, no sense of any difference. He was an educated Negro. Few Southerners ever meet or have any contact with educated Negroes. They only see a black anonymous mass threatening their way of life.

"Shelley was the dashing one," Misty went on. "I was the quiet one. While the town knew me as the editor's daughter, it knew Shelley at a distance. The Shelburns, the Templetons and the Talbots lived in a world apart, aloof from the village. They were gentry. And Shelley was instilled with the Southern attitude. I was the daughter of a literate and intelligent newspaperman and historian. And proud of it. What he did was more important than what his name was. This is not the way most Southerners think. Take Miss Abby Cooke, who runs Cooke's Store. Miss Abby's grandmother ran the store when it was part of the family plantation. Miss Abby runs it because it is in the tradition. She does not consider herself a storekeeper, nor is she considered one by the people who trade there. She is Miss Abby, a Cooke of Cooke's Manor. It's this, the Southern tradition, the exaggerated sense of family and rage for privacy, that insulates people like Shelley from reality. Now they feel it threatened by forces they don't understand. . . . I'm on a talking jag."

"Go ahead," Mike insisted.

She gazed into the orange-blue flames of the crackling fire. "It's like trying to give up smoking or drinking. On the one hand you cling to the delusion that it won't hurt you. On the other you yearn to be rid of the addiction. Rather than believe tobacco and alcohol are bad for you, you rationalize. The Southerner turns to any desperate rationalization to perpetuate the Southern way of life. He seeks to believe Negroes are happy, that they prefer segregation. It's a relief when the delusion is ended. Maybe the only way to learn compassion is to pull the wings off flies. Maybe you never know how badly you *can* feel until you discover that it's too late to put them back on again."

Misty studied the burned-out fire. "Shakespeare never had a lead that was poor."

"What do you mean?" There were times when Misty's logic left Mike groping.

"He never had a poor man for a hero. Plenty of minor characters, yes, but not in the lead. It wasn't done in his day. He probably wouldn't have been able to sell his plays if he'd written about peasants rather than princes."

"What has that got to do with Shelley?"

"Just that it's the way the South, the old South, thinks."

Misty spread out her hands in front of her. "Money has nothing to do with the attitude. Ever since the war, I mean the War Between the States, the lack of it has been a prideful thing. As far as the Shelburns were concerned, there were but two kinds of people—the aristocrats, and the peasants put on earth to administer to their pleasure. They saw life as Shakespeare did, in terms of kings."

Mike shook his head, baffled. "How unrealistic can you be?"

Misty smiled. "Nobody ever accused a Shelburn of being realistic."

Mike sighed and bowed his head. The sound of Misty's voice, the cry of the tree frogs coming from the moon-washed darkness beyond the open window, the feeling of peace which the room gave him, had eased his tension. He wished he could stay in the rocking chair, let his head fall onto his chest and sleep.

Misty reached out her hand, as if to touch him. At that moment the grandfather clock in the hall began its slow, ponderous chiming of the midnight hour.

Mike leapt to his feet. "I had no idea it was so late. No, don't come with me," he said as Misty grasped her stick.

"Don't forget to stoop," she said as he reached the doorway.

He turned to look at her, started to speak, and then did not. Quickly he walked to the front door. After a brief struggle it creaked open and he went out into the night.

The big hall clock at Shelburn Hall was slow. It had just finished striking midnight when Mike returned.

"Oh," he said, coming into the kitchen, "you're still up."

Now that he was home, all her hurt, all her frustrations hardened into antagonism against him. "Since when does Rotary go on all night?" she asked bitterly.

"I stopped by to see Misty. We were talking."

"Meanwhile, back at the ranch—" She sighed. "I'm going to bed."

"Don't." He put out his hand.

Her face, framed by loosened hair, had a lost quality that tugged at his heart.

"Talk to me," he offered. "Has something happened?"

"Lance killed Millicent's precious-darling-love." She stood rigidly, trying not to tremble. "She wants Lance destroyed."

Although the evening was warm the house suddenly seemed very cold.

"We can't do that. Lance is part of the family."

"I know that." She gazed at him miserably.

"Can't you explain to her?"

"I tried. She wouldn't listen."

"Come and sit down. What about some cocoa or coffee? A drink? A glass of milk?" He started toward the refrigerator.

"We're out of milk."

"Never mind. Just come and sit down."

Walking as though in her sleep, she returned to the leather chair. Lance lifted his head and then let it fall back down onto his paws.

"There were some phone calls, Mike." She told him about the anonymous caller.

He stared at the stem of his pipe. "I hoped it wouldn't involve you and Cam."

She noticed that his pipe stem was bitten almost through. He must be tired, too, she thought suddenly. It can't be easy for him either.

"I suppose you have to do what you think is right," she said finally. "You can't go back now."

"No. But I wish—I'd do anything . . . that is, to avoid hurting you and Cam."

The room no longer seemed so cold. She stood up. "They can't get away with it."

"Good girl." He smiled faintly. "Rise above it. Get some sleep. In the morning things will look better." He watched her walk to the door and pause. When she spoke, the set of her shoulders, the tilt of her head were all Shelburn.

"They can't hurt us. I won't let them. Mike, you better come to bed, too."

Cam was scrubbed and cleaned and fed. His hair was flattened down and parted on the side. He wore his new brown oxfords and long trousers from the Dependable Store.

While Shelley backed the station wagon out of the garage, he picked a handful of orange chrysanthemums from the plot by the old tennis court and several late-blooming roses along the fence. The colors were ghastly together, Shelley thought, but Miss May would realize that it was the intent that counted. Cam was one of her favorites. "So sensitive!" she told Shelley. "What the Irish call a soft child. And smart! I hate to think of his leaving me next year."

For years Miss May, an elderly spinster with graying hair

pulled back into a bun and a manner Mike described as Southern genteel, had maintained a kindergarten in the basement of her big brick house behind the Episcopal Church, where she lived with her invalid mother. Now on this first morning of the new school year, she was busy greeting old pupils and welcoming the new, assuring their mothers that everything would be fine as soon as they departed and the children got to know one another.

Cam darted ahead, clutching his bouquet.

"Miss May, I brought you some flowers."

"Thank you, Cam," the teacher said quickly. "Set them on my desk. I'll find a vase." She pronounced it vaaze with a long A. "In a minute."

Miss May had often told Shelley how nice it was to have a Shelburn of Shelburn Hall in her school. Now she greeted Shelley with a terse nod and "Good morning" and turned away to speak to Katie Schligman about enrolling little Augie, clinging to his mother's skirt of pink tweed. Shelley put Miss May's abruptness down to the general confusion of opening day, waved a final good-by to Cam, now happily greeting Buddha, and started back to the car.

Samantha Sue and Sion Atwell stood chatting in the parking lot.

As Shelley approached she heard Sion say, "She sat up all night with Mother's precious-darling-love. Then she wrapped the dead puppy in a plastic bag and put the body in her freezer."

"Hi," Shelley called out. "Lovely day, isn't it? Still too dry, but . . ." Her voice faded out. Was it her imagination or had they deliberately turned away, heading for their cars, when they saw her.

Hurriedly she got into the station wagon, started it up and drove home. They were probably in a rush, she thought. Mornings in The Valley with horses to be exercised and marketing to be done and households to organize were always chaotic. She mustn't start imagining things. Surely they knew by now that she wielded no influence over the *Sun* and its policies. Deliberately she forced herself to think about her morning's schedule. The mare she was boarding for the Martins could be lunged. The young horse she was schooling for Millicent could have a session in the ring.

Thinking about the stable, she forgot that she had not asked Samantha Sue if Buddha could come and play that afternoon.

It was still early when she rode out on Lookout Light. The fields were clotted with cobwebs, delicately strung from one tuft of grass to another. Along the woods path they hung at intervals, stretched from branch to branch, filigreed and shining in the sunlight that broke through the tops of the great trees. It seemed a crime to break them. Whenever possible, Shelley left the path and rode around them.

Purple thistles brushed against the colt's gray legs. The dogwoods were veined with crimson, leaves curled like fingers around their clusters of berries, which suggested Christmas boutonnieres. The ground was iced with a coating of lacy frost. The air was as clear as her Waterford glass and suddenly the day seemed filled with promise.

In the distance the line of Webster's woods was all reds, greens, golds and orange, and crimson-tipped as though dipped in a giant paint pot. Behind the camouflage of color rose the peaks of the blue-hazed mountains. Overhead a buzzard circled lazily and in the distance a dog barked.

She opened a farm gate and rode out onto the lane. Purple and white asters nodded alongside the drive and a furry black Angus calf stuck his head over the fence, causing Lookout Light to shy again.

Shelley jumped the colt over the coop into the field of cattle and cantered across it to a panel in the old wall that crested the ridge, rising against the skyline like a horse's mane. The way led past Mattie Moore's cabin perched on a rocky hillside. A crude walkway led up the steep incline. Mattie had placed rusted cans on either side and filled them with bulbs or seeds so that now the entire slope was a vivid mass of blooms—dahlias, chrysanthemums, asters and blue morning glories growing around the rotting pillars that supported the sagging roof.

Lookout Light snorted at the old woman's pigs rooting and grunting in their odiferous pen beside the cabin. Mattie was feeding her hogs. She wore a long skirt with a rip in it that resembled one Mrs. Dinwiddie had worn for years and then donated to the church rummage sale. A blue kerchief was knotted around her head.

"That you, Miss Shelley?" she called out, setting down her bucket of slops.

"Yes. Lovely morning."

"Deed so," Mattie agreed. "Comin' on cold though. Soon be hog-killin' time."

"Mattie, your flowers are beautiful."

"I'd like you to have some, Miss Shelley."

"Thank you. I'll bring Cam over some afternoon. Good-by." She waved and rode on.

She came out at Priscelly Gate, an estate now owned by T. Patterson Gibson of the Gibson Steamship Lines, who had renovated the manor house and the old slave quarters and refenced the extensive acreage for a breeding establishment.

Sidney Merrywood, her father's old trainer, lived in one of the cottages. Shelley saw him now, bending over the beds where he cultivated the flowers which he made into special bouquets for his friends, choosing blooms the color of their racing colors.

"Hi, Uncle Sidney," Shelley called. "Lovely morning."

He looked up quickly. At sight of her a welcoming smile spread over his face. He was a short man with a square, stocky body that had now put on its normal quota of weight, denied during the years when he had been the country's leading steeplechase rider. He had retired from riding races to become the Shelburn trainer. Shelley remembered him directing the operations in the big front field at Shelburn Hall when the schooling course had stood there. Always immaculate, he wore a covert coat and gray bowler and rode a gray cob. His Dalmatian trotted behind him. One of her earliest memories had to do with sitting on the pommel in front of him as he directed the race horses, never missing a nuance of their strides as they worked on the flat or over the fences.

After her father's death, when the race horses were sold, he had retired from training, devoting himself to adding to his sporting library and raising flowers. Here in her growing-up years Shelley had found solace, having tea in front of the fire after hunting, riding over in the summertime for a sandwich lunch under the maple in the garden, or seeking advice about her own horses.

"Say, that horse is coming along," he said admiringly.

"I know. But it's hard schooling him and keeping the stable going. There's just Virginia City, you know."

He nodded. "Everything's changing. Not the way it used to be.

Help is a terrible problem. Soon there won't be any open land at all. Nothing but housing developments!" The old gentleman snorted. "Strangers moving in. People like that foreigner with his airplane who bought Ballyhoura!"

The colt moved impatiently, chewing on his bit.

"I must be getting along," Shelley said quickly, aware that if he began on how it was in the old days the morning would be spent.

The old gentleman's words had brought Zagaran to mind. She had not seen him since the first morning of cubbing. He must still be away. She urged Lookout Light on faster, hoping that by increasing her speed she could drive the image of his dark face from her.

At home she schooled Millicent's young horse in the ring. He went well, jumping his fences safely and cleanly. Millicent should be pleased at his progress. If she missed seeing her at school, she would call her that evening, tell her about the colt and apologize for Lance. Maybe during the afternoon she would have time to do some painting.

"Shelburns don't apologize," her grandmother had always said. "At least not before noon."

Cam was waiting for her at the school entrance. Behind him she saw the other children coming from the school building, each carrying a cardboard clown with a red balloon attached to it.

"The invitations to Buddha's party," Cam said. He dug his fists into his eyes, attempting to stop the flow of tears. "I didn't get one."

By the time they reached home, Shelley's shock and hurt had turned to anger. As soon as she was inside the house, she telephoned Samantha Sue Buford. She gave her name to David and waited. It seemed a long time before the butler returned and told her that Mrs. Buford had gone to Washington. Shelley told him she would ring back that evening.

She did not have to telephone Millicent. Millicent called her.

"Shelley, I hope you've disposed of that dog," she said without preliminaries.

"Millicent, you know I can't destroy Lance," Shelley replied. "It would break Cam's heart."

Millicent cut her off. "The damn dog is dangerous."

"I know how you feel, Millicent, but I did warn you about bringing your dogs onto the place."

"Balls!" Millicent said.

"Millicent," Shelley cried, but the phone was dead.

She stood motionless, holding the receiver. Millicent couldn't mean what she said, not after all they had been through together. Millicent was her best friend. Probably she had been fighting with her husband. She was off her feed, or perhaps it was that time of the month. Tomorrow she would talk to her. Millicent loved dogs. She would understand about Lance. She would have to, Shelley thought, her resolve hardening. There was no way Millicent could force her to do away with the mastiff.

THIRTEEN

ON PRESS day Mike carried out the tradition begun by Charles Shelburne. Although the little colored boys hired to sell the newspapers no longer ran through the town waving copies of the paper and shouting, "*Sun's* out! *Sun's* out today!" Mike continued to hang out the carved wooden sign over the door. On it was written in gilt-painted letters: "Sun's Out Today!"

Mike looked at the clock. As yet the first run had not gotten off the old press. Pete was under it now, trying to figure out what was wrong with one of the rollers that kept breaking the web. If the old flat-bed wasn't fixed soon, they'd be up all night.

Somehow, by the next week, he would have to find the three hundred dollars that he owed for newsprint. If he did not, if he failed to get the paper out, he would lose his postal permit and be forced to sell out to Buford. Yet, if he took the money from the *Sun* account, he would not be able to meet the payroll. The preceding week the web had broken again. By the time the second-hand flat-bed press started running, overtime had canceled out the extra page of advertising Mike had sold the manager of the new shoe store which had opened next to the Fox in the High Hat.

Each week there was the same desperate circle in which his mind seemed unable to come up with any answer. Yet, somehow, by some miracle, the paper managed to be published, to come out on Thursday.

He did not know how much longer this would be possible. Now in October the financial damage suffered in canceled subscriptions and advertising was secondary to the emotional toll starting to take effect. Ironically, the civil rights situation was worse than it had been before Desegregation Day—the Sunday following Zagaran's ball.

In spite of Mike's arguments, backed up by Preacher Young, Washington Taylor had gone ahead with his scheme to "dry the town up." The Negroes living within town limits who had running water turned on all their faucets. By the end of the week, the town well had gone dry.

The powers reacted. Funds were voted from the scant emergency reserve to make a quick survey and engineers called in to lay out a new and modern water system that would pump water from Buffalo Run. Aware that they were fighting a losing battle, the Negroes turned off their faucets. Slowly the old wooden water tank began to fill up. Goodwill, however, had gone down the drain.

Polo Pete Buford ordered the iron jockey at the entrance to Silver Hill painted white, and evicted three Negro tenants who had attended Human Relations Council meetings. Tom Smith, a hard-working and responsible Negro who had been in charge of the broodmare barn for fifteen years, pleaded that it would take him a while to find living quarters for his wife and nine children. Polo Pete called Senator "States Rights" Talbot in Richmond, who got in touch with the state police. Papers charging fourteen-year-old Dicie Smith with soliciting jockeys and grooms from the training track were served. Tom Smith insisted this was a lie. Nevertheless, the family was forced to move and be separated, the Taylors taking three of the Smith children. Others were divided among relatives. Tom got a job in another part of the county driving a truck, and his wife, Loretta, went to work for the Schligmans.

The eviction accomplished the purpose Polo Pete had in mind, that of "scarifying the niggers" to the point where further agitation would be put down. For as Washington Taylor said, most Valley Negroes were Uncle Toms.

Those with the ability and the education to get higher-paying jobs went "down country" to the suburbs or got government jobs. Only the older generation remained. Uneducated past primary grades, the only jobs open to them were as grooms or as farm laborers, while the women worked as domestics. Washington Taylor pointed out that they had been brainwashed for so many decades that truth and the will to fight were no longer in them. Now they were too old to change, and when they saw what could happen to one who had been faithful to his job, they feared for their own.

Thus segregation, largely self-imposed by the Negroes themselves, returned to Shelburn. Yet feeling against Mike and the *Sun* did not abate. Instead it crystallized into a subtle kind of attrition —the silence that came over the people eating lunch at the Gone Away when he entered, the quickly averted faces at the post office, the crossing of the street to avoid meeting and speaking, the decline of dinner invitations.

He had expected ostracism. He had been aware that when his role in desegregating the community was made public the people who normally tolerated him because he was Shelley's husband would begin to back off. He had not expected it to include his wife and child. Yet the day after Shelley refused to obey Millicent's demand to destroy Lance, Dixon, her groom, drove up in the trailer with orders to take Millicent's young horse, which Shelley had been training, back to Last Resort; and Marjorie Martin moved her mare to Story Jackson's barn. Dooley Wright, the blacksmith, who had always come when Shelley needed him, put her off. The garage kept her waiting and then refused to put an inspection sticker on the station wagon unless she ordered four new tires.

When the telephone calls began to reach Shelley, when Cam was not included in Buddha's birthday, when he saw the numb look of hurt that came over Shelley's face when she heard about a party that they had not been asked to, he felt depressed to the point where, at night, as he sat alone setting copy on the linotype (in order to avoid paying overtime he had learned to operate the machine himself), and the tinkling noise of the slugs dropping down into the metal galley grated against his nerves, he was tempted to sell out and go back to the city.

He lit his pipe and turned doggedly to the mail. The first letter was from Frank Walker, a shy, soft-spoken man who operated a nursery near Bellevue. Frank's eight-by-ten ad for "box bushes, flowers, shrubs and on the mantel holly trees" had been running weekly ever since Mike bought the paper. Ads such as this, left standing from week to week and requiring no composition changes, were the financial backbone of the paper. As an advertiser, Frank was the answer to a publisher's prayers. Unlike the majority, he never telephoned the office or complained about typographical errors. Only last Christmas he had stopped by for his annual visit. After presenting Shelley and Mike and the staff with pots of poinsettias, he cleared his throat and then mentioned casually, apologetically, that seeing as his holly trees stood over seven feet high, it might make more sense if the ad was changed back to its original meaning—"ornamental," rather than "on the mantel."

Now, reading Frank's note attached to his check for the previous month's advertising, Mike felt as if all the mats from the linotype had crashed down around his head.

> Dear Editor: As you know, I've been waiting for my son, Jim, to graduate from VPI and take over the running of the nursery so that the Missus and I can move to Florida. Jim has a lot of new ideas about building up the business, advertising, and so forth. It's Jim's idea that we cancel our ad in the *Sun* and start advertising in the county paper and on the radio. I'm real sorry about this. I think you and the *Sun* have been doing a good job. But if the boy is going to run the business, I've got to give him a free hand. Please give my regards to Mrs. Latimer. I hope the plants I set out for her last spring are blooming.
>
> Sincerely, Frank Walker

There were two more cancellations of standing ads and five subscriptions, a terse directive from the County School Board that the contract to print the school paper would not be renewed. The few small checks for printing and classifieds came to but a fraction of the amount owed. Written on the bill for newsprint was a note to the effect that until the account was paid up, no more newsprint would be delivered.

He opened a smeared envelope on which his name had been written in pencil.

> I'm living in the same house now twenty years because no other place to go. Mr. Buford see to that. I told him I'm tired of living this way. He say I don't know when I'm well off. I say foxes come up on the porch and into the chimney. Mr. Buford tell me this is a lifetime home, but I don't like to live with foxes.

Mike decided he would print this letter along with the congratulatory letters, including one from Kevin Martin about the recent editorial he had written entitled "Rabies and Racism."

He picked up the last envelope. From the National Association of Newspaper Publishers. Probably a notice about the convention to be held in Washington in November. He almost threw it away without reading it. Then his name and the word "award" caught his attention. Quickly he scanned the letter. The press was running once again and he was needed in the back shop. The chairman of arrangements had written asking him to come to the annual banquet in order to receive a thousand-dollar award "for honest and courageous journalism . . ."

He dropped the letter onto the growing pile "to be answered," picked up his pipe and rose. As he walked to the back shop, he would gladly have traded the money that would pay for the newsprint for an invitation to Cam from Buddha for his birthday party.

On Friday when Mike went to pick Cam up from kindergarten he saw the children clustered at the gate. Party dresses and good flannel trousers showed beneath their coats and each held a brightly wrapped present.

"Hi," they chorused happily, "we're going to Buddha's party. There's going to be a clown."

"I see you are." Mike smiled at little Augie Schligman.

"Where's Cam's present?" Augie asked. "Oh, there's Mommy. She's taking us."

Cam stood to one side, alone, beneath the maple tree that shaded the play yard. He wore his last year's corduroys that were too short and the red sweater with a tear at the elbow that hadn't been mended. There was a smear of dirt across one cheek and his eyes were huge. At sight of Mike, he ran to him and buried his face against his khakis. He did not speak or look up. He simply stood, clinging to his father's leg, and it seemed to Mike that as he clung there his hurt flowed from the boy to mingle with Mike's own growing rage. When he looked up from his son's golden head, the children were piling, in a flurry of excited chatter, presents and gaiety, into cars that were drawing up for them.

Miss May came out the gate and shut it carefully behind her. She wore a hat and coat and carried a present. She started past Mike, then caught sight of Cam and paused. Mike saw the indecision written on her face. Obviously, she wanted nothing to do with the editor of the *Sun*. On the other hand, Cam was one of her favorites. And his mother *was* a Shelburn.

"I'm sorry." Her eyes dropped. "I tried, but—"

"I understand." Mike gazed back at her steadily. "Come along, Cam. Say good-by to Miss May."

Cam put out his hand and made his bow. Then, with astonishing adult dignity, he turned and put his hand in his father's. Together they walked past the cars.

Cam's asthma attack began shortly after lunch.

"Strange," Dr. Watters said, after giving him a shot. "He was doing so well." He took off his spectacles, held together with Band-Aids, and stared at her thoughtfully. "Has anything happened to upset him? All this is tied in with nerves."

"Not that I know of," Shelley lied.

Why had she come back to Shelburn, she thought, putting Cam to bed in the room that had been hers as a child. She had told herself it was for his good, and so she had persuaded her husband and son to return with her to find a past that perhaps had never been at all. The upstairs smelled of damp and mildew and in the corner of Cam's room sat a Georgian silver soup tureen set out to catch a leak. This reminded her that the roof had not yet been fixed and that the interest on Polo Pete's loan was due the following week.

Wildly she looked around at the hunting prints still on the wall, the birds' nests and bones, the colored stones and shells on the shelves, seeking in these familiars, in the things of long ago, to find again her roots and reason for being.

The dogs' frantic barking signaled the arrival of a car. Looking out the window, Shelley saw the crimson sports car shoot up the drive, slew around the corner, brush a box bush and then stop just short of the steps leading to the front door.

The top was down and her red setter sat on its haunches on the seat beside the driver.

"Kelley, stay!" Tatine Zagaran admonished as the hound puppies converged on the car and Lance left Cam's bedside, leaping to the window to glare out at the intruders.

"Hi," Tatine said, untangling herself from behind the driver's seat. She had on tan frontier pants and a heavy white ski sweater with a rolled neck. Round dark glasses covered the upper half of her face. In the afternoon light her flaming shoulder-length hair was the color of the changing red-gold leaves on the oak that shaded the front of the house.

"Dr. Watters told me your son was sick." She dove down behind the seat. From a miscellany of objects that included her battered straw hat with "Nassau" written on it, a white rabbit with one glass-bead eye missing, a beer can, wrench, a mug that said "Princeton, Class of '63," a torn book entitled *The Invisible Man*, a copy of *The Village Voice*, a pair of dirty sneakers, a hair brush, an apple and a bunch of orange chrysanthemums, she extracted a cage in which a small brown hamster was going around on a wheel.

"I hope you'll forgive me." She looked suddenly shy. "Cam said he wanted a kitten but that the mastiff would kill it. I thought maybe a hamster in a cage—"

Shelley was touched. "It's a wonderful idea," she said warmly. "He'll be thrilled."

Tatine put the cage on the ground, reached back of the seat again and drew out a pair of evening slippers. "I meant to return these ages ago. The maid said you left them at my party."

"I planned to come and get them and call on your mother."

"She's in New York. She's going to have some treatments." Tatine picked up a leather shoulder bag the size of a mailman's pouch. She gazed at the tops of the Doric pillars supporting the roof over the stone-floored porch where the old wicker furniture stood at crazy angles, needing paint and to be put away for the winter. "What a lovely, lovely place," she said, speaking in a small awed voice.

"Do come in," Shelley urged quickly.

"Oh"—Tatine stood in the shadowed hall, looking at the circular staircase—"it's beautiful."

"Would you like to see the rest of the house?"

"Yes," she breathed. "Oh, yes."

Shelley led her through the musty-smelling elegance of the closed-off rooms, showing her the piano and the portraits, the Waterford decanters and Lafayette's warming pan and the pane of glass where the French general had carved his name with his diamond ring, the bed Dolly Madison had slept in and the other historical items mentioned in the book of *Great Virginia Houses*.

Afterward she led her down to the kitchen.

"This is where we live." She shoved the pile of bills aside and put the hamster cage on top of the old iron stove. She then went to the gas stove and switched on a burner. "Tea or coffee?"

"Tea, please," Tatine answered politely. Sitting down in the rocking chair, she glanced about appreciatively. "What a super room. That old fireplace and the hanging things, the curtains and that wonderful old table—our kitchen at home is about as cosy as an operating room."

After Tatine had drunk her tea she reached into her enormous bag and began riffling through its contents. "Damn," she said suddenly, upending it onto the pine table. "Excuse me, I can never find my cigarettes." She indicated the pile of miscellany that had fallen from the bag. A handful of balloons, a United States Equestrian Team cigarette lighter, a bag of gum drops, a compact, several lipsticks, a perfume atomizer, a comb, keys, pad and pencil, part of a pearl necklace and one gold earring, a dried leaf pressed into her address book, and finally a package of filter cigarettes.

"I don't know why I carry all this junk around with me." She smiled at Shelley. "My security blanket, I guess. I understand you teach Sunday School," she added unexpectedly. She lit her cigarette and clicked shut her lighter. "Do you need an assistant? It looks as if I'm going to be around for a while, and I'm crazy about kids."

"I think it would be great," Shelley replied sincerely. "I was considering resigning."

"You mustn't do that," Tatine cried. "Look. I'll be glad to help."

Cam called out then and Shelley took Tatine and the hamster in the cage upstairs. His face lit up at sight of the girl and her gift. "Thank you," he cried delightedly, holding the soft furry animal gently in his hands.

He smiled at Tatine. Again Shelley sensed the strange rapport that the girl projected.

"Better put it back before it gets away," Tatine advised. "I lost it in National Airport when I brought it on the plane from New York. Sweepers and passengers and airline people were looking everywhere. We finally tracked it down in a corner of the news-stand."

"Is it a he or a she?" Cam asked.

"I don't know. Let's make it whatever you wish."

"A she." Cam gazed at her. "I want to call her Pansy."

"That's a perfect name."

Shelley saw the two smile at each other and realized that the friendship begun in the orchard was ripening like the fruit left in the mellow holes in the old wall.

They left the hamster continuing its aimless rounds on the wheel. Shelley held off the hound puppies, threatening in their exuberant friendliness to knock Tatine down before she could clamber into the low-slung driver's seat, where the setter began licking her face.

"Go away," Tatine said, pushing him aside. "You're squashing Softie." Reaching down, she held up the white rabbit with the missing eye. "Silly, I know," she explained to Shelley, "but I take him with me wherever I go. Thank you for the tea."

"Tatine," Shelley called, "will you be hunting tomorrow? Your father—"

"Zagaran's on a cruise," Tatine answered indifferently. "Somewhere in the Caribbean. Don't know when he'll be back." She put the car in gear. Shelley reminded her that part of her seat belt was hanging out the bottom of the door, but the noise of the high-powered engine drowned her out. Tatine backed expertly, twirled the wheel around and waved. With a roar the car lunged forward, sideswiped a bush and vanished down the drive in a cloud of gravel and dust. Much too fast, Shelley thought, praying nobody was coming along in the opposite direction.

While Cam was ill, Tatine came every afternoon, bringing him a different present, a small stuffed animal, a puzzle, a coloring book, a marble and a chameleon from the Firemen's Carnival.

When he was over the attack, Tatine took him fishing. During the long, golden afternoons of Indian summer they sat on the edge of the pond at Ballyhoura, dangling their lines in the water and catching an occasional sunfish. That this curious girl with her flaming hair and lawless nature should devote so much time and thought to a small child was a source of amazement to Shelley. One Saturday afternoon Tatine had the children—little Augie Schligman, Jimmy Jones and Cam—flown to Washington to supper and the movies in her father's plane for what she called Cam's pretend birthday party. Shelley knew she had been invited to a University of Virginia football game by Sandy Montague. When she suggested to Tatine that she might prefer to go to Charlottesville with her own crowd, Tatine shook her head emphatically. "I'm doing what I want to do. Don't you see," she added softly, "I was never a child myself."

It was Tatine's idea that Jimmy be included.

"He'd be crushed, and so would Cam, if we didn't take him."

Jimmy had never flown or been farther from Shelburn than Bellevue, where he'd gone once or twice when his father was arraigned in the county court. His eyes were as round as brown pennies and when the plane took off he became very silent, sitting tensely, his fists clenched to his lap. Nervously fingering his frayed but immaculately clean clothes, he looked at everything, and his only comment as they drove along Constitution Avenue to the restaurant where they ate was to ask if the Washington Monument had been erected by the Ku Klux Klan.

In early October the Episcopal Church had what was called the Christmas Bazaar. Millicent Black had originated the idea after the war. She wrote to various posh shops and asked if they would be interested in sending salesmen and setting up booths and selling their wares during the three-day period. The Bazaar was an immediate success. An assortment of well-known firms came from New York, Philadelphia, Wilmington and Washington. After the church women decorated the parish house, shops selling everything from children's toys to fine lingerie, men's toiletries, gifts of all varieties, suits, dresses, fine sweaters and ski clothes were set up, and people traveled from as far away as Wilmington and Washington to do their Christmas shopping.

All the women in the congregation worked at the Bazaar either as salesgirls, waitresses or in the kitchen, where Misty Montague presided over Linda Taylor and Community Brown, who cooked the food and baked the rolls served at the daily luncheon. Samantha Sue Buford had been chairman of the benefit for the past two years. She ran it efficiently and well. This year, at the last minute, she had gone on a Caribbean cruise, leaving Millicent Black as her vice president in charge.

At noon the rush began. The queue lined up at the door to buy two-dollar luncheon tickets stretched to the street.

Each of the round tables in the dining room seated eight, and by noon almost all were full. Shelley lost track of the number of plates she filled with roast beef, scalloped potatoes and rolls to serve to the diners. She was so rushed that it was a while before she noticed a well-dressed dark woman standing quietly by herself, waiting to be shown to a table. Glancing around the crowded room, she saw that the only available seat was at Mrs. Dinwiddie's table. Quickly Shelley directed the stranger to it. The woman nodded and politely thanked her. Shelley noticed that she was striking. Wings of blue-black hair protruded from beneath a smart green hat that matched her emerald green suit. Although she seemed totally self-possessed, Shelley sensed a certain nervousness in her manner, in the way her eyes canvassed the room, in the slight hesitation that preceded her taking her seat.

"I'll serve you right away," Shelley told her, smiling. She looked over at the Beast. "I see you're ready for coffee. I'll bring it as soon as I serve—"

"Never mind coffee," Mrs. Dinwiddie snapped. "I've had quite enough without it." She gazed directly at the stranger, who sat motionless, her head bowed, her hands folded in her lap. When she spoke again, the Beast's eyes held the same hard blue glitter as the sapphire horseshoe pin decorating the lapel of her tweed suit. "My dears," she said imperiously to her companions, "let's leave."

The stranger did not look up as they left. She continued to sit motionless, her head bent slightly, a strange faraway look in her eyes, as though listening to fine music. All the other tables were full and the line at the door stretched from the dining room to the entrance of the parish hall. There were seven empty seats at the table where the stranger sat.

Yet none availed themselves of them.

318

PART THREE
THE CHASE

FOURTEEN

THAT fall the foliage had never been more beautiful. By mid-October the splendor of woods and fields was breathtaking. The gum trees turned a vivid scarlet. The maples and tulip poplars were gold tinged with orange, and the oaks a deep rich red, the color of blood. Shelley rode through the woods and over the fields high in goldenrod and feathery sumac, beneath a cloudless sky, and wondered why, during this favorite season, there was no joy, only a heaviness that settled down on her like city smog.

She had always had the feeling that she belonged everywhere. Now she felt that she belonged nowhere.

It was as though a curtain had fallen, separating her from all that was around her. More and more she felt out of contact with her family, in the supermarket and in the hunting field, where people suddenly seemed overpolite, and yet when she sought to join them in coffeehousing, chatting over the usual trivialities, she had the feeling of breaking into a conspirators' meeting where there was no intention of including her. The feeling that had begun growing the night of Tatine's coming-out party was now perpetual, blurring her relationship to all that was around her. Day-to-day activities had lost all meaning. Underneath, where the foundations of family should have sustained her, there was a void of loneliness. Somewhere, somehow she had failed and she did not know how or why. She had heard nothing from Zagaran—and nothing about him, except that he was out of town.

In desperation, she turned to the thing she knew best, the hunting field. Here, if nowhere else, she felt herself to be invulnerable.

In order to rebuild her confidence and shake off her depression she rode with new recklessness and abandon, as though in speed and fast galloping and high fences she could escape from the growing sense of apartness, blend the two levels of living together. Dreading the moment when it came time to step down off her horse and face the routine of daily life, she stayed out until hounds went home.

Although the time of the meet had been raised to nine, it was still the cubbing season. This Saturday meet was at Last Resort, a good hour's hack from Shelburn Hall. Shelley prayed that Suellen would not keep her waiting when she went to pick her up.

It was a lovely morning. Overhead the sky was a deep blue. The woods were brilliant, the gums and oaks a deep crimson, the maples the rich gold of creamery butter. As she drove to Muster Corner the fields were misted, the hollows obscured by pockets of silver.

It had rained the previous week, yet woods and fields were still dry. Later, when the sun burned away the mist, it would be hot.

At Muster Corner she banged on Suellen's unpainted door. After what seemed an interminable wait the door opened to disclose Suellen, eyes red-ringed, the corneas streaked with fine red threads. Bare feet were sticking out from beneath a soiled flannel nightgown and her hair was in pink plastic rollers. Behind her, Shelley saw a rumpled bed covered with a faded patchwork quilt. A rat ran across the floor and vanished under a peeling lopsided bureau. Stockings and lingerie hung from its half-opened drawers and its top was loaded with open jars of cosmetics.

"I'm coming, Miss Shelley." Suellen stifled a yawn. "Me and Eddie went down country. We was late gettin' back. I'll just get my clothes."

Suellen looked as if she might be pregnant again, Shelley thought as the girl backed inside and closed the door. Suellen already had one child, a daughter, presumably by Eddie, one of the Smiths from Muster Corner. Although Eddie was a raging drunk and would not marry her, she refused to leave him. She had told Shelley that Eddie once took time out from beating her to pay Chester Glover fifty cents to go away. From then on, whenever Shelley saw the policeman, she wondered how he could tolerate the sight of a huge Negro male brutalizing his woman, allowing her to be pounded unconscious in return for a fifty-cent piece. But when Shelley sympathized with her, Suellen turned a hard, sullen face to her and retorted, "What you expect—shit like that?"

Now it was almost eight. Mike and Cam would be waiting for breakfast. Suellen came finally, her hair still in rollers, half the hem out and two buttons off the soiled blue cotton uniform Shelley had bought for her at the Dependable Store. There was an angry-looking burn festering on her forearm and she smelled of grease. Without saying anything, Shelley put the car in gear and drove back to the highway.

"Mr. Latimer will pick up Cam at school. He can have a peanut butter and jelly sandwich for lunch and there's some Jello."

Suellen yawned. "Yes'um."

Shelley, determined to control her annoyance, said, "The children waiting for the bus—do they go to the Shelburn school?"

"Nome," Suellen replied. "They go to the colored school out to Bellevue. Way bus travels takes most an hour to get there."

"Aren't they supposed—I mean—don't they want to go to the white school?"

Suellen shook her head. "I don't want my baby goin' to school with whites."

"You don't?" Shelley stared, puzzled.

"My baby is getting along just fine," Suellen said emphatically. "You get white children in school and she going to ask herself what they talkin' 'bout! No, sir, I don't want my baby getting no complex."

"How is Melusina?" Shelley asked, quickly changing the subject.

Suellen hiked up her skirt and scratched her thigh. "Her mind wanders a lot. She right old. Reckon won't be long now 'fore she passes."

I must go see her, Shelley thought with a twinge of guilt. Sudden longing swept over her. She wanted to climb into Melusina's lap and rest her head against her shoulder. She could hear Melusina saying, "There, there, child. Melusina get you some candy. Melusina will make it right."

As she drove into the courtyard she saw the red-painted plane circling for a landing.

Mike and Cam were eating toast and jam.

"Cam," Shelley ordered, "drink your milk."

"There isn't any," Cam said. "Me and Daddy fixed toast."

"Daddy and I," she corrected, hugging him.

"My Boy Hambone just called," Mike said. "Something about Fax wanting you to take the field this morning. Hey, aren't you going to eat?"

"I'll just make it if I leave now. Good-by," she called back. "Have a good day."

Jimmy Jones was sweeping the stable aisle. His five-year-old brother Bardy was running his toy truck on the hard-packed clay. Bardy now lived with Simeon Tucker's brother's family, who had agreed to keep him for a weekly fee that generally came out of Mike's pocket. He smiled widely in response to Shelley's greeting.

Virginia City's rheumatism was worse. It was becoming difficult for him to handle billets and buckles, so Jimmy had tacked up Lookout Light, with the noseband twisted and the girth backwards. Silently she set about adjusting the tack. "Miss Shelley," Jimmy began tentatively, "mind if I ask you something?"

"Oh, Jimmy," she answered, "I'm in such a rush."

He reached out a hand as she started to lead Lookout Light from the stable. "Miss Shelley, I carved a horse for you."

"Jimmy, will you get me my whip—please—"

"Yes, Miss Shelley." He pulled his hand back and went to get her hunting crop from the hook by Lookout Light's stall. " 'Bye, Miss Shelley, have a nice hunt."

"Thank you." She looked down at his upturned face. "Jimmy, I'll see your carving as soon as I get back. O.K.?" As she rode away she felt as if his fingers were clinging to her, holding her back among the trivialities, the threads of responsibilities that were her life. When the woods finally closed around her it was as though she was going on a much-needed vacation.

With an eye out for beer cans and broken bottles, she kept Lookout Light at a jog until they reached Silver Hill. Here she decided to leave the road and cut across country.

As Lookout Light's stride lengthened and feathers of crimson sumac brushed his legs, the remembered childhood feeling of escape and adventure, when Saturday was a timeless day filled with wonder and Monday weeks away, stole over her, replacing her tensions. If she rode through the Gibson farm she would still be on time.

When she tried to cut through the farm she found the gate

onto the lane on the far side had a big padlock attached to the chain wrapped around the post. There was no way to unlock it. She looked around but nobody was in sight. She would have to remount, return the way she had come and go around by the road.

Lookout Light was reluctant to stand still. Each time she tried to get her foot into the stirrup and swing up onto his back, he sidestepped out from under her. When she finally managed to remount it was half an hour after the time the meet had been called for. Somebody would take her place, she thought. Still, the idea of hounds moving off without her was annoying.

The sun was up now and the day became increasingly warm. She was hot and irritated as she pulled up on the top of a rise to listen.

Lookout Light pricked his ears. The cry of hounds came like church bells pealing across the fields of plumy sumac and golden broom sedge. In the distance she saw horses outlined against the sky. She began to gallop.

As she jumped into the old eroded cornfield behind DeLong Manor, she met My Boy Hambone. Wearing Fax's British-made handed-down riding clothes, the groom was riding one of the Schligmans' young horses which he was introducing to the excitements of the chase, taking him hilltopping in a hackamore. After a year of My Boy Hambone's unique schooling, the "green hunter" would be "made."

My Boy Hambone told her hounds had found back of Last Resort.

"I got your message," Shelley said. "I couldn't get here any sooner. Who has the field?"

"Reckon Mr. Zagaran took it."

"Mr. Zagaran!"

"Yes, Miss Shelley. Mr. Dinwiddie say for Mr. Zagaran to take it."

"Well I never!" Shelley said, imitating the Beast. "Where are hounds now?"

Simultaneously the pack broke from the woods, noses close to the ground. Sending out a great cry, they began running across country to the towers and turrets of Ballyhoura. Lookout Light leapt into a gallop to follow.

Hounds crossed the lane behind the house and streamed over the Valley floor. Shelley saw a horse and rider coming toward her, their identity unmistakable. He sat erect and easily, his figure tall and graceful, his narrow face made leaner by the visored hunting cap. The mare moved smoothly beneath him, her wildness disciplined and controlled, her black coat gleaming in the sunlight that touched the Ballyhoura Oak silhouetted against the sky.

The Hunt field and the staff had yet to catch up. There was nobody near. The sun and sky, the turf beneath their horses' feet, the hounds ahead and their cry belonged exclusively to them. It seemed to Shelley that Zagaran would hear the hammering of her heart, as loud as Lookout Light's vibrating beneath her knee. She saw him lift his cap in the traditional manner that indicated a view. Then she heard his exultant "Tallyho."

Following the direction in which Zagaran was waving, she saw the hunted fox, gray and furtive, fleeing toward the great tree. For an instant he paused, swiveling his head around to observe his pursuers. Then, aware of how close they were, he continued up the hillside, his brush, matted with mud and burrs, dragging along the ground.

The cry of hounds now seemed to fill the countryside with menace.

"Don't," Shelley heard herself call out. "Don't kill him."

She could not tell if Zagaran heard her or not.

The fox reached the foot of the oak. He gave a final despairing glance at the pack boiling up the slope behind him and flung himself at the Hanging Tree. Exerting the last of his strength, he scuttled catlike up the trunk.

Hounds, a seething mass of black and white, crying out in rage and frustration, hurled themselves against it, falling back on top of one another. High above them the fox lay flattened against a branch, gazing down. His lips curled back from his teeth and his eyes filled with fear and hatred as the terrible noise persisted beneath him.

The riders caught up and pulled their panting horses to a stop. The Old Huntsman peered up at the fox, partially hidden by October leaves, yellowed and flecked with crimson like drops of blood.

"Reds don't climb trees," he said to the Young Whip. "On the other hand, gray foxes don't run straight the way this one did. They must have changed foxes."

"Well I never!" Mrs. Dinwiddie said, leaning forward and resting her forearm on the pommel of her mud-spattered sidesaddle. "Dinny, didn't you say you viewed a red?"

"Yes, my dear," replied Beauty, who had come around by the lane on his cob and looked as fresh and free of mud as he had when the run began. "He popped out of the covert directly in front of me."

Polo Pete Buford dismounted and turned his horse over to Roy, his groom.

"We don't want grays in our country," he said grimly, picking up a piece of dead wood. Leaning back, he hurled it upward. It struck the branch on which the fox lay and fell back downward. "They should all be destroyed," he muttered, going to retrieve the stick.

Millicent was not to be outdone. She jumped off her horse and gave it to her daughter Merry to hold. "Come along, Bones," she cried, picking up a stone from the pile the workmen had made when they cleared the race course. "Help us shake him loose."

Her husband pretended not to hear her and rode over to join Cosy Rosy, the Dinwiddies, Betsy Baldwin and some of the children, who were bored now that the run had ended. While the grown-ups, their faces rapt and intent, sat silently gazing upward, the Young Entry talked among themselves, letting their ponies graze at random.

Dash-Smythe and several grooms also dismounted, handed their horses over to others to hold and looked around for wood or rocks to throw. The fox clung desperately to the branch, moving its head to one side and then the other as the barrage continued.

Tatine rode up alongside Shelley and sat silently smoking a cigarette.

Other members of the field stood about in groups discussing the situation, occasionally glancing at the tree and shaking their heads. A few hounds, losing interest, wandered away and lay down. The rest remained, whining and staring upward.

"We'll get him," Polo Pete called out confidently, as a stone struck the branch.

The Old Huntsman appeared not to hear him. "I don't like it." He spoke as though to himself. "Something strange." He turned to the Young Whip, who had gotten off his lathered horse and was walking him around in a circle to cool him out. "Let's see if we can get 'em away from here."

While the Young Whip set about persuading the pack to leave the tree, issuing terse commands, "Leave it, Barber. Let's go now, Bouncer," brandishing the thong of his whip, the Old Huntsman put his horn to his mouth and began to blow hounds home.

"Hounds need to be blooded," Polo Pete insisted. "We haven't had a kill this fall." He looked around at the assembled riders. "Somebody go to the house and get a gun."

Zagaran had been speaking to Simeon, who had come from the barn. Now he rode over to where the fat man stood beside the pile of missiles he had accumulated. The two men exchanged a long, meaningful look and then in a voice so low that only Polo Pete heard it, Zagaran said, "This is my property. I give the orders here."

Without waiting for a reply, he wheeled his mare around and rode her beneath the hanging branch. Beckoning to Simeon to come and hold the mare's head, he shook his feet free of his stirrup irons and dropped his whip onto the ground. Then letting his reins go free, he shrugged out of his coat and vest and tossed them to his groom. With a quick agile movement like that of a circus rider, he drew his legs up alongside and jackknifed himself upright, standing with his feet planted one on either side of the saddle. Reaching overhead, he grasped the branch and vaulted up onto it. Before any of the astonished spectators could move or speak he began climbing slowly and steadily upward toward the fox, still as death, on the branch above.

Shelley sat motionless, watching the drama being played out before her eyes. She had always hated this final end to the chase.

Zagaran had almost reached the branch where the fox lay. It seemed to her that he was smiling as he stretched out his arm.

"I think I'll go home," she said, pulling her horse away. "I really hate this."

"We all do," Tatine said, throwing down her cigarette. "But nobody does anything!"

There was a sudden drawn-out "Aaaaah" and Shelley turned to see the fox hurtling from the tree. Then all other sound was drowned by the fierce and terrible cry of hounds as, wild with the lust to kill, to taste blood, they broke from the staff seeking to restrain them and fell upon their quarry.

Zagaran came down out of the tree. When the Old Huntsman failed to move, he plunged into the sea of foxhounds. Legs spread wide, he held the bloody fox high above his head. Seemingly unaware of the warm blood dripping from it, he swung it around in primitive triumph.

Shelley's joy in the morning's gallop was gone, like the blood running from the remains of something that moments before had been proud and gleaming and alive. At that moment she had a clear view of the brush. The Old Huntsman was staring at it with horror. She understood then the reason he had tried to whip hounds off, why now he sat like a statue, his face white beneath its tan.

She had almost reached the Valley road when Zagaran caught up to her. He stopped the Jaguar beside her and got out.

"I have something for you." He drew the matted, blood-caked brush from his pocket. "You were first at the kill."

"You mean I reached the Hanging Tree first. I don't want it."

"Why not?" His voice compelled her to look at him. His coppery skin, daubed with blood from the fox, the scar over his left eyebrow now raised in inquiry, made violence, even tragedy, seem consistent with his actions.

"You wouldn't understand," she said helplessly.

"You think I climbed that goddam tree, scraped my hands and tore my new breeches to throw the fox to the hounds? Is that why you won't accept the brush?"

"The brush is black." She looked directly at him and again she felt the strangeness, the fascination of his foreignness, which, like the Hanging Tree, the wandering wood itself, had to do with past mysteries, things whispered about and never wholly explained or understood.

"It may look black to you." He held it up. "Actually, it's dark gray. You heard Polo Pete. Grays are inferior. They're to be done away with."

"People say that they're not purebred, that they're a mixture. I only like thoroughbreds." She reached down and patted Lookout Light's neck. "But that doesn't mean I believe in killing. Anyway, there's an old superstition in this country that to kill a black-brushed fox means death to the killer."

"Surely you don't believe that nonsense," he said scornfully.

"The Old Huntsman does."

"That's why he didn't want it killed?"

She nodded. "Nor did I. It's macabre and bloodthirsty to throw a fox down into the middle of the pack. It's the chase that counts, not the killing."

He gave her a long look. "Someday, Miss Shelley ma'am, you'll learn that you can't run with the hare and hunt with the hounds."

She had gone some distance before she dared glance around. He was standing beside the car staring after her. She could tell by the way he held himself and the brush that he was coldly furious.

FIFTEEN

THE long twilight of Indian summer had ended. The days held a clarity, a brilliance, like the shine on the horses' coats and the deep blue color of the mountains. At night a full orange moon, the hunter's moon, rose in the Virginia sky. Round, luminous, so near you could almost read the expression on its face. There was magic in it. It glinted over the fields, making paths of gold where foxes played, field mice skittered and deer grazed.

Pumpkins lay on the ground and were piled in front of the supermarket. The Queen Anne's lace that faithfully lined the roads from early spring until late fall gave way to frost that came during the night, silvering the early morning fields and byways.

Soon it would be November. The wind blowing the dying leaves to the ground. The smell of wood smoke. Frosty mornings and fresh horses, newly fit for hunting. A tension in the air, a quickening tempo as the season approached.

The Saturday before opening meet was Mike's fortieth birthday. The Jenneys, Misty Montague and Fax Templeton were coming to dinner.

"No civil rights," Shelley said at breakfast.

"Right," Mike agreed. "And no horses."

They smiled at each other and for a while the golden quality of those first months at Shelburn, when they had sat across from

330

each other at the old pine table, with the bright sun coming through the trees and past the red-checked curtains into the big white-painted room, was back. Briefly the tensions of past weeks were replaced by memories of the time they had drunk coffee and planned Shelburn's future, the rebuilding of the house and the newspaper. For a moment all was right with their world and the grayness they had come to struggle with daily seemed unreal.

Even Zagaran, whom she had not seen since the day the gray fox had been killed cub hunting, seemed as remote as a childhood dream. She had taken the field on several occasions when Fax failed to appear. Zagaran had not been hunting. He was away on business, she heard. Andrea was in Connecticut taking a cure and Tatine came and went with breezy irregularity.

The morning of Mike's birthday she rode out on Lookout Light. Her boarders had melted away. Millicent's young horse and the Martins' mare had returned to their own barns, and the two horses she had taken on in order to help out Story Jackson when his stable became overcrowded had both been sold. Although this left her with less pressure and more time, her finances were in such dismal shape that the last check she had made out to cash at the supermarket had bounced, and she had had a difficult time persuading the manager to give her credit until the end of the month. In order to buy two bottles of champagne for Mike's birthday, she had been forced to borrow from Cam's piggy bank.

It was too beautiful a day, she told herself, to worry about money. As she rode out onto the lane that ran back of Ballyhoura, the feeling of the horse beneath her and the sight of the countryside she loved began their magical process of renewal.

She was singing softly to her horse and herself when she met Bebe Bruce riding the spotted horse she had bought from Fax.

After commenting on the weather, discussing their horses and the guest house the Schligmans were building, Bebe said she would see Shelley at the meeting that afternoon.

"What meeting?" Shelley asked blankly.

"The Hunt meeting," Bebe replied. "Polo Pete's secretary telephoned yesterday."

"She didn't call me."

"Maybe you weren't home."

"I was home all last night. Suellen was there during the day."

"The meeting's at Ballyhoura at five," Bebe volunteered.

"Ballyhoura? Why Ballyhoura?"

"P. P. suggested it. I suppose with Samantha Sue away he didn't feel he could have it at his place. You know she always puts on such a show. Shelley, you'd better come. I understand they're fed up with Fax. There's to be a motion to make Zagaran Master."

Shelley stared at her dumbfounded. "Zagaran! Now I know you're joking. Why, he's only just started hunting with The Hunt. He doesn't know the country." She shook her head, unable to continue.

Bebe gave her a long, level look. "Dear Shelley, you must know by now that money will get you everywhere." She wheeled her grass-fat gelding around and started down the lane. "Be sure to come," she called back. "Fax needs his friends."

Since her return to Shelburn Hall Shelley had, because of her name and her heritage, been permitted to hunt without paying a subscription. Samantha Sue had called her prior to each Hunt meeting and asked her to preside at the tea table. But Samantha Sue had not returned from cruising the Caribbean. Meanwhile, Polo Pete was drinking more heavily than ever, spending less time in his office at the bank and more time on the Valley road making visiting rounds.

Shelley thanked God that he had shown no inclination to drop by Shelburn Hall. For once he settled in with a toddy in one hand, a cigar in the other, there was no getting rid of him until he became so abusive and befuddled that it was necessary to call his chauffeur to bundle him back into his limousine, drive him home and get him to bed.

She had managed to meet the interest payments due on his loan with the money from the sale of one of the ancestors. The painting was a Gilbert Stuart, and a Washington gallery was happy to buy it.

Debby Darbyshire and Millicent Black were waiting at the front door when she reached Ballyhoura. They seemed surprised to see her. Debby concentrated on taking off her string gloves and Millicent rummaged through her bag of needlework for her cigarettes. How dare they act as if she didn't exist, Shelley thought angrily. It was the way they behaved toward Katie Schligman and

Negroes, people they considered inferior. She was about to speak when Zagaran opened the door. Simultaneously they pushed past him and began speaking at once.

"Gorgeous day . . . glad to be able to come . . ."

He looked past them at Shelley, standing on a lower step. "Why, Miss Shelley, I'm honored. What brings you here?"

She lifted her chin. "Why wouldn't I come? It's a meeting of The Hunt, isn't it?"

"The Hunt, I should have known." He stepped aside. "Do come in."

Someday I'll get even with him, she thought, passing from the bright October afternoon into the long, paneled hallway lined with mounted heads. Although for what, exactly, she couldn't say. He wore what Debby described as his safari suit. Highly polished brown boots, breeches and tan khaki jacket. He explained he'd just returned from shooting deer over the land he had bought in the Free Zone.

Shelley had heard Debby tell Millicent that the hunting box he'd fixed up resembled a World's Fair version of a Virginia farmhouse. "All comfy chairs, decorated chintz and a big open fireplace."

He led the way to the den, where guns were racked along the wall and a portrait of Andrea looked down from over the fireplace. "Straight Cecil B. De Mille," Debby whispered sotto voce as he took his place at the head of the long table. With anyone else, the theatricality of his clothes and manner would have seemed ludicrous. Yet it did not occur to anybody to laugh.

The pine-paneled den resembled a company board room. Leather armchairs surrounded the refectory table, centered by a silver bowl of hothouse roses. A heavy round Steuben glass ashtray, a pad and carefully sharpened pencil had been set at each place.

Bebe Bruce, immaculate in lavender tweeds and looking as if she had just come from her hairdresser in "Wash," sat next to Polo Pete, his face blotched and his clothes rumpled. The Dash-Smythes; Cosy Rosy, baby-faced and braless in a thin striped turtleneck; and the R. Rutherford Dinwiddies were already at the table. Shelley waited politely for Debby and Millicent to be seated. She was about to sit down beside Millicent when Zagaran beckoned her to the chair next to him. She waited for a sign from Millicent or Debby, but neither of her friends acknowledged her.

"Is everybody here?" Zagaran asked.

"Everyone but our Master." R. Rutherford Dinwiddie's waxed mustache ends seemed to become more rigid.

"Now, Dinny." His wife put a restraining arm on the sleeve of his tailored tweed. "Muddy Watters warned you not to get excited."

"I am excited. Yesterday was the last straw."

"What happened?" Zagaran asked calmly.

"I had a call from Chester Glover asking me to come and get our Master." The old gentleman's voice quavered with indignation. "I had been about to leave for Washington. I canceled my appointments and drove to the jailhouse and what do you suppose I found?"

Debby Darbyshire obliged. "The dear boy, in his cups!"

R. Rutherford Dinwiddie threw her a dark look. "Our Master, the Master of *The* Hunt, was sitting in a cell in full evening dress, playing poker with that no-account darkie who works for the *Sun*." He glanced at Shelley. "Jubal something or other, who's always standing on the corner by the liquor store."

"Jones," Shelley said faintly.

"Yes, Jones. Fax did not seem at all concerned that I had been forced to change my plans. He had the nerve to ask if I m-m-m-minded w-w-w-waiting until they finished the g-g-g-game."

It seemed that instead of going straight home from a dinner party, Fax had gone to Muster Corner to buy some bootleg whiskey.

At Delia's Kitchen he began drinking with the colored people. He got into an argument with Jubal that developed into fisticuffs when Fax called him a bastard.

"The policeman was called in to separate them. After Fax slept it off in jail, he persuaded Jubal that bastard was a term of endearment. 'You know how c-c-c-close My B-b-b-Boy H-h-h-Hambone and I are,' " R. Rutherford continued in imitation of Fax. " 'Not a d-d-d-day p-p-p-passes I don't call him b-b-b-bastard. And this m-m-m-man here'—he actually jabbed me in the ribs—'why this old b-b-b-bastard was one of my d-d-d-daddy the Judge's oldest f-f-f-friends!' "

It was all Shelley could do not to laugh. The others, however, looked serious.

"The dear boy goes too far," Debby murmured disapprovingly. "Such goings-on give The Hunt a bad image."

"Fax is a First Family of Virginia," Dash-Smythe said defensively.

"You mean his ancestors came over on the *Mayflower?*" Cosy Rosy asked.

"Unfortunately, it was a one-way trip," her husband replied darkly, puffing on his pipe.

Many things were moving through Shelley's mind at once. Briefly she felt wordless and immobilized. Then she rallied her loyalty. "Fax is a good Master. He knows horses and the country and he goes like a bomb. The farmers like him."

"He's fall-addled and he drinks too much." Millicent bit off a length of wool thread and began to work on the tapestry she was doing for the church.

"Business," Polo Pete said briskly, rapping on the table. "Let's get to the business at hand. Dudley, you have a report to make?"

Dash-Smythe set his pipe down in the heavy ashtray. "We have a problem. Groundhogs. The country is riddled with holes."

"Groundhogs and gray foxes," Polo Pete said. "I suggest we get rid of them."

"I spoke to the county person," Dash-Smythe said. "It is possible to blow up the dens. Or they can be filled in."

"Let's take it under advisement," R. Rutherford Dinwiddie said.

Dash-Smythe picked up his pipe, which had gone out, and started methodically to refill it from the tobacco pouch he brought from the pocket of his crested blazer. When he had finished, he picked up one of the notes he had placed on the table in front of him and peered at it.

"I've been told by an informant who shall be nameless that the chickens The Hunt puts out for the Silver Hill foxes are being caught and eaten by members of the Muster Corner community." He looked over at Polo Pete. "Apparently, some families have been existing on the Bounty due our foxes."

"I'll look into the matter," Polo Pete promised, his face reddening with annoyance. "What other problems are there?"

335

"It's time we weeded out some of the dead wood." Dash-Smythe drew a list of Hunt members from his briefcase on the floor beside his chair. "Some that have been dead for years are still getting fixture cards. Others haven't paid a subscription." He glanced pointedly at Shelley. "We have a large deficit. Those of us who have been making it up each year feel that we should no longer be called upon to carry The Hunt."

"I'm a newcomer, an outsider." Zagaran emphasized the word "outsider." "I don't want to seem presumptuous. But it appears to me that some things could be done to make the operation of The Hunt more efficient."

"How?" R. Rutherford asked.

"Sell the present site," Zagaran replied. "I'd like to buy the land as an investment. Move hounds and staff horses back into the original kennels here. It will take very little to put them in shape once again, and I'll gladly do this as my contribution to The Hunt. Of course," he concluded quickly, "this is just an idea, but I believe it would help to put The Hunt on a sounder financial basis."

"Let's face it," Mrs. Dinwiddie said flatly, "The Hunt needs money. The kennels are a disgrace. The other day Dinny and I took Lord and Lady Willoughby-Walloughby from the British Embassy to see the hounds. I was ashamed. Runways hadn't been washed down. The Old Huntsman's kennel coat was filthy. The only one on his toes was that new Young Whip, Doyle, isn't that his name?"

Shelley was used to speaking out concerning The Hunt and to being deferred to by the other members. "I think Mr. Zagaran's idea is excellent," she said spontaneously. "The original kennels were here at Ballyhoura. They were moved when the place was shut down. The Hunt could also take in additional members." She suddenly felt as though she were in a room full of strangers. Why was it that they all seemed to be looking at her as if they had never seen her before? All but Zagaran, who sat relaxed, smoking one of his Turkish cigarettes and gazing out the window.

"Foxhunting has already become very common," Dash-Smythe said.

"Let every Tom, Dick and Harry into The Hunt and the field'll be so big you'll never see a hound," Polo Pete offered.

"It wouldn't surprise me to find nigras hunting with The Hunt," Mrs. Dinwiddie said pointedly, looking at Shelley. "Now,

Indians, mind you. There is something to be said for Indians. They know about horses—"

"Please excuse me," Zagaran interrupted. "I see that groundhog that's been tearing up the Cup course!"

He rose and went to the gun rack. Nobody moved as he lifted down a rifle, walked to the big window looking out onto the field below and slid it open. Then, adjusting the gun to his shoulder, he squinted through its telescopic lens, sighted and shot the groundhog.

"I left then," Shelley said as they were having cocktails in the library that evening. "The shot not only killed the groundhog, it killed the discussion."

From five, when she returned from the Hunt meeting, until seven, when the guests were due to arrive, there had been the usual rush.

She had just put the casserole in the oven and fixed the cheese tray when the Jenneys arrived. By the time Mike had made them a drink and poked up the library fire, Fax and Misty were at the door.

"That couldn't be Fax," Hunter Jenney said. "Why, he's practically on time."

"Fax goes by SPT," Shelley explained to Enid. "Southern People's Time." She started for the door. "I told him to pick up Misty an hour ago so he'd be here by seven-thirty."

"This is about the only house in The Valley that I know of that doesn't have a bar in the living room," Enid commented when they were all seated in the den. "I'm told the Schligmans have torn out an entire wall and put in a bar as big as the altar in Washington Cathedral."

"They probably need room for the horses to turn around after they deliver the beer," Mike said. "Shelley, pass the cheese tray."

"How's the colt going?" Misty asked Shelley.

"Wonderfully," Shelley answered enthusiastically. "Polo Pete wants to buy him back. God knows we need the money, but I can't bear the thought of selling him. Personally, I think he's a Shelburn Cup horse."

Fax had been staring into the fire. Although he was dressed as nattily as ever, green velvet dinner jacket and his needlepoint fox-head slippers, he seemed strangely downcast.

337

"You're very quiet," Misty remarked, not unkindly. "Are the Schligmans getting you down?"

He turned to her without smiling. "P-p-p-people like that shouldn't move into The V-v-v-Valley. This is g-g-g-good whiskey. Not as g-g-g-good as my corn likker from the F-f-f-Free Zone, but g-g-g-good s-s-s-sippin' whiskey."

"I think they're good people," Misty said. "You can't maintain the status quo forever."

"Sure c-c-c-can't," Fax agreed vehemently, looking at Shelley. "Mine's f-f-f-finished, thanks to your n-n-n-neighbor up the r-r-r-road."

"What are you talking about?" Shelley asked.

Fax stood up. He drank the last of his drink and extended his glass to Mike for a refill. "The l-l-l-last of the Templetons has gone down the d-d-d-drain," he said dramatically.

"What do you mean?"

"After you left, they held a s-s-s-secret m-m-m-meeting," Fax said, his stammer more pronounced than before. "They d-d-d-decided I was g-g-g-giving The Hunt a b-b-b-bad i-i-i-image. They elected Z-z-z-z-z-Zagaran M-m-m-m-m-m-Master."

"So Zagaran got what he wanted," Hunter Jenney said softly to no one in particular.

"What do you mean?" Shelley asked.

"Nothing, really. Just a feeling I have about him. It began when I sold him Ballyhoura."

"Are you going to let it just happen?" Mike asked the room in general. "Why not a letter to the Hunt members or a petition?"

Fax leaned back wearily. His face looked suddenly lined, almost old. "I n-n-n-never did hold with f-f-f-fussin' and f-f-f-feudin'. Tell the t-t-t-truth, I'm tired."

Shelley stood up. "I'm going to do something about it. I'll write a letter and get the Hunt members to sign it. Come along, we'd better eat before I get too wound up. Bring your drinks with you."

It had been coming, she told herself. Fax had been lax, late for meets, rarely visiting the kennels, leaving more and more up to the Old Huntsman. Yet they shouldn't have done it this way. They should have had an open meeting, with all the Hunt members present.

In the kitchen, warmed by the old-fashioned wood-burning

iron range, they sat down at the long pine table, covered now with a red-checked tablecloth. In the candlelight the silver gleamed. From the stove came the savory aroma of the casserole. With a sigh of contentment, the dogs took their places by the hearth.

"This is nice," Enid said appreciatively as she accepted a plate piled high with the chicken, rice and red wine mixture—a form of chicken cacciatore that Shelley called her chicken catch-all—green salad and garlic bread. "Shelley, you do so much, cooking, coping with Cam—"

"Not as much as you do, Enid," Shelley answered sincerely.

"She's good on C's," Mike said. "Cam, casseroles, canned soup, chocolate—"

"I was going to set the table in the dining room," Shelley said, "but it's so cold, and my basic black is costing more and cleaning less."

"Who do you have?" Misty asked.

"Suellen Smith. She's surly and unreliable. She just asked for a raise. At the same time she announced she was pregnant."

"My!" Enid exclaimed. "Who to?"

Shelley shrugged. "I think it's Eddie, who, as she puts it, 'does her over,' but if you spend your time in a briar patch, how do you know which briar does the scratching?"

"Must be one of the Muster Corner Smiths," Misty said. "The ones born on the dark side of the moon."

Mike pushed back his chair. "I'll get another bottle of wine. Enid, what do you think about the population explosion?"

He had no sooner finished speaking than there was a loud bang, followed by a sizzling sound.

"The champagne," Shelley cried, springing up. "I put it in the oven and forgot it."

Mike gazed around at the surprised faces. "We always have our champagne fresh from the oven. Served at room temperature."

"F-f-f-frankly, old m-m-m-man," Fax said, "ah prefer m-m-m-mine cold, say the c-c-c-correct body temperature of B. Z-z-z-Zagaran."

"I forgot to chill it," Shelley apologized, laughing. "So I put it in the freezer compartment. We took so long over drinks that it froze solid. So I thought I'd just put it in the oven for a few minutes to warm it up." She opened the oven door. Steam billowed out and the oven was filled with broken glass.

For the remainder of the meal and the ceremony of the birthday cake, they discussed country topics, the growing number of rabid foxes and the water shortage, plans for the School Fair. "We're putting on an art exhibit," Enid said. "Lucy Mae Taylor has done a marvelous painting of her great-grandmother, Melusina, and the Day School children did a collage. Each child drew a series of figures and pasted them up. You won't believe it, but Buddha Buford's was black."

"Poor Fax," Shelley said as the sound of the last departing car died away. She started emptying ashtrays and turning off lights. Mike came up behind her and put his arms around her. "The world's in flames and we worry about The Hunt."

"Please, Mike, I'm too tired." She smiled shakily. "The dishes. As Suellen says, shall we stack them or is we gentry?"

"Stack them!"

"I can't." Shelley began pushing them in the sink. "There's too much to do in the morning. I promised to see Melusina. Damn, the drain's clogged again."

Mike turned to her helplessly. "Shelley, what is the matter with us? The Hunt and the horses? Now the drain?"

Her feeling of annoyance returned. "What do you think I've been doing, feeding it oats?"

"We the undersigned members request that the President of The Hunt call a special meeting of the members as provided by Article VII of The Hunt Constitution.

"We feel that the peremptory appointment of a new Master should be considered by the Board of Stewards and nominations submitted by the membership of The Hunt Club to a nominating committee of these Stewards, elected by the Board and voted on by the entire Board of Stewards, a two-thirds majority being necessary."

The letter that Shelley drafted to Polo Pete Buford was never sent. No signatures were forthcoming. When it came to actually signing their names, the landowners refused. "Lot of things I don't like about Mr. Buford," Ambrose Webster said, "but I can't rightly go against him. Ten years he been holding the mortgage on my farm and he ain't never raised the interest rates. Most every bank charges seven per cent. He's stayed at four."

So it went on down the line. Finally Shelley realized that nothing could be done to keep Fax Templeton in office. B. Zagaran was the new Master of The Hunt.

Several days after the Hunt meeting and Mike's birthday Shelley received a call from Millicent inviting her to meet "the girls for a sandwich at the Gone Away." It was the first time that Millicent had telephoned since the matter of Mother's precious-darling-love. Shelley, hoping she had undergone a change of heart and decided to end the feud, was glad to accept.

After picking up Cam, she drove to the drugstore. In Millicent's Rolls two terriers were barking frantically at Butch, Debby Darbyshire's guard dog, who was restrained from leaping at smaller dogs by the wired windows of her dusty pickup truck.

Shelley parked behind it. Quickly she glanced in the rearview mirror. Wisps of hair had come loose from the bun at the nape of her neck. Maybe she should cut it, she thought. It would be easier to wear under her hunting cap.

Mike's old Army rucksack that she used as a shopping bag disclosed a confusion of bills, a notice from the bank in reference to her overdrawn account, Suellen's shopping list that she hadn't been able to find when she went to the supermarket, two small trucks and a cardboard submarine that Cam had extracted from a cereal box, an assortment of Green Stamps, a comb and compact but no lipstick. She needed a new one anyway, she thought, re-fastening the rucksack. Her old one was worn down to a nub. She'd buy one now in the drugstore, and charge it.

Grabbing Cam's hand and pulling him along behind her, she crossed the street and entered the Gone Away.

Millicent, Sion Atwell and Samantha Sue, who had just returned from her cruise, were seated at their usual table by the cosmetic and lotions cases. Merry Black and Buddha Buford were devouring hamburgers at the adjoining table.

"I'm late," Shelley said breathlessly. "Sorry. Just as I was leaving the house Suellen called and gave me a long explanation about how she couldn't come back to work until Monday."

"Don't give it a thought," Millicent said serenely. "Cam, go and sit next to Merry. Shelley, here's a seat for you."

"Hope you don't mind," Samantha Sue said, taking off her

wraparound dark glasses and eying Shelley up and down. "We went ahead and ordered." She was still tanned from the Caribbean sun.

Her hair and face were perfection and her smart blue tweed skirt and round-collared shirtwaist were immaculate. Sweetly she went on: "Shelley, you do look tired. It must be dreadful having to do all your own work. Me-mah always said we shouldn't worry about the morals of our cats or our darkies, but when they begin to interfere with the job— Ah mean I think you should take Suellen to the clinic and have her *spayed* . . ." Shelley but half listened. This was Samantha Sue's way of reaching the point she wanted to make. "You'd think you of all people wouldn't have help problems," Samantha Sue continued. "Way you feel about nigras and all." She waved one brown, beautifully manicured hand. "Anyway, you always look divine. Tell me, dear, who's doing your hair? Still Miss Esther, or are you doing it yourself?"

What is Samantha Sue gunning for now? Shelley thought, mystified, knowing her hair looked windblown and uncombed. Samantha Sue's new hair-do, short cropped curls carefully streaked and crowning her head like anchovies, was the latest creation of Mr. Alphonse, who maintained his own establishment in Washington, where Samantha Sue and some of the other Valley women went once a week, driving the hundred and twenty miles to and from the city.

"I'm lucky I don't have to do much to it," Shelley said pointedly. "You see it's still its own color."

"Shelley, what'll you have?" Sion asked. "We've ordered hamburgers."

"I'm going to have a club sandwich and coffee."

"But it takes hours, sweetie," Samantha Sue protested. "Mrs. Winecoop, bless her lil ole heart, is slow as molasses in January. Now that she's back on the job and the counter's closed to nigras, she's positively rushed off her feet."

"I'm hungry," Shelley said briefly. She looked over at the postman's wife behind the counter, but both Mrs. Winecoop and Ethel were busily taking orders and failed to see her.

"Ah reckon you'll just have to wait, sweetie," Samantha Sue continued. "Times change and all. First come, first served."

With a deliberate gesture Millicent ground out her cigarette.

"By the way, Shelley, we've just been talking. We decided that as long as you don't have any help to speak of and you're so busy, it really isn't fair to ask you to take on Pony Club again this year."

"But Millicent," Sion flattered, "you can't do everything. Red Cross and PTA and all those committees."

"I'll manage," Millicent said confidently. "There, now that's settled. Shelley, you real-ley must be starving. Here comes Mrs. Winecoop. Oh, she's going to that other table. You were here before Herm Gillespie and Greg Atwell came in. Oh, Mrs. Winecoop," she called out, "we have another order."

"Don't bother," Shelley said tersely. "I'll wait." Slowly she glanced around at Samantha Sue carefully fitting a cigarette into her Dunhill holder, at Millicent caressing the puppy that had replaced Mother's precious-darling-love lying in her lap, at Sion staring at her with disbelief. There was a sameness about them she had not noticed before, a certain hardness, an air of self-righteousness.

"Here's Mrs. Winecoop now," Millicent said. "What was it you wanted?"

"A hamburger and a glass of milk for Cam," Shelley said, noticing that the waitress had not once looked at her. "And I'd like one of your club sandwiches. That is, if it isn't too much trouble. And coffee, please."

"Hamburger-glass-of-milk-one-club-'n-coffee." Mrs. Winecoop scribbled quickly. She looked down at Millicent and smiled. "You ladies look as though you could stand some more coffee. I'll bring some hot soon's I finish waiting on Herm and Greg over there."

"Thank *you*, Mrs. Winecoop." Millicent smiled. "And do see if you can hurry up Mrs. Latimer's order. She's positively starving."

"Sweetie"—Samantha Sue took her long holder out of her mouth—"you haven't told us about your party."

Shelley looked slowly around the table. "I had a small dinner party," she said pointedly. "Black tie. It was Mike's birthday."

"You mean you didn't have any colored people?" Millicent asked. "Of course, you know how gossipy The Valley is. Really, the things you hear. For instance, somebody told me you had Muster Corner children at Cam's birthday."

Shelley leaned her elbows on the table and looked directly at Millicent. "And just exactly what else did you hear?"

"Why, I heard you invited Linda and Washington Taylor and people from Muster Corner and that woman from the N double-ACP that you served at the Church Bazaar."

Shelley stared at her blankly. "What are you talking about?"

"Why, sport, the one you put at Mrs. Dinwiddie's table." Millicent smiled around the table.

"You can't honestly mean that you thought I planted her there purposely? When I showed her to a table I didn't even realize she was colored. Later I heard she came with a group from one of the South American embassies."

She looked at Samantha Sue. "What about those people the Martins brought? Nobody made a fuss about them."

"You mean those black people in sheets?" Samantha Sue replied. "Why, sweetie, they were Africans. That's different!"

Shelley gazed at them helplessly.

"Sport, you know we're your friends," Millicent said soothingly. "But if you can't stand the heat in the kitchen you should get out."

"What does that mean?" Shelley asked.

"Well, you'd have been the logical person to take over as Master."

"Real-ley," Shelley said, imitating Millicent's drawl.

Millicent shrugged. "Obviously you're much too controversial. So it had to be Zagaran. There just isn't anybody else with the time or the money."

"Shelley," Samantha Sue said sharply, "Cam is keeping the children from finishing their lunch."

Shelley had forgotten the children at the next table. Now it appeared to her to be the other way around, as though Buddha Buford was poking Cam.

"Cam," Shelley commanded, "stop it."

"But, Mommy," Cam wailed, "Buddha's hitting me."

"That's what my daddy does to niggers," the older boy said, jabbing his fist at Cam's ribs. "Pow! Pow!"

"Buddha, you musn't do that, baby," Samantha Sue drawled. Her mouth curved into a candybox smile. "America is the great melting pot."

"It's a damned slow melting pot," Shelley said, standing up. "Come on, Cam."

"But, Mommy," Cam mourned as she took his hand and pulled him toward the door, "I didn't do anything."

"Hush," Shelley said with helpless fury, "just hush."

She drove home blindly. In the distance rose the blue mountains, jagged against a cold sky. She saw them through a haze, a haunting sense of sadness and nostalgia that their very beauty seemed to accentuate.

She was, as Melusina used to say, "all in pieces." She did not know why. What Millicent had said, the fact that she was no longer head of Pony Club, was not that important. It was true that she had no longer had the time. Lately she had not had time to work on the paper or paint. Hunting three days a week, exercising the horses, maintaining a big rundown house without adequate help kept her in a continual state of tension. She felt burdened with failure. She had thrown herself wholeheartedly into doing the things she was sure of, the things she really knew— horses, foxhunting, and the life that went with them. Now it seemed to her that she had not only failed in her human relationships but at those things which, as a Shelburn, she had been brought up to excel at. As a child she had been the leader. Whatever the others could do, she could do better—ride a more difficult pony, jump a higher fence, swing the farthest out over the quarry swimming hole.

Now the lines were drawn, the duel forced upon her. The day she had picked Cam up at school and found him fighting back his tears as the other children ran to their mothers to show off their invitations to Buddha's party she had been aware of beginning anger which had slowly hardened into anger against Mike. He had involved them, committing Cam to an adult war he could not possibly understand. Well, the Shelburns were fighters. She could feel guilty about many things she had done, but she wasn't going to assume an additional burden of regret for Mike's activities. Let him fight his own battles. She would take care of her own, if she could just find out what the lines, the issues were . . .

Millicent and Debby were sorting their mail at the high wooden desk by the post office window. Shelley was about to stop and speak but they deliberately averted their eyes and began riffling through their mail. As she bent down to open her box she overheard Millicent say, "The fixture cards are out. Opening meet's at Ballyhoura. B. Zagaran, MFH. Let's go to the Gone Away for coffee."

"Can't." Debby gathered up her mail. "Got to take the dogs to the vet for shots, get the horses out, breed a mare, buy groceries." She strode toward the door. "See you at Sion's cocktail party."

Shelley stuffed the mail into her bag. Nothing from The Hunt. Just bills and another anonymous letter warning her that if she persisted in her activities to BEWARE! This was followed by a line or two of obscenities. She tore the letter into small pieces and dropped it into the wastebasket.

The following day her mail still failed to yield an invitation from The Hunt. She was sure it was a mistake. Bitsy Baldwin, who acted as Millicent's secretary and was paid by The Hunt to send out the cards, was notoriously vague.

The Saint was tied to the parking meter in front of the Gone Away. A moth-eaten monogrammed sheet was thrown over the saddle and tied around his neck.

Fax came out of the drugstore, checked the meter, and then crossed the street to Herm Gillespie's. The leather saddlebag his grandfather had carried when he rode with Sean Shelburn's Raiders was under his arm. His silver hunting horn was thrust between the buttons of his tweed jacket, edged and patched with chamois and boasting a rosebud in its frayed buttonhole. A red silk kerchief, listing the names of the Grand National winners since the beginning of the great race, was knotted around his neck. His breeches fitted like Cosy Rosy's turtlenecks, and his boots gleamed from the elbow grease My Boy Hambone always expended on them.

Fax threw Mike, who was checking an ad, a toothless grin and turned back to the proprietor. "Just need a smidgen of paint. And a roasting pan. Mattie Moore brought me a ham. Ah need sumpn' to cook it in. Been using mah other one to make mash for The Saint."

"Be glad to let you have one," Herm said, "but Fax, if you could just advance me something on account."

"Herm, you-all know ah can't afford to pay out anything now," Fax said. His elongated drawl and stammer indicated he had been drinking. "Ah got to go and get me some new dentures. Man can't go around without no teeth in his head." He lowered his voice and went on confidentially. "Just might be getting hitched someday soon. The Duchess, you know." He reached into his saddlebag and extracted the silver flask one of his girl friends had given him. "My Boy Hambone just fetched me a batch of sippin' whiskey from the Free Zone."

Herm shook his head. "That stuff's strong. Makes my head sore!"

"Corn whiskey don't give you no headache," Fax scoffed. "Mike here'll back me up."

"Well, maybe a little taste," Herm said doubtfully. "You're sure now it won't give me no headache? Got to have me a clear head to go over accounts." He gazed pointedly at Fax. "Got a lot of outstanding accounts."

"Course it won't," Fax interrupted quickly, pouring from the flask into a Dixie cup. "This likker ain't got any of those old chemicals in it."

"All right," Herm said nervously, "but best make it quick. Can't afford to have Mrs. Dinwiddie or Miss Letty or one of them white ribboners coming in here." He took a long swallow. "Not bad," he gasped, when he could speak.

They sat in Herm's back room drinking and discussing the rabies problem. The wife of a Buford tenant farmer had opened the door to let her dog out and been bitten by a fox which had been lurking on the porch. Another, a woodcutter timbering around the old quarry beyond Webster's woods, had looked up and seen a fox coming toward him. Before the man could defend himself, the fox had bitten through his pants leg.

The Health Officer suggested that state trappers be invited into the county to reduce the wild-animal population, that contaminated dens be blown up, and that a concentrated effort be made to avert what could become a full-scale epidemic.

Mike repeated the statement from the county supervisors, who said that because of opposition from landowners the board had postponed making a decision until an opportunity to assess public reaction to a trapping program presented itself.

"Folks always r-r-r-rantin' 'bout r-r-r-rabies," Fax deprecatingly. "Every year s-s-s-somebody gets b-b-b-bitten. That don't m-m-m-mean all the foxes have gone m-m-m-mad." He refilled Herm's paper cup. "Mostly just g-g-g-grays get r-r-r-rabies anyhow!"

After Herm had another refill, Fax had his paint and his roasting pan without having advanced anything other than the charm of his presence and personality.

"Got to go p-p-p-put m-m-m-money in the meter," Fax said at last, picking up his bundles. "So long, H-h-h-Herm. So long, M-m m-Mike." At the door he paused. "If you could spare a dime, I'd appreciate it. Ah got to stop by and see Tina Welford. I baked her some cookies. And I've got some of my t-t-t-tomato r-r-r-relish for Linda Taylor." Herm reached into his cash register and brought out a dime. "Thanks, H-h-h-Herm." Fax took the proffered coin, inclining his head graciously. "Tain't right to cheat the town out of its revenoo way some folks do."

They watched him cross the street. "I declare—he could steal all the apples off your tree and then make you believe he'd been polishing 'em," Herm said wonderingly.

Mike nodded in agreement. Fax, he thought, was like the ships in the bottles in his parents' house. A kind of ancient art. He was of that class of men who are never conscious of not having money, who consider it beneath them to pay bills. The last of the big rakes, he thought, smelling of old leather and bourbon, who kicked dogs and debauched the upstairs maid.

Mike said good-by to Herm and set out on the rest of the advertising rounds. He was halfway to the Fox in the High Hat when he noticed Miss Kitty having difficulty circumventing the puddle where she was attempting to cross the street. Turning back, he walked to where she stood hesitating on the curb and took her arm.

"Young man, that was kind of you," she said when they were across the street. "I'm an old lady and I can't get used to the traffic. The cars go so fast." She turned to enter her antique shop and then paused. "I been meaning to call the *Sun*. Reckon you might as well put that standing ad of mine back in the paper. Course it doesn't bring me any business, but I do believe in supporting my home-town newspaper."

Shelley came out of the post office and started along the sidewalk to the drugstore. She saw Mike ahead, assisting Miss Kitty across the street. She started to run after him and then did not. He was always rushed the day before the paper went to press and never seemed to listen when she tried to tell him anything. She felt her hurt and anger blending into one emotion directed at her husband. Helping old ladies across the street when he was in a hurry—the very things that annoyed her most were his special qualities, gentleness, awareness, sensitivity.

She knew how illogical her feelings were and yet could not seem to help herself.

Fax Templeton was inserting a dime into the parking meter. The Saint, all but his head shrouded in the Templeton brown sheet with the T on his flank, stood patiently, one hind leg resting against the other.

"Fax," Shelley began, and found suddenly she could not speak.

He turned and saw her. "Miss Shelley, honey, you look a little u-u-u-upset."

"I'm a lot upset."

"Come along. I'll buy you some coffee."

Mrs. Winecoop, who was behind the counter, looked past Shelley to Fax and gave him a wide smile.

Shelley took off her long woolen scarf and stuffed her rucksack under her chair. After Fax ordered two coffees she told him about not receiving her invitation from The Hunt.

Fax looked uncomfortable.

"You knew," Shelley cried accusingly. "Why didn't you tell me?"

"Well, Miss Shelley, honey, I thought it would all b-b-b-blow over." He began searching the pockets of his tweed jacket for one of his whiskey-soaked cigars. "Look, Miss Shelley, honey, just tear up that c-c-c-card and you'll get your invitation to h-h-h-hunt."

"What card?"

"Why that C-c-c-Communist c-c-c-card, of course."

"I'm not a member of anything," Shelley cried.

Fax lit his cigar. Gazing dreamily through the smoke at the front window decorated with its bottles of blue water, he commented, "M-m-m-mighty d-d-d-dry. If we don't get r-r-r-rain—"

"Fax." Shelley looked at him helplessly. "I thought you were a friend."

Fax set his cigar down and studied it. "Folks around here feel pretty strong 'bout what you and Mike have been doing. S-s-s-

349

stirring up the n-n-n-nigras and all." Mrs. Winecoop set their coffee down in front of them. Fax beamed up at her. "Mr. Winecoop sure is a lucky man. He's married to the b-b-b-best coffee maker in Northern Virginia."

"Fax," Shelley said disconsolately, "you haven't heard a word I said." She paused. "When Zagaran was made Master, I wrote a letter."

"Didn't do a mite of good," he interrupted. "M-m-m-money t-t-t-talks. Miss Shelley, honey, you know how The V-v-v-Valley is. Reckon now they're afraid you might bring one out foxhunting."

Shelley looked at him as though seeing him for the first time, the once good looks blurred, frayed like the buttonhole where the rose was wilting. The outrage that she had been keeping under control erupted.

"Right now I'm not sure what to think," she said, standing up. She picked up her scarf and flung it around her throat as if it were a banner. "One thing I do know, and that is that The Hunt can't do this to me. *I'll* close my land—"

"Miss Shelley, honey," Fax said reasonably, "you ain't got no land to close, no more'n I have."

"I've got Shelburn Hall," Shelley said. She picked up her rucksack. "On second thought, closing my land's too common. Anybody can do that! I'll pave mine and paint it green! So long, Fax. Thanks for the coffee."

"Miss Shelley, honey—"

She paused halfway to the door. "Yes?"

"Miss Shelley, honey, would you mind?" He lifted the bill for the coffee that Mrs. Winecoop had set down beside him. "Just so happens I'm a little short."

That night she told Mike she had not received a fixture card, an invitation to hunt.

"You're not going to let that upset you!" Mike answered. "Now you can paint, have another child—"

"How can I sell horses when I can't school them or show them off in the hunting field?"

"Laugh it off. Rise above it." He gave her a long look. "Remember that phrase of John Buchan's, when Hannay speaks of his wife? 'She didn't scare and she didn't soil.' That's how I think of you."

. . .

Support came from unexpected quarters. Ambrose Webster stopped Mike on the street and told him to relay the message that Shelley was welcome to ride over his land any time. Miss Letty Miller deplored the Yankees who felt that just because they had money they could run the country any old way they pleased.

Nevertheless, Shelley felt as if she had acquired an infectious disease that no one would mention or discuss with her. It was as though overnight she had become nameless, a nonentity in the world of The Valley, someone who no longer mattered.

When the Hunt's Stewards had originally voted against inviting Augie Schligman to join The Hunt, saying that "if you let one in pretty soon you'll have 'em all," she had sat mutely by. When Katie asked her if she could do something about making it possible for Judy to hunt, she had said quickly that the decision was in the hands of the Stewards. Now she recalled the look that had crossed Katie's face and in retrospect she remembered seeing the same expression on Cam's face the day of Buddha's party, on Jimmy's when he reached out to touch her and she moved aside, on Miehle's when she shut the dog outside, refusing him the run of the house.

That those she had considered friends failed to lift a finger in her defense seeded her self-doubt. The fact that they would not face her with their accusations or permit her to discuss or defend her so-called "activities" for which she was being blackballed seemed the most unfair thing of all. She began to understand what Mike was experiencing, the sense of being condemned as a criminal while striving to behave as a Christian.

"Now you know how Negroes feel," Enid told Shelley.

The dawning of compassion and awareness should have given her relationship with Mike a new closeness and meaning. But the process of desegregating her mind and heart was slow, and there were times when she hated herself and those around her. Although Mike sensed her desperation, he was too tired and overworked to offer sympathy for matters he considered so far removed from the mainstream of life that they were not worth mentioning.

"I feel like a living Balkan State, fighting over the same ground," he said wearily.

She wanted to shake him into a violence that matched her own.

Instead of platitudes, she would have liked him to fight a duel on her behalf.

"It's like swimming underwater," she told Enid Jenney. "I don't know what I'm fighting. Samantha Sue thinks it's all right to entertain Africans but not Negroes. Mrs. Dinwiddie is all for the Indians."

"Neither Africans nor Indians are here," Enid said. "They're not a threat. The Negroes are!"

Shelley grinned crookedly. "It's making me miserable. Most of the time I feel like a peasant. The only time I don't is when I ride Lookout Light. Then I feel like a queen."

Enid shook her head helplessly. "There's little logic in the way most people think."

"But I'm one of *them*."

"They're striking back at Mike through you."

"What can I do?"

"Ignore it," Enid advised. "Rise above it. By the way, who are the landowners threatening to close their land?"

"Probably Polo Pete," Shelley said. She was aware of sudden panic. Unless she found the money to pay the interest due on his loan, he could take Lookout Light from her.

"Why don't you speak to Zagaran?" she heard Enid say. "Isn't he the new Master?"

Shelley shook her head. "I'd rather die first."

SIXTEEN

IT WAS the morning before opening meet. The warmth of Indian summer had given way to a sudden cold spell. The first frost iced the fields. Dark clouds scudded over the mountains, deep purple now against the leaden horizon. A cold wind swept across The Valley, blowing a swirl of leaves across the old lane in back of Ballyhoura as Shelley rode Lookout Light toward Muster

Corner to see Melusina. The morning news had reported snow in Maine and a freak storm moving south. If it continued to blow, scent would be poor. It was to be Zagaran's first appearance as Master of The Hunt. Everyone would be watching. If sport was bad, there would be I-told-you-sos from the Fax Templeton faction.

Briefly she had forgotten that she would not be there. In her mind's eye she saw the brilliance and the pageantry, felt the suppressed excitement and anticipation of the riders and their horses. Then she remembered she would be in Washington, at the Press Association banquet where Mike was to be presented with his award. She should be proud and happy. Instead she felt as if she had fallen off Lookout Light and the horse had stepped on her body, leaving it bruised and aching.

Lookout Light's head came up. He took a sudden dancing step. Shelley looked past his pricked, curving ears and saw Mrs. Dinwiddie riding along the lane toward her. The older woman wore hacking clothes, brown boots, brown sidesaddle skirt and matching tweed coat. Her hair was hidden under her felt riding hat with its brown grosgrain ribbon and narrow brim.

William Tucker, Simeon's brother, who had been hired as groom to replace Dixon, rode behind her, maintaining a respectful distance. Suddenly Shelley could not bear the idea of encountering the older woman.

A large new chicken coop with a pole across the top of it led off the road into the old Atwell property that Mrs. Penneck, a rich recluse from Rhode Island, had recently bought. The field was planted in fall wheat, but she could ride around the edge.

Lookout Light was very fresh. She could feel him tense, anxious to leave the lane, jump onto the inviting green and gallop. It was a simple matter to jump the coop. Yet something held her back. The colt was still inexperienced, she told herself, the coop with the rail on it was too high. None of her excuses were valid. The thing riders fear most had happened. As she stared at the fence, the pounding of her heart, the dryness in her mouth and a shortness of breath told her she had lost her nerve.

Nonsense, she told herself, riding up to the fence. She would drop the rail and jump the coop. As she leaned over to lower the bar, she saw it was wired to the posts. There was a gate down the fenceline, but Mrs. Penneck, who raised sheep and was feuding with The Hunt because the hounds had chased her lambs the previous season, had earned the name of Mrs. Padlock by padlocking her gates.

As she debated what to do, Mrs. Dinwiddie jogged past. She saw William glance in her direction and start to pull up, but the Beast beckoned to him to catch up with her. The groom turned his head away and urged his horse on after its stablemate.

At sight of the horses traveling away from him, Lookout Light swerved away from the fence. Shelley, who had been leaning over to investigate the wired-up pole, was caught off balance. The colt's enormous leap over the ditch onto the lane unseated her and she found herself in the muddy ditch while Lookout Light raced to catch up to the riders. She had fallen against a blackberry bramble and torn the corner of her mouth. Tears of frustration scalded her eyeballs as she suddenly became conscious of the sound of hoofs. Black Magic was galloping across the wheatfield, kicking up clods of tender jade spears. Without pausing, the mare cleared the high fence and came to a stop beside her.

"You're bleeding. Shelley, are you all right?"

He looked brown and fit and completely at ease. His eyes with the amber lights in them were like bits of glass, driving holes through her defenses.

"It's nothing." Her hand trembled as she lifted it to her mouth. "A long way from my heart. I tried to lower the rider and Lookout Light swerved out from under me."

"Since when do you lower fences?" he asked, his eyes not leaving her face.

She was appalled at the thought of how she must look, blood and tears streaking her cheeks, her hair loose and wild and hanging below her shoulders. She, who didn't soil and didn't scare, now both soiled and scared!

"I don't know what is wrong with me," she choked, digging her fists into the corners of her eyes the way Cam did when he was hurt.

Dismounting, he pulled a crimson handkerchief from his pocket. She noticed the bold Z embroidered at its corner as very gently he began wiping her face.

The silence stretching between them was like one of the shining webs strung between the blades of wheat, needing only the warmth of the sun to break it.

It was Mrs. Dinwiddie's groom who broke it. "Here's your horse, Miss Shelley." He handed her Lookout Light's reins. "I told the Madam it was only fitting I should catch him and bring him back to you."

The Negro gave her a leg up. She thanked him warmly and he rode away. Zagaran remounted and smiled at her.

"I'll give you a lead." Without waiting for an answer, he turned Black Magic around and jumped her back over the big coop with the rail on top of it. He had thrown a gauntlet down between them. The fact that he had come upon her in distress and disarray was bad enough. But to have him see her funk at a fence was unbearable.

Shelley took a deep breath and picked up her reins. Just before the panel she grabbed a handful of mane, clinging to it for security, the way she had when following her father over obstacles above her pony's head. Lookout Light, anxious to catch up to the mare, took off a stride early and cleared the fence by a country mile. Shelley reached down and patted his neck.

Black Magic's ears went back as the colt came up beside her. Her head snaked out like a bee set to sting. Zagaran pulled her aside. "She almost unloaded me in the stableyard." He laughed. "Simeon warned me. He told me she would teach me humility."

He didn't look humble, Shelley thought. His skin was burned almost the color of Simeon's and his eyes were like the whirling leaves without their dryness. He had, she realized, rescued her from fear and for this reason if for no other she turned to him gratefully. "Thanks for the lead."

Then she remembered that he was now Master of The Hunt.

Putting down her instinctive resentment, she forced herself to say, "It'll be cold tomorrow and it's still too dry. The rabies epidemic has killed off a lot of foxes. Still, I hope you have a good season."

"I intend it to be," he said quietly. "If necessary, we'll bring in foxes."

"Dropped foxes?" she cried involuntarily. "It's illegal and dishonest and not fair to the foxes."

"To have sport you have to have foxes. As Master of The Hunt it's my job to show sport."

"By importing foxes you endanger the native ones. It's the foxes from outside that bring in the rabies. And when you drop a fox in a strange country he doesn't know which way to run, where to go to save himself." She reached down and flipped over a handful of mane that had fallen on the wrong side of Lookout Light's neck. "By the way, what's happened to the fox you told me you were trying to tame?"

"There were three in the litter. One's dead. One went away. I have one left."

A covey of quail rose from the underbrush bordering the wheatfield. Lookout Light leapt sideways at the sudden whirring noise.

"Have done with it," Shelley admonished. "You've seen birds before."

The quail skimmed away toward a neighboring wood. All but one, which lay on the grass border beside the seeded ground.

Zagaran was off in a flash. Kneeling down beside the small bird, he lifted it into the palm of his hand. "I thought it might still be alive," he said softly, "but it's dead."

Just when she thought she had him classified as cruel and unfeeling he did something to confound and change her image of him. Now as she watched him lower the quail gently back down onto the ground, it was as though his hand that had been holding it was slowly squeezing the blood from her heart, leaving her as lacking in will, as helpless as the bird.

The motion of the horses, the scuffing sound of hoofs against falling leaves, the jangle of bits and creak of saddle leather enhanced the sense of intimacy as they rode on.

"My father used to bring me here," Shelley said. "He liked to shoot and this country is full of grouse, pheasants and wild turkeys. I hated the killing and the noise. I made him promise to tell me when he intended to fire his gun. Then I'd run behind him and put my hands over my ears."

"You thought a lot of your father?"

She saw him look down at his knee touching hers and wondered if he was as aware of her as she was of him.

"Yes," she answered. "I loved my father."

The lane funneled down an incline to a clearing where abruptly the stream spilled into the quarry pool Shelley had swum in as a child. Into her mind flashed the image of the figures lying on the grassy bank by the pool that long-ago day.

"Once I saw a couple here making love on the ground under

that old tree—" She broke off, embarrassed, wondering what had prompted her to speak out in such a way.

The stream had narrowed now, becoming more urgent, rushing downhill, tumbling over and around the rounded boulders that rose like the backs of animals in its demanding path. Once again it reached a clearing, a grassy cul-de-sac, on the green slopes of which nestled the little house, log barn and assorted outbuildings.

Compared to the shanties that the people of Muster Corner lived in, Melusina's house was a castle. The main part, built of hand-hewn logs, chinked and perched on a fieldstone foundation, was as it had been in the days of slavery. Her son, Washington Taylor, had added a stone wing and a bathroom. The "flush toilet" was Melusina's pride. Shelley had helped furnish it, providing fixtures, monogrammed towels and a fluffy pink rug. When it was finished, Melusina's neighbors came for a viewing. Although nobody was allowed to use it, the children, wide-eyed with wonder and delight, were each allowed to flush the toilet as they filed past.

A yellow dog, part hound, part collie, rushed out to meet them. He was followed by Melusina's great-grandchildren, who seemed to come in all sizes and shapes and from all directions, shinnying from the tree house in the maple, running from the meadows where they had been gathering nuts, emerging like dryads from the pile of leaves where they had been jumping.

At sight of the horses, the dogs set up a great clamor. Running to the house, the children cried, "Miss Shelley's here. Miss Shelley's here."

Melusina came to the gate. She was almost ninety. Her face, all bones and wrinkled skin, mirrored her delight. She wore a blue gingham dress that reached to her ankles. Her white hair rose like a spun sugar cloud from her ancient creased face. Her steps did not falter and she stood erect.

"So you come up that little dog path road to see Melusina," she cried, extending her arms.

Shelley's reaction was immediate and sincere. Dismounting, she handed Lookout Light's reins to one of the barefoot boys and ran into the old woman's embrace. Zagaran's face softened. Checking the restless mare, he listened while Melusina recited Shelburn history, how it had been at the big house, as though it had all been yesterday. She wanted to know about Cam. "'Bout time for him to come see Melusina and get some pears for his mellow hole." About Virginia City and Suellen. "That girl don't have walkin'-around sense," she said scornfully. As she talked she gazed into Shelley's face, as though Shelley was one of her children who had returned home after a long absence.

Melusina paused finally. "This your husband?" she asked, turning her almost sightless eyes toward the other rider.

"No," Shelley replied, "this is Mr. Zagaran of Ballyhoura."

At the word "Ballyhoura" an odd, almost frightened look came over the face of the old woman, and she made a quick gesture, as if crossing herself.

"Why did she do that?" Zagaran asked as they rode away.

"I think she mistook you for my grandfather. Sean Shelburn of Ballyhoura. You look like the painting."

The sun was high now. From the old wall, draped in honeysuckle, that led to the Valley road, came the drone of bees. The sun on Shelley's back, the sound of the bees, the motion of the horse brought on the euphoria that riding gave her.

"I—I must get home," she said, forcing herself to break the languid sense of timelessness. "It's late."

Zagaran's smile was gentle, the way it had been when he knelt over the dead bird. Black Magic stretched out her beautiful head, baring her teeth at Lookout Light. And as suddenly as the smile had come it was gone, like the sun obscured by a passing cloud.

"Why do you hurt her?" Shelley asked as he snatched the mare's head up.

"Magic? I don't hurt her. We understand one another. As I think you and I do."

"How was your trip?" she asked, shifting to safer ground.

"Which one? I've been on several." He leaned forward in the saddle. "Why the hell are you so afraid to talk to me? You're a Shelburn. You know your world. Your place in it."

"I thought I did until I was told people would close their land to The Hunt if I rode over it."

"What do you mean?"

She told him about not receiving a fixture card.

"When you're happy, singing happy the way you were that first day I saw you, your eyes are deep blue, like the mountains on a clear day. Now they're dark, almost purple. The changing colors of iris."

"I'd forgotten you were a gardener." Before, she would have been indignant at what she considered his overfamiliarity. Now that she herself was so uncertain, his very certainty was a rock she yearned to reach out and cling to, the way she had clung to her horse's mane over the big fence.

The roadway ran from under the shoulder of a rocky slope into the open. Below lay The Valley, a checkerboard of soft gray-green fields wreathed in the pale shine of the fall day. There was no plow or wire to be seen, nothing but fair hunting country, bounded by post and rail fences and stone walls.

"I'd get up in the night to jump those fences." Shelley pointed to the land stretching below. "Once all of that was Shelburn—"

"You're lucky. I never had a country."

"Now you do. You're Lord of Ballyhoura and Master of The Hunt."

"You didn't want me to be Master."

"I was afraid of what it would do to Fax."

"I didn't ask for it. But now that I have the job I intend to do it as well as possible."

They had reached Ballyhoura's back gate, opening onto the Cup course. "I've unlocked all my gates," he said, bending over to unlatch it. "That doesn't mean you can't jump them if you want to."

They rode onto the Shelburn Cup course. Some of the fences had sunk deep into the ground and were rotting away. Those that remained still looked big, brown and forbidding.

"The course needs to be rebuilt," Shelley said.

"I was thinking the same thing myself." He pointed his whip in the direction of a group of surveyors, measuring the distance between the fenceline along the lane and the one that separated the concrete landing strip from the skeet-shooting area.

"I'm having the property surveyed. I don't think it's been done since Washington's time. There's some confusion over boundary lines. Once we finish the survey, I'll get on with rebuilding the course. You wouldn't have a picture or a diagram of the way it was, would you?"

"Yes"—she nodded excitedly—"there's one on the wall in the den."

"Done." He grinned at her. "Come spring, we'll have the seventy-fifth running of the Shelburn Cup. Now I should speak to the men. I'll see you tomorrow. At Opening Meet. I'll close my land if you don't hunt!"

She could no longer fight him. He had given her back her nerve and her pride, her most priceless possessions.

Four wild ducks rose from the farm pond beyond the runway where the crimson plane stood parked. The ducks flew off toward the great gaunt stone edifice that rose gray and forbidding atop the hillside. The sun touched its windows, turning them to flame. Beside it stood the Hanging Tree, where the black-brushed fox had been killed. She thought of the curse that had followed the Shelburns to the New World, destroyed Sean Shelburn and reached out to all who inhabited the house. Would it affect Zagaran? As she said the name to herself she was conscious of a shivering anticipation not unmixed with apprehension that had nothing to do with the growing chill in the fall air.

At Shelburn Hall she went straight to the wall in the ballroom and took down the Peale portrait of Hugh Shelburne, the philosopher. Without bothering to wrap it up, she drove directly to the bank. It was noon and Togo Baldwin told her that Polo Pete had just left to go to lunch.

"May I write a note?" Shelley asked.

After Togo supplied her with a pen and some paper, she wrote: "Here is the painting you wanted. It was valued at $4000 when my father had it appraised. It should be worth double that now. Unless I hear from you, I will assume that this takes care of my debt to you and covers the purchase price of Lookout Light." She signed it and then added a PS: "I'll see you at Opening Meet."

She had finished putting dinner on the table when the doorbell rang. She opened the front door to find Sam, holding his cap in one hand and a large bunch of iris in the other.

"Compliments of Mr. Zagaran, Miss Shelley." He handed her the flowers and a note.

"Iris!" Shelley exclaimed. "This time of year. Where on earth—"

"Don't rightly know, Miss Shelley. He sent off the plane for them."

After he had departed Shelley opened the envelope. A fixture card for The Hunt, giving the time and place of meets for the forthcoming month. There was no writing on it, but Ballyhoura and the date of Opening Meet had been encircled with red ink.

SEVENTEEN

IN THE VALLEY there was an air of suppressed excitement. Since before dawn lights had burned. In the kennels where the hounds to be hunted that day had been culled out and fed. In the stables where the hunters were being cleaned and their manes braided. In the big houses where the foxhunters had been shaking their heavy formal habits out of summer mothballs, setting out their silk hats and boned black boots.

"For God's sake!" Mike Latimer exclaimed, throwing back the covers. "Must you make so much noise?" He sat upright. "Shelley, what are you doing?"

"Trying to find my hunting underwear." She tugged at the bottom drawer of the mahogany chiffonier. A knob was missing and the drawer was stuck.

"But it isn't daylight yet. I thought you said you weren't hunting."

The drawer came open. "I changed my mind." Mothballs showered onto the floor as she pulled out the long underwear. "Weatherman says it's going to be cold. A freak storm—"

"Then you're not coming with me?"

"No." She stood up and began pulling on the undershirt. It fitted like a leotard. She was thinner than she should be, the rounded curves of summer dissolved by hard exercise. Her body was flat and hard, like a small boy's. In the dim orange light from the lamp he could see how she would look when she became old.

The skin drawn tight over the fine angular Shelburn bones, eyes darkened and huge, burning with that controlled intensity.

She saw him looking at her. "Mike, I have to hunt today. I have to show them." She began rummaging in her jewelry box. "I'm sure I put them here. I can't find my gold stockpin or a collar button."

She had forgotten him already. The stab of disappointment was like a sharp pain. It surprised him. Over the past weeks he had become conditioned to rejection. He had been too busy to think about anything but the newspaper and too tired to feel beyond a numbing sense of loss. He realized now that he had been looking forward to the holiday, counting on it to restore some measure of communication, or at least slow the sense of separation that seemed daily to be accelerating.

Shelley cooked breakfast, sent Cam out to feed the chickens, and drove to Muster Corner to pick up Suellen, who kept her waiting while she finished dressing and collecting her belongings for the night. When Suellen finally appeared, lipsticked and not the least bit apologetic, Shelley forced herself to be pleasant. She couldn't afford a fight this morning. It would be just like Suellen to say she had a date and couldn't stay the night after all.

Even though she wasn't planning now to be away with Mike, Suellen's staying would leave her free to go to the Dinwiddies' annual hunt breakfast after Opening Meet.

Mike was in the hall when she returned. He wore his dark city suit and the blue shirt that made his eyes seem more blue than gray. The suit looked slightly rumpled and too large around the waist. He would never achieve the tweedy London-tailored elegance of Zagaran or Fax Templeton. Nor was he interested in doing so.

"Sure you won't change your mind and come?" he asked.

His eyes were as direct as his question. Fine honest eyes. Honor was the word that came to mind. There was honor in them and humility. They were not the eyes of men who rode blindly through wheat and over people's lawns and knocked down their fences.

Suddenly she wanted to go with him. Forget the problems of finding collar buttons and stockpins, planning lunch and supper for Cam, making sure Virginia City put the running martingale on Lookout Light. Follow the dictates of duty. End the pull.

"I called Misty," he said. "I thought she might enjoy the banquet and meeting the Shapiros."

It was like coming to a big barway and being all prepared to jump it when somebody beat you to it and dropped the top rail.

"In that case," she said, "you don't need me."

"But I do. Shelley—"

The clock in the hall bonged the half hour, drowning out his words. If she didn't hurry she would be late.

"Don't rush back," she said quickly. "It'll do you good to get away. Stay in town overnight and don't worry about the *Sun*."

"I may just do that. Good-by, Shelley. Have a good hunt."

She did not see the look in his eyes as he went out the door. She was wondering where she had mislaid her stockpin.

Shelburn was clogged with traffic. Horse vans and trailers rumbled through the town. Major Southgate DeLong eyed them resentfully. In his day people did not van to meets. They rose before dawn and rode long distances, usually hacking their tired horses home the same night. When the meet was in the distant mountainy country, he had ridden over the day before, put his horse up at the old Mellick farm, hunted all the next day and ridden home again on the following. People no longer did this. The Free Zone country was rough and overgrown and no longer hunted, and that foreigner Zagaran had bought up the Mellick farm and was buying more land to use as a shooting preserve. Now people drove to the meet in heated limousines, and grooms delivered their horses in padded horse pullmans. Soft, the Major thought. The people and the country. Everything changing. His fault, he thought bitterly, noticing Mike Latimer drive into Gilbert's filling station. Writing those editorials. Mixing things up. Black people and white. Opening up the country to foreigners. Bad enough when a Yankee took over The Hunt. That had been the beginning. But Cameron Fitzgerald had been a gentleman. Not like these new people, lacking manners and respect.

The Major pulled Artaxerxes to a halt in the middle of the street. Brakes screamed as an out-of-state car stopped just short of hitting the buggy. Oblivious of the traffic jam he was causing, the Major maneuvered the old horse into a space opposite the post office, in front of Miss Letty Miller's neat tree-shaded yard.

"Morning, Major." Old Nat looked up from weeding Miss Letty's border. He got to his feet with difficulty and hobbled to the gate. Leaning on his hoe, he squinted up at the Major. "Sho is a fine hunting mawning."

The Major looked up at the sky. "If the wind drops. Coming on cold." Slowly he clambered down from the buggy. "Time was when we'd be going out hunting," he said, giving his old horse a slap on its rump. "Those mums look well."

"Thank you, Major." Old Nat bobbed his head gratefully. "Tain't easy weeding with mah rheumatism, but long's ah can, ah intends to do mah best."

The Major finished tying Artaxerxes to the parking meter. "I'm sure you will. I'm sure you won't let any outside agitators start agitating you. Communists! All of 'em. Dirty Reds!" The Major spat emphatically onto the curb.

The old Negro shook his head violently. "Nah, sir, Major, sir, no agitator goin' agitate Old Nat."

Satisfied, the Major shook his finger at Joe. In the same tone of voice he admonished the hound to guard the buggy. By way of reply, Joe opened his almost sightless yet still baleful yellow eyes, gave his tail a perfunctory wag and went back to sleep.

Walking with military erectness, oblivious of the cars honking at him, the Major made his way across the street to the post office.

Old Joe lifted his head. Slowly he rose. Then, for the first time within memory, he abandoned his post. In the manner of his master, without looking where he was going, he jumped blindly down onto the highway.

Possibly he sensed his end was near. Or, like those who are old, he may suddenly have been afraid of being left alone. Whatever it was that prompted him to leave the buggy spelled his demise. There was the sound of brakes, then a thud as a station wagon loaded with visiting foxhunters slammed into the old dog.

"Don't stop," the woman next to the driver said urgently. "We're late now."

"Christ," the driver said, "I better—"

"Keep going," the woman commanded. "Hounds will move off without us."

Mike had just pulled away from the filling station when he saw the accident. Driving to one side he parked the car, jumped out and ran to the dog. As he reached him, the old hound's body twitched in a final spasm and lay still.

In the way of small towns, where any tragedy, large or not, immediately attracts a horde of onlookers, people came running from all sides. Chester Glover materialized from the Gone Away, where he had been having a cup of coffee, and stopped traffic. As Major DeLong came out of the post office he saw the crowd. Then he saw Mike lift Joe, carry him off the highway and gently lower the dog down on the grass between the sidewalk and Miss Letty's white picket fence.

The Major let out a cry. Pushing past the people obstructing his way, he reached Joe's side and went down on his knees. Taking the hound's battered, bleeding head in his lap, he broke into anguished sobs.

"You killed him," he choked, looking up at Mike. "Ran over my dog."

"No, sir, Major DeLong, sir." Old Nat stood by Miss Letty's gate. "I was weedin' this here border." He stood tall and erect, no longer bent over and his voice when he spoke was strong and forceful. "I seen it all. Mr. Editor didn't hit Joe. 'Twas some folks in a station wagon."

The Major appeared not to hear him. The hatred in his eyes as he continued gazing at Mike was terrible, so all-encompassing as to seem ancient, animal-like in its fierce immediacy. "You killed my dog," he repeated, heartbroken. "Killed my Joe."

Later it was not the hatred in the Major's eyes that Mike remembered. Instead the picture that came to mind was that of the old aristocrat in his worn frock coat and frayed Panama hat weeping over the body of his dead hound.

Shelley found the stockpin (she remembered using it to hold up Cam's blue jeans) in the laundry. By ten-thirty her starched white stock was tied and secured with the straight gold pin and she was booted and spurred, fully dressed in her best cream-colored breeches and the formal black coat with the Hunt's collar and raised buttons. The coat, made for her when she was fourteen, still fitted her to perfection. Her hair was netted and neatly secured under the velvet hunting cap which, as a former Field Master and honorary whip, she was entitled to wear. Astride the beautiful thoroughbred—despite his crippled fingers, Virginia City had managed to braid the colt's mane, and Jimmy had rubbed him until his coat shone like polished marble—Shelley looked cool and contained, with an elegance matched only by Mrs. Haliburton Harcourt, Millicent Black's aunt, who came from Massachusetts to hunt during the season and had two grooms, a personal maid to lay out her clothes, and a chauffeur to drive her to the meet.

The morning was raw and colder than was usual for this time of year. The night before snow had fallen on the mountains, now streaked with white. The Ballyhoura Hanging Oak stood gaunt, its remaining leaves clinging with a kind of shriveled desperation against the wind.

Shelley felt the same desperation. As she rode past the rhododendrons Zagaran had planted on either side of the avenue, shyness and a sense of panic gripped her. She should have gone with Mike. Instead, she had deliberately chosen to cling to a past instinct told her was no longer valid, but which her heart had yet to relinquish.

It was to be one of the more crowded opening meets. There was a steady stream of cars and trailers and horse vans. A long line of grooms leading horses and children on ponies moved along the side of the driveway. Connie Jackson, looking officious, was carrying a pad and pencil and pointing out the gentry to a photographer who had been sent out from the *Capital Courier*, and there was a strange-looking contingent of dowdy women who resembled refugees from the Salvation Army and of long-haired youths passing out leaflets. These, Shelley discovered later, were members of the Anti-Blood Sports League and had driven out from the city to distribute their material at the meet. At sight of them Lookout Light began to prance and chew on his bit. Added to the usual anticipatory excitement of a new season beginning was the interest aroused by the new Mastership. As it would be Zagaran's first appearance as Master of The Hunt, a large number of visitors had come from as far away as Pennsylvania and Delaware. Some of the members of the rival hunts hoped he would be incompetent. Jealous of The Hunt's reputation, resentful of its exclusiveness, they would not be displeased if sport turned out to be bad.

Shelley saw the Jessups and the Greens from Maryland and the Sit-Tight sisters from the Suburban Hunt near Washington. The Sit-Tights—their name was really Sitovski—were big on dressage.

Now they pranced down the driveway on their matching chest-nuts, sitting deep in the saddle, looking elegant in show-ring shad-belly coats, canary yellow vests and high silk hats.

Shelley nodded and spoke to them and rode on by. A sharp-featured woman wearing the color of New Commonwealth was getting out of a station wagon.

"Imagine a foreigner as Master of The Hunt. I'm told he learned to ride in a riding school."

"Fax Templeton wasn't perfect," the man with her replied.

"But Fax is a gentleman," the woman said. "And the Temple-tons have been here forever." She glanced at her watch. "I do declare. We made it after all. Never thought we would. After that dog—"

Shelley did not hear any more. Lookout Light, wildly excited by the other horses and the activity, required all her concentra-tion. Betsy Baldwin, surrounded by her children on their ponies, caused him to snort and try to buck.

"Watch out," Shelley warned. "He's full of gelignite this morn-ing."

"What?" Betsy looked vague and harassed. Wisps of hair es-caped from beneath her slightly dented derby, and her old black hunting coat was now too small for her. Still, she was one of the few people with whom Shelley still felt at ease. Submerged in her world of children and domesticity, Betsy remained untouched by gossip and the tensions that swirled around her.

"Dynamite!" Shelley smiled and snatched the colt's head up. "Look out for Lookout Light," she warned Buttons Baldwin on her spotted pony. "He's full of himself this morning."

"He's so pretty," the child said admiringly.

"It would be nice if he'd stand still." Shelley smiled at Buttons and felt better.

A Master should have flair, Shelley thought. Starting with Sean Shelburn, Masters of The Hunt had been noted for their daring and style. And she'd have to give Zagaran full marks for putting on a super show. Ballyhoura, now that it had been completely renovated, its lawns and outbuildings repaired, statuary and gar-dens replaced and replanted, looked like the etching of the origi-nal Ballyhoura. Were it not for the cars parked along the drive it could have been a lawn meet of old. As an added touch, Zagaran had invited the farm children to hand out yellow chrysanthemums tied with green ribbon to match The Hunt's colors.

To the right of the great arched, crested entrance, on either side of which two carriage lamps gleamed against the grayness, a long table covered with a damask cloth had been set up. There Manassas Brown and Billy Joe Wilkerson were serving port and brandy stirrup cups, sherry in small glasses, Irish coffee and hot pastries. The Four-H girls stood smoking and drinking. Their rigid black-clad backs, the way they stood animatedly gossiping, the sense of intimacy they projected, had the air of a conspirators' meeting. Katie Schligman stood to one side, her mink coat clasped around her as though for protection.

Story Jackson rode up on a new horse he had bought while judging a recent horse show in the Midwest. "Got just the horse for you," he said to Katie. "Best I ever had in the barn. Dead quiet. Come right up and sit in your lap if you asked him to."

All of Story's horses were always the best he ever had in the barn. He really believed this, Shelley thought, and his enthusiasm was so infectious that he sold horses that were half blind and had bows and bad feet and stifle problems for gigantic prices to people from Pittsburgh, Philadelphia and even Palm Springs. But after her cubbing experience he was not going to snare Katie.

"If you cut off its legs, put wheels and white-wall tires on it and painted it pink," she said, shaking her head vehemently, "I still wouldn't ride it."

Story was about to say something more when one of the Anti-Blood Sports people tried to give him a leaflet. At the sight of the paper, the "dead quiet" horse swerved away, almost unseating him.

At the far end of the table the Bentleys and a group of official-looking guests were sampling the fare. The Senator wore loud tweeds and a green-checked Sherlock Holmes hat. Maggie had on a pale blue suit and a sheepskin coat. Their guests were equally well attired. They looked, Shelley thought, like the people in the ads depicting a gleaming new car drawn up before a great country house. She would have liked to join them, but there was nobody to hold the colt and he was becoming more excited each moment. In order to keep him from kicking or trampling anyone, she started back along the drive. The Dash-Smythes were getting out of their English Rover. Dudley looked splendid in his black shadbelly coat and high silk hat. At sight of Shelley his bulldog pipe almost fell out of his mouth. He managed to rally, however, and tell Shelley how well both she and the colt looked.

"Did you ever see such a crowd?" Cosy Rosy cried out, and fluttered off to the house to use the plumbing.

Shelley saw Telly Talbot coming toward her across the lawn. Since he had been appointed to fill out his late father's term in the State Senate he had become even more portly and pompous. His recent pronouncements and the newsletter mailed out each month to his constituents made the old Senator's "States Rights" policy seem New Era liberal by comparison.

Shelley observed that he was more country squirearchical than ever. Overly long tweed jacket, lapels, elbows and cuffs lined with chamois, and an old-fashioned wide-brimmed planter's hat on his head. She saw him pause to speak to Dudley Dudley-Smythe and wondered if he was going to acknowledge her. She knew he recognized her as she rode by, but he did not nod or pause in his denunciation of the present administration.

Shelley moved aside to make room for Fax's My Boy Hambone coming along the drive. Hambone had his hands full. He was riding Fax's Saint and leading Bebe Bruce's spotted horse on one side, Dickie Speer's Mister Ed on the other.

Somehow he managed to touch his fingers to his cap. "Nice mawnin', Miss Shelley." In the midst of a blizzard, Hambone and the other grooms would say "Nice mawnin'," Shelley thought.

"Kind of cold." She shivered under her vest. Even though the extra clothing might cause her hunting coat to wrinkle, she wished she had worn a sweater. "Hambone, your horses look beautiful."

Hambone observed his neatly braided manes and gleaming tack with the same Old World pride evinced by Virginia City. "I try, deed, Miss Shelley, I try." He indicated the young white boy Debby Darbyshire had hired to replace Roosevelt. The teenager wore dirty khakis and there were wisps of straw in Debby's horse's tail. "Now they're some," he muttered darkly, "who just don't care how their horses look."

Shelley was saved by the Dinwiddies from further observations on the part of the groom. She restrained Lookout Light, smiled and said good morning.

The Beast's habit, made at the turn of the century, was overly long and fitted at the waist. Age and weather had given it a faintly greenish tinge and beneath her old-fashioned wide-brimmed derby her face was pointed like a spade. Beauty, however, was turned out like a figure from a Munnings painting. Scarlet coat, and his doeskin breeches, washed and dried on special wooden stretchers, fitted like gloves. His boned boots and high silk hat, steamed over a kettle, held a sheen that was almost blinding. Whereas the Beast would ride at anything—wire, five-barred gates, and had once led an intimidated visitor off the side of a bridge, down a four-foot drop into a stream—her husband had hunted almost fifty years without ever jumping a fence. Always immaculate (Millicent Black reported that he put his mustache up at night in something that resembled a jock strap and walked around stark naked, wearing a bowler hat fitted to bring out the wave in his white hair exactly where its brim tipped his ears), he had an uncanny instinct for pursuing young girls and knowing which way the fox would run. Thus no matter how hard or long hounds ran he inevitably turned up at the end of the day, astride his bay cob with the docked tail, looking as cool and unruffled, the ends of his mustache as carefully waxed, as when he had arrived at the meet.

"Shelley, is it?"

Since her most recent fall the Beast had all but lost the sight of one eye and had double vision in the other. Now she stopped just short of walking into Lookout Light.

"Shelley, I didn't expect to see you here."

"Now, dear," her husband interrupted, "you mustn't excite yourself. We're going to have a devilish fine go and I'm sure Lord and Lady Willoughby-Walloughby aren't interested in our petty hunt problems." He turned to the visitors, introducing them to Shelley. The Englishman was tall and thin and as straight and spare as the pipe in his hand. His wife was almost as tall and spare, with a rosy outdoor face that bespoke mists and moors.

Both smiled and said, "Howjado."

"What a smashing-looking horse," Lord Willoughby-Walloughby said. In response, Lookout Light spun around and stepped on his foot.

"Oh, I'm sorry," Shelley apologized, pulling the colt to one side.

"Zingy, what!" His Lordship gave her a wry smile and jerked back his foot.

"I don't see the Master." The Beast, who wouldn't admit her eyesight was failing, made a pretense of studying the crowd. "Nor his wife." She turned to the Willoughby-Walloughbys. "Such a shame she's not well. She's a lady, whereas her husband—Dinny says— Dinny, where are you?"

"Coming, my love," R. Rutherford Dinwiddie replied. "I believe the Bentleys are here and your nephew Telford. I say, there he is with the Bentleys." Now that he had an authentic Lord and Lady in tow, R. Rutherford was more British than ever. "Let's move along. What ho! Cheerio, Shelley."

Shelley watched them troop over to the table where Telly Talbot, beaming and seemingly the soul of affability, was deep in conversation with the Senator he had but moments before been reviling.

The *Capital Courier* photographer was taking pictures while Connie Jackson hovered in the background taking notes.

"You did get my invitation to breakfast afterward?" Shelley heard the Beast say to Maggie Bentley. "In years past I simply gave the field a blanket invitation. But now, my dear, servants are so scarce and costs so high I've had to limit the guest list. I know there will be hurt feelings . . ."

As Shelley rode away she realized that she had not been invited.

It was almost eleven now. Yet hounds had not come from the kennels. Nor had Zagaran appeared. People began moving away from the long, white-clothed table. They were drawing on their gloves, setting their hats at the proper angle and looking around for their horses.

Shelley saw Millicent loping toward her. Late as usual, and wearing what Fax called her loose horse look, a slightly wild-eyed distracted air. Shelley raised her whip to wave but Millicent's eyes slid past her to Bones, riding Nautilus around the field with the other race riders—Sandy Montague, home from the University for the weekend, Freddy Fisher's son, Tommy, and young Tiger Talbot, Telly's son, who had dropped out of college to break yearlings at the training track. They were all on long, leggy steeplechasers who pranced and cavorted and were already dark with sweat. Although they wore hunting clothes, their stirrups were shortened and they rode with a relaxed hunched-over nonchalance that emanated an air of daring and glamour. Molly Atwell and the other teenagers gazed at them with shy admiration.

Bones rode over to the fence.

"Cripes almighty!" Dixon, the groom, called out as Nautilus went up in the air and came down again in a bone-shattering buck. "Better tighten yerself, Mr. Bones."

"He needs another jockey," Millicent said grimly, taking her bay mare, Sabrina, from Merry, who had been holding her.

Millicent, who could have bought any one of the horses in the field, paying Story Jackson-type prices, had been riding the mare for years. Sabrina had been bought off the half-mile track at Charlestown. Never particularly manageable and always a chancy jumper, she had given her owner numerous falls. Yet Millicent continued to ride her, as though driven to prove that she could bring the mare to some kind of terms. In order to do this, she alternately talked baby talk and swore.

"Come along, love," she said, taking the mare from Merry and leading her to the mounting block. "Mama's sweet, adorable darling is going hunting today."

But "Mama's sweet, adorable darling" had seen Nautilus and would have none of it. At sight of her old stablemate, from whom she had been separated since Bones had moved out of Last Resort, the mare began to whinny and pull away from Millicent.

"Damn and blast!" Millicent exclaimed as Nautilus replied with a shrill whinny. "Sweet, adorable darling's herdbound!" She gave the mare a vicious jerk. Then her voice softened. "Mama's ittsy bittsy mare wants her big handsome Nautilus."

"Sweetie," Bones said placatingly, "the mare hasn't any emotional problems." With a mischievous twinkle in his eye, he went on teasingly, quoting his wife's words. "She just doesn't like to be alone. Horses and husbands. They're all alike. All they need is some TLC."

"I'll tender loving care you," Millicent said furiously as the horses' nickering affinity for each other drew amused glances.

"That nutty mare has given her so many falls you'd think she'd stop riding her," Bones said aside to Sandy Montague. "Sweetie" —he turned to his wife—"you might as well give up and get on."

"Damn it, I can't," Millicent replied helplessly. "The bloody mare won't stand still and I'll split my breeches."

Shelley was about to offer assistance, when Dixon came to the rescue and gave Millicent a leg up.

Then Polo Pete blocked her view. His port wine complexion was the same shade as his pink coat, strained at the seams. His eyes filled with greed as he gazed at Lookout Light. For a moment Shelley thought he was going to speak, but he did not. Turning away, he rode up beside Millicent.

"Morning, Milly. If the wind slacks off, scent should be breast-high."

Millicent turned. "Say, did you see . . ."

Shelley felt as if a steel band were tightening around her chest, sucking her breath from her. Below she saw the first fence on the Cup course. The fear that Zagaran had helped her to put down returned. She wished she had a glass of sherry. Perhaps that would refire her blood. The longer she waited, the colder it became.

"Oh, Mrs. Latimer, you look beautiful."

It was Judy Schligman. As her mother had not hunted since the disastrous cubbing morning, Judy, home for the weekend, was riding Katie's horse.

"Why, Judy." Shelley managed a smile. "How nice to see you."

"Oh, Mrs. Latimer"—Judy indicated the Christmas card panorama of pink coats and gleaming thoroughbreds—"isn't it glorious? This is my first hunt and I'm so excited."

"I hope we have a good run for you."

"It's enough just to be out at last," Judy enthused, looking starry-eyed.

She feels the way people should feel, Shelley thought, gazing at the young girl's flushed, excited face. The way one should feel about foxhunting and marriage, full of anticipation and wonder.

Again she wished she had a stirrup cup. Yet nobody offered to get her one and if she got off she would have trouble remounting. The colt would not stand still. She would have to ask somebody to hold him. The sense of apartness returned. Before, she would have been one of those around the lawn table. Again she had the feeling she fitted nowhere, neither with the gentry nor the grooms.

At that moment Fax drove up in the Rakish Stud pickup. His face was flushed. His cap was at an angle and his white stock was loose and askew. Bebe Bruce sat beside him. She was staring straight ahead, her classic coin-cut features wearing an ice-maiden look. As soon as the truck stopped she opened the door.

"Honey baby," Fax implored, "if you-all just wait for lil ole Fax—"

"Honey baby yourself," Bebe answered, getting out of the truck without waiting for his assistance. "Why don't you just cut out that Deep South *Birth of a Nation* crap?" Slamming the door of the truck shut behind her, she walked quickly to My Boy Hambone, standing like a maypole festooned with reins belonging to the horses he was holding.

Now that Fax was no longer Master he was rarely sober. Before, he had restricted his serious drinking to non-hunting days. Now while hunting he took constant nips of corn likker from his flask. When not foxhunting, he rode The Saint into town, tethered him to the iron jockey in front of the Halter Club and spent the remainder of the day in the bar. There he talked and drank and planned projects that he never completed. Currently he was painting the kitchen floor and touching up the fox on the front door of his stable apartment. Originally, Fax had painted a life-size mask, with bared teeth and a ferocious expression, designed to frighten off bill collectors. Nights when he was drinking he repainted the mask. From the resulting expression of the fox's face it was possible to gauge Fax's mood. If the fox's mouth was closed and wore a benign expression it meant that Fax was manic and had gone to bed peaceably. The opened mouth, bared teeth and savage expression indicated a depressive phase, brought on by a fight with Bebe or his creditors, and usually meant that My Boy Hambone, Wiley Matthews, head of the local AA chapter, or Preston, the Halter Club bartender, had been called upon to subdue him and put him to bed.

Now he slowly disembarked from the truck. For an instant he stood swaying slightly. The drunker Fax got, the more elaborate his courtesy became.

"Mawnin', ladies," he said, doffing his velvet cap with an exaggerated gesture. Shelley looked away and My Boy Hambone busied himself tightening Bebe's girth. "We who are about to ride s-s-s-salute you!"

Fax put his cap on his head and walked to his horse. As he did so a sudden hush descended on the crowd and all eyes turned toward the house, where the heavy front door had just opened.

"Aha," Fax cried in a loud voice, "the Master c-c-c-cometh. The sh-sh-show is about to begin!"

The new Master was framed in the doorway, directly under Sean Shelburn's great carved crest. For an instant he stood motionless, a tall figure in perfectly cut scarlet, white breeches, gleaming boots, his spurs and buttons shining like the metal fox-head knocker on the door. His cap was under his arm and he looked like the portraits such people as R. Rutherford Dinwiddie and the Dash-Smythes ordered painted to hang over their fireplaces. Shelley had the distinct impression that he had timed his entrance to the moment, had in fact been waiting behind the door to enter the stage on cue. And that as he looked down at the crowd of upturned faces, he was inwardly laughing.

The Bentleys and their guests came forward and Zagaran went down the steps, walking with the careful precision that new hunting boots require before they are broken in. Then he was nodding and smiling, his whip under his arm, its lash hanging down. The pale sun moved from behind the massed clouds and its light struck his dark head, turning it to silver. His eyes met Shelley's and it was as if a star had glanced off the brilliance of his shining boots, buttons and spurs and shot into her, igniting a spark of excitement, of challenge.

Hunting cap and whip in hand, he stood with Senator Bentley on one side and Telly Talbot, who had hurried forward to stand on the other side. While the photographers from the county papers and the *Capital Courier* took pictures, Connie Jackson, notebook and pencil in hand, queried Maggie Bentley, busily taking down the names of the weekend guests.

Shelley saw him coming toward her and the Beast moved forward to intercept him. Zagaran stopped.

"Good morning, Mrs. Dinwiddie."

The Beast's smile looked as if it had been sewed on. "Young man, there are some things about The Hunt you should know."

"Some other time, Mrs. Dinwiddie. If you'll call my secretary and make an appointment I'll be glad to discuss matters pertaining to The Hunt."

The Beast was not used to being cut off. Beneath her black hunting veil her face tensed with anger. "Young man, as The Hunt's oldest living member, I'm not accustomed to having my word disregarded."

Zagaran bent his head and smiled. "Nor am I, Mrs. Dinwiddie."

"You mean you—"

The expression on the Master's face froze the words she had been about to speak. "Civility, madam, is common property," he said formally. "I suggest that as the oldest living member of The Hunt, Mrs. Dinwiddie, you avail yourself of your share at the earliest opportunity."

Without giving her a chance to reply, he strode over to Shelley. "I'm glad to see you," he said in a voice that carried to the Beast and the others watching. He grinned and his eyes looking into hers were filled with a kind of mischievous glee. "It wouldn't be proper, now would it, to have an opening meet without a Shelburn."

Shelley found herself smiling back. "All this time I've had the feeling that chivalry was not only dead but decomposed."

"A picture, sir?" It was the *Capital Courier* photographer. "One with the lady."

"Of course," Zagaran answered graciously. "I guess it won't matter if we're late starting."

Shelley felt suddenly wonderful, as though she had drunk the stirrup cup after all.

"Miss Shelley, ma'am, ah declare, pretty as ever. B., this hee-ar was the prettiest lil ole girl in all of Virginny—" Telly Talbot ran on, blocking the photographer's view.

"All right, Senator," the photographer said wearily. "Now if you'll just stand there, to one side. The lady in the middle."

Fax Templeton took off his polo coat and handed it to the over-burdened Hambone. He was about to give Bebe a leg up onto the spotted horse when he noticed the tableau taking place. At sight of Zagaran he stiffened like a pointer in the field at sight of its quarry. There stood the man who had cut the country from under his boots. The damn Yankee who had usurped him as Master of The Hunt.

"Son of a bitch!" he muttered, balling his hands into fists.

"Fax"—Bebe reached out to restrain him—"don't be a bloody fool."

"Damn Yankee," he continued furiously. "Thinks he can run The Hunt like Wall Street, by computer. Buy everything in sight."

It was not like Fax to be aggressive, Shelley thought. But now she saw that a combination of things, including Bebe's scorn, had ignited his anger, already fueled by numerous nips from his flask.

"I had two Yankee wives that bossed me most to death," he said thickly, shaking Bebe's hand off his arm. He let out a giant hiccup. "From now on, nobody's gonna tell ole Fax what to do."

Telly Talbot was grinning fatuously into the camera. Neither he nor the photographer saw Fax advance. Zagaran was holding Lookout Light's bridle to keep the horse steady. Shelley turned to smile into the raised camera and heard a loud hiccup followed by Fax's cry.

"Goddamn foreign b-b-b-bastard!"

Zagaran pivoted, fast as the camera shutter.

Fax's roundhouse swing missed, but Zagaran's counterpunch caught him right on the jaw, with precision and strength. Fax lost his balance and stumbled into Dash-Smythe, knocking his pipe out of his mouth and silk hat off his head.

"Dudley Dudley D-d-d-Dash-Smythe," Fax choked. "Son of a b-b-b-bitch-bitch!"

"Get up, Fax." Zagaran stood grinning down at him. "Your hiccups are gone!"

While Telly Talbot pleaded with the photographer not to print the picture of the State Senator in a brawl with the scarlet-coated foxhunting fraternity, Dash-Smythe led Fax back to his pickup. "Oh, Mr. Fax," My Boy Hambone cried, coming to help Fax into his truck, "you done ruint your appearance. That Mr. Zagaran ain't no gentleman," he continued darkly. "He didn't even wait to pick Mr. Fax up after he done knock him down."

Shelley had a final glimpse of Fax, slumped against the seat of the truck in an attitude of defeat, the former Master's old-young face as white as his loosened stock.

Dickie Speer broke the tension. Tall, gangling and loose-jointed, wearing black coat, boots, and derby perched on the back of his head, he stood in the center of the turning place wringing his hands in mock despair.

"I've lost my horse. Shelley, presh, have you seen Mister Ed? I don't see Hambone anywhere."

"Right here." Shelley pointed to the brown, now being held by one of Zagaran's grooms.

"So it is." Dickie gave his infectious laugh. "Presh, I wouldn't recognize my own mother this morning. I'm that dead."

"Bet he never had one," Debby Darbyshire muttered. Dickie had once cut her off at a fence and she had yet to forgive him.

Then everybody seemed to be getting on at once and the air was filled with the sounds of horses moving and people giving final instructions to their grooms.

Hounds were coming now, heralded by excited cries from the foot followers, a moving black and white sea swirling around the hoofs of the Old Huntsman's wise, aged gray hunter.

Black Magic was led up. Fighting to escape from Simeon's hold, the mare towed the groom along, almost jerking him off his feet.

"I'll take her," Zagaran said.

With the agility of Sandy Montague or someone much younger, Zagaran vaulted onto her back. As Simeon leapt aside, Magic reared like a circus horse and when she came down again Shelley saw the new Master was laughing.

Then he turned the mare around and rode over to where the Old Huntsman, hounds grouped around his horse's feet, waited beneath the Ballyhoura Oak for the picture taking to be finished and the chase to begin.

Debby and Mrs. Dinwiddie had ridden up behind Shelley and were conversing with one another.

"That's Mrs. Doyle," Debby explained. "The Young Whip's wife. They live in the cottage by the kennels. She's a Mellick from the Free Zone. Her brother is with her. The one that pitch-forked Black Magic. He tried to get a job with me after he was fired. But he's a nasty piece of work. I didn't want him on the place."

While they had been talking Shelley observed the girl and the man hovering by the entrance to the kennels. The girl's lips were parted and her eyes were focused on her husband as he rounded up a stray hound investigating one of the rhododendrons bordering the drive.

The man with her was short and stocky. He wore farm coveralls and a cloth cap and his hand under her elbow was protective. There was a marked similarity in their features, the too-narrow eyes and heavy lips, and on their faces Shelley recognized the same sullen, dulled and animal-wary expressions as those worn by the Free Zoners who came to town on Saturday nights.

At that moment Tatine Zagaran rode up with Sandy Montague

on his race horse. In her beautifully fitting black coat and boots, her flaming hair held in place by a net, she reminded Shelley of the courtiers painted by Bronzini that she had studied in History of Art at Miss Shelburne's.

Tatine turned to speak to the Young Whip. Sandy looked after her, his face wilting like the chrysanthemum in his buttonhole. A flush rose on Richard Doyle's dark cheeks. Hastily his eyes swept the crowd, lingered for an instant on his wife, and then returned to the Master's daughter.

"Well, I never," the Beast exclaimed. "You'd think they'd have some discretion."

"I saw them riding yesterday," Debby said. "I must say, he's rather sexy."

"Debby, really," the older woman admonished. "There, finally we do seem to be moving off."

The Old Huntsman moved up the drive, his hounds foaming about the legs of his gray horse. The Young Whip rode behind, flicking his whip at lagging hounds. Then the Master, tipping his hat first to one side then the other, saying a word here, a word there to the car and foot followers. Something about the way he sat his horse, the aura of drama he projected, caused them to fall silent, staring after him as he went past. Despite their grumbling about the damage The Hunt did to their property, the expression on their faces was one of awe not unmixed with pride.

Lookout Light arched his neck and chewed on his bit. Aware of the admiring glances that followed his dancing steps, Shelley thought that no matter how unreal, how temporary, how wrong it might seem, one could not help but enjoy this momentary sensation of power and well-being.

Mike was on his way to pick up Misty and drive to Washington. He pulled the station wagon to one side in order to let The Hunt go by. Mr. Winecoop stopped behind him. He remembered asking the postman once why the mail on the rural routes was often late, and Mr. Winecoop had replied it was because much of his time was spent waiting for The Hunt to permit him to go by.

Polo Pete Buford pulled his horse to a standstill in the center of the highway. His air of self-importance was as obvious as his scarlet hunting coat as he raised his arm to stop oncoming traffic.

As though it was their divine right to ride down the center of the interstate highway, the field filed past. A few gave noblesse oblige nods to those standing or parked along the roadside. Most, however, were tense and unsmiling, concentrated on controlling their horses and not sliding on the slippery asphalt.

Bebe Bruce took the trouble to lean down and call to him. "Hello, Mike old boy, you should be glad you're not out. Opening day is always such a scrum. Like a big cocktail party. Tallyho, old boy. 'By now."

Mike had to admit that Shelley and Lookout Light stood out in the scrum. In foxhunting jargon, they were beautifully turned out. He was used to seeing Shelley ride in a ragged tweed coat and khakis or blue jeans. Now she was all black and white, her hunting coat well fitting and workmanlike. The gray was as clean as castile soap could make him and Shelley sat him exactly right, her reins and stirrups long and her back as straight as the hunting whip in her string-gloved hand.

She smiled down at him sitting in the car beside the road and waved, looking very slender, almost fragile, as she rode past. His heart gave an odd lurch. Even in riding clothes, her hair pulled back under her cap and a stiff white stock binding her neck, she gave an impression of strong femininity. By contrast, Debby Darbyshire's face looked brown and wrinkled, like a potato left too long in the oven; and her square, solid, shapeless figure, rising like an upended brick and spilling over from her saddle onto the back of her too-small cobby-type hunter led Connor, the Dash-Smythes' groom, riding behind her, to comment to Roy, the Bufords' man, that "the joint was too large for the platter."

Hounds clambered up the bank, wriggled through the rail fence and fanned out over Ballyhoura's freshly planted wheat. The Old Huntsman on his gray horse followed while the Young Whip stood to one side, flicking his whip at the stragglers. Then Zagaran rode the black mare up the bank and jumped the fence. The field followed, their horses snatching at their bits, frantic to be over the fence and away.

The drivers of the trucks that had been halted by Polo Pete waited impatiently, anxious for the last horse to leave the road so they could continue on their way. Mike wondered what they thought of this archaic sight, the Old World pageantry of horse and hound and scarlet-coated riders, as they watched the riders canter across the field, moving spots of color against the bleached gray-green November countryside, the horses' hoofs pressing down the tender shoots in the newly seeded field.

As the last of the riders filed off the road into the field, the driver of the lead truck began gunning his motor loudly. Polo Pete, waiting for a stray hound to cross, did not move from the center of the highway. The truck driver did not see the hound. Fed up with waiting, he put the truck in gear and began to move.

Buford's face purpled. Raising his arm he indicated to the driver that he wanted him to stop. The man grinned insolently and speeded up. Polo Pete slid his feet from his stirrup irons and slipped one of his leathers from its safety catch on the flap of his saddle. As the truck approached he swung the leather with the iron on the end of it around his head and then threw it at the windshield. The driver ducked instinctively, and as the iron bounced off the shattered glass he put his foot down hard on the accelerator and headed the truck directly for Buford's horse.

The big hunter swerved sideways onto the shoulder of the highway and slid into the ditch that ran alongside it. Polo Pete narrowly avoided falling off. As Mike drove past he saw Buford shaking his clenched fist at the receding truck.

Shelley watched hounds spill down the slope, the Old Huntsman galloping in their midst as they fanned out over the grass.

Into the Valley rode the six hundred, she thought as the field surged after them.

The big fence loomed ahead, the traditional first fence on the Cup course. Four rails, standing four foot six inches, with the posts cemented into the ground. The Old Huntsman was not young and Shelley could tell by the way he was riding that his bad shoulder, the one that the horse the Baldwins had given to The Hunt had fallen on, was bothering him. Still, Shelley saw him sit down in the saddle and boot the old hunter on into the fence. There. Although a bit sticky, the gray cleared the fence. Then the Young Whip, giving his young horse a beautiful ride, landed safely and it was Zagaran's turn. Standing well back, Black Magic made a spectacular jump that brought a wave of sound from the watching crowd.

Shelley wanted to give her colt plenty of room. It was the kind of fence a young horse could easily funk. She did not want to permit him a chance to stop. Should he choose this time to refuse, in front of the people on the hillside and those in the field who had pulled aside to watch, it would be embarrassing as well as difficult to get him going once again.

Now the crowd had thinned out. Shelley saw a panel that was clear and turned the colt at it. Leaning forward, she drove him up into the bit. She knew he could jump out of his stride, and the faster she sent him on into the fence, the less chance for him to shy or duck out. "Come on, Lookout Light," she whispered urgently. "Show them what you can do."

She was concentrating so hard on the fence ahead she did not see the surveyor's stake in her path until Lookout Light was almost upon it. At the last minute she pulled him to one side.

"Oy-ee!" Bones Black's high Rebel yell was earsplitting. "Ride, Red, ride!"

On came the race riders abreast, Bones, Sandy and Tommy Fisher bringing up the rear. Disconcerted by the pounding hoofs threatening to overtake him, Lookout Light got it wrong, hit the top rail a terrible clap, twisted over it and managed somehow to land still on his feet.

"Hang in there," she heard Bones shout. "Gallop all day, jump fences—"

"Bones," Shelley cried, "you almost knocked me down. This is a green horse. Thank God he seems to have a fifth leg."

"That'll learn him," Bones called back cheerfully. "Ready him for the Shelburn Cup."

"Bones! Bones!" Millicent cried. "Sweet, adorable darling—"

A sudden cry from the crowd caused them to look back. Millicent's mare, frantic to catch up to Bones's Nautilus, had hooked the top rail with her knees, sending Millicent planing through the air. Lord Willoughby-Walloughby, unable to control his borrowed mount, narrowly missed landing on top of her and Augie Schligman, whose new horse pecked badly, fell off beside her.

"Christ." Bones jerked Nautilus around. "It's the Madam. Damn it, I warned her not to try that fence on that nutty mare."

As he spoke, one of the Sit-Tight sisters roared past out of control, and Tommy Fisher cried that he had staked his race horse on the surveyor's marker. Shelley saw him trying to pull the crippled horse out of the path of the oncoming riders.

Millicent was on her feet. "Sweet, adorable darling" lay on her side, the wind knocked out of her. Millicent began kicking her horse. "Damn you, mare. Damn you!"

"My God, sweetie," Bones exclaimed, shocked, "you musn't do that!"

"Turnabout!" Millicent cried gleefully. "It's the first time I've ever gotten up before her!"

Meanwhile, Augie Schligman, wildly excited and anxious not to be left behind, caught Castle Irish, the Dinwiddies' big brown horse that his Lordship had been riding. Thinking it was his own Drum Major—aside from the fact that Castle Irish had two white stockings behind rather than one, the horses were dead ringers for each other—Augie led the hunter up along the fence, where he remounted.

By the time Lord Willoughby-Walloughby had retrieved his topper, brushed the mud from his scarlet coat and picked up his whip, Augie, bouncing on Castle Irish's kidneys, was well away.

"I say," cried his Lordship, "that bloke's got my horse!"

"I'll get him back for you," volunteered Sandy Montague, and galloped off after Augie.

"Mr. Schligman," he cried, coming up behind the beer baron, "his Lordship would like his horse."

"This is my horse," Augie replied with some asperity. "I bought him from Story Jackson and paid six thousand dollars—"

"I'm not interested in the price," replied Sandy, "just the horse. That, sir, is Castle Irish. I should know. I was second on him in the New Commonwealth point-to-point."

"Couldn't be," Augie answered stubbornly. "My God, man, don't you think I know my own horse when I'm on him?"

Sandy appealed to Shelley, who had ridden up alongside and was doing her best to keep from laughing outright.

"Cousin Shelley, please tell this gentleman that he is on Castle Irish and not Drum Major."

At that moment Staunton, the Schligmans' groom, appeared, crimson-faced and breathless, leading Drum Major.

"Well, I'll be damned." Augie Schligman began to laugh uproariously. "So I was on the wrong horse. No shit!"

"Holy gee," Sandy said wonderingly as they rode on after The Hunt. "How could a man as stupid as that about horses be so smart about making money?"

. . .

The first draw proved blank. The Old Huntsman lifted hounds and proceeded to Webster's woods.

"I'm enjoying your lovely country," Shelley heard Lord Willoughby-Walloughby remark to Zagaran. "It reminds me of Liecestershire." He gazed around at Bebe and Debby crowding up on their heels. "In England it isn't considered correct to wear a velvet cap unless one is a member of the Hunt staff. Tell me, are all these women Masters?"

Zagaran grinned. "No, just mistresses!"

Cosy Rosy took a perfumed silk handkerchief from her pocket and blew her nose. "Think I'll go home. It's getting colder by the minute."

"Maybe now scent will improve," Debby said in a low voice to Millicent.

"It may be lousy on the ground," Millicent answered, "but it's sure as hell breast high around here. No wonder hounds can't smell out a fox." Raising her voice, she called out to her rival, "Dahling, you smell divine."

"Usually I smell like a horse," Rosy replied succinctly, lowering her incredible eyelashes.

"Did you say horse?" Millicent asked sweetly.

"Yes, I said horse. Want me to spell it? H-O-R-S-E, horse."

"Oh," said Millicent. "I thought there was a W in front of the H."

Lookout Light had settled down now and was walking peaceably. The woods path widened into a grassy glade where the Young Whip stood watching to see if a fox broke out of the cover to the west, by the Websters' farm pond. Tatine paused to speak to him and as Shelley rode by she saw them exchange a look, a look that lasted but an instant but spoke of so much naked longing that Shelley felt her heart fill with envy.

At the head of the column filing through the woods she saw Zagaran's straight back, and the melting sensation she had experienced at the meet when he spoke to her returned.

The sky was darker now, the air turning colder. They had drawn the cream of the country and the most reliable covers had proved blank.

The new Master must be worried, Shelley thought. On his

shoulders rested the responsibility for providing sport. And although she had heard rumors that many foxes had been imported and put out, none, on this vitally important day, seemed abroad. Now, after riding around in the cold for three hours, the novelty of hunting a new country had worn off and many of the visitors were pulling out.

After telephoning from nearby houses for their grooms and trailers, they had climbed into heated cars and driven back to the Dinwiddies', where the bar and buffet of sausage, scrambled eggs, dry paper-thin Virginia ham, smoked turkey, hot rolls and other Hunt breakfast delicacies had been set out and Raymond Hoe would be tuning his guitar in preparation for rousing renditions of "D'Ye Ken John Peel" and "Drink, Puppy, Drink" and the other old songs that the foxhunters, relaxed and uninhibited after a day in the open and numerous bourbons, called for.

Bones Black and the racing boys, who found hunting tame, had left shortly after noon. The Pony Clubbers had gone home to be on time for the Disney film being shown that afternoon at the Halter Club. The Dinwiddies had reluctantly departed in order to host their party.

The diehards who were left were buttoning the top buttons of their coats to ward off the wind, lighting cigarettes with numbed fingers and apologizing to the remaining visitors, still hoping to get their capping fees' worth of sport, for the lack of a run.

Yet while there was light there was hope. To the true foxhunter it was this, the never knowing, that provided the sport's fascination.

At that moment there was a burst of sound from the woods. While the field waited for the Master to signal which way to go, the music grew in volume. Then, as suddenly as there had been sound, there was silence. Moments later the Old Huntsman rode out of the woods and up to the Master. Moving up within earshot, Shelley heard him say that hounds had jumped a fox lying beside a log and chopped him. "He was full of mange," the Old Huntsman said darkly. "Might be a good idea for Buck to go back and get the mask. Send it to the Health people to be checked for rabies. We don't want none of the dogs to get it."

Zagaran's face tightened. "Draw the old Talbot place. If we don't get anything there, start toward home."

Swinging his horse around, he cantered off to confer with Buck, the foxman who followed The Hunt in his Jeep loaded with shovels, spades and the two tan terriers.

The way out led through the rotting gate to Major DeLong's driveway. Richard Doyle got off to open it. As he undid the baling wire loop that served as a latch, the gate disintegrated in his hands, falling to a heap in the grassy cart track. The Major's old hunter, Artaxerxes, stood with his head over the pasture fence observing the proceedings.

The Young Whip pushed the pile of boards aside. The Old Huntsman, his hounds grouped around him, rode through. Then the remaining field crowded past, a jumble of mud-splattered horses, sweat drying on their necks and loins in ridges like those left on a beach after the tide has gone out.

Shelley nodded and said, "Thank you, Richard." The Young Whip, leaning against the gatepost and holding his horse, jerked his head up in surprise. "Easier to build another gate than put that one back together," Shelley continued, indicating with her crop the collapsed boards and baling wire.

"Yes, ma'am." The Young Whip smiled and touched his fingers to the brim of his hunting cap.

While the others rode ahead she waited for him to put the gate back up and remount. At close range his rugged maleness suggested a simplicity and violence of the senses she found disturbing. However, he seemed to be working out well. The Old Huntsman, something of a martinet in his old age and not easily pleased, liked him. The Young Whip was hard-working. He had a pleasant smile and a nice manner. And there was something else— kindness and a certain intuition and sensitivity. Horses sensed this and went well for him.

Major DeLong stood in his overgrown yard. He wore torn, stained farmer's coveralls and a raveled broad-brimmed planter's hat, and although shapeless and shabby he somehow retained that intangible air of the aristocrat.

A rusted icebox leaned drunkenly. In the turning circle in front of the crumbling, dilapidated mansion stood the "marriage car," the grass around it reaching to the tops of the doors. For almost forty years the old touring car had stood there in preparation for a honeymoon which had never taken place. The Major's young daughter, Annie, had died of a ruptured appendix the morning of her wedding. Grief-stricken, the Major had left the car where it now stood, still packed with its moldering suitcases of trousseau finery.

As she rode through the high grass to speak to the Major, Shelley thought of something her father had said shortly before his death. He had been in one of his depressed periods following a drinking bout. "Shelley, my girl, people are like lawns. Without effort, they go to seed."

The Major had obviously gone to seed, becoming senile. Although she rode directly up to him and said, "Good morning," he did not acknowledge her existence. Turning his back, he limped toward the house.

I mustn't start imagining things, Shelley told herself, riding away. He's old and half blind, like his dog, and probably didn't recognize me. Briefly she wondered where Joe could be. The Major was never without the dog at his side. Perhaps he had locked him in the house when he saw hounds coming through the property.

"I'm calling it a day," Millicent said. "I'm freezing, and my hemorrhoids hurt."

"I think I'll pull out, too," Debby said. "See you at the Dinwiddies'."

Shelley watched them go. She found it hard to believe that the Beast would deliberately exclude her. The Beast had been one of her grandmother's closest friends, even after the scandal caused by her mother's elopement. Yet the older woman had obviously had something to do with her failure to receive an invitation to hunt. It doesn't matter, Shelley told herself positively. She didn't want to go to the breakfast anyway, stand around and watch Fax, Dash-Smythe, Polo Pete and the others get drunk. When The Hunt was over she would go home and spend the evening with Cam.

Now Polo Pete—all day he had ridden on Lord Willoughby-Walloughby's scarlet coattails, dropping names whenever the Englishman was within earshot—pulled out. His Lordship had settled his differences with Augie Schligman and was discussing the merits of Bavarian hops as opposed to the U.S. variety. Judy Schligman, the sharp-faced woman from New Commonwealth, Tatine, Shelley and a handful of grooms were all that remained of the original field of seventy.

Shelley had purposely avoided speaking to Zagaran. She knew how anxious he was to show sport to the large crowd. To be defeated by the vicissitudes of nature, to be touched by something beyond his control, would seem to him to be a weakening, despicable thing. From the set of his shoulders and the apprehensive manner in which he kept glancing up at the sky, she realized he was angry and ashamed of his powerlessness to provide a run. And yet, as she found herself alongside him, it was as though all the hours she had been riding over the countryside had been meaningless until this moment, when his eyes turned to meet hers.

"Sometimes when it matters the most you have the worst days," she said sympathetically.

He glanced around at the members of the field who remained. "I wonder where the hell all the foxes are."

"My father once said that he hoped when he died he would find out where all the foxes he had lost went to."

"Good question, and one I suppose that has haunted huntsmen since the world began." With a gesture of resignation he drew back the cuff of his scarlet coat. "Almost three. Might as well call it a day. Any minute now it's going to snow."

Suddenly, unaccountably, she did not want The Hunt to end. She saw the Hunt members trooping gaily into the Dinwiddies' house, filled with light and music, and herself riding home in the cold to a sullen Suellen and Cam, with whom she could not share the day's experience. She glanced at Zagaran's profile and realized he was not thinking of her. The understanding that had run between them the day before was, because of the weather and lack of foxes, disturbed and wanting.

"So you're giving up?" she said tauntingly. "You never did draw Ballyhoura. We used to always get a fox out of there." She looked at the Old Huntsman trotting up the road, the hounds jogging behind him. "We're almost back now."

"Aren't you in a hurry to get home?" he asked. "What about that husband of yours?"

"He went to Washington to a press dinner. They're giving him an award."

"Congratulations." His face lightened. "What the hell, we might just get a three o'clock fox out of Ballyhoura after all!"

It was clear from his expression that the Old Huntsman was not pleased about making a final cast. His back registering disapproval, he blew the pack into the woods. The pack, too, seemed disinterested. As they crashed through the underbrush only a few of the old hounds had their noses to the ground and were working. Then suddenly Barber opened. The pack's disinterest vanished. Within seconds they came together and their high shrill voices reverberated through the wood.

"Come on," Tatine cried, her face radiant. "That's what we've been waiting for."

Shelley hesitated. To her trained ear the cry of hounds was too shrill, too high-pitched, too excited. "Sounds like deer to me," she said doubtfully.

But Tatine was already galloping along the path down which the Young Whip had vanished.

The sky was very dark now, ominous, and the air becoming more frigid. Shelley felt trapped in the dark wood, held by a strange fear, as though if she followed Zagaran now she would be lost in some dark wood of her own.

Lookout Light shook his head, frantic to be away.

Then she heard the Old Huntsman's spine-tingling Rebel yell. Despite his weariness and aching shoulder, once hounds were away he could not keep the exultation from his high-pitched "Oy-eeeee." Then the Master's shrill "Gone Away." So it was a fox and not a deer!

Suddenly all the parts fragmented by the weather, the torn relationships, the loose ends she felt her life had become, came together to make an integrated whole. In that exultant cry lay the violence, the passion, the exhilaration, the release. Image of war without its guilt.

The Jenneys' new wire fence stopped them. Finding the barway wired up, the Old Huntsman ordered the Young Whip to dismount and take it down.

"Get out of the way," Zagaran cried and sent Black Magic speeding into it.

"It's too high for me," said the woman from New Commonwealth and pulled aside.

For an instant, as the barway rose black against the sky, Shelley felt the same fear that had come over her the day before when Zagaran had found her. Then as Black Magic landed and kept on galloping, her hesitation vanished. An overwhelming determination not to be left vanquished the fear.

"Lookout Light," she whispered, "I hope you learned your lesson this morning."

Lookout Light had. Standing back, he cleared the high unyielding barway with inches to spare.

"You love." Bending low on his neck, Shelley gave him his head and let him race on in the wake of Black Magic.

Hounds flew through the Jenney farm, past Enid and the children waving from the porch, and headed west toward the Free Zone.

Shelley had forgotten the wind, the cold. The weeks of exercise were paying off. The colt was galloping easily, fencing brilliantly. Caught up in the excitement, the urgency of the chase, she did not realize how long they had been running until they labored up Hunting Hill to the high ridge overlooking the wild mountainy country, the Free Zone, now no longer hunted. At the summit the Old Huntsman pulled up his horse.

As the field stopped behind him, the only sound that came to their ears was that of their own and their horses' breathing, that and the creak of saddle leather and the moaning sound of the wind.

"We seem to have lost hounds," Tatine whispered.

Holding up his hand, Zagaran signaled them to be quiet. "I don't hear hounds." He looked down the long slope and across the rocky uneven fields stretching to the blue mountains.

"We're a long way from home and it's beginning to snow." He turned to ride up to the Old Huntsman. "I guess we might as well call it a day."

EIGHTEEN

THE Old Huntsman sat motionless, listening too. As Huntsman for the past forty years, he carried each of his hounds on his back, in his mind, in his heart and in his dreams. And this responsibility, together with the pressure from his followers to furnish sport, caused the lines in his face, the body hunched with thought and the eyes which looked off into the distance where hounds stretched forever on the line of a straight-running fox.

Around his neck, like an extension of himself, was hung his old-fashioned Virginia-type hunting horn. Instinctively, without thinking, he raised it to his lips. Then, with a feeling close to shame, he lowered it again. Despite the ache in his bad shoulder that told him weather was coming on, he could not bring himself to blow hounds home.

In his time he had seen many huntsmen. A few had been good. Many had been bad, and some had been downright dishonest, to their hounds and to the field. A bad huntsman refused to give his hounds a chance. If they came to a loss, he would show off his ability on the horn and get hounds' heads up. Generally his whippers-in finished the job by unnecessary rating and whip cracking. By this time the pack would be thoroughly rattled and would have lost whatever interest it once had in pursuing the fox.

Nowadays, the Old Huntsman thought, so few people understood the art of venery that they became impatient with a huntsman who did not "blow his own horn" and put on a show of bustling about.

For this reason it was difficult not to become a faker, not to lay drags, drop foxes at the end of the drag lines and make the field believe they were hunting fox when in reality they were hunting the huntsman. When hounds ran mute, as apparently they were doing now, it would be easy for him to lift the pack and fool his field. Yet despite his weariness, the growing cold, the snow, the Old Huntsman could not bring himself to do this. In his opinion, a deliberately dishonest huntsman not only ruined his hounds and deceived his followers, he did something worse. He ruined and deceived himself.

Taking one hand from the reins, he cupped his ear, every sense, every nerve straining to hear. I must be deafer, he thought sorrowfully. I should hear something. Then a chilling thought struck him. Could he have miscalculated? Could hounds have swung back to Ballyhoura instead of turning west toward Hunting Hill?

If he lost hounds this day he'd be pensioned off for sure, put out to pasture like his old horse. Just let me hear one hound speak, he prayed, old Bouncer say, or Barber. Then I'll know which way they've gone.

Suddenly the full weight of his accumulated exhaustion swept over him, like the wind coming from the north. That and a terrible sense of aloneness. Where in tarnation was the Young Whip, he wondered angrily. For the past month he hadn't been worth the salt that was put out in the pasture for the horses. If he didn't have the Master's daughter on his mind instead of his job, they might not be in this predicament.

He did not hear the Young Whip canter up.

"I don't hear anything from the other side," the Young Whip said carefully, letting his reins go slack. "I've been thinking. The fox could have turned back, toward Ballyhoura—" At sight of the Old Huntsman's face, he broke off. "Like as not," he finished lamely.

The Old Huntsman felt his irritation rising, like scent on a still day following a night of rain. Antagonism, like the hated wire now replacing the old walls and rail fences, the barbs of which caught and tore at his hounds, rose between him and the Young Whip. Young whippersnapper, he thought angrily, that's what he is, thinks all you have to know about hunting hounds is how to ride and crack a whip. He wanted to tell the Young Whip that when he had been hunting over forty years and had come to know foxes, which were local and which were visiting, and which way they ran, depending on the terrain, the direction of the wind and innumerable other factors known only by experience coupled with instinct, then he, the Young Whip, would have the right to tell him, the Old Huntsman, which way hounds had gone.

"I'll do the deciding," he said sharply, by way of reply. "Long-as-I-am-Huntsman! Now ride over to the south side and listen some more."

The Old Huntsman watched the Young Whip gallop off. His relaxed suppleness, the ease with which he drove his horse over the uneven ground, the unthinking fearlessness with which he jumped the wall into the woods made him resent the Young Whip even more.

There he goes, he thought, butting his bullheaded way through the trees, drunk with power, galloping first one way and then the other, not saving his horse. God, he concluded, there must be better things to do than break my back and my heart teaching a green boy the ways of a fox and hounds.

Yet even as he thought this, he knew it was not true. As the Young Whip vanished from sight, he was aware of a terrible sense of loss. In the Young Whip, in the jaunty angle of his cap, the wonderful unshaken confidence with which he rode, he saw himself, the way he himself had been when he first started whipping in for Cameron Fitzgerald.

He had forgotten the field. Glancing back, he saw the few who were left coffeehousing, circling their steaming horses, lighting cigarettes. Convinced that it destroyed one's "nose," made it impossible to smell out a fox—something he believed he could do almost as well as a hound—the Old Huntsman abhorred tobacco and considered people who smoked in the field on a par with loud conversation when he was trying to listen, or wearing velvet caps when not a member of the Hunt staff. "Bad form," the old Master would have said. "Bad form."

Now he was aware that the longer he waited, pretending to listen, the more impatient the field would become. Already they had suffered through the long morning hours, traversing the fields and woodlands that hounds had drawn blank. Aside from the mangy fox which hounds had chopped down, they hadn't spoken until Ballyhoura cover. Then hounds had gone away so fast that for a moment he had thought they were on deer. He'd ridden after them, sending the old horse on as fast as he could. Yet now it appeared that somehow they'd gotten away from him. Instinctively he knew that he must keep going, that the moment had come when the run must begin again, before blood turns cold, energy is dissipated, and the grumbling begins.

"Well?" The new Master sat motionless on his black mare, waiting for a reply.

"Reckon it'd be best to try and horn 'em in." The Old Huntsman gazed up at the sky. "Snow's coming on, too."

Putting the treasured horn to his lips, puffing out his cheeks, the Old Huntsman began to blow. As the mellow rising and falling notes echoed out across the countryside, a thrill ran through the hearts of the true foxhunters in the field. For in The Valley it was said that the Old Huntsman's capacity with the horn was equaled by no man.

As the last pure note died away and no hounds were to be seen emerging from the wood or coming across the Valley, the Old Huntsman was filled with a sense of hopelessness. He saw the Young Whip returning at a gallop, shaking his head, and knew that he would have to ride farther.

Gathering up his reins, hating to force the old horse to additional effort, he urged him into a stiff-legged trot. As the pain in his shoulder grew in proportion to the horse's jarring downhill gait, the Old Huntsman knew with sudden, terrible certainty that he had guessed wrong.

From the Valley floor came not a sound. The cattle, grazing unconcernedly, had not been disturbed by fox or hounds running past. No crows circled overhead. Riding blindly on because he had to do something, go somewhere, the Old Huntsman realized that the Young Whip had been right. Whatever it was they had bolted out of Ballyhoura had probably gone back to the cover.

The Old Huntsman skirted a seeded field, jumped a small snake fence into a pasture, on the far side of which stood a high stone wall. Beyond it lay the Free Zone, a wild mountainy country where hounds could become lost for days. With a quick, furtive glance he looked around. The Young Whip rode easily to one side. The new Master and the field were practically in his pocket.

It was too late to turn and go back. He must keep on, driving ahead. If only by some miracle he could be proven right, find hounds had run this way.

"Any sign of hounds?" The new Master's voice was as cold as the November air had become.

Despair swept over the Old Huntsman. Lifting his arm to blow his horn was agonizing. He knew he was slumping, but his back was too cramped from the hours in the saddle to straighten.

In desperation he looked at the Young Whip. He was sitting very erect, staring past the cattle munching silage at the woods to his right.

"Hark!" he cried suddenly, leaning forward to listen. "I think I hear them." His voice quickened with excitement. "It's Bouncer, with Barber chiming in!"

As his horse's ears lifted and his heart began to hammer, the Old Huntsman realized he'd been proven right. Still, it was a hollow victory. Because the Young Whip had thought hounds had gone the other direction, he had deliberately brought the field all this long way. Now by some fluke, one of the variables that gave fox-hunting its fascination, his reputation had been saved.

"Yonder he goes!" Standing up in his stirrups, the Young Whip swept off his cap and swung it high in the air. "Tallyho!"

Simultaneously the Old Huntsman saw the fox. Tired now, his brush heavy with mud and burrs. Could it be, or was his eyesight failing him? The fox was coming toward him now. Tongue lolling, he trotted slowly through the herd of cattle.

Suddenly, with a shattering sense of shock, the Old Huntsman knew what it was that, all during the strange run, he had subconsciously been afraid of. His instinct had been right. It was no ordinary fox. The brush, drooping now, dragging behind, was black.

Then he heard hounds bursting from the woods, giving tongue with the ringing, exultant cry that moments before he had longed to hear.

He whipped the horn to his mouth and urgently, desperately, he began to blow.

Jerking his horse to a stop, the Young Whip looked at the Old Huntsman as though he had lost his reason.

"Stop them," the Old Huntsman cried, taking the horn from his mouth. "For God's sake, whip them off!"

"Have you gone mad?" The new Master's voice was as hard, as unyielding as the wall over which the fox had disappeared. "The fox looks done in. Go put them on the line."

"It's a black-brushed fox," the Old Huntsman said.

"That crazy superstition!" With a threatening gesture, the new Master raised his hunting whip. "Let this one get away and you're finished as Huntsman!"

The Old Huntsman's shoulders straightened. His head went up.

His eyes as he gazed at the new Master were as blue, as cold as the distant mountains. "Perhaps it's you who's finished," he said softly. "You and the others who care but for the killing."

As he spoke, he realized that the fear, the indecision were past. Now he knew what he must do. Slowly, carefully, the Old Huntsman lifted the heavy unwieldy horn over his head. As he held it out to the Young Whip, touching the curling cow's horn, feeling its mother-of-pearl smoothness for the last time, he had the feeling that he was surrendering a part of himself.

"Take it," the Old Huntsman ordered. "It's what you've been wanting. Well, here it is."

The Young Whip's baffled expression gave way to wonderment. "You want me to carry it?"

"You heard what the Master said. Blow hounds back on the line." And then because he had to, because he couldn't quite relinquish everything that he was, that had given his life meaning, he added gruffly, "It'll be years before you learn to blow it proper like."

The Young Huntsman's eyes dropped. His color heightened.

"However, I'll do what I can to teach you how," the Old Huntsman concluded.

As the Young Huntsman proudly lifted the horn to his lips, the Old Huntsman felt the first flakes of snow.

As the Young Huntsman took the horn his confidence was shaken. With the eyes of the field boring into his back he suddenly felt weighed down with responsibility. For the first time he, alone, was responsible to The Hunt. From now on, rather than being relatively free to ride where he chose, he must always be in front, alone with hounds.

With a show of bravado, he put the horn to his mouth. Desperately he hoped that the time he had spent learning to sound the basic calls would result in clear melodious sounds rather than the muffled ugly toots of the amateur.

He heard the proper notes coming from it with relief. The hounds that had automatically followed the Old Huntsman halted. Lifting their heads, they gave the Old Huntsman a final lingering look. Then, in response to the short imperative commands, they turned back to the Young Huntsman.

Deliberately he cast hounds. He must, he thought, do this right.

Yet his concentration was divided. Instead of hounds he saw her, the new Master's daughter, back there in the field watching, judging, that amused mocking look in her green-yellow eyes.

At that moment when, at long last, he had achieved his lifelong ambition, he felt himself to be in mortal danger.

Tatine was becoming careless, talking to him at cubbing meets, lingering behind in order to ride home with him. Now they went to the farmhouse almost every afternoon.

It had never occurred to him that a lady could make love the way she did, talk the way she did. At first he'd been shocked, appalled at the things she did and the things she said, things his wife, even the whores he'd known when he was in the service, could never have imagined. It was as though she wanted to confront him with all the dimly hinted sins which his upbringing, his background had endowed with fear and retribution. There was a cruelty, a feline streak about her, and the aftermath often left him stricken with a sense of guilt and horror.

He had never dreamed that anyone could kiss the way she did with her teeth, her tongue, her whole body moving, twisting, her nails digging into his back, moaning noises coming from her throat. When he touched her breasts she went into a frenzy.

And one long afternoon after they had made love once and were waiting to begin again she told him about a place in New York.

"It's a kind of beauty salon," she said in her husky whispering voice. "They give you special treatments." As she spoke, she began caressing him. "They give massages and if you're willing to pay the price you can have the full treatment."

"What's the full treatment?" he asked lazily, loving the tingling sensation caused by her long nails against his body.

"I'll demonstrate. Roll over on your stomach." Kneeling over him, she ran the palms of her hands up and down his back. "They massage you like this. With special creams and lotions. You can have one man or two—"

"Men!" He twisted around to stare at her.

Except for the earrings she always wore, she was naked. Her beauty, the firmness of her pointed breasts and the ivory flatness of her stomach made him draw in his breath.

"Of course, silly." She reared back on her heels, taunting him. "You don't think I'd do it with a woman, do you? Well, they just keep on doing this for a long time, until you're all warm and relaxed and sexy. Then they turn you over. Now." She flopped down on her back. "You do it. One works on top. The lotion makes you all smooth and slippery. The other works down below. God"—she began to writhe—"I'm starting again!"

"So am I," he admitted, catching one of her moving breasts with his teeth. Lifting his head, he asked, "Are they always the same men?"

"Oh, no. After you've tried out a few you get to know the ones you like best. I had a truck driver. A Negro. He was so big and pressed down so hard it lasted for ages. He went back to driving his truck. Nobody's ever made it last like that," she added wistfully. "You're almost as good but not quite!"

"Jesus," he said.

"I shock you, don't I? I'll bet you never knew anybody like me," she said.

"No, I can honestly say I never did."

"Do you think I'm sinful?" she asked afterward. "Do you wish I were nice? Demure, like other girls? Like your wife?"

"No." He was unable to help himself. He knew only that she had a hold on him, a hold so openly, so blatantly sexual that she was ruining it for him with any other woman.

"Well"—she smiled happily—"you know I could get pregnant. Think what a juicy scandal that would make. It would set the bitch pack up for months."

The thought appalled him so that for a moment all desire ceased. "Don't say that," he begged. "Please."

"Well, I might. We've done it so many times this afternoon I haven't got any stuff left."

"Then we'll stop."

"The hell we will." Bending over, she put her mouth against him.

By now, no matter what she did, what eroticism of mind and body she revealed, he could not leave her without an aching desire to return. She had awakened his sexual hunger to such a pitch he could repeat the experience over and over without a sense of repetition. Now he no longer cared that his work was slacking off, that his wife was beginning to look at him curiously, ask where he went every afternoon. All that mattered was being with Tatine.

The last time he had been with her, just yesterday, there had been a difference. All the way to the farmhouse she had seemed remote, preoccupied. On reaching it, she had suggested having a drink.

"I don't want a drink," he said, noticing the line of her breasts stretching the fabric of her jersey. "We can have coffee afterward."

Walking over to the fireplace, she stared at the gray charred remains of the fire they had built the last time they were there.

"I want you now," he said hoarsely. Taking her arm, he pulled her toward the stairs.

"How dare you push me around?" she asked coldly, holding back. "Who do you think you are?"

Dark anger flooded through him. "This time you're doing it my way." Picking her up, he carried her upstairs and threw her down across the bed. She lay motionless, staring up at him wordlessly. On her face was a half smile and in her eyes a strange triumphant glitter.

He was filled with sudden rage. Pinning her beneath him, he took her with a brutality that caused her to cry out with pain. When he released her, ashamed of his savagery, there was a soft, bemused look about her. With a gentleness he had never seen her display, she reached up and touched his cheek.

"Do you really hate me?" she asked.

"No," he murmured desperately. "My God, no. I'm sorry if I hurt you."

Pressing her face against his shoulder, she whispered, "You didn't hurt me."

He almost said it then: "Tatine, I love you." Instead he said miserably, "I haven't anything to offer you."

"You really want to offer me something?" She sounded surprised.

"Yes."

Looking at her unlined face, without make-up or need of it, the clear, creamy skin faintly dusted with freckles, he realized with shock how young she was.

Abruptly she said, "Let's not pretend this is anything more than fucking." As though determined to hurt him, to spoil the tenderness that for a moment had existed between them, she continued, "What else is there in life but that?"

Suddenly she began to cry bitterly, wildly, with the shuddering, sobbing violence of a brokenhearted child. "It's all hopeless." She dug her fists into her eyes. "You do hate me. Just like everybody."

Not knowing what else to do, he put his arm around her. Drawing her to him, he felt her warmth and softness and was aware of the wonderfully clean scent about her skin. The last of his violence drained away. He felt protective, gentle.

She clung to him, seeming to want to lose herself in his body. "Richard, I want to be with you." Her voice was almost inaudible. "I lied about those men, about feeling that way. Richard, don't you see? It never happened to me before."

"I haven't anything—"

"So you said." She flung her head back and he saw the long white line of her throat. "Darling, I have enough for both of us."

There was a slow thudding in his chest, a feeling of growing excitement, as her meaning became clear.

It was snowing now, icy pellets striking his face and bouncing off his horse like wedding rice. The new Huntsman was momentarily at a loss. Like hounds, he sought the correct line to follow. She had said she would meet him that night, after the Hunt breakfast. By then he must reach a decision.

When hounds spoke he almost wished they hadn't. He couldn't quite discount the Old Huntsman's warning. He had been brought up on the tales and superstitions that the mountain people spoke of nights, sitting by the hearth when the wind moaned in the chimney and rattled the eaves. His generation, he told himself now, did not believe in haunts, curses and old wives' tales. What if the fox did have a black brush? Lots of foxes, grays in particular, had brushes that looked black and in this light you couldn't tell anyway. The Old Huntsman had fallen on his head so many times he was punchy. And his eyesight wasn't too good any longer.

Yet as he rode off to encourage hounds, he was filled with dread.

· · ·

Shelley had seen the look on the Old Huntsman's face. The sense of strangeness she had experienced at Ballyhoura returned. It was as though The Hunt was compelling those who were left to some final decisive action as unaccountable as the storm.

The raw cold struck her. Particles of snow stung her cheeks. They had run out of The Hunt's country and it would soon be dark.

"Isn't it glorious?" Judy Schligman rode up beside her, and at sight of the young girl's shining eyes and ecstatic face, Shelley was reminded of herself, the day she had ridden The Gray Goose on their first great hunt.

Richard Doyle and Zagaran cleared the high wall. Lookout Light, settled now, his mind on his business, jumped perfectly, extending himself in mid-air to clear the ditch on the landing side.

"Bless you," Shelley whispered. Despite the distance traveled, he did not seem tired. As he set off across the rough, rutted field his stride was strong and he was not blowing enough to snuff out a match.

Glancing back, she saw Lord Willoughby-Walloughby come to grief in the ditch. Polo Pete and Augie pulled up to avoid jumping on top of him and Judy's mare, dead tired now, refused.

Satisfied that his Lordship had help, Shelley rode on. Hounds were screaming now. In the misted snow-filled world through which they were passing their voices held an eerie, almost unearthly quality.

The Hunt's manicured fields and well-paneled fences lay behind them. They were in the Free Zone and the country was becoming wilder by the minute. "Hairnet country," Shelley called it as a branch slammed across her face and brought her hair cascading down her back.

It was a mountainy country, rocky and unkempt, made up of cider-colored fields and weathered snake fences as old as the original settlers who built them. It was the domain of the Mellicks, who had settled there when the first pioneers built their cabins. Until the thirties it had been a feudal domain presided over by the descendants of Black Horse Harry Mellick, who had ridden with Shelburn's Raiders. The people who lived in the Free Zone were violent and uncouth. During Prohibition it had been alive with stills, and any law officer or unauthorized person who wandered into the area ran the risk of being shot. During World War II the

Free Zone had been depopulated. The men had gone to war and the women had drifted down to the towns. The small farms had gone to ruin and the land had reverted back to its original state.

Zagaran seemed to know where he was going, and then she remembered that she had heard he had begun buying up additional land to use as a shooting preserve, and that somewhere in the area he had renovated an old farmhouse.

They traversed a rocky pasture. Zagaran and the Young Huntsman galloped just ahead, Tatine to the side. Black Magic was still going strongly but the Young Huntsman's horse appeared to be laboring.

The horses slowed. The ruins of an abandoned farm were to their right. In the failing light rose a rusted wire fence. No gate or barway was visible.

If they had to backtrack they would lose hounds altogether, and the way the pack was running, straight for the mountains, it might be days before they found them again.

An old plank gate opened into the adjoining farmyard. If the gate was leaned back along the wire, the fence might be jumpable. She hailed the others. Quickly she explained what she had in mind.

For a moment they stared at it doubtfully. The horses, glad of a respite, stood with their heads lowered, steam rising from their heaving sides. It was snowing harder now and the light was diminishing. Ahead the cry of hounds was fading. Every second lost meant less chance of catching them.

"I saw my father jump a gate like that once," Shelley said. "He was trapped in a field surrounded by wire when hounds were running."

Her hair that had come down was blowing in the wind. Her eyes blazed with excitement and her color was high. The fever, the passion of mind and body and effort that constitutes the chase, was upon her. That and a vital necessity to prove something, not only to Zagaran but to herself. She saw him catch his breath as he looked at her and suddenly she was laughing with utter and complete delight in the day, the way it had gone and the challenge it offered.

Zagaran's smile flashed white. "One of your ancestors must have been a pole vaulter." He turned to the Young Huntsman.

"I'll hold your horse while you lift the gate over against the wire.

"—Shelley, wait!"

She heard his shout, but nothing could stop her now. Lookout Light was speeding over the rapidly freezing ground. The faster you go into a fence when it's slippery, her father had told her once, the safer you are.

From the takeoff out of the old cart track the gate looked close to five feet. In daylight it would have given pause to all but the bravest of the field. At dusk, with the ground becoming more slippery by the minute, it was a terrifying obstacle. Should their tired horses hit it, breaking the rotting planks, they would fall and become entangled in the wire.

In the dark and distant past there had been the Pilot, who had beaten the fastest horses of his day. His progeny had been famed for their speed and valiant hearts. There had been Beacon, who won the Virginia Hunt Cup on three legs, refusing to give up when a tendon bowed five lengths before the finish. Channel Light, Sea Buoy and scores of others, the cream of a great line tracing directly back to the Darley Arabian, this blood had been distilled into the veins of Lookout Light, giving him the thoroughbred courage to gallop and jump until his heart ceased to beat.

His faith in Shelley was complete and now that her need was transmitted to him in her voice, her hands on the reins and her knees pressing against his sides, he did not hesitate. As he landed safely, avoiding a boulder she had failed to see, Shelley's heart filled with love and pride.

Now she knew she had a Shelburn Cup horse.

Letting the wet, slippery reins go slack she leaned forward, resting her cheek against his wet mane.

Black Magic would have swerved had Zagaran not driven her into the fence with the same strength and determination with which he had driven himself to wealth and fame. The mare had no choice but to jump, and although she hit the gate with her hind legs, she negotiated it safely.

Not so the Young Huntsman. In order to round up stray hounds, and in hopes of viewing a fox, his young horse had been forced to travel twice the distance that the others had. Now, although he made a gallant effort, he hit the gate with his chest.

The gate, old and rotten, collapsed and the exhausted horse, his front legs caught in the fence, fell in a tangle of broken boards and wire.

Richard was thrown clear. The horse lay where it had fallen, its head twisted beneath it.

"Richard," Tatine cried, sliding down off Warlock and turning him loose. Scrambling over the remains of the fence, she ran to him. "Richard," she cried again. "Oh, Richard."

The Young Huntsman struggled to his feet. "I should have pulled up," he said brokenly. "I shouldn't have made him go on."

Tatine put her hand on his mud-covered arm. "Are you sure you're all right? Richard . . ."

His eyes were on her face, wet with snow. "I'm all right. You go on ahead."

"No," Tatine said positively. "We'll find our way together."

"Take Lookout Light," Shelley volunteered, knowing the proper procedure was to offer her horse, but praying the Young Huntsman would refuse.

"That won't be necessary," Zagaran said quickly. "Don't you come from around here somewhere? Find a house and telephone the stable. Be sure to take the tack off your horse when the van comes and take it with you. Now give me the horn."

The Young Huntsman's eyes did not leave Tatine's face. With the slow, deliberate motions of one moving in a dream, he lifted the leather thong over his head and handed the horn up to the Master.

"What the hell you done to mah gate?"

They had not noticed the man who had been leaning on the pitchfork observing them from the falling-down barn. Now he emerged from the shadows and came through the broken fence to face them. A short, stocky youngish man wearing coveralls, a cloth cap and a mocking sneer about his mouth. With his hands clasping his pitchfork, he gazed up at Zagaran. "This heah's Mellick land. Land you ain't got aholt of yet. Now, Mistuh Zagaran, suh, how long you figgah on breakin' down mah fences, lettin' mah cattle go loose, without no good ree-turn?"

"My fault, Tom," the Young Huntsman put in. "I broke the fence. Didn't know you'd moved here or had any stock. Place looked empty to me."

"'Tain't likely you'd know, busy like you've been." Mellick's eyes slid to Tatine, whose hand still lay lightly on Richard's arm. "I say this for you, Richie-boy, you sho know how to pick 'em," he observed with a leer and a snicker. His voice took on a whining note. "We'se kin, Richie-boy. How come you stand by and let this man here take our land from us'n. Now all we Mellicks got left is this trashy old piece and here you-all come through breakin' up mah gates."

"I bought the land from the bank," Zagaran interrupted, restraining a fidgety Magic anxious to be off in the wake of hounds. "If you'd help Richard here find a telephone—"

"Ah ain't helpin' Richie-boy find nuthin'." Mellick took a step toward Magic. "Richie-boy doin' right well by hisself. Now Mistuh Zagaran, suh"—he lifted the pitchfork threateningly—"you ain't gwine no place till you pays me for mah fence."

"Somebody will be over in the morning to repair your fence and replace the gate," Zagaran promised. "And if any cattle get out, The Hunt will see to it that you're reimbursed." He raised his hunting whip. "Move, Mellick, before I split your skull!"

Mellick's eyes gleamed with fury. "You can't talk to me that-away. You on mah land. Mellick land. Time was Mellicks owned everythin' round here." He broke off, screaming with terror, as Black Magic, who had caught his scent, reared and then lunged at him. Dropping the pitchfork, Mellick turned and fled. From the safety of the barn lot he bellowed his wrath. Shaking his balled fist at the departing riders, he delivered a string of epithets.

Tatine and Richard did not seem to hear him. They were standing hand in hand, their heads bowed over the dead horse, as the new snow fell on its motionless body, covering it like a shroud.

Shelley and Zagaran were alone now with hounds.

It was snowing harder, a slanting, swirling mist out of which the walls and snake fences, built long ago when the fields had been cleared and cultivated, loomed dark and forbidding. Shelley's fear was gone, the qualms she had felt back at the meet. The great leap had restored her confidence, given her back the courage without which she had not wanted to live. This was survival hunting. Hunting in the old-fashioned sense, before the artificiality of a pampered country and made fences, when all one's forces concentrated on simply staying with hounds, wherever they happened to lead.

The going was treacherous. Vaguely she was aware that they

were deep into the Free Zone. Seen through the veil of snow and oncoming darkness, it was a bleak, haunting country, holding a dreamlike fascination, not unmixed with a sense of the supernatural.

The encounter with Mellick had shaken her. Yet she could not think about it now. All her concentration was needed to stay up with the new Master, not lose him on the winding overgrown woods paths that required all of Lookout Light's ability and agility to navigate. She marveled at the certainty with which he drove Black Magic into the walls of trees and along tracks being obliterated by the snow.

As the grueling pace continued and hounds' voices continued to shriek through the gathering dusk, the knowledge was brought home to them that this was no ordinary fox. Running in a direct line to the mountains, it was more like some strange unearthly quarry, as freak as the early November snowstorm.

Reason told Shelley that Lookout Light was tiring and she shouldn't push her luck. But her blood was racing. The urgent, striving cry of hounds was a lure reeling her on against judgment. Taking the big black fences, the hairy overgrown walls, leaping ditches and fallen trees, plunging down into streams and up out of them, it was as if they were being carried along together toward a joint destiny.

Suddenly, directly ahead of them, they saw hounds. In the eerie visibility they looked like a ghost pack, larger than life-size and as white as the snow driving against them. Behind them, dimly discernible in the dusk, rose the black outline of the mountains.

"They've lost," Zagaran said.

"I'm glad," Shelley answered. "It was a brave fox."

She let her reins go loose. The gray's head dropped and he stood wearily, sides heaving, catching his breath. The night and the snow were all around them and it was suddenly very cold.

"Some day all of this will be mine," Zagaran said. "They'll call me Mr. Free Zone! In another ten years The Valley will be a suburb of Washington. The land we've just ridden over will be worth a fortune."

"Surely not. Not in our lifetime."

"You're living in a fool's paradise. I wonder where the rest of the pack is."

His words hit her like the darkness and growing cold, forcing her back to reality.

"I must get home."

"The farmhouse I've done over isn't far. We'll put up the horses and have dinner there."

Shelley felt a powerlessness, as though she were one of the snowflakes being blown by the wind without will or entity. She had no choice, she told herself as they came out onto the frozen cart track, but to follow where he led. In the snow and darkness she could not ride her tired horse home. Nor was there anywhere that she could telephone for a van.

Coat collars turned up, they jogged along the lane. The tack was black with water and freezing. Magic, the fight taken out of her by the long day, no longer laid back her ears at the colt. Instead, the two horses now accepted each other as though they were stablemates of long duration. Around their feet bobbed the tired hounds, beginning to limp as the ice cut into their pads.

The wind hurled the snow against them with new ferocity. Shelley was conscious of the ache in her back and legs, the numbness of her face and hands. At the same time she almost relished the discomfort. Somehow the long hack home through the cold of oncoming night was as necessary to the sense of conquered danger as the physical effort that preceded it. Without the cold and discomfort, the thought of home and fireside and shared companionship would not seem so inviting.

As they turned into the yard at the farmhouse the old feeling of blissful completion, of homecoming, swept over her.

Inside, the barn looked as if it had been vacated but yesterday. Fresh straw and hay had been put in the stalls and the water buckets were filled. Barricading themselves behind the sliding doors they untacked the tired horses, rubbed them down until they were dry, found blankets for them and turned them into stalls. Zagaran brought grain from the feedbox and poured it into their mangers. Picking up a hay bale as easily as though it was a lightweight bag, he shook it out for the horses. After counting hounds they discovered all but two and a half couple accounted for.

"Nothing we can do about them now," he said. "They'll probably find their way back to the kennels."

Assured that all the necessary things had been done and that the hounds, sprawled in the aisle and extra stalls, were secured, they slid open the doors and inched out into the tingling cold. Zagaran pulled the door shut behind them and they ran across the yard, their boots leaving imprints on the new-fallen snow.

Then he had the front door open and they were inside, the cold and wildness of the storm-filled night put behind them.

The small stone farmhouse had a luxurious simplicity, a cosy cheerfulness of bright curtains and matching chintz. The walls were covered with hunting prints and there was a wide comfortable sofa and slipcovered armchairs. In the fireplace lay the remains of a fire and in the air lingered the smell of coffee.

"Tatine comes sometimes when she wants to be alone," Zagaran explained. "I send people over once a week to see that the house and stable are in order. During the dove and quail season I bring friends out to shoot."

"The house is charming."

"Samantha Sue did the decorating. Here, let me have your coat and your cap. Your hair—" He watched her as she pushed it back off her face. "It's wet."

"No matter. It's drip dry."

She felt his breath against her cheek as he helped her off with her coat. Again she felt herself warming to him, melting like the ice turning to water on her hair.

"In a minute I'll have the fire going. Then I'll get you a drink."

Everything he did he did well, she thought, watching him build a fire that blazed into crackling warmth the instant he set a match to it. While he went to provide drinks she knelt before it, holding out her frozen hands.

"Now I know why people have hideaways," she said when he returned, carrying a tray of glasses and bottles.

"You do?" He sounded surprised.

"As long as you know you have a place to go to you can do the things you have to do in order to be free to go to it."

"I never thought of it that way." He set the tray down on the coffee table in front of the fire. "But you're right. What'll it be? Scotch, bourbon?"

"Do you have any sherry?"

"You don't drink?"

She shook her head.

408

"Are you afraid to?"

She stared up at him defiantly. "Let's not go through that again."

He stood very still, looking down at her. His eyes were the color of firelight on the bourbon bottle. "Then we'll celebrate. We'll have she-crab soup and champagne."

Sitting tensely on the edge of the sofa, she accepted the proferred glass. As the fire began to warm her outside, the wine set up a tingling inside. Slowly her hands and feet and body began to thaw. A longing to be rid of her muddy boots, her sodden breeches, shirt and stock and to lean back against the sofa became stronger.

With great effort she roused herself. "I must telephone Virginia City to come and get me."

"In that jalopy of his?" Zagaran refilled her glass. "He won't be able to get in. By now the lane will be a quagmire."

"But I must try." She stood up. The wet leather of her boots seemed to have grown to her skin. "Where is the telephone?"

He took a long swallow from his glass. His profile made her think of a Rembrandt, the same dark, rich quality, softened now by shadows.

"I had it disconnected," he said slowly, looking at her over his glass. "One of the reasons for a hideaway is to escape from things like telephones."

For an instant the wind was the only sound.

"I see." She started toward the closet. "Then I'll have to ride."

He turned, pivoting with the same quick animal-like grace that had saved him from Fax's wild swing. "You don't really want to go home."

The sound of the wind seemed louder. She turned and opened the front door. All she could see was a swirling mist.

Zagaran reached over her shoulder and slammed it shut.

There had been a time when she had been able to let things go. When nothing other than foxhunting had seemed hurried or immediate. Now decisions seemed continually to be confronting her. It was like being in the alien country over which they had come that afternoon. She had no precedent to follow, no knowledge distilled from experience. Because there had been no previous experience. She had prided herself on being inviolate. Now it seemed that the principles, the guideposts of her life, had changed. For a time that day the decisions, the pull, had been left in abeyance. Now once again she was trying desperately to orient herself in a strange territory where there were no signs to follow. And as Zagaran's hands tightened against her shoulders she felt as though the last lines mooring her to reality were about to slip, sending her coursing down some unexplored channel.

Curiosity stirred and with it a kind of recklessness. It was the way she had felt when she turned Lookout Light at the gate.

As though reading her mind, he said, "There are two kinds of people. Those who choose the gates to go through. And those who jump the fences. Those who play safe or"—he reached up with his index finger and gently touched her cheek—"those who take their chances." He turned her around slowly. "You might as well drop your boots and stay awhile. You'll find everything you need upstairs. Look in the drawers and closets."

Two of the upstairs bedrooms had been carefully arranged. One for men and one for women. Going into the men's room by mistake, she found the drawers of the mahogany bureau filled with neat rows of multicolored Brooks Brothers shirts, all with a tiny crimson Z monogram on the pocket. The bathroom closet held bottles of men's toilet water and aftershave lotion. Unscrewing the top of one, she recognized the distinctive lemonlike scent that Zagaran used.

In the bedroom designed for feminine use Samantha Sue's touch was apparent. No detail had been overlooked. There were china bibelots on the mantel, sachets in the drawers of lingerie, pomanders hanging in the scented closet. The huge four-poster was adorned with pink sheets, the softest imaginable blankets and the sheerest silk monogrammed spread.

In the closet she found a tweed suit she recognized as belonging to Tatine, several pairs of pants and a long red woolen robe. A chiffonier was loaded with lacy nightgowns and lingerie and the bathroom shelves held cosmetics and a jar of pink bath salts.

As she luxuriated in the steaming scented tub, she decided that a life of leisure, of luxury could be wonderfully inviting. Facing the full-length mirror, she observed her long, slender body, naked but for the Band-Aids worn on the inside of her knees to protect the places that became raw and rubbed during the hunting season. She bent down, peeled them off and threw them into the wastebasket.

Modesty caused her to cover her breasts and turn away from the mirror. Yet a feeling of erotic excitement persisted, becoming a wildness that was like the wind battering the foundations of the old house.

On the dressing table she found hairpins. Quickly she wound her hair, still damp from the snow and her bath, into a French knot and pinned it up. A pair of long, gold earrings had been carelessly left lying on the tray with the hairpins. She screwed them into her pierced earlobes. Then she stepped into the monk-like robe, zipped it up to its high rolled collar and tied the tasseled cord around her waist. She did not let herself dwell on the fact that Andrea Zagaran was short and the robe had obviously been designed for someone tall. Sliding her feet into high-heeled back-less slippers she had found beneath the bed, she went downstairs.

He had been bending over the fire, blowing on it. At the sound of her step he straightened up.

"You should always wear red. Gold earrings and the look of happiness . . ." He reached for the bottle of champagne on the table and filled a glass. "Here." Her hand curled around the stem of the glass, meeting his with a sudden tingling shock as they stood looking at each other.

"To us," he said, lifting his glass to drink from it.

Somehow, along with preparing the soup, tossing the salad, setting the table and icing the champagne, Zagaran had also managed to shower and change. Now he wore gray flannels. A red silk scarf was knotted around his throat and his beautifully tailored Bond Street blazer completed the impression he gave of casual elegance.

Quickly, efficiently, he cleared the card table he had set up in front of the roaring fire. She offered to help but he wouldn't let her. After putting the table away he turned on the record player and shoved the sofa closer to the fire.

He sat down beside her and they were silent, staring at the blazing logs, listening to the symphony of the wind blending with Beethoven's Ninth. The sensations of her body, languorous now and relaxed, mingled with the memories in her mind of riding Lookout Light over that wild snow-filled landscape.

She was afraid to speak, afraid to break the spell. The sense of completion, of having gone the length of the run, finished out the day with hounds, and the resultant sense of well-being on returning to warmth and fireside were as old as the blue mountains from which the wind swept down across The Valley, assaulting the walls of the ancient farmhouse. The beauty of the chase, a beauty she had never been able to communicate to Mike, lurked in her mind, leaving her detached, dreaming, until once again it became necessary to eat, sleep and pick up the threads of responsibility.

Now, slowly sipping the wine, feeling the fire against her cheeks, she thrust back all thoughts of existence beyond the walls of this room, knowing even as she did so that if she remained, if she succumbed to this growing lethargy of thought and action, she would inevitably become lost, ineffectual, like somebody outside adrift in the storm.

Zagaran sat deep in the chintz-covered couch, stretched out and relaxed. Yet even in relaxation there was a tautness, a stillness that seemed but a prelude to the violence she sensed was his natural being.

"Would you like more wine?"

"I'm afraid I'll fall asleep. That soup was delicious."

"I have it flown up from Charleston, where it's made." Reaching over, he took hold of the knot at the back of her head. As her hair came loose from the pins, falling around her face, he said, "It's better that way. Makes you look softer, younger." His hands moved gently through her hair. "More approachable."

Above the sound of the wind came the long, mournful baying of a foxhound.

Shelley tensed. "One of the missing hounds. We better go and let it in."

"Damn." He stood up and started toward the door. "Wait here. It's bloody cold."

"I want to see Lookout Light."

"All right." He reached into the closet. "Here's a coat of Tatine's and some boots."

The tingling cold struck them like a blow. The wind whipped the skirt of the robe around her, pushing her backward. Zagaran grabbed her hand and pulled her along behind him.

Outside the barn a hound stood, its nose lifted toward the sky, baying. From inside came a growled response. Zagaran slid the door open.

The hound, in a frenzy to join its fellows, pushed between his legs. Zagaran reacted, giving it a sudden hard push that sent it scuttling into the barn whimpering.

"Stupid animals," he muttered as though to himself. "Like women—always whining about something."

The hound's entrance roused the others, lying in various attitudes of rest. As Zagaran switched on the light they lifted their heads inquiringly. The two horses moved in their boxes. Shelley slid her hands along Lookout Light's tendons. They were cool and free of filling. She lifted the blanket and felt his back where the saddle had been. When he didn't flinch she replaced the covers and put her lips against his gray-pink nose.

"You love," she whispered.

"Bitch," Zagaran said as Magic flattened her ears, snaked out her head and grabbed his shoulder. He reached out to touch her scarred chest but she reared, striking out at him. He stood his ground, smiling at her, mocking her. It seemed to Shelley, watching them, that an unearthly, almost sinister, understanding existed between them, an emotion not far removed from love, binding man and animal together in a terrible fascination.

Before he could stop her she pushed back the stall door he had pulled shut and walked into Magic's stall.

All of her faculties were concentrated on the horse. Stepping closer, she blew softly against Magic's muzzle. The horse studied her, making up her mind. Then slowly, hesitantly, her ears crept forward. Finally, lifting her head she made a noise like a long sigh and her escaping breath brushed Shelley's cheek.

"Don't ever do that again," Zagaran ordered when she was outside the stall.

"And why not?"

He latched the door shut. "Because it's not safe."

The same reckless confidence and elation that had stirred her to jump the Ballyhoura gate swept over her. "Who wants to be safe?"

He moved so swiftly that her next awareness was of the strength of his arms around her and the hardness of his chest when she rested her cheek against it. There was no violence in his kiss. Instead there was a gentle certainty about it, more devastating than passion.

It was a long time before she opened her eyes. She saw the way his hair grew back from his forehead and his eyes, open and probing into hers. She was suddenly conscious of the mouse that skittered across the aisle and vanished under the feed bin, of the odor of dogs and horses, wet leather and well-cured hay, over all of which lingered the haunting astringent scent of Zagaran's expensive lemon lotion.

A sense of wonder and womanliness began stretching to all her nerve centers and then because she had never felt this weakening, this losing of herself from herself, before, she sought to escape. Trembling, she stepped backward, stumbling over a hound. There was a yelp of anguish and the pack awakened as one. Pointing their noses skyward, they filled the stormy night with their lonely spine-tingling cry.

In the instant before his arms closed around her she saw Cam's face, heard her child calling for her in the night. She tried to draw away but something had happened to her body and it would no longer obey her.

Her instinct had told her he knew everything there was to know about making love and her instinct had been right. It was as if he had grown up in the land of her body and, just as he had known the land over which they had ridden that day, he had known its geography by heart. His hands played over her as deftly as the flickering firelight.

"I want to look at you," he murmured when she tried to switch off the lamp.

She shut her eyes and saw the couple in the glade beside the pool, the girl's fingers digging into the man's muscled back. The gold earrings dropped to the floor and then there was nothing but desire as blinding as the snow, forcing her for the first time in her life to reach out to a man.

"Please. Oh, please."

She opened her eyes to find him looking down at her, studying her in a curious impersonal way, as if he had held himself separate from the coming together that had just taken place. He reached down and drew the curtain of hair back from her face.

"Most women would have cut it off."

"I'm not most women."

"No." He bent his dark head and kissed the corner of her mouth. "You're not most women."

Far away, above the noise of the wind and his breath against her ear, a fox barked. In reply, a hound raised its voice to the night.

He lay beside her, asleep, one arm flung over his head. It had stopped snowing and in the white light that came in through the window glass of the bedroom his dark face remained taut, strained, as though even in repose it continued to reflect some inward battle of his own making. They had gone upstairs to bed, where he smoked one cigarette and then unpredictably, the way he seemed to do everything, he had gone suddenly to sleep. She lay beside him wide awake, marveling at what had happened, feeling a tingling excitement and new-found awareness, wanting to talk about things she hadn't thought of in years or ever intended to tell anyone about.

So she watched him, longing to caress him, and yet restrained by an instinctive fear that came from not knowing how he would react. He moved restlessly onto his side. The urge to touch him became irresistible.

"No!" He lashed out at her so suddenly and with such violence that she recoiled, retreating to the far side of the bed. He sat up and glanced around dazedly. "I was dreaming."

"A nightmare?"

"Yes." He reached for his cigarettes. "It's always the same dream. I'm being tagged and put on a train." He reached out and drew her to him.

"Tell me about it."

"Not now."

In the vacuum that followed pleasure came panic. Desire appeased, conscience regained. Never having known ecstasy, she had never known the need for it. Now that she knew him to be the instrument of it, she must flee before she became dependent.

In the morning she found the telephone. It had been lifted from its stand and shoved on the floor of the closet under the coats. Impulsively she lifted the receiver. As the dial tone sounded in her ear she felt betrayed.

NINETEEN

THE Young Huntsman, out looking for hounds in the hound truck, found them riding home in the bright sunlight of the clear November morning, already melting the unseasonable snow. He told them that he had walked with Tatine until they found a telephone. The truck and trailer had come from the kennels to pick them up and collect the dead horse. He had taken the liberty of reimbursing his brother-in-law for the fence. He apologized for Mellick's truculent attitude. "It pains me to say this," he explained, "but he's mean as a Free Zone copperhead."

After loading the hounds into the truck he politely tipped his cap to them and drove off to Ballyhoura for the horse van.

"We could have called from the Hunting Box," Shelley said. "I got a dial tone."

"Then somebody's had it reconnected," Zagaran answered blandly. "Possibly Tatine. She's been spending a lot of time there lately."

She realized he was not going to make any admissions and suddenly she did not want him to. It had happened, and there was no going back to what had been before.

Virginia City was waiting at the stable door when the big red Ballyhoura van with the blue lettering on the side drove up.

"You all right, Miss Shelley?" he asked worriedly as they opened the door to unload Lookout Light. "We've been anxious."

She explained about being caught in the storm and staying overnight with friends on the far side of the hunting country. "The way we used to in the olden days," she said.

The old stableman was reassured. After checking Lookout Light to see if he was sound and unharmed, he led him off to do him up.

Cam and the dogs rushed to meet her. "I cried and cried," he said accusingly. "There wasn't anybody to hear my prayers and cover me up. Where were you?"

"Darling." Kneeling down, Shelley took him in her arms. "Why aren't you in kindergarten?"

"Wasn't anybody to take me," Cam said.

"I never dreamed I wouldn't get home. It was the snow." She turned to Suellen. "How are you, Suellen?"

"I'se feelin' mighty gaseous," Suellen replied, patting her swollen stomach. "Mrs. Baldwin called. Wanted to know where you were. Said she didn't see you to the breakfast. Mr. Latimer called from the city. He'll be home this afternoon. Mrs. Jackson wants to know 'bout writin' a story 'bout this house. I done fall over dat dog." She pointed to Lance accusingly. "And hurt mah leg sumpn' awful!"

"She did." Cam nodded. "She cussed sumpn' awful!"

"Cam!" Shelley exclaimed.

Suellen tossed her head. Her eyes flashed angrily. "Ah could a had a missed carriage due to dat old dog." She glared at Shelley. "Plenty a places where the pay's bettuh and ah won't be tre-eated like a slave."

Shelley bit her lip. She was about to tell her to go and pack and get out when the thought struck her that if she didn't have anybody to replace Suellen she would be tied to the house, unable to hunt—or be with Zagaran.

"I'm sorry, Suellen," she apologized. "I'm tired and edgy. Please stay. We need you. Now tell me what you want and I'll go to the supermarket."

Suellen sniffed. "I just want to be treated human-like," she said, heading back to the kitchen.

When Shelley returned from the store Suellen handed her the note that had come from Ballyhoura: "You have only been gone an hour but it seems like a lifetime."

That afternoon Shelley drove along the Valley road once again. The mountains were still dusted with the sudden snowfall. At the Jenneys' the field that Hunter had plowed lay veined with a thin coating of snow. The barn stood weathered and gray in the background, like an Andrew Wyeth painting.

"I lost my marbles under the seat," Cam said as they pulled up in front of the house. "Augie Schligman gave them to me. I wanted to show them to Rob-Rob."

"I daresay they'll turn up. Now why don't you head on out and play with the boys while I talk to Mrs. Jenney."

Enid was stirring up a cake, her eyes as blue and direct as her china bowl. Shelley expelled two cats curled into orange balls on the rocker and sat down in front of the kitchen fire. The apple-wood logs cracked and the kettle hissed on the stove. Enid with her children and her cats, her hearthside and devoted husband, would not know what it was like to be torn, pulled one way by passion, another by responsibility.

"Tea?" Enid offered. "Shelley, you look as if you could use some."

"Thanks." Shelley nodded.

"Shelley," Enid asked, starting to pour the tea, "what's wrong?"

I can't tell her, Shelley thought. Unburdening herself to Enid would draw a curtain between them that would afterward be difficult to penetrate. It was like her feelings about her painting. The more she cared, the harder it was to talk about it.

"I'm all right. Just tired. We had a long day yesterday and when I got home I had a go-around with Suellen."

Enid handed her a cup of tea. "I understand you were caught in the storm?"

Shelley's hand holding her cup wobbled. "Where did you hear that?"

"Mattie Moore. I gave her a lift into town. She said she saw you riding home this morning—with Zagaran."

Enid waited, and when Shelley didn't speak she went on. "Shelley is there anything you want to tell me? That's what friends are for. Are you having trouble with Mike?"

"I'm not having trouble with Mike," Shelley answered sharply. "Why should I be?"

Enid returned to her mixing bowl. "I know it's none of my business. Mike's been working so hard. Why don't you let me keep Cam so you can go on a vacation, a long weekend?"

Shelley bent her head. "You're good, Enid. So kind. Forgive me. I'm tired."

"Remember, you can count on me." She began pouring the batter into a pan. While she busied herself with the cake she told Shelley about the windows that had been broken at The Valley Day School.

"The private school children are supposed to be well brought up," Enid said. "Still they run wild. Take Tatine Zagaran, bombing up and down the road in that five-thousand-dollar sports car—a mother who's a lush, a father like Zagaran." Enid banged the oven door shut and stood up. "Shelley, what would you do? How would you change your life if you believed in the devil, if you thought of him as a living entity here in this valley?"

Shelley glanced quickly at Enid. It was as if her friend suddenly knew, without being told, as if some new look or mark had given her away. She tried to laugh. "I suppose I'd exorcise him."

"I think about these things a lot," Enid continued. "I see The Valley, what's happened to it, I hear the way people talk to and about one another. Shelley, look out the window at the sky, the fields and meadows and woods. We have this fabulous land. Yet it's a country without compassion or kindness. How can a sport as beautiful as your foxhunting, as soul-satisfying as you say it is, breed such cruelty, such vindictiveness?"

"It isn't the sport that's at fault," Shelley answered defensively. "It's the people."

"Little people," Enid said. "Spoiled little people who climb up on big horses and think that gives them power, the prerogative to look down on others. Yesterday when you came through somebody took down the barway and didn't put it up again. The ponies got out." She poured more tea. "How can people with no respect for the property of others teach their children to respect established laws?"

"Why blame Zagaran?" Shelley flared. "He didn't leave the barway down. We jumped it." She stopped, remembering what he had said about the people who choose to go through gates or jump them.

"No, but as Master he's responsible."

"Enid, I'm confused," Shelley admitted. "When I'm with you I know you're right. You and Hunter stand for the good things and somehow you never seem to doubt. When I'm away from you I waver. I'm torn between your world and that other."

"All women want a Zagaran," Enid said perceptively. "A knight on a white horse to come riding by. Often the women here get to care more for the horse than the man. Shelley, Zagaran isn't the knight in shining armor you think he is. The true knight is Mike, your husband."

. . .

When he returned late that afternoon Mike seemed very tired. "I missed you," he said. "I called last night to see if you had gotten home safely from hunting."

Cam saved her from having to explain. "Suellen was sick," he said clearly. "She said she had dire-rear and went and lay down on your bed."

"She said she had what?" Mike started to laugh.

"Diarrhea," Shelley said. "Feeling gaseous."

"I had fried eggs for supper." Cam made a face.

"What's the matter with fried eggs?" Shelley asked. She must take him to the barber. When he bent over his plate the hair that grew in the hollow at the back of his neck curled over his red turtleneck sweater. She reached out and touched it, marveling at its texture, soft as the down on the speckled hen's newborn chicks in the box beside the stove.

"The middles are squishy." Cam moved his head away from her hand. "Yuk!"

"I think I'll hit the sack," Mike said when dinner was over. "Tad kept us up most of the night—talking."

"Is that all you did? Talk?"

"Well, we did do some drinking," Mike admitted.

For a long time, unable to sleep, Shelley lay beside him, staring at the darkened ceiling overhead. Her relief when he did not try to make love to her was an additional guilt suffocating her.

In the days following the Opening Meet she made a determined attempt to forget what had happened at the Hunting Box. Yet she could no more do this than she could forget the crimson roses that came the next afternoon with the earrings, gold foxheads with ruby eyes, buried in their midst, or the daily notes.

She was absorbed by her happiness and unhappiness, her exultation and her shame. She wondered why it was that to others, Samantha Sue for instance, who had known many lovers, it was part of a pattern of life, whereas to her it was a kind of agony.

Perhaps it had begun the night of the ball when, unconsciously, she had first begun to reject her husband. Hers was a heritage of rebellion and rejection. A heritage that rejected reality.

Now Zagaran was becoming her only reality. At night she lay rigid, unable to sleep. She prayed Mike would not touch her, and the fact of her shrinking from him added to her shame and guilt.

The abstinence that had come to characterize her relationship with Mike now served as a potent aphrodisiac. Nothing had prepared her for the desire that had overcome her that wild snow-filled night at the Hunting Box. Yet instinctively she knew that to continue her relationship with Zagaran would be to cut off her way back to sanity, to that world where Mike and Cam lived, and wherein lay her security.

Wednesday night Mike stayed late at the *Sun* to wind up the week's rewrite. Tonight he was later than usual. The one naked light bulb hanging on its long cord outlined his shirt-sleeved figure hunched over the battered portable which seemed an extension of himself. The typewriter that skipped letters and made a loud clatter had been to Korea with him, to Asia when he did the series on postwar Japan, and the unpublished novel that lay in the bottom of the filing cabinet had been written on it. The typewriter, with its margins that kept slipping and its keys from which the letters had been worn away, seemed a human thing with whom he had communed for long hours in this dim dust-ridden place. To discard it or turn it in on a new one would be like turning his back on an old friend.

In the corner Miehle, curled on a pile of moldering newsprint, lifted his head. As the footsteps outside the plate-glass window went on past, the Labrador sighed and went back to sleep, his black jowls slack over his crossed paws.

Illuminated by the orange glow of the hanging light bulb, the editor was easily seen through the unwashed window. In the past Doc Dickerson and other businessmen walking home from work had often stopped in for a cup of coffee, "bringing news off the street." But now, for weeks, nobody had stopped in.

Once Mike had dreaded the drop-ins. Now he found himself lifting his head in the manner of the Labrador to listen, unconsciously hoping for the interruptions he had formerly found so frustrating.

He missed, for one thing, being able to talk to the Reverend Chamberlain. He had been one of the few people in The Valley with whom Mike felt at ease. However, the minister had stopped by the week before and announced he was leaving.

"I have no choice. Togo Baldwin came to see me. He was apologetic but firm. Said a new pastor was coming from the seminary. I'm tired, Mike," the minister concluded. "I haven't been feeling well. Going to Florida and sit in the sun and fish."

Now the dark, shadowed office, smelling of ink and newsprint and molten metal, which had once seemed an oasis of friendly warmth, seemed merely drafty, dusty and cluttered, and as the night hours wore on, infinitely lonely.

He looked at the pile of releases he had written and thought of going home. Then he remembered he still had an editorial to write. Ambrose Webster had telephoned to report that one of his steers had died. Laboratory tests had proved the animal to be rabid. This had thrown the farmer into a panic. Now, he determined to shoot all the foxes he could find.

"Those damned foxhunters," he exploded. "I've tried to go along with them. Even after the hounds got into my pigpen, scared the shoats to death and killed one of my turkeys. That redheaded Zagaran girl was real apologetic. I agreed to put in a gate and a panel so that The Hunt could get through my big pasture. Not now. No sir. Land's closed. The old Master used to go around and visit the landowners. Take the farmers a bottle and have a drink with 'em at Christmastime. Work with people 'stead of runnin' over top of 'em."

Mike thought about the farmer's words. Work with people instead of running over them. Rapidly he began to type.

Suddenly he paused. As sometimes happens when one is very tired, the spelling of the word "epidemic," a word he had been writing almost daily for months, evaded him. Groggily he rubbed his forehead with the back of his hand. As he did so he realized that his pipe, clenched between his teeth, had gone out. Swiveling his chair around, he reached for the can of tobacco holding down the papers in the copy basket.

The explosion, followed by the sound of splintering glass, was deafening. The can dropped from Mike's hand, spraying tobacco over the papers on the desk. The Labrador, panicked by the noise, ran behind the filing cabinet, where, whining and scratching, he tried to dig a hole in the concrete floor in which to hide.

Mike stared at the spilled tobacco. Automatically he began to scrape it up. As he turned he saw the bullet imbedded in the beaverboard partition directly in front of where his head had been.

．．．

Aware that the case would drag on indefinitely and that he would be fighting a losing battle in the county courts, Mike did not try to have Major Southgate DeLong prosecuted. He asked that he be taken to the Veterans Hospital, where he was given a psychiatric examination and diagnosed as suffering from hardening of the arteries and senility. Greg Atwell, the longtime family lawyer, holding power of attorney, signed the papers that committed him to the institution. DeLong Manor and its remaining run-down eroded acreage was bought by Zagaran's recently formed Ballyhoura Land Corporation.

Naomi went to work for the Schligmans. But after years of employment without supervision or schedule, she found herself unable to adjust to accepting orders. Routine and the predictability of a large weekly paycheck that came on time proved too boring to put up with. Naomi retired to Muster Corner, where she helped Delia turn out the chitterlings and greens that were cooked on an old wood stove in the kind of kitchen she was used to, without the modern appliances and insistence on cleanliness that had characterized her brief sojourn at the Schligmans'.

Artaxerxes was put down and sent to the kennels for the hounds, and seven truckloads of rubbish—yellowed newspapers dating back to Reconstruction days, tin cans, bottles, empty cartons of shells, cracked, broken riding boots and shoes and pieces of tack—were carted away from the crumbling manor house.

"My father used to say that the definition of aristocracy is the length of time it takes for a family to disintegrate," Shelley told Mike. "The DeLongs were a great family once. Now there's nothing left. Thank God he missed you," she added, realizing that she meant it. Briefly the bullet had penetrated her self-absorption, and she put aside her pleasures involving meetings with Zagaran to collect copy from the country correspondents and help out on press night.

For although the Major was put away and the plate-glass window repaired, memory of his bullet and the closeness with which it had come to ending Mike's life stayed with her. It also touched off a chain of circumstances that was to make it no longer possible for The Valley to disassociate itself from the civil rights problem.

The Major, previously denigrated as a crackpot and a bore, suddenly became a hero. Lines firmed up. Opposition solidified.

"Like I say, the Major now, he was just doing what he considered his Christian duty," Doc Dickerson pontificated from behind his empty lunch counter. "Doing his duty as he done seen it," the druggist continued, leaning his elbows on the marble countertop and lifting his voice so that those sitting at the tables could hear him. "Them interferin' nobodies from up No'th just don' understand. Our nigras are happy nigras. They know we take care of 'em."

"You're right," Charlie Woodruff from the news store said emphatically, joining the conversation. "Our good nigras ain't gonna make no trouble. It's them agitators like that Martin Luther Coon and that preacher that runs the school!"

"Do-gooders and bleeding hearts like Latimer," Polo Pete chimed in, "coming down here and messing up a relationship that's been good and beautiful for hundreds of years."

Public school integration ground to a standstill.

Senator Telly Talbot made an impassioned speech in which he said that county schools would be closed rather than integrated and promised that state funds would be provided to open private schools.

Shelley and Mike attended a PTA meeting at The Valley Country Day School. Shelley had been a member of the first graduating class, and as Cam would enter first grade the following year they were prospective parents. It developed into a stormy session. Mike had promised Washington Taylor to find out if Lucy Mae Taylor, who met all the qualifications in the bylaws and had been found to have an IQ superior to that of any of the Valley Day School children, could enter in the fall. When he raised the question as to whether or not a qualified Negro child would be accepted, he was met with a shocked silence. Finally Millicent Black, who was president and chairman of the board, rose. "How much is the N double-ACP paying you?"

Before Mike could reply, Togo Baldwin was on his feet. Pointing his finger at Mike, he cried, "Some of us Virginia gentlemen think it would be a very good idea if you Yankees went back home and let us alone. Then we might have a chance to solve our own problems in our own way."

Mike glanced hastily around. Aside from Greg Atwell, Hunter Jenney and Togo Baldwin, he did not see any others in the audience who qualified as Southerners.

"That might be a good idea," Mike replied calmly. "Of course," he added, "it would be expensive. The Virginia gentlemen might have to buy up some of the valuable property in the county that's owned by Yankees." He looked around at the Northerners in the room, the people who had moved to The Valley from Boston and New York, from Long Island and New Jersey. "You might have to build a high wall," he went on quietly, "a kind of Berlin barricade to maintain your own private Confederate enclave."

"Gentlemen!" Crocker Stephens rose to his feet. Knowing which side his intellectual bread was buttered on, the headmaster smiled his nervous, conciliatory smile and said, "I suppose that if I were to visit the parents of these Negro children I would find sets of encyclopedia in their libraries." He paused, and then glancing around for approval, delivered his punch line. "In irregular plural, you know."

This bit of erudition was lost on all but a handful.

Millicent grabbed the floor again. "We're not beholden to the Supreme Court. *We* don't have to lower our standards to accommodate them."

Mike controlled himself. "Integration is bound to come. By integrating the lower grades, having white and colored youngsters go to school together as a matter of course from the beginning, the evolution will take place naturally."

This brought Polo Pete to his feet again. "You want your son to go to a decent school or a progressive school?" He glared at Mike. "What happens when they get to be teenagers? They might get to like one another!"

"It might be wiser to start them off in, say, eighth grade," Connie Jackson said seriously. "By then we'd have taught our children enough about niggers for them to know not to mix."

Mike started to say more, but a glance at the faces around him stopped him. Whatever he said would be of no avail. It was as though a door had been slammed shut and locked, a wall built between himself and those looking at him.

"If you ask me," Millicent said positively, ending the discussion, "the trouble with the children today is that none of them are brought up with proper nannies!"

Millicent had made clear that if any serious consideration was given to the possibility of admitting a colored child, she would cancel her gift to the building fund. As the new building was considered essential and the contribution from Millicent's grandfather's foundation substantial, nobody dissented. Mike's own particular area of hypocrisy kept him from speaking. Cam would enter first grade the following fall. In principle, Mike should have put him in public school. But this would have caused a complete schism in the family. Shelley would never have consented to it and Cam would have been distressed at being separated from his friends. Perhaps this very thing was at the bottom of the world's problems. Fear of speaking out. Fear of taking a stand. Fear of being cut off from one's fellow men.

Because it was not fair to use Cam as a scapegoat for his beliefs and because he was afraid to jeopardize Cam's chances of going to The Valley Day School, Mike remained silent. To each his own Achilles' heel. It was, after all, but a matter of degree.

"Damned if I know what this valley is coming to," grumbled Pete as he set the head for the lead story. "Rabid fox situation worse," he quoted. "In the country you got to carry a stick to beat off foxes. Here in town you need a gun to protect yourself from people. Listen, Editor"—he turned to Mike—"you better start toting a gun."

Mike did. For a week he carried the pistol he had worn in Korea. At the end of the week he took it home, put it back in its case and locked it away in the bottom of his footlocker, where it would be safe from Cam.

"Why did you do that?" Pete asked him curiously.

"I'm not sure," Mike said. "Except that carrying it gave me a funny feeling. It was as though I was no different from them, the people who call up and write letters. It made me feel dirty."

"Sorry, Mike," Herm Gillespie told him when he stopped by the general store. He did not look at Mike. "I've been going over my books. Decided to cut down on advertising for a while."

"Cut down or cut out?"

"Well, as long as you put it that way, I guess what I mean is that I'm going to try the *Daily* for a while. They've got that new offset process and they sure do make my ads come up nice."

"You told me that last ad I made up for you brought in four new customers."

"Could be," Gillespie replied evasively. "I just feel like making a change."

Mike decided to stop off at the Covertside Inn and have a beer before starting to make up the paper. Jake Bronstein was at the bar. Jake was editor of the Buford-owned *Daily*. Once he had been bigtime, a political reporter for the *Capital Courier*, but age and alcohol had taken their toll. Now he wore the breezy, cynical air of one who has stopped caring, as indicated by his rumpled clothes and flab and nicotined fingers that trembled when he lifted his glass.

"If it isn't William Allen White himself," he said by way of greeting. "Sit down and tell me how it feels to be the John Brown of Bellevue County. Christ, Mike, why don't you quit?" He shoved aside a quarter-page ad that Herm Gillespie had given him. "You can't buck Buford. And you know something? He may be right. Take this integration thing. You and I come from the North. Now people here in the South feel differently. September when Shelburn desegregated, I had the story set up for the front page. It was already locked up, ready to go onto the press. In comes the publisher. I said the story ought to stand. It was running in the Washington papers. It was news. Buford blew up. He shouted and pounded the desk. Then he fired me. Told me if the story was run, so would I be—right out of town."

"So that's why you didn't publish it?"

Jake looked away. "What could I do?" In one long gulp he drained his beer. "Say, how about another? Damned blue laws. Can't buy anything stronger."

"No, thanks." Mike stood up. "Got to go see the advertisers." He looked down at Jake. "Not that it'll do any good. Your boy was in Shelburn yesterday." He dug into his pocket and brought out some change. "Here's for the beer. When you set up Herm Gillespie's ad, remember there are two L's."

"I'll be at the farmhouse tonight." The note came the day before Thanksgiving.

"You're late," he said when she came in. He was standing with his back to the fire and his face told her nothing. As the shadows played across his features she could not tell if he were sorry or glad. The fox he had tamed curled in the chintz-covered chair in the corner. In the shadows it looked black and its eyes, open and watchful, held a baleful, menacing light.

"I almost didn't get here," she answered, feeling rebuffed. "I mean it's been weeks." She shrugged out of her sable coat and flung it on a chair.

"That is a coat!" His voice was admiring. "Wherever did you get it?"

"It was my grandmother's. One of the things she left me, along with a strong sense of guilt. The coat and the guilt counteract one another." She walked over to the fire. "I can't stay long. There's only Virginia City at home."

He smiled then and with a slow certainty reached out and drew her to him. "I've been away. Setting up a new corporation. I've missed you."

She buried her face against the shoulder of his jacket, smelling the familiar smell of Turkish tobacco and lemony aftershave lotion. His arm tightened around her, drawing her closer.

"Did you miss me?"

"Yes," she whispered. "Oh, yes."

She rubbed her face against his chest and then, because she was suddenly filled with so much unaccustomed emotion, pushed away from him. She went to the sofa and sat down, her back straight, her feet flat on the floor, feeling suddenly shy and ill at ease.

"Champagne?" he asked, lighting one of the Turkish cigarettes that were especially blended for him. "I put some on ice."

"Nothing." She clasped her hands around her knees and stared into the fire.

"So you don't want a drink," he said with sudden irritation. "Damn it, we both know why we're here!" He threw his cigarette into the fire and went to her.

"If you would just turn off the light—"

"I like to look at you." He began unbuttoning the vivid Pucci blouse Millicent had given her for Christmas the year before.

"My grandmother used to say that baring one's bosom in public was like giving away family secrets. I wonder what she would say if she could see me now."

"I'm not the public."

The wind swept down from the mountains, rattling the eaves of the old house, blowing smoke into the room.

"A sullen fire." Zagaran rose and went to shake it up. The fox's eyes followed him, gleaming like the sparks that shot out as the poker struck the charred logs.

When the fire was burning properly he went to the refrigerator for more wine. Shelley watched him return and uncork the bottle. The wind, the firelight, the fox in the corner, the dark face added to the strangeness and mystery that surrounded him and which she had yet to penetrate. Whenever she tried to question him, find out where he came from, why he had come to The Valley, he put her off, sending out sparks of anger and bitterness that seared her like the fire. The more she was with him the less she seemed to know him, and because of this she continued to persist, thinking that if she could discover the secret of his being, the thing that drove him to greater ambitions and extended efforts she could find some justification for the hold he now had upon her.

She looked at the special label on the wine bottle, on which his name and that of Ballyhoura had been printed.

"You've never told me what the B stands for."

"Bastard," he said, handing her a glass.

"No, seriously."

"Seriously. All I knew for a father was a jaunty man in a high silk hat, sitting on a coach, flourishing a whip in a faded photograph on my mother's dressing table." He stopped abruptly and drained his glass. "Once you told me you only liked thoroughbreds. What do you say now?"

Shelley pretended not to have heard. She took a swallow of her drink and reached for a cigarette in the silver box on the table. Automatically he brought out his lighter and lit it for her. The unaccustomed smoke made her cough. He took the cigarette from her and ground it out in the ashtray.

"Beauty and the bastard. What would your father say now?"

She gazed at the fox, its eyes fixed on them, watchful and wary behind their phosphorescence.

"Zagaran, what makes you the way you are? Trusting nothing and nobody, like your fox?"

He refilled his glass. "The stink of poverty," he said bitterly. "Cabbage cooking and musty rooms where the shades are never raised so you won't see the dying, day by day. My stepfather was a choreographer who escaped from Russia after the revolution.

My mother, who was French, danced in his ballet company. When she became ill with TB he abandoned her. My mother lay in a room under the eaves in a Paris pension. I took care of her—" He broke off and lit a cigarette. "After her funeral the nuns wrote my destination on a tag and pinned it to my jacket. They asked me my name. It was then that I realized I had none."

"That's the dream that makes you cry out in the night."

His body stiffened and when he did not speak she put her hands on his shoulders.

"Zagaran—" He twisted violently away from her. She sat up straight and defiant. "Zagaran, it's not who you are, it's what you do that counts." She didn't realize until after she had spoken that she was quoting Mike.

With the devastating suddenness with which he changed moods, he drew her close. "You've lost an earring," he said, his lips against her throat.

"I'll find it later." Her mouth moved against his. "Bastard!"

"What did you say?"

"I said bahstard." She pronounced it with a broad A. "It's a term of endearment in the South."

When she arrived home she looked in on Cam. Briefly the sight of her child, his profile pressed against the pillow, the frayed Kitty-Kat cradled against his chest, restored her balance. Certainly she had never meant to let herself fall in love with B. Zagaran. In the beginning she had intended to humble him, show him up as the raider she had taken him to be. When she found herself becoming involved she had thought she could still remain safe. Now she felt herself unable to stop. It was like riding a runaway. She should jump off and save herself yet she remained frozen in the saddle, powerless to avert whatever fate awaited her.

Gently she moved her son's small fist so that she could cover his chest. Bending over the side of the crib, she kissed him on his forehead. As she did so, the smell of fresh soap and clean skin and woolen sleepers assailed her. It was, she thought, the smell of innocence.

TWENTY

AFTER Thanksgiving, the social tempo of The Valley accelerated. Plans were made for holiday hunt breakfasts, dinners and open houses. Every year the Bufords organized a party around a certain theme taken from a contemporary film or play. The year before it had been *My Fair Lady*, and guests had been invited to come in appropriate costumes, and the orchestra had concentrated on the score of the musical. This year Samantha Sue decided to give a *Tom Jones* party, and The Valley was agog over the costumes that Mrs. Waller, the local dressmaker, had been asked to make.

Aware that her food and drink and entertainment were second to none, Samantha Sue could afford to be selective about her guest list. Each year she carefully culled out those who had offended her in any manner.

Now word went around that Connie Jackson, who had alluded to the dinner after Tatine Zagaran's ball in her column, commenting that "certain members of the Go-Go set conducted themselves in a manner hardly to the manor born," would not be invited. Nor would Debby Darbyshire, who had said that the Peale painting Polo Pete had bought for a high price was a fake; or the Latimers and their coterie, which included Misty Montague and the Jenneys, who, it was believed, had betrayed The Hunt by fencing off their property with hated wire. Following Samantha Sue's lead, several other hostesses crossed the Latimers off their list. Thus, as the Christmas season approached, the engagement pad beside the telephone remained blank, and the invitations on the board in the hall were no longer stacked one atop the other for Connie Jackson to ogle enviously when she stopped by to collect for the ASPCA.

It was hard for Shelley to understand that she was no longer in a position to choose. That the Schligmans, whom she had made jokes about, should now be among the few to include Mike and herself at one of their parties was a blow to the special status quo she had been brought up to believe nothing could ever topple.

Now, although she dreaded facing the people she had considered her friends and felt herself a hypocrite for accepting the invitation, she determined to go to the party, wear her best dress and pretend everything was as it always had been.

Zagaran would not be there. The new construction corporation was requiring a great deal of his time. When not foxhunting he was traveling. In the hunting field they spoke to each other casually, in passing. It gave Shelley a perverse satisfaction to wonder what people would think or say if they knew his background and their real relationship to each other.

Shelley had not been to the Templeton house since the Schligmans had bought it. In The Valley, nobody ever called on anybody else. This, the residents claimed, was part of the Valley mystique. Unlike Greenwich or Lake Forest or others of what Mike called sub-bourbon communities revolving around the country club and committees, one could live here for years without encountering one's neighbors. People moved in, stayed a year or two, and moved away without anyone being the wiser. Occasionally somebody asked what happened to the Warners or the Thompsons or the Byrneses, but unless they had undergone the curious assimilation process and achieved acceptance in the In Group, they faded from the communal stream without a ripple.

The Schligmans' invitation was for dinner the Saturday before Christmas. Roosevelt and the air-conditioned crested passionate pink Cadillac drove to each house with a six-pack of Schligman beer (the new-type can with the pop-up top) accompanied by the party booklet called *Parties with Pizazz*, recipes for food cooked in beer, which Augie boasted of having put together himself.

Mike was enthusiastic when Shelley showed him the invitation. "I like Augie. There's no nonsense about him. He came into the office and took out three subscriptions. One for himself, one for a married daughter in Milwaukee, and one for My Boy Hambone in the stable. I thought it was damned decent of him. Then he began talking about his horses, laughing at how he'd been taken by Fax and the locals. He's one of the few foxhunters I've met who can laugh at himself. I asked him why he moved here. He

432

said because he liked the country and his daughter Judy was crazy about horses."

The night of the party was bitter cold. Snow had fallen the day before and in the evening light the fields lay blue-white. Trees and walls and the flamingo pond fronting the house stood out starkly against a milky cloud-scudded sky. The winding drive to the house was icy.

The turning circle had been graveled and widened and a parking space squared off in what had been Fax's mother's cutting garden. The old house, which had weathered until it seemed a natural outcropping of the hillside on which it was built, had been painted the color of the Schligman beer cans and racing colors. Shelley called it hippopotamus-mouth pink (the trade name was flamingo). On the left of the house the old stone barn, where in Shelley's childhood the Rebs had hidden out from the Yanks, had been transformed into a glass guest house that glittered in the moonlight. The homely, hospitable porch had been torn away and replaced with a flagstone terrace, and the front door was flanked by two giant Ali Baba jars.

My Boy Hambone, who doubled as butler when the Schligmans entertained, opened the door.

"Good evening, Hambone," Shelley said politely. "How is your race horse doing?"

"He's a morning glory horse," My Boy Hambone replied, ushering them into the hallway. "Runs real good in the morning."

"I thought racing took place in the afternoons and evenings," Mike said.

"That's the trouble, Mr. Latimer," My Boy Hambone said sadly. "He don't like to run in the evening."

Community Brown accepted Shelley's coat. The hall, formerly a repository for boots and skates, coats and hard hats, whips, bridles and occasionally a saddle, had, like the rest of the establishment, been completely redone. The fine old paneling had been ripped out and replaced with mirrors. An elaborate ebony table stood along the wall with a huge silver bowl of pink hothouse carnations in the center.

Shelley glanced at herself in the mirrored panels. Her reflection was reassuring. She had had her hair done. Now it waved about her face, softening it. There was a restrained excitement

433

and brilliance in her blue-violet eyes which matched the velvet of her long evening skirt. Mrs. Waller had made the skirt from material found in the attic that her grandmother had bought many years ago. It was rich and beautiful—blue, jade and soft pinks against a purple background. The bottom of the skirt was banded with sable. It was very narrow and split up the side. With it she wore a plain black jersey. She had looked around for the gold foxhead earrings Zagaran had given her, but could find only one. Then she remembered she had left the other at the Hunting Box. In place of them she wore her sapphires. She knew she looked well. Still she was nervous. She saw Mike coming from the men's room and turned to him gratefully. Together they walked between the two life-size statues of turbaned blackamoors guarding the entrance to the living room.

The living room was famous. It was forty feet long, with fireplaces My Boy Hambone had used to smoke hams at either end. Now it looked like a Lord and Taylor's showroom.

"Upper class, my dear," Mrs. Dinwiddie murmured to Debby Darbyshire, "but still display."

The fine old woodwork had been replaced with pecky cypress, and although Shelley knew the wormholes to be natural they looked as if each had been carefully drilled. The room, with its fluorescent lighting, had pink wall-to-wall carpeting, pink satin chairs and divans and what Katie would call drapes, but which Shelley had been brought up to call curtains. Hothouse flowers in arrangements and family photographs in massive silver frames stood on the tables.

The wall next to the fireplace at the far end of the room had been knocked out and an enormous mahogany bar erected. The space behind the bar was mirrored like the hall, and shelves had been built to hold an astonishing array of glasses and bottles.

Their host came to greet them, Roosevelt a step behind carrying a large Steuben glass ashtray in which he endeavored to capture the ashes that fell from Augie's wildly animated cigar.

"Look!" Augie exclaimed proudly as he pushed a button in the wall beside the fireplace and the bar, like a revolving stage set, vanished. "Presto!" He pushed another button. Slowly the wall swiveled around once again, disclosing Manassas Brown and Billy Joe Wilkerson working behind it. "How about that?"

"Flairy, don't you think?" Dickie Speer came up behind her.

434

"Don't those drapes grab you? I picked out the brocade in Hong Kong. Sweetie, if you look closely you can see concubines, flying fish, bridges. Real jazzy, sweetie." The decorator's eyes traveled up and down her, taking in the luxurious material and her jewels. "Sweetie, you do dress a room. Tell me, what *is* this I hear about you—"

Shelley was never to know what he intended to say, for the decorator's attention was grabbed by Bebe Bruce wearing a gold dress so skin-tight it left nothing to the imagination.

"She cuts holes in her bras," Millicent said as Dickie bounded past to greet Beebe. "So the nipples show."

"Fat lot he cares," replied Debby Darbyshire.

"Mama isn't down yet." Augie glanced toward the entranceway. "Can't imagine what's keeping her. Let me get you both a drink. Editor, what'll it be?" He lowered his voice. "Say, I liked that editorial about human rights." He glanced quickly around. "I realize you've gotta be careful around here."

Shelley saw Enid Jenney sitting on the sofa and went to join her.

"Good evening, Mrs. Dinwiddie," she said politely, passing in front of the Four H's sitting to one side. The Beast, droopy in purple crepe held together with a large opal brooch, gave her a frozen smile and turned to Debby. "When are we going to eat?"

"Mama hasn't shown yet," Debby said. "Probably can't get her eyebrows on straight." Shelley remembered hearing that Katie sometimes took as long as an hour to put on her make-up.

Although they were discussing their hostess, she felt their eyes following her. "Whew, I feel as if I'd just run through a brush fire," she said as she sank down next to Enid.

Enid didn't hear her. She was watching Katie Schligman, poised hesitantly in the doorway. She looked as if she were about to go on stage to take a bow and was not sure how she would be received. She wore floor-length pink satin with a wide full skirt, and on her low-necked bodice diamonds glittered, as well as along her arms, on her fingers and in her hair. This was meticulously piled into a high pompadour, resembling a pouf of pink cotton candy, and her theatrical make-up gave her face a painted, expressionless look, as if a smile might cause it to crack. There was a queer bright shine in her eyes, and when you looked closely it was possible to see how pale she was beneath her pancake and that the perfect line of her left eyebrow was marred by an almost imperceptible squiggle.

"Poor thing," Enid said, "she looks scared to death."

"My God, she won't be able to lift her arms with all that jewelry!" Millicent exclaimed loudly. Then she was advancing on Katie crying, "Katie, darling, how lovely you look. What sweet little diamonds. Do you buy them by the bushel?"

"What a marvelous bracelet," Dickie Speer said to no one in particular. "I *do* like money!"

Shelley got up, crossed the room and, ignoring Millicent, said warmly, "You look lovely. It's good of you to have us here tonight."

Bebe was behind her. "Darling Katie," she said, embracing her. "I understand you've got music coming. You must sing 'The Rosary' for us."

Some color came into Katie's cheeks. "I'm afraid I'm late. I had trouble dressing. Has Dad given you a drink?"

Katie had expended every effort toward making this, her first dinner party in The Valley, memorable. Not a detail, from the flower arrangements to the beer cheese bisque and chive butter, to the *Apfelstrudel*, to be followed by a recital in the new conservatory, had been overlooked. It was to be, as she told her husband, an evening of culture. "Genteel. I want people to know that we're refined, not just bourgeois beer people with money." Tossing her cotton-candy head, Katie had added, "We'll show them, Dad, that Augie Schligman and Katie O'Connor are just as good as they are."

As it turned out, the evening *was* memorable, in fact unforgettable, but not for the reasons Katie had intended.

After dinner everyone was ushered into the conservatory, where potted palms and a string quartet, imported from New York, were set up. Chairs had been borrowed from Wilbur Robertson, the undertaker, and were ranged in rows. When everyone was seated, programs especially printed for the occasion were distributed.

"I don't d-d-d-dig this M-m-m-Mozart fella," Fax whispered to Bebe. "Give me 'That Old Black Magic.'"

Most of the audience agreed with him. They stirred restlessly, crossing and uncrossing legs, rustling programs and whispering to one another.

"You needn't be so bloody rude," Bebe said to Fax as they headed for the bar during intermission. "The least you could do is sit still."

"People in the hunt country can't sit still," Fax answered bluntly.

"In God's name, why not?" persisted Bebe.

"Why, honey"—Fax turned to her in surprise—"all h-h-horsey people have h-h-h-hemorrhoids."

Shelley went to the ladies' room. As she entered, she heard Millicent's strident "Shit! I'm surprised she didn't ask the Schligmans if she could bring some of her colored friends, the ones she's always shaking hands with in the supermarket."

"Shelley wouldn't do that." Shelley recognized the voice as that of Tina Welford. "She's a lady."

"So is Misty Montague," Millicent said. "And she goes to all those meetings with Mike Latimer. They're inseparable."

"Yes," Tina admitted. "I saw them on the way to Washington, the day of the Opening Meet."

"Serve Shelley right," Millicent said meanly, "if Mike left her. She's always listening to Bones at parties, taking his side against me, then pretending to be so pure. If you ask me, Andrea Zagaran should have taken up foxhunting. Even if she just hilltopped, she could at least carry a pair of binoculars!"

"Whatever do you mean by that?" Tina sounded mystified. "You can't mean—I never heard of Shelley being involved—"

"Just wait and see," Millicent hinted darkly.

They hate me, Shelley thought, appalled. What have I done to make them hate me so? She heard the door open and then a gasp. With a meaningful glance at Tina, Millicent cried, "Shelley, we didn't know you were waiting."

"Obviously."

"Must be time for more of that ghastly music," Millicent said, unabashed. "All I can do to sit through it. Coming, Tina?"

"Just a minute," Shelley said to Millicent. "I've been a good friend to you, Millicent. I've kept your children and your horses and cooked casseroles and I've listened to your marital problems. Now I've had it. If I hear of you shooting your horses with a BB gun to make them jump, or teasing your mares with a baseball bat to get them in foal, I'll report you to the ASPCA."

I wonder why I didn't report her long ago, Shelley thought, as Millicent swept out. She found her hand was shaking so that she was unable to put on her lipstick. She was also so unnerved that she forgot to look at the life-size oil of a nude over the toilet and the two sunken tubs, side by side, with pink hyacinths planted around them.

Shelley sat next to Enid, waiting for Katie to sing "The Rosary." She was afraid the tears of angry hurt burning her eyeballs would spill over and disgrace her. She had told Enid what she had heard. Her friend, sensing her distress, reached over, took her hand and squeezed it.

"Look at them," Enid said suddenly, violently. "There they sit, smoking and smiling, waiting like beasts to pounce on anybody different, ganging up like Dante's furies, sitting like some court of social judgment, issuing edicts of the most lethal snobbery against anyone who does not accept every one of their midget-minded mores, or taking it out on their children, excluding them, destroying their confidence, talking out of the corners of their mouths to one another, using a different tone to anyone else, and almost everyone else is considered an inferior—"

"Why, Enid," her husband said mildly, "I didn't know you felt so strongly."

"Darn right I feel strongly," Enid said. "The Hunt's had it in for us ever since we complained about the foxes eating our chickens and built the wire fence without leaving room for the foxes and hounds to get under it. An oversight, but they think we did it on purpose." She took a deep breath and continued. "You can play musical beds or get divorced or mistreat your children and horses and dogs and nobody gives a damn. But try doing something for mankind, writing a book or painting a picture and you've had it!"

Shelley felt better. Enid's vehemence mirrored her own. She accepted a glass of draft beer from one of the pitchers being circulated among the guests and settled down to listen to Katie's singing, which brought barely stifled giggles from some of the guests. Katie had a lovely clear contralto but nervousness brought on by the audience's lack of enthusiasm caused her to miss some of the notes.

Shelley realized later she should have asked Mike to take her home, but there was that thing in her, that determined defiance, to show The Valley that she didn't scare and she didn't soil. Had she done so, she might have avoided the advances that suddenly appeared from the most unlikely sources. Bones Black, who, despite her attempts to shut him up, proceeded once again to give her chapter and verse of his marital problems; Fax, who insisted she had always been his one true love; and Greg Atwell, who lunged at her when she went into one of the side rooms in search of Mike. It was as if somehow, in some subtle, intangible way, her status had changed and she was now, due to gossip and conjecture rising around her, suddenly fair game.

She found Mike with Augie, talking animatedly, while Roosevelt darted around him attempting to catch the ashes from his wildly waving cigar.

"I was asking your husband if he thought you'd do me a favor," the big man said.

"Of course," Shelley answered. "What is it?"

He looked away and then went on shyly. "I'd like a painting to hang over the fireplace. You know, a big one, in my new red hunting coat."

"In scarlet," Shelley said, "with perhaps a hound at your feet?"

"That's it, Shelley," he said enthusiastically.

"I'd be glad to, Augie. When would you want it?"

"You mean it?" he cried "You'd do it?"

Shelley smiled at him gratefully. "As soon as the holidays are over we'll get to work."

"That'll be great."

"It was a wonderful party," Shelley and Mike said in unison. "Thanks so much."

Augie's face glowed like the end of his cigar. "You really think so?" he asked eagerly. "No shit?"

As Christmas came and went and the January snows brought hunting to a halt, Shelley became more committed, both obsessed and possessed. Away from Zagaran she felt as though she were moving underwater, going through the days with a remoteness and a detachment that bore no relationship to reality.

Each time she saw him, the guilt that she was able to control through constant activity rose up to smite her with new violence. She told herself that he had lied to her, that he had not been faithful to his wife and was not being faithful to her. When she questioned him about Andrea, still in the sanatorium in Connecticut where she was being treated for acute alcoholism, or Samantha

Sue, who had been on the Caribbean cruise with him, he retorted, "I don't ask you about your husband"—he never mentioned Mike by name—in such a way that she did not dare to query him further.

She sensed that in the power he had come to exert over her and the community lay evil. At times when she was riding, or during the night when she lay awake beside Mike, she remembered the soaring joy of that wild and windswept first night that had made of her body a new thing, cherished and responsive, something wanted and womanly.

They agreed to meet every Thursday. It was a non-hunting day and the day the *Sun* went to press, which meant that Mike would not get home until late. It took but a few minutes in Zagaran's private plane to reach the airport and then to drive to his penthouse in the recently completed apartment building his development corporation had built.

The lower floors were taken up with dentists' and doctors' offices. Zagaran went up ahead of her, warning her to wait and then take the elevator.

"What'll I say if I meet someone?" she asked him.

He shook his head wonderingly. "Miss Shelley, how you can have lived so long! Just say you're going to the dentist."

One day in the lobby she heard a voice call out. "Why, Cousin Shelley, fancy meeting you here." And found herself face to face with Misty Montague. "Shelley, you look so smart. Wherever did you get such a pretty frock?"

Frock, Shelley thought disdainfully. She hadn't heard the word in years. She was conscious of her new black wool, bought at the Fox in the High Hat after Zagaran mentioned seeing it in the window and that it would look well on her, and the earrings he had ordered designed for her in New York, which were intricately made of silver with blue stones to match her eyes. She had also paid one of her rare visits to Miss Esther's beauty salon. From beneath the beret she had bought to match the dress her hair fell in shining waves from her small elegant head.

Shelley, conscious of her new clothes, observed her cousin critically. Beneath her old polo coat Misty wore her brown tweed suit, an inch too long to be fashionable, her "sensible" shoes, brown oxfords with tongues, a yellow cashmere sweater, her pearls and her brown felt riding hat. Very country. Very vicarage, Shelley thought. She felt the way she had when her older cousin had come upon her smoking her first cigarette behind the barn. Misty had not looked disapproving. Nor had she tattled to Miss Marlee or Melusina. All Misty said was "Don't let it become a habit, because it will cut your wind." It was this quality in Misty, her lack of malice and failure to correct or criticize, that made Shelley additionally conscious of her guilt and wrongdoing.

"I had to come to the dentist." Feeling called upon to explain further, she added unnecessarily, "Zagaran was kind enough to give me a lift in his plane."

"Do you go to Dr. Kirkman, too?" Misty asked. "I've just come from him. If you like, I'll wait and give you a lift home. I promised Mike I'd help fold papers." There was a slight pause and then Misty added, "You know Pete is sick and Mike has to run the press."

"Thanks, but no." Shelley forced herself to smile. "I have some shopping to do. Clothes for Cam. I loathe coming to the city. Now that I'm here I want to get everything done that I can."

Misty's face was unreadable. "In that case, Cousin Shelley, I'll be on my way." With the aid of her cane she took two short steps and then looked back. "Any messages for Mike? Will you be coming in later, to fold?"

Shelley felt her cheeks flaming. "No. No messages. Suellen is off. There's nobody to leave Cam with."

"Where is Cam now?"

My God, Shelley thought. Why doesn't she go? "Enid Jenney is picking him up and taking him home for the afternoon." She didn't add that Enid had also agreed to keep Cam for the night.

Zagaran opened the penthouse door. "Darling, you're late." He gave a quick glance at the elevator door sliding shut behind her. "Quick, come in. I've champagne on ice and she-crab soup."

As she shrugged out of her sable coat she realized that she had forgotten to take the price tag off her new dress. Before she could thrust it back out of sight, he ripped it off and dropped it on the floor.

"You're careful about how you're turned out in the hunting field," he said, taking in every detail of her appearance, "yet so careless about how you look when you meet me."

"I suppose you'd like me better if I spent all morning putting on my make-up and having my hair frosted like Samantha Sue."

He pretended not to hear her. "And you should never wear a hat." Reaching up, he snatched the beret from her head and sent it planing across the room.

"Zagaran," she said resignedly, "give me back my hat."

"Why do you need a hat? It's bad luck to wear one in bed."

She laughed. "I need it to throw over the windmill." She told him about Misty.

He shrugged. "Why should you care about her opinion or anyone else's?"

"I value public opinion," Shelley answered. She smiled ruefully. "When I'm about to do something disastrous, like jumping a gate, it generally holds me back." She took the glass of champagne he offered her. "Somehow the old checks and balances don't seem to be working."

"Other people's opinions don't matter," he said stubbornly.

She thought of Cam, how he was at night, buried under the covers, Kitty-Kat clutched to his chest, the gossamer texture of his hair, like milkweed gone to seed.

"Zagaran, they do. People do matter."

"They don't." He spoke with a kind of dogged determination, as though it were necessary to follow the conversation to its conclusion, as if it were important for him to win something from her. "Come here." Taking her hand, he led her up the winding stairs to the great glassed-in bedroom. The curtains had not been drawn and the room was flooded with the pale gray light of the late winter afternoon.

"This is all that matters." He put his hands on either side of her face. "You and me. How we feel about each other."

Shelley walked to one of the great glass walls of the bedroom and stood staring at the lights below. The bedroom was built on the roof of the new apartment building erected by the Zagaran Corporation. He had shown her his plans for further high-rise apartments in the cities, modern communities in suburban areas.

"There's never been building like this before," he told her enthusiastically. "It will make all other housing obsolete." His ideas as he outlined them to her staggered her imagination, like the room in which she now stood.

When the heavy crimson curtains were drawn back they disclosed three walls and a ceiling, all made of glass. Standing in the center of the floor or lying in the vast king-size bed, it was possible to see the Capitol building shining like a jewel against a velvet background studded with stars. From it, the eye moved to the blazing milk-white shaft of the Washington Monument and the Lincoln Memorial, a curving panorama that seemed designed as a spectacular extension of the astonishing room.

"It's as though you ordered Washington, the world, built around you!" Shelley exclaimed the first time she saw the view.

"A wraparound view." He laughed and began to sing, "A wraparound view, designed for you—"

"You didn't know me then." She drew in her breath, smelling his individualistic male smell, Turkish tobacco and the lemony aftershave lotion that somehow became mingled with the scent of wood smoke and roses, hounds and horses and new-mown hay whenever she thought of him.

He stood smiling down at her, the scarred eyebrow giving him that faintly quizzical, mocking look. "I've always known you."

"You don't know I hate turnips. My grandmother used to make me eat them—that was after Melusina began growing them in the old tennis court. I never could get rid of them. Dogs won't eat turnips and the toilet was too far away."

"I don't want to talk about turnips," he said, starting to undo the buttons of her high-necked dress. "I want to know what you do when I . . ."

Later she asked about the painting. It was the only painting in the room, hung on the only available wall space above the bed.

"What is it? Surely not one of your wife's?"

"Of course not. Andrea has never been here. It's called 'Bird Maddened by the Sound of Machinery.' "

Her eyes remained glued to the bird disintegrating beneath waves of red. The painting held a power, a horrible beauty that made it an effort to turn away.

"That's the way you feel, isn't it?"

He nodded. "Either we do the crushing or we get crushed, like the bird."

The buzzer sounded. "What the hell?" He glanced at his watch. "Stupid son of a bitch should have been here hours ago."

"They're the wrong color," she heard him saying angrily to somebody at the entrance. "I ordered red. I always order red.

These are pink." She heard the door slammed shut and then the sound of the departing elevator.

Suddenly the glass room seemed garish, in poor taste. There had been moments when his tendernesses were not for the retelling or even for remembering in the light of day. Then the tautness would come into his face. It would become blank, still, as if something within him were holding its breath. She would sense a kind of wary eagerness and then those strange burning eyes—Heathcliff eyes, she told him once—would darken. His nostrils would flare and she would see the face of the hunter the way it had been when he swung the fox over his head, the way he had looked at her in the gazebo the night of the ball.

There was in him, she realized, a streak of the common, the crude and the earthy. His buccaneering manner, which made her think of men storming the gates of walled cities and standing on the bows of sailing ships, added to the impression that violence, even tragedy, was an acceptable part of the action that surrounded him. The way he talked to people, ordered them around, was part of this pattern. It explained why the turnover in help at Ballyhoura was great. It wasn't just superstition on the part of the Negroes that kept them from applying for jobs, it was the way the Master spoke to them. They had argued about this. Richard Doyle, the Young Huntsman, had lost hounds one day and Zagaran had called him down in front of the assembled field.

"You shouldn't have spoken to him like that," Shelley said when they were riding home. "He's new at the job. Give him a chance."

"He needs to learn his place."

"Zagaran, it's a matter of common courtesy, the difference between—"

"Us!" he finished for her. "The difference between a Shelburn and somebody with a name like Zagaran. The difference between making a name and being born with it."

"My father used to say there aren't good and bad manners, just manners, and manners are the same for everybody, whether prince or pauper."

"Fuck your father!" he said deliberately.

The more he angered her the more she wanted him. He represented a force, a dominance and certainty lacking in the men she

444

had known. Whereas Mike was gentle, humble, wearing his humility the way he wore his torn shirts and the ink on his hands and forehead, Zagaran was arrogant, positive, and it was as though the very things she most deplored, his violence and occasional vulgarity, unlocked a sensuality she had not known she possessed.

She went into the mirrored bathroom and turned on the water in the tub. She loved to luxuriate in the steaming scented water. At home there was rarely the time, and sometimes when she came in from hunting, longing for a bath, Suellen had used up the hot water doing the wash.

A bottle of pink bath salts stood at the edge of the tub. Unscrewing the glass top, she turned it upside down. The granules, like pink sand, spread, turning the water to rose.

Lying back in the scented tub she gave a long sigh of pleasure. The tinted water swirled and foamed around her breasts, the tips of which matched its color. She thought of Zagaran and what he did to her and the things he whispered to her and again felt the quickening of her desire.

"You look like those paintings people hang in guest rooms, Watteau, I think. With your hair pinned to the top of your head and your skin all rosy."

He stood beside the tub looking down at her. He wore his blue silk dressing gown with the flamboyant crimson Z embroidered on the pocket. It was belted around his narrow waist, and his feet were bare.

She sat up slowly, languorously. There was a small sound as he drew in his breath. Turning abruptly, he went into the bedroom. Then he was back, carrying the flowers that had been delivered that afternoon. Standing on the thick blue rug in the center of the bathroom floor, he began tossing roses into the tub.

"I ordered red," he said. "I was going to throw them out. But now I see they match."

"Hey, they've got thorns!" Laughing, she put up her hands to protect herself.

"Shelley—" There was a sudden break in his voice.

The robe fell to the floor. She was agonizingly aware of his body, of the white gleam of teeth against dark skin. Then he was pulling her up from the tub. Her hair came loose and cascaded

445

down over her shoulders. The roses were mixed up between them, and his bare chest was wet from her dripping scented breasts pressed against it.

He picked her up as easily as he had lifted the hay bale the first night at the Hunting Box and carried her into the glassed-in room, dropping her onto the great bed.

That night the shame and guilt that lingered in Shelley's memory after they had made love gave way to rapture, remaining with her like the scent of his shaving lotion, the cigarettes he smoked in bed, and the roses.

The curtains were open. "I hate darkness and to be closed in," he said. "That's why I put in the glass."

Sometime during the night the snow began, hurling itself like shining splinters against the windows. In the great bed they were an island of love and warmth in the midst of the blizzard. The snow smashing against the panes seemed a part of the wildness, the onslaught of sensations his touch aroused, making her a trembling supplicant.

"What would your father have done," he demanded, "if he could have seen me do this and this? Would he have challenged me to a duel?"

"The words alone would have been enough to make him chase you out of town with his hunting whip."

They lay in the immense bed, drinking champagne and watching the snow, falling softly now.

"I never liked to be touched before," Shelley said. "When Fax, Togo Baldwin and the other boys I grew up with tried to lure me into dark corners and parked cars, I felt revolted. They all thought me frigid!"

"Fire and ice," he murmured, his hands moving over her as lightly as the flakes outside.

"I guess I was afraid of what would happen if the fire was ever ignited. So I built a wall around myself, as high as the old wall around Shelburn Hall."

"Are you still afraid?"

She took his hands and turned them over. Then one by one she placed them on her breasts.

The snow had stopped and the sky through the glass windows held the leaden weight of dawn.

"Where did you go when you were put on the train in Paris?"

446

He reached for his cigarette case on the bedside table and extended it to Shelley. "You're learning all kinds of bad habits," he said as she accepted one. Then he paused and looked at her fiercely. "I took my stepfather's name, but my father was Galtee Buford. I'm Polo Pete's half-brother."

She sucked in her breath. "I don't believe it," she said.

"Nobody knows except P. P., and he's not about to tell anybody he has a bastard half-brother. The British Bufords took me in. My mother had written to them before she died. Anthony Buford, that's Polo Pete's uncle and the head of the British firm of Buford and Company, agreed to let me come and live with them. I was overjoyed. Then I found out I was only the foreigner, or the boy, asked to do things nobody else wanted to do and the servants wouldn't because it wasn't their job. One day Uncle Tony took me into his office. A man was sitting there. A professorial type in dark clothes with a pipe and a briefcase. 'This is Mr. Perrin,' Uncle Tony said. 'He's headmaster at St. Vincent's School for Boys. You're to enter St. Vincent's in the fall.' The headmaster looked at me and then back at Uncle Tony. 'What education has the boy had?' he asked stiffly. Uncle Tony looked across his desk at me as if he'd never seen me before. 'Why, boy,' he said at last, 'come to think of it, what education have you had?'

"I told him I hadn't had any other than what I'd given myself. Uncle Tony looked back at the headmaster and said, 'I'm afraid the boy is right. We'll have to do something about it before fall.' I know it sounds strange," Zagaran said, "but I hadn't been to school. My mother taught me to read and when she became ill I read to her. I had to learn about money in order to go to the market and buy food for us to eat. The rest I picked up for myself.

"My mother used to talk endlessly of The Valley," he said. "She spoke of the Shelburns and Ballyhoura and the feud that existed then between the Bufords and the Shelburns. I had a set of blocks and I spent hours building Ballyhoura, its towers and turrets and outbuildings. Every man has a dream," he concluded simply. "The Valley was mine. I determined to make enough money to buy into it."

"Money isn't everything," Shelley said.

"Money is power," Zagaran replied. "Money and land." Then, as if he had said too much, he turned to her and kissed her, his violence turning to tenderness until she could think no more.

. . .

Shelley arrived home to find that Pansy the hamster had died. Cam was in tears and Virginia City, an apron tied over his jodhpurs, was trying to comfort him.

"Where is Suellen?" she asked, looking at the dishes piled high in the sink.

"She went home when the lumpy fog began," Cam said.

"But the snow didn't amount to anything."

"Suellen isn't ready for integration," Virginia City muttered darkly. "No sense of responsibility. I put the wash in the machine and was about to do the dishes." In reply to her unspoken question, he added, "I turned the horses out."

"I guess that really is the end of Suellen," Shelley sighed, hanging up her coat. "We'll bury Pansy as soon as I change. Cam, I'm sorry." She leaned down and kissed him.

"Lance did it. Pansy got out of the cage when I was feeding her."

Later, after the sun had thawed out the ground, they dug a hole and placed Pansy, "asleep" in a shoebox, in the ground under the magnolia. Shelley made a cross out of sticks, covered it with tinfoil and put it over the animal's grave.

Snow was still on the ground when word reached The Valley that Andrea Zagaran had died in the Connecticut sanatorium of an overdose of sleeping pills. Shelley's first thought was that now Zagaran was free. But when it was time for her to return home from the Hunting Box, she left him without any promises, nothing but the memory of his lovemaking.

TWENTY-ONE

IT WAS press day. Pete Saunders was making up the sports page, his face as dark and set as the imposing stone over which he was working. Pete had a shrewish wife who called him constantly at the office to tell him her domestic problems and recount the misdeeds of their children. He had monetary problems, a bad hip and matching disposition which he compensated for by long hours spent making up type forms and feeding newsprint into the flat-bed press.

Nobody, Mike thought, but idiots, incurable idealists, alcoholics or religious fanatics stays in the weekly-newspaper business. In the face of broken-down machinery, almost human in its foibles and eccentricities, that he was forced to coddle and cajole each press day, Pete's temperament was understandable. Before Pete they had had a journeyman printer who had gotten down on his knees in front of the press and, like an Arab saying his prayers to Mecca, had exhorted God whenever there was a breakdown. In a business that left no room for moderation, Pete was the most moderate he had known. He did not drink or smoke and his only interest outside the shop and his peony bed was in the volunteer fire company. His pride lay in being first on the scene at each fire and his passion, aside from making the cranky press respond, was in handling fire-fighting equipment.

Sitting down at his desk, Mike decided he'd better call home. Shelley had told him she was going to Washington to see an old school friend and might spend the night. He knew from the way she spoke that there was more to it than that, but he had been too weary, too troubled by what was happening to them, to want to pursue the truth.

Virginia City told him, "Suellen has gone home and Mrs. Jenney is bringing Cam from school and keeping him for the night."

Putting down the phone, he forced himself to concentrate on

the stories for the front page. Fifteen of Silver Hill's prize cows had fallen into the swimming pool and drowned. The dairyman at Silver Hill had not broken the ice in the watering trough and the pond was frozen. The frantic cows had finally found that the gate to the pool area had been left unlatched. They pushed through it and plunged into the water. A maid in the house saw their frenzied thrashings and called the *Sun* office. Pete suggested calling out the fire trucks and apparatus, but it was Bobby Gilbert and his wrecker from the filling station who finally managed to extricate the cows, dead from drowning and from cutting their own throats with their hoofs in their frantic efforts to escape.

Mike went on to the next story. The Board of Supervisors had met and discussed the comprehensive plan for county zoning submitted at a previous meeting. Apparently they were still dragging their feet about drafting new zoning ordinances that would support the master plan and channel development in an orderly fashion. Delay, delay, Mike thought, was the order of the Valley day and could prove disastrous. He had written several editorials warning the supervisors that some kind of overall plan should be passed to avert the haphazard and ill-conceived plans for subdivisions and housing developments mushrooming around Washington and slowly spreading into the rural areas. Only a few days previously Hunter Jenney had mentioned mysteriously that he'd been approached by some corporation or other and asked to find out about available properties in The Valley.

While Pete went home to supper, Mike kept on working. With Shelley in the city, Suellen gone and Cam at the Jenneys', there was no reason to go home. Nor did he want the time and the solitude in which to think.

He had not paid any attention to the first anonymous letter warning him to watch out for his wife and Mr. Zagaran. Recently one had come almost daily, reporting on when and where they had been seen together. Mike meant to show Shelley the letters and talk it out, but every time he tried she was in a rush to work on the portrait of Augie Schligman she had promised to deliver by early spring, or out riding. Nevertheless, the time was coming when they would have to have a showdown. It was he who would have to go away, if it came to that. Shelley belonged in and to The Valley. And now, oddly, he did not want to leave. Somehow The Valley had taken hold of him. Nor could he contemplate life without Shelley and Cam. The brightness would be dimmed, like the lights when the roar of the old press shook the building and the antiquated circuits became overloaded.

About eight o'clock, when he was struggling to replace the mats that had fallen out of the linotype, Herm Gillespie walked in. In his hand he carried a grimy sheet of brown wrapping paper on which he had jotted down a long list of items and their prices.

"Changed my mind," he said abruptly. "Here." He shoved the paper at Mike. "Figured it's my duty to support my home-town newspaper."

Too bad you didn't decide before this, Mike thought, aware that Pete would have a breakdown, like the press, when he saw the additional ad with lines of fresh type to make up. Already the press was running off the first section of the paper.

"What made you change your mind?" Mike asked, supporting himself on the edge of his desk.

"Got to thinking." Herm took a cigar from his pocket and lit it. "Miss Misty used to give me free space when I was getting my business started. I thought of how the *Sun* worked last year to raise money for a new truck for the fire company, and what you did for my son Larry. I dunno, Mike. Mostly I decided that we need somebody like you in town. Somebody who's not afraid to speak up for us small businessmen, not that I agree with some of the things you do, understand?"

"Thanks, Herm." Mike took the ad. "I'll lay it out. You want Bodoni or Cheltenham?"

"Any way you think it looks best." Herm started for the door.

"Hey," Mike called after him, "what size?"

"Make it a quarter page. Got a lot of new stuff in." At the door he paused. "Hell, it's been a good year. Make it a half page."

After that the linotype no longer spewed mats across the cement floor and Mike was able to set a galley of type with almost no typos.

Halfway through the evening folding session, the fire whistle went off. Flipping off the switch that stopped the press, Pete leaped down from the platform on which he'd been standing feeding pages of newsprint into the maw of the Miehle. Like a ball player sliding home, he drew himself to a stop in front of the chart tacked to the wall.

"Two longs and a short," he cried. "Out of town." He grabbed his jacket from a peg and ran out of the shop.

"Wait," Misty cried after him. "I'll take you."

"It's a bitter night and God knows where the fire is," Mike said. "Might be hours before we get back."

"I want to go."

"All right." Mike held the door open for her.

"Thank you, Michael," Misty said graciously, accepting his proffered hand. As he assisted her into her dilapidated pickup truck he was reminded of a queen being helped into a sedan chair.

"Like old times," she said as they roared off into the night. "I haven't been to a good fire since I sold the paper."

As they drew up in front of the firehouse the new hook and ladder outfit the *Sun* had helped to promote emerged from the building. Clinging to its rear, along with the other volunteer firemen, was Pete, his plaid cap on the back of his head and a wide anticipatory grin on his ink-smeared face.

"A good fire is what he needs," Mike said. "It'll keep him on an even keel for a week or so. It's practically impossible to get people to campaign for clean streets or good government, but blow the fire siren and the entire population turns out."

"It's something to do," Misty answered. "Instead of sitting and watching the cars rust. Look, already there's a line behind us. Where they come from and how they got here so fast is always a mystery."

Suddenly Mike found himself caught up in the excitement. He realized he didn't want to lose sight of the screaming fire engine any more than did Misty, gripping the wheel like a race car driver.

The engine screamed past Shelburn Hall and Ballyhoura and then swung left, onto the Muster Corner road.

"I hope it isn't the church or the new school," Mike said worriedly.

The road, unpaved and deeply rutted, required concentration. Mike watched as Misty deftly maneuvered the truck, avoiding the spring-breaking potholes or scraping the high frozen banks. The night was frigid, starless. Ahead the glow in the sky became larger, more brilliant. With a sinking sensation Mike realized that it must be the church school.

By the time the firemen were able to begin pumping water

from the pond, which was the only source and too distant to be effective, nothing could be done. The volunteer firemen and onlookers stood by helplessly as the combination dormitory and classroom building became a flaming holocaust. The anguished faces of the students standing within the perimeter of the fire and illuminated by the leaping flames were plainly visible. Some wept openly.

"Don't rightly know how it started," Preacher Young replied in response to Mike's questions. "One of the boys started yelling, 'Fire! Fire!' Next thing there's smoke everywhere. Thank the good Lawd all my boys got out."

At that moment there was a crash. The second floor caved in, showering sparks on the assembled onlookers.

"Back, everybody. Step back," commanded Pete briskly. Grabbing the nozzle of the big hose, he directed it at the flames. A tiny stream of water trickled out, sizzling as it struck the flaming debris showering from the burning building.

Mike was aware of a small hand seeking his. Glancing down, he saw that it was Jimmy. His eyes were wide open and white-shining. Tears ran down from them, dropping onto his striped jersey.

"Jimmy," Mike exclaimed, "this is terrible! Were you able to save anything?"

The boy shook his head, unable to speak.

"Don't understand how the fire could have gotten going so fast," Preacher Young repeated dazedly. He looked at the caldron of twisted iron cots, flaming bedding, chairs, tables, desks, books. "All my books," he said sadly. "And the boys' wood carvings."

"I lost my horse," Jimmy choked. "Full year I've been carving." He gazed shyly up at Mike. "A horse like Lookout Light. I was going to give it to Miss Shelley."

Mike put an arm around the boy's thin shoulders. "How would you like to come home with me? The horses will be glad to see you."

"All my books," Preacher Young repeated. His shoulders sagged. It was as though the hopes that had sustained him over the years of building and hardship were going up in smoke, along with the hard-won possessions belonging to the boys and their teachers who had lived in the building.

While Mike worked to help salvage books, charred clothing and a miscellany of articles from the smoking ruins, Misty and the Muster Corner women served coffee and sandwiches. They had prevailed upon Preacher Young to sit down and drink a cup of coffee when Pete returned from investigating the premises.

On the end of his fireman's hatchet dangled a rag. "Know anything about this?"

"What is it?" asked the preacher.

"Rag, soaked in kerosene. Found it out back. Looked as if somebody had a bunch of 'em and dropped one by mistake."

Preacher Young looked aghast. "You mean somebody set the fire?"

"Looks like it," Pete said.

"It isn't fair," Misty cried angrily. "Who would do such a thing?"

"I don't know," Mike answered wearily. "I never thought anybody would shoot at me, either."

"It's incredible. Something like this happening in our valley. Do you think they can catch whoever did it?"

Mike shook his head. "Chester the Arrester will pretend to put on a big campaign. That's about as far as it will go."

"Reckon Miss Shelley let me ride Lookout Light someday?" Jimmy sat on the edge of the seat between them, small and thin in his zippered jacket.

"You'll have to ask Miss Shelley," Mike answered. He wondered if she was at home, but when they reached Shelburn Hall the house was dark.

Mike wrote an editorial hinting that Preacher Young's school had been deliberately fired by an arsonist. Chester Glover pretended to investigate the matter. Shelley, Misty and Katie Schligman began collecting clothes for the preacher to distribute to his boys, most of whom had been relocated with Muster Corner families until money could be raised to rebuild the school. Then, as February faded into March with snow flurries and high winds, the rabies epidemic again began to dominate the local news.

Now the country people carried sticks and cudgels to protect themselves from skulks of rabid foxes, skunks and other diseased animals. The week after the fire a Mellick child from the Free Zone was bitten by a fox while waiting for the school bus, and

My Boy Hambone shot and killed a groundhog he found behaving strangely by the stable door.

"For months we've been printing releases from the Health Director and the Game Commission," Mike told Misty as he drove her home on press night. "Yet this afternoon Togo Baldwin issued a statement that the attack on the Mellick child was an isolated case. As you know, he's the new president of the Breeders' Association. He said the story I ran last week about the stallion that had to be destroyed was detrimental to the breeding program, that people from out of state might stop sending mares to The Valley to be bred."

"People are always worrying about the breeding program," Misty retorted. "Too bad they don't give as much attention to their own breeding as they do to that of their animals."

Mike laughed. "Have I told you? A broker called me from New York. Said he had a buyer for the paper. He wouldn't tell me his client's name. It was a damned big offer."

"Do you want to sell out?"

"I don't know," Mike answered slowly. "Depends—" The rest of his words were lost in a sudden shattering clap of thunder. For an instant the wildly blowing trees and the undulating sweep of the countryside were illuminated in white light. Then the crooked fork of lightning vanished and the storm was upon them.

Miehle pressed himself against Mike. Trembling with terror, the Labrador tried to burrow down into the seat between them.

"Whenever he hears a loud noise he goes into shock," Mike said. He gazed across the dog to where Misty was wedged against the door. Her profile was tense and one hand lay on the handle as though poised for flight. "He doesn't do anything," Mike continued. "He just wants to be with people. With Shelley away so much I have to keep him with me. Good thing. If I'd left him at home the front door would be gnawed through by now, or a window broken."

"I wasn't thinking about Miehle." Misty put her hand on the dog's trembling body and began to stroke it. "I don't blame him. The thunder scared me, too."

The rain hammered against the windshield. Sheets of water, like gelatin, obscured the road.

It had been close to midnight before they finished delivering the newspapers on the back porch of the post office for Miss Letty to sort and mail out in the morning. Back in the closed-in intimacy of the cluttered press room, an atmosphere of ease, of unspoken accord had prevailed. Now, along with the driving rain, tension seemed to have arisen.

Mike turned the station wagon into Fairmont's long, rutted drive. He stopped the car in front of the walk.

"Michael, would you come in?" Misty asked. "I know it's late and I shouldn't invite you, but just for a little while. You can have tea or coffee or a drink."

"I just remembered," he answered, "I haven't eaten. Would a sandwich be too much trouble?"

"Of course not."

"What about Miehle?"

"I'll shut the dogs in my bedroom. The cats can take care of themselves."

After the darkness and driving rain outside, the lamplit living room with its faded chintz, leather armchairs and wide, sagging, yet infinitely comfortable sofa looked wonderfully inviting. Gratefully he sank down into it.

The thunder had stopped. Now the only sound was that of the rain against the windows, the crackling of the fire. Slowly the Labrador eased himself down onto the hearth.

"While you have a toddy," Misty said, "I'll make sandwiches."

Mike opened his eyes. Misty stood in front of him holding a plate of roast beef sandwiches. He had not realized he was so hungry. While he ate, she sat beside him. In the lamplight her face looked softened, youthful.

"Michael," she said when he finished, "you're staring at me."

"I've just realized what it is that makes you different from the rest of the Valley women."

"Oh?" She arched her eyebrows. They were thick and curving and completely natural.

"Compassion. You have compassion."

"Oh?" She sounded disappointed. "I thought you were going to tell me I was sexy in my inkstained dungarees."

"You are. Sexy. Compassionate."

"It's the roast beef talking." She smiled at him. Then, suddenly,

456

her mouth tensed. A look of pain crossed her face. She stood up and limped to the fireplace, detouring around Miehle stretched in her path. For a moment she stood with her back to him, her forehead resting against the pine mantel.

"Misty," he asked, "what is it?"

"It was a mistake to ask you in." Her voice was muffled. "No, let me finish. I'm ashamed of myself. Shelley is my cousin." Nervously she fumbled for a cigarette. "No, don't get up. I have a match."

"If you're trying to tell me about my wife and Zagaran," he said slowly, "I know . . ."

She lit the cigarette, blew out the match and tossed it into the fire. "No, it wasn't that." Quickly she hurried on. "What I wanted to tell you was, well, how happy I've been these past months. I've felt more useful than at any time since my husband died. If you hadn't come along and given me a job I might have become an alcoholic, like Andrea, or over-devoted to animals—you explained it once. Something about those without proper love in their childhood devoting themselves to horses and dogs. Animals being less demanding than humans, with less chance of hurt or involvement."

"Misty." Mike's voice caught in his throat. In one long bound he crossed the room. Roughly he pulled her to him. For a moment he was aware of her response, as urgent, as demanding as his need. Then she pulled herself away.

Mike sank down on the sofa beside her. "Misty." He stretched out his arms to her. "You're beautiful. Sexy. Beautiful. There's nothing to stop us. You know about my wife and—"

"Yes," she said quickly. "But I wasn't sure *you* knew."

"Has Shelley talked to you?"

Misty shook her head. "Shelley could never talk about things. Everything got frozen inside her back when she was a child, after her mother left." She glanced at the clock on the mantel. "It's late."

"Damn it," he said violently, "I don't want to go home. I am tired of being Miss Shelley's husband and living in a house full of ghosts. There's no reason why I shouldn't stay."

"There is every reason. When reason fails, decency should prevail. I am not geared to passing involvements. That's why I've been alone so long."

He could not look at her, standing in the doorway, a smudge on her forehead and her shirttails loose from her jeans. The tension built up over the months of restraint clamored for release. With great effort he controlled himself and went to the door. He was halfway to the car when he remembered Miehle. Looking back, he saw Misty framed in the doorway, the light from behind her making her seem smaller, somehow more alone.

"Call your dog," she said softly.

"Maybe you're right," he said as though to himself. "Maybe I am just a back-sliding monogamist."

The rain had stopped and the moon was out. The air was moist, soft, carrying on its breath the promise and urgency of spring.

When he got back to Shelburn Hall the house was dark. Going into Cam's room, he looked down at his son, asleep in the moonlight streaming in through the half-open window. Lance, on the floor, lifted his head from his paws, saw who it was and let it fall back down again.

Shelley had returned from wherever she went most nights. She lay on her side, one arm cradling her head, her long hair massed against the pillow. The way it grew in the hollow at the back of her neck made him think of Cam. When he got into bed she did not move. Her back turned toward him was like a wall he dared not breach.

PART FOUR
THE CUP

TWENTY-TWO

SPRING came late that year, like a slow smile, a promise that manifested itself in the buds on the dogwoods, the shoots of crocuses and daffodils thrusting upward through the semifrozen ground. As the ground thawed and the grass began to come in, people's thoughts turned to the Shelburn Cup.

Zagaran had rebuilt the course from the original plans drawn by Sean Shelburn which Shelley had lent him and revived the race meet that was always the highest point of the spring point-to-point season. Since the announcement that the race would take place, people had talked of little else.

When Andrea died it was assumed that the ball, which as Master of The Hunt Zagaran had planned to be held at Bally-houra, would be called off. But Zagaran insisted that he wanted it to go on. "I wouldn't want personal problems to interfere with The Hunt," he told the committee. As the ball was a subscription affair necessary to The Hunt's financial well-being, people excused themselves, saying it wasn't as if Andrea's death had been unexpected. She had not been well for a long time and although it was a terrible thing to say, it must have come as a relief to Zagaran, who had proved himself to be a devoted husband, flying to Connecticut to visit her at least once every week.

When Shelley volunteered to have the dance at Shelburn Hall he accepted her offer with alacrity. Shelley was disappointed. The idea of taking Andrea's place had crept into her mind, slithering in and out of her thoughts like the long black snake that lived in the stable and emerged every spring. Zagaran's failure to admit any change in the status of their relationship was be-

461

coming as frustrating to her as the continued cold of the gusty March weather.

When Millicent, Debby and the others on the committee suggested alternatives, Zagaran remained firm, saying that Shelburn Hall would provide the most beautiful as well as the most traditional setting for the ball.

With Zagaran behind her there was nothing they could do about changing its location. Mike was appalled.

"Good God!" he exclaimed. "We can't pay our bills now. What are we going to do about food, liquor, the help? We can't afford any part of it."

"I'm having local help," Shelley told him. "And Zagaran is paying for everything."

"Not in my house," Mike said vehemently.

"I didn't know it was your house."

Mike's hands clenched around the stem of his pipe. "Shelley, don't you remember the things you said last year, the night of the ball? You can't have changed so much. Shelley, what has happened to us?"

"I've got to go to market," she said as the clock in the hall chimed. "And then pick up clothes I've collected for Preacher Young's boys." She looked at him defiantly. "You should be happy to know that since the fire we've gathered seven truckloads."

"Shelley, I'd be a lot happier if we could sit down and talk."

She started toward the telephone. "Some other time. Right now I've got to get hold of Dooley Wright to change Lookout Light's shoes."

He shook his head helplessly. "You make me think of the Red Queen, who kept running faster and faster just to stand in one spot."

"Instead of being so erudite, why don't you fix the washing machine?" Shelley called over her shoulder. "It's been out of commission since Monday and still nobody's come to repair it."

"Maybe if you'd stay home . . ."

She did not wait to hear any more.

The Shelburn Cup steeplechase is an oddity in racing. There is no money for it. Only glory, heartbreak and a silver goblet that hasn't lost its shine since 1889, when Sean Shelburn designed the first flagged course.

Since the initial race run over this course, a number of horses have died and two riders have been killed endeavoring to capture the replica of the Cromwellian goblet that Sean Shelburn ordered from Tiffany's following the first moonlight steeplechase. After that first race he had the twenty-four fences built on the valley floor in order that the spectators, picnicking on the hillside or sitting in their conveyances drawn up along the finish line, might view the entire race.

Despite decades of breeding horses that would stand up over the grueling course, no Shelburn horse had won the Cup. Cameron Fitzgerald tried several times during his career, but never finished better than third. When he became too old to ride the race, he pinned his hopes on Fermoy, the handsome chestnut descendant of Galway Pilot, who had an unbeaten record at the Hunt meets. Fax Templeton rode him. Fax was in his prime then, young, bold and brash. Instead of rating Fermoy as the horse galloped into the fence aptly known as The Coffin, Fax had sent him on, urging the tiring horse past Bold Tribute, the Dinwiddies' old campaigner. Fermoy misjudged the takeoff and dove through the fence, breaking his neck.

Shelley would never forget the sight of the fallen horse, lying motionless, blood coming from his half-opened mouth while Fax, tears running down his cheeks, cradled the horse's head in his lap. Shelley was thirteen that year and the romantic race rider with his golden head, flashing smile and devil-may-care attitude had been her idol. She yearned to go to him and try to comfort him, but Taffy Carlisle, down from New York for the weekend, had beaten her to it. So she had stood on the sidelines while Virginia City took Fax's racing saddle off Fermoy and Sidney Merrywood, his trainer, ordered the crowd away. Doc Black had been young then, and new to his profession. His hand trembled as he lifted the revolver to destroy the horse. Shelley, unable to watch any longer, ran blindly off the course. Huddled behind the Ballyhoura Oak, she heard the sound of the shot.

Twice The Goose, with Fax riding, had put up a good try. The first time the gray was knocked down at the Terrible Tenth. The second time a horse from Maryland nosed him out of the finish. During the intervening years the striking Shelburn-Fitzgerald colors had been absent.

With something close to reverence Shelley extracted them from the bottom of the old tack trunk and sent them to the cleaners. Then she went to see Sidney Merrywood.

She found the old trainer tending his rock garden.

Even in his Montgomery Ward overalls with a dab of dirt on his cheek there was an air of distinction about him, and although his hair was as white as his azaleas, his blue eyes held a youthful alertness and vitality. He beamed with pleasure at sight of Shelley.

"I have some yellow tulips just starting to bloom." After Shelley had admired the garden and exclaimed over the tulips, she told him what she had in mind.

"Well now," he said, "I would like to win a Cup Race before I die." He looked out across the fields, where, in his mind's eye, horses moved forever at a gallop. "There's not much time. We'll have to work hard. Now how about a spot of tea?"

That night, thinking over what she had done, Shelley had qualms. The old trainer was a martinet. He belonged to another era, that of Ambrose Clark and Harry Worcester Smith, of braided stalls and gaslight. She remembered how he had forbidden electricity in the racing barn, saying it kept the horses awake and both horses and men should go to bed with the sun and rise when it rose. And he had insisted on rain water from the green-and-yellow-painted barrels that stood in the stableyard instead of tap water for the horses. Yet, in his time he had been tops and there was nobody else, aside from Fax, who knew and understood the temperament of the Pilot strain.

Now it was necessary to find a rider.

On the morning that Shelley went to see Fax, wisps of black rain clouds moved across the tops of the blue mountains. The snow that had disrupted hunting, causing the horses' hoofs to ball up and slide, had melted, giving way to what Shelley called the mud season. The ruts in the clay lanes and byways deepened and the fields, starting to emerge from their drab gray-green garb, were so deep that hunting was further postponed.

The fox that Fax had painted on the door panel grinned at her. A good omen, Shelley thought as she climbed the stairs and knocked. From within came the sound of barking and then a shout.

"Shut up, God damn it. Come in, whoever you are."

Shelley opened the door and was promptly converged upon

by the foxhounds, puppies, grinning their slobbery welcoming grins and buffeting her with their heads.

"God damn it," Fax roared, coming from the kitchen, a cigar in one hand, a spatula in the other. "Frisky, Fanciful, git!" He swatted them with the spatula, and the puppies, howling in pretended pain, ran and leaped onto the sagging sofa.

"Miss Shelley, ma'am. A pleasure." He wore jodhpurs and bedroom slippers, and a torn stable sheet in Templeton brown with a black border was wrapped around his waist in place of an apron. "Come into my parlor," he urged with a sweeping bow.

Fax's parlor, where he ate, slept and entertained, was hardly large enough to turn around in. Saddles and old hunting boots were piled on the floor. Mothy fox masks grinned from the mantel festooned with a frieze of old hunt fixture cards. Sporting books from Judge Templeton's library, empty mason jars and bottles lined the shelves. On the dining-room table newspapers and unopened bills were piled high. Bridles hung from the light fixtures on either side of the stone fireplace, which was stuffed with trash. Photographs—horses racing, horses jumping, horses standing still—were tacked to every available inch of wall space. In almost all of them a round hole, where Fax's head had once been, had been carefully cut out by the girls who pursued him when his trademark was the gleaming blond hair which he refused to cover with the conventional cap or derby when he rode in the show ring.

Mixed with the smell of dogs, dust, leather and cigar smoke came the odor of fresh baking.

"Wait here while I check the oven." Fax turned to display the T monogram on the old sheet decorating his left buttock. "Having a party for little Augie this afternoon. Hope you'll bring Cam. The Duchess is coming with some bloke from the Shires who's visiting her. I'm baking cookies. Soon as I get out the ice we'll have us a little l-l-l-libation."

"Fax, the sun hasn't even begun to cross the yardarm, whatever that means." Shelley laughed. "Besides, I have serious business to discuss."

"Miss Shelley, ma'am, ain't nothing serious good s-s-sipping whiskey won't fix." In the kitchen she watched him lift the pan of cookies from the oven, separate them with the spatula he had used to discipline the dogs, and slide them onto a cracked Canton platter. "Coffee, then?" he asked, turning the burner on under the rusted pot in which egg shells floated with the grounds. "Set," he said, noticing she was still standing. "Coffee'll be h-h-h-hot in a minute."

Shelley detoured around the hand-sewn double bridle hanging from the hook fastened to the ceiling over the table, where My Boy Hambone cleaned tack in cold weather. She sat down and Fax poured out her coffee. Then he took a tarnished silver cup from the shelf. Reaching for the bourbon bottle under the sink, he poured himself a generous amount. While he drank, she told him she wanted him to ride Lookout Light in the Shelburn Cup.

When she was finished he sat very still. The puffiness around his eyes and chin no longer seemed so pronounced. The slouch went out of his shoulders and his body straightened. Slowly he set down the silver cup and stared at it. Then with a sigh, he picked it up again and the lean beauty that for an instant had flickered across his face was replaced by the tired pouched lines of resignation and self-indulgence.

"If only I could solve my p-p-p-private life."

"What's the matter with your private life?" Shelley asked, surprised. Fax looked so woebegone that she began to laugh.

"I don't have any."

"What about Bebe?"

"I'm cold-trailing there."

"Try going on the wagon and cutting out those awful cigars," Shelley said. "Fax, remember Fermoy?"

"I remember Fermoy."

"Fax, I'm offering you another crack at the Cup."

"There are only so many shots in my breech."

"Surely you don't want Zagaran to win?"

His head shot up. For an instant hope gleamed, then, like the mangled cigar in the ashtray, died.

"I sure would like to beat the son of a b-b-b-bitch," he stammered. "But Miss Shelley, honey, I'm aged. Like The S-s-s-Saint out there. I'd be riding against the sons of my friends. Like Sandy Montague. Just the other day I was asked to be a patrol judge. They only ask you that when you're over the hill."

"Settle down, Fax," Shelley said. "Bones Black is almost as old as you are. Zagaran is older."

Fax got up, went over to the sink, started to pick up the bottle

466

of liquor and then did not. For a moment he stood staring at it. Then, slowly, he lifted it and poured its contents down the drain.

"You think I can do it?" he said without his usual stutter. "You really believe I can, don't you?"

In the early March sunlight filtering through the grimy windows she saw the Fax she had once known. "I know you can," she said quietly.

They made an incongruous trio. By comparison to the modern trainers, hard semiprofessionals, and the new breed of owners like Augie Schligman, who drove to the schooling sessions in heated limousines, they resembled characters out of one of Fax's dusty sporting tomes.

Where Fax was slender and long-legged—now that he was no longer drinking and had gone on a crash diet his leanness and good looks were returning—Sidney Merrywood was short and bandy-legged. Yet both had the same courtly Old World manner. It was an intangible quality, something that even Zagaran, with his dark dramatic looks and beautifully cut London-tailored clothes, failed to achieve. It was the same quality as that displayed by Lookout Light, an aura of aristocracy bred and distilled over the centuries, something that could not be bought or sold in terms other than those of time and tradition.

Mornings the hillside was covered with owners, trainers, grooms and riders—the latter living now on lemons, Melba toast and bouillon—and interested spectators like Mr. Winecoop, the postman. The women, with long, elegant necks and long, elegant legs, wearing suede sheepskin-lined coats over their jodhpurs or corduroys and scarves tied around their heads, huddled in groups, discussing their horses' chances with their grooms and trainers.

Bones Black and Millicent had agreed on a truce until after the race. Every morning now he could be seen in his rubber reducing suit jogging behind Millicent's Rolls as she drove it along the Valley road, holding the wheel with one hand, clocking him with the other. Jointly they fussed over Nautilus, the big-boned, big-striding brown horse Bones would ride in the Cup Race, Millicent crooning endearments to her horse and cursing her husband.

Augie Schligman had entered Drum Major, the big brown he had bought from Story Jackson. Shelley had finished painting Augie and the horse, and the handsomely framed canvas now hung over the fireplace in the great front room at Templeton. Augie had paid Shelley a generous sum, most of which had already been spent on further repairs at Shelburn Hall, buying a new washing machine and the additional stable supplies incurred by Lookout Light's training.

Polo Pete was running My Paramour, a French import he had acquired off the flat track for a price said to be exorbitant. He had planned to start the horse in Samantha Sue's name, but on the day that the entries closed she had announced that she was divorcing him. The story spread by Millicent over the produce section at the supermarket was that Samantha Sue had told Polo Pete that from now on he was to "keep his cotton-gloved hands off her, pick up his pants and get going!"

Mrs. Dinwiddie had asked Sandy Montague to ride her Contender, and Rosy Dash-Smythe had put her good hunter Samson into training for the spring circuit and hoped that after his initial start at New Commonwealth he would prove up to the big timber of the Cup course.

Added to the local horses were several out-of-state entries. Keystone, the Pennsylvania point-to-point champion, and Rocket Man from Maryland. Essex Lad was the New Jersey hope and there was a possibility of some starters from Ohio and Kentucky. If all the horses went to the post, the Cup Race promised to be better filled than in many a past year.

But it wasn't the additional number of entries that was creating the intense interest centered around the Cup Race. It was the rivalries involved. The fact that Zagaran was going to ride (many of the Old Guard felt he should be in mourning for his wife) and compete with the man whose place he had taken as Master of The Hunt gave the competition an added excitement. Further talk had been caused by Tatine, who had entered Warlock—it was to be the horse's last race before retirement—and asked that Richard Doyle be permitted to ride.

In the heyday of the Hunt meets when Fax, Bones Black and the other young men in the area had been in their prime, amateurs had been plentiful. There had been no guilt attached to being subsidized by the long-stemmed heiresses with racing stables, whose horses they rode in return for gold cufflinks and platinum cigarette cases and fornication behind the closed doors of the country houses they visited weekends.

Some had died in Korea. Others, like Freddy Fisher, had taken to the bottle. Bones remained, and a few younger men like Sandy Montague, who managed to combine college and working at a job, but the day of the true amateur who had made sport a way of life, an end in itself, was past. Because of this the National Hunts and Steeplechase Committee had been forced to rewrite conditions, thus making it possible for any rider who was not directly paid for riding and who proved acceptable to the committee to compete.

"Why shouldn't Richard ride?" Tatine asked defiantly when Polo Pete had protested. With Samantha Sue in Vegas, he now began drinking at breakfast and continued all day.

"Doyle is a paid professional," he insisted angrily.

Tatine gazed into his bloodshot eyes and said impudently, "Mah pappy used to say, 'Ain't no moh difference 'tween an amateur and a professional rider than they is 'tween a lady and a whore.' "

When it came up for a vote the majority of the committee members, aware that the race was run over Tatine's father's property and that Zagaran was in large part financing it, voted to permit Richard to ride.

Time shortened. Tension increased. During the training sessions Shelley saw Zagaran almost daily. Nights when Mike was working they went to the Hunting Box. Sharing the tensions and the zest of being in competition seemed to draw them closer together.

Shelley realized that Zagaran was determined to win the Cup, that for him it was the equivalent of winning The Valley. The fact that he would be one of the oldest riders lent a note of gallantry to his attempts.

The routine of early rising, the scent of coffee before sunup, the horses emerging from the mist as they danced across the cobwebbed grass, and the visible development of Lookout Light, changing daily from mere hunting fitness to the lean, muscled hardness of the thoroughbred in training, were positive realities for Shelley. Mornings when Fax overslept she worked Lookout Light. Galloping her horse the required lengths that would bring him to his peak and seeing that all the necessary things were done during the course of each day left her too tired by evening to worry about Mike or Cam or finances. That her marriage was rapidly deteriorating, that Mike ate the majority of his meals away from home, and that Cam spent most of his time with Jimmy Jones, who was living at Shelburn Hall while the new school she was helping to raise funds for was being built at Muster Corner, were facts she refused to face.

"We're more in debt each day," Mike said at breakfast one morning. "Why don't you send your horse to the track where he could win some money? You'll break your heart and your back, for what? A silver cup? As if we didn't have enough of them already."

"That reminds me," Shelley said, "I'll have to get somebody in to clean and shine the silver before the ball. I sent the gilt chairs to be repaired. They should be picked up—"

"You're really going through with it." He began filling his pipe. "In spite of everything I've said."

Shelley looked past him at the window where Virginia City's "ladies," including the proud little banty hen and her chicks, were lined up on the sill. "Augie paid me for the painting. I delivered it to him the other day. Thank God he liked it. I put all the bills in the hat and paid all but that man we had working on the roof. He still hasn't fixed the leak in Cam's room."

She watched the familiar motions, the way he held his pipe and tamped the tobacco into the bowl with his index finger. She wanted to rip it from his hands, force him to some kind of action, some violence of emotion that would match and in some way justify the antagonism inside her.

"You haven't asked me if the paper is alive or dead," he said bitterly. "And you don't seem to care whether I am or not. I get shot at, a school burns down. People get hurt, like the Jenneys. All you think about is your horse."

She knew he was right, that she was becoming more neglectful of her family and household. For a long time now she had failed to stock his humidor with the pipe tobacco he liked or check his drawers to see that his socks and shirts were darned. Subconsciously she had detoured the usages of kindness, the small courtesies that cement a relationship. Their birth had come naturally. Their death could be irreversible. Yet she was too intensely involved with Zagaran and her horse, in the compulsive effort expended in preparing for the race, to have room for anything else. Always this had been her escape—to look to the physical as an answer to problems of the mind or spirit, to lose herself in what was familiar rather than voyage into the unknown nuances and complexities of human relationships.

"This is the fourth time I've asked you to buy sugar," Mike continued. "There hasn't been any for coffee for five mornings."

"I forgot. I took the last lumps for Lookout Light."

"Mommy, Daddy, don't fight." Cam gazed at them pleadingly.

Mike rose to leave, patting the pocket of his khaki work shirt to make sure his pipe was there.

"Connie Jackson called me at the office last night. Said she'd been trying to track you down for days, something about a feature on Shelburn Hall. Debby called, too. She said the McFarlands, those people from Minnesota who bought the Warner place, didn't get an invitation."

"For good reason," Shelley interrupted hotly. "They didn't invite us to their open house."

The hall clock struck eight. Her sense of pressure returned. "I must hurry. Fax is schooling Lookout Light. Cam, eat your cereal."

"If you're determined to go through with this, I'd appreciate it if you'd write to the Shapiros and invite them for race weekend. Tad has an assignment to do an article on what he calls the horsey-doggie set."

"The Shapiros!" Shelley exclaimed, forgetting Cam. "Marina here? In the country? In her mink and spike heels? Tad is contemptuous of people with money and horses. I don't want to find myself being made fun of in one of his articles."

"Damn it, they're my *friends*."

Then the thought struck her that the presence of the Shapiros would serve to hold off their growing friction, help to stabilize their relationship, which each of them knew without saying would have to be resolved soon.

"I'll write to Marina." She smiled at him. "But about the article —you know how The Valley feels about publicity!"

Shelley felt the world of the household closing in on her. Now along with the race and putting on the Hunt Ball, she would have to do something about entertaining the Shapiros.

There was Millicent's annual prerace luncheon, generally a chaotic affair complete with masses of visiting celebrities. Millicent had recently been overly friendly, asking what she could do to help with the ball. "You must come," she had said the other morning in the post office, "and bring your guests." Mike, she knew, would call her a hypocrite. On the other hand, it was a way to entertain the Shapiros and nobody should visit The Valley without seeing Last Resort.

Maybe Misty could be persuaded to give a dinner party. Dining at Misty's would provide local color, grist for Tad's article. She made a mental note to telephone her. And she must see about renting the round tables from the Halter Club and check with the new Ballyhoura gardener about flowers, order candles, masses of candles—

"Miss Shelley, sorry to disturb you, ma'am." Jimmy stood in the doorway, twisting his cloth baseball cap in his hands. "Ain't no more feed for the chickens and Virginia City say to tell you he's out of bran."

It was a bog, Shelley thought. Each time she tried to extricate herself, she sank deeper into the morass.

"Mike," she called to him as he was putting on his jacket, "I asked you to order some scratch feed."

"And I asked you four days ago to get sugar."

Jimmy lingered in the doorway. His face wore its habitual wistful, pleading expression. "Miss Shelley, sorry to disturb you, ma'am, but I was wondering—"

"Yes, Jimmy?" She was in a fever of impatience to be gone.

"I was wondering if maybe you might advance me some money. You see, Miss Shelley, I kind of needs some clothes, a shirt and some socks. Course if it's any trouble . . ."

"But I—" She broke off, seeing him suddenly as a small black boy, holding himself straight and tall in order to seem older than his twelve years. Clean, yet his sockless feet were loose in broken too-big men's shoes, and a too-large jacket with the padding coming from a rip at the shoulder was all he owned to keep out the cold of the March morning.

"Of course, Jimmy," she said gently, starting past him. "I'll call Mr. Matthews at the Dependable Store and tell him it's okay for you to charge the clothes to my account."

Impulsively he darted his hand out to touch her, then quickly took it back. "Thank you, Miss Shelley!"

Shelley turned to Cam. "Eat your oatmeal while I call the feed store."

Cam's face wore the same look that Lance's did when there was no meat mixed with the dog meal. "There isn't any sugar. It's yuk!"

The morning of the last school over fences Shelley awoke to find the daffodils in bloom. The air held a new softness and the bleached-out fields of winter were turning green. White apple blossoms and lavender-pink Judas spread delicate lacy outlines over lanes and byways.

Now, a week before the great race, there was added excitement and an increase of tension. The world of horses is never without anxiety. The more valuable a horse, the greater its potential for injury. Story Jackson's entry had broken down the preceding week. Rosy Dash-Smythe's Samson had been kicked on his way to the post at New Commonwealth and was a doubtful starter. Augie Schligman worried about his horse's condition and ordered My Boy Hambone to mix eggs and beer into his feed. Tatine prayed that Warlock's bad tendon would hold up until after the race, when she planned to retire the old steeplechaser.

Because of Sidney Merrywood's careful training, Lookout Light had survived without a scratch. The trouble lay with Fax. Years of self-indulgence had taken their toll. Lookout Light was still young and inexperienced. The tall unbreakable timber was new to him. He needed a strong rider to give him confidence over the big fences. When Fax tensed and froze, refusing to allow the necessary speed and length of rein for the horse to extend himself, Lookout Light remembered the pain suffered at the hands of Polo Pete Buford. He became wary of his mouth, began to check himself and lose his rhythm.

When he was schooled over the big fences the first time, three of Millicent's terriers ran out onto the course, causing the gray to swerve at The Coffin. Fax's heart had gone out of him and he was unable to throw it over the fence. The horse had known it and refused.

After several tries it became obvious that even with Warlock's lead, Lookout Light was not going to jump. Fax, head down and shoulders slumped beneath his tweed jacket, had ridden back to where Virginia City waited to take the horse. Dismounting quickly, he slung his polo coat over his shoulders and walked off to the Rakish Stud pickup.

Sidney Merrywood put his hand on Shelley's arm as she started after him. "What matters more," the trainer asked, "winning the race or saving the man? For Fax's sake, let's give him another chance."

Now on this last day of schooling the sun was drinking away the remaining dew clotting the clumps of grass. On the hillside the horses waited, tossing their heads and pulling against their shanks, their bright-colored sheets tied high on their necks and blowing in the fresh breeze.

"You all just look out," Virginia City boasted. Involved in training a Shelburn Cup horse again, he walked erect and looked a dozen years younger. "Look out for that Lookout Light!" He put up his hand to stroke the colt, and Black Magic, standing nearby, rolled her eyes and pulled backward.

"My mare'll be hard to beat," Simeon said. "She's some fast but there's no way to rate her. She's got to break in front and stay there. Lucky the Cup course is left-turning. Ever since that jockey at the track hit her 'longside the head, she most always jump to the left."

Simeon's son, Junior, holding Warlock, looked around. "Miss Tatine say she be here by seven o'clock sure."

"It's gettin' on," Virginia City said worriedly. "Wonder where Mr. Fax is at?"

Zagaran leaned against the paddock fence. During the weeks of training he had become thinner, harder. In his skin-tight white racing breeches and jersey, there was about him a sense of controlled, almost animalistic, strength and grace not unlike that of Black Magic. He had cut down on his smoking and drank only champagne. Now he exuded health and by comparison to some of the spectators, say Polo Pete with his soggy mind and soft body, the aura of the physical, the magnetism that surrounded him, was accentuated.

He glanced at Shelley. "Are you missing your jockey again?"

She gave him a long, level look. "He's probably been held up."

"At the Halter Club?"

Shelley turned away. He was in one of his scoffing, jeering moods. It was the same compulsion to criticize, to make fun of Valley mores and attitudes that at times came over Mike. It was when she liked him the least. Others reacted the same way.

Sidney Merrywood, for instance. When Zagaran came over to speak to Shelley, the trainer invariably walked away or directed his attention elsewhere. The other riders did not include him in their easy badinage. Those who were dependent on him for their livelihood were overly respectful. The power of his money, plus his foreignness and the mystery that surrounded him, made people wary. Because she was the only one to have penetrated the mystery, Shelley felt compelled to defend him.

"Why don't you like him?" Shelley asked her trainer. "He rebuilt the Cup course and Ballyhoura. He saved The Hunt. You admit he's a superb horseman."

"He is that," Sidney admitted, "but I don't like to see a man brutalize animals. I would never train at the big tracks because I saw too much of it."

"I've never seen him brutalize a horse," Shelley protested.

"You will. Someday he'll forget himself. A man who would keep a wild animal shut up, like that fox, and the way that mare behaves . . ."

"But she was always like that."

"He could have gentled her," the trainer said. "He has a liking for the way she acts. She sets him off. And while we're on the subject, what he did to Fax is hardly a thing to be proud of."

"Zagaran had nothing to do with his being put out," Shelley argued. "Fax kept being late at meets, drinking too much—"

"Fax is one of us," Sidney Merrywood said. "That man Zagaran is not."

As Lookout Light was led out quietly, confidently, with a new sheen to his gleaming coat, an admiring gasp went up from the onlookers on the hillside.

Sidney Merrywood took out the round gold stop watch Cameron Fitzgerald had given him. "Any idea where Fax is?"

"He was at the Halter Club last night," Zagaran volunteered. "I saw his horse tied to the hitching post."

"I'll go call him," Shelley said.

My Boy Hambone answered the telephone. "I woke him like you said, Miss Shelley."

"Are you sure he woke up?"

"He seemed like he woke," the groom answered defensively.

"Better go check."

"Miss Shelley, he ain't here," Hambone reported when he returned. "Truck's here but The Saint, he gone."

"I counted on this school," Sidney Merrywood said when Shelley got back.

"I'll ride."

"You?" The trainer shook his head. "You've got responsibilities. A husband. A child. You could be hurt."

"The horse is mine. I know him better than anyone."

The trainer recognized the look in her eyes. "Virginia City"—he snapped his fingers—"bring up Lookout Light."

"Yes sir, Mr. Merrywood, sir." The grin on Virginia City's face was wide and happy.

Dixon gave her a leg up.

"Stay clear of Magic," the trainer warned. "Remember she swerves to the left."

Shelley smiled at him. "We'll be so far ahead there won't be any problem." Holding the snaffle rein in her teeth, she finished adjusting her stirrups and directed the groom to let the colt's head go free.

"I'm going to beat you," she warned, riding up alongside Zagaran.

"Try." He laughed. "Just try."

They broke head and head. In the distance the sun rolled away the last of the mist from the blue mountains. Then there was the pounding of hoofs, the rush of wind against her face.

As they came into the first fence Zagaran deliberately sent Magic shooting ahead. Shelley was vaguely aware of Sidney's voice carrying across the course. "Rate him. Rate him. You've got four miles."

But at that moment there was no way on earth to slow Lookout Light. All Shelley could do was sit in the saddle and pray that Magic would not swerve across the fence in front of him.

Now the first two fences were past. As they straightened out for the third, Shelley felt her heart pounding, her breath coming in gasps. She knew it was a moment such as this, with the rushing, surging power of a good horse beneath her and a big fence looming in front, that made all the falls and broken bones and the heartbreak of horses worthwhile. This was what spoiled men for other sports and made the love of racing a breathing, vital thing, understood only by those who belonged to that small exclusive group of horse people. This was what could not be put into words —the danger and driving exultation that made men like Bones Black slowly rebuild their nerve after the bad spills and go back for more, always more, until they grew too old and arthritic to hang up their own tack or got the one-too-many that led to a wheelchair by the fireside.

They swung left and headed down the long slope toward The Coffin. Suddenly Shelley felt a shudder pass through the horse's body. Here was the place where he had refused with Fax. Perhaps he remembered the sharp hurting jabs on his mouth as Fax, unable to control his fear, had tried to stop the horse. His ears went back. He began to slow down.

Using her head and her heart and her hands, Shelley urged the horse on, calling to him not to fail her. There was a second's hesitation. Then Lookout Light's ears went forward once again. His tail ceased to go around. He went back to running.

When they pulled up after the finish line, Lookout Light was in front.

"What are you going to do about a rider?" Zagaran asked her after they had dismounted and the horses, blown and steaming, had been led back to the stable to be cooled out and done up. "Surprising Fax stayed sober as long as he did. A man who's lost his nerve."

Sidney Merrywood gazed at him steadily. "I never knew a good man yet who didn't have a fit of nerves before a race or facing the enemy on the battlefield." He turned to Shelley and, although he had not indicated it in word or manner, his dismissal of Zagaran was apparent. "I want to see Virginia City about putting Lookout Light up in bandages."

Zagaran stared after him. "Fact remains that Templeton is yellow, as yellow as your silks, and you're out a rider."

"Fax will be back," she retorted with more confidence than she felt.

"Even if he sobers up long enough to ride, he'll funk." He hiked his sheepskin coat collar higher against the brisk wind from the mountains and began walking to his car. "I don't suppose I'd qualify to ride a Shelburn horse."

She couldn't believe she'd heard him correctly. "But what about Black Magic?"

"I'd scratch her if you wanted me to ride your horse."

Shelley was dumbfounded. Was it for her? Or to ride a winner? "I can't scratch Fax."

"All right, hang onto your gentleman rider." He opened the car door. "I'm good enough for you but not for your horse!"

"Zagaran, don't. People will hear."

He took her arm roughly. "Get in the car."

"No." In the bright morning light her profile was as clear, as sharp as a mirror. People and horses went by, leaving the course. The grooms nodded respectfully. The gentry gazed in the other direction.

His grip on her arm tightened. "Get in."

She made a last desperate attempt to break free. "I have to find Fax."

"Suit yourself." He released her so suddenly that she staggered against the car. She looked at him, saw the cold anger on his face. She bent down and got into the car. The noise of the starting engine drowned out his laughter. He put it in gear as she pulled the door shut behind her.

"Champagne breakfast at the Hunting Box." He shifted down in order to turn onto the highway. Tatine's sports car, coming from the opposite direction, roared past. Richard Doyle sat beside her, eyes intent on the road ahead. Neither waved or acknowledged Zagaran and Shelley.

"They're late for the school," Shelley commented.

Zagaran's jaw tightened. "This time she's going too far."

"Maybe they had to pick up something in town, or see about a horse," Shelley said defensively.

"At eight o'clock in the morning!" The powerful car shot forward, past the familiar fences and fields.

She saw from the expression on his face that he was very angry. At any moment the violence that lay so close to the surface could erupt, using her as target. The qualities that drew her to him, she realized, were those that instinctively, by nature and heritage, she should deplore. His physical hold over her was a shaming of herself to herself. When she liked him least, she wanted him, with a hot aching want she had never known with another man. The car seemed to be carrying her to a strange and unknown country of mind and body from which there might be no way to return. Suddenly he turned off the road into a lane.

"Where are you going?" she asked.

He drove the car into the clearing by the quarry pond and stopped. Turning off the ignition, he swung his body around and faced her.

"You're no different from that girl you told me about, the one you saw here lying on the ground making love. Behind that cold morning manner you're sensual as hell."

He reached over and tugged at the gold stock pin fastening the fly of the men's jeans she had bought at the Dependable Store. The pin opened as his hand slid between the material and her skin.

"You told me how shocked you were. People making love, like animals, on the ground."

"Zagaran, it's only eight o'clock in the morning. Somebody might come by."

"They can start selling tickets!"

His hands moved against her. "Do you know what happens to a man when he's on a horse, when he feels contact with the saddle and at the same time sees a girl ahead with a beautiful tight bottom jumping fences? Here, let me show you."

"Please," she begged with mounting desperation, not knowing whether to make him stop what he was making her do or end the anguish of her desire. Throwing open the door, she jumped out of the car.

He caught her at the edge of the pool. With the abruptness and strength that was so much a part of him, he picked her up. She landed in the pool with a splash. When she surfaced, thrashing wildly and pushing her hair away from her face, she saw him standing above, grinning down at her. She scrambled up the bank.

"You bastard!" She stood before him, wet tangled hair falling to her narrow waist, jersey and jeans clinging to her soaked body. The repressed furies and frustrations of their relationship surfaced, as she had from the frigid water. She picked up a stick lying on the ground and started toward him.

He fended off her blows, laughing. "Such conduct for a lady, a Shelburn. What would Mrs. R. Rutherford Dinwiddie say?"

The stick broke against his chest and just as suddenly his savagery became gentleness. With a whimpering cry she was in his arms. The fact that at any moment they might be discovered added a leaping excitement to the encounter. Desire mounted as she pressed her body against his.

The painting of the fox on the door was smeared and barely discernible. While she waited for Fax to open it that afternoon, Shelley watched My Boy Hambone riding one of the young horses in figure eights around Katie Schligman's box bushes. As the horse wove in and out, the groom swung the polo mallet he always carried in order to get the colts he was breaking used to a hunting crop.

"Now, hawse," he said, maintaining a running monologue, "you behave. See here, hawse," he said reprovingly as the animal shied at Judy Schligman's collie that ran out from behind a bush, "cut that out. There, now. That's a good hawse."

Fax opened the door finally. His eyes were bloodshot and the puffed, pouchy look of defeat had returned. The chamois patches on his jodhpurs had ripped loose and there was a tear in the neck of his jersey. He looked as seedy and unkempt as the apartment.

"Miss Shelley, ma'am, d-d-d-do come in." His stammer was worse than ever. "May I offer you a d-d-d-drink? This weather. Unpredictable. D-d-d-daffodils be d-d-d-damned. It'll be raining or snowing Saturday. Shelburn Cup weather."

"Do you still want to ride?" she asked wearily.

Fax gazed out of the window. "There was a time when I felt like a mighty eagle. Riding races. Flying a plane. Up high. Looking down. Fast horses and high fences, Taffy and Caribbean cruises. Then suddenly, it's gone. Other day The Hunt went by. People sitting there on their tall horses looking down at me. Now I'm nothing but a grubby worm." He picked up the glass from the table and drank from it.

"Fax, what is this grubby worm bit? I thought you and Bebe were, as Connie Jackson would say, an item."

"The Duchess won't change monograms. Marries nobody but B's."

"You can still be a mighty eagle." Shelley leaned over and took the glass from his hand. "Please, Fax, for old times' sake. For Uncle Sidney. For me."

He looked up. "You mean it? You'd still t-t-t-trust me to ride your horse? Think there's t-t-t-time for another round?"

Shelley nodded. "A clean round, Fax. No ticks this time."

TWENTY-THREE

SHELLEY felt as though she were on a seesaw. For months she had been in social limbo, in the purgatory of ostracism. Now suddenly she found people angling for invitations to the ball. Patiently she explained she had nothing to do with the guest list and referred them to Sion Atwell, who was in charge of the invitations.

Shelburn Hall had been restored as well as possible. Zagaran had sent over a man to mow the grass under the oaks in the park. Shelley had weeded the flower borders, and fresh geraniums had been put in the pots in the stableyard and on either side of the front door. Only the ruined wing with the tree draped with wisteria growing out of it remained the same. At night, when the moon shone down upon it, it was a dead and soundless place bearing the chilling smell of cold stone and past mystery.

Inside, the Race Ball Committee had transformed the long, dimly lit drawing room and the pine-paneled dining room into an elegant eighteenth-century ballroom. The crystal chandeliers and Tiffany lighting fixtures had been carefully cleaned and candles installed to replace the light bulbs. The old square mahogany piano had been tuned. Samantha Sue Buford, who had returned from Nevada and was staying with Debby Darbyshire until after the race, had made her usual clever flower arrangements for the tables set up in the hall and around the edge of the space cleared for dancing.

"The room looks handsome," Mike commented, "but why the blank spaces? Where is great-great Uncle Hugh?"

"I sent some of the ancestors off to be cleaned. Enid knows somebody who restores paintings for the National Gallery. Uncle Hugh was all cracked."

"I miss him," Mike said. "He's my favorite ancestor."

"If the paintings don't get back before the ball I'll fill in the blank spaces with sketches, different scenes of the chase."

I should have told him, she thought, as Mike turned away. Yet now her guilt went deeper than paying off Polo Pete with the painting. What is to be done? she asked herself. What is it that I want? She watched him get into the Jeep and drive away, leaving the unspoken question between them like a division of the heart.

Melusina, Shelley's old nurse, did not live to see another spring. Her funeral was on Friday, the day before the Shelburn Cup. Linda Taylor set about notifying the immediate family. It took some time to reach them all—Melusina's relatives were scattered throughout the country.

After the funeral arrangements were made—it was decided that the service would be held at Muster Corner Church at two P.M. Friday afternoon—Linda telephoned Melusina's white friends.

The list was long. The Taylors were as closely intertwined with Valley families as the telephone lines linking their houses. Yet the Latimers and Misty Montague were the only whites at the funeral.

One reason was that the time coincided with that of the annual Hound Show. This was an important event on the sporting calendar posted at the Halter Club. To members of The Hunt and those concerned with becoming members, the Hound Show was a must. Only the most dedicated cared about seeing the Young Entry, watching the hounds led around by the Huntsman in his long, white kennel coat as the puppies struggled to get free of their couplings and lifted their legs on the chairs set out around the roped-off space at the newly rebuilt kennels (the previous year a hound had deliberately lifted its leg on that of Mrs. Dinwiddie while she was being sharply critical of Fax's Mastership, and several of those watching had teasingly accused Fax of putting the dog up to this gesture of disdain). Aside from the Hunt staff and a handful like Fax and Shelley who really knew hounds, the onlookers came to be seen by those who were prominent in sporting circles, make knowing remarks (most of which had been read in books) about bone and pads and proper sterns, and partake of tea and drinks served afterward in the striped tent put up alongside the ring. Zagaran had asked Shelley to pour tea.

"What shall I do?" Shelley asked Mike, following Linda Taylor's telephone call.

"Do?" Mike replied. "Go to the funeral, of course." He stared at her, astonishment and dismay written on his face. "Melusina was your friend."

"I planned to show Ballerina and Ballyhoura, the two bitches we had all summer."

"Shelley," Mike said, "what has happened to you? You've always said Melusina was practically a mother to you."

Shelley put up a warning hand. "I'll go."

"Then why don't you call Misty and go with her? I didn't really know Melusina. I don't want her family to think I've come to observe, as though they were a petri dish."

"But of course you should go," Shelley said. "If you don't, they'll think it's odd. Besides, if I have to come back and pick you up we'll be even later for tea."

"I'm not going to Ballyhoura," Mike said. "I'm going to stay here and wait for the Shapiros to arrive. Cam can help me rake leaves."

"He's going to the Jenneys'."

"Aren't we overdoing the Jenneys? Seems to me he's always at the Jenneys'. Why don't their kids come here?"

"Oh, Mike." Shelley turned to face him. "Enid is always home and the older ones look after the younger ones. She says she loves to have him. Mike, what is a petri dish?"

"A glass dish in which you study cultures."

It was late Friday afternoon when the Shapiros drew up in front of Shelburn Hall. The dying sun was slanting through the trees, misting the park with chartreuse-colored light. In the fields the grass, moving in the breeze, shimmered like silver, and from the chimneys of the house rose blue smoke.

"How beautiful it is!" Marina exclaimed, getting out of the car. She had on a mink coat over a tight red skirt and matching sweater. With her long black hair, high cheekbones and liquid Latin eyes, she looked exotic and citified, as foreign to the

483

countryside as the high-heeled brocaded boots she wore on her feet. She hugged Shelley and then lifted her sharp animated face to Mike. "So this is your little caseta!"

Tad Shapiro stood gazing at the great house. Slowly his head revolved as he looked around at the park, the overgrown terraces and broken, crumbling statuary, the stables and pastures stretching beyond them.

"My God," he said finally. "Mike, whatever do you intend to do with all this?"

"Pave it and paint it green!" Mike grinned and clapped him on the back.

They were going to Misty Montague's for cocktails and dinner. By the time Marina had decided to wear a black velvet skirt and a long-sleeved ruffled matador's shirt in place of the strapless satin gown she had brought for the ball, it was a good half hour past the time they had been invited for.

Tad gazed appreciatively at the countryside. "I had no idea there was country like this so close to Washington. Land must be very valuable."

"You're seeing the most expensive real estate in the country. The landowners and members of The Hunt live in terror that some smart operator will come along and subdivide. Most of it now belongs to a syndicate. A man named Zagaran heads it."

"The Zagaran of Zagaran and Company?"

"The same," Mike said.

The recent mud season had turned the rutted dirt lane that led to Fairmont into a morass. The station wagon labored through the liquid clay, spattering the banks with yellow clods. On either side of the lane rose the rotting rails held together with baling wire and bits of cord that served to keep Misty's collection of horses and cows from escaping onto the road. In the dusk the animals could be seen grazing along the banks of the shallow river. As they rounded the corner the old stone house, shaggy with untrimmed ivy, came into view.

The walk, bordered by overgrown box, was rough and uneven with weeds growing up between the millstones that led to the house. In the dark Marina did not see the fresh steaming pile of manure left there by Brighty, Misty's old mare, who had the run of the premises and enjoyed nibbling on the box.

There was a horrified cry as Marina stood on one high-heeled evening slipper, holding the other up to the light from the carriage lamps on either side of the door. Tad reached out to support her.

"Baby, you've just been initiated into the mink and manure set."

Misty, surrounded by a cordon of dogs, met them at the door. Her hair was braided around her head like a crown. She wore a long black dress, faintly rusty with age, and her pearls.

Fax Templeton, the Schligmans and their house guests from Greenwich, some people named Stowell, were gathered in the front room. Like everything about Misty, the room was slightly out of kilter. The low beamed ceiling slanted to one side so that, as Misty explained, it was necessary for tall people to stand at the "deep end."

At sight of Marina, Fax Templeton's eyes lit up. "Nice-looking f-f-f-filly," he drawled to Shelley. "Speaking for myself, I prefer good bone, bottom, like you, Miss Shelley, ma'am. But for a short sprint, these light-boned hotted-up foreigners make a hell of a run for it. Remember that little French horse—"

"All right, Fax," Shelley answered. She could tell he had been drinking and it annoyed her that he could go partying the night before he was to ride her horse in the Shelburn Cup. "I'll introduce you. But hands off. Incidentally, hadn't you better go easy on the grape?" She broke off. Fax wasn't listening.

"Honey," he was saying to Marina, "ummmm." He bent his head lower. "I surely would like to lay a drag with that scent."

"How was the Hound Show?" Shelley asked as Marina moved out of Fax's range to be introduced to the others.

" 'Bout like it always is." Fax blew smoke toward the ceiling. "The Young Whip, guess you'd call him the Young Huntsman now, was showing hounds. Tatine never left his side. Seems to me that little ole boy's got himself overmounted. Speaking of being overmounted," he continued, warming to his subject, "our Master was squiring Samantha Sue. They were sitting in her car, with the heater on. He had her pour tea—"

"Why, she's not his cup of tea at all," Shelley broke in and then realized that Fax, his hand holding his cigar poised in mid-air, had stopped speaking and they were all looking at her. "I mean, I can't imagine a man like that—" She broke off in confusion. Turning to the fire, she felt the hot flush mounting to her cheeks.

"Honey"—Fax gazed at her speculatively—"what would you all know 'bout a man like that?"

"I would think they'd be exactly right for one another," Misty said thoughtfully. "After living with Polo Pete, Samantha Sue would find Zagaran's maleness and magnetism irresistible. And Zagaran would find her a sexy little steppingstone on his way to the top." Misty shrugged. "When he's tired of her, he'll leave her."

"How do you know so much about him?" Shelley asked.

"I sense that he's utterly ruthless," Misty answered. "Certainly he's fascinating. A woman can tell that at a glance. I just have a feeling. I can't explain it." She glanced in the direction of the kitchen. "I wonder where the Jenneys can be. My spoon bread will be ruined."

As though on cue the front door swung open. "I thought we'd never make it," Hunter said, dropping his sheepskin jacket on the bench in the hall. "Enid had the steers mixed up with the cows."

"How on earth did you do that?" Misty asked, going to greet them.

"I was late picking up the children at school," Enid explained. "I didn't have a chance to look under them."

"Under the children?" Katie Schligman asked, mystified.

"No, the cows," Enid said.

Hunter rolled his eyes at the ceiling. "Some farm girl I married."

"I never pretended to be a farm girl," Enid retorted. "I was a writer, living in an attic in Greenwich Village, when you rescued me from a life of sin, suffering and repentance."

"Cosy Rosy is living in the tack room," Misty was saying to Tad and Mike. "She insists that Dudley tried to kill her by putting poison in her milk. But if she leaves him there's nobody to take care of the horses. Connor left, you know, to work for the Martins."

"She'd give up the children," Mike said to Tad, "but not the horses."

Misty ignored his aside. "I thought we should drink a toast to Lookout Light." She lowered her voice. "Mike, Jubal Jones came by. I loaned him some money. It left me with a dollar eighty in my account." She put a hand on his arm. "If we run short of champagne, add some white wine to each bottle. You'd be surprised how few know the difference."

Mike returned with the wine. The cork exploded with a resounding bang and bounced off the painting of Misty on her mare, Brighty, that hung over the mantelpiece.

"Old Colonel DeLong, the Major's father, lost his eye due to being hit by a champagne cork," volunteered Fax. "He g-g-g-got a g-g-g-glass eye and had the Confederate flag painted on it."

"Now, let's all drink a toast to the Shelburn Cup," Misty cried. "To the brave horses and the brave men who will ride them tomorrow." Draining her glass in one long swallow, she flung it into the fireplace where it splintered against iron tongs shaped like foxes. "No," she said quickly as Fax started to follow suit, "mine was a jelly glass. You've got one of the last good ones. I don't mind washing silver cups but washing cheap china seems a waste of time."

Mrs. Stowell was standing next to Shelley. She was a large woman in a print evening gown. Her features were heavy and undistinguished but her blue eyes were alert and intelligent.

"I find this a most unusual place," she said.

Shelley was automatically on the defensive. "More so than Greenwich?"

"I don't know many people in Greenwich who are living in tack rooms," Mrs. Stowell said thoughtfully.

Misty's dinner was memorable. Moses, who had grown up at Fairmont, had come in from the stable to serve. He wore an ancient black suit and cotton gloves. Somehow he managed to thread his way between the jam jars and empty egg cartons and pots and pans that stood in piles on the kitchen floor and overflowed up the back stairs and serve roast duck with oranges and a wine sauce, wild rice, string beans with toasted almonds, steaming spoon bread and avocado salad. All of this was eaten off the famous silver dinner plates that Misty's great-grandmother Shelburne had buried in the sand at the bottom of Buffalo Run when the Yankees raided The Valley.

"All my china is cracked or broken," Misty explained to Tad on her right. "These are the only plates left." She leaned forward to speak to Shelley. "Sandy is thrilled about riding Contender. He's been running around the rotunda in a track suit and living on lettuce. I hope he gives the old fellow a good ride."

"I'm sure he will." Shelley looked pointedly at Fax across the table, wishing he would stop asking for more champagne and go home.

"I'll be glad when the race is over," Mike put in dryly. "Lately it's been nothing *but* race problems."

Hunter Jenney took his wife's hand. "Time we went home to the kiddies."

"Wait," Fax said. "Speaking of trouble, Hunt, you remember our d-d-d-discussion about f-f-f-foxes?"

"About mange being the forerunner of rabies?" Hunter let go of his wife's hand. "Ambrose Webster killed a rabid fox on his place the other day, almost in his barnyard. He says the disease is being spread by the foxes The Hunt has brought in. They weren't properly inoculated. He went to a meeting of the game commission. He suggested to Pete Buford that The Hunt blow up the dens in the area where mange has been found. Otherwise the foxes will return to them when they breed again and become re-contaminated. Buford just laughed. He asked if Ambrose thought The Hunt would consider anything so unsporting as blowing up dens!"

Mike spoke up. "I thought I read somewhere that it's illegal to bring foxes in from out of state."

"They've been importing f-f-f-foxes and p-p-p-putting them out since I can remember," Fax said. "Polo Pete hauls them in from the West each spring. He p-p-p-pens them up in that old cabin in the woods back of B-b-b-Ballyhoura."

"I stumbled on them when I was out looking for my ponies that got loose," Hunt put in. "The foxes looked in bad shape. I called Buford. He warned me to mind my own business."

"Pete's nothing but a t-t-t-tool," Fax said bitterly. "Zagaran's the p-p-p-power."

"Tool or fool?" Enid commented.

"How did Zagaran get so much power?" Katie Schligman asked.

"Easy," Fax replied. "All you n-n-n-need is m-m-m-money. Money begets land, and in foxhunting country land is p-p-p-power."

Hunt said, "Many of the old families made the mistake of leaving their property to several different heirs. As a result, the places went to ruin. Like the Free Zone and that land the Talbots used to own."

"And the Shelburns," Shelley said bitterly.

"The bank's been selling farms at auction," Hunt continued.

"Now Zagaran has The Hunt." Fax stared moodily into the bottom of his glass. "And he owns the Shelburn c-c-course. Miss Shelley, honey, you and me, we used to be the haves. We ain't got it any more. We just ain't got it. Take what h-h-h-happened this afternoon."

"Come on, Enid," Hunt said. "We really must get home. Mike and Shelley are tired and Fax has to ride tomorrow."

"Game warden was at the Hound Show," Fax said casually. "Seems The Hunt's being fined for bringing out-of-state foxes into the county."

"No kidding?" The Jenneys sat down again.

"Apparently somebody let the f-f-f-fox out of the b-b-bag. The Beast and her b-b-b-bridge pals got it into their heads that Hunt here t-t-t-tipped off the sheriff. Probably because you complained about losing chickens. The Beast and B-b-b-Buford have made it their business to call all the Hunt m-m-m-members and ask them not to eat at the Inn."

"You must be joking," Mike said. "They better not call me."

"Or me," Shelley volunteered and then remembered that she was no longer a Hunt member, just a guest on Zagaran's sufferance, his personal invitation.

"Whatever makes The Hunt think I'd inform on them?" Hunter asked, baffled. "Not that I approve of bootlegging foxes."

"What a very strange place," the woman from Greenwich said wonderingly. "Do I understand you to say that the foxes are subsidized?"

Augie Schligman nodded. "They disallow the people. Yet the foxes are on welfare. A chicken in every den." He went on to tell about the Muster Corner families picking up the chickens set out for the foxes until Polo Pete put a stop to it.

"We better all have another drink," Misty said, going to the table where the liquor and ice had been set out.

"How could they do this to us?" Enid asked.

"It's the way The Hunt operates," Fax said. "They're p-p-predictably unpredictable. How do you suppose Zagaran got to be M-m-m-Master?"

"He's done a lot for The Hunt," Shelley said defensively. "Refinanced it. Rebuilt the old stables and kennels. Hired more help."

"Now almost everybody owes him something," Hunt added.

"Even the Dinwiddies," Fax said.

"In what way?" Shelley asked.

"He makes a fourth at bridge. Samantha Sue roped him into playing after his wife went away."

"Fax, why don't you go to Zagaran?" Mike asked. "Have him call a meeting. Tell him Hunter wants to face his accusers."

Fax drained the remaining contents of his silver mug. "It's n-n-n-not my b-b-b-business." He looked at Mike apologetically. "You know m-m-m-me. I hate to get involved."

"Never mind." Enid smiled around the room. "The new cook at the Covertside Inn will poison everyone who comes in anyway. Come on, Hunt. You were the one who wanted to go home."

Shelley was horrified at what she had heard. Then she thought, I'll speak to Zagaran. He'll put a stop to the boycott. She walked over to Fax, who had poured himself another drink and was sitting on the narrow love seat with Marina. She took the glass out of his hand. "Sorry, old boy," she said, as Marina removed Fax's other hand from her lap. "You've hit a cold line."

TWENTY-FOUR

AT DAWN Shelley crept out of bed. Quickly she pulled on pants and a turtleneck, grabbed her sheepskin coat and, without waiting for a cup of coffee, drove to the race course.

The day was cold and raw with a feeling of rain in the air. There was a silver coating of frost on the fields, and beneath the pewter-colored sky the mountains looked gray and distant.

As she drove to Ballyhoura, the marbles Cam had been looking for rolled backward and forward, grating against her nerves, like her anxieties, her worries about money and all the things that were painful in her relationship with Mike. Fists clenched around the steering wheel, she forced them from her mind. After the race she would think about them. Now all that counted was the outcome.

The gatehouse was empty. The entrance unobstructed. Zagaran had not hired anyone to replace Freddy Fisher. As she drove in between the stone gateposts, she remembered the day she had first seen the locked gate and despised its owner. In the light of early morning the things that had happened since seemed incredible. Then as she pulled up in front of the long, low racing barn and parked the station wagon alongside the line of horse vans, the old familiar atmosphere of Shelburn Cup Day caught and held her in the grip of growing excitement.

Although it was barely light the stable was astir. From somewhere came the sound of hillbilly music blaring from a portable radio. Smoke rose from a fire set in an empty oil drum standing in the center of the walking circle under the trees. Several grooms and exercise boys stood around it warming their hands. Keystone, the Pennsylvania horse, a big strapping bay with a blazed face, was being walked by a Negro groom who wore his cloth cap facing backward and a rub rag stuck in his rear pocket.

Dooley Wright's battered brown coupe was drawn up beside the stable. Black Magic stood cross-tied in the aisle. Simeon had hold of the twitch on her nose, and several onlookers, including the man Mellick she had seen the day of the opening meet, stood watching from the side. While the mare rolled baleful white-rimmed eyes, the blacksmith held one of her front hoofs in his lap against his leather apron. Using his pull-off nippers, he removed a racing plate that had been bent in order to replace it with a new one.

Shelley nodded and spoke to the men. "Mawnin', miss," they replied, doffing caps and ducking their heads.

"Magic looks wonderful," Shelley cried spontaneously, and indeed she did, her coat shining like water with oil poured on it, muscles rippling beneath it like a running tide.

Simeon responded with a proud and happy smile. "That's one thing can be said for this mare. She's always ready." Magic laid her ears back and tried to reach him with her teeth. The groom gave the twitch a jerk. "Always ready for some devilment!"

Shelley asked Dooley if he would mind looking at Lookout Light's hind shoe that seemed loose.

"I've got two other horses to do," he said around the nails in his mouth, "but you can be sure I'll get around to Lookout Light." He looked up at Shelley, a smile breaking through the dirt and grime and weariness on his face. "A long time since a Shelburn horse has run in the Cup. We don't want anything to go wrong."

Shelley thanked him and continued on down the line of stalls. As she did so, she noticed that the man Mellick had turned away and was walking quickly in the direction of Richard Doyle's cottage. She remembered the look of venom that had been on his face the day they had ridden over his land and the story of his pitchforking Black Magic. Briefly she wondered if he could be considering "doctoring" the mare, doping or damaging her in some manner prior to the race. Then she realized the horse was too well guarded for that. Zagaran had security men posted in all the barns and Simeon would not leave Magic's side until after the race.

The sound of Lookout Light's welcoming whinny wiped all thoughts other than those concerning her horse from her mind. Lookout Light stopped stall walking, and butted his head playfully against her. She lifted her hand to pat him and he grabbed it, holding it lightly in his teeth. Shelley put her arms around his neck and buried her face in his satin shoulder. She heard the stall door open and felt the horse start as Zagaran came up behind her and slowly turned her around.

His leather flying jacket was zipped halfway up over his crimson turtleneck with the blue stripe running diagonally across it. The color contrasted with his dark skin. There wasn't an ounce of excess weight on his body, muscled and disciplined by daily workouts and the exercise routine he put himself through. He looked wonderfully hard and handsome, masculine and very fit.

Shelley had never seen him so confident or in such high good humor.

She thought of Fax Templeton and the barely disguised panic held in check the night before by the innumerable glasses of wine. Would Zagaran be proved right? Would he funk and lose the race?

There was the smell of wood smoke in the air, that and the scent of strong tobacco and the clean pungency of hay being shaken out in stalls. She could hear the rhythmic clanging as the blacksmith hammered out Black Magic's racing plates on his anvil and from somewhere came the sound of a voice singing "Swing Low, Sweet Chariot." She felt completely attuned to her surroundings. The noises, the smells, the atmosphere of slowly building tension were things she knew and understood and at that

492

moment Zagaran, his confident devil-may-care attitude, his male vanity and the pride he took in his hard clean body, fitted into them in a way that Mike never had. They stood looking at each other and it was as though they were both holding their breath, as though each understood that all was being held in abeyance until after the race.

Lookout Light put his ears back and bared his teeth. Zagaran ignored him.

"I intend to win," he said to Shelley. "You know that, don't you? All's fair in love and war and horse racing!"

When Mike awoke, Shelley had already gone. The Shapiros were still asleep. Cam came into the bedroom, jumped on the great bed and announced he was hungry. Mike rose, pulled on his khakis and went downstairs to find Jimmy, back from feeding the horses in the stable, frying bacon.

Mike made himself a cup of instant coffee, fixed a bowl of cereal for Cam and had just sat down to toast and bacon when the telephone rang.

"Sorry to bother you on Shelburn Cup Day," Larry Gillespie said.

"No bother," Mike answered kindly, wondering if Larry was in another scrape. "What can I do for you?"

"Nothing you can do for me this time, Mr. Editor. Thought I might be able to do something for you." There was a brief silence in which Mike remembered the night he had spent persuading Larry to go back and finish high school after the boy had pilfered his petty cash box.

"I'm calling from the Gone Away," Larry said breathlessly, lowering his voice. "Mr. Baldwin asked me to bring your bank statement to his office. Mr. Buford was in there. They were talking about you. I heard Mr. Baldwin say something about five hundred dollars and Mr. Buford started to laugh. He said your wife had been trying to pawn off old paintings and that if you had five cents let alone five hundred dollars, he'd push a peanut the length of the Shelburn Cup course with his nose."

Reaction from the night before was starting to set in. Desperation coupled with an inordinate amount of Misty's champagne laced with brandy had not helped Mike's morale. As the meaning of Larry's words struck home, it became even lower.

"Mr. Buford looks over at Mr. Baldwin," Larry continued. " 'Togo,' he says, 'when Latimer comes in Monday no extensions, no loans, understand?' Just then he looks up and sees me standing there. I handed him the papers he wanted and he told me to go."

"I see," Mike answered slowly. "Larry, thank you. You know you could lose your job because of this."

"I realize that, Mr. Editor, sir. But I got to thinking—about the talks we used to have nights, folding the paper. Weren't for those talks I wouldn't have finished high school." He broke off. "I got to go now, sir, but I thought if I warned you maybe you could pay off the note this morning. They don't expect you until Monday. Time I get back to the bank they'll be gone."

"I'd come if I could, Larry," Mike said sadly, "but I haven't got the cash or credit."

"Must be some place you could borrow it," Larry said hopefully.

"I can try, Larry," Mike said and hung up.

Tad Shapiro was standing in the hall.

"I heard your end of the conversation, old buddy. I gather the heat's on. Want to tell me about it? If it's money, maybe I can lend you some. My last book's done surprisingly well. They're talking about a movie."

Tad's words helped to ease the hard cold knot that had been growing in his stomach during the conversation with Larry. For months he had felt that life had him by the throat. Even if he did manage somehow to collect the money he owed the bank and pay it before noon, the gesture would be but a finger in the dike of emotional and financial disaster destined to give way after the race, a race which now in the light of this gray March morning he felt bound to lose.

"Old buddy, is there any coffee?" Tad asked. "I need plasma. By the way," he continued as they went toward the kitchen, "you'll have to interpret some of last night's events. I sensed enough undercurrents to put the *Queen Mary* on the rocks. Speaking of rocks, from now on I drink Scotch."

Jimmy turned away from the stove and grinned at them. He had tied one of Shelley's ruffled aprons around his waist over his too-large hand-me-down work coveralls. He had on a checked shirt, newly purchased, phosphorescent pink socks and scuffed men's shoes. The weight he had put on since coming to Shelburn Hall was not noticeable. For a boy of twelve, he was painfully small and thin.

"Got some bacon and fried eggs comin' up," he said, giving the eggs an expert flip.

Mike put his hand to his head. "Jimmy, where did you get those socks?"

"You gentlemen sit down," Jimmy replied formally, "and I'll serve you. Reckon Miss Shelley went to see her horse and won't be back for a while." Holding up his spatula, he turned to Mike. "Is sumpn' wrong with my socks? I got them for Sunday meetin'."

"No, Jimmy, not a thing wrong with them." Mike shaded his eyes. "They're real Sunday-go-to-meeting socks." Indicating the wicker breakfast tray on the counter that Jimmy had set with the best green and yellow china, he asked Tad if Marina was ready for her breakfast.

"Jimmy's even put a yellow rosebud in a silver cup in Marina's honor," Mike said. "He must have gotten up before dawn to set the tray. For the past few months Jimmy's been doing everything," Mike explained after Jimmy, filled with self-importance, left with the tray. While they ate, he told Tad about the boy's background.

"It may not seem so to you, old buddy," Tad said slowly when Mike finished, "but the work you're doing here is a damn sight more important than you think."

Tad's words jerked Mike back to the present. The money owed the bank. Where was he going to get it?

The interest on the loan Mike had taken out on the *Sun* was due Monday morning. All Mike had to do was make out a check and hand it to one of the tellers. The problem was that he did not have the money. The five hundred dollars he had put aside had gone to pay for the newsprint needed for the first section of the Anniversary Issue that had been printed up the past week. He had counted on getting an extension of his loan until after publication. The Anniversary Issue would sell for a dollar a copy and county newsdealers had assured him of enough orders so that a good profit was indicated.

Now he knew, too, where the painting of Great-great-uncle Hugh had gone. Shelley had sold it to Buford.

Through the worry and fatigue dulling his mind and body Mike heard Tad say, "Old buddy, let's go to the bank. I'll make out a check."

At that moment Shelley returned. Cam and the dogs rushed to meet her. Simultaneously the telephone began to ring and Connie Jackson arrived with the final seating arrangements for the dinner.

An hour later the house was chaos. The ladies from Delia's Kitchen who were cooking the dinner had crowded into the kitchen, from which came peals of laughter. Enid Jenney was arranging fresh flowers in the silver bowls in the hall and Connie Jackson and Debby Darbyshire were arguing over the seating arrangements. This had been a running battle for weeks. Connie kept grabbing the list and rearranging it in order that the people she stood in awe of or wanted to be friendly with would have the best positions, while those she felt had slighted her would be "below the salt," delegated to the rooms opening off the ballroom.

"I've had it," Debby said, slamming a batch of place cards down on the table. She was in stained blue jeans, and a wisp of straw clung to her short-cropped steel-wool hair. "I'm putting my place up for sale. Paper work, paper work and no help and then getting a lot of lip from the stable. Yesterday I spent all day at the desk filling out forms for the Jockey Club. After I'd done all the colts in pencil I read the fine print and saw I was supposed to do their pedigrees in ink. I had to start all over again." She reached into the pocket of her pants for a cigarette. "Got a match?" She looked up and noticed Tad. "I'm Debby Darbyshire," she said, putting out her hand. It was stained with nicotine and spots of green paint.

"This is Tad—" Mike began and got no further.

"I'm going down on the Carolina coast," Debby ran on in her down-to-manure manner. "I'm tired of spending my life mucking out stalls or on a ladder painting the house. I want to be free to fish. So I'm selling the works. Mike, put an ad in that sheet of yours. Where's Shelley? That Fail Safe snob Connie has fucked up the seating again." She turned. "Shelley, we can't have Millicent in the same room with the Beast." She reshuffled the cards in her hand. "Tina Welford can't abide Katie Schligman, says she hired away her cleaning woman."

"You have to give Millicent a front row table," Shelley argued. "She's bought stacks of tickets and is bringing a lot of guests."

"She's sure to fuss wherever we put her," Connie said meanly. "She's been in a temper ever since Sailor died."

"That freezer must be awfully full," Debby commented. "Dogs, stallions—"

"I'm glad I'm not going to her luncheon." Connie sniffed. "I don't fancy fried dog or roast horse."

"I'm going downtown," Mike wrote on the pad in front of Shelley at the telephone. "You look very pretty."

"Just a minute," she said to the *Capital Courier* press photographer she was directing on how to reach Shelburn Hall. She turned, tossing her hair out of her eyes. "Mike, we're due at Millicent's at noon, to see the horses."

Mike groaned. "I thought we weren't speaking to Millicent."

"I met her in the post office. She invited us and I accepted. I thought the Shapiros would enjoy it."

"I've seen Millicent's horses," Mike said.

"You'll have to see them again or you won't eat."

"We won't eat anyway," Mike answered gloomily. "Millicent generally forgets to order any food. Is it all right if I take the station wagon or are you going out again?"

"God, no," she answered, shrugging out of her coat. "I've got to show the women how to cook the salmon Zagaran had flown from Canada, get Manassas Brown to ice the champagne, take Cam to the Jenneys', muck out the guest room if Marina ever gets up—getfoodforbreakfasttomorrow, pressmydressfortheball—"

"Enough," Mike said. "At that rate it will be next year before we see you again."

"Mike." Her eyes suddenly softened. "Oh, Mike, there never seems to be time any more. The race—"

Impulsively he leaned over and kissed her on the cheek. "Remember Scarlett O'Hara in *Gone with the Wind?* We'll think about it tomorrow."

He left her speaking rapidly into the telephone. "At Shelburn you turn onto the Valley road. What? What's the route number? I haven't the slightest idea. Everybody knows the Valley road. Mike," she called as he went out the door, "don't forget the extra case of champagne."

Mike gave Tad a rueful smile. "I don't know what we're doing buying champagne when we can't pay the mortgage, but then I keep forgetting—we'se gentry!"

The main street was clogged with traffic. From the lampposts fluttered the flags that are put out for race day: the town flag, a red running fox surmounted by a curving brush against a gold background; the stars and bars of the Confederacy; and the green and yellow Shelburn colors that adorned the finish stretch at the course.

As the vans carrying their cargoes of high-priced horseflesh drove past, you could see the horses' heads, veined, breedy, keen and excited. Their grooms leaned out over the opened upper half of the entranceway, teeth flashing white, grinning and waving to their friends on the sidewalk or lounging on the corner.

Out-of-state cars, station wagons, Jaguars and Rolls-Royces, with diagonal stripes painted on their sides and expensive intricately made foxes, birds, jumping horses and other sporting emblems drilled onto their hoods, lined both sides of the street. At the Halter Club owners, trainers and riders stood around the bar, animatedly discussing their horses' chances. Shelley was relieved to see that the Covertside Inn was also crowded. In spite of the boycott that had been proposed against it, both bar and restaurant were doing a booming business.

"Strange to be going to Last Resort again," Mike said as he drove onto the Valley road. "We haven't been there since the dog episode."

"Lance killed one of Millicent's terriers," Shelley explained to the Shapiros. "She was very upset. I can't say I blame her but she had been warned time and again not to bring her dogs on the place."

"We may end up eating Mother's precious-darling-love for lunch," Mike said, and explained about the dog being stored in the freezer.

"She always gives a luncheon on Shelburn Cup Day," Shelley said. "If you're going to write about The Valley, you shouldn't miss Millicent or Last Resort."

The long avenue wound around numerous barns, a pond and a mile-long race track. It was lined with yellow daffodils and forsythia. "Ours haven't started to come out yet," Mike said, indicat-

498

ing the yellow bushes foaming alongside the drive. "I wonder why Millicent's bloom so early?"

"They wouldn't dare not to," Shelley said wryly.

The great white-pillared mansion was full of people, standing isolated in bunches, like clumps of asparagus, or wandering about gazing at the priceless sporting paintings, part of the world-famous collection that Mason had left Millicent along with the house. Cracked and darkened with age, they were hung in improbable places, beneath the stairs and in the reeking bathrooms where batches of new puppies wriggled in baskets under the ringed and grimy wash basins and in the old claw-footed marble tubs.

Mike gave a relieved sigh. "At least we've escaped the stable bit. Millicent has three hundred and twenty horses by the latest count and if you don't oh and ah over each one, your food rations will be cut off." Gazing into the dining room full of fabulous old English soup tureens and racing trophies, but bereft of anything resembling food, he concluded glumly, "Not that we'll eat anyway. Millicent usually forgets to order any meals."

"Just so they don't cut off the liquor." Tad started toward the bar in the hallway. "By the way, is that our hostess?"

Heralded by a barrage of terriers bounding ahead, Millicent swept down the wide stairs. For luncheon and the races she wore dungarees and sneakers and a man's orange-colored shirt held together by a safety pin. On the bottom step she paused. Observing the throng in the hall and the huge sunken living room, she threw wide her arms in a gesture of welcome. "Where is everybody? Boojie, Terence. Hi, sports. Why, Shelley." Stepping down into the hall she went up to Shelley and took her face in her palms. "I kiss you on the nose. Sweetie pie, let's not fight. I was shitty to you. It's over now and forgotten. I took Mother's precious-darling-love out of the freezer yesterday and buried him in the dog cemetery."

"That's a relief." Shelley smiled and introduced Millicent to the Shapiros.

"You must talk to Terence," Miliicent said when Mike told her Tad was the author of a recent book about Spain. "Terence Glyndon, you know. He wrote *Summer in Sumatra*. Terry baby," she cried, looking around, "where are you? Timmy, have you seen Terry? I want him." With an imperious gesture she

499

beckoned to a distinguished-looking man with white hair. Mike recognized him from his press photographs as a Supreme Court judge who had been earnestly studying the Herring barnyard scenes in the hall.

"You really should have this restored," he said, indicating a hole in the corner of the canvas. "It's too valuable to let go to pieces."

"Rick, my third husband, shot it out one night. He was drunk and thought he was pig-sticking in Injah, yuh know. Terribly pukka sahib he was, especially when he was drinking, which was all the time. But stop looking at those dreary old things, Timmy. Come and meet the Latimers and Mr. and Mrs. What-did-you-say-your-name-was? Mike is the editor of our local newspaper and the sport here wrote that divine book about Spain, something about Iberia."

"I'm afraid you're thinking of someone else," Tad said modestly.

But Millicent was no longer listening. "Bones isn't here. He hates missing a chance to show off the yearlings, but he had to leave early to walk the course again. But come along, sports. I'll give you the tour. Shelley, wait until you see my Windswept filly. She's the last of the Sailors." Millicent's eyes filled with tears. "You heard—he died last week." She blew her nose with a man's orange-colored handkerchief and banged the Indian gong by the door. Dogs barked and people carrying glasses came from the living room, hall and dining room. Millicent led them out the door and down the drive, past lush paddocks and outbuildings. Fighting chickens scurried away in alarm and a flock of geese honked at sight of the dogs. In the long, low barn the terriers flushed a covey of colored grooms rolling dice in the tack room.

"What do you boys think this is, your birthday?" Millicent demanded. "Shooting crap on company time. Pick up dem bones and get moving. Lead out the Windswept filly and the bay Challenger colt. Step on it."

"You, Russell." She addressed a stockily built Negro with heavy jowls and a battered felt hat who was surreptitiously trying to sweep a pile of cigarette butts left by the crap players under the tack box. "You know the rules about smoking. If I find you boys lighting up here in the barn again you'll all be fired."

Whereas Millicent often quoted the remark made by a guest to the effect that you could plant potatoes in the house and they would sprout, she took a fierce pride in the fact that you could eat off the floor in her stables. The aisles were swept twice daily by a tractor with a broom attachment. The straw in front of the stalls was braided to avoid bits and pieces of bedding escaping onto the walkway, and the entire stable was sprayed several times a day with a scent called "Millicent's Own," especially concocted for her by a friend who was the manufacturer of a famous line of cosmetics.

After pulling on a pair of spotless white kid gloves that Russell handed her from the shelf in the tack room, she ran her hands over the buckets and halters, with shining brass nameplates, hanging beside each stall and along the backs and sides of the horses led out for her inspection. She then looked at her gloves. Any signs of dust or dirt caused what she described as a rocket issued to the groom in charge of the unclean horse.

Pausing in front of each stall, where a card fitted into a brass frame gave the breeding of each occupant, she crooned and patted, explaining that the colt was either the most precious she had ever owned or the most itsy-bitsy love of a filly ever dropped at Last Resort.

"Do they drop their babies?" Marina asked a man with a red tie with foxheads on it and a loud plaid vest with a gold watch chain. The man, said to have paid the highest price ever paid for a yearling at Saratoga, gave Marina a clinical, humorless explanation of horse obstetrics.

"In Ireland they say a shamrock grows up wherever a foal is dropped," Shelley explained kindly. "In The Valley, mint grows up instead."

"Speaking of mint, where are those juleps I've heard about?" Tad asked.

"When are we going back to the house?" Marina demanded plaintively. She looked back at the groom following with a rake to erase their footprints from the tanbark walkway. "It is hard to walk."

The Valley was the only place, Mike had said once, where you needed both blue jeans and dinner jacket on the same day. People dressed down in the daytime and up at night. Marina, a city person, did just the opposite. In her ornate high-heeled boots that sank into the aisle, huge gold circles in her pierced ears and gold necklace, she looked as alien, as out of place as a foreign object in the eye. She turned imploringly to her husband. "I am hungry."

As the extended tour continued, the Supreme Court justice mopped his face with the carefully pressed handkerchief that had been protruding from his breast pocket. Marina's expression of boredom deepened. Mike and Tad, wishing they could smoke, lagged further behind. Shelley looked at her watch. Only one o'clock. Post time was at four. Three more hours.

At length they reached the last stall.

"Come along and see the two-year-olds," Millicent said gaily, striding ahead. "Still plenty of time." She was so earnestly explaining the bloodlines of her horses that she failed to hear the almost audible groan.

The Supreme Court justice and several others managed to escape back to the house. Shelley and the hard-core horse aficionados, including the man in the plaid vest, were herded into Millicent's pink and orange station wagon with her emblem, racing silks and cap, orange polka dots with a pink stripe, painted on the doors.

"I'll come with you," Tad said, sliding into the back seat alongside Shelley. "Mike and Marina are headed for the bar."

Halfway across the first pasture they encountered two of what Millicent called her winged friends, two young men in plum-colored Nehru jackets, sideburns and pointed suede shoes.

"Loves," Millicent cried, slamming on the brakes, "where have you been? Hurry, get in. We're going to see the two-year-olds."

"We've seen the yearlings and the two-year-olds," they said in unison. "We've even seen the three-year-olds." They got no further. At Millicent's insistence they were crammed into the back with Shelley and Tad and a blond girl whom Millicent introduced as Miss Dimples from Louisville. "Bones asked her," Millicent whispered to Shelley. "He really is an indulgence rather than a husband, don't you agree?"

They traversed two more pastures, forded a stream and eventually came to the field in which the young horses were grazing. Tad started to jump out to open the gate.

"Sit still, sport," Millicent commanded sharply. "My boy Russell will be along in a minute."

"But it's miles," Tad ventured as she pointed to the Negro running up the incline behind them. Millicent looked hard at Tad.

"Hard enough to keep them in their places these days. I don't want mine spoiled."

Russell reached the gate. Without pausing, he unlatched it and swung it wide for the car to pass through. Glancing back, Shelley saw him slumped against it, catching his breath.

Millicent got out of the station wagon and walked up to the young horses. They crowded around her, nipping at one another and pushing against her. "There, loves," she crooned. "I kiss you all on the nose."

All but Shelley and the girl from Louisville looked terrified. The others hung back, planning to make a run for the station wagon if there was a stampede, as Millicent went into her ethnic dissertation on the bloodlines of each animal.

Much to Tad's discomfort, the winged ones wedged themselves up against him for the return trip. As they drove through the gate, held open for them by Russell, splashed through the stream and bounced back over the rutted track in the fields to the drive, he sat helplessly in the back seat, overly warm in his topcoat, unable to move away from their giggling advances.

"My God, old buddy," Mike exclaimed when Tad reached sanctuary by the bar, "you look done in!" He noticed the Nehru jackets making their way toward them. "Wherever did you find *them?*"

"Friends of Millicent," Tad replied dryly. "Picked them up in a field."

"Oh, I see." Mike cocked an eyebrow. "Fruits of the land."

Back at the house more people had arrived. There were people in tweeds and tartans from Long Island, Pennsylvania and Maryland. A scattering of local foxhunting types and some of the younger set home from school and college for the weekend, gaggles of elegantly dressed girls with long, straight hair, long legs and long, swanlike necks. They wore pastel-colored tweed suits, striped nylon turtlenecks with gold pins in the collars or on their lapels. They had finishing-school drawls and an air of infinite superiority. And when they moved, it was en masse, like lemmings, as though unable or unwilling to be separated one from another. Their long-stemmed elegance contrasted oddly with the retired jockeys with wizened old-young faces, the politicians and a scholarly-looking man with a magnifying glass examining the sporting

503

books in the library, who turned out to be a famous rare book collector.

As she almost never remembered names, Millicent never bothered to introduce anyone to anyone else. Thus, the people who knew each other banded together, standing by the bar or wandering through the house to stare at cups in glassed-in cases, ragged faded horse-show rosettes on strings tacked to the beautiful pine mantels, and dusty photographs of famous people, fading to a chocolate-pink in tarnished silver frames standing on the piano and antique tables.

In one of the drawing rooms, punch was being ladled out of a huge silver challenge bowl that Millicent's Windjammer, the first of her famous line of steeplechasers bred from the stallion Sailor, had won at Aqueduct.

"Have some punch," Millicent urged, picking up her needle-point.

"I never saw such a big bowl," Tad said. "You could take a bath in it." He took a sip of the dark foaming liquid.

"Better stick to bourbon," Mike warned. "It's champagne mixed with stout."

"Guess you're right." Tad set his glass down. "Looks like a long journey into night."

"I'm told this is a famous house," the elderly woman they had met at Misty's said conversationally. "George Washington is supposed to have slept here."

The living room looked and smelled, Mike thought, as though Washington had kenneled his hounds in it. Every chair was tenanted by little brown terriers, mournful-looking bassets, and an assortment of canines that appeared to have more mixed blood than a New Orleans prostitute.

Unable to sit down, the guests stood on the floor stained and littered with the white tissues which Millicent ripped from Kleenex boxes set on the tables and dropped onto the puddles made by the dogs lifting their legs on the priceless period furniture. As people spilled drinks and ground cigarettes out on the beautiful pine floor, Mike decided that some of the humans were as unbroken as the dogs.

Leaning against the mantel, he listened to the pair of flat-chested raw-boned women from Pennsylvania discussing the race.

"Black Magic is the favorite," one said. "B. Zagaran rider."

"Who is this Zagaran?" her friend asked. "Ever since I've been in The Valley I've been hearing his name."

"He's a bit of a mystery. Very rich. Very good-looking. Said to slay foxes and women. By the way, what do you think of Sailor?"

"I don't think much of his get."

Her companion thought a moment. "He throws good bone!"

"What are they talking about?" Tad whispered to Misty. She had just come in and made her way across the room to speak to him. She looked clean and workmanlike. In answer to his question, she let out an unladylike hoot. "They're talking horse talk. Sailor is Millicent's stallion."

"I feel like George Orwell," Tad said, "or as if I'd gone through the looking glass for the third time."

One of the farm women, in a stained Mother Hubbard, entered carrying a silver tray. Pushing aside the used glasses on the refectory table, she set it down. The contents of the elaborate antique trophy won by a Last Resort horse were open-faced sandwiches, bread spread with cooked meat and cut into stars, moons and other designs with a cookie cutter.

"Lunch!" Millicent caroled. "Help yourselves."

"I'm famished," Marina said. Reaching for a sandwich, she popped it into her mouth. "Good!" she announced when she finished chewing. "May I have another?"

"Of course." Millicent beamed at her. "I'm glad you like them."

"Very much," Marina replied. "Tell me, what is this spread?"

"A Last Resort specialty," Millicent explained. "We cut some colts yesterday."

"I don't understand."

"Testicles," Millicent replied succinctly. "They're called Montana oysters on our ranch. We cook them and grind them up— Why, sport, is something wrong?"

Marina was suddenly very pale. "Excuse me," she gasped. "I must find a bathroom."

The drive to the course was agonizingly slow. Horse pullmans honked impatiently. Limousines, farm families in pickups from the Free Zone, and a busload of students wearing funny hats and drinking mint juleps out of Mason jars were bumper to bumper. Planes and helicopters circled the course, waiting to land on Zagaran's airstrip.

"I hope the fog doesn't get worse," Shelley said worriedly. "If it does, we won't be able to see anything."

"Relax," Mike urged. "It's still a good hour before the race."

Shelley had an impulse to shake him out of his controlled calm, and Marina, with her flirtatious manner and facetious chatter and constant questions, increased her annoyance. Tad, with the benign fatherly air of an amused parent, patted his wife's mink-clad shoulder and gazed at the passing parade of racegoers.

Finally they reached the entrance onto the course allotted to owners, trainers and riders. Herm Gillespie, in charge of the gate, waved them through.

The hillside sloping downward from Ballyhoura House was black with people. Around the paddock and along the snow fence, designating the finish stretch, flew flags in the colors of the participating stables. The scarlet coats of the hunt staff and members serving as patrol judges and the red and white flags marking the fences stood out against the green of the carefully maintained course.

It was forty-five minutes to post time. The wind had risen and the air carried an ominous chill as though rain or even snow might come at any moment.

Mike parked the station wagon in the lot. Then the Latimers and the Shapiros fought their way through the crowd flowing courseward like a multicolored river. Many had been on the hillside since noon, muffled in sheepskin and polo coats, enjoying tailgate picnics ranging from hot dogs bought at the stand set up by the Ladies of the Shelburn Fire Department Auxiliary to elaborate buffets served by liveried butlers.

The best vantage point was on the hill in front of the Ballyhoura Oak. The spaces had been assigned according to heredity and longevity, and, in the words of Dash-Smythe, "old friends who have physical ailments such as the gout." This allotting of hallowed ground to a chosen few had caused no end of division and squabbling. People who had contributed heavily, like the Martins and McFarlands, were excluded because they were new people, whereas the Dinwiddies, who contributed nothing, had the number one spot beneath the tree.

The Webster family was nearby, devouring massive helpings of fried chicken. Next to their pickup, David, the Buford butler, had set up a card table covered with a white cloth and centered with fresh-cut flowers and a silver candelabrum. "Polo Pete's Pub" was parked alongside. From the back of the Volkswagen bus, in which there was an electric stove, a refrigerator and an ice-making machine, Buford affably dispensed drinks to his luncheon guests. Zagaran was there. Over his white breeches, racing boots and silks he wore his polo coat. Against the shelter of his turned-up collar his profile was as sharp and clear as his eyes when he saw Shelley.

Shelley did not want to meet him. Now, before the race, there was nothing further to be said to each other. And not with Marina observing them. Marina in her high brocade boots and her mink, with her white skin, mascara and long, thick black hair, looking like something out of the Chinese theater. But she had no choice.

"Isn't that your Mr. Zagaran?" Marina demanded.

"Not *my* Mr. Zagaran." Shelley pulled away and tried to hide behind the Websters' truck. But Zagaran had seen her and was coming toward them.

While Mike and Tad stood stiffly to one side, Zagaran smiled down at Marina, who said she thought the fences looked very high and the men who rode over them very brave. At that moment Raymond Hoe, who had been sitting on a nearby rock, raised his guitar and began to play. For years the blind Negro had existed by playing his guitar at horse shows and race meets and private parties. At the Shelburn Cup he was as much a part of the scenery as the Ballyhoura Oak. When he finished "Carry Me Back to Old Virginny," Shelley reached into her shoulder bag and brought out some change. She leaned down and put the money in the tin cup on the ground beside the old man. The blind man stared up at her.

"Who does Uncle Raymond have the honor of playing for?" he asked politely.

"Shelburn Latimer."

"I knew your grandmother," the old Negro said softly. "The third Missus Shelburn. And I played at your mother's wedding."

"I am Zagaran of Ballyhoura," Zagaran interrupted. Coming forward he dropped several bills in the old man's palm. The Negro held the money in his palm. "Mister Zagaran, you big rich"—his sightless eyes peered up—"but you can't buy one poor old blind man." Slowly he turned his hand over, letting the bills fall onto the ground. "I don't play for anyone from Ballyhoura."

No emotion showed on Zagaran's face. Yet for a moment as he stood there, there was something cold and terrible about his stillness.

"What did the man with the guitar mean?" Marina asked after Zagaran had gone to see about his horse.

"The colored people have a superstition about Zagaran," Mike answered. "Washington Taylor told me they believe he is the devil, or Sean Shelburn returned to life. They think Ballyhoura is haunted. During Reconstruction Sean Shelburn hunted down and lynched Negroes. In the minds of the old-timers the legend lingers on."

"He's very handsome," Marina said softly, stroking her mink.

On Shelburn Cup Day the paddock is the mecca of the sporting world. There the same people who had come together in the past had returned for the renewal of the race, a little older, a little more weatherbeaten, but with the same unchanging eagerness for sport, clean competition between thoroughbreds and men with the courage to ride them.

Here the high and the mighty, the poor and the lowly were bound together, accepted by one another within the framework of their mutual enthusiam. R. Rutherford Dinwiddie, Esquire, resplendent in London-tailored tweeds and gray bowler, shooting stick and binoculars, studied his race card in the company of farmer Webster and Bob Gilbert. Bebe Bruce, her two greyhounds on a leash, asked My Boy Hambone what he thought of Keystone, the Pennsylvania horse. Owners, trainers and riders stood about, individual islands discussing their horses' chances. The sheepskin set had surfaced. The women wearing tweeds and brown walking shoes and a knowing, confident air, that look of conformity and inborn certainty that bespoke Foxcroft and Farmington, Long Island, and Lake Forest, and made them hard to distinguish from one another.

Clustered around the Ballyhoura Oak were the Negro exercise boys, swipes and grooms, discussing the merits of the entries, doffing their caps to the passing gentry.

Now the horses were coming, being led single-file across the

Valley floor. Their vivid monogrammed sheets tied high on their necks and blowing in the wind caused them to look medieval, as though setting out for a tournament. Grooms clung to their heads, leaning their weight against their shoulders, crying, "Heads up, heads up, let the horses through."

Lookout Light came quietly, confidently. From the tips of his curved, pointed ears to his shining tar-painted hoofs, his breeding was apparent in the way he carried his proud, beautiful head. Looking over to some distant place of the mind, he set up a singing in the heart. Virginia City walked alongside, holding the horse's shank in one hand, waving and bowing to acquaintances and well-wishers with the other. The old man had said he wanted to lead in a Shelburn Cup winner before he died. He had bought a new suit for the occasion, and his battered black bowler sat squarely on his grizzled white head. In spite of his crippling rheumatism he walked proudly, holding himself erect, his ebony face wreathed in smiles as he nodded to admiring onlookers.

Jimmy trotted alongside, pulling his small brother Bardy along with him. Jimmy's pink socks and Bardy's crimson overalls, which had originally belonged to Cam, shone through the growing gloom of the darkening afternoon.

Tatine's chestnut, Warlock, was second in line. The old steeplechaser was a favorite with the crowd. With bowed tendons and timber knees, his swollen, battered legs looked like champagne bottles. He had a past and a presence, an intangible quality of gallantry. His coat, rubbed by Simeon, held a gloss like copper wire, and as though sensing this to be his last great effort, he pranced and chewed on his bit.

Black Magic came next, plunging and lashing out at the crowd. Then the bay Keystone, winner of several good races the previous year; the Dinwiddies' wise old hunter, Contender; Nautilus with Millicent, vivid in the orange horse blanket she had tossed over her shoulders, running alongside, offering admonitions mixed with baby talk ("Bones, remember sweetums likes to run on into his fences, Mama knows what sweetums likes, so don't take back too much"); Augie Schligman's Drum Major; and Rocket Man, the entry from Maryland.

The paddock was packed now. Between the clusters of owners, trainers and riders and members of the United Hunt's Steeplechase Association, with their gold badges in their lapels, there was hardly room for the horses to parade. "Heads up," pleaded the grooms. "Heads up, puleese!"

Tatine stood alongside the fence. She wore green tweed, simple as a boy's suit and worn as though for protection rather than effect. Her flamboyant hair blew wildly, an orange pennant with the wind whipping against it as she turned her head to speak to Richard Doyle. Shelley saw a long look pass between them. Simultaneously she noticed the Young Huntsman's wife standing on the other side of the paddock fence. The inevitable hair curlers protruded from beneath her loosely tied bandanna, and her vapidity, her slackness, seemed an insult to the handsome, expensively dressed people surrounding her. The man Mellick she had seen that morning was with her. He wore coveralls and an old crushed felt hat.

His eyes, Shelley noticed, were set close together and he had a mean varminty look about him. Now, as he stared at Tatine, his face took on a twisted, vindictive expression. Something about him, the way he slouched against the fence, the malevolent look in his eyes, was familiar. It was the same as that which had been in his eyes when he stood in the barnyard shaking his fist at them for breaking down his gate the day of Opening Meet.

She started to turn away, but something in the man's eyes held her rooted in her tracks. They were focused on Black Magic and the look in them was one of sheer cold hatred.

The moments now until post time seemed endless. Shelley smiled and spoke automatically to those who came up to wish her horse luck. She looked at the rain clouds gathering overhead and tried not to notice Zagaran standing near his horse, his dark head inclined as he stood with his arms crossed over his silks, talking to Samantha Sue Buford.

In the striped tent the scales waited for the riders to weigh out. One by one they came, staring past and beyond the people who crowded around them, with that wintry unseeing look men wear before going into battle or riding a race. Carrying their weight pads, toylike saddles, numbers and girths, they vanished into the tent where the clerk of the scales waited to write down their names and weights.

"Where can Fax be?" Shelley asked Sidney Merrywood. "You don't suppose—"

510

"Surely not." The trainer's tone was reassuring but his eyes as they scanned the crowd around the entrance were worried.

Fax Templeton felt nausea creeping like cold fingers toward his stomach as he made his way to the paddock. The fingers became a hard clenched fist, squeezing his nerve into nothingness. A sharp wind blew across The Valley, whipping his polo coat around his knees. Under it his silks felt cold and slippery against his body. People nodded and waved and called out to him, "Hi, Fax, here's luck." He made himself reply, forcing his face into a smile. Now was the time before the race when everything seemed unreal, horses and people, the flags flying along the snow-fence finish stretch fluttering from the brown toylike fences in the distance.

Lack of food and sleep made him feel lightheaded. That morning when he weighed himself he'd still been two pounds overweight. He'd put on Bones's rubber suit and gone out and steamed himself in the manure pile behind the barn—the poor man's Turkish bath. He'd lost one pound. No breakfast, no liquids, and he might be able to make it.

For the past week he'd been unable to sleep, dozing off only to awaken with that frightening sensation of falling, then lying awake, jumping the course over and over again, seeing the great fences rising in his mind's eye, growing higher as the long hours of darkness crept toward dawn. Always, as he rode the course in his mind, the horse's pace accelerated, faster and faster, until they reached the Coffin fence, his heart pounding in concert with the roaring of wind and hoofs in his ears. Then the crash—

If only he could have a drink.

He made his way to the scales. Sandy Montague came out, looking young and strong, fit and anticipatory. My God, Fax thought, to be twenty years younger, to be going out for my first Cup Race—to know once again the leaping, tearing, heart-pounding excitement, the sense of strength and aliveness and anticipation. No fear then—nerves, yes. But not this cold, sickening sensation of tension and breathlessness. Did it show? he wondered. Could Sandy see what he was feeling? He felt the trembling in his knees and body and hands—maybe if he had a drink.

Tiger Talbot and Tommy Fisher were waiting to weigh out.

They looked calm, confident, saddles and weight pads draped over their arms, joking easily with each other. Once he had been the focal point, the rider whom the new jockeys looked up to with awe and admiration. They nodded and spoke, but with a difference—the innate, insensitive superiority of youth and male fitness.

He was caught now, trapped in the crowd around the paddock entrance, where Wiley Matthews, hired to man the gate for the occasion, struggled to keep those without the proper badges from crashing the inner sanctum.

"Heads up," Fax pleaded. "Heads up. Please let me through."

"It's one of the jockeys," someone said. Then Wiley saw him.

"Make way for Mr. Templeton," he commanded. "Let him past."

Inside the paddock he paused to let the horses go by. He saw Virginia City leading Lookout Light. Lookout Light's ears were pricked. His big intelligent eyes roamed over the crowd. He seemed to be taking in everything that was around him. Fax's heart leapt. For an instant he forgot his fear, remembering how once it had been, when he'd been young and bold and the opportunity to ride such a horse as this had been the only thing on earth that mattered.

Somehow he got weighed out, made the proper-sounding remarks to the other riders, gathered up his tack and made his way back in the darkening afternoon. The sky was even grayer now, the air colder. Dizziness overcame him. He began to shiver. A drink—if he could just have a drink.

In the olden days there had always been somebody with a bottle. "False courage," Freddy Fisher used to say, taking a swig and winking at My Boy Hambone or one of the other blacks behind the barn. "Who needs it?" And in those days they hadn't needed it. They'd kidded each other and gone out to ride, hearts and spirits high, not from alcohol but from love of the game, swaggering and showing off in front of the sleek, beautiful girls from Far Hills and Old Westbury, Ligonier and the Green Spring Valley, who had rich daddies with racing stables. Freddy, Dave Montague and himself, driving all night in Freddy's old Ford touring car to race at Middleburg or in Pennsylvania or Maryland, riding all day, drinking all night. The Three Musketeers of the Hunt meets. Now Freddy and Dave were done, the one from cirrhosis of the liver soon after losing his job at Ballyhoura, the other killed in the war . . .

Only Bones was left.

Jubal Jones and a crowd of Negroes huddled behind the tent where Misty's Moses had his shell game going. They knew they couldn't beat Moses at his own game. Yet year in and year out they clustered around him, hypnotized by his hands darting over the board balanced on his knees, putting out their money, lured by the eternal hope that their eye would prove quicker than the old Negro's nimble fingers.

At the sight of Fax they straightened up. Moses sought to cover the board with his ragged sleeve.

"Jubal," Fax ordered, "come here."

"Yassir, Mr. Fax, yassir."

"Jubal," Fax stammered desperately, "you g-g-g-got a bottle? I got myself some kind of v-v-v-virus and I got to r-r-r-ride."

"Yassir, Mr. Fax." Jubal's eyes were knowing and sympathetic. "It's coming on mighty cold." Reaching into the pocket of his ancient overcoat, he brought out a fifth.

Fax took the bottle. He glanced around, then quickly lifted it to his mouth and took a long swallow. The cheap, harsh liquor burned down his throat and into his empty stomach, hitting it with what seemed an almost audible thud. For an instant he swayed, clutching Jubal's shoulder to keep from falling. The wave of nausea subsided. His head began to clear. "Just one more and I'll be okay. This wind—"

"Sure, Mr. Fax." Jubal nodded somewhat reluctantly as he eyed the rapidly depleting bottle. "Help yo'self."

As Fax was about to hand the bottle back to Jubal, a passerby joggled his arm. The bottle slid out of his hand, and as Jubal watched with a horrified expression, it crashed against a rock and broke, spilling its remaining contents onto the ground.

"Jubal, I'm sure as hell s-s-s-sorry," Fax stammered. "I'll m-m-m-make it up to you."

"Good luck, Mr. Fax," Jubal said resignedly. "I shore hope you win." As Fax departed he stood mournfully gazing at the liquor trickling from the broken bottle. "There goes my Saturday night," he said, shaking his head sorrowfully.

"Where *is* Fax?" Shelley asked desperately. "Uncle Sidney, he promised."

"Here he comes now," replied the trainer.

"Fax, you're late," Shelley exclaimed. She looked at his drawn face. "Fax, are you all right?"

Fax put his hands in his pockets to hide their trembling. "S-s-s-sure I'm all r-r-r-right."

"Now listen, Fax," Sidney Merrywood said, "remember Magic's habit of jumping to the left. You'll have to steady the colt at his fences. Be sure you give him his head and plenty of room—"

A bell jangled. The stentorian voice of Togo Baldwin, the paddock judge, rang out. "Now then, gentlemen, everybody up."

While Simeon held Black Magic on one side and another Ballyhoura groom took hold of her bridle on the other, Zagaran vaulted onto her back. After standing up and testing his stirrups, he gathered up his reins and ordered the men to let go. As they jumped backward, Black Magic shook her head, snorting. Sidney Merrywood checked Lookout Light's overgirth. Then My Boy Hambone gave Fax a leg up. As Fax sought to knot his reins, My Boy Hambone took the rub rag from his back pocket and gave his gleaming boots a quick dusting.

"Stay on the inside," Sidney Merrywood repeated for the final time.

Fax's fingers felt swollen and numb. He could not get the knot right. Shelley's worried face swam before him. "Don't worry about winning. Just stay out of trouble."

"Have a good trip, laddie," the old trainer said softly and turned away.

"Thanks." Fax felt himself sway in the saddle. He took a deep breath, seeking to steady himself and put down panic. Desperately he prayed he would not be sick.

Lookout Light lunged forward. Fax managed to regain his balance and pick up his reins. All those people on the hillside, watching. Fear rode with him, riding like a thin layer of ice on top of the warmth of Jubal's bourbon burning his empty stomach. The hopes and fears of all the years. Fifteen minutes from now, he told himself, it would all be resolved, one way or another.

Now the ride to the post, the last interminable minutes ticking away until flag drop. The wind that whipped the flags flying from the paddock slashed against him. His legs felt rubbery, without

514

strength, his arm muscles were already aching and he could not seem to get the air from his opened mouth down into his lungs. He tried to swallow, but his mouth was so dry he could not. He'd never known a rider yet who wasn't nervous going to the post unless it was Bones, slightly punchy now from all his falls. It was normal to be nervous, to have that feeling that you had never been on a horse before, as though each arm and leg and muscle was a separate untried entity instead of part of a coordinated whole. But then, once the race began, those last awful moments were forgotten. The training and reflexes that came with youth and experience took over and the glory began. You began to ride. Ride, Red, ride.

But that had been when he was young. Would it work now? Would the words "They're off" serve once again as the catalyst to courage?

He noticed the flags lining the snow fence bending in the wind. Crimson, the same color as Zagaran's silks. Zagaran and Black Magic. That was the combination to watch for. With great effort, he forced his mind to focus on the silks worn by the competing riders, committing them to memory. There was much more to racing than just being a good rider. You had to think, too, know your competition. Once again he ticked off the things he had learned about the horses. Keystone was a careful jumper who lost ground at his fences, gaining it again on the flat. Drum Major was chancy and could fall. Warlock was a good one to follow, safe and steady as a church. Rocket Man was erratic and hard to hold. Best to stay away from him, especially as he was being ridden by young Tommy Fisher, the son of his old friend Freddy, riding his first race.

Aside from Bones and Zagaran, the rest were all young riders, rank gung-ho kids who hadn't learned to think a race through beforehand. Riding races was alien to what they would normally be doing these days, sitting in a bank or selling bonds. Their only consideration would be to get the race over with some way and get on home. Once they were away they got all excited, lost control and traveled all over the place, endangering those around them.

The horses were peeling off now, some jogging, their jockeys standing high in their stirrups, some circling the field, having

515

what the British called a brief pipe-opener. Lookout Light tossed his head and leaned his youthful exuberance against his snaffle bit, yearning to be off and running.

Weakness assailed Fax. The liquor hadn't helped, only made it worse. He'd been wrong to agree to ride. It wasn't fair to the old trainer or to Shelley. Too much had happened. Too many years of overindulgence. Oh, God, he thought, tomorrow at this time it will be all over.

Visibility was getting worse. The sky was dark and glowering. Any minute now it would open and spill its contents onto those below.

The horses were being led to the post by the Old Huntsman on his gray. Keystone, the Pennsylvania horse, went first, a big, raking bay with a long, flowing tail and bandages on all four legs. Then Contender, Warlock, Rocket Man and Drum Major, Nautilus—Bones, in the shoulder pads that he wore to protect his smashed collarbone, looking topheavy. As the brown horse pranced past, Millicent called out, "Bones, don't let my sweetums get hurt. Bones, remember what I told you!"

Black Magic plunged after him. Froth spewed from her open mouth.

Lookout Light came last, walking calmly and easily now, ears pricked, eyes intent on the scene around him.

Fax sat clumsily. The saddle was hard and unfamiliar, as slippery and unfriendly as glass. His legs felt cramped and powerless, refusing to meet the leather and blend into it. His hands on the snaffle rein were numb and heavy, without lightness or flexibility.

Sidney Merrywood stared down at his highly polished chukka boots. He's drunk, the trainer thought miserably. Whatever made me think he'd be able to ride?

Shelley stood on the rock that was her special vantage point on the hillside. As always in those last tense moments before the tape went down, she felt detached and alone. Now it was as though all her life had been aimed toward this one race, the outcome of which would determine her future.

The years blurred and ran together. Her first Shelburn Cup, clinging to her father's hand as he pulled her up onto the rock. The year Fermoy fell. The years afterward, the waiting-to-be-grown-up years when she would no longer have to go home to early supper with Melusina. Then the finding herself grown and that it was all illusion. Outwardly she looked like the other long-stemmed, elegantly clad girls the race riders clustered around. Inwardly, she was as shivering and unsure as she had always been. It was only when she was with Fax that she felt whole, able to compete. Fax, with his golden head, his swagger. Wonderful grin and lust for life. Standing in the familiar paddock, she remembered how it had been watching him win his first Shelburn Cup on that horse of the Carlisles' nobody believed could go a yard, the tremendous ovation as he rode back to the judges' stand, laughing and waving to everyone, the great party that night when Freddy Fisher and Dave Montague picked him up and dumped him into the old claw-footed bathtub at Templeton, which they had filled with champagne. Shelley and Fax had become engaged that night, and life had become a succession of hillsides on which she had stood, her heart in her mouth, as Fax galloped and jumped his way through life, as lighthearted and carelessly as he had gone off to Korea, telling her before he went that he could not marry her—that he was going to marry Taffy Carlisle.

The horses were turning now, breezing off at a gallop toward the hollow where the race would begin. Beyond them the new fences Zagaran had ordered built were brown against a background as smooth and green as a polo field. From a distance they looked deceptively easy, but Shelley knew that close up the Terrible Tenth came to her shoulder and that there wasn't a horse living that could break the top rail of The Coffin.

They had almost reached the post when the rain began. Quickly the gay tweeds were disguised by yellow slickers and tan mackintoshes. Umbrellas bristled like multicolored mushrooms from the hillside.

The ambulance from the clinic and the Jeep carrying the judges bounced over the open field on the way to their stations on course.

The horses were under starter's orders now, circling and moving up in a line where Dash-Smythe held the big square canvas flag tacked to the end of a stick. Pink-coated patrol judges wheeled and circled like sheepdogs. Toward them, through the cold rain, drifted a handful of balloons that had broken away from the children carrying them.

At the post the horses swayed backward and forward, held

against an invisible force. Forward, false start, go back. Now, once again. They're off. No. Something's happened.

"Looks as though Magic has kicked Nautilus," Sidney Merrywood reported. His eyes were glued to his binoculars and his brow was furrowed with anxiety. "Yes. There. Bones is getting off and leading the horse away. He's lame."

Millicent, surrounded by her entourage, stood in her minicoach drawn up by the finish line. She was pointing and gesticulating.

"I'll bet the air around her is so blue you could blister a horse with it," the trainer said as Nautilus left the course. Doc Black, the course veterinarian and Bones's father, bent down to examine the horse's leg. Straightening up, he held up a hand and shook his head. Millicent's horse was out of the race.

Once again the horses lined up.

"Why can't that fool Dash-Smythe get them away?" Sidney Merrywood asked.

Lookout Light stood quietly now, waiting. Fax looked at the curved ears in front of him and felt his heart go out to the young horse. Pray God I don't let him down, he thought.

The rain pounded against them, turning the colt's gray coat dark. The ground where they continued to circle was becoming cut up, slippery.

The line evened and then fell apart as Keystone bolted for the first fence and had to be brought back. The starters swore and strained to keep the horses in position as the will to go forward swelled and grew to the point where it could no longer be borne.

"They're off!"

Excitement spread through the crowd like brandy warming the blood after a cold ride on a winter day.

The first fence was a blur, all of them going at it together, a bunched kaleidoscopic mass of moving horses and multicolored silks, shouting, swearing riders, then the zap zap of flailing legs against rails, slamming them front and back.

As a young rider, once the race began, Fax's instincts, his reflexes had taken over. The business of riding the race became all-absorbing. He became wholly concentrated. His body relaxed, began to move in rhythm with the horse's stride. The tension, the nervous fear became but a necessary preliminary to the pounding exhilaration, heightening awareness, providing the reason that men climbed mountains, went to war and rode steeplechases.

But that had been when his body had been fit and flexible, his mind clear and keen, when it was as though no amount of alcohol could bloat his body or blur his brain. Fax Templeton, they used to say, why he's so cool he could make out his income tax going over the Coffin fence.

Now they were swinging right, heading into the third, rising through the thickening curtain of rain driving against them. A timber wall growing higher and higher—Fax felt himself sliding, lurching. Desperately he tried to balance himself, his hands on the reins becoming rigid, pulling back, interfering, throwing the colt off stride.

Sidney Merrywood's eyes were glued to his glasses. Through the mist the racing horses, the shining silks looked dwarfed, artificial, like a theatrical illusion.

The trainer groaned. "Leave Lookout Light alone. For God's sake, give him a chance."

Shelley's nails bit into her palms. "Fax, oh, Fax, don't—" She turned her head away, unable to watch any longer.

Marina chose that moment to ask why some of the horses ridden by the patrol judges had red ribbons tied to their tails.

"For God's sake, Marina," Shelley exclaimed, "it's to warn people not to come close! Because they kick, that's why!"

"Shelley," Mike said quietly, "it's only a race."

She had been so completely absorbed in memories of the past that she had forgotten his existence. Now she turned toward him, saw the tiredness, the strain on his face, the intangible difference in his manner and his clothes, the tweed coat that she had made him buy that he almost never wore and as a consequence looked too new, the raincoat that was not stiff like the British-made mackintoshes. Instead it came off the rack at the Dependable Store. It looked too shiny, too new. Something rose in her throat, guilt, sorrow, anger, anger at herself, her inadequacies and loss of honor, and this anger focused on her husband.

"I think I go to the car," Marina said. "My mink is wet."

"Must you?" Tad asked. "At a time like this?"

"I go," Marina said imperiously. "I read my book and wait in the car."

Mike looked around at the people on the hillside in the downpour. They were huddled under horse blankets, rain gear and umbrellas, their faces red and pinched from the rain and raw air.

"This craving for discomfort is astonishing," he said casually. "We'd all be wise to go to the car and turn on the heater."

Shelley faced him furiously. Her face was wet, from rain or tears he knew not which. "Then why don't you?" she demanded. "Instead of standing here being superior and supercilious?"

Mike saw that the people around them had turned and were listening. "Not so loud. No need to make a public display."

"I wish that just once *you'd* make a public display," Shelley cried vehemently.

"I should have known Fax was over the hill, beyond recall." Sidney Merrywood sighed and lowered the glasses.

Lookout Light fought for his head. He changed leads. Fax saw the horses ahead leave the ground. He felt Lookout Light rating himself, judging the fence, then rise into the air. Making a mighty effort he twisted over the fence. For an instant Fax could not believe they were back on course and racing on. In that instant he said a prayer of thankfulness to the Pilot, the blood and sinew and great heart that the sire had projected to his progeny.

"Forgive me," he whispered, leaning low on the horse's neck. Lookout Light gave his head a shake and extended his stride.

They were starting to string out. Black Magic, still in front, was setting a killing pace. Contender was falling back, Rocket Man moving up. Fax saw Warlock on his right.

Now that the hold on his head was relaxed, Lookout Light's stride increased, covering the wet grass with a wonderful even precision and power. Suddenly Fax felt the blessed sustaining confidence starting to come, the sense of intense excitement and glory that made all that had gone before worthwhile.

Fence after fence swept by. Fax was aware of the rain against his face, of the white puff of blossoms on the old apple tree that marked the farthest point on the course. "Ride, Red, ride." He was riding now, helping rather than hindering, rating, easing, getting Lookout Light in right and giving him his head over the big fences, and the colt was responding, fencing flawlessly, without thought of funking, the weeks of schooling and preparation paying off. Fax's heart swelled with love for the horse, gratitude for the colt's courage and ability.

Contender went down at the tenth. Lookout Light twisted in mid-air, missing Sandy Montague, who lay motionless like a broken toy on the ground. Black Magic's burning pace was starting to tell. Drum Major was lagging and Keystone, the pride of Pennsylvania, fell at the fifteenth. Rocket Man was dropping back and Warlock was coming on strongly. At the twenty-second, Drum Major pecked and went down in a heap.

Two more fences to go. The racing began.

They started down the long slope. Black Magic was still on top, with Warlock in second place. Lookout Light's long stride lengthened, passing Rocket Man, bringing him up between Warlock running on the inside, Black Magic on the outside.

Now the three horses were head and head, driving downhill through the rain.

"Uncle Sidney," Shelley said urgently, "where is Lookout Light? How is he going?"

"He's going very well." The trainer sounded excited. "Fax seems to have pulled himself together. It's just possible that—" He shook his head. "That blasted fog's made it impossible to see, just when they're running down to The Coffin."

Suddenly Fax felt exhaustion, an overwhelming weariness that made his knees turn to water, his arms and body limp, muscleless. Through the rain and the fog and the fear of failure came Sidney Merrywood's words out of the past. The smart rider saves his horse on the level and lets him gain ground downhill. Send him on, Fax. Send him on. "Ride, Red, ride." In his mind's eye he saw the young Fax hunched over, driving Fermoy on down the hill, laughing as he did so, calling triumphantly to Freddy on one side, Dave Montague on the other. He remembered going into the fence, hearing the roar of the crowd, then the crash, blackness.

Lookout Light was dead fit and still full of run. Extending his nose, he leaned against the bit, fighting for his head. Fax was aware that they were almost abreast of the wing that sloped inward to the end of the four-panel fence set in the field. It was the narrowest fence on the course, barely wide enough for three horses to jump it abreast, traveling straight ahead, nose to nose, shoulder to shoulder. At this pace the slightest miscalculation or interference could cause a horse to misjudge the fence, get in wrong and go down.

Out of the corner of his eye Fax had a fleeting glimpse of Richard Doyle's face, strained and anxious, dead white beneath the mud spattered on it. Concern overrode his fear. He must leave room for Warlock on the inside. The Young Huntsman was inexperienced. Too young and inexperienced to realize the chance he was taking by making for the hole on the inside.

Memory of Fermoy, fear of falling, was blotted out. In the final crucial second before the fence he was aware of the growing roar from the hillside and the people knotted in the field, the pounding of hoofs, the creak of leather and his own sobbing breath.

All his concentration lay in holding Lookout Light straight and steady. At the very last second he saw Black Magic on his right and remembered the mare's tendency to swerve toward the inside.

The bump caught him unawares. Then he saw the distended nostrils, heard her panting breath and saw the flecks of foam from her opened mouth mingled with that on Lookout Light's neck, felt Lookout Light stagger as the mare swung sideways, cutting him off, blacking out the fence ahead.

"Watch—" The rest of his warning was lost as Lookout Light, knocked off stride, banged into Warlock, causing the horse to crash into the wing.

Above the sickening noise of splintering boards came the sound of a spectator's scream.

Fax felt the reins jerked from his hand as Lookout Light rose, felt the post graze his ankle. For an instant it seemed to him that Lookout Light hung in the air, directly over Warlock's wildly thrashing legs. He felt the colt twist under him, make a kind of flying change in mid-air, causing him to land free of the fallen horse and rider. Then Lookout Light was skating along the ground on his nose, struggling desperately to regain his feet.

Suddenly, miraculously, the colt was upright once again.

A rush of love enveloped Fax, an emotion of such piercing intensity that all he fancied he had felt for Taffy and the other women he had known was but the brittle dust of winter leaves as compared to the love he felt for this horse.

The sound of the ambulance clanging across the field and the sight of Black Magic galloping ahead brought Fax back to the reality of the race. As he reached for his reins, he saw Zagaran glance back over his shoulder. It seemed to Fax that he was laughing.

Rage engulfed him, an all-consuming anger that left no room for fear or exhaustion. It was possible that the swerve had been deliberate. It was something no gentleman rider would do, but then he had never considered Zagaran a gentleman. The will to win was necessary to make a good jockey. But not at the price of deliberately maiming a rider or a horse.

In a flash he had the reins gathered up. "Now!" he shouted as Lookout Light leapt back into his stride.

A broad back blocked Shelley's view. She heard the crowd gasp, then a stunned silence.

"What's happened, Uncle Sidney, what's happened?" Desperately she plucked at the sleeve of his mackintosh.

"Something happened at The Coffin. I couldn't see. Ah, here they come. Warlock must have fallen. Just two horses on course, Magic leading."

Across the Valley floor they went, Fax bent low on the gray's neck, driving him on, riding with the verve and dash and drive of old—

"My God," Sidney Merrywood exclaimed, "look at Fax!"

Over the small depression at the foot of the hill, and then the gray's stride was eating up the distance between himself and the black mare, tiring now as she went into the last fence and starting to stagger as though after setting that burning pace for all of the four miles her great heart was beginning to give out.

Lookout Light's nose was abreast of her withers when she took off. The gray rose with her, jumping a stride before it was necessary.

Shelley's fingers dug into the trainer's arm. She couldn't speak. Not even in the old days, when he was the country's leading amateur rider, had she seen Fax ride as he was riding now, bent low on the gray's neck, his legs moving like pistons, riding with all of himself. Riding to win.

Zagaran went for his bat.

Lookout Light's nose moved beyond the mare's withers, to her head.

"My God," Sidney Merrywood repeated, "even Freddy Fisher never rode a finish like that!"

"Black Magic," screamed the crowd. "Lookout Light."

Shelley clutched his arm. "Did we win? Did Lookout Light win?"

"Can't tell. We'll have to wait for the judges' decision."

Zagaran rode up to the hay wagon where the judges stood in the rain. He waved his bat and was given permission to dismount. Tossing his reins to Simeon, he threw his right leg over the mare's withers and slid to the ground. Then Fax received the judges' nod, slid off Lookout Light and began to loosen the horse's girth. The colt stood still, head down, sides heaving, sweat pouring from his belly like rainwater.

Shelley, Sidney Merrywood and Virginia City converged upon him simultaneously. "What happened?" they cried in unison.

"Got bumped," Fax answered clearly. He still hadn't got his breath back. His face, behind his triumphant grin, was wet with sweat and spattered with mud. His breeches were split at the knee. He put his hand up to stroke Lookout Light's lathered neck and when he spoke it was with his old golden-boy bravado and confidence and without a stammer. "Miss Shelley, honey, this hyar is a horse!"

"Fax, hey Fax." Greg Atwell was beckoning to him. "They want you in the judges' stand on the double."

At The Coffin, Warlock struggled to his feet. A horrified gasp came from the onlookers as they saw his left front leg dangling brokenly like a rag doll's. Richard Doyle stood by the horse's head, his face twisted in anguish.

"Where is Doc Black?" Tatine cried, flinging her arms around her horse's muddied, sweat-soaked neck. "Please God, somebody get him." Tears running down her cheeks, she stood holding Warlock, seeming to support the exhausted horse and keep him from falling.

On the hill beside his sound truck, Lou Dawson from the county radio station was broadcasting in staccato tones. "We're waiting for the race to be declared official. Nobody seems to know just what has happened. In the judges' stand there seems to be a violent argument. Now the riders and patrol judges have been called in. The problem seems to be who fouled whom. Whether Black Magic or Lookout Light interfered with Warlock at the Coffin fence, or whether the favorite fouled both horses. Visibility was so poor we couldn't see. The rain is turning to sleet and the fog is worse. It looks as if Warlock went through the wing and is hurt—"

At that moment the sound of a shot rang out.

"Ladies and gentlemen," Lou Dawson cried, "Warlock is dead."

The judges had questioned them, Fax told Shelley. Zagaran had merely shrugged. "I can't tell you what happened," Fax reported him saying. "All I remember is jumping the fence in the fog and going on." Fax told her that Zagaran had glanced around at the faces sitting in judgment on him. Lowering his voice, he had added slowly and distinctly, "If you want to think I deliberately fouled my daughter's entry, that is up to you. Everyone is entitled to his own opinion." He refused to say anything more.

The committee was at a loss. Because of the fog, the patrol judges had not been able to see what happened. Nor had the riders. Fax admitted he would have enjoyed telling them that Zagaran had deliberately pulled Black Magic across his path, but it wouldn't have been honest or sporting. At such a pace, anything could happen.

So the judges had let their first decision stand, that Black Magic had won. "Why make trouble, stir up controversy?" said Togo Baldwin. "Black Magic was first across the finish line. She's the winner."

Zagaran had stood up then. "If it's going to be that way, I don't want the Cup. Unless the committee is in complete agreement, I will not accept the award. Give it to the second horse. Good day, gentlemen."

"Wait," R. Rutherford Dinwiddie cried, "we didn't mean to imply—" but Zagaran was out of earshot.

"Well, what do we do now?" Togo asked helplessly.

"Sounds to me as if he's guilty," Dash-Smythe said. "I vote to give the Cup to Shelley. A Shelburn horse—"

A Shelburn horse and local rider had won the Shelburn Cup and there was no joy in it. No one knew what had happened out there on the misted course. Had Zagaran done something no gentleman, no sportsman, would do?

"Congratulations, Shelley," R. Rutherford said as he presented her with the Cup. Sidney Merrywood and Fax stood on either side. As the photographers tried to shield their lenses from the deluge and take pictures, the smiles remained fixed and artificial.

Zagaran came out of the stand. His cap was tipped back on his head and his racing bat was under his arm. People turned to look at him. A few plucked at his arm, asking what had happened. He paused, shook his head and continued on his way, swinging his racing bat as if slashing at weeds. Those he had spoken to looked after him with expressions of sudden resentment for which they could give no specific reason.

Shelley caught up with him on his way to the house. They stood under the Ballyhoura Oak, the homeward bound racegoers streaming past in the rain.

"Zagaran, what happened?"

He spun around. "What do you mean, what happened? What in hell do you think happened?"

"Did the mare swerve?"

He had thrown a polo coat over his mud-spattered silks and his face was cold, closed in. "Are you saying, on purpose?"

Shelley shook her head, waiting for the current of understanding, of sexual oneness to assert itself. Before, when surrounded by people, she had known a sense of possession not possible anywhere else. Now there was a difference, a distance between them as long as that covered in the race.

"No," she said miserably. "I mean . . . I don't know. Zagaran, tell me—"

"There's nothing to tell." He inclined his head in a slight bow. "Congratulations, Miss Shelley, ma'am. You won."

"Young man!" Mrs. Dinwiddie stood in front of them, leaning on her shooting stick. She wore tweeds to her ankles, thick woolen ribbed stockings and heavy shoes with fringed tongues, now covered with mud from the course. "I don't approve of you. Your wife hardly cold in her grave." She peered at him nearsightedly. "Did she tell you I warned her, the night of the ball?" She lifted her shooting stick and waved it in the direction of Ballyhoura. "Bad luck house. No happiness there. I don't know what you did today," she continued disjointedly, "but I have a feeling—"

"My dear," R. Rutherford said, materializing out of the crowd and taking his wife's arm, "we must go. The car's blocking traffic over there."

"Dinny, one moment. I was just saying that I think—"

Zagaran cut her short. "Mrs. Dinwiddie, you are welcome to think whatever you wish. Good-by, Mrs. Dinwiddie. Good-by, Shelley."

"Zagaran, wait." Forgetting the Dinwiddies, Shelley started after him.

He paused. "You won. What more do you want?" He began walking toward the house. His shoulders rose higher than those of the people around him, and the back of his head, the way the hair grew in the hollow of his neck, made Shelley swallow against the ache in her throat.

Augie Schligman clapped her on the back, almost knocking her over, and then caught her in a bear hug of congratulation. When she was able to get her breath and speak, Zagaran had gone.

"Beastly weather," Bebe Bruce said conversationally, clinging to the leashes on her greyhounds. "My goodness, Augie, you certainly are well plaided. We could play checkers on that reversible mack of yours."

The big man beamed with pleasure. "You mean it, Duchess? No shit?"

"There's Fax now," Bebe said. " 'By all. See you later."

Fax drove up in his pickup. Jumping out, he shooed Bebe's greyhounds into the back, then with a flourish he opened the door for the Duchess to get into the front seat with him. In the late afternoon light the lines of dissipation were erased. He looked tall and slender and dashing and twenty years younger. Now he stood erect, the rain falling on his bare head, and his eyes had lost the dulled lowly-worm look of past months. He bowed the Duchess into his truck as though it were a sedan chair, his new teeth flashing white in a wide victorious smile, and when he spoke it was without a stammer.

"Hop in, Duchess." He waved to Shelley and Tad Shapiro, waiting for Mike to bring up the car.

"You all go on to the cocktail party," Shelley told them. "I have to go home and see about things."

Marina shook her head. "My hair. I must do something to it. And my mink." She made a face. "It is soaked."

It was, as Bebe said, a beastly night. Raw, cold, sleeting. The windshield wipers hummed and scraped the ice into little piles against the glass. Mike leaned forward, peering at the Valley road.

"I'm not clear about what happened today," Tad said. "People seem divided. Did this man Zagaran commit some kind of crime?"

"Funny thing," Mike said thoughtfully. "For a time he could do no wrong. Then something happened. I'm not sure I can explain it," he continued, "but I think it has to do with the race. Cheating on one's husband or wife is par for the course, but cheating in a horse race, an amateur race at that, is something else."

"Are we sure that he pulled a fast one?" Tad asked. "I thought nobody could see."

"Nobody knows," Mike replied. "They just suspect, because of what he is. He has three strikes against him. He's an outsider, he's arrogant and worst—he's successful!"

Shelley sat frozen against the window. She knew she should be exuberant and in a celebratory mood. A Shelburn horse had won the Shelburn Cup. At the same time her life lay in rubble around her. She had been rude to Marina, she had hurt Mike, she had swept everyone and everything from her path to victory and in the winning she had lost the things that made the winning worthwhile.

She suspected now that Zagaran was not a sportsman—a sporting man, perhaps, but not a sportsman. There was a difference. It was not *what* you won so much as *how* you won. His was a different code. The derisiveness of his smile, the mockery in his manner, the lofty assumption that nobody would or should question his actions, were those of a pirate, a raider. Instinct warned her that he was plundering both herself and The Valley. Yet at the same time that she told herself she hated him, she wanted him more than she had ever wanted anything or anyone.

She would see him at the ball. She would tell him—never mind the race—he had won.

TWENTY-FIVE

CAM was in his pajamas and plaid wrapper, watching television in the kitchen. Shelley wanted him to remember Shelburn Hall as it would be that night, as it had been when she had been Cam's age and had sat at the top of the stairs shivering in her long flannel nightgown, not from cold but from the excitement of seeing the men resplendent in scarlet evening dress, waltzing with the women who had replaced their familiar riding clothes with jewels and full skirts, investing them with new glamour. When Mike argued that it would be better for Cam to go to bed than see the guests misbehave, Shelley had disagreed. She remembered hearing about the time Bones and Fax got drunk and fought over Taffy Carlisle, and the incident of the drag, when Freddy Fisher let the hounds out of the kennels and they swarmed through the ballroom, lost the scent in the dining room, where they leapt onto the table and gobbled up the buffet, and then refound the line that led out of the downstairs lavatory window.

But when she thought about the past, the men were on their best behavior, the great dining room was alive with scarlet evening coats lining the long table over which bent numerous tail-coated waiters wearing the green and yellow Shelburn livery. The cracks in the high ceiling were magically healed and the holes in the faded curtains no longer apparent. The women were all gracious and beautiful, the men courtly and handsome. At those imagined dinners, drawn from childhood memories, the men had always before seemed slender and faceless. Now she knew how they looked. They had dark, sardonic faces, reddish hair that grew to a point at their foreheads, and a scar over their left eyebrow.

"Somebody's bound to get drunk and start breaking up the furniture," Mike said. "Isn't that the usual procedure at Hunt balls?"

Zagaran's face was erased from her mind. In its place she saw

Mike's familiar bony features. "They won't fight here. Not when the place looks so beautiful."

"Why would that stop anyone?" Mike asked.

"It would be like getting drunk at Mount Vernon or Monticello."

"I hope you're right. Nevertheless, I'd remove Lafayette's warming pan, the Waterford glass, the chair that Mrs. Washington sat in and the rest of the heirlooms." He paused. "Is Pete Buford coming?"

"He's a sponsor and President of The Hunt and on the race committee and paid for half the food."

"I asked you if he was coming."

Shelley looked away. "Yes."

"Then you're a fool not to put away the antiques," Mike said darkly.

"Oh, all right," she replied. "I'll lock up some of the glass. Right now I have to slice the bread for the salmon."

"Isn't it already sliced?"

"Yes, but not thin enough."

"As though anyone will know or care," Mike muttered.

"Did you put away the Waterford decanters?" Mike asked as he stood in front of the bathroom mirror trying to tie his black bow tie. He repeated the question.

"What? Oh, the decanters." Shelley looked at herself in the mirror. She had meant to get a new dress, but there had not been the time or the money. Now the old black sheath with the strapless fitted bodice that had seemed too tight the night of Tatine's ball had zipped up too easily. The hollows in her cheeks seemed deeper and her breastbone stood out.

"I left the decanters on the mantel, along with Cromwell's goblet. Part of the décor. Mike, can't you ever get your tie to stay straight?"

With a quick, angry gesture he took hold of one end of the tie and yanked it loose. "What the hell difference does it make whether it's straight or not, whether the bread is sliced or not, whether the champagne is iced or not, whether I go downstairs or whether I do not?" His voice, when he spoke again, sounded exhausted, drained of emotion. "It's been months since you've seen me, really seen or noticed anything about me."

She stared at him, aware of a deepening sadness. As he turned away, all her breath seemed gone from her. She knew how the fox must feel when the pack starts to gain on him and his strength begins to desert him.

He saw the planes of her face accentuated by her paleness. She had lost weight. But despite the hardness of her body that came from the riding, there was about her a new softness, a new womanliness. It was the way she had been before Cam was born. Although she led the same existence, spent largely out of doors, there was that quality of femininity, almost a fragility, that set her apart from the Millicent Blacks and Debby Darbyshires, the flat-chested, heavy-bodied women with their leathered faces, cigarettes and imperious speech drawled from the corners of their mouths. Even when wearing evening clothes, the Valley women walked with their legs apart, as though they had on boots.

Now as she sat at her dressing table adjusting the Shelburn Sapphires to her ears, there was a stillness about her. Yet behind the stillness he sensed a waiting quality, as though she, too, waited for an unknown but inevitable climax. With an almost imperceptible shake of her head she said with unaccustomed humility, "Mike, I am sorry. Lately I've been beastly to you and Cam."

"Beastly? You sound like Bebe. Frankly, I am no longer amused."

"No," she answered slowly. "I don't suppose you are." She stood up. "You better retie your tie. We should go down."

"What for? You know what tonight will be like. Everybody's half drunk already."

She turned and faced him. Her shoulders were back and now her color was high. Her eyes flashed dark like the sapphires at her ears and when she spoke it was with the haughty pride of generations of Shelburns. "It's a ball at Shelburn Hall, Mike. I think that means something in The Valley. It does to me, you know."

He watched her walk from the room, along the shadowed hallway to the stairs. Outside the storm still raged, and as he listened to the now familiar house noises he was aware of the sadness of the storms that divide a house and a family, put a sinister ring around its beauty, like that around the moon, now seeking to emerge.

Thoughtfully he returned to the mirror over the dressing table and carefully retied his tie, concentrating on getting it straight.

The storm had passed. The flares lining the drive had been lit. The rain had stopped and the fog lifted. Now a pale moon, veiled by scudding clouds, shone down on the white-pillared house. The shaggy grounds, ruined wing and overgrown gardens were disguised by darkness, the great hallway and high-ceilinged rooms transformed by candlelight and music to the storied enchantment of Old World glamour.

In the soft light the areas where the French wallpaper had flaked off, the rents in the Aubusson carpet made by the spurs of Sheridan's cavalrymen, the scars on the marble mantel where the Union soldiers had chipped off mementos, and the long scratch on the mahogany sideboard into which Cam had run his tricycle were no longer obvious.

Fires crackled in all of the fireplaces. Spring flower arrangements were on all the tables and windowsills. The antiques, thoroughly cleaned and rubbed with oil, reflected the light from the hundreds of candles Shelley had laboriously placed in the chandeliers and silver candelabra. Lafayette's warming pan, hanging on its hook beside the Parisian mantel, had been polished. The Lowestoft horses and the heavy historic Waterford glass decanters which the first Shelburn had brought with him from the Ballyhoura convent sparkled, adding to the atmosphere provided by what the newly printed Chamber of Commerce brochure boasted of as "generations of gracious living."

Community Brown stood in the hallway to accept women's wraps. Manassas Brown and Billy Joe Wilkerson and the other waiters took their places, waiting to serve the champagne.

"Shelley, it's beautiful," both Marina and Tad said sincerely when they came down the stairs.

Shelley stood welcoming people in the hall. As she listened to their exclamations she was glad now that she had let the ball be held at Shelburn Hall. If this was to be all, the end of a way of life, then let the evening be memorable, in the tradition of her forebears, with wine and candlelight and the throat-catching nostalgia evoked by the house and the things that had happened there.

There was a sudden stir. "My God," somebody exclaimed, "the Bentleys!"

The Senator and his wife smiled and nodded. Maggie Bentley commented in her soft, breathy voice that the house looked beautiful. She looked ravishing. In keeping with the black and white Hunt Ball motif expressed in the invitations, she wore a white chiffon gown that shrieked of Paris. Her carefully coiffed hair was studded with diamonds.

"It's actually a wig," she confided. "I no longer go to New York to Mr. Kenneth. I just mail up the wig when I need it for ceremonial occasions."

"Great for après hunting," Cosy Rosy Dash-Smythe commented. "I got absolutely soaked this afternoon and my hair is a mess."

Maggie Bentley turned to Shelley. "Did my secretary call about a table?"

"I'm sure she did," Shelley replied. "Connie probably got the message." She gazed into the big room where the tables were quickly filling up. "Why don't you take the one to the right of the fireplace?" She signaled. "Manassas will bring you champagne, or maybe the Senator would prefer Scotch."

"I would at that," the Senator said. "Mrs. Latimer, this is a beautiful house. Sometime you must tell me its history. Of course, I've read the historical marker on the road, but I'd like to know more about King Shelburn." He turned to Mike. "I've been reading your newspaper." He paused and stroked his chin. "Actually, I've been meaning to call you. There's something I'd like to ask your advice about. About a development in The Valley. I'll be home all day tomorrow. Would it be possible for you to drop by the house sometime?"

"Thank you, sir," Mike replied politely. "I'll come whenever it suits you."

Shelley glanced quickly at her husband. His tie was straight and he stood easily, with strength and confidence. She looked around at the people standing in the hall with a sense of déjà vu, as though she had stood there before, and as before there was a feeling of unreality. Again she was aware of that chilling sense of danger, of something ending.

Cosy Rosy was still talking to Maggie Bentley. Dash-Smythe

had agreed to escort her to the ball. "Just because we're divorcing," Cosy Rosy was explaining, "doesn't mean we can't still be friends."

The Schligmans had just come in, Augie florid-faced and proudly wearing a new scarlet tailcoat with The Hunt's colors displayed on its satin lapels; Katie, a new blond mink coat covering pink satin and diamonds.

By nine-thirty every table was filled but one. The table Zagaran had reserved remained empty. Community Brown came to tell Shelley that the ladies in the kitchen were ready for the dinner to be served.

"I'll let you know in a minute," Shelley replied, excusing herself from the Schligmans.

Tatine was standing in the hall with Sandy Montague. In her long white dress, Grecian and without ornament of any kind, she had the severity and simplicity of a marble figure. Her flaming hair, reflecting the candlelight, and her lips made the only note of color. She is really and truly beautiful, Shelley thought. No wonder that Sandy, who had regained consciousness after his fall from Contender and been released from the clinic with nothing worse than a few bruises, was looking at her with his heart in his blue Montague eyes.

The Dinwiddies entered and handed their coats to Community Brown. "Well, I never!" The Beast sniffed, staring at Tatine as she went by. "She can't wear a thing under that dress!"

Tatine overheard her. "I don't, I shave!" She turned back to Sandy. "Old bitch," she murmured under her breath.

"Tatine, please," Shelley heard Sandy say. "What will people think?"

"What will people think?" Tatine mimicked, her green eyes blazing. "All right to do what you want in the wings, as long as nobody finds out that you beat your wife, sleep with other women, cheat at horse races—just don't get caught." She put her hand up in a helpless fluttering gesture. Then in a lowered voice she continued. "What do I care what people say? Do you think they could say more about me and my family than they already have? My God, what do you think they're saying now? After this afternoon? Sandy"—she touched his arm—"find yourself some nice girl. I'm no good for you." There was a sudden break in her voice. "For you or for anybody."

"Tatine, you know how I feel," he said stubbornly. "I'd do anything."

"Good evening, Tatine, Sandy," Shelley said. "Tatine, I'm so sorry. Warlock was a wonderful horse. Sandy, your fall was tough luck. Why don't you go in and get a drink while I talk to Tatine a minute?"

Drawing the girl to one side, she said in a lowered voice, "We're ready to serve the salmon and I was wondering where your father is."

Tatine gave her a long, level look. "You know Zagaran and I go our separate ways, but I can tell you this. I heard him mention to Harrison—that's the new butler—to have the Jag brought around, that he was going to Washington. Shelley"—Tatine stopped abruptly—"you look pale. Is anything the matter?"

"No," Shelley replied. She took a long breath. Then she lifted her head. "No, of course nothing's wrong. I just wondered. He reserved a table—"

But Tatine was no longer listening. Richard Doyle, his hair freshly slicked down with water, like a small boy, was coming from the men's room. His black dinner jacket, with its too-square shoulders and indented waist, had obviously been rented. He looked shy and self-conscious. Tatine was smiling at him, and at that moment her beauty was staggering.

Shelley turned to Richard and extended her hand. "Good evening, Richard," she said warmly. "I want to congratulate you on the job you're doing as Huntsman."

"Thank you, Mrs. Latimer." He colored slightly as, inclining his head, he took her hand. "Ain't—I mean—there haven't been too many good hunts lately. A lot of foxes with mange. Then they comes on rabid."

"That's not your fault. Now that it's rained we should have a good hunt before the season ends."

"Ain't—that is—not but one day left."

"Plenty of people here," Tatine observed, standing in the doorway. "Paneling fund should make a pile."

"We need to panel that country we ran over on opening day, near your father's Hunting Box."

Shelley saw Tatine's quick questioning glance and the sudden color rising in the Young Huntsman's face. At that moment Larry Lester and his Red Coats launched into their first waltz.

"Come on, Richard," Tatine said quickly, taking his arm. "It's grown-up music, square, but let's try it anyway."

She remembered writing down the private number of the penthouse and putting it somewhere, in a bureau drawer, or her jewelry box. Frantically, while the kitchen ladies waited for word about dinner, she went through the drawers of her dressing table and the boxes full of safety pins and oddments on top. She found it finally, in the envelope in the rear of her handkerchief drawer where she had put his notes.

The telephone rang for a long time. Then, just as she was about to put the receiver down, she heard Samantha Sue's unmistakable drawled "Hello."

The main living room—the ballroom—looked transformed. The wall behind the orchestra had been covered with Shelley's sketches of the chase. Surrounding the dance floor were circular tables for eight. They were covered with scarlet cloths, set with silver and crystal goblets and wine glasses and centered with the bowls of flowers. The best tables, those bordering the space cleared for dancing, had been reserved for The Hunt's board members and stewards and members of the race committee.

By the time dinner was served, the rounds of cocktails, augmenting those drunk early in the day at luncheons and tailgate picnics, followed by further rounds at the Baldwins' and other after-the-race cocktail parties, had created an atmosphere of conviviality.

Mike and Shelley, the Shapiros, the Jenneys, Fax and Misty were seated together.

"Isn't that the Young Huntsman?" Misty asked. "Dancing with Tatine?"

"The girl in white with the red mane?" Tad asked.

Following the direction of their gaze, Shelley saw Tatine, her figure molded indiscreetly against her partner's. Richard's face was flushed as, with an air of defiance, he held Tatine too close for the comfort of the elderly onlookers.

"Ah declare," Fax said wonderingly, "her ass ain't any bigger than a hummingbird's."

"I think she's done it," Misty observed quietly. "This time she's gone too far. She *is* the Master's daughter. As such, she's placed one of his employees in an awkward position."

536

"Ah wouldn't mind being in his position," Fax observed.

For a moment the candles seemed to flicker out, leaving the table in darkness. Shelley bowed her head. Tatine's a better person than I am. Braver and more honest. If only Zagaran had come. If only—

"Come on, Miss Shelley, drink up." Fax refilled her glass. "Don't forget you won the Shelburn Cup."

In that instant something happened to Shelley. She looked around at the expectant upturned faces. Most were people she had always known and considered friends. It had not occurred to her to probe beneath the surface, demand that they voice their values or prove their loyalty. She had automatically assumed it to be there.

Then they had tried to put the *Sun* out of business, and because they assumed that she believed in the things that her husband did, and was therefore, as Mrs. Dinwiddie put it, a traitor to her class, they had set about with conscious intent to punish her. This they had done by excluding her from their activities, by attempting to cut her off from the sport she knew and loved. Now, strangely, the pendulum had swung back. Either because they had found they needed her, or needed Shelburn Hall for the ball or for any one of the intangibles that bring about a reversal in the herd attitude, she had been reinstated to her original position as one of them. Instead of gratitude, she felt contempt. As she gazed at the sea of faces, she was aware of a growing anger.

She lifted her champagne glass and drained it.

"I used to think you were behind the bit," Fax said, staring at her strangely. "Now I'm not so sure. Lately—"

"Lately what?"

"Lately you're different. Up in the bit. On contact. For instance, I never knew you to drink like this."

"I used to drink to get to people," Shelley said bitterly. "Now I drink to forget them."

"Shelley, you know me, I hate to be involved. But I've got to tell you this." Speaking with his new-found confidence, Fax continued, "You've got one hell of a good man there in that husband of yours. Okay to have a little pipe-opener. Sometimes it's good for the long haul. But don't let yourself get run away with." He stopped, embarrassed at having said so much, and turned to Marina on his left, who was yawning.

"Poor baby," Tad Shapiro said. "All that fresh air. She's positively stunned. Now that she's back breathing good clean smoke, she'll wake up."

"Maybe she'll terpsichore with me. How about it, Miss Marina?"

"I'd be delighted," Marina answered, staring straight at him, "if you'll take your hand off my thigh."

Fax jerked his hand away as though she had dropped her cigarette on it. "You're the first girl I ever met who didn't like it," he said in honest amazement.

While the salmon was being served, Tad escorted Shelley onto the floor. A flock of teenagers in billowing skirts were huddled in a corner. They reminded her of the Baldwins' sheep in a storm, as they focused their longing gaze in the direction of the bar, where Sandy, Tommy Fisher and the other young riders, celebrating now that the race was over, hovered like bees around a hive, oblivious of everything but their drinks and conversation.

Cam sat perched on the steps, his chin in his hands, mesmerized, as the orchestra leader led his Red Coats into the traditional waltzes and dances.

Members of The Hunt circled the floor, elbows bobbing and extended, their pink coattails flying. The Dinwiddies were a sight to behold. Beauty looked magnificent, gold buttons and patent leather pumps shining, mustache waxed to perfection. He was dancing with Lady Willoughby-Walloughby from the British Embassy, a tall, angular woman with frizzed yellow hair turning gray and an arrogant air. Mrs. Dinwiddie, wearing a shapeless purple garment that looked as if she had made it herself from an old bedspread, and several strings of round amber beads, was dancing with Lord Willoughby-Walloughby. He was tall and attractive, whirling the Beast about with dash and certainty. Shelley wondered how it was that his wife could be so drab. Probably they had met in the hunting field. As was so often the case with this segment of British society, Lady Willoughby-Walloughby went like a bomb, and her spare flat-chested build and canary-thin straight-up-and-down legs, which, like her body, lacked all shape, made her look smashing in hunting clothes. Yet when these women turned out in the evening, they gave the impression that they considered it sinful to look smart or feminine.

As Lady Willoughby-Walloughby danced by, Shelley overheard her say to her partner, "I find The Valley a most un-American place, so quiet . . ."

Tad Shapiro led Shelley back to the table. She had the feeling that he was relieved now that his duty dance was behind him. She knew Tad had tried to dissuade Mike from marrying her, that he had insisted Mike could never be happy in a place like The Valley. That afternoon she had sensed his disapproval more keenly than ever. The critical way he had looked at her and the way his eyes were now circling the people in the room reminded her of the group from the city that had picketed Opening Meet, pressing anti-blood-sports leaflets on anybody who would accept one.

Dinner was being served. Shelley had wanted only local help and rather than have a buffet, she had ordered the food served at the tables. Bearing the salmon on silver platters decorated with slices of lemon, capers and parsley, the local waiters Manassas Brown had rounded up began passing the first course. Jimmy, carrying plates, brought up the rear. Dressed in a black suit bought at the church rummage sale, he watched the other waiters, doing exactly what they did. Handling the gold-rimmed china with infinite care, he set it down in front of the diners, speaking to them as he did so. "Evening, Mr. Jenney, sir, Mr. Baldwin, Mrs. Baldwin." When he reached the Dinwiddie table, where his Lordship was sitting, he said, "Here's a plate for you, Mr. Lord."

The salmon, served with the extra-thin brown bread it had taken Shelley so long to slice, was superb. So was the main course, rare roast beef, shoestring potatoes, fresh green beans and Linda Taylor's fresh-baked rolls. This was followed by green salad with Shelley's wine dressing. The molded dessert, the traditional charlotte russe that Shelley had insisted on, topped off the superb meal. Even in The Valley, a sit-down dinner for one hundred guests, served on fine china with crystal goblets and an array of silver at each place setting, was a rarity. Those who had complained about paying twenty-five dollars a couple were aware that they were getting their money's worth.

The excellent food, washed down with the champagne Zagaran had contributed, had put everyone in a mellow mood.

Enid Jenney spoke across the table. "A beautiful party, Shelley."

"Yes," Misty agreed. "You were right, Shelley, to do it up this way. Usually on race weekends there are a lot of drunks by this time. Instead, after that marvelous dinner, everyone is well fed and happy. Shelley, you've even left the curtains undone." She turned to Tad Shapiro. "In the olden days, the curtains were left open so that the servants could look in on the gentry disporting themselves."

"Shelley's theory is that shoddy surroundings create shoddy behavior," Mike explained. "And that an atmosphere of elegance makes for sobriety and good manners." He lifted his champagne glass. "Shelley, here's to you. Let's hope your theory holds water rather than wine."

"I remember the year we had the ball at Templeton," Fax mused. "Major Southgate DeLong fell into the cellar when the floor gave way. It had been declared unsafe after the mares foaled in the downstairs bedroom, but nobody paid it any mind."

"Miss Marlee had the theory that you should move everything of value to the upper floor and barricade it with barbed wire." Shelley laughed. "But then why bother to have nice things? It's like Katie Schligman's diamonds. Why not wear them if you have them, instead of keeping them in a safe deposit box?"

Fax looked over at the Schligmans' table, at Katie, all pink and gold and glittering. "Ah declare, I asked if I could take a look at the lil ole diamond she wears on her hand. I clocked myself. A minute and a half just to cover the course."

The waiters opened additional bottles of champagne and began passing them.

"Time for a toast," Fax said, rising to his feet. He hammered on his wine glass for silence. There was the sound of chairs being pushed back and a chorus of "Hear, hear."

"A toast to our hostess," Fax said when there was silence. From the corner of her eye Shelley saw Cam peering around the door-way, his eyes huge in his excited face. Jimmy stood behind him, his face black and glistening.

Fax raised Cromwell's intricately chased silver goblet. "A toast to Shelley and Lookout Light."

"To Shelley and Lookout Light," echoed the voices in the room as the goblet was passed from hand to hand.

Dinner was over and the dancing had begun when Millicent made her entrance. Dolly O'Day, the movie star who had flown from the coast for the party, followed behind her.

Shelley looked around the room. All the tables were full. To make things worse the Bentleys, Polo Pete Buford and Bebe Bruce were sitting at the most prominent table by the fireplace.

Millicent was wearing a floor-length coat of orange-colored fur over an orange caftan, gathered at the waist with a pink sash that made an incongruous contrast to the famous necklace her first husband had given her. A red bow perched crookedly at the back of her head.

"The bow in her hair," Marina asked innocently, "that means she kicks, yes?"

Fax nodded soberly. "Bites, too."

As the orchestra launched into her theme song, "Horses, Horses, Crazy over Horses," Millicent started across the floor. In her wake came Bones and guests: the tall keen-faced man who was said to be one of the President's closest advisers; Timmy, the Supreme Court justice with his thatch of white hair and horn-rimmed spectacles; and a famous and diminutive jockey, less than five feet tall. Dolly O'Day, with palomino-colored hair and a bosom eulogized by the world's press, was escorted by her current lover, the cowboy hero of a popular television series, whom her husband was threatening to strangle with his own lasso, presuming he could get his hands on him. Twittering in the rear were Millicent's winged friends. Wearing wine-red satin dinner coats and lavender shirts, they looked straight out of the cast of *West Side Story*.

Millicent paused, blocked by the couples dancing. After nodding to Larry, gray-haired now and portly, but whose Red Coats were still able to provide that special rhythm that was traditional at Valley parties, she started on past. By chance, Pete Buford and Cosy Rosy danced across her path. Millicent stopped dead. Momentarily she stood as though transfixed. With a ruffle of drums announcing intermission, the music ceased. In the ensuing silence the distinct sound of hissing could be heard coming from Millicent's mouth.

"Why, Millicent," Cosy Rosy said, stopping directly in front on her, "what a beautiful coat. Is it Sailor's?"

Millicent glared at her rival. "Mink pussy," she said succinctly, "dyed orange!"

"Time to fasten our seat belts," Misty Montague whispered.

"There'll be more fireworks when she finds her table," Shelley said worriedly. "I better go see."

She was too late. Ignoring the half-empty glasses, evening bags and furs, Millicent sat down at the largest table beside the dance floor. After shrugging out of her coat and piling it on an empty chair, she placed both feet squarely on the floor and rested her elbows on her knees, "as though sitting on the toilet" was the way Fax described it. "Jesus," she said loudly, "I'm hungry as a horse."

Her guests had just settled into their seats when the original occupants of the table returned from the dance floor.

"I'm afraid you have our table," Senator Bentley said politely, indicating the evening bags and furs that had been piled on an empty chair.

Millicent realized suddenly who was speaking, "That Bentley," who was to blame for the recent civil rights legislation. In a tone of outrage that could be heard over and above the sounds of the waiters clearing away the dessert plates, she answered icily, "There's no law you can pass to make me move."

The Presidential adviser studied his wine glass. The Supreme Court justice, looking as if trying to reach a decision, stared at Lafayette's warming pan, his brow furrowed in thought. The jockey's simian face was split in a wide, anticipatory grin. The star, diverted from sliding down the shoulder strap of her gold lamé sheath, clutched her lover's arm. The cowboy glanced quickly around. He had originally been a body builder before breaking into the movies. Aware of the men gazing with awe at Dolly's famous body, he scowled warningly. The lavender shirts giggled.

Russell Grimes was bound kitchenward with a loaded tray of dessert plates. He had grown up in one of the tenant houses at Last Resort, where he worked in the yearling barn, and this was his first experience as a butler.

Fax chose that moment to head for the men's room. Mesmerized by what he later described as Dolly O'Day's "well-developed mammary glands bursting from her dress like overripe Camembert," he did not see the waiter in his path.

As they collided, a landslide of half-eaten charlotte russe descended onto the table. Millicent was doused with whipped cream and Dolly O'Day's dress was decorated with ladyfingers.

What happened after that was never quite clear. Later, Tad Shapiro described it as being like the last hours of Pompeii. The walls stood, but not much else. Some insisted that Pete Buford rose like an avenging angel with a ringing "You clumsy son of a bitch" and tried to hit Russell, the heavyset waiter, on the jaw. Others maintained he did no such thing. What he actually said was "You nigger bastard, get out of my way" in order to avoid a fight and reach sanctuary in the men's room. Simultaneously, Millicent recognized one of her grooms. This attack on one of "her boys" triggered her off. "Bones," she shouted to her husband across the room, "go get 'em!"

Galvanized into action, Bones vaulted over a chair and let fly with an uppercut that sent Buford reeling backward into the debris of smashed crockery.

By now Millicent was standing on the delicate gilt chair that had been in Martha Washington's bedroom, screaming, "Bones, Bones, let 'em have it! Atta boy, Bones, you show the bastards!" The remainder of her cry was lost when, with a crash, the priceless antique collapsed beneath her. Down she went, like Humpty Dumpty in his great fall, taking the Presidential adviser with her and dislodging the Supreme Court justice, who ended on the floor, his white head encircled by the flower arrangement that had been on the table.

About this time the lavender shirts were seen scuttling for safety in the direction of the doorway. The cowboy lover gripped Dolly O'Day by the shoulders, inadvertently dislodging the upper half of her dress, which descended to her midriff. If anything, the sight of the star's famed superstructure should have stopped the free-for-all. The fact that it did not showed the extent to which things had gotten out of control. For by now, the majority saw a chance to rid themselves of the frustrations and insults suffered during the foxhunting season.

"I daresay there hasn't been anything like this since Waterloo," Lord Willoughby-Walloughby cried delightedly. "Clear the ride. I'm coming through."

Dash-Smythe, shedding dignity along with his coat, rolled up his shirt sleeves, grabbed the tails of Bones Black's new scarlet coat and accused his friend of taking his wife from him and creating the third of a triangle. As the new coat Millicent had bought for him began to rip, Bones cried aggrievedly, "What you trying to do, rub out one of the corners?"

"You're damned right, old boy," Dash-Smythe said, giving a yank that split the coat down the middle.

"You can't do that to my husband," Millicent cried, and hit him on the head with one of the gold Shelburn plates.

As R. Rutherford Dinwiddie, Esquire, tried to escape from the flying fists and crockery, someone's elbow connected with his jaw and sent him crashing to the floor. The Red Coats, following the tradition of the sinking of the *Titanic,* broke into "D'Ye Ken John Peel," playing it as loudly as possible. "I always hoped to go with the cry of hounds in my ears," R. Rutherford muttered sadly. "Instead, broken glass—"

"Like many of the upper class, he liked the sound of broken glass," Tad Shapiro quoted, watching the gentry gaily crowning one another with ashtrays, plates and whatever they could get their hands on, while the Latimers, Misty, the Jenneys and a handful of others looked on, helpless and appalled.

Fax was enjoying himself thoroughly. In past years the hunt balls had degenerated into dull, prosaic affairs during which few fights occurred. This he blamed on the new element that had moved into The Valley and did not understand the necessity of a good free-for-all to clear the air for the coming foxhunting season. Thus, he waded happily into the melee, hitting people at random, without rancor, merely as a means of working off the energy he had rekindled after the race with numerous bourbons followed by celebratory champagne. Now he resembled a battered survivor of a television Western after single-handedly fighting off a band of Apaches. Donnie Welford had tackled him for making a pass at Tina behind a box bush the night of Tatine Zagaran's coming-out party. Before he could properly defend himself, Donnie had closed one eye and yanked his dress shirt almost off. The Judge's gold foxhead studs with the ruby eyes had been torn from his shirt and had rolled under a table. Going down on his hands and knees, Fax began searching through the debris of flowers and crockery. Huddled in a corner, barricaded by overturned chairs, he came across the movie star, gold lamé torn, hair awry.

"I can't find my eyelashes," she cried tearfully. "I'm so mortified."

Fax saw only her bare breasts. They were, he thought, the most luscious he had ever seen. Better than Taffy's, better even than Bebe's. Then he remembered the size of her lover's muscles, the way he had glowered. At that time, in that particular place, Fax

544

decided that discretion was the better part of valor. Fumbling in his pocket, he brought out a frayed linen handkerchief on which years previously his grandmother had embroidered a T. Very carefully, and with the utmost delicacy, he placed the handkerchief lightly over the girl's chest. Although still on all fours, he managed the semblance of a bow. "My dear, if you'd be good enough to help me find my studs, I'd be delighted to help you up."

"Fresh!" The palm on her hand met his cheek with a resounding blow.

Briefly the mood of the melee had been one of relative fun. It would, Misty commented, give The Valley something to talk about for at least a week. Then, suddenly, the mood changed, shattered like the dessert, its curlicues of whipped cream and extravagant towers fallen.

"Mike," Shelley cried desperately as one of the young riders from Pennsylvania put his foot through Lafayette's window, "Mike, do something!"

Manassas Brown and Billy Joe Wilkerson had been trying to put out the candles. "I never seen nothing like this," Billy Joe commented, "not even at Delia's Saturday night."

"High class, low class," Manassas muttered, "it's all the same when there's women and drinking."

The Bentleys had fled when the brawling began, but the photographer from the *Capital Courier*, who had been unobtrusively taking pictures during dinner, had now thrown discretion to the winds and was standing atop a table, indiscriminately photographing everything in sight.

Shelley was sick with shame. When the fighting began she observed Cam and Jimmy peering wide-eyed from the hall. She had practically dragged Cam upstairs. There she had left him with Jimmy, who had been equally reluctant to leave the ballroom. Now she saw the look of appalled wonder on the faces of the Shapiros. She had boasted to them of the beauty of the country, the color and vividness of its personalities. She had wanted to impress them, prove to them that their impression of The Valley and its way of life was wrong.

In her youth the feuds, the fights and the violence that too much money, leisure and time spent in the open chasing foxes seemed inevitably to foster had somehow seemed glamorous. Now suddenly they seemed barbaric. R. Rutherford, for instance, had been a friend of her father's. She had revered him, looked up to him with awe. Now he lay in the corner where he had fallen, his eyes closed and his hands clasped. Somebody had put a rose on his chest and he no longer conjured up awe. Lying amid the debris, he merely looked ridiculous.

So did Fax, now no longer dashing and dramatic. With one eye almost closed, blood coming from a cut on his lip, and his shirt opened to disclose a ragged undershirt, he simply looked silly.

At that moment it seemed to Shelley that her house, her treasured possessions, everything on which she had based her life and had believed in, was smashed, like the gold-rimmed plates, the crystal and antique chairs lying broken on the floor.

Mike returned with Chester Glover and two state troopers who had been directing traffic. With the arrival of the law, some of the waiters prepared to wade into the melee.

Community Brown clung to her husband's arm. "Don't," she warned. "This is white folks' business." The big man shrugged away from her. "Manassas," she cried, "be careful."

What took place happened so fast and was so shocking that all who saw it were stunned and disbelieving, unable to move until Mike, calling for Dr. Watters, broke the spell. Community Brown insisted afterward that Manassas leaned over to tie his shoe and that Polo Pete Buford thought he had deliberately tripped him. Whether this was deliberate or accidental was never to be known. For Buford got up off the floor and saw Manassas kneeling. Inflamed by drink and the previous violence, he lurched backward against the mantel, grabbed one of the cut-glass decanters that had somehow remained in place, and brought the heavy glass crashing down onto the colored man's skull.

TWENTY-SIX

THE Shapiros left early Sunday morning for New York. Marina announced that the country was giving her claustrophobia, that the crowing chickens and clanking radiators would not let her sleep, and that Tad had to be back for a party his publisher was giving him that afternoon in honor of his new book. Shelley was relieved to see them go. Her pride lay in pieces, like the broken glass and crockery on the floor. There was no way to explain, nothing she could say.

As soon as they had driven away, Mike departed for the office. Shelley went into the kitchen and stared at the piles of unwashed plates and glasses covering the table and the counters. The help had left during the pandemonium that followed the attack on Manassas Brown. She was wondering where to begin when Tatine came by to pick up Cam and take him to Sunday School. Shelley thought of leaving the dishes and joining her, but she had not been to church since the Reverend Chamberlain's departure. Each Sunday she managed to find an excuse, knowing as she did so that the real reason she could not force herself to sit in the Shelburn pew was her sense of wrongdoing.

When Tatine began teaching by herself, she introduced her own variations of Shelley's creative Sunday School. At Christmastime she baked individual cupcakes and gave one with a candle on it to each child as a "Jesus Birthday Cake." The children then knelt before an imaginary cross, made a secret wish for Jesus, blew out the candle and ate the cake.

"Pagan!" snorted Mrs. Dinwiddie. "Positively pagan. I'm surprised she doesn't have the children smoking pot."

Most of the members of the Vestry agreed with Mrs. Dinwiddie. However, as none of the volunteer teachers were able to control the pupils, it was decided to overlook Tatine's unorthodox methods and ask her to stay on.

"All right," she agreed, "but only on my own terms and without interference."

547

"Honestly, Tatine, you're the world's most unlikely Sunday School teacher," Shelley said now as she opened the door for her. "Haven't you got a proper church hat?"

"What's wrong with my hat?" Like a man entering the house, Tatine pulled off her battered straw hat and sent it sailing across the hall, where it landed on top of the pile of scarves, evening bags, unmatched evening slippers, jewelry and other paraphernalia left over from the ball.

"Nothing, really," Shelley answered. "It's a beautiful hat! Come on into the kitchen. I'll see if I can find a clean cup for coffee."

"Tatine, Tatine," Cam cried breathlessly, bursting through the door, "can we go fishing?"

"Of course, my little suckling fuckling." As Tatine spoke she looked impersonal, chaste, as untouched and innocent of the words she pronounced as the golden blue-eyed boy. Lifting Cam up onto her lap, she hugged him. "I promised, didn't I?"

"Tatine, you needn't use four-letter words all the time," Shelley remonstrated mildly.

"The new minister is trying to break me of the habit." Tatine grinned. "Goddamnedest hardest habit I ever had to break!"

"You mean words like shit?" Cam asked. "Little Augie says shit all the time!"

"Cam!" Shelley admonished, "I'll have to wash out your mouth with saddle soap."

"You say damn when you have to put money in the parking meter," Cam answered accusingly.

Shelley looked at Tatine helplessly. "We'll discuss it some other time. Now, Cam, while Tatine and I talk, you go upstairs and get your piggy bank and bring it down to me."

Tatine sat down in the rocking chair and began rummaging in her bag. "I think this is yours," she said, extracting one of the gold foxhead earrings Zagaran had given Shelley.

Shelley's hand holding the coffeepot shook, almost spilling its contents. The earring had dropped off at the Hunting Box and she had not realized it was missing until she reached home. She had intended to go back and find it. "Thanks," she said, setting the pot on the stove. "I'm always leaving them around."

Tatine slowly drew a cigarette from the package. "I have some just like them." She lit her cigarette and stared thoughtfully at Shelley through the smoke. "Zagaran gave them to me."

"Tatine, do you take cream or sugar in your coffee?" Shelley asked, feeling Tatine's eyes pressing against her, as though the tip of her cigarette had been placed against her back, causing a burning sensation.

"Neither," Tatine said abruptly. "I take it black." She took a long pull on the cigarette and asked, "Where is Mike?"

"Working. Always working." Shelley ran a cup under the tap. "The phone started ringing at daybreak. About Manassas."

"Simeon told me he's in the hospital with a fractured skull. They don't know if he'll live. He's in intensive care." Tatine stared at the ceiling. Swinging one of her long, slender legs back and forth, she asked, "Did the Waterford break?"

Shelley spun around. "Heavens, no. Just Manassas's head." She stared at Tatine. "What did you mean by that remark?"

"I'm not quite sure." Tatine peered at the tip of her cigarette. "I probably shouldn't say it."

"Go ahead," Shelley urged, "say it."

"Sometimes I get the feeling that I'm one of your token young people. That things, the Waterford for instance, mean more to you than people. Even your husband." She stood up and ground out her cigarette. "Now I've said too much. I better go," she added, pushing back her hair. "I don't suppose anything will happen to Mr. Buford. He'll promise the people of Muster Corner indoor toilets and buy Community Brown a color television set. Nothing will really change. Well, I better be off."

"Tatine, wait, your coffee." Shelley extended her hand holding the cup.

"I changed my mind," Tatine said. "I don't want any."

"Tatine—"

The younger girl paused. "If it's what I said, forget it. Maybe I only spoke the way I did because you are so damned decent. You and your husband. What the hell do you know about—" She clapped her hand to her mouth. "There I go again. Cam," she called, "let's be off. Time I repented for my sins."

"Sins?" Cam peered around the kitchen door. "What are sins?"

"Sins are things you wouldn't know about. Black things like worms, that wiggle inside you and impel you to do bad things."

Suddenly her face twisted. Impulsively she grabbed the little boy to her, pressing her cheek against his. "I wish I could go back, be all new again, like you."

Letting him go, she strode ahead into the hall, grabbed her hat from the pile on the floor and started out the door.

"Tatine, wait—"

"Yes?" Tatine turned.

Shelley did not look at her. "I wondered when your father would be home. I need to ask him about some Hunt matters."

"God knows. You know Zagaran. Here today—" The expression on Shelley's face stopped her. "You might call the house. Maybe they've heard."

" 'By, Mom," Cam said, going to the car.

"Good-by, Tatine." Shelley stood in the doorway, still holding the coffee cup. "Good-by, Cam. Don't forget to make your manners to the new minister."

She watched Tatine move Softie, the stuffed toy that traveled with her wherever she went, off the low-slung seat so that Cam could sit down. Then the high-powered sports car burst into a roar. It leapt forward onto the drive, slewed around the box bushes and sped down the avenue at a speed Shelley estimated to be close to fifty.

Chester Glover would say that Tatine was scratching gravel. She would have to speak to her about driving so fast on the narrow avenue, especially with Cam in the car.

Shelley went into the house. She picked up the earring from the kitchen table and carried it upstairs and she put it in the back of the handkerchief drawer, where she had hidden the notes signed with the slashing crimson Z.

Mike spent Sunday talking with and attempting to calm down the Negroes who came to see him at his office.

The Valley was made up of people who, because they were rich, were considered to be privileged beyond the normal bounds of behavior and thus exempt from the laws which govern the behavior of others. The community assumed automatically that Pete Buford belonged in this category and was therefore unpunishable.

The Negroes knew this, and Mike sensed that whatever punishment was meted out, if any, would be sparked by Mase Brown, who had been in Mississippi conducting a demonstration concerning school integration when the news about his father reached him. Mase, Mike understood, was on his way home and would be at the emergency meeting of the Human Relations Council that had been called for that night.

It was late when Mike reached home and there was barely time to wash, change his shirt and grab a cup of coffee.

"Don't bother about dinner," he said as Shelley started to take the casserole she had put together from the leftover salmon out of the refrigerator. "I've got to go to a meeting."

"Surely not tonight," Shelley cried. "Mike, you need to get some sleep."

He set down his coffee cup and stood up. "They've called a special meeting at Muster Corner. I must go."

"Oh, Mike, why?"

"Maybe by being there I can do some good. Maybe if a lot of white people would start showing a little concern the problem would stop being a problem. Anyway, since when have you cared whether or not I get any sleep?"

"Mike," she said impulsively, "let me go with you."

He shook his head. "It's too late." He spoke without conscious thought. He was too tired to know if he meant too late at night or just too late—too late for everything.

It was raining. He went to get his mac. As he got into the car he realized that he had been in The Valley so long he had begun to think of a raincoat as a mackintosh. He heard Shelley call, "Mike, I wish—" and did not wait to hear what she wished.

He drove slowly down the long drive, past the slanting burned-out flares. Several had been flattened, and an unknown car had been abandoned when it had veered off the road, crumpling the box bushes. The shrubbery still hadn't been cut back. A wonder there hadn't been an accident last night. He'd do it himself, he thought, and then he realized that he might no longer be living at Shelburn Hall.

Buford could have the paper. Shelley could keep the house. Or, and his heart veered like the car that had gone off the road, she would marry Zagaran, be the wife of the Master of The Hunt. The only thing he would fight for would be Cam. In his mind's eye he would always see Cam, all pink and gold and blue, so very fair by contrast to Jimmy, and the pair of them sitting on the steps leading into the ballroom and gazing with wide-eyed wonder at the orchestra and the dancers. Then the look of horror that had come over their faces when the brawling began. The Valley was no place to bring up a child.

As he drove through the rain-filled darkness he tried to put the whole business of the race, the ball, the wreckage in the house, what had happened to Manassas Brown and the last hour out of his mind. It was not easy. Even after years of practice, his brain still persisted in working on its own, seeking to find the missing pieces to the puzzle, where the slow degeneration, the gradual attrition had begun.

The rain came at him, a shower of silver quills glancing away from the windshield. Each one seemed to pierce his chest, where there was a terrible tightness. He had yearned for escape, escape from Shelley, from the house and from The Valley. Now that it was possible, something held him back. It was as though the vast unwieldy house with its ruined wing and its ghostly noises had, in some curious way, entwined itself around his heart, like the wisteria that circled the pillars and was forcing its way through the wall into the den. As with the newspaper, he had given so much of himself to it, so many nights and holidays and Sundays of painting and repairing and pruning, that now a part of him belonged, and this part would never again be free of the nostalgia instilled by the old brick and crumbling pillars and clanking radiators.

Generally the monthly meetings of the Human Relations Council were routine. Hymns were sung, a portion of Scripture read and reports rendered. Tonight promised to be different. Manassas Brown, who, ironically, had refused to join the Council and become involved, was in critical condition.

It was important, Mike thought, for the white community to show their concern and sympathy. He had telephoned the Jenneys, the Martins and Tatine. Misty was the only one able to attend.

Mike saw the light streaming from the opened doorway of the church. He drove into the parking lot and stopped.

"I don't want to face them," Misty said suddenly.

She turned to him helplessly. "I feel guilty. Guilty for us all."

The rain was softer now, more of a drizzle, blurring the outlines of the little church, causing the light from the windows to glow faintly pink. He was aware of her scent, so distant that it seemed imagined, like that of lavender in old linen.

He did not want to move from the warm safety of the car. His fingers touched her neck, a soft tendril of hair that had escaped from the thick, lustrous coils brushed upward and held in place with amber hairpins. As though by themselves, without conscious direction from him, his fingers moved up and around, toward the line of her face. Suddenly his weariness and loneliness and sense of exclusion were overwhelming. Desperately he held her close, hearing the comforting sound of the rain against the car roof.

"Michael." Her whisper was barely audible. "Oh, Michael."

Past the dark cloud of her hair he saw the figure of Preacher Young standing in the doorway. People were trooping into the church. Reluctantly, he drew away. It was time for the meeting to begin.

Before, the majority of Valley Negroes had been too fearful of losing their jobs to participate. Tonight the scarred wooden pews were filled. The men were immaculately clean, in dark suits and ties, white shirts and polished shoes. In spite of the chill of the early spring evening, the women wore flowered dresses and hats. Mike saw Misty's hands go to the scarf covering her hair and saw that she was embarrassed she had not worn a hat.

Quickly he helped her into a rear pew. But before she could lean her cane against the back and sit down, Preacher Young rose from his seat at the table holding a cut glass vase of paper roses and beckoned them to come up front.

Mike would have preferred to be inconspicuous. But Preacher Young was insistent and by his insistence, his deference, he underlined the very "difference" the Human Relations Council had sought to overcome. As he followed Misty up the aisle to the place that had been saved for them, there was a flurry of movement, a respectful inclining of heads. Linda Taylor, John's wife, showed them into the pew. A silver web stretched from the back of it to the rack holding the worn hymnals and gaudy cardboard fans that Wilbur Robertson had made up and donated to advertise his undertaking establishment. Linda started to brush it away.

Misty grabbed her arm. "Look, the spider is busy weaving. Nobody can make a web like a spider. Let's leave him alone."

"If you say so, Miss Misty." Linda gazed doubtfully at the silvery substance, in the center of which the spider was at work. "Myself, I don't think much of spiders."

Although it was damp and raw outside, the inside of the little church was overly warm. The stove sputtered and hissed and rain dripped from a crack in the ceiling. Misty leafed through the hymnal and found the assigned hymn. Linda went to the old upright piano and "Pass Me Not O Gentle Savior, Do Not Pass Me By" filled the building. In the warmth of feeling that rose with the voices lay beauty, Mike thought, the true beauty of brotherhood.

"We'd be happy if Missus Montague would read to us from the Scriptures," Linda said when they finished singing.

Misty, startled, glanced around. But Linda had already moved from the piano and was holding the Bible out to her. Misty rose. In her clear, melodious voice she read the passage from the Psalm of David in the wilderness of Judah, "These also that seek the hurt of my soul, they shall go under the earth. Let them fall upon the edge of the sword, that they may be a portion for foxes."

Mike looked up and saw that Mase had arrived and joined his mother in a front pew.

When Misty was seated, Preacher Young quickly waived "the old business and the new business." He gazed down at Community Brown, flanked by her children. Mase sat next to her, his face twisted and bitter as he stared at the paper flowers in the vase on the altar.

"My heart goes out to Sister Brown and her family, to those who suffer because of the sins of others. But this isn't the time for my speechifying. Our president is here." He inclined his head in the direction of Washington Taylor. "He is a good man for making us do right. It would be hard to find another to step in his footsteps. He will push you farther than you'd push yourselves." He gazed around at the congregation and then went on.

"I see a lot of new faces and some of our good white friends. It kind of boosts you up. Church is the best place to meet and learn our people. Not only a place for preachin' and healin' and singin', but a place to teach. And now I'll turn the meeting over to our president, Brother Taylor."

The preacher moved to a chair at the end of the table. Setting the vase of paper roses to one side, he put his Bible down in front of him and then sat down himself. Behind him, the water from the ceiling dripped steadily.

Washington Taylor stood up slowly, giving as he did so the impression of controlled power. The way he stood silently observing the crowd made Mike think of a loaded shotgun, with the safety catch held in careful check. In the flickering light from the weak bulbs set in the old brown lamps originally designed for kerosene, his face, the prominent bones and straight, slightly arched Shelburn nose, was the reddish-brown color and texture of the Virginia clay from which he sprang. As he lifted his great lionlike head, his eyes flashed with blue fire.

"We know there's two kinds of law," he said with his careful diction. "When a white man kills a Negro the book's opened to a different place than when a Negro kills a white man. Words mean different things, too. On the Valley road, where the roof keeps the rain out and there's inside plumbing, 'murder's' an ugly word, like 'rape.' Murder becomes an accident, or a man protecting his honor. Rape—we know what they call rape." His voice became bitter. "The white man's privilege." He paused, and in the silence it seemed to Mike he could hear the spider weaving its gossamer web. There was a muffled sob and soft murmurs of sympathy from the women who sought to comfort Community.

"It's your fault," he said distinctly, jerking his finger at the crowd. "You and you and you. All of you who are whiter than white people. All of you who have been brainwashed until you can't even ask Mister Charley to let you live like a human being instead of like a fox. 'Tired of living with foxes,' you say. Look at those of you who live at Muster Corner. One pump for thirty-two families. Walking a quarter mile for water, to do your tub washing with a washboard." He paused and then said coldly, distinctly, "Is it any wonder white people say we stink—stink like foxes?"

Community Brown gasped and buried her face in her hands.

Washington Taylor's eyes raked the congregation. "My friends, you reap what you sow, and it's hard reaping."

Mase Brown stood up. His voice rose above the sound of his mother's sobs. "My father taught us to do right. What good did that do?" he asked contemptuously. He looked over at Washington Taylor and the scar across his cheek twisted like the crack in the ceiling overhead. "I am warning you, Mr. Taylor, sir, that if my father dies I plan to take matters into my own hands."

Billy Joe Wilkerson rose up. "He's right. Brother Brown never went against Mister Charley. Manassas and me, we worked parties twenty years or more. Manassas never wanted trouble." He nodded emphatically. "Time we showed the white folks where we stand."

From the back of the room came a loud "Aaaa-men!" Mike turned and recognized Fax Templeton's My Boy Hambone. He had never before seen him out of his handsomely made, handed-down riding clothes. Now he wore a custom-made tweed jacket with chamois patches that Mike had seen Fax wear, a dazzling white shirt and a black tie.

"Don't do no good to put old wine in old bottles. Gotta put new wine in new bottles."

"Yassir, yassir," echoed the crowd. "The brother's right. You gotta put new wine in new bottles—"

"Mister Charley can put your shoes on," Hambone continued, "but he can't tie 'em for you. You gotta do that yourself."

As he spoke, Mike had a mental picture of Hambone dutifully polishing Fax's boots, then giving them a final going-over with his rub rag when Fax was mounted in the paddock before the race.

Mike had not realized that Simeon Tucker was in the congregation until he rose.

"Our school has been burned. And some of our people beaten. We've been told it's too soon. We must wait." He looked at Washington Taylor. "Well, I say we won't wait. Not any longer. They say separate but equal facilities. We all know what that means. Hot water coming out of the toilets or no water at all. Secondhand desks so beat up you can't write on 'em. They spend more on their horses than on education. They takes better care of horses than they does of people—"

"Hear, hear," echoed the congregation.

Looking around, Mike saw the dazed, scared eyes of the women. Misty touched his arm. "They mean it. I've never seen them like this."

Washington Taylor leaned forward challengingly. "And what does our good friend, Mr. Latimer, think?"

556

Mike stood up. Briefly he was aware of Misty gazing up at him, a look of confident expectation on her upturned face. At first he had no idea what he intended to say. But somehow her faith transmitted itself to him. The words began to come, slowly at first. Then with ease and force.

"What's surprising to me is that you have refrained from violence and rebellion. If the color of my skin was the same as yours I doubt if I would have the faith and courage to endure. There would be rage in my heart. I would want to avenge Manasses Brown, and the countless wrongs against my people."

He glanced over at Preacher Young, who sat with his head bowed. Behind him the water dripped down from the ceiling.

He looked past the upturned faces, at the crudely painted windows covered with animals and angels, done by the Bible children.

"In Kansas the prairie stretches for miles, a sea of grass as far as the eye can see. Once a small child was lost in the grass ocean. The men for miles around went out to search for the child. They searched all day and far into the night. Then somebody suggested that they join hands and march together through the grass. This was done and the child was found. But it was too late. The child was dead. Let us not be too late. Nor let us destroy that which we seek with hatred and violence. Let us join hands and march together. In this way, We Shall Overcome."

Community Brown was looking at him. Her eyes were dry and her face mirrored a faith as strong and as old as that of which he spoke. "Mr. Latimer is right," she said clearly. "We must walk peacefully hand in hand. We need more love for one another. More doing for others and forgetting self."

Beside her, Mase sat motionless, his chin sunk in the palm of his hand, hiding the scar on his cheek.

Linda went to the piano. The people in the pews joined hands. Together they swayed from side to side, singing.

As they came out of the church, Jake Bronstein was standing on the steps. The reporter had a cigarette hanging from his mouth, a pencil stuck behind his ear. In his hand was a sheaf of notes. It seemed to Mike that he could almost see his nose twitching as he scented out scandal for Buford's *Daily*.

"Well, well, well," he greeted them cheerfully, "that was quite a speech." He waved his sheaf of notes. "I got most of it down.

My publisher will be interested." He turned to Misty. "Tell me, Mrs. Lincoln, aside from that, how did you like the play?"

Mike clenched his fists and unclenched them again. Had he been in any other place, he might have given way to the temptation to bash in the reporter's face. He thought of his conversation with Jake at the Covertside Inn, and he wondered if the reporter had come to believe the poison he had originally been ordered to write. Now it seemed to have become second nature. He had heard that Jake was drinking heavily, and his face, even in shadow, had the puffed, mottled look of the alcoholic.

"How did you know I was here?" he asked, before Misty could reply.

"Instinct!" Jake replied airily. "I figured the tribes might be restless."

"I assume you'll report in full what happened on Saturday night," Mike said, emphasizing the "full."

Community Brown, assisted by Corinna Wilkerson on one side and Linda Taylor on the other, came down the church steps.

"We'll put it in if we have the space." Jake spat the limp butt of his cigarette from his mouth and ground it under his heel. "Other things are happening in the county besides the beating of one nigger."

Community Brown paused. She lifted her head and stared directly at Jake. Then her eyes, filled with contempt, passed over him and settled on Mike. Instead of turning left toward the parking lot, she came toward him. With an odd, almost hesitant, gesture, she reached out and touched his arm.

"Mr. Latimer," she said softly, "no matter what happens—" She broke off, unable for a moment to speak. She took a deep breath, swallowed and then concluded, "I want you to know, 'fore I leave. I don't mind white folks at all."

"I feel sorry for you, Jake," Mike said slowly, watching Community disappear. "I'd rather wake up in the morning and see that my skin had turned black than be you and look in the mirror and see the color yours has become."

"Ugh." Misty shuddered when they were in the car. "He reminds me of a ferret. Jake used to be a good man, a decent citizen. Michael"—she turned impulsively—"you were great. I was so proud of you."

558

"I'm not sure what I said," he answered. "I just started talking."

"They know it came from the heart." She put her hand on his arm. "What happens now?"

He drove out of the parking lot. The rain had stopped and a thin moon raced behind a veil of clouds. There were people walking on both sides of the road. They turned and waved as the Jeep went past. "If Manassas Brown dies—" He shook his head. "Anything may happen." He bit his lip. "All any of us can do is keep working, keep trying to build a bridge of understanding."

"You said you were going to sell the paper."

"I don't know— Look, there's a fox."

Misty sat up. "Where?"

"He's gone now. Into the bushes. The night of Tatine's ball Shelley and I saw a fox. Somehow it began then. All the trouble."

"A portion for foxes," Misty said slowly. "Will they let Buford off?"

"Probably. This is the South. It's not what you do that's important, it's who you know! He's buddy-buddy with everyone at the courthouse. He owns land, the newspaper. You heard what Jake said."

The rain had stopped. The trees and bushes in the park trembled, sending the drops of water that decorated their greenery shivering into the night air. The park smelled of fresh damp earth and the clean astringency of sassafras.

Richard Doyle felt a quietness of mind and body. The delight, the ecstasy of the past hours with Tatine were still upon him. The anguish and the peril and the guilt would come later. Now it was enough simply to experience the repose, the drained, unthinking emptiness that was the aftermath of their lovemaking.

"Well?" Tatine stopped the car behind the rhododendron bush and turned to him. She had on narrow whipcord trousers and a tan sweater with a high rolled collar. Above it swam her face. In the light of the dashboard it looked strangely pale and pinched.

"Well," she repeated, "say something."

Richard roused himself. "What did you say?"

"I said, I'm having a baby."

He was not surprised. He had always expected this, that they would pay the price, the wages of sin, his mother would have said.

She was looking at him steadily, but in her eyes was a look of fear he had not seen before. Reaching out, he took her wrists in his big square hands. They felt small and fragile and it was easy to circle them with his thumb and forefinger. He thought of her breasts, how when he first touched them they felt like the small helpless birds that fell from their nests in the stable rafters and which he tried to save, cupping them in his palm and feeding them with an eyedropper until they gained strength, like her nipples that became erect and exciting under his touch. He thought of what they had been to each other, and in spite of his exhaustion he felt the familiar stiffening.

"I love you, Tatine," he said.

"Do you?" Her low voice throbbed and the look in her eyes changed to one of hope. "Richard, do you really? Richard, marry me!"

"Marry you?" he echoed miserably. "I *am* married."

"You don't love your wife. You can get a divorce."

"She won't divorce me. Not in a million light-years."

"Did you tell her? About us?"

"I just said I thought it would be best if that brother of hers came and got her, and took her and the baby home for a while."

"You must have given her a reason."

"She knew," he said bleakly.

He didn't want to remember the scene with his wife. She had cried and threatened to go to Mr. Zagaran. She had called Tatine terrible names and when he slammed out of the house she had yelled that her brother Tom was going to come down off the mountain and kill the people who had done this to her. Then she'd grabbed the hunting horn off the wall and thrown it after him. When he'd picked it up off the stone walk he noticed the end was chipped. He'd gone back inside and taken hold of her with one hand and started to rip out the hair curlers with the other. She had struggled and screamed. He wondered if he had hurt her, and then he realized he didn't give a damn. Now it seemed incredible after what he had known with Tatine that he could ever have conceived a child with a woman who smelled faintly of grease and went to bed with plastic rollers on her head.

He looked into Tatine's eyes and saw that they were very wide and the pupils dark. Tenderness came over him like a wave. Leaning over, he buried his face in her thick sweet-smelling hair. He kissed her ear and her neck and felt her warmth and the pressure of her hands against his back.

"I love you, Richard, so much. I know it doesn't make sense. That it's mad and hopeless and crazy. But I do. Do you know—I don't use four-letter words any more? Richard"—her voice was urgent—"if she won't divorce you, we'll go away together."

"What about the hounds? I have to stay until your father finds another Huntsman."

"Oh, The Hunt," she cried bitterly. "Always the bloody Hunt. The Hunt comes before bed or The Bomb. The Hunt makes me sick."

"You said you didn't swear any more."

"Bloody has six letters. Hell, I mean sorry about that."

"I can't leave without giving notice."

"I can't go tomorrow anyway," Tatine said. "I promised Cam I'd take him fishing." She drew a package of cigarettes out of her leather shoulder bag. After she had lit one, she said, "Let's aim for the end of the week. Hunting will be over then. Richard"—her voice was suddenly jubilant—"just think of having a child of our own. Oh, Richard, I'll love him so much, be so good to him. Know something? He's just going to be allowed to have one stuffed animal. Just one, all his own, to take to bed at night."

He gazed at her, baffled. There were times when she went off, riding her own conversational line, into a country where he could not follow. "Why only one stuffed animal?"

"Because when I was little I had a whole roomful. Shelves and shelves of stuffed animals. Can you imagine anything more decadent?"

He still didn't get it. "What's wrong with that? Most kids never have any."

"That's the whole point," she said intensely. "Most kids never have any. So one means everything. One animal to be all your own. One man. Not six dozen."

Shelley was awake when Mike got home from the meeting, sitting in the kitchen rocker. She was in her work clothes, corduroy pants and turtleneck. Still the beauty and elegance that had always intrigued him were apparent. Somehow she was more beautiful now, since her loss of innocence, and this added to the anger about the shambles the house and his life had become.

"Why aren't you in bed?" he asked, going to the refrigerator to get some milk.

"I waited for you to come home."

"Why?" He slammed the refrigerator door shut. "A little late for that, isn't it?"

"I wish—" she began, and clapped her hand over her mouth.

"What do you wish?" he asked wearily. They had been out of communication for so long it was an effort to try now.

"Nothing, really— No, that's not true. I wish life was simple once again, straight."

"Where the hell's a glass?" he demanded. "There aren't any clean ones on the shelf."

"I'll get you one." She handed him a jelly glass from the table.

"Shelley, there's so much wrong that once we started, it would be as if somebody began uncovering all the beer cans and bottles Buford's men mow over when they clip the rides on either side of the Valley road."

"You know what a compulsion is?" she asked suddenly.

"Yes."

"One was marrying you. The other was coming back here."

He heard Miehle whining at the door to be let in. Still he did not move.

She sat staring straight ahead, her feet flat on the floor, twisting her thumbs in her lap. "It's like going down to a big fence on a horse you can't hold. You find yourself sitting back, sort of outside yourself, watching yourself, knowing you're going to crash." She took a cigarette from the package Tatine had left on the kitchen table that morning.

"When did you start smoking?" he asked. "Never mind. I know. Zagaran."

Her hand holding the cigarette stopped in mid-air. The name lingered between them like a sword.

"Do you want to talk about it, or not?"

"I don't know if I can," she answered miserably. "You remember I told you once it was hard for me to talk."

"I know. You were brought up to eat your turnips and like them. Nobody asked you what you wanted or what you thought,

562

and when you did speak your grandmother rapped the back of your hands with the silver handle of her knife." He drank the last of his milk. "I'm sorry, Shelley, but I've had enough."

Like all men of honor, there was in Mike a streak of stubbornness. He could be pushed so far and no farther. In hopes that Shelley would see reason, he had let her play out her rope to its end. She had taken his love and flouted him and made him laughable. All of this he could have endured, even forgiven her for, but for one thing. She had abandoned Cam, his son, left him to go to Zagaran, night after night, when his son needed her.

He ran his glass under the spigot to wash it. As he did so, he wondered why he bothered. Trash, dirty dishes and glasses were piled everywhere.

He remembered her compulsive neatness when they'd first been married, the pride she had taken in keeping the apartment and his clothes in order, in her cooking and her painting. For weeks now her housekeeping had been as desultory as Jubal's sweeping at the *Sun*.

He turned around slowly. "Why aren't you with him now? You're free to go. I'll pick up Cam in the morning."

"Mike." She ran after him as he headed for the front door. "Where are you going?"

He gave her a brief smile. "I reckon I'll turf out with Fax Templeton. Isn't that the standard operating procedure?"

"But then everyone will know—"

He shook his head pityingly. "Poor Shelley, still worrying about what people might say."

"Mike," she cried desperately, "I'm probably all the awful things you think I am. But Mike, don't take Cam from me."

"You left him," he answered coldly. He went on out the door. "You've lost all honor, decency. I don't want my son with you."

"What about school?" Shelley cried.

"Spring vacation starts the end of next week. It won't hurt him to miss a few days."

"But where will you take him?"

"Home," he answered. "To the farm. My mother will take care of him until I decide what I'm going to do."

"Mike, please don't take him from me."

Mike gazed at her for a long moment and then slowly climbed into the Jeep.

"Mike—" She started after him and then stopped. By her actions she had forfeited her rights to her child.

Mike came and took Cam before school started on Monday.

"Aren't you coming with Daddy and me?" Cam asked as Shelley handed him his canvas bag.

"I can't for a while. You'll be with your grandmother and grandfather. Darling, it won't be for long. You'll have fun." She sank down onto her knees and held him against her.

"Come, Cam." Mike lifted his son to his feet, and beneath its layer of tan his face was bone white.

"So long, Mommy," Cam said, straightening his shoulders.

She watched him walk with his strut, self-confident, unafraid, to the car. When it was out of sight she realized she was clinging to the newel post, bending over it as if seized by a cramp. After a while, moving heavily, dully, without real awareness of what she was doing, she went upstairs. In the bathroom she sat on the edge of the sunken tub. She remembered the flowers that had filled it, the daffodils the night they had moved into Shelburn Hall. In her mind's eye she saw Cam running through the flowers in the green-gold light, and the dark, black misery she knew then was worse than anything she had known before.

For a long time she crouched there in the silent house. After a while she forced herself to lift her head and move from her cramped position. She rose shakily and went into her room and then out into the hall, opening each door as she came to it. Mike's dressing room, shirts and socks piled on the chest where they had rested for months, waiting to be mended. The guest room was in disarray, the shades still drawn against the daylight Marina hated, the huge bed unmade, the towels piled on the clothes basket in the bathroom, tissues stained with Marina's magenta lipstick on the floor. Cam's room with the pictures and books that had been hers as a child, the bones and marbles and miscellany of boyhood piled in profusion on shelves and floor. She continued down the back stairs and into the great high-ceilinged kitchen, where the baby chicks scratched in their cardboard box and a field mouse ran behind the stove.

She walked through the front rooms, where the curtains had been drawn, groping her way in the dark, and then she went back upstairs to her own room and thought, Surely he'll come home today.

A strange male voice answered the telephone. No, Mr. Zagaran was away on business. No, there was no word as to when he would return. Tomorrow was the last day of the hunting season. Surely he would be back to take his place at the head of the field.

She looked out the window. It was raining so hard that the water lay across the glass like moving sheets of plastic. A good day to stay indoors and get things done, she thought, and everywhere she looked there were things that needed doing. The house looked as if The Hunt had run a fox through it. Empty champagne bottles were piled in corners and mountains of trash had yet to be evacuated from the kitchen. There was broken glass everywhere and she didn't dare assess the damage to the antiques, the gilt chairs that had been smashed, the gold service that had been a wedding present for Miss Marlee, the crystal champagne glasses, the floor where people had ground out cigarettes and the rents in the damask curtains that had been laboriously mended before the ball. The washing and ironing had yet to be done, and her desk was piled high with bills to be paid.

She must pull herself together, force herself to bring some kind of order out of the chaos her house and her life had become.

She gazed at herself in the mirror. Face white and pinched, eyes huge and the hair—she ran her hands through it, feeling its thickness, its heaviness, and shook her head violently, as though to ease pain.

"I'll chop it off," she decided. "Right now, as long as I'm changing my way of living, my point of view, like the song."

Miss Esther told her she had a cancellation due to the weather and could take her immediately.

An hour later she looked at her hair, piled on the floor of the beauty salon. Miss Esther had been reluctant to cut it. "Are you sure?" she had asked. "It's so beautiful." Now she stood caressing a length of blue-black hair and asked, "Do you want to keep it? Make a fine fall."

"I never want to see it again," Shelley answered adamantly.

When she came out of the beauty salon, Debby Darbyshire didn't recognize her. "Shelley," she cried finally, "all those twists and twirls. What have you done? Are you going to a party?"

"No, I'm going home and feed the horses."

"When the horses see you, they'll flip," Debby said.

Tuesday morning Shelley awoke to a brilliant blue sky and a splitting headache. Toward morning she had fallen into a dream-wracked doze. In her dream she saw Zagaran coming toward her, arms outstretched. She started to run to meet him, and as she did so his face suddenly became that of the fox that had climbed the Hanging Tree, twisted and filled with hate. She had called for help, but there had not been anybody in the house to hear her.

Lookout Light was sound and dead fit. He needed exercise badly. Jimmy was back in school. Since the race, Virginia City had been more crippled than ever, as though once his big effort was finished his body had reverted to its former state of age and debility. This meant that she was doing most of the stable chores, mucking out and feeding, and had not worked Lookout Light since the race.

A button was off her best breeches and the tab inside her left boot had broken. She had to tug and twist the boot on without using her pullers.

She heard the plane come in, circle over the house and then head downward toward the landing strip. She began to hurry.

After the days of raw, cold rain the color of the country moved Shelley to think in terms of oil paints, thallo greens and yellow ochers. The sky was cobalt mixed with white and the air held that undefinable softness that, along with the gentle cooing of doves, signaled the coming of a Virginia spring.

The meet was at the Dinwiddies'. Most of the field had already assembled when she arrived. The atmosphere was tense and sub-dued as they stood around the long table set out on the lawn, sipping their port or sherry. It was as if after Saturday's race and the ensuing events nobody quite knew what to say or expect.

Millicent Black shrugged. "Don't know why I bothered to get dressed up. Might as well go for a hack. It's been weeks since we've had any kind of a hunt."

Shelley wondered whether the attitude toward Zagaran would have been different if the Master had shown the sport he had promised. But that had not been the case. When the strangely severe winter that seemed to have been preordained by the freak snow on the day of the opening meet finally concluded and hounds were able to go out once again, they had drawn cover after cover which either produced a fox diseased and unable to run, so that the pack chopped him down, or was blank. Now the old-timers grumbled that they couldn't remember a worse fox-hunting season.

"Hounds should be here," R. Rutherford Dinwiddie volunteered, riding up on his cob. He glanced at his watch. "The staff is late. Bad enough having a bounder as Master, let alone one that's not punctual—"

The rest of his sentence was lost in the sound of the crimson XKE with the blue stripe painted diagonally across the door swirling to a stop in front of the house. Zagaran emerged from behind the wheel and straightened up. Shelley had a glimpse of his face as he gave the field a brief nod and beckoned to Simeon to bring up his horse. It was dark and closed in, the way it had been when she had last seen him beneath the Ballyhoura Oak.

As the groom started toward him, leading Black Magic, a young woman climbed down from a pickup truck parked alongside the drive. A faded khaki Army jacket was thrown over her soiled gingham house dress, and a blue bandanna covered the rollers on her head. Her face was pinched, sad-eyed, and in her arms she held an infant wrapped in a soiled pink blanket.

" 'Scuse me, ma'am," Simeon said politely, pulling the mare to one side.

The woman ignored him. Not taking her eyes from Zagaran, she stood facing him. "He's going to leave me and baby. You gotta stop him." The nasal voice and the toneless yet melodramatic words shook the already electric silence.

Zagaran recoiled, both from the words and from the rancid smell that rose in the fresh morning air from the baby.

"He said he was sorry. Sorry! It's you, Mr. Zagaran, and that daughter of yourn that's gonna be sorry."

Zagaran's face was as still as a death's head. "Mrs. Doyle, I'll look into the matter and get in touch with you. Now, if you don't mind—"

"No, you won't." The defiance she had been holding onto as desperately as she was now clutching the baby gave way to great choking sobs. While the people on their horses and on the ground tried not to look at one another, she gave a garbled account of her former state of marital bliss, the baby's birth, how it was sickly, that the roof of their cottage needed repairing and other irrelevant items of information, all pointing to the fact that Tatine Zagaran had wrecked her marriage and her life.

Shelley was horrified. Yet something in the girl's despair and sense of rejection mirrored her own, and this prompted her sudden impulse to dismount, hand Lookout Light's reins to My Boy Hambone and go to the Young Huntsman's wife.

"Come along with me, Mrs. Doyle. We'll have some coffee and you'll feel better."

"Yes," Zagaran urged, looking relieved. "I'll be in touch." He reached into his pocket and brought out a roll of bills secured by a clasp made in the form of a gold Z. With a quick darting gesture she knocked the money from his hand.

"You think money will bring my Richard back? Well, Mr. Zagaran, you can keep your money. All I want is for my husband to come home. Leave that woman, that whore!" Twisting away from Shelley, she ran along the road toward the Young Huntsman, who was trotting up to the turning circle, his hounds bobbing at his horse's feet.

Richard Doyle's face went white as his wife grabbed his horse's reins and forced it to stop. "Tom," he appealed to the man in coveralls who had gotten out of the pickup parked by the drive, "for God's sake, take your sister home."

"The woman must be having a breakdown," Zagaran said to the appalled field and as Shelley looked at him it seemed to her that his dark, handsome face had become suddenly old. Then some auxiliary discipline was brought into play and the emotions that had been momentarily chalked on it, as though on a blackboard, were with one swift stroke wiped clean. He smiled at the people grouped around him. "Is there any sherry left? I could stand a drink." He drained the glass that was handed to him and set it down. "Time we moved off. Country around here is supposed to be alive with visiting foxes from the Free Zone."

Shelley purposely did not go up to him or speak. There was so much they had to say to each other that it could not be said here, where emotion could spill over into the public domain. The appalling exhibition the Young Huntsman's wife had put on prompted her former sense of decorum to assert itself. Although she yearned for a word, a gesture that would still her panic, she forced herself to ignore him.

A number of guests, including Lord and Lady Willoughby-Walloughby, had stayed over to hunt and a big field had turned out. After drawing several covers, it looked as though, despite Zagaran's promise of foxes, the day was to be another blank. As the field moved from cover to cover, without going out of a walk or jumping a fence, the Master's ill-humor increased. When Lady Willoughby-Walloughby commented cheerfully on the weather, his reply was barely audible and when Cosy Rosy rode up on his heels, he barked at her not to ride in his pocket.

It was well past noon when the sound of a hound opening in the Ballyhoura wood signaled the start of a run. To everyone's astonishment they heard the Young Huntsman's horn, blowing hounds off.

"Must be deer," said Debby knowingly. "I saw one here when I was out hacking the other day."

"That was fox," Fax said positively. Following his ride in the Shelburn Cup, a noticeable change had taken place. For the first time in years he had arrived at the meet cold sober. His stock had been properly tied, his boots polished to their old sheen. Now he spoke with a touch of his old authority. "If it had been deer, hounds would have been long gone."

"A rabbit, maybe," hazarded Cosy Rosy.

"There you go, splitting hares," Dash-Smythe muttered. He glanced around, but nobody was paying him any attention. The field was looking after the Master, who had suddenly spurred his horse into a gallop and gone after the Young Huntsman walking slowly along the edge of the cover, blowing his horn.

"What the hell do you think you're doing?" Zagaran's furious voice echoed across the meadow.

Richard turned in his saddle. "Sir, that was a dropped fox."

There was a sudden flash as the sunlight caught the silver band below the bone handle, followed by the cracking sound of the whip as the Master lashed his Huntsman across the face. Then, while Richard Doyle sat stunned and robbed of speech, Zagaran said in a low warning voice, "You do what I say and leave my daughter alone." Then he spun his horse around and faced the assembled field.

"If anyone here thinks I ordered a bagged fox dropped today or any other day, he or she is free to leave."

Nobody moved. Even the young horses seemed stilled. The visitors looked from one to the other and then back at the Master. "I know goddamn well he dropped a fox," Bones Black whispered to Cosy Rosy. "I saw the kennel Jeep down by the swamp, where hounds found."

The early afternoon sun blazing down from the benign sky glanced off the Young Huntsman's gleaming brass buttons. As he walked over to the Master, leading his horse, the hounds that came reluctantly from the woods followed uncertainly, baffled by the peremptory horn that had torn them away from their quarry.

Richard Doyle stood now, gazing up at Zagaran's livid face. "The Old Huntsman learned me," the Young Huntsman said doggedly. "He told me never to hunt a bagged fox. A fox dropped out of a sack don't know which way to run. He ain't—I mean, hasn't—no chance. Sir, you'd best start looking for another huntsman." Slowly, lingeringly, he lifted the old horn on its leather thong over his head. "Take it," he said, holding it up to the Master. "Best take your horse, too."

Zagaran accepted the horn and hung it around his neck. Then he took the reins Richard handed him. As the field watched, mesmerized, the Young Huntsman turned his back on the Master and began walking purposefully toward the lane that led out to the Valley road.

The hounds that had come out of the woods followed. "Go back," ordered the Young Huntsman. "Bouncer, Braggart, go back."

Hounds paused, confused, looking questioningly from the Young Huntsman back to the Master. Richard began walking once again. After a second or more, hounds continued in his path. Again he stopped, ordered them back, and again the original hounds, augmented now by the others pouring from the woods, refused to obey. For although he no longer carried the horn, no sounds, no blown commands, no mellow long-held notes were forthcoming from the Master, who, despite his puffed-out cheeks and straining vocal cords, lacked the long practice, the knowledge and ability to make the familiar music.

With the help of some of the grooms, Zagaran managed to collect hounds and while the members of the field trailed silently along behind, he began to hunt them, drawing the remainder of the cover with an intensity of purpose that left no room for conversation.

With startling suddenness, hounds opened. Zagaran spurred Black Magic after them. As Shelley prepared to follow, Lady Willoughby-Walloughby's horse stepped in a groundhog hole and fell, throwing her Ladyship directly in front of Lookout Light.

Shelley stopped to help and by the time the horse had been caught and the visitor had remounted, hounds had left Ballyhoura wood and were streaming southwest toward the quarry country.

Shelley gave Lookout Light his head, urging him to catch up, as hounds, screaming like banshees, vanished into Webster's woods.

Fax, riding The Saint, pulled up. "Go ahead." He indicated the path that led through the forest, ending at the abandoned quarry.

"Are they on deer?" Shelley asked, marveling at the hounds' cry.

"Why, Miss Shelley, ma'am," Fax said, glancing around, "where have you been? They're running Zagaran's house fox. He broke out of the house and the whole pack took off after him."

"Who let the fox out?" Shelley cried aghast. "Fax, we've got to stop them."

As The Hunt rarely hunted through the thick wood, the path had not been cleared. It was narrow, twisting and studded with loose rocks. Lookout Light plunged through the briars, sent stones rolling from beneath his hoofs and ignored the branches tearing at him.

The formless, frightening thought that had lain in Shelley's subconscious surfaced—the story of the tame fox, black-brushed, that portended death. She knew she was upset and overwrought and that since the race she had not been thinking clearly or logically. Still, a terrible urgency drove her on to pass the remaining members of the field.

Ahead a fallen tree blocked the path. Black Magic refused. At Shelley's signal Lookout Light bounded forward, passing the mare. Shelley had a momentary glimpse of Zagaran's face, a look of surprise mingled with anger as the colt flashed past. Then the gray was in the air. Shelley's leg scraped against a branch. Another tore her hair net, almost causing her to lose her cap, loose now without its padding of long hair.

From ahead came the cry of the pack, heading for the old quarry. If they were not turned, hounds would continue on over the edge, dashing themselves to pieces on the rocks below.

Shelley urged Lookout Light through the sun-dappled wood. She was panting now, like the colt. Each labored breath became a prayer. The path, no wider than a child's tricycle, plunged downward. The crossing at the bottom, made long ago when the quarry was in use, had been washed away. Water moved between the sheer banks.

Shelley pulled the colt sideways, to the right where the banks seemed more solid, less choked with underbrush. Branches slapped at her face and caught at her clothes. At the last minute the colt saw the chasm. Boldly he pushed off from the crumbling bank, caught the far side with his forefeet and, with a goatlike thoroughbred agility, scrambled up through the wall of green.

Over and above the creak of leather and panting sounds of exertion she heard a noise like the swish of a whip, followed by sudden searing pain. Blinded, stunned by the blow, she momentarily lost her reins. If her physical reaction from years of riding had not been quick, she would have fallen. As the dizziness and pain subsided, she saw Black Magic drawing ahead. Then the hounds, surging, boiling, jostling through the thick underbrush with frantic rapacious leaps as the heady scent heightened.

"Stop them!" Shelley screamed.

Zagaran looked back. She could not hear what he said but above the noise of the pack it seemed to her that she could hear his laughter, taunting, triumphant.

Shelley crouched forward. Hands draped in the colt's mane she sought to balance herself, stay on against the onslaught of branches and vines tearing at her. As though sensing what was at stake the thoroughbred responded, lengthening his stride, striving for greater speed.

Suddenly there was blue sky overhead. A few more yards and they would be at the precipice.

She saw it then. The fox she assumed was Zagaran's pet. A fox strange to the country. A fox that had never before been pursued and was therefore incapable of the instinctive wiles and protective measures which the wild foxes resorted to. A fox that did not know of the awesome drop ahead. A fox about which there was something strange.

It was almost to the edge of the abyss when one of the lead hounds reached it. Zagaran pulled the lathered Magic to a panting halt and jumped off. Reaching down, he grabbed the fox by its brush and drew it snarling and wildly twisting out of reach of the hound. Then as Shelley watched, speechless with horror, twelve couple of foxhounds burst from the underbrush and poured over the man and the fox in a surging mass of black and white, made wild and savage and uncontrollable by their lust to kill.

Only then, when almost submerged by the wave of hounds, did Zagaran let go of his prey.

Shelley rode Lookout Light into the melee and began flailing the avid hounds with the thong of her hunting whip. But the pack, wild in its savagery, was not to be diverted.

The glad, exultant cries changed to yelps of disappointment. There was a sudden profound silence as the last hounds drew back. Wearing hurt, chagrined expressions, they slunk into the underbrush. Shelley slid off her horse. She put her hand up to wipe away the sweat and mud, and when she drew it down again her white string glove was red with blood.

"That's one brush nobody is going to get," Zagaran said, pushing it aside with the toe of his boot.

"That was your fox." Pain from her bruised, battered face, shock and exhaustion combined to make the involuntary statement sound more accusing than she meant it to be. "Don't you care?"

Zagaran stiffened. For a moment he stood regarding her, tall and straight in his mud-spattered scarlet. The way he stood, and his silence, stubbornly forbade explanation or apology or appropriate denial. Then his eyes, which for an instant had gone dark with pain, as if mirroring some deep and nameless hurt, moved away from her. Reaching upward, he adjusted his hunting cap to its usual rakish angle. Pulling the reins over Magic's lowered head he advanced toward her.

Shelley saw the angled cap, the mouth and eyes. Then his features seemed to swim before her. To her left was the quarry, a sheer black drop. To her right the hunter, advancing slowly, purposefully.

"It's the chase that counts," he said, continuing toward her. "That's what you told me. Remember?"

In that moment everything seemed to go to pieces inside her. She had done this to herself, brought herself to the edge of the

573

precipice. His face, seen through a haze of red, was mocking her, menacing her. She saw him reach into his pocket and felt herself sway.

"You look as if you'd been blooded," he said, bringing out his handkerchief.

A sudden noise in the underbrush caused the horses to start.

"Presh," cried Dickie Speer, emerging from the woods, "am I glad to see you. I've been lost for absolute hours, trying to find my way through this loathsome jungle. Surely The Hunt could clear a path." He indicated a tear in his breeches. "I'm shredded. Positively shredded." He looked at the remains of the blood-soaked brush lying in the dirt. "Sorry about your fox."

"My fox!" Zagaran stared at him.

"Yes," Dickie replied. "I got lost and came out by the house. A woman opened the door and I saw the fox pop out. Just then the pack burst out of the woods."

"What woman?" Zagaran's voice was barely audible.

"She was in hair curlers and had a baby. I supposed she was one of the maids." He broke off, gazing at Shelley. "My God, presh, what happened to your face?"

After they collected hounds Shelley, Zagaran and Dickie Speer rode home. Zagaran hardly spoke, answering Dickie's questions in monosyllables. When Shelley suggested he might have difficulty finding a new huntsman and that possibly if he apologized—

"Zagaran doesn't explain or apologize," he responded coldly, cutting her off.

She started to mention the fox again and then did not. As they rode through the quiet countryside, the sun shining on fields and fences and farm ponds, it was hard to retain a sense of violence and tragedy. Just as she had mistakenly thought he had lashed out at her with his whip, she had been mistaken about the fox. He had not deliberately set out a fox. Its struggle to escape from the man and the hounds had not been the strange and awful thing it had seemed. Zagaran had tried to rescue his pet, save it from the rapacious pack. Could she have been mistaken about the race? Had Magic's swerve indeed been unintentional?

"Will you be going to the Schligmans'?" Shelley asked.

He shook his head. "As soon as I change, I'm flying to New York."

"Will you be back soon?"

"I don't know. I have urgent business to take care of first."

He touched his cap in a gesture of dismissal. "We'll call it a day. All things end. A race, a hunt, a season! So long, Miss Shelley."

There was a finality in the way he spoke. That and the rigidity of his back as he rode between the entrance posts, past the iron gate, kept her from calling out or following him. With a terrible sense of desolation, bereft of anticipation and fulfillment, she saw horse and rider disappear behind a screen of green. Turning to Dickie, she forced herself to talk of trivialities as, on this last day of the hunting season, they rode their tired horses slowly home.

PART FIVE

THE DEATH

TWENTY-SEVEN

MIKE had never imagined that he would end up sharing quarters with Fax Templeton at the Rakish Stud, but when Fax mentioned that the Blacks had been reconciled—Millicent had been so upset when her husband was beaten up at the Hunt Ball that she had paid his back bills, bought him a new scarlet evening coat and made him a present of Nautilus—and that Bones's quarters had been vacated, Mike accepted gratefully.

"I'm glad to be back home with Millicent and the children," Bones confided to Mike. "I was getting mighty tired of that triangle. Happy to have this corner rubbed out, even if it did mean ripping my new evening coat."

Now that he was ensconced in the room cleared of Bones's clothes, shoulder pads and racing saddle, some of Mike's loneliness was dispelled by Fax's easy confidence and likability. Fax was everything Mike had always supposed he was. Yet he was so happy-go-lucky and honestly dishonest that Mike could not dislike him. Although they had nothing in common, there was a relaxed ease in their relationship.

Now Fax was talking about horses and women, as usual. "The Duchess bought her off the track. Charming! It's just her legs."

"Legs?" Mike looked up. "The horse's legs?"

"No," Fax replied, "the Duchess's legs. Haven't you noticed? In jodhpurs she's so bowlegged Judy Schligman's collie dog could run between 'em and never ruffle a hair."

Mike laughed. He watched Fax carefully adjusting a rosebud in the buttonhole of his ancient but wonderfully tailored dinner jacket. "Straight from the gee-yarden," he said, standing back to admire himself in the cracked mirror almost obscured by snap-shots and invitations.

"You mean the Schligmans' garden?" Mike asked.

"Well, yes, now that you mention it. But then it was my gee-yarden before it became theirs. Actually, these are from the con-servatory. I had My Boy Hambone slip in there and cut me a dozen or so for the Duchess. Ta, ta, ta." Fax gave his tie a final tweak and did a dance step. "Say, you better change. Aren't you joining the gentry at the big house?"

Mike shook his head. "I'm taking Misty to dinner and then I have to work. Keep your shirt on, old boy," he called as Fax went out the door.

Speaking of shirts, he thought when he was in the Jeep, I better stop at home (in his mind he amended it to Shelburn Hall) and pick some up.

Shelley opened the door. Lance growled and then, recognizing him, rushed at him and stood on his hind legs, his great paws pressed against his chest.

"Down, Lance. Shelley, call him off."

"Here, Lance." Shelley stood with her hand on the newel post, feeling the amity button with her thumb. She was dressed in her long velvet skirt, a high-necked jersey top and the Shelburn Sap-phires. There was a jagged scratch across her cheek and then he saw what it was that seemed totally strange.

"Your hair!" he exclaimed, horrified. "What have you done to your hair?"

"I cut it," she said flatly. "Time I did, don't you think? As long as I'm changing my way of life."

"But your hair—" He turned away. Her appearance was changed so radically that it was hard for him to look at her. The cap of curls, frosted and brushed up from her face, made it seem thinner, accentuating the fine bones, the Shelburn nose. "You're all dressed up," he said finally. "Going out? Don't let me hold you up. I just came by for some shirts."

"I haven't done the ironing." She grasped the newel post more firmly. "Sorry about that. Maybe tomorrow. I'd press them now, but Katie asked that people come on time."

"You're going there—with him?"

She lifted her chin. "Why not? Who's to stop me?" Her hand clenched around the newel post.

Point of Satisfaction, he thought grimly. What satisfaction had it brought the Shelburns? He shook his head helplessly. "If you don't understand why you shouldn't be seen with *him* until after the divorce—"

"Divorce?" Her hand went to her mouth. Above it her eyes were huge. "You're divorcing me?"

He sighed. "Shelley, what in hell do you expect me to do? It's what you want, isn't it?"

"I wasn't going with Zagaran," she answered defensively. "He's away—on business. I just didn't want to stay here in the house alone."

She stood there clutching the post, as though in some way the amity button put there by her great-great-grandfather spelled the security she felt being taken from her. In the dim light she looked fragile. And yet he knew her physical strength to be extraordinary.

He turned away. "Zagaran is what you want, isn't he? A jet plane and horses and no maintenance problems. Think what you can do to Shelburn Hall with all that money. Rebuild the wing. Make it a real show place."

Without looking at her again, he went out the door and climbed into the Jeep.

Since Mike had left, Shelley had lived through her days with an emptiness, a frozen numbness which, suddenly, the word "divorce" had penetrated. It was as though all at once, with the full realization of what she had done, things that never in her wildest imagination had she ever contemplated were now being brought home, one by one. Then she remembered the party. Time enough tomorrow to think of what she must do. If she was to go down in defeat, it might as well be with the Shelburn Sapphires in her ears and a new hair-do.

At the last minute something prompted her to give the stable a final check.

When she turned on the light, she saw at once that something was wrong. Instead of the contented chuffing noise that usually came from Lookout Light's stall, there were odd grunting sounds.

The horse was circling his stall, seeking to lie down. She would have to call Doc Black or go to his house for colic medicine. The spring grass was coming up thick and juicy and lush. Lookout Light must have eaten too much of it when she turned him out after hunting. She would have to watch him all night. There was always the chance that a colicky horse would get cast and not be able to get up.

So, she thought, walking back to the house in her long dress, she wasn't going to go to the Schligmans' party after all.

Shelburn Hall rose dark, lightless, as though its honor had been forsaken. Steeped in night, it seemed unfamiliar to her and unforgiving, its welcoming peace shut away from her. She had a sense of fatalism, as though the destruction she had brought on herself had been preordained.

Lance followed her into the drawing room-ballroom. In the dim light the desecration, the tears in the curtains, the marks on the floor and woodwork, the dented warming pan and the tarnished brass and the bloodstained Waterford decanter seemed lost in a ghostly mist of departed glory. The fragile gilt legs of the chairs seemed barely to touch the floor, and the faint scent of the roses that had come from Ballyhoura conjured up an aching nostalgia that caused her to flee, back through the black hall and up the stairs, where silence closed like the door Mike had shut when he departed.

She called to Lance and the long, dark passages took up her voice and answered, echoing through the rooms, empty and forsaken like the paintings whose contents faded blackly against the walls. Without people, without a child, Shelburn Hall seemed like an abandoned ship.

Lance came to her. The rabies tag hanging from his studded collar made a jingling noise. He shoved his great fawn-colored head against her. Wearily she patted him, feeling his short wiry hair, aware of his snuffling detachment, more healing than human sympathy in its lack of understanding. Thank God she had not permitted him to be destroyed. Now he was her only bulwark against loneliness.

"I'm late," Tatine said, stopping to pick up Richard, who was waiting behind the rhododendron bush. "Hurry. Get in. Quick, stow your bag in the trunk."

Somehow he was able to stuff his Army duffel bag into the small space the manufacturers of sports cars had allotted for luggage. Tatine's red leather cosmetic case and sheepskin coat took up most of the space. With difficulty he managed to fold his angular six-foot frame into the bucket seat.

"You don't like my car much, do you?"

"Getting into it is like pulling on a pair of pants," he said stiffly.

"You're funny." She smiled at him, a smile of such tenderness and guile that his anger at her for keeping him standing in the dark for the past half hour vanished.

"Actually, I was doing my nails. It isn't every day a girl runs away with her father's huntsman."

"I'm no longer your father's huntsman. I was fired this morning. Remember?" He tugged at his seat belt, part of which was caught in the door. "The seat belt's caught."

"You and that old seat belt." She tossed her head impatiently. "You weren't careful today and I loved it." She reached over and gently touched the welt her father's whip had left across his face. "You were great when you told Zagaran off."

His qualms, his apprehensions receded in a rush. Suddenly he was happy. What did anything matter as long as this girl cared enough to go away with him? Giving up the horn was a small price to pay for winning the Master's daughter.

"Richard, let's go—"

"Wait." Reaching out, he pulled her to him. He saw the stars twinkling beyond her head and smelled the odor of her hair and skin, sweet-smelling and clean, like good soap and new-mown hay.

"We better scram," she said, freeing herself reluctantly.

"Where are we going?"

"Surprise." She switched on the ignition and gunned the powerful motor. "You'll see when we get there."

"But—" A rush of wind as the car leapt forward took the words from his mouth. No matter. What did anything matter as long as they were together? Now she was the present and all the future he would ever have.

Without coming to a full stop, the sports car slewed out onto the Valley road. There was a screech of brakes as a furiously driven pickup truck, deeply encrusted in mud, swerved to avoid it. In the second before the truck continued on its way along the avenue to the kennel's cottage, Richard saw the driver's angry face and recognized his brother-in-law.

"Son of a bitch!" Tatine exclaimed. "That truck almost creamed us."

Tom's face indicated he'd been drinking and when he drank he was, as they said in the Free Zone, a mean drunk. Well, Richard thought, he was no longer his problem. No point in telling Tatine.

"A close shave," he agreed. "But then you shot out in front of him, Tatine. You needn't drive so fast."

"I want to get the hell away from here," she said.

"So do I, but in one piece. Tatine, you said you'd stop swearing."

"I forgot, damn it. Sorry," she shouted above the sound of the wind rushing at them, "but you must admit Zagaran's a devil."

When she spoke this way he was afraid of her. Again it was borne in on him what different worlds they stemmed from. Brought up as he had been to believe in authority, to respect his God-fearing family, it was hard to accept the loathing and contempt with which she spoke of her parents.

"You shouldn't talk that way," he admonished mildly. He thought of the car in which they were racing through the blue-black night. "Your father's given you a lot."

"Zagaran has never given me a bloody thing," she cried bitterly. "Nothing that mattered. I mean like love or listening. When I was a kid I used to beg him to take me riding, or just to listen to me. Do you think he would? 'Now be a good girl. Stay with Nanny.' Then he'd go out and take over another corporation or chase a seladang, or somebody's wife. Now he's hell-bent on adding Shelley Latimer to his collection, putting her up on the wall along with his masks and brushes. They've been together at the Hunting Box. I found one of her earrings."

Richard felt a sudden sadness. He liked Mrs. Latimer. She always spoke politely to the Hunt staff and was never foul-mouthed like some of the other women. She went like a house afire in the field and he would always appreciate the fact that she, along with old Mr. Dinwiddie and Mr. Templeton, had been the only people at the Hunt Ball who had spoken to him. When the grooms and country people got together Saturday nights and gossiped about the hunting people, her name was never brought into the conversation. In his estimation, she was one of the few in The

Valley who conducted herself the way a lady should, not overriding hounds, always saying "Thank you" when he opened a gate for the field. Fact was that when he'd come upon the Master and Mrs. Latimer riding home that morning from The Hunting Box, he'd been shocked. He'd wondered—though he had never spoken a word about it to another living soul.

"I don't think she's that kind," he answered. "She seems like a real nice lady to me."

"That's what's so tragic. He'll destroy her. The way he did my mother. Once he gets what he wants he doesn't want it any longer. He has some strange power— Oh hell, let's not talk about him. We've got us to talk about. Give me a cigarette."

As his match flared for her cigarette, her features were sharply etched, her body a series of soft curves.

"Where's Softie?" she asked.

"Here, on the seat."

"And my bag?"

"Here."

"I'll bet I forgot my wallet," she said. "Oh well, we can cash a check."

Rich people are amazing, he thought. All his life he had worried about money. About getting in over his head, not being able to meet the payments on the deep freeze and color TV his wife had bought on the pay-as-you-go plan. Yet as long as he had known Tatine he had yet to see her carry any money with her. Whatever she wanted she charged, and when she needed cigarettes he was the one who bought them for her.

"I can do over a hundred," she said as the road leveled out. "I'm in a hurry, aren't you?"

He started to argue and then did not. With sudden anguish, he was aware that just as that day he had handed over the reins to her father, he had in the same way handed over to her the reins to himself. From now on he was in her power, destined to be little more than a possession, like the car, roaring its song of power through the night. Now he was all hers, a machine for her to manipulate and control.

At that moment he would have turned back. Then he remembered that his bridges were burned. When he turned his back on Ballyhoura, he had left his wife and his son and all that he had known in the smoking ruins of what had been his life.

Tatine threw her head back and he heard her exultant cry. "Oh, darling, darling Richard, we're together, at last."

Her lips parted in a pleased, secretive smile. Impulsively she reached out and touched his knee. Wearing her best-for-last expression, she put her hand back on the wheel. Grasping it firmly, she pressed her foot down hard on the accelerator. The car shot forward, thrusting him backward against the seat. The speedometer needle moved slowly upward.

Richard tightened his seat belt.

Walls, trees, gate posts whipped by. They were approaching the entrance to Shelburn Hall. Tatine decelerated slightly, then jammed her foot down hard, accelerating. The car shot over the top of the rise.

Suddenly he saw a pair of headlights leap from the shrouded mystery of the woods. The high growth made it almost impossible for anyone driving out of the entrance to see oncoming cars. Mrs. Latimer really should trim the bushes away from the drive.

It was the last thought he was ever to have.

There was a scream of brakes, followed by the ghastly sound of a collision.

Mike and Misty heard the siren in the distance. Then the mournful wailing sound became deafening as the ambulance, its red unicorn light whirling like a baleful eye, passed them leaving Shelburn.

"Must be an accident," Mike said as it vanished over a hump in the Valley road. "Hope it's nobody we know."

Long before they got there, they saw the lights.

"My God," Mike cried involuntarily, "it's Shelley!" He put the accelerator down to the floor. The Jeep lurched and then leapt ahead. Misty's hands holding onto the seat tightened. She turned and saw his profile and knew with sudden deep certainty that the dream she had indulged herself in was hopeless.

There was such a crowd gathered around the entrance to Shelburn Hall that they were forced to park at the end of a line of cars some distance away.

"Wait here," Mike cried, jumping out of the Jeep.

At sight of Tatine's car his fear gave way, briefly, to relief. Then as the red rays from the police cars crossed and recrossed it like long, bloody fingers he was aware of growing horror. Looking like a child's toy flung aside during a tantrum, it lay upside down in the ditch, crumpled and broken and completely crushed. Half across the road lay the remains of Virginia City's ancient coupe.

"What happened?" Mike asked Chester Glover.

"Tatine Zagaran," the policeman said, shooing onlookers out of the way of the traffic. "She was scratching gravel, musta been traveling close to a hundred miles an hour as she come over the rise." He jerked his hand in the direction of the mangled car. "I almost gave her a ticket the other day and then she looks at me in that way of hers and says, 'Chester, you wouldn't do that to me, now would you.'"

"Is she—?"

"She come over the rise," Chester continued methodically, "and she hit the nigger. Sorry, Editor. The nigra—he pulled out of the driveway there, and she hit him broadside."

Mike tried again. "Is she—?"

"The nigra's hurt bad. The boy was killed."

"Boy?"

"Richard Doyle, his name was. Worked up to Ballyhoura as huntsman. Funny thing. He had his seat belt fastened and he was crushed. Tatine, she didn't have no seat belt. She was thrown clear."

"Alive?"

The policeman nodded. He shook his head wonderingly. "She was conscious. 'Softie,' she says to me, 'Chester, find Softie for me.' I don't know what the hell she's talking about. Then she asks about the boy—"

Mike turned away. The crowd had thickened. He recognized the Websters and the Free Zone families, returning from shopping at the supermarket, arguing and gesticulating as they discussed the accident. In the eerie moving light the faces of those hurrying to the scene were excited and animated, while those who had gotten there wore smug looks of satisfaction at being able to impart the gruesome details. Mike started back to where he had left Misty in the Jeep. In order to let a car go by, he moved to the edge of the macadam. In the beam of the headlights, he saw something white lying beyond the wreckage. Softie, Tatine's stuffed toy that she always took with her.

Mike picked it up carefully. One ear was ripped almost off and one glass-button eye was missing. The other eye, caught in the lights from a passing car, gazed up at him with an air of secret mockery.

He heard the ambulance start up and jumped aside. The back was lit and as it sped past, gathering speed, he saw Shelley bent over Virginia City, lying on the stretcher. She looked grieving and defenseless, her unfamiliar cropped head giving her the appearance of one much younger, one whose haughty pride has all departed.

Mike watched the receding red light and felt suddenly stricken by the senseless tragedy, by the waste and confusion and emotion all around him.

In The Valley, Tatine Zagaran had been like the flame of her cigarette lighter, a brightness that flared and then was gone.

Now her beautiful body was broken and paralyzed. She would never know the comfort a mother gives to her child, the love of a man reaching for a woman in the night.

"They've decided to operate," she told Mike when he went to see her. Softie, the stuffed rabbit that he had picked up, lay beside her. Her hair, spread against the white sheet, framed her face. That and her jade eyes provided the only color.

"You'll come out of it," Mike replied as the nurse came in to ask him to leave.

"I want to be useful," Tatine murmured weakly. "I'd like to help you with the paper."

"Welcome aboard," Mike said.

After leaving Tatine, he went to see Virginia City, who had a broken arm and leg but otherwise seemed as indestructible as ever.

"I'll be back on the job before you know it," he promised. "I don' like to think what a mess that stable's gonna be neither. Yessir." He nodded emphatically. "That old pine box is gonna have to wait a while longer for Virginia City."

Mike asked if there was anything he wanted.

"Miss Shelley gone home to fetch me my Bible," the old Negro answered. "She gonna feed my chickens . . ." He closed his eyes, and as Mike slipped out of the door he heard him mumbling the Lord's Prayer.

. . .

Mike found the brochure on his desk when he reached the office. It was printed on heavy expensive paper, decorated with a border of red foxes against a white background.

With growing amazement and disbelief, Mike read:

> The Zagaran Development Company, Inc., takes pleasure in presenting completed Phase One of the Urban Design Study for the historic property of Ballyhoura and the town of Shelburn. We hope that this study will prove useful in stimulating consideration of the potential benefits of the proposals by you and your fellow townsmen. This study is conceived as part of an ongoing process of community planning and as a catalyst for concerted town action to channel the growth and strengthen the character of Shelburn, and as a guide for the subsequent development of your property.
>
> Shelburn is a beautiful town, in a beautiful country with a rich and historic heritage, located so as to benefit from the vital economy of the Washington area . . .

Mike went on reading. What the stilted prose boiled down to was that Zagaran, with the cooperation of Senator Bentley, who had talked to Federal Housing officials, had put through a plan for the twenty-year development of Ballyhoura's five thousand acres. The western portion of the estate bordered Muster Corner. The Negro community was to be leveled and would become part of the Ballyhoura "Planned Cluster Community, eventually to include six thousand homes and a population roughly estimated at twelve thousand." The brochure went on to say that the community "will provide everything needed for a well-rounded life. This will include a shopping center and cinema, restaurant and beauty salon."

Wow, Mike thought, wait until the local merchants got wind of that! He could hear Herm Gillespie: "We don't want or need change here. None of them newfangled centers like they're putting up at Bellevue. Folks here like things to stay the way they are, the way they've always been."

He went on reading. The master plan called for open space to be preserved through the clustering of dwellings. Focus of the layout was a five-hundred-acre lake to be known as Lake Tatine. The map showed that the lake was to be constructed where the Shelburn Cup course now stood.

"Buffalo Run, fed by a twelve-thousand-acre watershed, runs

north to south through the tract and when dammed will provide water for the lake and the dwellings, to include not only single-family homes but town houses and apartment buildings."

Thanks to Zagaran, the people of Muster Corner would have adequate housing and would no longer live like foxes.

Mike read on. "The Manor House will be renovated as a country club. The historic forty-room house was originally the seat of Sean Shelburn, famed leader of Shelburn's Raiders in the Civil War. Recreation facilities are a principal objective of the plan. The plan calls for an equestrian center, foxhunting with The Hunt . . ."

At thought of Mrs. Dinwiddie's face when she picked up the *Sun* on Thursday morning, Mike experienced his first moment of real enjoyment in many months.

"Swimming pools, one of Olympic size, eighteen-hole international golf course, miniature golf, skeet shooting, tennis courts, a series of trails for hiking and riding, an amphitheater, arts and crafts pavilion and other facilities."

"Hey, Editor." Pete stuck his head around the door. "Time to start making up the front page. Shall I put in the regular—Chamber of Commerce, Board of Supervisors, and so forth? Or do you have a lead story this week?"

Mike dropped the brochure on his desk and reached for some paper to put in his typewriter. "It just so happens that this week we have a lead story!"

It is doubtful if any news since the announcement of Virginia's secession from the Union had as much impact in The Valley as the *Sun*'s story that appeared under the headline, "Zagaran Announces Plans for Housing Development and Recreation Area at Ballyhoura. Shopping Center, Lake and Six Thousand Homes to Be Built in Near Future."

The story and map of the proposed development covered almost all of the front page.

An hour after the *Sun* was on the county newsstands, it was sold out. The phone in the office rang without stopping. The weekly had gotten a clean beat on the *County Daily* and Jake Bronstein called to find out why he had not been notified.

"Ask your boss," Mike replied. "He must have known about it."

"Hell," Jake answered disgustedly, "he's drying out at that

place up north where they send the drunks. We haven't heard from him."

"Then find out for yourself," Mike said and hung up.

The Chamber of Commerce called an emergency meeting to see what steps to take in order to prevent the building of the proposed shopping center.

R. Rutherford Dinwiddie, Esquire, was named to represent The Valley Conservation Association, hastily formed at a meeting called by Dash-Smythe.

People were united in denouncing Zagaran. "Edwardian turncoat," R. Rutherford snorted. "I always said he wasn't a gentleman."

"That means the end of The Hunt," the Beast said philosophically as she waited at the supermarket to buy ground round steak for her dogs. "Hunting's gotten to be like meat," she confided to the butcher. "So expensive only Yankees can afford it."

Shelley read the *Sun* with horror mingled with disbelief. And yet, as she sat holding the paper in her hand, she had a feeling of inevitability. Zagaran had begun the process of dissolution, the tearing down, as if he had pushed over the first row of a line of the blocks he told her had been his only playthings as a child. One by one they had begun falling. This past week the last of them had tumbled in a heap, bringing the established order, the structure, down with them.

Since the Hunt Ball Shelley had forced herself to continue maintenance, the mechanics of existence. In the days following Mike's and Cam's departure she had tried desperately to stop feeling and thinking and living, making herself move from chore to chore. When not working in the house—Linda Taylor had rounded up some women who had slowly brought order from the chaos left over from the ball—or stable, she had been at the hospital visiting Virginia City.

She had not seen Tatine or her father. Tatine had been flown to a New York hospital to be operated on by the country's leading neurosurgeon. Now that Tatine's restless, seeking body was stilled, the people who had heaped the most vituperation on her flaming head pretended to be the chief mourners.

"So tragic," Mrs. Dinwiddie said, dabbing at her eyes with a torn mauve handkerchief. "So young, so vital, so much to live for."

"Yes," Debby Darbyshire agreed as they stood talking at the checkout counter in the supermarket. "I wonder if she'll ever ride again."

"It's a fifty-fifty proposition," Doc Watters told Shelley when he came by to see Virginia City. "If the operation is successful, she'll be able to walk. If not—well, that's the way the cookie crumbles. The girl's got guts. She announced that if she couldn't walk or ride again she was going to study and read books, become 'a goddamned intellectual' was the way she put it."

The least she could do for Tatine, Shelley decided, was to go to Richard Doyle's funeral, held on Saturday afternoon at the funeral home. The service, hurriedly read by the Baptist minister, sounded harsh and unsympathetic. His wife was not there, nor his child. Shelley was told that Mrs. Doyle had packed up her belongings, taken the baby and returned to her family in the Free Zone. The rendering of flowers was sparse. A wreath in the shape of a horseshoe in chrysanthemums the color of Tatine's racing silks, a basket of the daffodils still blooming in the park, from Shelley. And the Old Huntsman had placed a small bunch of violets and the cow hunting horn, the rim of which was chipped, on top of the casket.

"I loved the boy like my own son," he told Shelley. "If he hadn't had woman trouble, he'd still be alive. He would have been a great huntsman. I kinda thought of the flowers as symbolic." He indicated the violets. "Your pa used to call them 'those stinking violets.' Hunting's over when they start to bloom!"

Shelley did not remember falling asleep and yet she must have, for when she awoke Sunday morning it was to a world that seemed unbelievably young and new and shining. There was the faint cooing of doves from the pastures, turning green from the spring rain. A hawk in one of the oaks was etched against the blue sky, puffed with clouds. For a moment her heart, like her body rising from bed, arched in anticipation of the slowly silvering day, and then it struck her what was missing from it. Aside from the sound of birds and the wind there was no other noise. In the house all was silent, and as the morning's quietness stole over her its very beauty seemed a desecration.

At least there would be somebody at the stable. Although Jimmy had returned to the temporary school Preacher Young had set up in the church while the new building at Muster Corner was being built, the boy still came Sundays, bringing Bardy with him. Generally they arrived by eight and Jimmy would begin mucking out the stalls while his baby brother played in the pile of clay used to pack the stalls, or drove his toy truck up and down the aisleway.

But this morning the stable was as quiet and empty of human activity as the house. The only sound came from the sparrows nesting in the rafters and Lookout Light, nickering eagerly for his breakfast.

Shelley found herself subconsciously listening for the sound of Preacher Young's old truck. Jimmy's ambition was to be a jockey and ride Lookout Light. She decided to let him practice in the ring today. While she waited, she might as well begin cleaning out the stalls. Pitchforking the used straw into the basket and carrying it out to the manure pile was good exercise. Best of all, it left little time for thought.

It was not yet nine when she finished. Still no sign of the Negro children. This was strange, for they had yet to be late or miss a Sunday. Now the day stretched before her, as empty as the ruined wing. How would she fill it? Maybe church would help her to solve some of her problems, to begin refinding her way. Then she would go and see Virginia City, perhaps the Jenneys. With a start she realized she had done nothing about the boycott of the Covertside Inn. She had intended to speak to Zagaran, but that had been before the news of the development. Still, she could use the issue of the Jenneys as a reason to see him.

She went to the house to change, dressing with greater care than usual. The black dress he liked, that she had worn the day she had gone to the penthouse and he had spoken to her of things he had not told anyone before. Spotless white gloves and the heavy silver earrings he had given her.

She put her hand up to her hair and patted the careful waves Miss Esther had put in place. Zagaran had teased her so often about her clothes, her refusal to smoke, called her old-fashioned, dated. Somehow she would show him she could be modernized, be as fashionable as Samantha Sue, entertain as well, be adept at making love and a new life.

She was about to depart when she heard a car drive up and recognized the veterinarian's ancient black coupe.

"Why, Doc Black," she said, opening the front door, "how nice of you to come by. Lookout Light cleaned up all his feed. He seems fine—Doc Black, you look ill. Come in the house. Let me get you some coffee or tea."

"I've just come from Ballyhoura." The veterinarian opened the car door, got out and began walking dazedly toward the house. "Shelley," he said when he was in the hall, "I have to set a spell."

"Zagaran—" She could hardly say his name. "He's all right, isn't he?"

"Sit down, Shelley." Doc Black patted the seat beside him.

"What is it?" she cried, seeing the anguish on his face.

"It was the worst thing I ever saw," the old vet said quietly.

Simeon Tucker found Black Magic when he went in to feed her. Usually when he did this she nickered and pawed, flattened her ears and came at him with teeth bared. Then Simeon would dump her feed in her manger and exit as fast as possible.

Ever since the man Mellick from the Free Zone had stuck the pitchfork in the mare's chest, Simeon had been the only groom brave enough to handle her. It fell to the old stableman to feed her, muck out her stall, tack her up and take care of her, and in the doing he had come to feel a closeness and affection for the beautiful black thoroughbred that he had never felt for another horse. After the Shelburn Cup he had led her back to the barn, spent hours cooling her out, cleaned her and then treated her to a good hot mash. The mare had thanked him by lashing out with her hind legs and trying to catch his shoulder with her teeth. He had laughed at her, knowing that she knew as well as he did this was a game they were destined to play.

"Come along, hawse," he said now, letting the breakfast slither into her manger. Still she did not come. Stranger still was the sound of her heavy breathing. Simeon turned.

Black Magic stood facing him. Her legs were set wide apart and the white rims of her eyes were red and anguished. A film of sweat lay over her satin coat.

When he saw the bloody foam coming from her half-opened mouth he thought she was having some kind of fit. Or that perhaps she had been bitten by a rabid animal.

"When she didn't come at me or try and bite," he told Doc

Black, "I knew sumpn' was wrong. She just looked and her eyes were awful.

"Mr. Zagaran had come home from seeing Miss Tatine in the hospital late Saturday," the groom continued with difficulty. "He was still asleep when I got to the big house. The new butler didn't want to wake him, but I told him it was an emergency."

When Zagaran came downstairs, wearing his dressing gown, Simeon reported what had happened. Zagaran ordered the butler to telephone the vet. Then, without pausing to change, he went and got a gun from the rack in the den.

Doc Black turned to Shelley and laid his hand gently on her knee. "When I got there the mare was dead. Zagaran was standing over her, wearing his bathrobe, holding a gun. I didn't know at first what had happened. I thought maybe the mare had savaged him. She had the reputation of being a mankiller. And he had shot her. Then I saw his face. He was weeping." The vet paused and swallowed. "I looked down at the horse. I saw the blood coming from her mouth. Then I saw the blacksmith's pull-off nippers lying on the ground beside the door. Somebody had pulled Black Magic's tongue out with the nippers."

TWENTY-EIGHT

ZAGARAN had made no effort to see her, had not called, sent flowers or a note. But now with the news of this final tragedy, on top of what had happened to his wife, then to Tatine, she had to go to him.

As she drove through the brilliant early morning light, past the Bentleys' chauffeur on his way to the Gone Away to get the Sunday papers for the Senator, Polo Pete, who had come home from the drying-out place, and Misty, on her way to church, she had no thought other than to be with Zagaran, to hold him in her arms, comfort him as she would have comforted Cam.

The countryside had never been more beautiful. The bleached-out look of winter was giving way to the glory of Virginia spring. The fields were a lush, inviting green, cushioned with thick clods of grass, calling to be galloped over. Flowers bloomed along the entrance lanes and avenues, where they had been carefully culti-vated to resemble the results of nature rather than of the hot-house. The woods were carpeted with tiny star-shaped blossoms, and clumps of May apples spread their parasol heads like scatter rugs.

In the fields bordering the road, newborn foals lurched drunk-enly on long, untried legs as they ran after their stately mothers. Calves lay in meadows where the colored people hurried to pick dandelion plants in order to "cook up a mess of greens" before the yellow blossoms came, like pats of butter turned rancid, render-ing them sour and inedible.

She turned into Ballyhoura, past the great stone crested en-trance posts surmounted by their stone foxes, and the crimson mailbox with the blue stripe. The gate had been removed and the gatehouse appeared empty.

The floor of the wood was spread with the butter-colored light from the daffodils Zagaran had set out that spring morning a year ago. Soon the ground in which they grew would be violated, the rich earth holding the tiny wildflowers and the golden clumps, "spinach and eggs" the country people called them, would be up-turned. The wood that had belonged to the wild creatures would be given over to matchbox houses, a country club and a shopping center.

No smoke came from the great turreted house. It seemed sunk into the earth like the Ballyhoura Oak. Would the tree be cut down, the gazebo destroyed?

Below stretched the match-stick tracery of the steeplechase course. Within weeks the fences Zagaran had so carefully rebuilt would be removed, the turf made springy by two hundred years of careful cultivation would become a lake, surrounded by roads and ranch houses with little metal signs reading "The Smiths" and "The Joneses."

Was it this, the rape of The Valley, or was it what Mike had called the turning away from responsibility, that had brought violence into their midst? Or had the violence always been there, mowed over like the beer cans on the side of the road? Had it come with Zagaran, the foreigner, with his dark, taciturn looks, the air of mystery that hinted of tragedy and evil and the strangenesses of the past?

Somebody new opened the door, a white butler Shelley had not seen before. His manner, as he told her Mr. Zagaran was in his den, was one of thinly veiled insolence. As she went down the long hall beneath the mounted heads, she felt his eyes boring into her back and the soiled, shamed feeling that had become familiar over past months returned, spreading over her like the bloodstains on the floor at Shelburn Hall where Manassas had fallen.

"Did your husband send you?" he asked. He wore a single-breasted gabardine suit, a crimson foulard and black patent evening pumps. A white handkerchief, the tiny crimson Z monogram showing in its corner, rose an inch above the breast pocket of his coat.

"No, my husband didn't send me," she answered defiantly. "When I heard—I had to come. Zagaran, who would do such a terrible thing?"

"Mellick. Doyle's wife's brother. Chester Glover picked him up. He was drunk at Delia's Kitchen. He was boasting that he'd fixed that mare of Zagaran's that savaged him. Doc Black said that at one time he'd worked as a forest ranger on the mountain. He knew about tranquilizing animals. Somehow he managed to shoot a tranquilizer into her."

Zagaran repeated what the policeman had told him, how in the Free Zone memory and the desire for revenge lie generations long. As the jug was passed around while the men sat by the campfire listening to their hounds running in the blue mountains, the old story of how Sean Shelburn debauched and deflowered a Mellick woman was told and retold, to simmer and fester in minds made murky by ignorance and superstition. As they thirsted for the raw liquor they made in their mountain stills, the Mellick men, ruthless and unforgiving, thirsted for revenge.

"Some of them mountainy men are mighty mean," the policeman explained. "And Tom's as mean as they come. Many's the time of a Saturday night when he's likkered up, I've had to take him in for goin' after some nigger with a knife."

Chester told Zagaran that the idea of revenge had been in Mellick's mind ever since the mortgage was foreclosed on the family farm. That, coupled with what had happened to his sister, which was somehow interwoven with the old story of Sean Shelburn and his great-grandmother, was enough to cause Mellick to steal the blacksmith's nippers the day of the Shelburn Cup, when Simeon had seen him skulking around the barn.

Zagaran went to the bar and took down a silver cup. He scooped up a handful of ice cubes from the bucket on the bar table and began breaking them into his glass with the handle of an ice pick.

"Black Magic." His hand shook as he poured himself a stiff drink. "Proud, beautiful—" His voice broke, and Shelley remembered what Doc Black had said, that Zagaran had wept. Now as she stared at him the thought struck her that, like her father, he was vulnerable after all.

She started toward him, but he turned away. She followed his gaze out the window. A cloud of pigeons rose from the stable, their wings silver in the sunlight, like those of the plane waiting on the runway. In the meadow, mares and foals grazed. A breeze blew through the Hanging Oak, slowly refinding its spring greenery. The pastoral scene made the violence, the tragedies of long ago, seem dreamlike, as unreal as the destruction awaiting the landscape.

He reached into his pocket for his cigarette case. "Still smoking?"

"Yes." She took the cigarette he held out to her.

"I always liked that dress," he said conversationally as she bent her head to accept his light, "but what have you done to your hair?"

She realized he had deliberately avoided touching her hand holding the cigarette. "I had it cut."

"In God's name, why?"

Her cigarette suddenly tasted foul. "I was tired of being *Mädchen in Uniform.*"

He began busily sorting bottles in the liquor cabinet. "I'm flying to New York. Tatine's being operated on tomorrow. Somebody's been into the Scotch. Must be the new man. Lucky I won't be needing him much longer."

She put out her cigarette, wishing she hadn't smoked it.

"Zagaran, I—"

He whirled around. "Still Zagaran, is it? As if I were the butler or the groom? Zagaran, even in bed."

"I just always thought of you as Zagaran," she said miserably, "as someone strong." She did not know how to go on.

He lit another cigarette. In the flickering light she saw the planes of his face, every inch of which she had traced with her fingers.

"You told me how much The Valley meant to you. Why have you sold out?"

"I prefer to think The Valley sold out." He extracted an empty bottle from the cabinet. "I know what The Valley means to you. Let me tell you what it means to me. Money timid. Minds as narrow as their Brooks Brothers ties. Pink coats and pass the port. Bloody Marys and sex on Sundays. Polo afterward."

"Damn you, Zagaran! We were happy!"

"Shit! Rundown farms, overgrown fields. And The Hunt. Hounds sick and starving because Fax Templeton never went near the kennels. The Old Huntsman trying to make do. It isn't in any one of you to face facts. Christ, Shelley, for every fucking one of you to whom vulpicide is a way of life, there are millions of the great unbooted who never heard of this valley!"

She hated him then. He had outraged her instincts, her background, upbringing and sense of decency. He was crude in manner and in speech and had violated everything she considered of value. He had destroyed her. Now he would destroy The Valley.

"I should have known the kind of man you were the day you climbed the Hanging Tree and threw the fox to the hounds."

"That was one of the gray fox cubs from a Ballyhoura den. Polo Pete wanted them destroyed, said they would spoil the cover for decent foxes. Red foxes. I knew that if I didn't rescue the fox in the tree he would shoot it down. When I reached up to grab it, the fox jumped. I tried to catch him and missed." His voice dropped. "By the time I climbed down it was too late. The pack was on him."

She stared at him aghast. "But you were the hunter." She gestured toward the hallway. "The heads. The seladang. The groundhog you shot the day of the Hunt meeting. The deer in the Free Zone."

"The Hunt was anti-gray fox, anti-groundhog, anti-deer. Anti-anything that interfered with the chase, its way of life. I played the game. I wanted to be accepted. To be somebody."

"But you are somebody," Shelley said.

"I mean somebody in The Valley. Being somebody in New York or San Francisco is different from being somebody in The Valley."

"You were Master of The Hunt. Still are, in fact. In this country, that means something!"

"When I became Master I thought I had it made. I planned to make it up to Andrea for the grief I caused her in the past. Tatine would marry a nice boy like Sandy Montague and inherit Bally-houra. There would be children. I envisioned a kind of dynasty to be handed down from one generation to the next." He gazed at the empty fireplace. "A house where the chimneys would never grow cold."

"You told me you loved The Hunt, the chase."

"I loved the challenge, the excitement and the country. I found I did not love the people who pursued this sport, this way of life." He drained his glass. "I won't hunt any more. I won't kill any more."

"But I thought—" She could not go on. The look he gave her made her feel burdened with loss, confidence gone, replaced with deadening self-doubt.

"You thought what you wanted to think. The way all of you wanted to believe I cheated in the race." He sent the bottle crashing into the wastebasket. "I knew then I would never be accepted. Only mistrusted. The Valley doesn't like anything that isn't pure-bred. Foxes or people."

"The swerve wasn't deliberate? You didn't foul Fax?"

"No." He looked directly at her and his eyes were like pieces of black ice. "But you assumed I did, and that made all the difference."

"You're wrong," she cried. "I tried to tell you after the race, under the oak, that I would go away with you."

"Shelley." He turned to look at her and for an instant his eyes were the way they had been when he spoke of Black Magic. "The first time I heard you singing, saw you ride up, the day you jumped the gate—" He paused and then added softly, "Shelley, you were The Valley to me."

Desire swept over her, melting her anger. She longed to hold his hand against her cheek. "And now?"

He did not seem to have heard her. "I must leave," he said, starting to put the bottles he had been counting back in the cabinet.

The life she had known with him flashed through her consciousness. She saw him as she had that first day, the uplifted eyebrow and mocking smile, and in the distance she heard the sound of music becoming louder, sweeping over them, the way it had been when they danced together the night of Tatine's ball.

"Zagaran—" She reached out as though to stop him. There was a clinking sound as one of the heavy earrings he had given her fell to the floor. He bent down to pick it up.

"Still losing earrings, are you? Here." He did not look at her as he handed it to her. "You'd better go. Samantha Sue will be here any minute."

"Samantha Sue!"

"I'm taking her with me," Zagaran said. "We're going to be married."

Shelley's hand went to her mouth. She did not know until later when she saw the toothmarks that she had closed her teeth on the skin at the wrist, biting down hard, weeping silently for the candy Melusina would no longer make, for the Shelburn Cup horses that had stopped moving single file across the horizon, for the music now silent and the hunting horn, its mellow notes stilled.

"That bastard of a butler," Zagaran said. "All the Scotch is gone."

It was after eleven when Shelley drew up in front of the church. She parked the station wagon, got out and walked toward the gate in the spiked iron fence surrounding the yard. The Sunday traffic that came with fine weather streamed past, bound from the city to the mountains. A robin flew out of the magnolia tree by the door, open to allow in the soft spring breeze. From inside came the sound of the organ as the service began.

Shelley was about to turn onto the flagstoned walk when the opening hymn ended. Main Street was strangely quiet. For a moment nothing moved and then the sudden, startling silence was broken by the sound of chanting.

As Shelley stood riveted by the fence the source came into sight. Turning onto the street from the square came a massed line of Negro marchers, blocking the cars queued behind them. On they came, six abreast, the sound of their feet against the pavement adding reality, a meaning and purpose like the background beat of drums.

Jimmy Jones marched in the front line. His plaid jacket was too small and bunched around the waist. His brown corduroy trousers were too short and his pink phosphorescent socks had slid down over his scuffed shoes. But his shoes gleamed with polish, like his face, shining with new-found pride and purpose. Mase Brown walked on one side, Preacher Young on the other. Washington Taylor, his tall figure and white-crowned head rendering him unmistakable, walked alone.

Behind the leaders Shelley saw row upon row of faces, as familiar to her as her surroundings. Smiths, Taylors, Wilkersons, Tuckers. My Boy Hambone, elegant in Fax's old tweeds, a yellow rosebud stuck jauntily in his buttonhole. Jubal Jones, miraculously sober, wearing his tattered frock coat. Even Suellen was there, her pregnancy well advanced, walking proudly alongside her Eddie.

They did not glance away from Shelley's gaze. Instead they returned it, their expressions grim and unsmiling, as strange to her as their pretended lack of recognition, ignoring her as they were ignoring the reporters and photographers trotting alongside.

"Washington." Her voice was that of Miss Shelley of Shelburn Hall. The Negro leader continued on down the street. "Washington," Shelley called sharply, "what's going on?"

Slowly his head swiveled around. Reluctantly he detached himself from the column and came toward her. "Mrs. Latimer." He had never called her Mrs. Latimer before. "Manassas Brown is dead. We've come to ask for our rights. We've drawn up a set of demands. Your husband is to deliver them after the service. Meanwhile, we're going to pray for Mr. Buford."

Shelley glanced toward the church. Through the open doorway she could see the congregation standing.

"What if they refuse to meet your demands?"

"No telling what will happen then."

"But why?" Shelley whispered. "Why now—after all this time?"

"We waited for the law," Washington Taylor said. "The law didn't change things. Mrs. Latimer, we've waited a long time. We thought the hating would end. But it hasn't. It's still here after hundreds of years. And now the people who do the hating have made haters of those they hate." He shrugged. "Your husband tried. It wasn't enough. Not enough people tried!"

The marchers halted in front of the entrance to the churchyard. Shelley noticed Mase, the bitter, scarred face, the eyes fixed upon her. Unaccustomed fear knotted her stomach, sweeping through her blood in waves as cold as the organizer's eyes, filled with contempt and rage.

"Where will it end?" Her voice was barely audible.

The tall Negro shook his head. "Who knows? This is only the beginning." From the distance came the wail of a police siren. The marchers moved restlessly. "Mrs. Latimer, go home." Washington Taylor's voice matched his eyes, distant, icy. "You'll be safe there." He turned, signaling the demonstrators to follow him.

Jimmy came behind Mase. Shelley thrust out her white-gloved hand. "Jimmy, I missed you this morning."

"Miss Shelley, ma'am." His eyes lighted with pleasure. "I was going to let you know. I won't be coming no more."

"Why, Jimmy?"

He moved out of the way of the marchers filing in to the churchyard. "We're organizing," he said proudly. "Mase is telling us what to do. We learning to demonstrate. Mase is teachin' us how to protect ourselves, how to handle tear gas and dogs."

The last of the women and children entered the churchyard. They did not look to the right or the left as they took their places, standing in uneven rows. The sun slanted down on their bowed heads and clasped hands as their low voices rose and fell, softly, melodiously, like the gentle wind against the magnolia leaves.

The sound of sirens shattered the prayer-filled Sunday quiet as a car carrying Chester Glover and four state troopers roared down the street. Behind it came additional police cars, red lights whirling.

They double-parked in front of the church, clambered out and started toward the praying Negroes. They wore white crash helmets and hip-holstered guns, and in their hands they carried nightsticks.

Equally suddenly the street was filled with townspeople, pouring from the buildings and side streets, running along the pavement in the wake of the uniformed police.

Shelley was aware that she was clinging to Jimmy's hand. She did not know she was squeezing it so hard, holding on to it as though for support, until he sought to draw it away and as he did so she felt the bones beneath the flesh, noted the thinness of his face and shoulders, the hole in the heel of one gaudy sock. In that instant it was as though his fist, twisting in her hand, had twisted its way into her heart, opening a door that had long been locked.

"Good-by, Miss Shelley," Jimmy said and broke from her grasp, running to join the ranks of praying people.

Mike was walking along the sidewalk with a photographer. She watched him come toward her and like everything else on this strange Sunday, she saw him as though she had never seen him before. The thought flashed through her mind that she would like to sketch him, the lean figure and well-defined features, the set of his finely shaped head and shoulders. She wanted to capture the quiet face with its strength and dignity and humility that was not so much humility as an absence of arrogance, as well as that other quality she had never been able to define, a sense of rightness somehow allied with kindness and decency.

Something else struck her, a new certainty she had not noticed before. It was in his walk and in the way he held himself. Because of what she had done, she had caused him to grow and find himself whereas she, herself— She could not continue. Remorse for the ruin she had made of her marriage froze her instinct to run to him, the way Cam would have run to him in order to have him hold him close and make everything all right again.

Now she saw him pause and incline his head in the direction of Chester Glover, who was directing the men from Bellevue Barracks into the churchyard. The photographer lifted his camera.

Simultaneously the police chief whirled. "We've never had no trouble in this town." He raised his nightstick threateningly. "We ain't about to have none now. We don't want no trumped-up pictures."

Mike stepped between the two men. "Chester, for God's sake!"

"You stay out of this," Chester roared. "No outside agitators gonna get away with stirrin' up trouble in my town. I'll teach 'em. Lay down the law here and now. As for you and you—" He glared at Mike and the photographer. "White niggers. Goddamn Commies!"

Mike pulled a paper from his pocket. "Chester, if you'd just listen—"

"I was fool enough to listen once. I should a given 'em what-for the day they tried to demonstrate at the edge of town."

"If we could just discuss—"

"You think we're gonna listen to outsiders?" He jerked his club violently in the direction of Mase. "We'll talk to ouah nigras!"

"You call Mase an outsider?"

"Goddamn right he's an outsider," Chester continued explosively. "Anybody startin' trouble in my town is an outsider!"

Shelley stepped forward. "Chester, if my husband is an outsider, then I'm one, too."

The police chief's manner, that had been hot with antagonism, suddenly became servile. "Now, Miss Shelley, that was a manner of speaking." He turned, adjusting his chinstrap. "You just leave it to me. We'll have 'em cleared out of here in no time."

Mike swung around to face Shelley. "Stay out of this. I've managed this long without your support, I don't need it now."

In the churchyard, the police were rounding up demonstrators, waving their weapons and crying, "You niggers, break it up, y'hear!" Now the troopers were herding the leaders ahead of them. The first lot went peaceably, filing back through the narrow entrance in the spiked iron fence. Then one of the Tucker women suddenly broke away and began running toward the church. "Robbie!" she screamed, as a small child in a red playsuit darted toward the open door. "Robbie, you come back here!" As though on cue, the women around her began to shout and struggle to reach the gateway. A state trooper raised his nightstick and struck one of the Smith boys who had broken out of line.

The city photographer cried out, "My God! Look what they're doing!"

Blindly Shelley reached out to Mike. She felt his arm stiffen and heard him snap, "Shelley, go home. You've no business here."

Then he was running toward the churchyard, forgetting her in the hell of flailing clubs and screaming women and children that, within seconds, the area had become.

As though on signal the townspeople crowded through the opening, trapping the demonstrators, now a milling, screaming melee of black faces, eyes white-rimmed with fear.

In the shock of the moment, a series of images recorded themselves on Shelley's eyes and ears, mind and heart, standing out like the stained-glass window over the church doorway, its every detail etched in glass, as sharply defined as the words inscribed upon it: "Lord grant that I may seek rather to comfort than be comforted."

The stunned faces of the congregation looking out at the scene in the yard seconds before the door was slammed by Fax Templeton, acting as usher. The Smith boy, impaled on an iron spike as he sought to escape by climbing the fence. The Tucker child running frantically through the crowd screaming, "Mama, Mama!" Simultaneously, Charlie Woodruff plunged into the mob. She had always considered the news dealer the mildest of men. Now she saw that he was carrying a length of two-by-four and on his face was an expression of murderous rage as he slammed into Mase, knocking him to the ground. "Get that nigger!" she heard him shout as Mase tried to roll out of range of the club.

Briefly Shelley had felt as bewildered, as terrified and disoriented as the Tucker child. Then it was as though the violence had ripped a veil from her eyes, leaving her with new-found clarity of vision. It was as if all her life she had suffered from a form of deafness that permitted her only to hear what she wanted to hear. Then, on that tranquil, sunlit morning that had become a hell of animalistic violence, an operation had been performed which now allowed her to hear and understand things she had shut her ears and awareness to before. Katie Schligman's hurt, despairing face the night of her dinner party. The boycott against the Jenneys. Hounds tearing apart the fox at the quarry, a surging mass of black and white, wild, savage and uncontrolled. A ganging-up, no different from that taking place now.

She heard Mike calling, "Jimmy, Jimmy!" as the boy went to help Mase and was struck down amidst the flailing clubs and frantic feet. She saw him struggle to his knees and then fall again as a booted foot struck his ribs.

The fury that had been building up inside her struck like the blow that had felled the child. Without conscious thought, she was battering her way through the crowd. She felt her pocketbook being torn from her and her skirt rip and heard Mike's sharp "Shelley, Shelley, I told you not—" as her body collided with another and she hit the ground.

Mike was saying, "Shelley, Shelley," and she was being carried to safety.

"Jimmy?"

"A lump on his head. Possibly a cracked rib. Doc Watters is looking after him."

"Mike, I tried." She buried her face against his chest, fighting back the tears she had always before managed to repress.

"Shelley, I know that."

She lifted her head. Over his shoulder she saw the street, a chaos of whirling forces powered by men like Chester Glover and Charlie Woodruff, herding sobbing women and terrified children back toward the square.

"Oh, Mike"—tears she could no longer hold back started to fall—"I want to try again."

He slid behind the wheel and turned on the ignition.

"I'll drive you home."

She reached over and switched off the motor.

"I'm involved now, too." Her eyes looked into his, burning them with their blue-violet intensity. "Do you have a handkerchief? I've lost mine, along with my pocketbook."

Begun Woodstock, Vermont, 1963
Finished Macdowell Colony,
Peterborough, New Hampshire, 1970